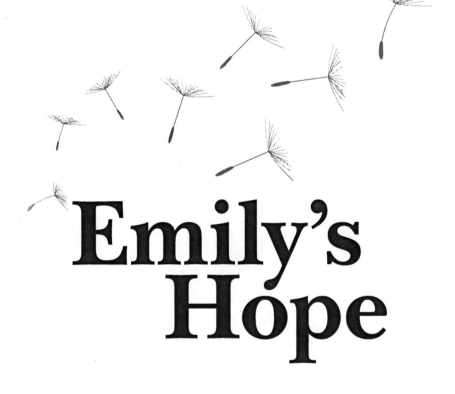

Emily's Hope

Printed in Charleston, South Carolina, USA by Create Space

Emily's Hope

by C. Scoushe Rosa

A STARRY MIND Publication, USA

For Lisa Steinberg (aka Elizabeth Launders) and
all the young innocents who could have continued
to be diamonds in the sun.

Introduction

---◇◇◇---

This book is not intended for young readers or for persons who may be offended by sexual and/or violent content. The story follows the lives of the benevolent O'Gorman family, with particular attention to young Katie, the victim of physical and sexual abuse, and the dynamics that she shares with her adoptive mother. In 1987, I was shocked when I heard of little Lisa Steinberg's tragic death at the hands of her foster father, an attorney. Lisa was tormented, tortured, and apparently sexually abused. There have been too many similar cases since then, which, I once erroneously believed, involved only children of low economic backgrounds. Because Lisa's case dealt with an educated middle class family, I decided to set this story at a more affluent level; child abuse can occur anywhere and observers, as in my case, can easily perceive what isn't real. While being mindful of the tragic lives and/or untimely deaths of children who are inexplicably born or introduced into vile or aberrant environments, I hope the reader will enjoy this tale and have a good cry or laugh with the O'Gormans and Katie. – C. Scoushe Rosa

One

⬦⬦⬦

March 2005

It was an activity-filled month for the O'Gorman family. March was not only the St. Patrick's Day month, but it was also the month for the opening ceremony at Emily's Hope, an O'Gorman wedding anniversary, and Easter Sunday. It was the second week of March. There was a chill in the air. However, if the weather prediction was correct, it would be a summery day. Twenty-five-year-old Dr. Katharine O'Gorman, PhD, aka Katie, stood on her Westchester County house deck. Above two layers of clothing, she wore her University College Dublin sweatshirt. She was sipping her morning coffee and observing the boats on Byram Lake, New York while the sun rose over the horizon. In a few minutes, Katie would take her own small yacht out, accompanied by Lolo and Lolita, her two German shepherds. Each dog would carry a bucket full of fish grub. Right now, the two dogs waited patiently on the house deck while Katie finished her hot beverage, the last of her breakfast. Katie and her dogs didn't always go on the boat during the early morning. Sometimes, they walked by the shore or hiked in the woods. Katie loved it here. *Life couldn't be more perfect*, she thought.

Life hadn't always been that way. Very early in Katie's life, when she was only four and had a different last name, she had a life-threatening experience. Doctors, as well as laypeople, believed the child would be traumatized for life. Up until that horrific determining point in time, for at least half of her short life, she had often heard her father yelling at her mother. Katie witnessed him beating his young wife and dragging her by the hair across the floor. At times, he was also cruel to his small daughter. Finally, when Katie was a couple of months past her fourth birthday, she saw the man she and her mother feared with every ounce of their souls grab a knife and repeatedly stab Katie's young mother. He finished the job by slashing her throat from ear to ear. When he turned, wiping the sweat from his upper lip with his bloody left hand, he noticed his wide-eyed, terrified little daughter staring up at him less than a foot away. As his hand cleared his lip, he forcefully swung his arm and slapped Katie clear across the room with a back-hand to her small cheek. She passed out. When she came to, her daddy was gone. Katie walked over to her mother, unaware of the blood trail she left behind and oblivious of the numbing pain. She slipped on the blood-soaked floor and fell headfirst on her mommy's chest. Time stood still as Katie tried to shake her mommy awake, asking her to please wake up. She lifted her blood-soaked body off the floor and walked to the phone, which was next to an armchair in the living room, and dialed 911. In a pained little voice, she said to the operator, "My daddy cut my mommy. She won't wake up."

The police alerts went out immediately. Two state lines away, in Cuyahoga Falls, Ohio, a state trooper spotted Lyman's dark blue sedan at a rest stop. The lawman called for backup and stood by the side of the building at the rest stop, waiting for the owner of the car to emerge. When the perpetrator approached his car and fished his keys out of his pocket, Officer Thomas walked behind him, gun drawn, and yelled, "Step away from the car, Doc; you're under arrest for murdering your wife, Emily Lyman," just as three police cruisers arrived.

* * *

At ten knots, the now older Katie guided her small yacht, *Ekaterina*, to a favorable spot. She traveled slowly because her dog Lolita was standing on the bow, her favorite spot, and Katie didn't want the animal to lose her footing. Byram Lake was immense and deep, with varying currents and eddies. Katie brought the boat to a stop at one of the more isolated areas. As soon as the boat stopped, Lolita walked down and joined Lolo, who was sprawled on deck. Katie secured the helm and ordered the dogs to bring the buckets of fish grub. The canines obeyed and soon joined her as she reached starboard. There, she secured each bucket of bait to a winch and lowered them to the water. With a remote device she kept on her waist-belt, she activated the bottom of each bucket to open, exposing graduated sieves. Using the same remote, she pressed a second button, and the boat started to move slowly forward. Lolita quickly returned to her place at the bow. As the boat moved, the buckets filtered out their contents through the water, releasing the fish grub through the sieves at the bottom of each bucket. When the food particles entered the water, the fish rose to eat. Lolo stood next to Katie, watching the feeding with her and barking as he caught sight of the fish. Katie stroked him behind the ear and smiled. Lolita took no interest and continued to enjoy the cool breeze sifting through her teeth. Although Katie worried about her pet's safety, the canine made a good copilot by barking whenever she spotted something of interest ahead. If anything went wrong, Katie hoped Lolita's lifejacket would afford her enough protection.

Katie's cell phone rang. She recognized the caller ID and responded with "Hi, Daddy." It was her adoptive father of twenty years.

"Hi, princess. Your mother and I were wondering at what time you plan to arrive for the opening ceremony. I hope you're done feeding the fish."

"I'm done, Daddy. I'll be there around nine o'clock. It's about seven now. Do you need me there earlier?"

"No. Nine o'clock is fine. Your mother and I will be there in about an hour so we can deal with the caterers or anything else that comes up. Hey, bring me some fish for lunch," he laughed.

"Dream on. I keep telling you, I don't fish them, I feed them. Ask your heartless fisherman son to come murder them for you. He's the one who likes to fish."

"It's a good thing your mother didn't hear you say that about her baby boy. She would be very upset, and so am I. Anyway, we'll have plenty to eat at the ceremony."

"I'm heading back to shore now, Daddy. I'll talk to you later." As soon as she broke off communications, she yelled to Lolita, "Off the bow, Lolita." Lolita complied and Katie was soon returning to port at thirty knots.

* * *

Back at his house, Matthew O'Gorman placed the cordless phone in its base and turned to his wife. "Katie will be at the academy around nine, Carolyn. She's still out on the boat, but she's on her way back to shore."

"What did she say now about my baby boy?" Carolyn asked.

"She referred to him as a heartless fisherman who murders fish."

Carolyn gave a sigh of annoyance and said, "I think I'm starting to lose my patience with her. Kieran's just a child, and she's a young woman. It's time for this sibling rivalry to end."

"Don't get upset, Honey-Lyn."

"I try not to, but when will she learn?"

"Carolyn, she is over twenty-one, and she is independent. The bird needs to fly, but you won't let her go. Then there is the other side of the coin. Katie doesn't want to change her ways because she knows it gets your attention. You've spoiled her, and you can't stop."

"So, it's my fault. Is that what you're saying?"

"I didn't say that. Don't twist my words around."

"Perhaps you should be more explicit then. So, what are you saying?"

"Katie loves to be the center of your attention. She'll do anything for it. She only knows one way to do that. She and you are like the boy and the little pigtailed girl. It's too difficult for him to say 'I love you,' so he pulls her hair instead. Katie has been pulling your hair since day one. And that poor sap Luis is another victim. Boy, does she have him under control. She has him...well, you know."

"Henpecked?"

"I was thinking of a stronger adjective. However, henpecked will do. I'm too much of a gentleman to say anything stronger in your presence," he said, feigning innocence while adjusting his collar.

"Of course," she said, putting her arms around him. "I bet you enjoy a little henpecking yourself."

"As a gentleman, I can't lie. Yes, I love it when you henpeck me. It's even better when I peck you," he responded with a sly smile.

"But you still blame me for spoiling Katie and allowing her to push my buttons."

"Boy, a man can't win. I never should have married a lawyer. Engineers don't put words in a man's mouth."

"I didn't put words in your mouth. You blurted them out. So do you want to file for divorce and marry an engineer? I'll draw the papers up right now."

He smiled down on her. "I might find an engineer, but she probably won't be as sweet or as pretty as you."

"Nice save. Besides, I would never divorce you or permit you to divorce me."

"Neither would the Church. I'm honor-bound and extremely henpecked."

"I'm glad to hear that."

* * *

Twenty-one years earlier, Philip Garrity was assigned to the O'Gorman/Lyman case. His police chief had received an interdepartmental call from the Rochester police department. They explained that the Ohio police were holding Dr. William Lyman. "Lyman will soon be brought back to Rochester. It appears," said the detective at the other end, "that the deceased wife's family lives in your area. I was hoping you'd swing over there and break the bad news to them." Phil's chief wrote down the details and passed the case to Phil. Phil asked James Esposito to join him; Garrity was never comfortable with this part of the job. It was heartbreaking to deal with a victim's surviving relatives. Esposito had a psychology degree, so Phil believed his coworker would do a better job at addressing the relatives. James agreed to do his good friend the favor. It was less heartbreaking to talk to a sibling than a parent, so they decided to visit the victim's brother, Matthew O'Gorman. Garrity sighed and thought of the case of a young boy named Luis Walker and other children like him. *"When will it end?"* he asked himself. *"Why are adults abusing children? It's a damn epidemic."*

* * *

Matthew answered his doorbell when the two detectives arrived.

"Are you Matthew O'Gorman?" the taller one asked, holding up a badge.

Matthew, looking perplexed, confirmed that he was. The officers introduced themselves as Detectives Philip Garrity and James Esposito.

"Can we come in, Mr. O'Gorman?" asked the tall one, Detective Garrity.

"Yes. Sure." Matthew motioned them to step forward, and he led them to the living room. He felt ill at ease, wondering if something bad had happened to his parents or another member of the family. He knew he had not done anything wrong. Carolyn had just come downstairs, after putting their infant son to sleep when she heard the doorbell. Matthew introduced his wife to the two men.

"Mr. O'Gorman," Detective Esposito said, looking Matthew in the eye as he sat across from him. "This isn't going to be easy." Matthew swallowed in anticipation, and Carolyn slipped her hand into his. Intuitively, Matthew covered her hand with his other hand and gently squeezed hers. Esposito continued to speak. "Do you know a Dr. William Lyman?"

"Of course I do. He's my sister's husband," Matthew responded, shooting Esposito an inquisitive look.

"I already said this isn't going to be easy," Esposito repeated without taking his gaze off Matthew. "I have very bad news to disclose, and I apologize for having to bring it to you. William Lyman is under arrest for murdering your sister."

Matthew paled. His eyes glazed. Carolyn's hand, in his two hands, was suddenly drenched with his perspiration. His mouth was dry. Esposito noticed the sudden change in Matthew's complexion and continued to watch him. He thought that if Matthew had been standing, he probably would have dropped to the floor. James Esposito waited for Matthew's demeanor to change, to give him an indication that Matthew was capable of hearing the rest of the bad news.

The indication came with, "My parents and I have unsuccessfully tried to contact Emily for at least a few months now. My father considered hiring a private detective because there has been a disturbing pattern to our lack of communication. Shortly after Emily married William, we would call and leave a message, but we wouldn't hear from her until weeks later. Then she wouldn't respond at all, so I stopped calling for a while. I should have known better. That son of a bitch moved her out of the family's reach two years ago. First, they went to Georgia," he said and detached himself from Carolyn. He started to pace, rubbing the back of his neck. "Then, they moved to Maryland. Last month, according to my parents, they called at their last residence in Pennsylvania. That's the number I had recently been calling. When my parents called, they discovered that the number was disconnected. That's why my father wanted to hire a private investigator. *William killed my sister, his own wife!* We should have hired someone years ago! I can't believe this shit!" He wanted to kick something, but he restrained himself. "Where is Emily now?" he almost whispered, turning to Esposito.

Esposito rose and said, "She and her husband were living in Rochester, New York."

"So the bastard moved them back to New York. What about Katie, my baby niece? Is she okay?"

"They have her in ICU. He nearly killed her too."

"What did he do?" his voice was hoarse. His face was very close to Esposito, eyes fixed on eyes.

"Emily and Katie's bodies both show signs of abuse that had been going on for some time. More recently, Katie's cheekbone is fractured. She shows signs of sexual abuse, and her private area has been mutilated. She almost bled to death."

"What did he do?" Matthew asked again, now almost shouting.

"He cut her clitoris." At this point, Matthew took a few steps back and sank into the sofa, next to his wife. Carolyn, troubled by the conversation and empathizing with Matthew, grabbed her husband's bicep and pulled herself closer to him.

When Garrity and Esposito left the O'Gorman home that evening, Matthew picked up the phone.

"You're not going to give your parents the bad news over the phone," Carolyn said in an admonishing tone.

"I'm not calling them," Matthew informed her, "but I do need to call Patrick and Neil." Patrick and Neil were his older brothers. "Tonight, I'll allow my parents to have a restful night's sleep. My brothers and I will visit them tomorrow to break the bad news. Then I need to make arrangements to go to Rochester. I need to bring Emily and Katie home."

"What can I do, Matthew?"

"You? You need to pack for yourself and Stevie so you can stay with my parents while I go to Rochester. I don't want you staying alone in this house while I'm away."

"I'm sure your parents will want to go with you."

"I think it's best if they don't go. That's it—I'll tell them I need them to keep you company while I go. Otherwise, they'll want to come. Is that okay with you?"

"Yes, of course," Carolyn said. Then she added, "We should call my mother and Paul Sheridan."

"Who's Paul Sheridan?"

"He's my parents' attorney. Mom can prevent a possible media frenzy. We can't have reporters breathing down our necks while we're handling a family crisis. The media love stuff like this, and it won't be fair to Momma and Papa. I also don't want you traveling back and forth between downstate and upstate New York for the impending trial. Paul is the man who's going to convince the Rochester district attorney and William Lyman's attorney that it's in everyone's best interest to hold the trial in Westchester

County. He'll also let you know who to see in Rochester to facilitate Emily and Katie's return home."

"He sounds like a very nice man."

"Yes, he is," she said.

She and Matthew came from wealthy families. However, compared to the O'Gormans, Carolyn's family was considerably wealthier, came from old money and had unlimited resources. Carolyn soon explained the situation to her mother Margaret. Then Margaret spent the evening communicating with the individuals who were needed to make things happen.

* * *

Carolyn Josephine Reilly-O'Gorman had never planned to be a stay-at-home mom. Like many wealthy, intelligent women her age, she had planned to have it all: a career, success, and a family. She was one quarter of two sets of twins who had been born to Margaret and Harold Reilly. Harold Reilly was the descendant and sole heir of Donovan Daniel Reilly, the pharmaceutical baron. Margaret was a learned physicist and experienced chemist who was also one of two heirs of the Galway Financial Services and the Muir (short for Ó Muircheartaigh) Hotel chain.

When young Carolyn Reilly finished law school, she landed a job at a prestigious law firm. She moved into a Soho apartment and cycled to and from work each day. As she was returning home one evening, a bus nearly hit her bike. She lost control of the bicycle and hit the curb. She envisioned herself flying over the handle bars and possibly hurting herself and a few pedestrians in the process. It never happened. A tall, athletic young man braced the incoming bike with one hand and her shoulder with the other. They gazed into each other's eyes, and Carolyn nearly fainted on the spot. In that instant, she met and fell in love with Matthew Thomas O'Gorman. In less than a year's time, they married. Carolyn soon took maternity leave and returned to work two weeks after giving birth to twins, Seán Patrick and Harold Ignatius O'Gorman. Life was wonderful; everything was falling into place. The twins had an excellent nanny, a college grad herself, who was fluent in French and German.

Carolyn's family owned pharmaceutical companies in the United States, Ireland, New Zealand, Malaysia, and Puerto Rico. As a child, she had visited the foreign lands with her family, sometimes for extended stays. As a result, she had learned to speak Spanish, Malay, and Irish. Her Spanish was honed further during a year-long stay in Puerto Rico as a graduate law student. *My sons*, Carolyn thought, *will learn to speak all those languages, travel the world, and maybe become foreign correspondents or diplomats.*

Sometimes, plans have a way of not coming to fruition. At the age of nine months, for some inexplicable reason, Seán Patrick and Harold Ignatius developed high fevers on a Saturday night. The pediatrician advised Carolyn to rush them to the hospital, where he met the young parents and cared for the children. The diagnosis horrified them; the twins had bacterial meningitis. Despite the doctors' efforts, the children died within three days and three hours of each other. For Carolyn and Matthew, time stood still. Suspended in that timeless abyss, they moved through empty space while burying their beautiful, red-haired baby boys. Physically and emotionally, they detached themselves from the world.

Unable to look at the children's pictures, Carolyn placed every photo she had of them in a plastic container and stored them in the attic. In his wallet, Matthew always kept pictures of the twins by themselves or them and Carolyn together. Over the years, he would open his wallet and quietly love his firstborn sons. During those early painful days, however, he was in a fog of his own. Matthew occasionally heard his wife weeping while he sat listlessly. Finally, one evening, his mind cleared as he listened to her sorrowful cry. Tenderly, he came up behind her and wrapped his arms around her. "I'm sorry, Honey-Lyn," he spoke hoarsely. She needed that tender hug to purge herself of the pain. Her subdued weeping became a wail of grief as she sobbed uncontrollably. He continued to hold her as she cried into his shoulder. "Life," she said between sobs, "is not fair. They were so little. They were so little." They continued to cry until they had no more tears.

While the sorrow was always palpable, the couple learned to cope and face the world again. They returned to work and learned to communicate with one another and the world around them in a different manner. In grief, love and lovemaking took on a whole new meaning. The gentle, tender moments became selfless between them. Each was silently saying, "Please accept my love as my gift to you," and "I give it to soothe your pain away." And so it was that on a quiet and gentle night, Steven Christopher O'Gorman was conceived.

As soon as Carolyn discovered that her next child was on his way, she left her law career to become a stay-at-home mom. In her heart, she now knew that caring for her family was the most important thing in her life. She would treasure every moment she had with her children.

There would be no nannies in their lives. She would be their protector. She would guide them. She would love them while they were unfertilized eggs and cherish them from conception to adulthood. She realized that throughout human history, poor women without any means of support had done what she yearned for. Being wealthy was no excuse to surrender the duties of motherhood to someone else and deprive herself of what she believed to be a woman's greatest joy: basking in the affection she felt for her children. She continued to keep a pulse on law and politics, but for the selfish knowledge that they could always be used as avenues to strengthen and protect her family. With the terrible news that the two detectives brought into her home, it was time to follow those avenues.

* * *

As Katie brought her boat to dock, she saw her boyfriend, Dr. Luis López, playing with his two rottweilers, Onyx and Amber. Luis heard the boat's engine shut off, and he turned to face the recent arrivals. Katie waved to him, and he returned the wave as he jogged toward the dock. He got there in time to help her tie the boat and secure the plank for the dogs and Katie to walk down. The four dogs greeted each other in regular canine fashion.

Katie tossed her life jacket to the ground and wrapped her arms around Luis's neck. The two kissed each other affectionately. "You're here early," she commented in Spanish. Katie enjoyed practicing her linguistic skills whenever she had the chance. She had a good ear for foreign languages, and she also spoke French and Russian. She had a very rudimentary understanding of Irish, but that understanding didn't come until later in life. Luis also enjoyed practicing Russian and Spanish with her. After they greeted each other, they called the dogs. As Luis removed the life jackets from Lolo and Lolita, Katie bent down to pet and talk to Amber.

"Have you been behaving yourself, baby? I hope you haven't gone off exploring on your own again," she said to the dog.

"So far, so good," Luis commented. "She hasn't run off again since the last time. I'm still trying to figure out how and why she undid the latch and got out. If she does it again, I'm going to put in a dead bolt. I don't want her to wander into the woods and encounter a rabid animal."

Katie turned to Onyx and petted him too. "You're a good boy," she cooed. "You don't do bad things like that."

"Maybe he's as lazy as Lolo," Luis commented as they started to walk toward the house and the dogs romped. Luis then explained that his mother had spent the night at his house in order to be closer to the day's activities. She had sent Katie a Caribbean style breakfast. Katie saw the food on the kitchen counter when they entered the house.

"Oh, the guys from the pet store dropped off your order of bone meal and meal worms and all that other stuff you get," Luis explained as Katie removed a jar from the refrigerator to make room for the food. "I had them put everything in the storeroom."

"Thanks, I don't want the raccoons to be enticed to a smorgasbord," she said as she handed him the nearly empty jar of juice left over from her morning breakfast. "Throw that out for me, please."

Luis took the jar and proceeded to drink its contents. "This is greener than usual. Did you add something to it?" he asked and burped.

"I added broccoli and extra wheatgrass."

"You're back on the health kick again?"

"Well, yes. And, you apparently don't give a damn about yours. You weren't supposed to drink that, you idiot," she said as she draped her jacket over a chair. "With your health problems, you don't need any extra vitamin K in your diet."

Placing the jar down on the counter, he said, "I'll live," and quickly changed the subject with, "Those people made me an offer of forty-five million for the Web site, but I did what you and Susan Sheridan suggested. I held out. They increased it to seventy-five."

Katie smiled and said, "That sounds good. What did you decide?"

"I asked them to meet with Sheridan and me prior to Easter, perhaps on the twenty-second. I spoke with Sheridan last night."

"What did she say?" she asked brushing his hair back.

"She'll call them today and set up an appointment. I'd like you to come with me to that meeting, if you don't mind. For moral support and input. You know?"

"Of course I'll come, but you really don't need me there. All you need to remember is not to answer any questions. Let Sheridan do the talking. She knows what she's doing, and she's good at it. She learned from her father, and he's a shark. You can relax."

"Katie, we're talking seventy-five million here. I've never been offered that kind of money. I'm nervous. What do you want from me?" he asked as he leaned against the counter.

"Act like you deserve it. You deserve whatever people believe you're worth, and more. You get thirty million hits a week on that site. Whenever people see a dog or are given the opportunity to talk about their pets, they can't resist. You did a great job by adding music and animation. I'm very proud of you, baby. The economy can't continue to spiral like this much longer. Homes that cost sixty thousand dollars worth of materials are selling for eight hundred and sixty thousand or more; it's insane. So if someone thinks your web site is worth seventy-five million today, then take their money and run before we realize inflation can't continue at this rate."

"We did this together. The Meerkat helped too." The Meerkat was Luis's pet name for Katie's younger brother Kieran.

Katie replied, "No, it's your baby. You conceived it. Kieran did help, so if you want to offer him something, I suggest you talk to my mom first. You know how she is about her children and money. As for me, I simply helped you iron out the kinks. You take the money and invest it."

"You also tell me to keep my head under the radar. Will seventy-five million keep my head under the radar?" Luis asked.

"Yes; these days, *Fortune* is profiling billionaires. You don't have a billion and you don't want your face on any cover because people won't leave you alone. Sometimes, you need to make your presence known. At other times, it's best if you stay in the shadows. In the business world, you need to know when to be where. You can choose to be a high-visibility rare orchid that everyone is dying to possess, or you can be a summer zephyr, welcomed but invisible."

"You're my orchid in a zephyr, Katie."

"Aren't you the poet," she said as she looked at the kitchen clock. "It's getting late. You better go home and get dressed. I'll do the same."

"What are you wearing?"

"The blue with the scoop collar," she said as she started to see him to the door.

He suddenly turned and said, "I like to see you in the green with the straps. The green makes your blue eyes turn green; I love how your eyes do that. Then, the way that dress flares out at the hips, you remind me of hot Rita Moreno from the movie *West Side Story*. Except she wore red. Oh, Mama!"

"You're starting to sound gay, Luis," she said. "Besides, I saw that old movie. I don't believe Rita wore red. One thing I've learned from Momma is that color is important to a story line—it lends to the plot, so she couldn't have worn a provocative color like red. It would have been out of character."

"Well, the color doesn't matter. Rita was hot—hot, I tell you. And you know I'm not gay; I like women," he said, standing close to her and locking his gaze with hers.

"You like women?" she countered menacingly.

"Well, I like you. I don't like *women*; I swear I don't. I like, I love you, Katie. When I first saw you, I went gaga," he said as he leaned over and kissed her neck.   "You were hot then, and you're really hot now." He kissed her again.

Katie pushed him away. "We don't have time for this now, *don Juan*. It's twenty to eight, and we have to get ready."

"Katie, Katie, Katie, Katie."

"What? Luis, Luis, Luis."

"We have time for a quickie." He locked his mouth over hers.

"Mmmm," she said when their lips parted.

He smiled because he knew they reacted to one another in a mutual fashion; Katie was ready to give in. He pinned her against the refrigerator door and thrust his pelvis forward into hers. As she gasped and closed her eyes, Luis suddenly yelped in pain.

"What's wrong?" she asked with alarm as she watched him double over while his face contorted in pain and turned crimson. "Oh, no; not again?"

"Yes, yes," Luis gasped as he held his pelvis. "The pain is back. Augh, God!"

"See? This is one reason why I didn't want you to mess with me, Luis. God, you never learn, do you? I swear, if we don't get to the academy on time, I'm going to kill you!"

Before she could continue, he whined, "Katie, it's getting worse. Please get me some ice. You can kill me later, but not now, please."

Katie quickly opened the freezer door and grabbed a bag of frozen carrots while Luis struggled to get to a chair.

"Don't sit," she warned him. "Can you remove your pants first? It's probably best if you place the bag directly on your skin. I'll help you."

She set the bag on the table and started to help him with his pants. The undressing required delicacy, for Luis's pain was centered on his privates. Due to a childhood injury, he sometimes experienced painful erections during lovemaking.

"I'm sorry, honey," Katie said, sounding concerned while handing him the frozen carrots, which he draped over his penis. "Relax. Don't let your blood pressure go up, or it will get worse."

"I know; it's my penis," he cried. "Katie, it really hurts."

"I'm sorry, Luis. Did you bring a hypodermic with you?"

"No, I didn't bring one! Would I be sitting here with a bag of carrots if I had one with me?"

"Well, I don't know, Luis. I guess you didn't plan this properly."

"I didn't plan anything. I didn't come here to seduce you; I came here to bring your breakfast."

"Evidently, you shouldn't have strayed from your mission."

"Katie, Katie! You're making it worse. Oh, God," he cringed, and his face flushed again. "God, I promise not to hump another woman again if you stop the pain now."

"Hump another woman?" she asked with a raised eyebrow as she punched him in the arm.

"It's the pain talking, baby. The things one does for love."

"You mean the things you do for lust, you damn fool. You couldn't leave well enough alone! You drank that damn juice, you damn idiot! You should know better than that; a person with circulation problems has to watch his intake of vitamin K, which green juice is loaded with, you damn tuit"

"Katie, please go home and get my medication. We can argue later—if I survive the pain."

Katie's compassion kicked in again. "Well, all right." She retrieved his house keys from his pants' pocket, and dashed to the garage.

Luis's problem could be traced to his childhood. When he was three years old, his biological mother, Lucy Walker, a crack addict, accidentally put him in a tub of hot water. The baby shrieked in pain as he was immersed up to his waist in scalding water. Luckily, Lucy reacted quickly enough to pull him out. Unfortunately, he developed third-degree burn blisters all over his lower body and spent most of the day sobbing in pain. Frank Gomez, the next-door neighbor, couldn't take the baby's crying any longer, and he started to kick the door while frightened neighbors called 911. By the time the fire department and the police arrived, two other men had joined Frank in his endeavor. The door was a mess, but the lock would not give way. The firemen gained entry by using a crowbar. The men were brought to tears when they found the helpless baby on the floor, too tired to cry anymore, with his lower body covered with oozing and scabby blisters. Lucy was literally dragged and pushed to jail.

Luis spent weeks in intensive care. The doctors had to scrape his skin to help him heal. With a tiny catheter, they had to force an opening through the tip of his penis and into his bladder in order to save his life. The scalding water had literally cauterized a third of his small penis shut, making it temporarily impossible for him to pass urine.

His rescuers stopped by daily to check on his progress. Because so many strangers flooded the hospital's switchboard with concerned calls about the child, the hospital turned to the daily press to report the baby's progress. His torment brought him fame at a very early age. Miles away, detectives Garrity and Esposito were among the many concerned citizens who read the daily reports. They were the two detectives who later brought sad news to Matthew O'Gorman, who was now Katie's adoptive father.

In the meantime, his mother died of an alleged over-dose while she was in jail and unable to post bail. Luis suffered through many operations. His tiny testicles were fused to his penis and torso. His small toes were also fused together. The doctors had to perform microscopic surgery to separate and reconstruct the fused body parts. Over the years, Luis underwent many operations to correct the deformities, and he developed hideous scar tissue throughout his lower body. Well into adulthood, he had to lubricate his skin daily and wear a body stocking from waist to toes to keep his skin from chafing. He didn't always wear the stocking because he considered it a nuisance. The scar tissue on his penis sometimes caused a problem with blood circulation when he experienced an erection. The results were sometimes painful and, he also reminded himself, possibly crippling or fatal.

As he now sat in Katie's kitchen, holding a bag of frozen carrots over his genitalia, he thought about a lot of things. He wondered if it would help if he wore the stocking more often. Would he eventually have to live a life of celibacy? Would he ever get better? God, it had to get better. Katie was hot. Katie was always hot. And she understood him. He understood her; they were like peas in a pod. They fought, but they always made up. He moaned, partly due to the pain and partly due to the image he had of Katie in his mind. He sighed. He remembered the first time he kissed her. He believed it was the year they met. They were about five or six then. He had leaned over and landed a wet one on the corner of her mouth. She knocked him to the ground. "You got spit on me," she complained. "Yeah," he said, smiling. He was thinking of that when Katie returned. He was grinning, and she noticed.

"Are you feeling better now?" she asked.

"Sort of; I was thinking about us when we were kids, you know. The first time I kissed you, and you pushed me; I landed on my ass."

She smiled. "As I've said before, you're incorrigible." She washed her hands. "Do you still need this?"

"I'm afraid so," he said, removing the carrots to reveal his penis still at attention.

Katie swabbed him down with antiseptic. She was used to the routine by now. As she introduced the needle, she commented, "I hope this will finally teach you not to leave home without your medication."

"I'm learning, I'm learning." He cringed with pain as she forced the last drops of the drug into the site. "Oh, God, I'm learning."

"Do you want me to kiss it to make it all better?" she teased him.

"Lord, mercy, no! If you do that, I'll probably get horny again. I'm going to get another bag of vegetables and lie down in the den. You know," he said as he struggled to walk, "one of these days, you're going to be in pain, and you're going to beg me for a painkiller, and I'm not going to give it to you."

"Are you sure you're a pediatrician? You whine like one of your patients."

"Don't start!"

"Go lie down. I'll bring you a bag of ice."

"Thank you, thank you," he said, placing the bag of carrots back on his member and walking as stiffly as a robot.

Katie joined him later in the den. After handing him the ice and covering him with a throw blanket, she laughed and commented, "It's a shame the little peppermint stick didn't behave well today. I could have eaten you like a praying mantis."

"Oh," he moaned and trembled. He drew the blanket closer to his neck. "I'm too young to die."

Katie left him alone as she went into hyperdrive, readying herself for the day ahead. When she returned to the den, he was asleep. She gently lifted the blanket and removed what was left of the melting ice. His penis was normal. As she placed the wet bag on the floor, he awoke and sat up.

"You're wearing the green with the straps."

"Yes," she said with a smile, looking up at him from a squatting position, resting a hand on his knee.

"You look great," he said, looking down at her and holding her hand.

"Thank you. Your kilt, stockings, and beanie are laid out on the bed."

He got up and started walking to the door. "Katie, you know I only use that at holidays and funerals, out of respect for the deceased. I hate it when people see my scarred knees and start asking me silly questions about the scars. I don't have the patience for that kind of nonsense. Besides, the fabric irritates my skin."

"You look cute in a kilt; I love it. Besides, Stevie and the other guys will be appropriately dressed. You'll be the only piper without it. And I brought you your tighty whities. It's less traditional, but you'll feel less irritation."

"Well, I guess I have no choice now."

"Your guitar and bagpipe are in the van."

"I also need the speakers and amplifier."

"You won't need them. You can hook the guitar to the equipment on stage."

"I'm not familiar with the equipment on stage."

"You are a regular pain in the ass," she said, sounding irritated. "By the time I finish loading all that in the SUV, I'll need another shower."

"We all have to make sacrifices for the greater good," he said. As he exited the room, he heard a wooden sculpture crash against the door frame. She had purposely aimed to miss him, but to make a point, nonetheless. "I love you too!" he yelled from the corridor.

Two

They were finally en route. Luis drove down the private road of the estate he shared with Katie. He drove past his house and eventually came to the gate, which was programmed with computer sensors to allow entry and exit of the O'Gorman family automobiles and local emergency units. Vehicles that weren't part of the database had to receive permission to enter. As the gate opened and closed behind them, it displayed both the Reilly and O'Gorman family crests next to one another.

"It's already nine fifteen," Luis said as he pulled onto the roadway that was part of Katie's private cul-de-sac road and fed onto a main road. "Did you call your parents?"

"Of course I did."

"What did you tell them?" he asked.

"I explained we would be late because you tore your pants."

"That's the best you could do?"

"Well, you did try to screw their daughter." She said, and he laughed as she added, "Then you had me lug those heavy, dusty speakers into the van. Don't you ever dust anything in your house?"

"The vibration from the music shakes the dust off."

"Like hell it does. But it's okay. I wore your trench coat."

"The new coat you gave me for my birthday?"

"Yes, the new coat I gave you for your birthday."

"That's okay," he said with a shrug. "I didn't like that coat anyway."

She glared at him. "What do you mean, you didn't like it?"

"Aha! You thought you would upset me by telling me you used my new coat as a smock. Who's upset now?"

"You never told me you didn't like my gift!"

"I'm teasing! I like the coat, but it was childish of you to select that particular coat and use it as a smock. Don't you agree?"

"No. Ooh, slow down," she said, tapping his leg and changing the subject. "What's going on over there?" She alluded to a situation at the opposite side of the road. A police car with flashing lights had stopped the driver of an SUV. A third car, a Town Car, was parked in front of the SUV. The driver of the Town Car was a plainclothes officer, and he stood by with his hand on a holster while the patrolman frisked the detainee. "That looks like Garrity," she commented about the plainclothes cop. "Let's see what's going on."

"We're running late, and you want to know what's going on?"

He continued driving and immediately turned right. A large blue sign with gold lettering surrounded by yellow forsythia and topiary read "Emily's Hope Academy." The entry gate hedges had been brought directly from the nursery and planted the day before. They had been chosen for their full bloom and were the final touch to showcase the beautiful landscape for the day's occasion. March could be a fickle and ruthless month for plants. Katie had wanted everything to be perfect and hoped that the night's chill would not damage the plants' blooms. Luckily, the yellow blossoms were perfect.

The young couple had arrived at the facility, but they still had about a mile of road ahead of them. The two guards at the gate waved them in, clearing them to continue.

As they drove up an incline, surrounded on either side by well-planned landscaping, Luis asked, "Is your uncle the monsignor going to be here?"

"I'm sure he will be. After all, this is basically a family affair."

"I get so nervous when he's around. I can't look at the man in the face. Every time he looks at me, I feel like he's saying, 'You're living in sin with my niece. You know you're going to hell!'"

"Uncle Patrick would never say anything like that to you."

"Well, he's a holy man. I'm sure he's thinking it. I can't even go to confession with a clear conscience anymore. I feel so damn guilty saying, 'Forgive me, Father, for I have sinned. I spend my life fornicating. When I'm not fornicating, I'm dreaming of fornicating.'"

"You dream of fornicating with me?"

"You don't know the half of it. It's really hard for me to concentrate on my work when I'm daydreaming of me and you. Why don't you marry me, Katie?"

"Please don't start this again. How many times do I have to explain it to you?"

"Your reasoning doesn't make any sense, woman! You love me; I love you. We're constantly horny for one another. And, I don't want to end up in hell!"

"Neither one of us is going to hell."

"How could you say that? We're confirmed Catholics. We're living in sin."

"For God's sake, Luis, everyone knows that we're screwing each other, and no one cares."

"God cares!"

"How do you know, Luis? When did He last talk to you?"

Luis stopped the car and put the gear in park. He turned to her and said, "Woman, that's blasphemy!"

"You know, if you feel so strongly about this, why don't you stop fornicating and get yourself ordained as a priest?" she said. He was about to interrupt, but she continued. "If it's a sin to express our affection with sex, why has God made it so pleasurable for us, for everyone? Despite our own personal mutilations, Luis, sex is good. Do you think that a caveman said, 'Woman, we must marry before I can hump you?' No, he pounced, probably when she wasn't looking, and discovered that it was a great thing. And it's a great thing for two people who love each other. God didn't come down and smite them. If He had, neither one of us would be here."

"That's rape. You're insane. You know you are definitely insane."

"Call me insane one more time, and the door will be closed the next time you come knocking. And I know you'll come knocking."

Luis sighed with exasperation and put the car in gear again. As he continued driving, he muttered, "I'll bet you'll knock first." Katie ignored him, and he continued to fume. After a few seconds of silence, he said, "I just want you to make an honest man of me."

"Honesty is a choice you make. Guilt is a choice you make. If you feel guilty or dishonest, it's your problem, Luis."

"In the eyes of the Lord, we're both dishonest. And we're both guilty of not abiding by Church law."

"I don't remember seeing or hearing you pray whenever we go at it. So add 'hypocrite' to your list. You certainly aren't fooling me. You'll use any argument you can find to arrive at your goal. My answer is still no. We don't need to be married."

As if he hadn't heard a word she said, he muttered, "God, I hope I don't run into the monsignor."

Katie decided to ignore him. It wasn't the first time she had heard what she perceived as illogical thinking. They arrived at their destination, and Luis eased the van into a parking spot. As they stepped out of the SUV, they observed that several of the guests had already arrived. Kieran and Stevie, Katie's brothers, stood by the family's parking area.

"Yo, sis," commented Stevie, the older of the two boys. Stevie was twenty-one, four years younger than Katie. "You look great!"

"So do you guys. You two always look adorable when you're dressed up. Stevie, that kilt really complements your gorgeous legs," she said, kissing him on the cheek and turning to do the same to twelve-year-old Kieran, who was wearing a blue suit and a pink pastel shirt with a striped pink and blue tie. Despite the differences in their age, Katie and young Kieran were sibling rivals. However, the rivalry had diminished slightly over the years. It was now more of a "pick and choose" battle of wits. After Katie kissed each of them, the boys then gave Luis a bear hug.

"Where are the folks?" Luis asked.

"Your mom," Kieran responded, "is in the cafeteria giving the caterers a hard time."

"I think my grandparents are out here somewhere, and my parents," Stevie added, "are in the auditorium giving the stage hands an equally hard time."

"They hired stage hands?" Katie asked.

"Yeah. Somebody has to dim the lights, check the sound system, and so on," Kieran added. "You guys need help setting up? We have about a half hour before everything starts."

"Yes," said Luis. "Can you guys give me a hand with my speakers? I'll get the amplifier and the bagpipe. Katie, could you please get the guitar?"

"Do it yourself. I've done enough schlepping for one day. I'm going to thank your mother for the breakfast she sent me. I'll meet you later in the auditorium." She walked away.

"She must really be pissed at you, Luis," Kieran said. "What did you do?"

He shook his head. "The list is too long for me to start," he said.

* * *

As Katie entered the building's lobby, she was greeted by a ten-foot painting of a young woman holding an infant. It hung in the center of the lobby, where no one could miss it when they entered the building. The young woman was her biological mother, Emily O'Gorman-Lyman; Katie was the infant in her arms. The painting was an enlarged version of a photograph her grandparents had at their home. Every time Katie encountered it, she got a pang in her gut. She wanted to walk past it as quickly as possible.

"Katie," a small child's voice called.

Katie turned to see seven-year-old Siddharth walking toward her. He was carrying a guitar case that was much too big and heavy for his small, slender frame.

Siddharth caught up to her and said, "I haven't seen you in a long, long time, Katie. You haven't been to the old school."

"I know," Katie commented, squatting down to make eye contact with the small child. "I've been working here."

"You've been working here? This is a nice place. We're going to be having all our classes here from now on."

"Yes, I know. Several people and I have been working here to get the place ready for you."

"Oh," he said, looking up at Emily's painting. "You look nice in that picture. It's very big."

"That's not me, sweetie. That's my mother, Emily."

"She sure looks like you," Siddharth said, straining his neck to look up at the large painting.

"Yes, she does. I hear you and Luis are going to perform for us today."

"Yes, we're going to sing and play guitar."

"Siddharth! Siddharth!" he heard his mother, Anika, calling from across the lobby.

"That's my mom. I better go. See you," he said with a sparkle in his eyes.

Katie used a stairwell near the rear of the auditorium to get to the cafeteria. When she entered, she paused to admire the table settings and decorations. The décor was important to the motif of the facility and this commemorative day. Everything at Emily's Hope, including the tablecloths, lattices, statues, and canvas art that appeared through-out the facility, was all designed by Emily, who had been a successful artist prior to her marriage to William Lyman. Katie and her team of architects and contractors worked meticulously at incorporating Emily's designs within the school that now paid homage to her departed mother.

Katie walked up to one of the tables and picked up a crystal wine glass, which had been specifically designed not to be top heavy. It was a small chalice. Instead of a stem, the cup was enveloped in a delicate lacy design that resembled the trimming of the green tablecloths, which were overlaid with a second white lacy cloth. Etched atop the lattice area, in a downward curve, sparkled the crystal lettering, "Emily's Hope Academy." For this special occasion, these delicate wine cups were being given as favors to the attending guests.

From across the large room, Nydia noticed Katie. Instinctively, Katie, with cup in hand, turned to meet Nydia's gaze. Katie put the cup down in its place, and the two women started to walk toward each other. When they met, they smiled and pecked each other on the cheek.

"This is beautiful," Katie commented, admiring the cafeteria setup. As she looked around, she noticed a large banner with a gold motif that read "Emily's Hope Academy."

"I didn't notice the banner when I came in." She suddenly had tears in her eyes. She bit her lower lip, trying to stifle the tears. "This is great. This is really great. I hope my mother is looking down from heaven and seeing all this."

Nydia reached for a napkin and quickly handed it to Katie. "I'm sure she is," she said as Katie wiped her eyes. "Emily has witnessed the opening of both academies from up above—Emily's Hope I, and now Emily's Hope II."

Katie took a deep breath, stifling more tears. "I was too young to comprehend what Emily's Hope I was or what it meant at that time." The first school was simply called Emily's Hope; the new facility now sported the word "Academy." "Now, it all suddenly hit me. I came down to thank you for breakfast. Now I thank you for this. You've done such a terrific job."

"You've done a great job too. You've designed a beautiful facility in your mother's memory. As magnificent as it is, however, the true Emily's hope is standing right in front of me. I'm sure Emily is very proud of you and all you've done; I certainly am. You have accomplished so much in such a short time. You have also motivated my Luis to be a fine young man. If it were not for you, he wouldn't have gone to college. Remember, he wanted to be a rock musician."

"I don't take credit for any of that. You, Felipe, and my mother, Carolyn, convinced Luis to go to college. Mom gave him a good chewing out when she heard he didn't want to pursue a higher goal; I suspect you did the same. As for this facility and the meaning of Emily's hope, there are numerous souls involved in inspiring us, beginning with Emily, Papa, and Momma, and so on down the line."

"Luis does have a great deal of respect for Carolyn. Even if she weren't his godmother, I don't think he would ever do anything to disappoint her. However, he also tends to follow your lead."

"Yeah, well Mom also read me my rights; I had no choice but to meet her demands. No one messes with Miss Carolyn. Now," she said, half beaming, "Luis is a doctor. He loves kids, and *he's a doctor*. I can't ask for anything more."

"Well, both Emily and Carolyn are very, very proud of you today. Now, wipe your face, and let's get upstairs. I don't want to miss the dedication ceremony."

As they walked to the exit en route to the auditorium, Nydia said, "I thought of something when you said you did not comprehend the magnitude of Emily's Hope I because you were so young. I have to tell you a story." Nydia intertwined her arm with Katie's to draw her closer. "We were all there at the school, Emily's Hope I, so Carolyn can verify what I'm about to say because she was there too. You probably don't remember. Well, I heard a child crying. I was on my way to the kitchen, and you little ones were in one of the rooms when I heard the shriek. The adults were alarmed, so we all came running. Zoe Epstein was the child who was crying. When we investigated, we discovered that you had bitten her arm."

"I bit her?" Katie sounded amused. "Why did I bite her?"

"Honey, you were always good at biting. The first time I met you, you bit your cousin Shannon. You also left her with that scar she still has on her chin today. That's a different story. You bit Zoe, and here's where it gets interesting. When Carolyn asked why, you said, 'She wanted to play with Luis. She can't have him because he's mine.'"

Katie laughed. "How old was I?"

"Well, you must have been five, maybe six—I don't recall. Emily's Hope had been open for a very short time, and we barely knew each other. Well," she continued as they started walking up the stairs and she released Katie's arm, "the thing is I spotted Luis, seated in one of those tiny chairs that they have in daycare or kindergarten. He was pouting, with his hands between his legs, and looking very uncomfortable. I asked him, 'What's the matter, Luisito?' He told me he needed to go to the bathroom. 'Well, why don't you go, my son?' 'I can't go because Katie told me to sit here and not to move. I can't play with Zoe, and I'm not supposed to move. I can't go to the bathroom.'" At this point Nydia couldn't control her laughter. "He said, 'But I can't hold it. I have to pee.' He started to cry. You came over and started to push me away, and you commanded me, 'Go away. Leave him alone. He's mine!' You pointed a tiny little finger in my face and gave me the sternest look I've ever seen on such a tiny child."

"I really did that to you?" Katie was stunned.

"Oh, yes. You were adamant, and poor little Luis was sitting there, terrified to move. Of course, that's when I finally realized you were a very strong-willed child, and audacious to boot. Carolyn picked you up and carried you away, as she often did whenever you got into trouble. You were always getting into trouble. As Carolyn whisked you away, I took Luis to the bathroom. Before I could get his body stocking down, Niagara Falls broke loose. He looked so embarrassed."

"Oh, my God. I was a terrible kid. Poor Luis. Poor Zoe. Poor you. I'm sorry."

"The point I'm trying to make is you knew what you wanted. You went for it, and you still go for it. You have set your goals and accomplished much. You're a wonderful young woman. I'm glad you succeeded at influencing Luis. He's done well, he's happy, and he continues to follow you wherever you go."

"Well," Katie responded, looking sullen, "evidently, I've been controlling him all his life. Maybe that's not such a good thing. Sometimes I think I can make him do anything. I don't want to control him. I just want him, but I want him to maintain his right to free will."

"He has free will. Don't you think he loves it when you grab him by his tie and drag him along like a puppy? I've watched the two of you when we have a party or important function. You grab his tie, and he follows with a big grin on his face. Why do you suppose he doesn't object?"

"I don't know. Why?"

"From day one, the two of you had a mutual attraction. Around you, Luis doesn't fear rejection. No one wants to be rejected. When you pull him by his tie, he knows he has an audience, and he's being accepted. He follows along, and he's saying, 'Look at me; she wants me.' For him, that makes up for all the teasing and abuse he endured. That's why he always has that victory grin on his face when you're around."

"I hope I won't pull him in the wrong direction."

"I doubt you ever will."

"Well, we had the usual argument on our way here, and I don't think Luis is very happy with me right now."

"My child, in that, you need to ask Little God for guidance," Nydia advised. For Nydia, "Little God" was her way of saying "the Baby Jesus." People who knew her understood what she meant. Nydia was literally translating from the diminutive and endearing Spanish word *Diosito*, and in her heart and mind, she always pictured God as the infant Jesus. The image of Baby Jesus and His mother Mary had become more important and endearing to her during the barren years when she had unsuccessfully tried to become pregnant. She continued advising Katie by adding, "With Little God's help, you and Luis will hopefully make the right decisions. No one else can do that for you. We love you, honey. And I love my Luisito with all my heart. There is so much good in you, but you really need to do some reflection so you can resolve this between you and him."

"I know. I know, but it's hard for me to do that."

They arrived at the front of the auditorium. The guests were starting to take their seats. The first two rows were reserved for the immediate family. That included Nydia, her husband Felipe, and Luis. Carolyn and Matthew were already in the first row with their sons, Kieran and Stevie. Carolyn's parents and Katie's other two grandparents occupied the first four seats. Monsignor Uncle Patrick was also in the first row, dressed in a suit and tie.

"I better greet the folks," she informed Nydia. "I haven't spoken with them yet."

"Well, I see my husband; I'll sit with him. I'll see you later, Katie."

Katie started kissing and greeting her family. Uncle Neil was there with his wife, Camille. Their three daughters were in the second row, along with their husbands. Soon, everyone was seated, and the guests started to quiet down, waiting for the show to start. Katie sat next to Uncle Patrick in the front row. Expecting Luis to join them after his performance, she held the adjoining two seats, in case Siddharth needed to sit with them.

The lights dimmed, the audience hushed, and a twelve-year-old emcee walked to the podium and introduced Dr. Ernestine Holder, the president of Emily's Hope. Dr. Holder welcomed the people in attendance, thanked several individuals, gave a brief description of the eighty-five acre facility, and introduced Mr. Sean O'Gorman as "the founder whom we all know as Papa Sean."

Papa Sean took his place at the podium and thanked Dr. Holder. "A forest burns," he started, "and the fire and embers kill everything in its path. A few years later, you return to the spot to find beautiful wildflowers and strong young trees that withstand the winds of a winter's storm. And so it is with Emily's Hope. For those of you who don't know the history, my only daughter, Emily, was killed in 1984.

Her only daughter, Katie, almost died that same night. As my wife Momma Ellen and I struggled with the loss of our young daughter and prayed by my little granddaughter's bedside, we realized that spousal and child abuse has become an epidemic. We believed we needed to do something to right this wrong. That way, Emily's death would not have been in vain. At first, we wanted to do something to help the children who are victims of child abuse. However, we realized that you cannot focus on them alone. The entire family unit needs to be nurtured. It was a tall order, but with the help of family and friends, Momma Ellen and I succeeded at getting our project off the ground. We sought and found an excellent staff, many of whom have been working with us these many years. We do concentrate on the children, but we do not limit the resources to them. The younger ones receive all of their care and education here. We have an afterschool center for our students. Children who attend school elsewhere may also partake in our afterschool activities. Our doors are never closed to anyone in need. In the audience now, I see several young adults who were once students at Emily's Hope. They come back from time to time, and I hope they will continue to come back. After all, we are all family."

Sean paused to clear his throat and wipe his eyes. "Those children, and the many children I see here today, are the beautiful flowers and strong trees that rise out of my Emily's ashes. With time, many become diamonds in the sun, spirited young men and women with strong and lovely souls. We have had many such successes. Several of our alumni have fine careers today. I understand that two of them, Dr. Luis López and Dr. Zoe Epstein-Katz, will be performing for us today. Dr. López plays a mean guitar, and Dr. Epstein-Katz is an accomplished violinist. I hope we can take the credit for some of that because here our children are exposed to academics and numerous enrichment activities—from art to martial arts, from music to meditation, ballroom and international dancing, and a lot of other wonderful activities. I'm going to get off the stage and turn your attention to our entertainers in a moment, but first I must say something about Emily's daughter, my granddaughter Katie. Katie is a bit like my wife, Momma Ellen. Neither one of them likes to take center stage. They are quite reticent when it comes to that. But for those of you who know Katie, you know how dynamic she is. She is a force to be reckoned with. I want to thank my granddaughter for all the work she has done because she is the power and foundation of this newest facility. I also thank her wonderful crew. Katie designed our new Emily's Hope, incorporating a lot of Emily's art within the facility and the adjoining grounds; she also supervised every aspect of the construction. Thank you, my darling." He bowed in her direction, and Katie blew him kiss. "I also thank Mrs. Nydia López, who is responsible for today's luncheon arrangements. Mrs. López is our daytime dietician and head of food services. She has asked me to inform those of you who submitted the form for your particular dietary needs to consult your waiter when you get downstairs. Now, let's get on with the show."

Luis was among the first to perform. He and Stevie were part of the bagpipe quartet that played a traditional Irish reel. Later, he performed with Siddharth Choudury. They were accompanied by nine-year-old Tameeka Jackson at the piano, twelve-year-old Parizad Ibrahim on drums, and a string sextet led by Zoe, who played her violin. Siddharth introduced each of the performers while standing on a portable platform in order to make up the difference in height between him and his partner, Luis. His large guitar hung from a broad strap on his left shoulder.

"The first song that we're about to perform is dedicated to Papa Sean and Momma Ellen," the small boy announced. "That was Luis's idea; it's a song from the olden days."

The adults in the audience burst into laughter. Luis joined the cacophony and faced away from the audience while shaking his head. When everyone had calmed down, Siddharth continued. "Luis likes old songs, and so do I. The second song was written by Luis. We dedicate that one to Dr. Holder, Carolyn, and the staff at Emily's Hope because you guys have helped us when we had little hope. Now we have lots of hope." The audience laughed again, this time in approval.

Zoe's string sextet and nine-year-old Tameeka on piano led the presentation. Siddharth waited nervously for him and Luis to join in as vocalists. Momma Ellen recognized the instrumental presentation immediately, and she gasped with swelled emotion before the lyrics began. It was the Tom Jones and Harvey Schmidt 1965 composition, *My Cup Runneth Over.* When the two vocalists, Siddharth and Luis, joined in, the older audience members exploded with applause because many of them were familiar with the lyrics. Tears welled in their eyes, Momma Ellen wept, and Katie leaned forward in her seat, for she enjoyed the touching song. When they finished the song, there wasn't a dry eye among the older adults in the audience.

"Next, we sing Luis's song," Siddharth said. "He wrote it especially for this occasion to honor the people who have helped us stand tall. It's called 'Cosmic Me.' Here goes."

Parizad, the drummer, and Tameeka, the pianist, did the percussion introduction to the song. Siddharth joined with bass guitar. Luis and the violin sextet entered with the remaining strings. Then Luis and Siddharth contributed the lyrics to the rock-and-roll composition.

> The sun is rising quickly, and I am walking tall.
> I'm walking towards that sunrise, escaping from a darkness
> That was yanking at my soul and causing me to fall.
> The light is growing brighter, diminishing the starkness.
> I can see the blue sky, the clouds are rolling by.
> If I reach a little higher, I'll surely reach that star.
> It will soothe me with its warmth and coo a lullaby.
> I'll veer its cosmic dust with a well-intended spar.
>
> I'm a child of the heavens; I'm a son of the earth.
> I'm part of the cosmos; I'm punting with the moon.
> No matter what is thrown at me, I'll always find my berth.
> Even when the ocean's rough, I'm sure to find my boon.
>
> When I was just a boy, my father beat me with a cane.
> My mother was so scared of him, for she often got the same.
> I whimpered and called for her, and I could sense her shame.
> My heart was full of hate; my soul cried out in pain.
> I wished I had the strength to slay that wicked man.
> He drank and staggered more each day as my pain became a rage.
> The day came for me to act and carry out my plan.
> But I was rescued from that wicked act by a truly selfless sage.

I'm a child of the heavens; I'm a son of the earth.

I'm part of the cosmos; I'm punting with the moon.

No matter what is thrown at me, I'll always find my berth.

Even when the ocean's rough, I'm sure to find my boon.

I'm a child of the heavens; I'm a son of the earth.

I'm part of the cosmos; I'm punting with the moon.

No matter what is thrown at me, I'll always find my berth.

Even when the ocean's rough, I'm sure to find my boon.

When the musicians were finished, the audience gave them a standing ovation. Luis pushed his guitar to rest on his back and lifted Siddharth above his head. He yelled, "Ladies and gentlemen, give it up for Mr. Siddharth Choudury!" The audience exploded, and Luis gave Siddharth a big kiss. "You're a hit, buddy," he told the now proud Siddharth. Luis then turned to the other musicians. They each bowed as they were showered with applause.

As they cleared the stage, Luis, with his guitar flung across his back and holding Siddharth's guitar in his right hand, carried Siddharth off the stage. Anika, Siddharth's proud mother, was waiting for her son at the foot of the steps, ready to take him from Luis.

"I have him," Luis said. "Where are you sitting? We'll join you. Was he a hit, or what?"

"You were all a hit," Anika corrected him with a smile, and she pointed to their seats. "That was a heartfelt song, Luis."

From her location, Katie watched as Luis disappeared up the aisle with Siddharth and Anika. She sat back, vexed and disappointed. From her seat, Carolyn noticed what had transpired. She noted that Katie had crossed her legs and arms, and her face advertised her emotions. During the rest of the performance, Carolyn continued to catch a glimpse of her daughter and instinctively knew that Katie's mind was definitely not on the performance. Carolyn let out a sigh of exasperation. She whispered something in her husband's ear. Matthew then looked at Katie, and said, "Oh, boy. Here we go again. One of these days, she's going to burst a blood vessel."

Carolyn sat back to try to enjoy the show and intermittently continued to eye Katie's expression. Eventually, she thought she had allowed Katie to stew long enough. She got out of her seat, walked over to Katie, and whispered in her ear, "Please come with me."

Katie did not budge. Instead, she rolled her eyes at Carolyn.

"This is not an invitation," Carolyn commanded in a whisper. "Get up now, and come with me."

Reluctantly, Katie rose from her seat. She followed her mother through a front exit. They walked to the elevators, and Carolyn activated one of them with a key. They were soon on the third floor, where Carolyn led her into a room. When they entered, Carolyn asked, "What's wrong?"

In the meantime, Nydia was also aware of the live show that was overlapping the stage performance. After Carolyn and Katie left the auditorium, she walked up to Luis, who was in an aisle seat, several rows up.

"Luisito," she whispered, "*Necesito hablar contigo./*I need to speak with you."

He quickly picked up his guitar and followed her through a rear exit.

Upstairs, Katie answered Carolyn's question with a sullen face. "Nothing's wrong."

"Look at you," Carolyn challenged her, "a twenty-five-year-old woman behaving like a child." The tears rolled down Katie's face, and Carolyn handed her a pack of tissues from her purse. "You have to stop being so insecure. If jealousy were indeed green, you would be a fir tree right now. Are you going to continue being jealous every time Luis is in the presence of another woman? When will you stop? When you're eighty?"

"He has been rehearsing with Siddharth for several weeks now. How do I know he hasn't been with her all this time? He just walked off with her, carrying the kid in his arms."

"For heaven's sake, Katie! Are you jealous of the child too? We really need to talk. I was too permissive with you when you were a child, afraid I might crumble a delicate flower. When you became an adolescent, I attributed your behavior to teenage insanity. Apparently, I have done something wrong; it hurts me to see you like this. Stop sabotaging yourself. Please, honey! You're hurting yourself. This is not healthy! I don't understand! Please help me to understand! You're an intelligent, talented, beautiful woman. You excel at everything, including this self-destructive behavior. It's a contradiction. At such a young age, you have three master's degrees and a doctorate, but you don't love yourself."

Katie turned her head to look away from her mother, and Carolyn continued.

"If you loved yourself, you wouldn't be this insecure. If you weren't this insecure, you wouldn't feel so threatened." She held Katie's face in her hands, attempting to look up into her eyes. "I love you, darling. You have so many people who love you and admire you. You don't need to be jealous or envious of anyone. I wish I could make you understand that."

"Why did he go off with them? He must have seen me in the front row. I know he saw me."

With jealousy, Carolyn thought, *logic and intelligence can apparently be overshadowed.* On tip toes, she kissed Katie on the cheek and said, "Oh, honey, you still don't understand. You're not hearing me. No one is going to steal Luis away from you, but if you continue to behave like this, you're going to lose to your own inner conflict. You aren't being honest with yourself, and you aren't being fair to Luis. You want to keep him tethered. You can't do that. The more you pin someone down, the more they'll want to fly away."

Carolyn's cell phone vibrated in her purse. It was Nydia.

"I saw what happened in the auditorium."

"I wonder who didn't," Carolyn responded.

"Has she explained it to you?" Nydia inquired. "If she hasn't, I have the other half here, and you are not going to believe this."

"I'm listening."

"Luis and Katie had an argument in the car, and he said he didn't want to run into the monsignor because he and Katie are living in sin, and Luis feels uncomfortable when Patrick is present."

"So of course, she sat next to Patrick, and Luis reacted. God, I love them, but when are these two fools going to grow up?"

"You've got me," Nydia replied. "I hope it's soon because I'm getting too old for this."

"You and me both. Let me please speak to your son."

Nydia handed the phone to Luis. "Carolyn wants to speak to you."

"Hi, Mrs. G."

"Hi, Dr. L. Katie and I are in room 317. For some strange reason, she's upset. Could you please come up here and help us out?"

"Anything for you, Mrs. G."

"Borrow the elevator key from Nydia or ask one of the guards to help you because the building is on lock-up above the auditorium floors."

"I have nothing to say to him," Katie commented when Carolyn flipped the phone off. She turned to stare out the large, heavily tinted bay window that permitted her to see out, but no one to see in. It displayed the willow tree fountain and the gardens below. On the other side of the gardens, she could see the Emily's Hope residential facility. It had been constructed to house families in transition. Carolyn grabbed Katie's elbow, coaxing her daughter to face her.

"You sat next to Patrick after Luis told you Patrick's presence makes him uncomfortable. Tell me what's wrong with this picture, Katie. I think you owe Luis an apology. Then you can go back downstairs and sit in the rear of the auditorium, if either one of you doesn't want to sit with the family. When we go down to the cafeteria, the two of you can sit at your own little table. We'll put one outside for you, facing China, if you want. I don't care where you sit, but you should be sensitive to another person's feelings, Katie." Katie rolled her eyes, and Carolyn said, "There you go again, rolling your eyes at me. That's really mature of you. You know, I'm going to discuss this with your father, and then you and I, and whoever else needs to be present, are going to talk about this until we get to the bottom of what's holding you back. You need some serious intervention. I'm done coddling you, and we're running out of time. You need to change course before you collide."

They heard a knock at the door. Carolyn responded, "It's unlocked; come in, honey."

Luis entered with guitar in hand. "I'm here," he said, shrugging his shoulders while he studied each woman's face. "I'm really sorry, Carolyn. I didn't mean to upset you and my mother. Katie and I had a little misunderstanding; you know how it is. Katie, I'm sorry. I didn't know you were going to get this upset. I told you I didn't want to run into Uncle Patrick because, well, you know. I thought you sat next to him on purpose—to irk me, you know." Katie continued to look sullen. "You do that kind of stuff all the time—like this morning with my coat." Her features softened. "Or last week when you locked me out of the car in the rain and feigned driving off. I figured this time was no different, so I decided to ignore you. I wasn't snubbing you, cross my heart." Katie sighed and Luis concluded with, "I'm sorry I upset you, honest."

Katie walked up to him and relieved him of his guitar. Then she pulled him toward her by grabbing the sash of his costume. He smiled as Nydia had previously described. "So we're okay?" he asked, and she nodded in affirmation.

"Don't start behaving like you need a motel room," Carolyn admonished them. "Katie, let go of his sash. Let's get back downstairs."

Katie released his sash, and Luis smoothed it back into place.

"Yes, Mrs. G.," Luis said, wrapping an arm around Katie's waist, ready to follow Carolyn out of the room.

Carolyn stood with her hand on the door handle, contemplating the two of them. With her high heels, Katie appeared taller than Luis. "Let me ask you something, Luis."

"Yes, Mrs. G.?"

"Do you still go to church on Sundays?"

"Well, of course, Mrs. G." He almost volunteered that he went to confession, but stopped short of saying it.

"Do you feel comfortable when you're in church—in the Lord's house?"

"I see where you're going with this." He held out his index finger.

Carolyn pushed his finger away. "Well, since you're a mind reader, Dr. L., tell me why you feel so uncomfortable around Patrick. Do you think you're so important that he came here today specifically to judge you?"

Luis's face dropped, and he looked very contrite. This was his godmother chewing him out, for whom he had tremendous respect. He was embarrassed to look her in the eye.

"You're usually the sensible one, but have you lost your senses too? This is Emily's day," Carolyn said. "It's a day for Papa Sean and Momma Ellen. It's not a day for either one of you."

Her stern look fell on both of them. Their faces were flushed, and they looked down at the floor.

"Look at me!" Carolyn demanded, and they complied. "Papa and Momma lost their only daughter at the hands of a very disturbed man. Neither one of you knows what it is to lose a child, especially in that manner. You also don't know what it is to live with the fear of losing one. Katie, I'm not diminishing your suffering or the contributions you've made. You have done a wonderful job making Papa and Momma's dream possible with this magnificent facility. Luis, you offered a lovely dedication, and your song is wonderful. However, for the rest of the day, don't either of you dare to make this about you, or God help me, I'll make it a living hell for both of you." She paused while Luis stood still, afraid to move a muscle. Katie was quiet and sullen. Carolyn continued the reprimand, adding, "And after you get out of church on Sunday, I want you both at my house for some serious talking. Do you understand me?"

"Yes, ma'am," was all Luis could say as he hung his head in shame. Katie said nothing and suppressed the desire to roll her eyes again.

Three

◇◇◇

1983-1985

In Harlem, they separated and saved some undamaged skin that the doctors had scraped from Luis's burn areas. From those scrapings, they succeeded in growing new skin tissue, which was later transferred with the toddler to Einstein Hospital in the Bronx, where they continued to incubate and harvest the skin for the many grafting procedures he would undergo in future years. When he was well enough to travel, they sent him to a rehabilitation center in Westchester County.

Before he arrived in Westchester, practically every staff member knew the three-year-old child was on his way and waited for him with anticipation. Nydia, a dietician, was no exception. When Luis finally arrived, the word went through the grapevine. The little boy had captured the hearts of practically everyone in New York and beyond. Adoption inquiries about him arrived daily by the hundreds. "How could anyone do such a terrible thing to an innocent child?" was a constantly asked question.

Detectives Garrity and Esposito were among Luis's numerous fans. Now that he had arrived at Westchester County, he was close to their hometown, so they visited him frequently. They were taken by the angelic-looking boy, who turned out to be quite precocious. Whenever Garrity arrived in the evenings, he was also taken by a woman in her late twenties whom he often found in the room rocking Luis or feeding him. Garrity and the lady got to know one another; she was Nydia López. Her husband, Felipe, was a radiologist at the same rehab facility. Nydia, Felipe, and Garrity's friend Esposito had something else in common. All three of them were musicians. They played acoustic guitar. Esposito, an avid rock fan, also enjoyed playing the electric bass guitar. Felipe's talent included bongos and keyboard.

Nydia was so engaged in daydreaming about having a baby that she could only see God as the Baby Jesus. Her home was filled with displays of Little God in pictures, statuettes, and stained glass. There were images of Jesus by Himself or with His Virgin Mother. Nydia had one lone display of the Sacred Heart of Jesus. "And," she would say, "isn't it a terrible shame that there are some parents in this world who don't appreciate the little living treasures the Good Lord blessed them with?" Garrity agreed, noticing the adoration she felt for Luis in her eyes. Nydia knew plenty about little living treasures. She had suffered three miscarriages and a hysterectomy. She remained long into the night, admiring Luis, God's most recent little living treasure. She returned early the next morning to make sure he ate his breakfast. She brought him fresh fruit and homemade cake, and her husband Felipe looked in on Luis in the middle of the day. The bilingual Dominican couple helped the rehabilitation staff to communicate with the Spanish-speaking child. And so it was that when Garrity discovered that Nydia and Felipe wanted to be the toddler's foster parents, and seven years later his adoptive parents, he put in a good word for them each time. Garrity, Esposito, and the Lópezes continued to be friends for many years to come.

When the Lópezes brought Luis home with them, Nydia checked on the toddler two or three times during the night. Felipe was amused by this, and he advised her, "Relax, honey. He isn't going to disappear during the night; he'll be fine. Get some sleep."

To be a full-time parent to the small toddler, Nydia quit her job and settled into that mode with fervor. She lovingly applied oils onto his rippled skin in order to keep it supple and encouraged him to do the painful exercises the therapist had recommended to loosen his tendons, sinews, and muscles. She dressed him with the greatest of care because she was afraid she might irritate something. She sang old Spanish and English songs to him while strumming her classical guitar and noticed that he enjoyed those sessions. At first, he stood in front of her with one small hand on the guitar, feeling the music's vibration as he listened. He started to imitate her singing. He pulled the guitar strings and giggled with delight. One evening, Felipe came home with a small guitar for the child. Luis squealed with joy as he took possession of his small instrument. Felipe started teaching him a few chords, and Luis played them perfectly.

Garrity and Esposito dropped by about once a month, and Nydia always insisted that they stay for dinner. While they sat in the living room chatting with Felipe, Luis showed them his guitar. In his still simple English, he said, "I play; I sing."

"That's terrific, buddy," Esposito commented. "I'm a guitar man myself. Let me hear what you've got."

The child did not understand, so Felipe explained in Spanish, "Detective Esposito asked you to play for him. Go ahead, my son."

Luis was delighted to honor the request and played an old Spanish melody.

"That was great," James Esposito complimented him. "I know that. It's *Cielito Lindo*/Pretty Sky. Lend me the guitar, pal. I'll teach you one from my grandfather's country. It's called Roman Guitar." He reached out for Luis's little guitar. Apparently, the child understood and gave him the instrument.

"No," Felipe told his son, "get him one of the big guitars." Luis ran down the hall and returned soon with his father's guitar; the instrument overwhelmed him with its size. He struggled to hold its neck above his head in order to keep it from scraping the floor.

Esposito played beautifully, and Luis listened attentively. "You show me?" he asked in broken English when Esposito was finished.

"It will be my pleasure. Come here," Esposito beckoned. In a short time, he was teaching Luis the proper chords. By evening's end, Esposito, Luis, Felipe, and Nydia were entertaining Garrity with their repertoire.

When Esposito returned again on a different night, Luis played "Roman Guitar" for him; Esposito commended him on an excellent job. Then he showed him the contents of a bag he had brought. "Roman Guitar and Pretty Sky are nice, pal, but you need a more modern mix. This," he said, going through a pack of tapes, "is a representation of the modern guitarists, including Les Paul, the father of the electric guitar, which is the heart of rock and roll." Sensing that Luis didn't understand a word he had said, Esposito added, "Never mind. We'll listen to this."

Nydia was very pleased with the interest Esposito had taken in Luis and his talent. During the day, she encouraged Luis to practice from the songbooks Esposito had given him. Because it involved the skill of reading, it was slow but steady. Luis was a tenacious student because the music was speaking to his inner being. There was something hovering in the distant reaches of his mind that he couldn't quite comprehend. The music teased a distant memory that would not break loose.

When Luis was almost five, Garrity stopped by with a job prospect for Nydia, if she was interested. He knew a family by the name of O'Gorman who wanted to dedicate a facility to their daughter's memory.

"Well, it so happens that they will need a dietician to work there. You can go back to work," concluded Garrity, "and still look after Luis. It shouldn't be a problem. I suggest you go down and see these people; I have his card here. Remind him that I spoke to him about you."

Nydia called, and Mr. O'Gorman invited her to interview with the O'Gorman family over brunch on a Saturday, at his residence.

"By all means," he said, "bring your family with you. I would love to meet you and your ward. Detective Garrity told me a lot about him. You and I may have something in common, so I would love to sit and chat with you and the boy."

The O'Gormans had a catered family brunch once a month on a Saturday in order to accommodate their son Patrick, a priest, who worked most of Sunday. It also gave the women time off because the men were in charge of the affair. At Momma Ellen's insistence, it had become a family tradition.

Nydia went without Felipe, who had to work that Saturday. When she arrived, Camille, Neil's wife, met her and Luis at the door and led them to the parlor. Nydia felt a bit on edge when she saw so many people gathered in one place. It was definitely a family reunion. Neil's three daughters—thirteen-year-old Shannon, eleven-year-old Elizabeth, and seven-year-old Courtney—were there. Little Katie, who was the same age as Luis, was in Momma Ellen's lap, and Carolyn was pacing back and forth with baby Stevie in her arms. When Momma Ellen and Carolyn saw the diminutive Luis, who looked more like a three-year-old, dressed in his smart gray suit with a blue shirt and a designer tie with matching handkerchief in his breast pocket, they were immediately taken with him. Without hesitation, the boy walked right up to Papa Sean, who was seated facing the door, and climbed into his lap. "Papa, Papa," he said to Sean in Spanish, touching his chin. Then he stood in the old man's lap and stroked his cheek a couple of times. He wrapped his arms around him and started to sob uncontrollably. Sean wrapped an arm around the child and stroked his hair in an attempt to comfort him.

The adults watched silently, all obviously taken by the poignant moment. Carolyn noticed that the boy had a dark pink birthmark on his neck that turned cherry red as he continued to sob. She felt ill as she stared at the birthmark and the child who couldn't stop crying. She wondered if it was possible for him to burst a blood vessel for he was wailing. He was also so small.

Elizabeth and Courtney were in awe. Shannon was moved by the incident. Katie watched solemnly. From his mother's arms, little Stevie pointed at Luis and said something that sounded like "Duh, duh, duh."

Carolyn held his extended little hand between her thumb and forefinger and agreed, "Yes, baby hurt." She kissed her son on the cheek and continued to study Luis with great concern. It was obvious that something had struck a chord in the young boy's mind. Katie left Momma Ellen's lap and walked up to Papa Sean's knee, where she continued to study the strange child with concern.

Unknown to everyone who was present, Luis was hit with the odor of English Leather aftershave the moment he entered the room. The scent produced a déjà vu moment, and drew him directly to Papa Sean, who brought him to an opaque memory of his grandfather. In turn, that opaque memory triggered a rush of distant memories of a doting grandfather who lifted him high and then pitched and rolled him like a barnstorming plane. It was a grandfather who handed him finger food and ice cream. It was a grandfather who carried him on his shoulders and floated tree leaves with him in a puddle of water. It was a grandfather who lulled him to sleep at night with the haunting music of his flute. The uncontrollable sobs Luis now wept into Sean's collar were the sobs that asked, "Where have you been? Why did you leave me to suffer so? Why didn't you come to get me?" But they were questions that were never asked because Luis did not know how to articulate them. He only knew how to cry them out to an old man who had died so long ago without ever saying good-bye to him. And he cried and wailed from the inner being of his soul into Sean's collar. All those memories had come in an instant flash, but the wails of a hurting boy continued to flow. Sean started to pat him on the back in an effort to soothe his pain.

Sean rose with Luis in his arms and gently shook him up and down, still trying to ease his obvious pain. Luis clung to him, catching the whiff of English Leather between sobs. Then he started to calm down, believing in the recesses of his mind that Nydia had brought him home to grandpa. He started to pant and hiccup as the tears subsided. "Papa," he was able to say once again, and he started to kiss his Papa on the cheek. The familiar taste and smell of English Leather was now on the child's lips. He licked his lips and smiled with delight, and again said, "Papa."

Nydia went to take the child from Sean, and he went into a tirade, screaming no and trying to kick her away while holding onto Sean's collar for dear life.

Sean calmly waved her away. "It's okay, Mrs. López," he said. Nydia stepped away, and Sean started to speak soothingly to Luis, rubbing his back and calming him down. When the boy was under control, Sean spoke to Nydia again. "I've had four children of my own, and my wife can tell you, they also had moments like this. Not as profound as this little guy, but they each had their share of a tantrum or two. This little guy, however, is trying to tell us something. Only God knows what it is. What's his name?"

"Luis José Walker."

"So, Luis, what's your story?" Sean asked.

When Luis did not respond and looked nonplussed, Nydia volunteered, "It's pronounced 'Loo-ees.' We call him Luisito."

Sean looked at the child. "What's your story, Luisito?" Again, the child did not respond and stared bewilderedly at everyone in the room. His small cheeks and ears were flushed. Someone handed Sean a tissue, which he used to clean the boy's face.

Matthew had entered to inform everyone that brunch was ready when the commotion started. Hearing the child's cry, Neil and Patrick had also rushed into the room. Now that Luis had calmed down, Patrick said, "Papa, the caterer has already prepared the dining table. We can start as soon as you're ready."

"What do you say we go into the dining room and have some brunch, Luisito?" Sean asked Luis. "All that crying must have used up a lot of energy." Then he turned to Patrick and said, "Please escort Mrs. López to her seat. The boy will sit with me."

"Yes, Papa," Patrick said as he volunteered his arm to Nydia.

In the dining room, Carolyn placed Stevie in a high chair and then looked for Katie to place her in a booster seat.

"Where's Katie?" she asked nervously when she realized the child was missing.

"She walked away from me," Ellen commented. "I thought she came in here."

"Matthew!" Carolyn yelled. "Don't just stand there. Look for her. Maybe she went outside."

"Don't get excited," he countered. "We'll find her. She's probably still in the parlor."

Just then, Katie walked in, carrying a furry stuffed toy. Carolyn breathed a sigh of relief. "Thank God," she said, remembering the last time the child had walked off. Matthew had found her a block away from home, en route to find her mother. At that time, he informed her it was impossible to walk to heaven, where her mommy was. This time, she had gone to the playroom to get the toy.

She walked up to Luis, who was sitting in Sean's lap, and held the stuffed animal out to him. The adults watched her with astonishment because Katie wasn't one to share her possessions. Luis still looked a little bewildered, his mind trying to grasp the memories that had flooded him and the belief that he and his grandpa were together again. He then focused on Katie and the toy, and he accepted it from her. He continued to stare at her, and he watched her silently as Carolyn led her to a chair and lifted her into a booster seat. Like Nydia, Carolyn took great pride in dressing her children, especially the cute little princess she had inherited from Emily. She was adorable, with her blond hair flowing over the dark pink sweater that covered a lighter pink and white plaid dress. She too was small for her age, but she was slightly taller than Luis. The family settled down to enjoy their meal. Sean placed a second plate next to his and started to serve himself and Luis. Now and then Katie would steal a furtive glance at the young guest. At times, he cauaght her staring at him, and they would momentarily and quietly lock in each other's gaze.

Celtic music filled the dining room as each person continued to pass one item or another. Over the sound of tableware, the soothing and ethereal music did not escape Luis's ears. He heard the sound of a penny whistle.

Luis reached for Sean's hand, and Sean allowed him to inspect it. "Where's the toot?" Luis asked in Spanish. He then turned to check Sean's other hand. "Where's the toot, Papa?" he asked him again.

Sean turned to Nydia, and she explained. "He's asking you, 'Where's the toot?'"

"Toot?" Sean asked, not making any sense of the question.

"Well," Nydia explained, "the word he's using can mean whistle or toot."

"Toot? Aha, you hear the penny whistle," Sean said, and he got up with Luis still in his arms. He walked to one of the wall speakers and pointed. "The toot is in there." He whistled the melody to Luis. Then he pointed to the speaker again. Luis smiled and hugged Sean's neck, for he was convinced that he had indeed found his grandfather.

"Is Luis a Spaniard?" Papa Sean asked Nydia.

"I don't know. All I know is that he speaks Spanish, but he doesn't speak Castilian Spanish, if that's what you mean."

"Well," Papa Sean responded, "I know they play the bagpipes in northern Spain, in the Basque and Galicean areas. In Peru, they play whistles that sound like flutes or penny whistles."

"He could be from the highlands of Peru," Camille volunteered.

"He looks Caucasian; he doesn't look Incan," Shannon said.

"Not everyone who lives in Peru looks Incan," Papa Sean corrected her. "Caucasians live there too. Well, we have a mystery on our hands. He speaks Spanish, but not Castilian. His last name is Walker, but I know several Latinos with Anglo-sounding names. He may have come in contact with someone who plays a penny whistle or flute or even a bagpipe. He has me confused with someone he knows. Who are you, little man?"

"Papa," the child said again.

Momma Ellen observed that Carolyn appeared nervous and was having problems getting Stevie to eat his baby food.

"A Carolyn Rua," she offered, speaking with a melodic Irish brogue, "trade seats with me, dear. I'll take care of the *buachaillin*." Ellen had lived in the States since she was thirteen, nearly forty years. She spoke American English as well as any American could possibly speak it. However, when she was with family, she reverted to her Irish brogue. When she didn't speak Irish, she sprinkled Irish lexicon into English. She referred to Carolyn as "Rua" or "Carolyn Rua," alluding to Carolyn's saffron red hair. The *buachaillin*, or little boy, was Stevie. She rose from her seat, holding her plate and utensils. As Carolyn reacted to her offer, Momma Ellen continued, "When rearing little ones, you must learn to take care of yourself first. My sons did not become self-sufficient overnight. You have to start teaching them early not to rely on you for everything. Now is as good a time as any. You sit and enjoy your meal. Stevie will not perish by waiting a few extra minutes."

"I'll try to remember that, Momma," Carolyn said as she walked past her, carrying her plate and utensils.

"Children need to be taught to honor their parents," Momma Ellen continued. "What better way to honor your parents than to serve them brunch on a nice Saturday morning? Look what a fine young man your husband has turned out to be. That didn't happen by osmosis, dear."

Matthew smiled at Carolyn from across the table and said, "I'm a fine young man, Honey-Lyn," and he held up his orange juice in a toasting gesture.

Carolyn smiled back and shook her head. "Don't encourage him, Momma. There are times he conveniently forgets to pick up after himself or to throw out the garbage."

"I'll tell you how to correct that later, dear," Momma Ellen replied. "I promise you he'll be more mindful, or he'll have to deal with me."

"You're in trouble, Mattie," Neil said, laughing at his little brother. "Trust me; I speak from experience. Never, ever cause your wife to complain to Momma about you. I advise you not to wait for the boom to fall before you change the error of your ways."

"I don't believe I have anything to fear from Momma. Do I, Momma?"

"I don't know, Mattie," Momma responded. "Why don't we wait and see?"

After brunch, Papa Sean and the women retired to the parlor with the three small children in tow. The older girls went out to play. The men were left to clean up and prepare the dining table for dessert, which would be served later. Katie left Momma Ellen's side and stood next to her grandpa, who had Luis in his lap. She took hold of Luis's hand.

"Come, Luisito," she invited. Luis looked timidly at his Papa Sean.

"Go ahead," Sean encouraged him, lifting him off his lap and onto the floor. Luis stood shyly by, first looking at Sean, then at Nydia, who also gave him permission to go and waved at him to move.

Katie grabbed his hand again, his other hand still holding the stuffed animal. "Can we go outside, Papa?"

"Don't ask me—ask Mommy," he said, turning to Carolyn.

"I'd rather you stay inside, honey," Carolyn informed her. "Go to the playroom."

Katie left, pulling her new friend behind her, and the adults soon turned to business. They shared each other's hopes about their future endeavors regarding a facility to help abused children and inquired about Nydia's qualifications to determine if she was the right prospect to fill one of the positions. As they were concluding their business, Carolyn recognized Katie's screeching coming from outside the house.

She handed Stevie over to Momma Ellen and quickly dashed out of the house.

Outside, Shannon was unsuccessfully trying to hold onto Katie while Katie cried at the top of her lungs, "Let me go!"

"What's going on here?" Carolyn demanded while other family members came up behind her.

"She bit me and hit me, Aunt Carolyn," Shannon complained, trying to prevent Katie from doing further damage by holding her at arm's length. "She bit me twice."

"Why?"

"She wanted to use the big kids' swing, Aunt Carolyn," little Courtney volunteered. "Shannon tried to stop her, and she bit her. She also hit her on the chin with the swing. She's bad, Aunt Carolyn, real bad."

"I'm bad?" Katie seethed. "Your mother, you fucking tattletale! I'll fucking kill you, you know!"

Courtney gasped and remained speechless upon hearing the tirade, and Carolyn grapped Katie by her elbows and looked into the child's pouting face.

"Katie, you can't say things like that."

"Oh, yes I can."

"Well, you shouldn't. And didn't I tell you not to go outside?"

"No."

"What do you mean no?"

"You said, 'I'd rather you stay inside.' You didn't say, 'Don't go outside.'"

Carolyn took a deep breath, expelled it, and said, "You know what I meant! Don't play games with me! You also need to apologize to Shannon and Courtney."

"No," she replied, pouting and glaring back at Carolyn.

In the meantime, Nydia retrieved Luis and led him inside the house. Camille inspected Shannon's bites and the bruise on her chin. The blow from the swing had peeled off a piece of skin. One of the bites on her arm had pierced her flesh.

Carolyn continued her discourse with Katie. "You don't hit people, honey. You are not supposed to hit anyone, and you have to stop using those hurtful words. Apologize to your cousins."

"No! Shannon got in my way. She better apologize to me, or I'll kick her ass!"

"Ooh!" Courtney cried out. "She said another curse word, Aunt Carolyn."

"Courtney," Camille interrupted, "Elizabeth, and Shannon, let's go inside. The show's over. Shannon, let's get you cleaned up."

The girls obeyed and followed their mother into the house. Courtney walked in backwards because she couldn't keep her eyes off the rebellious Katie, and Katie returned a menacing glare.

Carolyn picked Katie up like a bag of potatoes, balancing her on her shoulder and rushed into the house with the child. As she passed Matthew, she muttered, "Instead of a sweet little princess, I end up with Clarence Darrow and a shock jock!"

"Keep the bliss, Honey-Lyn!" he commented as an inside joke that only he and Carolyn understood.

Carolyn rushed past Camille and her daughters and carried Katie right into the playroom, closing the door behind her. She set Katie down on a small chair, sat on the floor next to her, and took a moment to compose herself.

"You know, Katie, you did a very nice thing today, and I'm proud of you."

Katie's pouting face softened slightly, but guardedly as she tried to understand what Carolyn meant by that comment. Afterall, she had just finished insulting and attacking her cousins. Carolyn thought she saw a spark of distrust or perhaps confusion on the child's face.

"You saw that little boy crying. What's his name?" she asked, as if she didn't know.

"Luis. His mother calls him Luisito."

"Yes, Luisito. You saw him crying, and you brought him a toy. That was very nice and generous of you. I'm very proud of you when you do good things. It's not a good thing to hit Shannon. It's not a good thing to say bad words or to threaten to kill Courtney. That makes me very sad. When you hit someone, it hurts. When you use bad words, it makes me feel bad. I don't want you to hurt anyone, and I don't want anyone to hurt you."

"She started it; she got in my way."

"If you use the big kids' swing, you can get hurt. Shannon was trying to stop you from getting hurt. Do you understand what I'm saying?"

"Yes," she replied with a much softer facial expression. Then she added, "But she was mean."

"What do you mean? How was she mean?"

"I wanted to show Luis the swing, and Shannon yelled at me."

"You mean she embarrassed you in front of Luis."

"Yeah, she embarrassed me, and she should not have done that. It's not fair," she said, crossing her arms.

Carolyn smiled and lifted her daughter off the chair and onto her lap. She kissed her on the forehead, and Katie felt better. Carolyn held her close and said, "You're right; it's not fair. I'm sorry you were embarrassed, but you know what?"

"What?"

"You embarrassed her back. You hit her, and you bit her hard. That wasn't nice, so I want you to do me a favor, please."

"What?"

"Could you please say sorry to Shannon? She was trying to protect you and made a mistake. You shouldn't punish her for making a mistake. Right?"

"I guess so."

"So could you apologize to her? You can say, 'Shannon, I know you were trying to protect me, so I'm sorry I hurt you.'"

"I guess so. Mommy?"

"Yes, honey."

"I have blood on my sleeve."

Carolyn examined Katie's sweater. "That's Shannon's blood, honey. It's a little bit. We can wash that out."

"Okay. Can we have dessert now?"

"After you apologize to Shannon and Courtney, we can have cake and ice cream."

"I don't have to apologize to Courtney. She's a tattle-tale. I'm not bad—she's bad. Tattletales die and go to hell. I'm going to kill her, just you wait!" she affirmed with a determined glare.

While Carolyn was not amused by Katie's belligerence, she was impressed by her verbal accomplishment. When she first met Katie at the hospital, the child had been taciturn and withdrawn. When she brought her home to be part of the family, Katie gradually exhibited the behavior of a child going through the terrible twos. She asked numerous questions, most of which were prefixed by "why." After a few weeks, her verbal abilities were comparable to her chronological age. She was now at the stage where her abilities displayed precociousness, but in a manner that shocked prim and proper Carolyn. Carolyn surmised that little Katie probably had a mental file of words and hostile expressions from her past turbulent life. None bothered Carolyn more than the ones that were combative or sexual in nature. *It's unjust for such a young child to know such rage*, she often thought as her disdain for William Lyman and his malevolent actions intensified.

"Katie, look at me," she coaxed her while serenely looking into the child's face. "I don't want you to kill anyone, honey. 'Kill' is a very hateful word."

"Well, I hate Courtney," she said, crossing her arms in front of her chest. "She's a tattletale. Tattletales burn in hell."

"That's not true, honey. Children don't burn in hell. Today, you don't like Courtney. That's okay. But remember, Courtney has done a lot of good things, and you don't dislike her for them. When you were in the hospital, she brought you some balloons. Last week, you were laughing and playing together. This morning, the two of you were playing in here and having a good time. If you forget and forgive what happened outside today, you can have more good times."

Katie looked about the room. Carolyn's statements were a lot of information for one little girl to take in. She started to play with her shoe strap as she tried to make sense of Carolyn's words.

"If I forget what she said, can I have more cake and ice cream?" she asked while holding up one finger for accentuation.

"You can have more cake and ice cream tomorrow. Today, you can have a normal portion."

"I like strawberry."

"You'll have strawberry."

"Do I have to apologize to her too?"

"That would be nice," Carolyn said and smiled at her. "Oh, and no more bad words. Okay?"

"Okay. Come on; it's time for dessert," she said, standing up and pulling on Carolyn's hand.

Carolyn rose to her feet, thinking, *One small victory at a time, but who's leading who?*

"Mommy?" Katie asked as she paused at the door.

"Yes, honey?"

"What's shock jock?"

Carolyn suppressed the urge to laugh. Evidently, Katie had heard what she had muttered to Matthew when she passed him in the foyer. With a straight face, she said, "It's a person who says bad things."

"Oh." She thought for a moment and then added, "So I'm not a sweet little princess."

"You will be if you stop saying things like, 'I'm going to kick her ass.'"

"Okay. What's Darrow?"

"You mean Clarence Darrow. He was a very smart man."

"Am I smart?"

"Well, you could be—if you go to school and study hard."

"Oh."

Four

<hr />

1986

Emily's Hope was in gear. As the word got out and the months passed, parents and grandparents in the area took advantage of the services offered. Classrooms were set up to educate the young children while attending to their special needs. During that first year, there were a small number of kids, and education appeared to be informal. Staff and children got to know one another as family, and the children often knew the adults by their first names. Nydia was hired to manage all food services, and she started with a small staff of only three people. Over the years, like everything else at Emily's Hope, the staff and services expanded.

Katie and Luis were placed in the same classroom with only four other children their age. Mary Robinson, a sweet young lady who had recently graduated college with a perfect grade point average, was their teacher. The children loved being with her, and when she sat them down to read to them, Luis listened attentively. He soon had an excellent command of English, but like most young children, he sometimes mispronounced a few words. Nonetheless, when he needed to speak, he turned out to be a chatterbox. He and Katie sometimes sat, head-to-head or close to each other, and spent hours talking about matters that concerned little children. "When I was little..." Luis would commence when he wanted to share information about his distant past. Katie listened attentively and started her own "When I was little" stories. They shared secrets. When they traveled out of the classroom, Katie would order him, "Come, Luis," and grab his hand to lead him.

One morning, before the ten o'clock snack time, Luis walked up to Katie with a pained look on his face. His brow was furrowed. He whispered something in her ear. "Come, Luis," she said and led him out of the classroom. Mary Robinson didn't see them leave; she was busy showing Howie Benjamin how to write the letter B.

Katie walked down the hall with Luis in tow. The two walked gingerly, but Luis was having difficulty keeping up with her. Finally, they reached a door, and Katie opened it. It opened into Carolyn's spacious office. Part of it was occupied by a kitchenette and most of the necessities a working mom needs, including an area for Stevie. There was a crib, a playpen, a swing, and a few toys to keep him entertained. He was on the floor, using a plastic hammer to force a square shape into a round hole. The rest of the room had a large conference table, several high back leather chairs, Carolyn's personal desk and chair, and two computer desks against a wall.

Carolyn heard the click of the door handle, and she and Dr. Holder turned and looked toward the door. The two women had been reviewing business related information on Carolyn's 386 edition computer. Carolyn now turned her attention to the two little people who had entered the room.

"What are you two doing out of class?"

"Luis is sick, Mommy." The two children continued to walk slowly up to Carolyn's side.

"What's wrong, Luis?"

He looked painfully at Carolyn.

"It's private, Mommy," Katie volunteered. She walked over to whisper in Carolyn's ear. "His pecker hurts and he can't pee."

"Luis, are you in a lot of pain, honey?" Carolyn asked him.

The walk down the hall to Carolyn's office had caused Luis's pain to intensify. Unable to speak due to the pain, he nodded in affirmation, and he looked as if he were about to cry. Unfortunately, the pain was so intense that he didn't have the energy to do that either.

Carolyn studied his features with great concern. She dialed 911, and then she called Mary's classroom to inform her that the children were with her. She called Nydia to her office and asked Dr. Holder to find someone who could lend an extra hand in the cafeteria.

"I'll take care of it, Carolyn." Dr. Holder rushed out of the office.

When Nydia arrived, Carolyn advised her to undress Luis and wrap him in one of Stevie's blankets.

"It will save time when the paramedics arrive. Come, Katie," she said, reaching for Katie's hand. "Let's give Nydia and Luis some privacy."

"It's okay," Katie interjected, looking at Luis. "I've seen Luis's pecker lots of times. Right, Luis?" With his furrowed brow, he nodded in affirmation, and Katie added, "With all the red lines, it looks like a little peppermint stick. Right, Luis?" Again, the boy nodded to confirm her description. "He lets me ride it all the time. Right, Luis?"

As Luis nodded in affirmation, the two women stared at each other in disbelief. Carolyn blushed, and Nydia turned pale.

* * *

After they arrived at the hospital, the doctors inserted a catheter above Luis' groin in order to drain his bladder and to prevent the urine from backing up into his kidneys. However, that was a temporary fix. They needed to remove scar tissue that had apparently grown within the urethra. The procedure was scheduled for the following morning and was espected to take less than a couple of hours. Felipe went to work that day, and Nydia sat alone in the waiting room while Luis went under the knife. She became increasingly anxious while the hours came and went, and she wondered if something terrible had happened. "Oh, Little God of mine," she murmured in Spanish, "help my little boy. Don't do this to me please."

By the fifth hour, Nydia was very concerned. Carolyn called to check on Luis' progress, and Nydia spoke to her on the phone at the nurses' station. Nydia was relieved when Carolyn said she was coming down to the hospital.

Carolyn hugged Nydia as soon as she arrived. "Have you learned anything yet?"

"No, no. I don't understand; he should have been in recovery hours ago."

"Well, let's see what the story is," Carolyn said as she guided Nydia to the nurses' station and calmly introduced herself to the nurse on duty. "I'm Mrs. López's lawyer, and we would like to know exactly what the status is for her ward, Luis José Walker."

"There's been a complication, Mrs. O'Gorman."

"Yes, we know that. Could you please define the complication? My client has a right to know."

"I'll page one of the doctors on duty. Perhaps he will explain it to you."

"There's no perhaps here. Someone has to explain it. Maybe you know."

"Ma'am, I will get a doctor for you right away. I don't have the authorization to disclose that information." She paged a Dr. Beck.

Carolyn stifled the urge to ask, "What, is this a case of national security?"

A short time later, Dr. Beck arrived at the station, and the nurse quietly relayed the request to him. He guided the women back to the waiting room and spoke with them in a concerned, respectful manner.

"Luis has a considerable amount of scar tissue that has protruded within the urethra. Because of his young age, the procedure is delicate and requires microscopic reconstruction."

"You must have known that before..." Carolyn countered.

"Of course we knew, to a degree. Please, let me finish. The surgeons are taking great care to make sure that we don't deform the child further. Obviously, he's been through a lot already. However, while we were seeing to this problem, his heart stopped beating momentarily."

"Oh, my God," Nydia gasped.

"Mrs. López," he said while he held her hand to comfort her, "we have it under control."

"What do you mean you have it under control?" Nydia asked. "He's just a tiny little boy. How could his heart stop beating?"

"We found a small hole between his left and right ventricle. Apparently, it's a congenital defect. The cardiologist sealed the hole. He'll be fine."

Carolyn tried to remain calm for Nydia's sake, but she too was visibly shaken. The two women needed to take the information in, but as the doctor continued to talk, they had difficulty listening. Finally, he ended with, "He'll probably be in the OR for another couple of hours. One of the surgeons will speak with you when it's over." He placed a hand on Nydia's shoulder as he rose to go. "He has an excellent team of surgeons in there. He'll be fine, Mrs. López." He then turned to address Carolyn and shook her hand, and he repeated, "He'll be fine. It was a pleasure meeting you, Mrs. O'Gorman."

Carolyn managed to thank him before he walked away. For an indefinite amount of time, the two women sat somberly, lost in their individual thoughts.

When Felipe arrived from work to join Nydia, Luis was still in the operating room, and Nydia and Carolyn were still distressed. All three of them were soon lost in thought or anxiously pleading with God.

A young woman approached them and introduced herself as Elvira Toscano, resident cardiologist. "Luis is out of the operating room. We've moved him to recovery," she said; Nydia gasped, and Dr. Toscano continued. "He'll be fine. From recovery, he'll be moved to intensive care. We want to keep him there for a few days to monitor him closely." She observed Nydia as the tears rolled down her face. She handed her a small box of hospital-issue tissues. "If you want to visit him in recovery, you can follow me."

"Thank you for saving my little boy, Doctor." Nydia said.

"Well, I'm one of a team of surgeons who worked on him," she humbly said. "We don't give up easily."

"Thank you, Doctor. God bless you, Doctor. God bless you," Nydia cried.

* * *

Luis's recent ordeal forced Carolyn to revisit the loss of her twins. In her grief, she had stored all memories of them in the attic. She now relocated their framed pictures where they had originally been. Matthew walked in on her as she was adjusting a picture on the wall, and she paused to finger her children's faces.

"I'm sorry," she said to Matthew. "I have been very selfish and self-absorbed. I also apologize to the twins. I had no right." She started to sob. Matthew wrapped his arms around her. "I had no right," she continued to cry, "to shut them out of our lives. They'll probably never forgive me."

Matthew looked into her face and wiped the tears away with his thumbs. "Like me, they understand that you were grieving their loss. Like me, they know you haven't forgotten them because you cry their names in your sleep. Like me, they love you all the more, my Honey-Lyn." And he hugged her again while she continued to sob.

That evening, Carolyn called her identical twin sister, Marjorie Louise, in Brussels and had a lengthy heart-to-heart talk with her. Carolyn and Marjorie had always been close, especially during Carolyn's college years. Carolyn shared recent events with Marjorie, including the ache and emptiness she still felt for her twin boys. The two sisters wept together on the phone and made a lifelong promise of commitment to each other and to family. For years, the sisters had shared a secret that continuously nagged Carolyn. She asked Marjorie to please help her by sharing their secret with their mother, Margaret, because it was time their mom knew.

Later that night, Carolyn received the dreaded phone call from her mother.

"I never expected either of my daughters to do that to me, Carolyn, especially you. You have always been so mature and rational, and I hear this now, under these circumstances? What were you thinking? Now you leave me with my back against a wall. We need to talk and reach a rational conclusion to this mess. At this point, I can only conclude that both you and Marjorie are certifiable and an utter disappointment."

The evening's two phone calls, first with Marjorie and then with her mother, led to a sleepless night and years of haunting uneasiness. The two events and a third she would experience nearly seven years later were painful, but instrumental in molding Carolyn into a strong, determined woman. We are all a total of our experiences. There are people who are weakened by pain and people who are strengthened by it. With time, Carolyn would become as strong as an oak that has been buffeted by many storms. Much of that strength was due to not wanting to be a disappointment in Margaret's eyes and a determination to be a model for her children. After her conversation with her mother, Carolyn decided to return to the hospital and share Nydia's vigil at Luis's bedside.

* * *

Katie missed Luis and had kept insisting to see him. Luis had also been asking about Katie whenever he awoke, so during Luis's second day in intensive care, Carolyn and Papa Sean arrived with Katie. Although Nydia was visibly worried, she tried to greet them with enthusiasm. She was also grateful that Carolyn had spent the entire first night after the operation with her and had taken the time to come each day. Sean or Ellen took turns accompanying Carolyn on the daily visits, and to see the boy who had touched their hearts. As for Nydia, she seldom left the boy's bedside.

Carolyn held Katie in her arms while the child examined Luis in awe. He was asleep, connected to an IV, a heart monitor, a tube down his nose, and a catheter. Katie whispered in Carolyn's ear with total fear in her voice, "Is he dead?"

"No, honey," Carolyn said as she kissed her. "He's asleep, but we better not wake him. He needs to rest."

"Can we come back when he wakes up?"

"Yes, but only for a little while because he needs to sleep a lot so he can get better."

"Okay, let's go," she whispered. "I want him to get real better."

Sean stayed with Luis while Nydia accompanied Carolyn and Katie to the cafeteria for a snack. When they returned, soothing Celtic flute music filled the boy's room, and Luis was moaning in his sleep. Nydia sat at his side again to continue her vigil and pray silently to her Little God. Carolyn took Katie for a walk around the hospital grounds for about a half hour before returning to the room. Luis was awake, and Nydia smiled at them; she hadn't budged from Luis's side. The boy looked pale. The Celtic music had been replaced by "Afternoon of the Fawn", and Luis was absorbed by the sound of the flute while Papa Sean held his small hand. Carolyn lifted Katie into her arms so she could get a better view of Luis.

"Hello, Luis," she said, slightly above a whisper.

He smiled and waved at her. "Hello, Katie," he said in a slight voice.

"Did you sleep okay?"

"Yes. I dreamed that you and I were at the park. We were on one of the rides, going up and down."

"Well, maybe we can go when you are better, right, Mommy?"

"That sounds like a good idea," Carolyn replied, "but we should wait until summer to do that."

"Well, I'm too tired to go now," Luis said.

"Katie and I will let you sleep, Luis. We'll come back when you're better, honey."

"Bye, Luis."

"Bye, Katie." He smiled and waved as Carolyn carried Katie out of the room.

Sean kissed Luis's forehead and also wished him good-bye, followed with "See you soon, son."

* * *

Concern for young Luis and his guardians extended beyond immediate friends and members of the Lopez and O'Gorman families. Shortly before Luis was moved from ICU, Carolyn stopped by with her parents, Margaret and Harold. Nydia had seen Margaret once before when she visited Carolyn at Emily's Hope. Harold traveled a lot, visiting his various corporations. Margaret, however, spent most of her time in New York. Now, accompanied by Carolyn, they stopped by to wish Nydia and her family well. Nydia thought it was very gracious of them and appreciated their good wishes. Harold and Margaret visited at least two more times before Harold left for Ireland. After that, Margaret and Carolyn often arrived together until Luis was finally released from the hospital.

Five

―◇◇◇―

2005

After the entertainment in the auditorium, guests of Emily's Hope were enjoying lunch.

"A penny for your thoughts, Honey-Lyn," Matthew said, kissing Carolyn on the cheek. "You've been very quiet."

She looked at him with a trace of sadness in her eyes. "I reprimanded Luis and Katie upstairs," she said. "He looked so contrite and embarrassed that he reminded me of the little boy he once was. I also remembered our twins. I thought of all four of them—when they were each at death's door. Do you remember that? First Seány and Harry. Then Katie. Then Luis during and after heart surgery."

"Of course I remember. I never forget the twins," he said, self-consciously touching his wallet pocket. "And I remember when they flew Katie in from Rochester. You were usually by her side. I remember standing next to you by her bed and hearing you say, 'I want her, Mattie. She's such a little angel.' I thought you were crazy. Stevie was a newborn, but you insisted you wanted her. She was so beaten up. But you can't dwell on that, Honey-Lyn. It's ancient history. She and Luis are both well now. They're no longer children."

"I know they're well, but there's something else nagging me now," she said with tears in her eyes. "Katie's very smart, but I feel as if she's rushing toward a train wreck."

"I know she has an overactive mind, but sometimes I think you worry too much."

"I disagree. I'm not overreacting, Mattie. I can't explain it. Perhaps it's a gut feeling. While I watched her and Luis upstairs, my mind wandered. I thought of Marjorie, and my blood ran cold."

When Katie was about twelve years old, a seemingly carefree, globe-trekking Marjorie overdosed on prescription meds. No one had expected such a tragedy. Carolyn always wondered if she could have prevented Marjorie's death. It had been a chaotic year for Carolyn, but not so chaotic, she thought, that she couldn't have interacted more frequently with Marjorie. Maybe, she thought, she should have been with her in Italy on that terrible day. Carolyn and Marjorie had always been close to the point of being confidants. However, if Marjorie's suicide was intentional, she failed or chose not to share that intent with Carolyn. Marjorie's final act became another indelible hollow in Carolyn's heart.

Matthew looked worriedly at his wife. She had expressed those feelings before, so he understood what was running through her mind. Numerous times, he had told her that she couldn't fix everything and that no one expected such a tall order from anyone. He believed that the best thing to do now was to distract her from her dark thoughts.

"Come on. Get up. It's a slow dance," he beckoned her, alluding to the band music, "and I want to dance with my wife."

He held her tightly as they danced. "You know, I have a few memories of my own. I remember you saying, 'I'm following my bliss, Matthew.'" He got her to laugh, and he repeated, mimicking her voice, "You said, 'I'm following my bliss, Mattie. I want lots of children—at least four.'" She laughed again. "Well, if we include Luis, we now have four healthy children, but not in the way you expected. After a few months with Katie, the usual expression was, 'That child is going to drive me to drink. By herself, she makes up for the total four I wanted to have.' Oh yes, I remember those days," he teased her.

"I remember them too. It wasn't Stevie who kept us awake nights. He was a calm baby."

"And Katie had the night terrors and the bed wetting."

"I remember those terrifying nights, Mattie, but they must have been a thousand times worse for her. Instead of getting a restful night's sleep, she screamed like a banshee."

"I'll never forget her eyes," Mattie said. "They were wide open and focused on nothing. Yet sometimes she appeared fine during the day, as if she didn't remember anything."

"She appeared fine, and we were exhausted from lack of sleep. That's when I went back to using the diaphragm for several years. However, I eventually thought it was safe to conceive Kieran, my darling little baby."

"Well, it's not too late to conceive another one. What do you think?"

She looked into his eyes and asked, "Another baby now? Are you serious?"

"Why not? You can't continue to put your life on hold on account of the kids. Katie will always be Katie. You've done all you can do for her: therapy, anger management, psychologists, psychiatrists. You know the cliché: 'You can lead a horse to water, but you can't make him drink.' The best we can do now is to catch her when she falls. She's a grown woman with unimaginable credentials. As for us, an empty nest is not too far around the corner. Stevie will be finished with pre-law next year. Kieran will eventually become a college student. You'll be following your bliss if you have another baby."

"I don't know, honey. Besides, I've probably missed that window."

"We can adopt another little angel. Is the bliss fading out of view?"

"The answer is no, but at my age I need to consider other factors. Besides, watching them grow has sometimes been harder than I expected. But they are fine kids, Mattie."

"If you don't like the idea of having another child, take some time to assess your life. Whatever you decide should be what's best for you. You are our helm, so you need to be the priority here. You know, I have other memories. I'm thinking of the times we've had naked yoga sex on the living room floor." She laughed, and he continued. "Oh, baby, those are sensual memories worth preserving. *Kama Sutra*." He thrust his pelvis forward.

"Stop that," she laughed, and she rested her head on his shoulder.

"We can plan future memories," he whispered in her ear. "When we get home, we'll send Stevie and Kieran to the movies, and I'll rub you from head to foot with lilac or lavender oil. Then we'll have naked yoga sex all night. Or we can send Kieran and Stevie to Costa Rica for the whole summer and spend the entire summer in *Kama Sutra* positions."

"Do you have any other plans, or is it all sex with you?"

"We can't procreate without lots and lots of sex. The more 'lots,' the better. Besides, I'm a man, and you're my woman. A man has to make love to his woman. Seriously, Honey-Lyn," he said, changing his mood, "I love you with all my soul. I'm married to the most beautiful, most intelligent woman on the planet. If someone offered me a million concubines for my wife, I'd say no way."

"That's because you would be a very tired man, my man. Besides, you wouldn't do it because I would have to castrate you first."

"So you're saying if you can't have me, nobody can."

"That's it in a nutshell," she replied.

"The woman loves me. My nuts are throbbing. What do you say we get down on the floor and start procreating right here?"

"Keep dreaming." She kissed him on the side of his neck. "Thank you," she said, feeling grateful because he had lifted her spirits with his banter.

"I'm here to serve and obey, my love. I'd be lost without you."

"I'd be devastated without you. After all, you're part of my bliss."

He held her tighter, and they continued dancing silently. She was lost in thought again, but for a completely different reason.

The music switched to a faster tempo. It was music that people of all ages enjoyed. Young and old poured onto the dance floor. The ones who were too young to understand the concept of dancing hopped up and down like kangaroos. Carolyn's parents and her in-laws were in the groove, doing the proper dance steps to music they were totally familiar with. The adolescents, including Kieran, improvised with modern variations. When it was over, everyone clapped. It was the perfect music to continue to lift Carolyn's spirits.

They returned to the table. As Matthew pulled the chair out for his wife, he said, "Don't let them get to you, Honey-Lyn. You deserve some 'me' time. The power is yours." He kissed her on the cheek and pushed her chair forward. The music continued to play at a quieter tempo as various conversations were struck around the table.

"Hey, Luis," Kieran called out to Luis, who was sitting next to Katie, across from him. "Pass the carrots, my man. Man, I do love carrots. Don't you love carrots, Katie?"

Katie smacked Luis on the head.

"Aught!" he complained. "Why did you do that?"

"You know damn well why," she yelled at him in Russian so no one would understand. "You told him."

Kieran burst out laughing. "Where are the carrots, Luis?"

"Shut up!" Katie countered.

"You all calm down," Matthew interjected. "You're not at a ball game here. And you're not children. Kieran, behave yourself. This is not the time or the place for this nonsense."

"You're right, Daddy. I apologize," Kieran said.

"Thank you," Matthew said as he crumpled a napkin.

"Katie," Kieran addressed his sister, "I also apologize to you and Luis. It's rude of me to behave like an oaf. I should be a model citizen, like Bert and Kurt."

"Why, you little piece of..." She rose menacingly while biting back the word "shit".

"Oops," Kieran said, leaving his seat. "Excuse me, folks, I have to go. I think my life depends on it." He dashed onto the dance floor while Katie glared at him.

Luis couldn't stop laughing, and Katie banged him on the head again. Calmly, with her head resting on one hand, Carolyn smiled at Matthew, and he smiled back. They didn't understand what was going on, except that twelve-year-old Kieran was behaving like a twelve-year-old, and he had managed to push Katie's buttons as he usually did. Apparently, Luis was in on the joke.

"Luisito," Nydia admonished her son from across the table, "you should be setting an example."

"We were just having a little fun, Mami. No harm done."

"The day isn't over," Katie warned him. "You'll find out what 'harm' means."

"Well," Momma Ellen announced, ignoring the infantile behavior, "it's time to mingle with the guests and thank them for coming."

"Yes, Momma," they all said in unison. They each parted ways and headed for a target location.

Luis didn't get very far before he encountered Garrity. He was with Cheryl Johnson, who had approached him earlier for help and advice. "Luis," Garrity greeted his young friend. "You remember Cheryl." It was a half question, half statement.

"Of course," Luis responded. "How are you, Cheryl?"

"Fine, thanks. Listen, Detective Garrity and I were hoping you could help me out with something."

"Sure, name it."

"Well," Garrity interjected, "Cheryl has an order of protection against her ex, but he seems to show up everywhere she goes. We stopped him a few hours ago just outside the gate here."

"Was that the blue SUV that I spotted this morning, around nine thirty? You were out there with a patrolman."

"Yes, that was his SUV. He's probably still out there. We couldn't do anything more than check his license and registration. He's more than five hundred feet away."

"I guess that's one of the terms on the OP, so he's not violating anything," Luis interjected.

"That's correct," Garrity confirmed.

"So how can I help? I don't know anything about police business."

"I was hoping we could take Cheryl's car over to your place so I could inspect it. I figure you must have the tools I'll need. I suspect her ex must have planted a GPS device somewhere on her car. That's how he knows where she goes and is able to follow her."

"You're probably asking me because I live within walking distance, but I'm the wrong guy, Phil. Matthew and Katie can help you with that. They can take anything apart and put it together again in the blink of an eye. Either one of them will most likely have all the tools you need. There's Matthew. Let me talk to him."

When Matthew heard the story, he quickly agreed to help. "If you want to wait until I finish mingling with the guests," he offered Cheryl and Phil Garrity, "we can take the car over to Katie's garage and do that for you."

The men patted each other on the back, and they and Cheryl went their separate ways.

In the meantime, in another area of the cafeteria, Stevie said, "Wait up, Sis," and Katie turned to face him. "I know you didn't ask for my advice…"

"But I'm going to hear it anyway," she completed his sentence.

He smiled. "You read my mind. Good for you."

"So what's the advice, Stevie?"

"Get rid of Bert and Kurt. You can't keep stuffed dummies in your car in order to drive in HOV lanes," he said. "It's illegal; high occupancy vehicle means exactly what it says. Dummies don't qualify as passengers, Katie."

"And I need an aspiring lawyer to tell me this. Gee, is that what tuition money is for these days? You're brilliant. Listen, when you need to travel from job site to job site to keep an appointment, let's see how many stupid laws you break."

"It may be a stupid law, but Mommy and Daddy aren't going to like it when they find out. Katie, if you get caught, it will cost you points on your license. If your license is suspended, you won't be able to get to any job site."

"Stevie, we're model citizens. At least, I'm a model citizen. I don't break reasonable laws; it's the stupid ones that are a problem. I don't drink and drive; I don't do drugs."

"Forget it. Keep deciding which laws are right for you and which are not. You're still committing a moving violation, no matter what you think. Eventually, you'll get the lecture from Mommy, Daddy, or a state trooper."

"If I count on you three stool pigeons," she said, referring to Luis and her two brothers, "I guess I'll hear it from Mom and Dad."

"Luis isn't a snitch. He didn't say anything to Kieran about Bert and Kurt, at least not intentionally. We saw your two dummies when we were taking the amplifiers and speakers from the car. Kieran figured it out."

"I guess the dummies must have introduced themselves to him."

"Well, Luis mentioned their names, but the guy didn't say anything else."

"What about the carrots?"

"I don't know anything about any carrots. I don't follow the little Meerkat around and take notes."

"Well, he embarrassed me in front of Momma and Papa. And Luis's mother was sitting right there."

Stevie started to laugh, and he shook his head while saying, "Katie, Katie. You embarrassed yourself by blowing Kieran's mocking out of proportion. Momma and Papa were probably not even paying attention to your little world. Kieran likes to mess with you and always manages to push your buttons. Then you try to act tough, but even he sees through your façade." She did not respond. Stevie winked into her pouting face and walked away.

Eventually, Katie did what Momma had instructed and started to approach people to thank them for coming. As she excused herself away from one of the couples, she turned to face Ekaterina Pinkhosova, aka Rina.

"Katie," Ekaterina said, "I've been looking for you. I'm sorry; we arrived late. This is my partner, Elena Morales."

"Rina! I'm so glad to see you," Katie commented. "I haven't seen you for at least eight or ten years. You look great! Nice to meet you, Elena. Rina and I were as thick as thieves when we were kids."

The three young ladies spoke for a while as the festivities wound down. Katie left a short time later with Matthew, Phil Garrity, and Cheryl Johnson. Nydia, Dr. Holder, and Carolyn had been the first to arrive, and they were the last to leave. Carolyn thanked Dr. Holder for her help and waved as she drove away while the boys started to reload the music gear into the van. Matthew had taken the car, so Luis had offered to take Carolyn and the boys home in Katie's SUV. Nydia and Felipe stopped to speak with them a while. While Luis said good-bye to his parents, Kieran stood by the van, engrossed in a video game when Carolyn approached him. She noticed he was disheveled, with his suit jacket unbuttoned, his tie loose, his shoes scuffed, and part of his shirt hanging out of his pants. She smiled to herself because halfway through any function, he always managed to look like an unmade bed. When he sensed her presence, he looked up from his game.

"Hey, Mommy, get a load of this," he said. "I said good-bye to Grandpa and Grandma, Papa Sean and Momma Ellen, and Meepa Felipe and Meema Nydia. If I get any more poppies, I could be arrested for drug trafficking. Get it? I have four poppies."

Carolyn nodded at Kieran's immature sense of humor. "Yes, honey, I get it. Do you also have a crypt of mummies?"

"That's a good one, Mommy. I like that."

Kieran had started calling Nydia "Meema" when he was a baby, when his young brain couldn't process Luis's Spanish comments correctly. Baby Kieran had heard Luis call Nydia "Mami," and he proceeded to do the same. Luis corrected him and said in Spanish, "*Es mi mamá, no tu mamá.*/She's my mother, not your mother." Kieran misunderstood Luis's statement and concluded the woman's name was Meemamá, which he reduced to Meema. No one bothered to correct him again. Hence, Nydia was Meema and her husband Felipe became Meepa.

"Did you have a good time today?" Carolyn asked him while running her fingers through his rumpled wavy dark hair.

"Yes, I did. It was fun."

"I thought you might have enjoyed yourself. I took a picture of you dancing with Supriya Singh. Do you like her?"

Kieran blushed. "Mom!"

"Ah, you do like her." She mussed his hair again and kissed the top of his head. "My baby has a girlfriend."

"Mom! Stop saying that! She's not my girlfriend." He had turned as red as a beet. "When I find that picture, I'm going to delete it."

"You can't. It's part of my memories. Besides, when you're old and gray, you'll probably show it to your grandchildren."

Knowing he couldn't win the embarrassing conversation, he said, "Okay, keep it. Besides, by the time I'm old and gray, I will probably have conquered lots and lots of women."

"Oh, so you think you can 'conquer' women. What century are you living in, Igor?" she asked, and he blushed again, realizing he had put his foot in his mouth. "Don't get me started because, in my world, men and women don't 'conquer' one another." She slipped her forearm under his chin and put him in a headlock to signal that she wasn't annoyed at him, but with his philosophy. "Couples love and respect each other. So don't let me hear you making comments like that again. Do you understand me?"

"Yes." He decided it was best to change the conversation to a matter he had been considering all day. "Listen, Mommy, may I stay with Luis tonight?"

Carolyn responded, "No. It's a school night, and Luis has to go to work tomorrow."

"Ah, Mom, come on. Luis won't mind."

"What won't I mind?" Luis asked as he approached them.

"Can I go home with you, Luis? We can take the boat out; Stevie can come too. It's still early; we can go fishing, the three of us."

"You can do homework," Carolyn interjected.

"I already did my homework." She looked at him suspiciously. "I swear, Mom. I finished it. I just have to print it out from the computer, and I can do that at Luis's house. Please, please."

"Carolyn," Luis said, "if it's okay with you, it's okay with me. A boat ride sounds like a good idea. Why don't we all go? Carolyn, you can use a little R & R. The boys can spend the night with me; I'll see that Kieran gets to school on time tomorrow."

"Yes, yes!" Kieran said. "See, it's a good idea."

"Well, fine. Luis, just drop us off at home, and I'll drive back later with the boys in casual dress," Carolyn said.

Six

Back in Katie's garage, Katie placed a couple of folding chairs for Phil and Cheryl to sit in while she and Matthew checked out the car. Their deductive skills paid off when they discovered two amateurishly soldered copper wires attached to the ignition system.

"They're the wrong gauge," Katie concluded. "And look at the soldering job, Daddy. It's messy and prickly."

Matthew confirmed her observation and suggested they take photographs in case they needed any evidence. After photographing the sloppy solder connection, they followed the wires under the carpet to the backseat that housed a cell phone, the device that Phil had hoped to find.

"This connection," Matthew said, turning to Cheryl, "could cause the cell phone battery to overload and explode. You're lucky it hasn't started a fire."

Matthew reasoned that whenever Cheryl started the car, she would activate and charge the phone, which most likely had a built-in GPS unit that Cheryl's ex-husband, Arturo Santillana, could use to track her.

"The good news is we found it," Phil started to explain to Cheryl. "The bad news is that we need to inspect it and link it to him. In order to do that, I have to remove it and send it to the lab techies to check. Once I do that, he'll suspect it either malfunctioned or you're onto him. We can go with the first option. If he thinks it malfunctioned, he'll probably try to break into the car again to correct the problem. Either way, we could stir up a hornet's nest."

"We might have a third option," Matthew volunteered. "It's a long shot, but my son could probably do that analysis for you right here in the garage. You won't have to take it anywhere."

"Stevie can do that?"

"Not, Stevie. Kieran can probably do that."

"Little Kieran? You're joking," Garrity said.

"It's not a joke. My little brother is a hacker. Annoying, but smart," Katie concluded, thinking of the time he broke into the computer system of her corporation and blocked her out of her own computer.

"Cheryl," Matthew said, "I advise you not to go home until this is resolved. You should stay at Emily's Hope."

"What about the car?" Katie asked. "If we leave the GPS in it, he'll know Cheryl is at EH."

"Once we have the information we need," Phil interjected, "I suggest she does go home and park the car there. Let him follow her. I'll be with you every step of the way, Cheryl. Go home, pack a suitcase, leave by the back door, and take a cab to Emily's Hope while I watch Arturo. Hopefully, he won't even see you leave, and he'll sit outside your home wasting his time."

Katie knew that Cheryl would need a car for work if she abandoned hers, so she offered Cheryl one of her vehicles. Katie and Matthew also offered to wait for Cheryl near her home, at the Bedford & Green parking lot, where Katie would transfer her car to Cheryl and Katie would return home with Matthew.

* * *

When Carolyn arrived at Luis's house with the boys, Luis informed them that Matthew needed to see Kieran ASAP. Stevie unloaded their belongings from the car, and Carolyn took Kieran straight to Katie's garage.

The garage was spacious and housed four cars, including Katie's SUV. Further in was her lab and a storage room where she kept the ingredients she used to concoct the fish grub she fed to the fish in the lake. A year earlier, she had sold the patent of a similar fish food to an industrial fish hatchery in Oregon. In the corner of the lab was a huge grinder that resembled a wood chipping machine. She no longer used the contraption, but she had used it to grind cattle bone she ordered from the butcher. It was part of the ingredients she included in her first fish grub recipe. Nowadays, she ordered ground bone meal from a local supplier. Beyond the garage and lab, there were four additional rooms and one and a half bathrooms on that level. Near the garage entrance, there was an elevator that was large enough to haul an SUV or a grand piano. At the far end, a passageway led to stairs and an indoor solar-heated swimming pool, which was adjacent to the inner courtyard. Everything, including the garage, was spotless and sanitary.

When Kieran arrived, Phil Garrity explained what he needed done, and Kieran said, "Piece of cake, Detective." He then climbed into the car to examine the phone.

"Katie," he said to his sister, "I'll need the wireless laptop and cables with the following connectors: one-fourth millimeter plug, USB, and micro alligator clips. Also, get me any soft media storage device you have and the printer."

As Katie scrambled for the things he needed, he said, "Gosh, it feels good to order her around."

Matthew admonished him, "You stop thinking like that, young man. I'm getting tired of the nonsense. Family is all you have, and in my family we respect one another. I strongly advise you to stop the hostility you hold and love your sister."

"Sorry, Daddy," he said. "I'm just kidding around. She does it to me."

"Well, it's time you both stopped. I will deal with Katie later because I've had enough of this nonsense. By the way, what do you have on your feet?" he asked Kieran, pointing to the holy sneakers the child was wearing. The canvas was so worn that it almost resembled gauze.

"It's just my sneakers, Daddy."

"A hobo wouldn't wear garbage like that. Why are you wearing them?" He turned to face Carolyn. "Didn't I see you toss them in the trash a few days ago?" he asked her in a near whisper.

"I did throw them out," she responded with the same tone. "Evidently, he dug them out again. It must be a fashion statement or a rite of passage. Let him wear them. One of these days, he's going to lift his feet at the wrong time, and his soles will detach from the threads. Maybe he'll step in some poop on the way home. That will teach him."

Matthew scratched his temple to hide his amusement from Kieran. "If only he would," he said to Carolyn; he then turned to face Kieran again. "When you get home, make sure you get rid of those things. I don't want you leaving my house again dressed like a bum. Do you understand me?"

"Yes, Daddy," Kieran responded with contrition in his voice.

Katie arrived with the supplies. She had heard Matthew's final statements to Kieran and smiled slyly at her brother. "You'll soon get yours too," he muttered to her in response. Katie ignored him and went to get two additional chairs for her parents to sit while they waited for Kieran's results.

In less than an hour, Kieran presented Phil with hard and soft copies of the information he had downloaded. He explained, "I checked the NAC and SIMMS. Their numbers are here." He pointed to the information written on paper. "The unit is for a pay-as-you-go cell phone, so he didn't have to provide any information when he purchased it or the service to use it. He probably paid cash, which allegedly keeps him anonymous. Except, he goofed. When he needed to purchase additional time on the SIMM, he used his credit card. That nails him for these dates." Kieran pointed to information on the page. "And the signal from this phone is providing a steady stream of information to a wireless computer listed in his name. Here are the numbers for that, along with the ISP, cell phone provider, and passwords he uses. Is this okay for you?"

"Kid, it's perfect. With this and pictures of the car's interior, I have enough to get a warrant to inspect his computer, request official information from the cell phone company and ISP, and arrest the SOB. You should work for us."

"Thanks, but I'd rather go fishing. If I hurry, Luis will still take me out on the boat. Katie, I need some worms."

"You know where they are," she said. "Get them yourself. And don't make a mess. If I have to clean up after you one more time, I'm going to make you lick the floor."

"Highly unlikely. Besides, Mommy wouldn't allow you to mistreat me." He ran into the lab. He returned quickly with a container of meal worms. He ran to Carolyn and said, "Mommy, let's go. I don't want Luis to leave without us." He grabbed her hand and pulled her toward the exit.

"We'll see you later," she called to Matthew as she allowed herself to be led away.

After taking additional photos, Matthew started to put Cheryl's car in order while Katie and Phil organized and e-mailed the evidence to Phil's headquarters. Katie allowed Cheryl to choose one of her cars to use. Cheryl chose a compact four-door BMW.

* * *

With fishing poles, tackle, a beverage cooler, and life vests on the ground next to them, Luis and Stevie were seated on the ground, back-to-back, leaning on each other and chatting while they waited near Carolyn's car. Lolo was lying on his back, next to Luis. Apparently, the German shepherd was enjoying the afternoon sunlight on his underbelly. Stevie was stroking Lolita behind her left ear while she lay near him. When Carolyn and Kieran approached, Stevie and Lolita quickly rose to their feet, and Stevie offered Luis a hand up. Carolyn noticed a grimace on Luis's face as he got up.

"Are you in pain, Luis?" she asked him while Stevie started to equip the dogs with their life vests. The two German shepherds wouldn't miss an opportunity to go on the boat. "You appear to be having some discomfort."

"My painkiller is wearing off. I just need a couple of Tylenol and I'll be fine."

"I have some in my purse. Kieran, get Luis a glass of water." Kieran ran back into the garage, and Carolyn leaned forward to whisper in Luis's ear. "It must have been some ordeal tearing your pants this morning."

Luis blushed, but he tried to maintain his demeanor. "Yes, it was," he replied.

"I'm offended that you two horny toads think I'm that stupid," she said, sounding amused.

"Actually, nothing sexual or unsavory happened, if that's what you're thinking, but I'll keep that in mind and try to be more open with you."

"Not too open, Luis. Games like this keep me entertained." She handed him the pills. "Sometimes, I believe that if I hadn't put Katie on birth control when she reached puberty, the two of you would probably have four or five children by now."

"You think so? That would be neat."

"That's because you wouldn't be the one carrying a child for nine months and finding it impossible to find a comfortable position to sleep."

"It can't be as bad as you women claim. If it were, women wouldn't keep having children."

"If you were my son, now would be a good time to wash your mouth out with soap and give you a good kick in the butt, smart-ass."

"Carolyn! Such language! I didn't think you had it in you."

* * *

Stevie and Kieran threw their lines over the stern of Katie's boat while Luis and Carolyn watched them from their seats a few feet away and chatted. Lolo was with them, occasionally looking over the stern, expecting the next catch. Lolita lay on *Ekaterina*'s bow.

"I've been made a seventy-five-million-dollar offer for my Web company," Luis explained to Carolyn. "I should have the deal sealed by next week. The Meerkat is entitled to part of that money because he helped me set it up."

"If your deal does go through as planned, you'll discover that money is a nice thing to have, if you use it wisely. Do you have any idea what you're going to do with that money?"

He shook his head. "Medical school was expensive, so, aside from paying off my debts, giving Kieran his share, and a gift for Stevie, I don't know."

"That's very generous of you, Luis. That being said, I don't want you to give the boys any money, unless it's ten or twenty dollars."

"Why not? The Meerkat earned the money. The company wouldn't be worth anything if it weren't for him."

She stared at him sternly. "First, that's an exaggeration. Secondly, you know me well enough not to ask me why not. Perhaps you've forgotten, so let's go over the drill again. Did you and Kieran negotiate a price before you accepted and he gave you his help?"

"No, but at the time, we were just having fun. We didn't know it was going to blossom out to this. Besides, I couldn't afford to pay him anything."

"You each should have thought of that before you started having fun. One thing I hope I have instilled in my children is that they must earn what they get. Part of the earning is to recognize an opportunity and envision its potential. You can't go through life expecting to have things handed to you. You plan and negotiate for them— you know that. The best work is the one that is thought through. If you anticipate pitfalls before they happen, you won't lose your footing. You also plan for success; Kieran failed to see an opportunity."

"He was only ten or eleven at the time. What does he know about money and opportunity, Carolyn?"

"Plenty. And, don't worry about him missing an opportunity. It's highly unlikely that the boys will ever use up what's rightfully theirs. Of course, if they marry the wrong women, they could lose it all in a blink. That would be a shame, especially if the money could be put to better use. However, it will be a lesson learned. Besides, every healthy human being is born with three assets: limbs, a heart, and a mind. My children have the added good fortune of having money, but that does not excuse them from using their given assets."

"What's better than sharing with Stevie and Kieran?"

"I don't know. That's up to you. However, because you failed to see the potential, before you seal this impending deal, you need to see a reputable financial advisor. Then, possibly after the deal goes through, because you don't have much time now, you could also speak with your mother. She's not a millionaire, but she has managed a successful food service for Emily's Hope for all these years. She can teach you about management and finance."

"What about you? What other advice do you have for me?"

"Haven't I said enough already, Luis?"

"I'm all ears, Mrs. G."

"I'll have to charge you to explain Reilly-O'Gorman Economics 101 to you, Dr. L."

"Name the price," Luis replied, grinning from ear to ear. "I'll soon be a rich man."

"I'm just kidding," she said while admiring his joyful grin. "However, that comment you just made informs me that you obviously need help. Being rich doesn't mean you should become a spendthrift. There's nothing wrong with a few indulgences, but you need to know how to safeguard yourself to guarantee a lifelong optimum quality of life for yourself and a future family. Do you know that 'need' and 'want' are two different verbs?"

"Of course I know that."

"Well, please remember that 'need' and 'want' don't necessarily complement each other. Sometimes they are in direct conflict. Except for special occasions, my family and I don't squander money," she said as she pulled a water bottle from the cooler. "I suspect most consumers do that because they allow themselves to be manipulated by the type of marketing practices that merchants employ. In this commercial world, you need to feel secure enough to disallow that manipulation. In other words, I don't need to prove anything to anyone."

"I'm not easily fooled into parting with money, Carolyn," he said as he leaned back in his seat.

"Only time will tell, Luis. On my side of the family, much of the family's wealth comes from astute marketing and retailing practices of our pharmaceuticals and managing the hotel chain, so we recognize the tricks and gimmicks that are employed to separate people from their money. Do you remember, 'Use Easy Passage, with GFL'?"

"Yes, I remember that slogan. It still comes on TV."

"Well, no one knows what the hell GFL stands for unless they take the time to read the fine print on the box."

"Gentle Fiber Laxative. I read the fine print."

"Evidently, you did. Placing ridiculous abbreviations on labels is a great way to entice buyers. My family made millions selling people GFL; it sounds cerebral; don't you think? We also sold them Soother with AFFC, Anti–Foot Fungus Cream. Or FFE, Fast Fire Extinguisher, made with witch hazel and aloe, for hemorrhoids. Using the letter F in our products has been very rewarding."

"You're on a roll, aren't you?" he asked, sounding amused.

"Absolutely," she laughed. "Anyway, that is how the Reillys have done marketing for generations. The latest approach is to invent diseases from symptoms that many people could remedy on their own if they took the time. If you make it sound like a disease, though, you create a whole new population of hypochondriacs. Then it's really easy to convince them to buy our product. The best part is when you get the medical community talking about it."

"How so?"

"Well, let's see. How about fibromyalgic induced bursitis?"

"FIB?" he asked with a laugh.

"The acronym says it all, don't you think? Air a nice commercial with an alleged doctor defining the new disease and endorsing the curative product, and everyone, including the health care providers, will believe that FIB actually exists. Then it's ka-ching!"

"It's an interesting composite. I thought you didn't know anything about medicine."

"When one's family is in the pharmaceutical business," she said as she brushed back the hair that the wind had blown into her face, "one tends to pick up a few useful expressions. It helps to know the lingo to fill your pockets."

"I never envisioned your family in that context. You've been duping people and I thought you were so nice."

"I'm nice when I need to be, Luis. What, nice people don't take advantage of opportunities? That being said, I'm also not an idiot. No matter what you do, people are always going to spend their money on useless stuff. At least, my family tries to use much of the profits for the general good," she said after sipping from her bottle. "Millions of our dollars go to productive charities, so we are redistributing the wealth that the common man was too foolish to retain. It's our duty to use riches wisely. It's hard not to be an idiot and squander your assets without thinking of your future and your obligations. If the deal goes through, how much will you owe in taxes?"

"Probably half, plus part of my actual wages. I'll still have over thirty-seven point five million."

"Which you're probably itching to spend, and you'll expeditiously put yourself into debt again. I've seen it done before, so you won't be the first fool I've encountered."

"I don't intent to be a fool, Mrs. G."

"I hope you'll prove me wrong. In terms of lifestyle, knowing how to protect your finances is very important. Will you still like where you are after the money is in your pocket, or are you going to be wasteful?"

"I like where I am," he said shrugging his shoulders. "Of course, where I am is living above my means because of the debts I've incurred. I borrow Katie's boat to enjoy an afternoon of relaxation; I accept gifts from her that I can't reciprocate. In essence, I'm a kept man."

Carolyn had heard him say that before. She was concerned that he might somehow feel inferior because he didn't have material wealth. "Trust me," she said, "if Katie didn't love you, she wouldn't be keeping you. Do you resent being 'kept,' as you put it?"

"Well, yeah; I have my pride. I wouldn't change any part of my life, except that. The impending money will take me out of debt and improve my life. However, I doubt it will improve the most important thing for me. I'd love it if Katie would marry me," he said sadly, speaking from his heart and recalling that Katie kept insisting it wasn't necessary to marry because she wasn't going anywhere. She would also state that marriage changes relationships. He couldn't understand what she meant. "It makes no sense," he said, thinking aloud and sounding frustrated.

"I'm sorry, Luis. Money doesn't fix anything like that. Katie will come around. She does love you; I hope you know that."

"I believe she does, but I don't know..." he said, looking away.

"I have women's intuition, Luis. You don't. Katie will do the right thing, and you need to talk to my financial advisor. I'll set up the appointment for you if you let me know your work hours for the next few days," she said as she rose from her seat. "Let's see how the boys are doing."

As they approached, Kieran was transferring a fish into the net that Stevie was holding.

"That's the fifth one," Stevie said. "We'll soon have enough for everyone."

"So, they're biting," Luis commented as he stood beside Kieran.

"The little Meerkat caught all of them," Stevie said. "They're just the right size, too, for individual serve. I can almost taste a Cajun-style fish fry."

"Who's cooking?" Carolyn asked.

"I'm cooking, Mommy," Kieran replied. "I'm going to smother them with hot sauce and paprika. It's going to be great—you'll see."

"I bought rotisserie chicken as backup," Luis said.

"You didn't think we'd catch anything?" Kieran asked.

"I know how much you like food, and I know you aren't going to say no to a drumstick while you wait for the fish to cook."

"We need corn on the cob, Luis."

"I'm afraid it's not the season for corn on the cob. We can make rice with a veggie gumbo. Simply open a can of corn and toss it in," Luis suggested.

"Don't get carried away," Carolyn cautioned them. "You're not cooking for an army or a church congregation."

"Mommy, speaking of church congregations," Stevie said, "I need to discuss something with you."

"What's up, honey?" she asked, looking up at him.

"I want to go to seminary school," Stevie said.

He was a tall young man, six feet five inches tall, a typical O'Gorman, with jet black hair, striking blue eyes, a defined jaw, and the body of a true athlete. Despite his good looks, he seemed to go through life unaware of the attention he drew. At times, Carolyn thought he was quiet and unassuming. At other times, she almost believed Matthew, who thought his son didn't have much sense about anything. "I love him," Matthew said on more than one occasion, "but I don't believe there's much hope for him. That boy is always in a fog."

Stevie's response caught Carolyn by surprise. "Where is this coming from, honey?"

"From soul-searching, Mommy," he said, and Carolyn smiled. Her maternal instincts made her suspect Stevie often tuned the world out because he was in deep thought and not because he was in a fog. After all, Dr. Holder had given him a battery of tests when he was younger, and she assured Carolyn that Stevie was both normal and somewhat special. "I don't think a law career is right for me," Stevie added. "I believe my bliss lies in the study of theology; it takes my mind to levels I never thought possible."

Carolyn brushed his cheek with one hand, and noticed a distant look in his eyes as she gazed up at him. She stood on her toes and kissed him on the cheek. "I will never stand between you and your bliss. Why haven't you said something before?"

"I needed to be sure, Mommy."

"Are you sure now, honey?"

"I believe I am," he said, gazing past her to the opposite shore.

She wrapped her arms around his waist and rested her head on his chest and could hear his heart beating. She thought of her son's probable life as a priest; it could mean months or years away from his family, away from her. "I love you, baby," she said.

"I love you too, Mommy."

"Stevie," Kieran said excitedly while Lolo barked over the stern, "I caught another one. Give me a hand."

A while later, Luis set up a table near the bank of the lake and dragged a hose line down the incline from the house. He and Kieran started gutting fish and placing the clean ones in a separate ice bucket. Luis was in shorts and flip-flops, exposing his scarred legs and feet with deformed toes, lifelong evidence of the burns he had gotten as a child. As Kieran separated each fish's internal organs,

Luis hosed out the viscera. They had done this numerous times before.

Inside the house, Stevie was getting the rice and the vegetable gumbo ready while warming a couple of rotisserie chickens, and Carolyn was on the front porch with Onyx and Amber, reading while she waited for Matthew and Katie, who had left with Cheryl and Phil and were due back soon.

Luis and Kieran finished gutting the fish. Luis had started to move the water hose back up the hill when he spotted Matthew and Katie walking round the bend on the footpath. He observed that they were still wearing their morning attire, Matthew in his suit and tie and Katie in the green dress and heels. Luis paused to admire her. Katie had a shapely body, and her full height of six feet enhanced her attractiveness. At that very moment, Katie pointed to Kieran, who was struggling up the hill with his bucket of fish.

"Dad," she said with alarm, and he looked to see what she saw. "Kieran!" she yelled. "Bear, Kieran!"

Near the bank of the lake, a large bear was following the smell of fish. He sniffed the air and headed for the area where Luis and Kieran had been gutting them. Disinterested in the intestinal waste that had been diluted with water, the bear sniffed the air again and headed toward the child who was struggling with the bucket as he tried to rush up the hill.

"Kieran," Katie called again, "drop the bucket!" But Kieran continued to struggle with his bucket. *Maybe he doesn't hear me*, she thought, and both she and Matthew started rushing down the hill.

Luis turned to see what the excitement was and yelled out as he dropped the hose to run to the boy. Carolyn rose from her seat and jumped over the porch's railing. The dogs trailed behind her, barking. Everyone was yelling, "Drop the bucket," and Kieran continued to struggle uphill while the bear was closing in on him. Luis got to him as Stevie came storming out of the house. Luis lifted Kieran up in front of him and turned to continue up the hill as Katie came between them and the fast-moving bear. She leaped into the air, spun, and landed the three-inch heel of her shoe in the bear's nostril. The bear whimpered and miraculously pulled away, taking her shoe with him. Onyx and Amber caught up to the animal as he turned to run. They continued barking and chasing him downhill and then across, toward the woods. On contact, Katie heard her foreleg snap and felt it go numb. She slapped the ground with her hand thereby cushioning her fall and allowing her to perform a partial somersault before she dropped to the ground with a final thump. Luis had continued running up the hill, holding Kieran attached to his bucket in front of him. Stevie and Carolyn caught up to them simultaneously, and Stevie took Kieran from Luis.

Matthew yelled out, "He's gone," as he squatted down to check on Katie. The others stopped in their tracks and looked back toward Matthew and Katie. With Kieran and the bucket in his arms, Stevie started down the hill. Knowing that Kieran was safe, Carolyn tagged along and tried to pry the bucket from his hand. It wasn't an easy task because Kieran's fingers were tightly wrapped around the handle. Carolyn noticed that a number of fish had fallen out while Luis was looking down at Katie with concern. He squatted next to her and examined her from head to foot while Matthew looked on anxiously and Carolyn joined them; Stevie continued to look in the direction the bear had gone.

"Amazingly," Luis said, "it appears you've only broken the talus and calcaneus. I thought there would be greater damage. Carolyn, give me the bucket."

"Why didn't you get rid of the bucket, you little idiot?" Katie asked Kieran while Luis started transferring ice from the bucket onto her heel and ankle. Kieran did not respond, and Katie added, "When I get up from here, I'm going to kill you, you little putz! And you owe me a pair of shoes!"

Kieran still did not respond. Stevie stopped holding him and stretched his arms out like a cross. "Luis," he said, "I think we have a problem here." Luis looked up to see Kieran clutching Stevie for dear life. Kieran had his legs wrapped around Stevie's waist, his arms holding onto his brother's neck like a boa constrictor, and his eyes tightly closed. "He's choking the life out of me," Stevie said.

Luis told Katie to continue packing ice around her heel and ankle, and then turned his attention to Stevie and Kieran. As Luis got up and the others watched Kieran and Stevie in dismay, Luis said, "Matthew, give me your jacket." Matthew complied, and Luis draped the jacket over Kieran. "Stevie, start caressing Kieran's back." Luis continued issuing orders while each person obeyed. "Kieran will be okay. Carolyn, there's some V8 in the kitchen cabinet near the door. Bring a bottle for the Meerkat; he's going to need it. Also, get me a vial of cortisone and iodine wipes. They're inside the refrigerator door, and the hypodermics are on top of the fridge. Get the large ones. Oh, and bring a sharp knife." As Carolyn rushed off, he turned to Matthew. "Matthew, I need you to get a few items from the garage.

There are some baseboards in there, near the entrance. We also need duct tape and rope to fashion a splint for Katie's leg, in case she has a fracture." Matthew headed for the garage.

Luis started whispering in Kieran's ear while Stevie rubbed his back, and Luis touched his clammy face. "Kieran, buddy, it's me, Luis. You're safe, little buddy. Everything is okay. Meerkat, open your eyes for me, okay? You're safe."

Kieran opened his eyes, but he looked dazed. "Do you know where you are?" Luis asked him as Katie watched with a worried expression on her face. The dogs had returned and were lying next to her, panting. She started to give them pieces of ice, believing them to be thirsty from the chase. Kieran did not respond to Luis's question. Luis examined his saucer-shaped blue eyes. They normally appeared luminescent and vibrant. They were glazed. Luis said, "It's okay, Kieran. Look at me, Meerkat. Look at me. You're in Luis's front yard. I'm Luis. Kieran, Kieran."

The child sighed, and his eyes started to focus. "Look at me, Kieran," Luis said again as Carolyn came racing up with the V8 in hand. "Talk to him," Luis said to Carolyn as he took the V8 and other items from her hands.

"Kieran, honey," she started to talk to him, touching his clammy face. "Are you okay, baby? Kieran, you're safe. Stevie is holding you, and you're choking him. Honey, let go of Stevie."

Except for the juice, Luis handed Katie the items Carolyn had brought. She looked at the sharp knife. "What do you intend to do with this?" she asked, sounding concerned.

"We need it to cut the rope and duct tape," he said, and she displayed a visible sign of relief. "And," Luis went on, "stop wasting the ice on the dogs. You need it to prevent swelling. Fill up the hypo with five cc. Can you inject yourself?"

"Hell no! Look at the size of that thing!" she said, looking at the hypodermic needle. "I've never used anything this big on you."

"Well, fill it up. I'll be with you in a minute." Luis then turned his attention to Kieran and Stevie.

Stevie had not stopped caressing the child's back, and he felt Kieran loosen his grip from around his neck. "Thank you, buddy," he said. "I can breathe again."

"See if you can set him down on the ground," Luis said, opening the small bottle of vegetable juice.

With Carolyn's help, Stevie was able to place him on the ground, and he held him against his torso. Luis examined his eyes again. "You're looking better," he said. "Can you drink this for me, please?" He held the V8 to Kieran's lips, but the boy still looked confused.

"Kieran, honey, drink the juice," Carolyn said. He looked around as if he had gotten off a roller coaster. He looked back in Luis's direction.

"Drink the juice, little buddy," Luis said, holding the bottle to his lips again, and Kieran started to sip. Luis squatted patiently as Kieran continued to respond in a more normal fashion. "Thank God," Luis finally said. "I was beginning to think he would need an IV, and I don't have any in the house. Kieran, who's that?" Luis asked, pointing to Carolyn.

"Mommy-Lyn," Kieran responded hoarsely, and Carolyn sighed with relief, although he had never referred to her in that fashion.

Luis made him take another sip of juice and asked, "Where are you?"

"In Luis's front yard," he responded.

"Who am I?"

Kieran paused a moment and looked around. Then he said, "Luis, why are you asking me such stupid questions?"

They all laughed, and Luis said, "Keep sipping slowly." He placed Kieran's hands around the bottle. "Don't lie down. I don't want the juice to come back up, okay?"

"Okay," Kieran replied.

Matthew arrived with splints and duct tape, and Carolyn removed his cell phone from his belt clip.

"I need to call 911 to inform them there's a wounded bear lose," she said. "Luis, should I request an ambulance?"

"Stevie and I can take Katie in her SUV. When you're done with the phone, I need to call and request the use of the MRI for her. I'll check Kieran out again in a little bit, but he looks good."

"My food must be charcoal by now," Stevie said.

"I turned the stove off," Carolyn responded. "On top of everything else, we don't need to burn the house down."

"Can we eat before we leave?" Katie asked. "I'm hungry."

"Can we move her, Luis?" Stevie asked.

"We need to keep her leg elevated and straight. Matthew, can you fashion a splint?"

"Sure, and I can carry her to the house when I'm done," Matthew said.

Carolyn finished with the phone and handed it to Luis.

"Meerkat, buddy of mine," he said to Kieran, who had almost finished the juice, "when your legs are functioning again, do you think you can pick up the fish from my front yard?"

"I don't want any fish," he responded, and everyone laughed.

"That's okay," Luis said, "but when I get back from the hospital, I want the Cajun-style fish you promised me. Besides, if you don't pick them up, their stinking little dead bodies will attract other predators."

"I'll help you pick them up," Stevie offered.

"What if the bear comes back?" Kieran asked.

"We'll get Katie to kick him again," Matthew said.

"Like hell I am! Luis, what happened to Kieran?"

"He panicked, and he was going into shock. That explains why he didn't drop the bucket."

Carolyn started to mess with Kieran's hair, mostly to calm her nerves. She kissed him on the cheek. "Are you okay, honey?" she asked him.

"My heart is going thump, thump, thump, but I'm okay, Mommy."

"My heart is also going thump, thump, thump, and I'm glad you're okay." She turned to Katie. "Katie, honey, thank you. How are you holding up?" Then Carolyn spotted Luis checking the hypo as he squatted next to Katie, and she reached out to hold her godson's wrist. "Hold it," she said. "We need to talk." He looked at her inquisitively. "Stevie," she said, "I need you and Kieran to go pick up the fish. Matthew, can you help them, please?"

Intuitively, Stevie picked Kieran up off the ground, and Matthew grabbed the bucket. They walked away, Stevie carrying Kieran in his arms.

"Luis," Carolyn said, "could you give Katie and me a moment? Get us more ice."

"Sure, but the sooner I give her the cortisone, the better," he said.

Carolyn mulled it over a second. "Okay—stay. There's no sense in putting off the inevitable, so I'll just say it. Carefully consider what kind of medication you're going to give her because she's pregnant."

"Mom!" Katie blurted out while Luis looked bewildered. "Where did you get that ridiculous idea?"

"Are you, or aren't you?" Luis asked Katie, conflicted with emotions.

"She is," Carolyn insisted. "I've been pregnant three times, so I know when a woman is pregnant. Perhaps it's not scientifically proven, but I saw it in her face this morning when I was speaking to her."

"How can you tell from looking at her face? I'm very confused and nervous here, Carolyn, so please don't confuse me further."

"Am I not here?" Katie asked. "I don't like being spoken of in third person."

"For now, trust me," Carolyn said to Luis, ignoring Katie. "I'll explain it later. Now you can decide what you want to do with any medication you want to give her. Give it to her if there is no risk. I'll leave you two alone." She kissed him on the cheek. "Congratulations, Daddy. You finally hit the jackpot. Katie, welcome to my world, honey." She kissed her bewildered daughter on the cheek, got up, and walked away.

"Wait, Carolyn!" Luis insisted. Carolyn paused and turned as Luis continued, "I'll give her an epidural, but I need your help. My hand is shaking!"

At that point, Katie grabbed him by the hair and pulled him toward her. Luis winced as Katie spoke vehemently. "Stop speaking of me in the third person. I'm right here, damn it! Talk to me! You want to prick me with a freaking needle, an epidural, and your hand is shaking? Are you out of your damn mind?" Luis continued to wince as she kept tugging at his hair. "And you call yourself a doctor. If there is ever another medical emergency, don't take command. Dial 911. If Mom is right, I don't want you in the delivery room when the baby comes. You're liable to drop him. Do you understand me?" Luis did not respond, and she pulled his hair tighter. "I asked, 'Do you understand me?'"

"Mercy, yes—I understand. Carolyn, help," he feigned distress. "She's going to kill me."

Katie loosened her grip on him. "I just want to make sure we understand each other," she said. "Luis, if Mom is right, is the news good for you?"

"Good? No—it's great! Katie, is it good for you?"

"Come, Luis." Instinctively, the two locked their mouths around each other to share a loving kiss while Carolyn stood patiently by. "You're going to be a daddy, Luis," Katie whispered in his ear. "Right now, I love you so much it hurts."

"That's the reaction from kicking the bear," he teased her. "Katie, I'm good now. My hands aren't shaking. See? I can give you the injection."

"If I hadn't permitted you to 'inject' me all those other times, I wouldn't be needing an epidural right now."

"Well, I wouldn't say that," he replied. "I blame the bear."

"The bear didn't knock me up—he knocked me down. Damn, it's starting to hurt," she said, holding her right leg above the knee, afraid to touch the painful area.

"It didn't hurt before?"

"Honestly, no. It felt numb. Now it's starting to hurt."

"Wait till tomorrow. It could feel worse then. Ignore it for now, and turn over on your side. I'll be gentle," he said, holding up the hypodermic.

"You're not going to poke me with that damn thing. Mom, get him away from me."

Luis and Katie looked up pleadingly at Carolyn, who had been waiting patiently and uncomfortably for them to finish their interaction. Luis said, "It could help reduce the swelling."

"Could isn't good enough in my book," Katie countered. "I told you, you're not sticking me with that damn thing. Just get me more ice."

Seven

◇◇◇

Stevie and Luis left with Katie to get the MRI, and Matthew helped Kieran prepare the fish. After they tidied up and prepared to leave, the phone rang.

"I'll get it," Kieran volunteered. "It's Meema Nydia," he announced, and he started a conversation with her. "Luis isn't here. He had to take Katie to the hospital because she broke her leg..."

"Let me have the phone," Matthew said to him, interrupting the conversation.

"Daddy wants to talk to you," he informed Nydia, and then he handed the phone to Matthew, who soon brought Nydia up to speed.

"What do you mean, she kicked a bear?" Nydia asked.

"Well, that's what she did. Short story. Long pain."

"Give me the phone, you fool," Carolyn said. She practically snatched the phone out of his hand. "Nydia, please excuse my foolish husband. He has a wry sense of humor and little diplomacy."

"Come on, Kieran," Matthew led Kieran into the living room. "When two women start to talk, there's no hope; we may as well watch a movie. And I was hoping to get home early."

He was wrong. Before he could thumb through the *TV Guide*, Carolyn was beckoning them to leave. She was just as anxious as Matthew to get home; it had been a long day for everyone.

As they walked back to Katie's house to retrieve their cars, Kieran, who was carrying his school knapsack, walked nervously, and looked around while Carolyn carried his overnight bag.

"Kieran," Matthew said, "the bear is long gone. Watch where you're going, or we'll never get there."

"He could come back, Daddy."

"He's probably up a tree, too afraid to come down," Matthew replied.

"Did you hear that?" Kieran asked, referring to a twig he had heard snap.

"For Heaven's sake," Matthew said in exasperation. "Carolyn, could you handle his knapsack? I'll carry him back to the car. I want to get home today."

"I can walk, Daddy."

"Well, speed it up; we don't have all day."

* * *

They were finally home.

"Are you tired, Mattie?" Carolyn asked, stroking his back and kissing him on the cheek.

"I'm beat. I thought we were going to have a nice, quiet evening at home tonight—just you and me and a bottle of wine. What a day!"

"I know, baby. I can tell when you're tired; you get cranky. I recommend a nice warm shower. I'm going to give Kieran some warm almond milk and cherries. That will knock him out and help him forget the bear. Do you want some too?"

"I don't need anything to knock me out; I'm beat."

"And you were hoping for the *Kama Sutra*. Go upstairs; I'll be up in a little while." She kissed him again. "If you're still awake when I get there, I'll give you a rubdown."

"I spoke with Katie today," he said, changing the subject, "while we were driving back from Cheryl's house. I told her it's about time she stopped bickering with Kieran. I thought I had gotten through to her until she called Kieran a putz."

"If I haven't gotten through to her in nearly twenty years, what makes you think you're going to do it during a leisurely ride?" she asked him while opening the refrigerator. "As for the name-calling, she just got through hitting a bear. I wasn't happy when I heard her say it, but given the circumstances, I decided to ignore it, especially after our talk this morning." She poured milk in a glass and placed it in the microwave. "If I don't react, maybe she'll stop. You're right—I need to let her be. It isn't going to be easy. Go upstairs, take a shower, and try to relax."

As Kieran ate a cherry, Carolyn said, "You need a shower. You smell like fish."

Kieran tried to smell himself. "I don't smell bad."

"Well, you do. When you get upstairs, shower from head to foot."

"Are you coming?" he asked.

Carolyn bent down to look him in the eye. "Kieran, honey, are you still frightened about what happened today?"

He nodded in affirmation, and his brow furrowed.

"Honey, we're miles away. There's no bear here."

"Intellectually, I know that, Mommy. But I can't get it out of my head. He was going to eat me, Mom."

"He was after the fish, honey."

"We picked up four fish from the ground, Mom. He could have stopped to eat those. He chose to chase me, and I couldn't run fast enough."

"Kieran, between you and me, honey, why didn't you drop the bucket?"

His eyes became watery. "I tried, Mommy, but I couldn't let go." He started to cry.

"I know, honey. Give me a hug?"

He continued to cry on her shoulder. She lifted him up and sat with him on her lap.

"I'm sorry, Mommy. I didn't mean for Katie to get hurt. Now she must be really angry at me, but I'm not going to tell her I was scared. She'll make fun of me."

"No, she won't. She was also scared."

"She wasn't scared. I saw her running towards that bear, and I was running as fast as I could, but I didn't run that fast. Mom, I saw her. Man, she can run fast, like a cheetah. I've never seen her run that fast. Honest, Mom, honest. And I thought that bear was going to eat me."

"Well, I'm glad he didn't eat you or Katie. She loves you. She teases you a lot, but today she proved she loves you. Of course, she'll probably not tell you that for the same reason you won't admit you were scared. You both need to learn to be honest with one another. There's no shame in love, and there's no shame in fear. I love all of you, and I was very scared."

"You were scared too?"

"I was terrified."

"You know, I need to get rid of these sneakers. They don't have any traction left."

Carolyn couldn't stifle a laugh. "I'm sorry, honey. It's not funny, but I'm glad you finally realize the sneakers have no traction. I bet now you wish you had left them in the garbage."

"Maybe. Maybe not. They still fit well."

"Sweetheart, it's time to bury them or write them a requiem. As soon as you finish the rest of these cherries, we'll go upstairs. I promise to stay with you until you fall asleep. No bear is going to frighten my baby boy and get away with it." She got up with him in her arms and deposited him back on the seat.

"Mommy, do you think we can trap the bear and send him to Yellowstone Park or something?"

"I don't know, but we can try. I'll have my secretary make a few calls tomorrow."

"That will be good. Do you think I'm ever going to grow? If I had been bigger, I could have probably kicked him myself."

"Oh, you'll grow. Boys don't grow the same as girls. I know several boys who go to bed one night, measuring less than four feet, just like you. The next thing you know, they're as tall as trees. Your uncles, Donny and Danny, were short too. Apparently, delayed growing runs in the family."

"You mean, I could probably be as tall as Stevie, taller than Luis?"

"Maybe. You know, Luis used to be very small. When I first met him, he was shorter than Katie. He was five years old, just like her, but he looked like a three-year-old baby. Then the doctors discovered he had a hole in his heart. They stitched him up, and he started to grow. Now he's six feet two."

"And Stevie is six feet, five inches. I'll settle for either. Do you think I may have a hole in my heart?"

"No, sweetie. Your heart is fine. You had excellent medical care as a baby. The doctors checked you from head to toe. Congenitally, you were compromised because you're a twin." It was a loss that Carolyn wished she could forget.

"My twin didn't develop, Mom. Maybe there's something wrong with me."

"There's nothing wrong with you, except your father thinks you're a cyborg—half human, half machine." Because of Kieran's fascination with electronic gadgets, Matthew had called him a cyborg on more than one occasion.

"I know what a cyborg is, and don't I wish! Then I really could have kicked that bear."

When they finally got upstairs, Matthew was fast asleep. Kieran showered and got into his pajamas. Carolyn asked him to type Luis's Web site on his computer, and she sat with him in her lap. His legs dangled over her thighs and the side of the chair. They clicked on an interactive tab. Here, they could select a breed of dog and dress him in costume. Kieran chose a Chihuahua and dressed him in a mariachi costume. Next, he selected a Mexican hat dance, and the little Chihuahua danced to the music.

"This is my favorite," Kieran commented. "And you can make it full screen if you click here." He clicked the full screen tab, and the dancing Chihuahua filled the entire computer screen. "Now watch this, Mommy." He hit another tab, and the dog started barking in tune to the music. They both laughed. "Isn't it neat, Mommy?"

"Yes, it is."

"You can send this to a friend as an e-card, or you can select it for wallpaper or a screen saver. There's a lot of other stuff. We can quit this," he said as he quit the subprogram and entered the main menu, "and we can go to Fashion Show. In Fashion Show, you can select a breed and dress him in an actual outfit. This is good for someone who wants to buy their dog a coat, a hat, or booties. Merchants can list their selections, and we dress the animal. Pick a breed, Mommy."

Carolyn chose a Labradoodle and dressed it in a tutu. She selected "Runway," and the dog appeared, walking on a fashion runway while wearing the ballet costume. Strobe lights blinked behind the dog, and music played in time with its walk. While she and Kieran enjoyed the interactive program, she took the opportunity to teach him some of life's lessons. As they perused the Web site further, she asked him to identify his contributions to the project. Then she queried him to identify the possible financial gains of a given application. She questioned him about freedom of liability, infringement of copyright, and marketing applications. She was pleased with most of his answers, and she coached him in areas where he was lacking.

Kieran yawned. "Can I go to bed now, Mommy? I'm sleepy, and this is getting boring."

She tucked him in for the night and continued to peruse the Web site and sent an e-mail while Kieran dozed. The phone rang. Not wanting the ringing to wake her son or Matthew, she quickly picked it up on the first ring. It was Luis. While listening to him speak, Carolyn grabbed Kieran's dirty laundry from the hamper and walked out of the room. She went into Stevie's room and removed his laundry as well. She then went down the stairs with both laundry bags in one hand and the phone in the other.

"We finally got home," Luis said from his bed. "We had to wait for the orthopedist. Katie is fine. On the MRI, however, it shows that she has a hairline fracture of the fibula. That's in addition to the calcaneus, which she totaled, and the talus."

"Stop showing off, Luis. I'm not a doctor."

"The calcaneus is the heel bone. The talus is the ankle bone. The fibula is the calf bone."

"Which one did she total?" Carolyn asked with concern.

"The heel bone."

"Oh, God. My poor Katie. How could you say she's fine? That's not being fine, Luis."

"Well, she's not in pain for now; she's comfortable."

"For now," Carolyn said, sounding annoyed at his cavalier attitude.

"Well, she said she's going to work tomorrow. We're about to turn in because we have to be up early. Stevie is going to drive Katie to work, although I told her to stay home and keep her leg elevated. She has one of those state-of-the-art casts that she can remove in case she has to scratch. And you're right. We did a pregnancy test. I'm going to be a daddy! How did you know?"

"I already told you. I've had a few kids of my own. After a while, you notice certain signs. Is Katie there?"

"Yes, she's right here." He was lying in his boxer shorts next to her. You want to speak to her?"

"Yes, please." Luis handed the phone to Katie.

"Hi, Mom. We're back. How's Kieran?"

"He's fine. How are you feeling?"

"Okay. Luis said I'll feel the pain tomorrow."

"Then why are you going to work?" Carolyn asked as she stuffed clothes into the washing machine.

"I'll be miserable here, and I'll be miserable there. So I may as well get something done."

"Listen, Stevie can't drive you to work. He has classes tomorrow."

"Yes, I know that. He'll come right back and get to school on time. I'll hire a driver for the duration of my recuperation. Mom, how did you know about my pregnancy?"

"Well, honey, as I told Luis, part of it is a well-trained eye. It isn't science, Katie. It's simply what I've learned from observation."

"Mom," Katie said irritably, "stop the suspense, please."

"When I stared into your face today, I noticed it looks fuller. Your nostrils are too, as if you crave extra air. You are also more emotional, as if that were possible with you."

"Mom, that's nonsense," she responded.

"I told you it wasn't science, Katie. The other part is you are still listed on my insurance policy. When were you planning to tell Luis?"

"I don't understand, Mom. What do you mean?"

"Oh, Katie, don't play innocent with me. I've been where you're going. As they say, I bought the T-shirt, I had a cup of coffee, and waited until you caught up. You're a few cups behind me, Katie," she said as she added the detergent to the machine and started the wash cycle.

"I still don't understand what that has to do with me."

"Okay, we'll play it your way. There are two things missing on the insurance statement, and there's something new."

"What's that?"

"You haven't purchased birth control or antidepressant medication for the last four months, but you did acquire a prescription for prenatal vitamins. Apparently, you've been taking them for months. You also updated your measles, mumps, and rubella vaccines."

"Oh, that," she said, sounding guilty as charged.

"The evidence is overwhelming. You've done every-thing you need to do for a planned pregnancy, but you overlooked the fact that you can't stop taking your anti-depressants at the drop of a hat. This is not good, honey. You don't do things without setting goals, dear. I know you. You're very meticulous and precise. You don't overlook the fact that I receive insurance statements with your name on them. What's the story?"

"You know, I really need to get some sleep. I want to leave here before rush hour so Stevie can get back to school. It's been good talking to you, Mom. Here's Luis." She handed the phone back to Luis.

"Did she tell you anything about her voodoo science?" Luis asked Katie as he took the phone from her.

"Nothing important," Katie lied, and she turned over on her side.

"It's me again," Luis said to Carolyn.

"Katie's right, honey; it's getting late. Go to bed. I'm sure you must be tired."

"Are you kidding me? I can't sleep now. I'm as high as a kite. Katie, my Katie, is having my baby. I feel like running the marathon."

"Go out and run then. I need my beauty sleep."

"So you're not going to tell me how you knew?"

"Eventually I will, but not tonight. Go to bed or get on a treadmill. I'm glad you're happy, honey. Congratulations and good night." Carolyn pressed the phone's *off* button to deactivate the call and soon decided to dial a new number.

In the meantime, back at Katie's house, Katie com-plained, "It must be really boring being that pedantic and living with yourself. Sometimes I really hate that woman!"

"Who?" Luis asked. "Your mother? You're crazy. You don't mean that. I think she's wonderful."

"Well, why don't you trade places with me?"

"Well, I also love my mother. I think she's great too."

"Of course you do. Everyone is great!"

Under the covers, she reached around to find the flap on Luis's shorts.

"Get your hand out of there, woman," he commanded. "You ain't gettin' any tonight."

"Luis," she said, kissing his neck, "I've never done it with a cast on. It could be fun."

"Not for me; I'm still sore from this morning. Get the hand out."

"Fine," she said, removing her hand. "Sometimes you're such a girl. I'm the one who broke her foot and leg, and you're complaining over a little pain."

"Little pain? Until you're there, don't compare my pain with your pain. Picking Kieran up with a ten-pound bucket and trying to carry him up the hill while wearing slippery flip-flops was no help."

"Why are you in bed with me then?"

"To help you. If you need something during the night, I'll be right here." Before she could interject, he admonished her. "Anything but *that*."

"Fine," she said, slapping her pillow and facing away from him.

He turned to face her and wrapped his arm around her. "We could snuggle," he said. "It might help me sleep."

"Go to hell!"

"Fine," he said, withdrawing his arm. "I'm going for a walk. If you need anything, get it yourself."

She turned and grabbed his forearm before he could get out of bed. "You're not going outside now. There's a wounded bear somewhere out there."

"So now you're concerned about my well-being? You just told me to go to hell."

"I didn't mean it. If you can't sleep, get a glass of milk."

"We have no milk; remember? You told me the dogs drank it all this morning. I'll tell you what. I'll get dressed and go buy some milk."

"No, no. Don't go. I don't want you to go. We'll get milk tomorrow."

"What's wrong with you, woman?"

"Fine, go! Go get your damn milk."

"Katie, if you don't want me to go, I won't go. What's the matter?"

"Nothing."

He reached over and hugged her. Her heart was racing, and his touch soothed her. He kissed her on the cheek, and she relaxed further. "I'm not making love to you to-night," he warned her, "but I'm not going to leave you." He kissed her again, and she breathed in his scent.

"I'm sorry, Luis. Why do you put up with me? Sometimes I get too selfish. Sometimes I get crazy."

"It's okay, baby. I know it's not easy staying off your medication. You aren't crazy, and you aren't selfish. You're just having a rough time." He put his forehead against hers, and they both sighed in each other's arms.

"Luis," she said, "you wouldn't be in pain if you hadn't insisted on a quickie this morning. You don't know how to do a quickie. When you're all better, I'll teach you how it's done."

"You are beyond belief, woman. You think you can teach me a better way?"

"I don't think—I know. Besides, I believe I have taught you all you know. You need a little spice in your life, my little grasshopper." She pecked him on the lips. "I'll show you how because I like having you around. Now that I'm impregnated with your seed, you'll be with me everywhere I go," she commented while touching her abdomen.

"You like that? I mean, being impregnated by me?"

"I love it. It's great. You have fathered my child."

"Our child." This time he was the one to kiss her lovingly.

She pushed him away. "Don't do that," she cautioned him. "You're asking for trouble because I'll be all over you and your pained peppermint stick in a second."

"Do I turn you on, baby?"

"You know you do. So stop asking stupid questions." Then she suddenly remembered something and exclaimed, "Luis! Oh my! My father gave me a gift earlier, with a card. I placed it on the dresser when I came up with Cheryl. With all the excitement, I forgot." She started to get out of bed.

"Don't move. I'll get it." He soon handed her a bent card and a small box.

"To our loving daughter," she read the card aloud. "Your father and I could not express in words how proud we are of you for the wonderful work you have done. You have designed and constructed a beautiful facility that not only honors Emily, but the entire family as well. We hope you like this gift as a token of our love and appreciation. Love always, Mom and Dad."

"She's right, you know," Luis commented. "You did a magnificent job. Open the gift."

"I am," she said, tearing the paper off and opening the box.

"Wow!" Luis commented when she revealed its contents. "That's some gift. Wow, I love you that much too, but I can't afford diamonds. That little bling must be worth as much as the egg Carolyn gave me when I was a kid. Wow!"

When Luis was twelve, Carolyn inherited her sister Marjorie's prized possessions. A Fabergé egg was among the items. During her time of grief, and believing no material things were worth the loss of her twin, Carolyn parted with several of those material items. After a plea from little Stevie, she agreed that the colorful gilded egg should go to Luis. Luis was too young to understand the value of the golden egg. He had given it a personally naïve value of one hundred dollars, which Carolyn found amusing. However, his foster father Felipe knew the true value of the egg and enclosed it in tamper-proof glass for the child. That glass was bolted to a metal panel in the wall of Luis's childhood bedroom.

When Luis asked him why he was securing the egg in that manner, Felipe said, "That egg is probably worth more than five houses and five cars."

"Really?" wide-eyed Luis asked. "Wow."

Katie smiled at him, holding the box between her and him. It contained a bracelet with matching diamond earrings. "That's half," she said. "They're a match to the necklace Papa Sean and Momma gave me. Aren't they beautiful?"

"They have a match?"

"Yes, they do," she said with a beaming smile.

"Promise me something," he said.

"What?"

"If you ever wear them in my presence, make sure you hire a couple of bodyguards. I don't want to put my life in peril in case someone decides to mug you."

Katie whacked him over the head and playfully scolded him, "Shut up, you damn fool!" Then she added, "You know, sometimes my mother gets on my nerves, but I have to hand it to her; she has exquisite taste. I'm willing to bet she's the one who picked out the entire set. Momma Ellen most likely consulted her, and Mommy picked it out. The woman is fabulous."

"A moment ago you wanted to trade her in. Now you're singing her praises. Diamonds sure make women fickle. Why do women like shiny rocks?"

"You like it too," she challenged him. "It left you speechless. How many wows came out of your mouth, girly boy?"

"One or two. It's a really nice gift; it deserves a few wows. I can buy you a chunk of coal and polish it for you if you like. Would you give me a wow?"

"Maybe I would. Let's see what you can come up with."

"You're on," he challenged her. Then he added, "By the way, this girly boy will be a father in less than nine months. My boys swim."

She pecked him on the cheek and said, "They do swim, and I'm glad they do." Then she added, "Luis, call Mommy back. She's probably wondering why I didn't mention the gift or thank her for it."

* * *

In the meantime, Carolyn was speaking to the party she had called earlier. "Did you get my e-mail, Mr. Haggerty?" she asked.

"Yes, I did. I was just about to call you, Mrs. O'Gorman; I apologize. Apparently, I misunderstood. I thought you wanted me to negotiate and that you were willing to go as high as one hundred and seventy-five, so I offered him seventy-five."

"I didn't tell you to take advantage of him. The Web site is worth a whole lot more, and you know it. As you said, I apparently did not make my wishes clear. Did you speak with his lawyer yet?"

"No, but she did leave a voice mail. I'll call her tomorrow."

"Then there is still a way to fix this. You will pay him one seventy five."

"It's your money, Mrs. O'Gorman. I simply follow instructions. I know it isn't my place to ask you this, but since the sum seems excessive to me, and my boss Mr. Harrington has entrusted me to handle this matter for you, as a precaution, I feel a need to ask you. Pardon me if I'm out of line, but why do you take such an interest in this young man? First, your family practically hands him below-prime interest loans for college, medical school, and his mortgage. Now you want to make him a millionaire overnight. He'll probably squander it all in a year. Why didn't you establish a fiduciary for him?"

"I do appreciate your concern. As for a fiduciary, don't you think I thought of that? It's too complicated a matter. He mustn't know the true origin of these financial arrangements. He needs to know he has earned the money. And he has. He put a lot of work into this project. I know there must be other speculators out there who would be interested in stealing the site from the unsuspecting young man. It has plenty of lucrative potential, and I don't want him cheated. I'm depending on you to make sure that doesn't happen, Mr. Haggerty. To ease him into his newly acquired wealth, arrange for installment payments at market interest."

"Yes, ma'am."

* * *

Not wanting to disturb Matthew by using their private bath, Carolyn decided to shower in the downstairs bathroom as soon as she finished talking with Mr. Haggerty. However, as she set the phone down and started to undress, the phone rang again. She recognized Katie's number.

"I was under the impression you were going to bed and didn't want to speak to me," Carolyn said as soon as she answered the phone.

"I always want to speak to you, Mrs. G.," Luis responded. "Hold on, Katie wants to say something." He handed the phone to Katie.

"Mommy!" Katie exclaimed, and Carolyn waited for the other shoe to drop. Through the years, she noticed that Katie would call her Mommy when it suited her to sugarcoat a situation, and she would revert to Mom whenever she didn't expect anything in return. Kieran and Stevie used either term randomly, without an agenda; Katie had a calculating nature.

"What do you want, Katie?" she asked.

"Nothing, Mom. Honest. I called to thank you for the very expensive, exquisite gift. I also apologize for not opening it earlier; I was distracted."

"That's understandable, dear. You tangled with a bear today and put yourself in harm's way to protect your brother. Thank you for that, and thank you for all the wonderful work you did in the construction of the new Emily's Hope. As for the other matter, I won't hassle you if you choose not to talk. I simply ask you to remember that I love you and I am proud of you. Do you understand that, Katie?"

"Yes, Mom. I do. I love you too. Honest. I don't purposely do things to irk you. I'm trying, Mom. I really am. It's very hard sometimes, Mommy. I'm sorry," she cried. Luis wrapped his arms around her and kissed her on the cheek.

"Katie, I know it's hard, honey. Sweetheart, you're very young and intelligent, but emotionally fragile. I know some things are difficult for you. I wish you would let me help. You are not alone, honey. Don't ever feel like you need to do things alone. From day one, I made a commitment and promise to you. You are my daughter; Emily is your biological mother. I want you to love and honor her memory, but you are my little girl. Together, we will find your light. Trust me."

"I do, Mommy. Thank you." The tears rolled down her cheeks.

"Katie, honey, don't worry. Okay?"

"Yes, Mommy. I'll talk to you tomorrow."

* * *

After taking her shower, Carolyn covered her nakedness with a bath towel. When she entered her bedroom with a basket of clean laundry, she stood by the closed door, waiting for her eyes to adjust to the darkness in the room. The moonlight filtered through the lace curtains. When her eyes responded to the dim light, she set the laundry basket down. As she walked to the bathroom, past Matthew's sleeping form, she noticed a second figure sleeping next to him. She shook Matthew and woke him.

"What is our son doing in our bed?" she asked.

Bleary eyed, Matthew responded, "He had a nightmare and was yelling in his sleep. I thought it would save me some sleep if I let him bunk with us tonight. Evidently, I was wrong because now you've awakened me again. You could have figured out the scenario without depriving me of my sleep."

"You feel deprived?"

"Yeah, I feel deprived."

"Well, come into Stevie's room, and I'll make it up to you."

The comment shook the sleep out of him. "Oh, Momma," he said, jumping out of bed. "Mattie is getting lucky tonight!"

"Hush. Don't wake him," she cautioned. "Let me get my diaphragm."

Eıght

◇◇◇

1986

In the vernacular of Carolyn's younger years, Katie's comment about riding Luis's pecker had blown her mind. Carolyn felt the detonation in her temples. It raced to her visual cortex, blew out through her ears, and almost caused her to lose her balance. While the news made Nydia turn pale, the explosion in Carolyn's head had made her light up like a ripe tomato. Yes, it definitely blew her mind. She walked back to her seat behind the desk and literally collapsed into the chair. As pale as Nydia was, she watched and heard Carolyn drop into the seat and then saw her drape her hands over her eyes. Katie also sensed something must be wrong, and she looked visibly frightened.

"Oh, my God, Carolyn," Nydia said nervously, trying to regain her composure. "Are you okay?"

Katie's eyes got larger, continuing to suspect that something was probably wrong. She asked, "Mommy, are you sick too?"

The explosion in her mind was so loud that Carolyn could barely hear Nydia and Katie speaking. Even with her hands over her eyes, she could see ripples, like water expanding in a pond. When she uncovered her eyes and opened them, most of the images in the room resembled a Cezanne painting, chopped up into jagged patterns immersed in a watery eddy. Carolyn was experiencing her first migraine headache. Everything looked geometric. She closed her eyes again and continued to see the ripples without the boxed patterns.

After a few seconds, she opened her eyes again and managed to say, "I'll be okay, Nydia." By then, Nydia was standing next to her, nervously holding a glass of orange juice that she had gotten from the refrigerator in the kitchenette. With her hand visibly shaking, Nydia handed Carolyn the juice.

Carolyn reassured her by repeating, "I'll be okay. Please keep your eyes on the children. Take care of Luis." She started to sip the juice as Katie stared at her.

Nydia grabbed Katie's hand and said, "Come on, honey. You can sit next to me while I get Luis ready to see the doctor." Katie allowed herself to be led away while watching Carolyn.

Carolyn said, "I wasn't expecting that."

Nydia understood and said, "Neither was I." In Spanish she added, "They're children. Children sometimes do these things."

Carolyn sighed and thought of William Lyman, Katie's biological father. "It's the father," she responded in Spanish so Katie would not understand. "He's scum."

Nydia understood. At Emily's Hope, every parent or guardian leaned on each other for support, so they had shared their stories with one another and learned from each situation.

Now Carolyn thought of leaving William Lyman without his manhood. *That bastard,* she almost blurted out. *Jail is too good for him.* She then said, "Katie, come here, sweetie." The sugar rush from the orange juice had helped clear her vision a bit.

Katie obeyed and went to stand next to Carolyn's seat. "Are you okay, Mommy?"

"Yes, honey, I'm okay." She picked the child up and put her in her lap.

"Why are you crying?"

Carolyn wasn't aware that tears had rolled down her face. Nydia eavesdropped on the conversation as she removed Luis's pants and body stocking. Carolyn reached for some tissues and mopped her face dry. "I'm angry, Katie."

"Are you angry at me, Mommy? I'm sorry."

"I'm not angry at you, honey. I love you; I love Luis. I could never be angry at you. I'm angry that sometimes bad things happen."

"Is Luis going to be all right?"

"Yes, Luis is going to be fine. Nydia is going to take him to the hospital, and the doctors will take care of him."

"Then why are you angry? Nothing bad is going to happen."

"It already happened."

"What happened?" Katie asked.

"I got a big headache," she said. Then she added, "But it's gone now."

"I'm glad."

"I'm glad too," Carolyn said, and she kissed Katie on her head. "I love you, my little angel."

"I love you too, Mommy," she said, fondling Carolyn's silk scarf.

Carolyn brushed Katie's hair back and looked into her face. She wanted to query Katie, but she didn't know how to phrase the questions or utter a statement. Finally, she asked, "Katie, why would you ride Luis's pecker?"

Katie shrugged her shoulders and then placed her hands over her mouth. She looked about the room, avoiding Carolyn's gaze.

"Katie, honey, look at me," Carolyn commented, looking into the child's face.

Katie's eyes stopped darting about the room, and she started to play with her shoe strap, digging the shoe's heel into Carolyn's thigh. Katie knew she had to avoid eye contact with Carolyn in order to evade the answer. In the innermost recesses of her young mind, she knew this was a taboo subject. It was also problematic because she did not have the skills to communicate that information to Carolyn. Katie knew she wasn't supposed to speak of such things because William always told her not to tell. "If you tell Mommy that Daddy loved you tonight, I will have to hurt Mommy. If I hurt Mommy, it's your fault." With her left hand, Carolyn was about to hold Katie's chin up in order to achieve eye contact. Katie grabbed Carolyn's hand in midair and examined it. Noticing something on Carolyn's finger, Katie knew she had the opportunity to skirt the issue.

"You have a heart," she said to Carolyn while holding her hand and gazing at her finger. She pointed to the claddagh ring on the palm side of Carolyn's finger. "The hands have a heart," she observed. "That's silly."

"Yes, the hands have a heart," Carolyn agreed while sizing her up.

"Why?"

"It's my wedding ring," Carolyn explained. "It means I gave my heart to my husband because I love him."

"You love Daddy?"

"Yes, I love Daddy."

At that moment, Katie experienced a flashback. Her senses recalled William Lyman's warm breath on her face. He had just finished rubbing his penis on her immature labia. His beard stubble scratched her cheek as he whispered, "If you tell Mommy, I'll kill her." Katie's eyes lit up and opened wide. Her little heart raced. She gasped and put her hands over her mouth again. She looked about the room once more. Carolyn noticed her increased agitation and observed her quietly while rubbing the child's back. After a few seconds, Katie uncovered her mouth and put a finger up to her lips. She then drew herself up to whisper in Carolyn's ear, "Daddy has a pecker." Carolyn turned crimson as Katie settled back into her lap. "Not this daddy," Katie said as she pointed to the ring. She held her finger back up to her lips. "If you talk, don't talk," Katie whispered nonsensically as Carolyn watched her with painfilled eyes. "Don't talk, okay?"

"Okay," Carolyn agreed. Katie put her thumb in her mouth. With the other hand, she grabbed Carolyn's blouse so tightly that she strained the buttons in their grommets. The top button popped open as Katie pulled herself to rest her head on Carolyn's bosom. Carolyn cradled the child's head in one hand and planted a kiss on her head.

"It's okay, baby, we don't have to talk." She wrapped her arms around her and turned her attention to Nydia. "Nydia, I'm so sorry about all this. It's surreal. Every time I think I've heard the worst, something eventually comes out of left field. I don't have the words to express the distress I feel about this latest turn of events. I sincerely apologize."

"Carolyn," Nydia said, "sometimes I think you worry too much. We can't fix everything. With time, Little God heals all wounds."

"Mommy," Katie asked, "why are you worried?"

Carolyn studied the child for a moment and said, "Katie forget about that, honey. I need to tell you and Luis something."

"What?"

"You can't ride Luis's pecker. You must not do that anymore."

"Why not?"

Carolyn was stumped. If she said that Katie could injure Luis by engaging in the activity, then Katie might conclude she was responsible for Luis's present predicament.

"When you are old enough to marry my son," Nydia interjected, "you can do that. Not now. Children are not supposed to do that because it makes God very sad. Do you want to make God sad?"

"No," Katie answered.

"Luis, do you want to make God sad and make him cry?" Nydia asked Luis, and his eyes opened wide as he stared up at her. He shook his head from side to side. Nydia commented, "Then the two of you must not do that again. Do you understand?"

Luis gave a fearful nod. Katie looked at Carolyn with eyes filled with guilt and fear. She didn't answer Nydia's booming question.

"Mommy, is God angry at me?" she asked.

"No," Carolyn murmured as the paramedics knocked and opened the door.

Katie and the two women turned their attention to the man and the woman at the door.

The paramedics quickly went into action while Katie soaked in all that transpired and was soon standing next to the male paramedic. She watched him examine Luis's abdomen.

"He can't pee, and he can't talk because it hurts so bad," she said.

"Katie, honey," Carolyn said, "the gentleman knows that. Come sit with me while he does his work."

"I want to stay with Luis. He's my best friend in all the world," she said, staring up at Carolyn.

"You can't stay with him. Come on," she said and went to take her hand.

Katie pulled away. "I have to stay with Luis," she insisted, crossing her arms in front of her chest and giving Carolyn a stern look.

"Honey, the longer we argue, the longer Luis has to wait. He's in pain, and these two nice people will take him to a doctor who can help him. They need to do it quickly, and you can't go with them."

Katie looked at Carolyn suspiciously. Then she turned her stern gaze on the paramedic. "You better take good care of Luis, or I'll kick your ass," she warned him.

"Katie!" Carolyn and Nydia yelled in unison.

The paramedic smiled and stifled a laugh. "We'll take excellent care of Luis," he said. "I promise."

"Well, you better 'cause I'm not kidding!" Katie said her final words without changing her menacing stare.

Nine

Later that day, Carolyn got a break from the kids and met Momma Ellen for tennis and dinner at the country club. Over the years, Carolyn and Ellen had developed a rapport with one another. Carolyn confided in Ellen, sharing personal information that she sometimes did not share with her own mother. At times, the two talked and giggled like schoolgirls and engaged in friendly banter. However, when Carolyn needed to have a serious conversation, Momma Ellen always lent a concerned ear.

"You didn't even let me work up a sweat today, a Carolyn Rua," Momma Ellen commented as they sat studying the menu. "I seldom beat you at tennis, but you seem distracted this evening. *Cad é tá cearr*/What's the matter?" she asked in Irish.

Carolyn explained that she hadn't gotten over what she had learned about Katie and Luis.

"Heaven knows how long this behavior has been going on. How could this happen?" she said to Momma Ellen.

"Are you sure you're interpreting this correctly?" Ellen asked.

"I don't believe I'm wrong about this. It's the residual effect of the monster she had as a father. Who knows to what extent that animal has damaged her? Then there are the ramifications, both legal and moral. I'm so embarrassed, angry, and upset; I could spit," she said vehemently. "Nydia doesn't have Luis attend Emily's Hope so he too can be made a victim. This could be very damaging for everyone."

"You think Nydia might sue us?"

"On the one hand, I don't think so. But I can't dismiss the possibility of it. She didn't seem that bothered by it, but who knows? I wouldn't blame her if she did sue on Luis's behalf," Carolyn replied as she unfolded her napkin. "What they did together could have a lasting effect on that poor boy. What if the state steps in? That could be a real can of worms. A few months ago, Katie bit that little girl in her class. Do you remember that?"

"Yes, Herself did bite little Zoe," Momma Ellen replied in her Irish vernacular, referring to Katie. "And she left a permanent mark on poor Shannon as well. Carolyn, children do things like that. It's their way of dealing with frustration. When they learn to vent in other ways, they will change. You probably bit or kicked a few kids yourself when you were her age."

"I don't think so."

"Check with your mother—maybe she can recall something. I'm willing to bet we all did it at one time or other. I can remember a few scrapes I had with my own siblings, including the lads. You couldn't have been such a perfect child," Ellen said and smiled at Carolyn. "Zoe's mother knew that, and that's why the matter was never blown out of proportion. Children heal and move on."

"I still can't help but worry about that and other things."

"What other things, dear?"

Carolyn took a deep breath and said, "If Katie did this with Luis, has she or will she do it with anyone else? Do we need to worry about other kids behaving in a similar manner in the future and victimizing other children? If I decide to raise Stevie or any child in this environment, will they suffer as a result of it?"

"You mean, will they be victimized by other victims?"

"Yes!"

"Calm down, dear. You think too much. Rein your imagination in a bit."

"I can't do that. That's how my mind works."

"I know—you have excellent foresight. It's a gift, but it can also be a curse, you know."

The waiter arrived to take their orders. Ellen requested a light meal. Carolyn ordered a medium-rare prime rib, baked potato with sour cream, broccoli in garlic sauce, and a papaya-coconut smoothie.

"My, my," Ellen said. "Are you throwing caution to the wind tonight, a Rua?"

"I'm having a rough day, Momma. It's either an increase in caloric intake or a margarita. Remember, I'm still nursing. I'm choosing the lesser of two evils. Today's little episode with the children has caused me to burn up more than the daily two-thousand-calorie requirement. I have to make up for it somehow."

"It's not wise to torture yourself, dear. First, put Stevie on more solid food, and then you can enjoy a margarita sooner than later. As for the day's events, I advise you not to permit anything to get the best of you."

"Easier said than done, on both counts. Today's events are augh!" she uttered in desperation. "And, I like nursing my son."

"I can vaguely remember the joys of nursing, so I understand. However, on both counts, you need to attend to your needs first. What happens when you're on a plane and it's about to crash? You are instructed to place the oxygen mask over your face first. Then you put the mask on your child. You understand the logic behind that, don't you?"

"Of course I do, but you're comparing oranges to apples."

"No, I'm not, a Rua. To be an effective mother, you need to take care of yourself first. If you get sick and, heaven forbid, have a nervous breakdown or weaken your immunity, who will take care of the children? The analogy is perfect. Give yourself the oxygen first."

"A margarita is not oxygen, Momma."

"I know that, dear, so don't get literal on me. You know exactly what I'm talking about. Are you still seeing that therapist, Dr. Shapiro? I suspect Katie's healing is going to be a lifelong, uphill quest for all of us. I don't want you to bear that cross alone, dear. We all need all the help we can get."

"Yes, I'm still seeing Shapiro. Katie's traumatic past is challenging, but I'm aware that I have issues of my own. So yes, I'm still seeing my shrink."

"You also have the burden of this job. I didn't ask you to take on the duties of CEO to make yourself sick. I asked you to do it because you have the qualifications and the heart for it. You are still young, perhaps too young to permit those duties to envelop you," she said and paused to take a few sips of water. "As far as the recent episode with Katie, you can pace yourself by viewing the scenarios as closed doors. Behind door number one, you anticipate a possible lawsuit. Behind door number two, you envision children molesting one another. What's behind door number three?"

"That's me fracturing a good relationship with people like Nydia because of door number two."

Ellen giggled. "I know it isn't funny to you, Carolyn, but it is to me. It's funny because I don't believe any of that will happen. However, I respect you, and I am extremely fond of you, dear. Listen carefully. It's wise to envision those doors, but until you hear someone knocking, don't open any of them. Also, rearrange them in order of importance. Which one do you view as potentially most threatening?"

Without hesitation, Carolyn said, "That would be door number two: children molesting children. That door has already knocked."

"Okay, good," Ellen said. "We'll step in there and have a look around. First, you need to realize that it isn't your responsibility to open any door alone. You're not Hercules. And, we're novices at this. First, we need to consult the experts and pray they know what they're doing. The puppeteers are also helpful in instructing the children and getting them to open up." Ellen was referring to a puppeteer group she had created for the express purpose of addressing difficult subjects with the children. They presented skits each month and met informally with the children at least once a week in the presence of two staff therapists. Katie was particularly fond of Fluffy, a squirrel that was brought to life by puppeteer Yolanda Martinez.

The waiter arrived with their salads and beverages as Ellen continued speaking. "We will open door number two together. After all, it's my granddaughter who's knocking. Pardon the pun, but she's knocking that cute little boy, Luis."

"Momma! This isn't a laughing matter."

"Lighten up, dear. You have to admit—he is a cute *buachaill*/boy," Ellen said. "I sensed Katie had the hots for him the minute she handed him a toy."

"Momma!"

"Try not to be so shocked, a Rua. It's not every day Katie parts with something she holds dear. I like Luis. Young Kate has good taste. The day they met, it was obvious she was flirting with him. Didn't you notice? Now we find out they've been experimenting. It's interesting."

"Experimenting? Interesting?" Carolyn asked in dismay. "It's disturbing; that's what it is. I don't care if he's a cute *buachaill*. Momma, we're talking about two little children. Children don't flirt; they don't know the meaning of it. She shouldn't be pining after anyone at her age. It's outrageous. She should be riding a rocking horse, not another child's...well, you know."

"I know, dear. It shouldn't be, but we're expecting two victmized children to view the world from a prism that they don't understand, and we, in turn, don't understand their confused and damaged little minds. That's why we're going to look into door number two. Don't worry about the other doors. If a lawsuit comes, it comes. We settle out of court. I wouldn't lose sleep over that. As for a rift between friends," she said about Carolyn's concern that Nydia could react negatively to the situation, "sometimes those things happen. If I were to worry about every friend I've lost or haven't seen in years, I could never rest. We lose friends and loved ones, and life goes on. They croak or live their lives—I live mine." She shrugged her shoulders, and Carolyn displayed a sad smile, for she knew how Emily's death had affected everyone, especially Momma Ellen, who continued her advice with, "Anyway, we are not here to speak about that. We need to speak of the children's future and ease the burden off your shoulders. I don't want you to worry like this. Making yourself ill is not part of the deal. If the weight becomes intolerable, you can bail out. Your well-being is more important than the job. Do you understand?"

"Of course I understand, but I'm not out, and Katie will continue to be with me, no matter what. I need to do the right thing for her. And you're right. I need to lighten up."

The waiter arrived with the rest of their meal and Carolyn made a comment about the single thin breast of tangerine chicken surrounded by a few apple slices and a side of spinach on Ellen's plate.

Ellen said, "I have to fly to Chicago next month. We're doing a shoot out there, and I don't want to put on any extra pounds. Vanity is my downfall. I try to look as good as those plastic Hollywood people I work with. I will not allow them to upstage me in the real world. Of course, if any of those young women were to wear the knickers of an average woman on a windy day, they would flap in the wind like a sail in a gale storm." Carolyn broke out in laughter. When she calmed down, Ellen continued. "It's unreal how skinny those souls get for the privilege of being immortalized on cellulose; they already look like walking bones, half dead."

"It's a good thing you're a producer and not an actress. Or as they're saying now, an actor."

"You're absolutely right. You wouldn't be able to stand me. Hell, I wouldn't be able to stand myself. My vanity would go into overdrive. However, keeping my figure keeps Sean interested and his eyes from straying."

"Do you believe Papa's eyes stray?"

"Carolyn, he's a man! Of course his eyes stray. It's probably not the only thing that strays. Men can't help lusting after lovely women. It's part of their DNA. It's written on the tip of their penis: Stray, boy, stray."

Carolyn spat her food into her hand, saving herself from possibly choking as she burst into laughter. Her dimples became more pronounced and her face flushed. As she calmed down, she said, "You're terrible, Momma. I could never imagine Papa Sean being like that."

"You don't know him like I know him, dear. He's great in bed; I didn't teach him all that. He had to learn it somewhere."

"I don't need to hear another word." Carolyn laughed. "Don't change my perception of you, of him. Please stop. I'll never be able to look him in the eye."

"Like I said before, you're still young. You have a lot to learn. Be sure to keep an eye on Matthew. He's my son, but he's also a man."

"No, no, no, no. I know how some men can be. Women too—there are no exceptions when it comes to lust. Matthew is different. You said so yourself—he's a fine young man. He tends to be shy around women; he was like that when we first met. His eyes may stray, and that's okay. But that's the only thing that will stray; I trust him to keep his pants on. I love him too much to think otherwise."

"I love Sean, but I still keep an eye on him. I make sure he keeps his pants on; I don't leave that to trust. There are too many young, slender women in the entertainment business, so I keep him close. Of course, when I have to leave his side, I call him and whisper sweet nothings in his ear. I do that because I love him—forget the trust. Jesus loved Judas, but he didn't trust him. I trust Sean with plenty, but not with his male DNA and his blinking penis seeking an entry gate."

"Do your sons know you think like this?"

"Probably not. However, if they're in tune with their DNA, they know from whence I speak. In my business, I see too much of that. True, women do it too. But I think the men outnumber us in that area. We have that fetal imprint to keep us in check and browbeat us till death. Most women first think of the children. We cannot hurt the little darlings. The men don't worry about the children and the consequences. If they're as shy as Mattie, chances are an experienced nymph will help them get over it; the pants will slip right off."

"Please change the subject," Carolyn begged her while feigning annoyance. "My poor husband is sitting at home with two very young children while I dine with his mother, and she's placing disturbing images in my mind."

"Matthew should sit home with his children. That helps him bond with them. Besides, he didn't spend several months sleeping uncomfortably as if he had a sack of spuds protruding from his belly. All he did was send his sperm up the canal in all of two seconds. It's only fair that he change a few diapers, and you shouldn't feel sorry for him, dear. Enjoy your meal, and we'll forget about this conversation."

"Thank you," Carolyn said as she cut her steak. Then she pushed the plate aside. "You know, I'm not that hungry anymore."

"It's a pity I don't have a dog; he would enjoy that," Ellen said. "You should try the chicken. It's quite good. Or did I spoil your appetite?"

"No, you didn't spoil my appetite. On the contrary, once again you have entertained me with your lies and ludicrous tales. At times you disturb me, but you're funny, Momma. Thanks to your canard, I don't need to drown my worries with these excess calories."

"Have you no respect for your elders, dear? Are you calling me a liar?"

"That's exactly what I'm calling you," Carolyn said as she took a sip of her tropical smoothie, "and I thank you for the effort to distract me."

"What gave me away?" Ellen asked with amusement as she forked a bite-sized piece of her chicken.

"A few months ago, you told me Sean has suffered from impotence for years. Now you claim he lusts after other women and he's great in bed. You should keep better track of your embellished stories."

"I do, dear. I was hoping you had forgotten about the impotent penis," Ellen said and made her hand go limp at the wrist.

"Have you no shame, woman?" Carolyn said, laughing and grabbing a napkin to wipe her eyes. "Of course I wouldn't forget a story like that. As for Papa straying, I know how much you and Sean love each other and how you adore your children. When I didn't know you very well, I used to fall for your ridiculous stories. Now I know better than to believe a writer-slash-movie producer. You're so full of blarney it oozes out your ears." Then Carolyn added in Irish for emphasis, "Óinseach mé/I'm not a fool."

"You have matured then, and you were leading me on with your feigned innocence. You should come and act for me, dear."

"I'm not falling for that either. You're the one who told me that in Hollywood the actors are the pawns and fools who do most of the work and the owner-producers reap the profits. Do you want to offer me your job?"

Ellen smiled at her. "You wouldn't take it."

"How do you know?" Carolyn asked while stirring her beverage.

"Because presently, you're like a pig in shit. You love what you do. It shows in your demeanor. I advise you not to play poker with me."

Carolyn smiled. "I don't know how to play poker. However, you're right. First, I don't have your creative genes. Secondly, I do love this job. It's almost like being a stay-at-home mom. I have my children near me, and I can also enjoy adult conversation. I come in contact with all those cute little kids; I like talking to them as well. It's fun, except for *the incident.*"

"Don't worry about that. My Katie, your Katie, is in excellent hands. You give her all she needs —acknowledgement, love, and affection, ALA. That's why Sean and I decided that you were the right person to adopt her. Losing Emily shattered his soul, and mine too, and we thought we should raise Katie. Then Matthew asked if the two of you could have her because you had fallen in love with her. I saw the look in Sean's eyes—he was torn. Then he asked me if I was willing to let her go. 'Carolyn exudes ALA,' he said. Then I knew I could say yes to Matthew's request."

"Thank you, Momma," Carolyn said with tears welling in her eyes.

"Before I forget, I thought you might be interested in this." She handed Carolyn a folder. "It's a background check on young master Luis."

"Nydia's ward?" Carolyn asked sounding surprised. "Why would you do a background check on him?"

"Isn't it obvious? I needed to know why the lad rushed into Sean's arms the day they met. In order to get the boy home, Sean had to accompany Nydia and him and assure the child that they would see each other again. He has apparently mistaken Sean for someone else. Luis's eyes sparkle whenever he sees his papa. His interest in the flute is also interesting."

"Is there anything of interest in here?"

"Everybody's life is relatively interesting," Ellen said, "but I didn't find anything that will make history. His birth and baptismal certificates are in there. Young Luis was born in Puerto Rico as a substance-abuse baby. He is a Puerto Rican of Scottish descent; I guess that could be considered interesting. His grandfather was Ernest Walker, a Scotsman who played the bagpipes and other woodwinds, including a flute. That could explain the child's interest in the so-called flute. Perhaps his grandfather used to entertain him with it."

"Well, that is interesting. What happened to the grandfather?"

"He was found dead in his bed, of an apparent stroke. There's a photograph of Ernest in there. I stared at it for a while to determine if Luis believes Sean to be Ernest. Ernest and Sean don't resemble one another, at least not when I compare Sean to that photo."

"Maybe Sean and Ernest were the same height or had similar stature. Maybe Luis thinks Sean is his father and not the grandfather."

"Perhaps," Ellen agreed.

"Is there any other family? Anyone who could come forward and claim him? I heard that his mother died while she was being detained. What about a father?"

"He died first, in a construction job. Apparently, that sent the mother off the deep end. It's all there in the report; you can read it all when you get home."

"Yes, I will, but I'm still curious. Isn't there anyone who can claim this child or cares if he's alive or dead?"

"Well, his foster parents care, and so do I. Obviously, so do you."

"That's not what I mean, and you know it," Carolyn corrected her. "I think it's sad that such a tiny little boy is suddenly left alone in the world. Surely he must have other relatives—uncles, cousins, whoever."

"Carolyn, there must be millions of children who are suddenly left all alone in the world. Luis, despite his misfortunes, is among the lucky ones. Evidently, the Lópezes love this kid. I have taken a shine to him myself, and I intend to keep track of him. If the Lópezes don't adopt him, he isn't going to fall through the cracks; I will see to that. Don't worry about him and Katie."

* * *

Matthew heard Carolyn's car coming up the driveway, and he flicked the kitchen lights on for her. He opened the kitchen door and waited there while she secured the car in the garage. As she walked in, he took the doggy bag from her and kissed her on the cheek. While Carolyn placed her bag on a chair and removed her jacket, he asked, "What did you bring me?"

"Key lime pie. However, you don't deserve it because I see the pizza box in the trash."

"What?" he objected. "Katie and I like pizza."

"We've been through this before. Pizza is a treat—not a meal. Don't eat the pie tonight because you're not getting two treats in one evening."

"Fine with me. We also had apple pie à la mode."

"Matthew! I left you chicken and vegetables. All you had to do was heat them up. You're supposed to set an example."

"I'll set an example tomorrow, Honey-Lyn." He placed the individual servings of pie in the refrigerator. "Can I have pie tomorrow? I'll let you have apple pie tonight."

"Don't get me started! Did you give Stevie his bottle?"

"Yes, I did," he replied and started to carress her bosom. "I gave him his mommy's milk at exactly eight o'clock. Are you pumping any more milk out tonight? I'm here to help." He kissed her cleavage.

Carolyn grabbed his hair and pulled him back. "Hold it right there, *don Juan.* Prove to me that you deserve mommy's milk."

"Well, actually, you're not going to be pleased. Come with me. First, we need a flashlight." He removed one from a kitchen drawer. Then he led her into the living room and up the stairs.

"What am I not going to be pleased about, Matthew?"

"Be patient. Come with me. You have to see this to appreciate it."

"Now I'm supposed to appreciate it." As they reached the landing, Carolyn caught a sweet odor in the air. "I smell perfume."

"Be patient." He opened the door to Katie's bedroom. The light from the hall flooded into the room. "Take the flashlight," he whispered, "and take a look at her face." Carolyn didn't miss the odor of saturated perfume as she reached Katie's pillow and briefly shined the light on her face, which was covered with lipstick, eyeliner, and mascara. Before Katie could react to the light, Carolyn turned off the flashlight. "There's more," Matthew whispered. "Follow me."

He led her across the hall to their bedroom. He opened the door, turned the light on, and announced, "Ta-rum!" while extending his arms.

Carolyn gasped. The air was heavy with different fragrances. There was a stream of toilet tissue everywhere. The walls were covered with lipstick as far as short little arms could reach. The bedcover was coated with powder. A couple of Spanish Lladró figurines lay at the foot of a Queen Anne chair, where they had each been shattered.

"What the hell?" Carolyn asked while taking in the sight. "Did Katie do this?"

"Who else? We don't have leprechauns," Matthew commented while smiling devilishly. "There's more."

"Matthew, I swear to God, I'm going to kill you and pull out your liver. What the hell were you doing? You were supposed to be watching her. She could have set the house on fire. What the hell is wrong with you?" She rushed to a window and said, "Help me open these damn windows to get this smell out of here." He complied while she continued to vent. "You damn idiot. And you tell me there's more. How much more could there be? What the hell were you doing?" she asked a third time. "Where were you while all this was going on?"

"I guess I better not tell you to check the bathroom," he said. Carolyn rushed across the room and flipped the light in the bathroom.

Their private toilet was stuffed beyond the brim with every toy imaginable. Soaking-wet towels were on the floor. Behind her, Matthew said, "You know how you tell me to check on her if it gets too quiet? Well, she wasn't quiet. I could hear her running around while I was being a good father and playing with Stevie."

"You mean you weren't doing what you were supposed to be doing. You weren't keeping an eye on her. She was unsupervised and playing with water—she could have drowned!"

"I was keeping an eye on her—sort of. I was in the nursery, and I could hear her. She was running around. Then everything got quiet; I came out to check. She had fallen asleep with the phone off the hook."

"Who was she calling?"

"I don't know. You know how the phone beeps when it's been off the hook for a while?"

"Yes." Carolyn crossed her arms in front of her chest as if to say, "This better be good."

"Well, it was beeping. Since I'm such a good father—I am a good father, you know—I put the phone back on the hook and tucked her into bed. It's just like you say, Honey-Lyn. She looks like such a sweet angel—at least, when she's asleep, you know."

"Oh, yes—I know, Honey-Matt," she said sarcastically. "You're such a good father; I know."

"Carolyn," he said defensively, "this is not my fault! I did follow your instructions."

"The only reason I don't kill you now is because I don't want to rot in prison. What is wrong with you, fool? You do not, and I repeat, do not leave children alone. You can play with Stevie, but you keep her by your side. You give her an activity book, Lincoln logs, whatever. You must keep her occupied and interact with her every few minutes. How long did it take her to do this?"

"Ten minutes, maybe. You see, it's not my fault." Carolyn shook her head and sighed. "I can make this right. I swear," he said, putting his hand on his chest while raising the other as if he were taking a Boy Scout oath.

She stared dubiously at him. "Stop trying to butter me up. How are you going to make it right? You were putting a child's life at risk, Matthew! And, look at this mess!" she yelled, unfolding her arms from in front of her chest.

"I swear; I'll never make the same mistake, Honey-Lyn. Tomorrow morning, Katie is mine. You can take her to school as usual, but I'll wake her in the morning and get her ready for school. At three o'clock, I'll leave work early and pick her up. The only afterschool activity she'll have tomorrow and this weekend is fixing this; I will supervise. Everything will be great—I promise. Cross my heart," he said, and he made the sign of the cross.

Carolyn sighed and glared at him. "You better get some blankets out of the linen closet. You're sleeping downstairs tonight, and I'll be in the guest room."

"Carolyn! Don't be like that," he begged, putting his hands on her shoulders and giving her a puppy-dog look. "You know experts agree that sex is the best way to get rid of tension. I know you're tense tonight. I only want the best for you. Let me help you get rid of all that tension." He moved in to kiss her, and she pushed him away.

"Well, I'm not a science experiment, and I'm in no mood to play doctor with you tonight. Did you remember to put her pull-ups on before she fell asleep?" She was referring to Katie's pull-up diaper. When they first brought her home, she would wet the bed and wake up screaming at all hours of the night. Between Stevie's midnight and three o'clock feedings and Katie's restless nights, Matthew and Carolyn experienced severe sleep deprivation. They toughed it out and were glad to meet the challenge.

The doctors attributed Katie's behavior to her traumatic history. After a few months, the nightmares diminished, but the bedwetting continued. In response to the look on Matthew's face and his guilty shrug, Carolyn muttered, "Oh, for heaven's sake. Come and help me put a pad under her. In the morning, you'll be washing dirty bedcovers. You're unbelievable!"

After they finished taking care of Katie, Matthew carefully closed the door behind him and said, "You need to pump your milk; I can help you. The weight of all that milk isn't good for your tense shoulders."

"I'm sure I can manage without you, thank you." She pushed him aside and started to walk away.

"Well, you can't stop me from watching," he replied, following behind her.

"You're not watching anything, voyeur. You're going to get a head start on tomorrow's work by vacuuming the powder from the bed. Then you're going to toss all those covers in the wash with plenty of baking soda in order to neutralize the odor. On the way out, leave the windows open an inch, top and bottom, and close the door; I don't want to freeze the rest of the house."

"Aye, aye, Captain Ahab."

"What did you call me?" she asked, turning to face him.

"Nothing, nothing—I didn't say a word. I'm simply clearing my throat. Ahem," he said, faking a cough. "That powder is making my throat itch, you know. I'm getting the vacuum right now."

* * *

When Matthew entered the kitchen en route to the laundry room, Carolyn was on the phone with Ellen. "Thank you, Momma. I'll talk to you tomorrow. I'm glad we both got home all right. Give my love to Papa, and thanks again." She placed the phone on its base. "Matthew?" she called as he went past.

"Yes?"

"I apologize for getting so angry at you. I'll have to learn to count to ten. You're not totally at fault."

"I keep telling you it wasn't my fault. I did everything you told me to do. You didn't tell me about the Lincoln logs or any of that. That child is too hyper for me."

"Don't blame Katie. That's what she is—a child. She's a child dealing with situations at a child's level. We're the adults here, and it's our responsibility to guide her in the right direction."

"In the meantime, do we let her destroy the house? She needs to accept some blame before I can guide her. The blame starts tomorrow because I'm going to be her guide. As a matter of fact, I'm setting this stuff down on the laundry room floor, and she'll stuff this heavy bedspread in the wash all by herself while I watch her and eat my pie. This little kid is not going to get the best of me!"

Carolyn stepped forward to relieve him of his load. "I'm not going to argue with you. I'll put these on the laundry room floor for you. You can get my breast pump and the milk bottles so you can help me pump my milk."

"Oh, yes! I knew you would change your mind."

"Matthew, I love you, but you are a very strange man. How many men get a kick out of milking their wives?"

"I'll bet most men get a kick out of milking their wives. Luckily for you, I milk you for milk and not for cash or anything else."

She studied him suspiciously for a moment and said, "You do milk me for sympathy, love, sex...the main reason you want to milk me now is because you know that it will lead to sex. Shall I go on?"

"No need—my blood pressure is rising; it's getting very hot in here. Are you saying that you're going to take advantage of me tonight? I'm not sleeping downstairs?"

"That's exactly what I'm saying. There's no sense in punishing myself tonight because Katie decided to trash my boudoir."

"Momma said something to you. Right? That's why you changed your mind. What did Momma say?"

"Your mother has no jurisdiction in my private affairs."

"What did she say? She sided with me, right? You called to complain about my ineptness, and she set you straight."

"She didn't set me straight, Matthew. The reason Katie had the phone off the hook is because she called Papa's house three times. I didn't know she knew the number. She knew I went to dinner with Momma, so she called the house three times asking for me because she couldn't get a hold of her little boyfriend, Luis. Papa told her that he's still in the hospital. She was worried, and she was annoyed at me because I wasn't here. In her frustration, she trashed the bedroom."

"So," Matthew said looking self-righteous, "it's your fault. It's not my fault. I didn't go out to dinner; I was here trying to be a good dad. Umm. Perhaps I'll have a headache tonight. Oh, this feels so good."

"Two things to remember, my love: First, you're the one who failed to keep an eye on Katie. Secondly, you better quit while you're ahead, or I'll have a migraine before your headache sets in."

Matthew smiled and reminded her, "But you don't want to punish yourself because Katie trashed the boudoir. I'll make you very happy tonight." He winked. Then he suddenly remembered something and rushed to the coat rack near the door. He started to put on his jacket.

"Where are you going?" Carolyn asked.

"Out to the shed. I need an old bucket I have in there; I'll be right back. Don't start the foreplay without me. I'm going to have such fun tomorrow. Where's the flashlight, Honey-Lyn?"

"I placed it back in the drawer."

Ten

◇◆◇

1986

The next morning, young Matthew was squatting by Katie's bed. "Rise and shine," he kept whispering in her ear until she opened her eyes. "Rise and shine, my little sunflower. Time for school."

"Where's Mommy?" she asked with half open eyes.

"Mommy is downstairs. It's my turn to get you ready for school. Come on—get up."

Groggily, Katie got into her slippers and headed for her bathroom. She turned the knob, but the door didn't budge. "Daddy, the bathroom is locked."

"I know," he said, towering over her. "I locked it. This is payback, kid. I can't use my bathroom, so you can't use yours."

"Daddy, I have to pee."

"I know," he said with a conquering smile. "I have just what you need. Come with me." He led her to the bucket that he had placed in a corner next to her play table. The table had all the toiletries she was going to need that day. "Here's your toilet." He pointed to the bucket. He had lined it with a plastic bag and one of Stevie's diapers. It was covered with a lid that had a hole in the center. "Here's your toilet paper." He handed her a roll. "Call me when you're done. I'll be right outside."

"I have to brush my teeth," she complained.

"Don't worry. I have that covered. Just call me when you're done with the potty."

"Potty! I'm not a baby."

"Well you have behaved like a baby, so I am treating you like one. Go potty before you have an accident." He stepped outside, leaving the door open a crack. "Call me when you're done," he called from outside.

Eventually, he heard, "Daddy, I have to poo-poo."

"Well, let it rip, princess. The bucket will hold it."

When she was ready to brush her teeth, he showed her the toiletries on the table.

"I have to spit," she said. "Where's the sink?"

"No sink, princess. You spit in the bucket," he explained as he poured water from a pitcher into a glass.

"That's all yucky. I can't spit in there. It smells bad."

"Well, when you don't have a bathroom, you have to make do. Make believe you're out camping. Come on—brush up. Then you have to look in the mirror so you can wipe all that makeup off your face. You can't go to school looking like a clown."

"I'm not a clown! You're a clown. And you're mean. I want mommy. I'm not going to spit in a dirty bucket." She started to storm out of the room, but he blocked her path.

"Here's the thing, my little sunflower," he said, bending down and holding her arms at her side. "Today, Mommy does not come to your rescue. You trashed our room last night, and that made Mommy and me very unhappy. So today, you deal with me. Mommy is not going to save you until you clean up all that mess. You cannot use your toilet until I can use mine."

"Mommy is mad at me?" she asked. Her eyes were large, and she spoke with a combination of contrition and dread. What Matthew did not comprehend was that children have difficulty separating emotions and understanding consequences, especially Katie. To her there was no difference between "unhappy" and "angry," or "tired" and "sleepy." For her those emotions sometimes went hand in hand because when she was angry, she tended to be sad. When she was tired, she often became tired to the point of being sleepy. The day before, Nydia had mentioned that Katie and Luis's actions made God unhappy. In her mind, the only thing that had registered from Matthew's speech was that Carolyn, her sanctuary, was unhappy. Therefore, Carolyn must be angry. In two days, Katie had managed to anger God and Carolyn. From her perspective, Carolyn was the only mortal soul on earth who protected her. In her mind, she was in a pickle, and she didn't know what to do. She looked up at Matthew, and the tears welled in her eyes. She realized she had been defeated by her own actions. "I'm sorry, Daddy. I'm sorry," she cried. "I promise I won't do it again. I promise, Daddy; I promise."

"That's nice, princess, but you still need to fix it. When you make a mess, you have to clean it up."

Katie looked at him, filled with desperation. The tears still flowed. "I'll clean it, Daddy. I promise. I'll clean it."

"In that case, I'm willing to make a concession," he said, although Katie didn't understand what "concession" meant. "I'll replace the dirty bag in the bucket with a clean bag. That way, you can spit. Okay?"

Katie nodded in affirmation as her tears mixed with her makeup. She returned to the table and waited patiently to follow directions while Matthew dealt with the waste in the bucket. She then finished her morning routine to the point of getting dressed while Matthew patiently guided her through each step, including removing the make-up. Matthew walked her downstairs and into the living room, where Carolyn sat nursing Stevie.

"Carolyn, we're all done upstairs. She's dressed. Now we're going to have breakfast. Will you be joining us?"

"I already ate. Your breakfast is on the table; I need to finish with Stevie."

Katie observed Carolyn from a distance, not knowing if she should speak.

"Good morning, Katie," Carolyn said.

Katie remained silent, hung her head in shame, and walked toward Matthew. She fit her hand into his and eyed Carolyn shyly.

Matthew said, "Come on, Katie. Let's see what's for breakfast."

Before she entered the next room, she looked at Carolyn one more time and dropped her head again. In the kitchen, she was sullen and barely ate. Instead, she cut morsels of zucchini bread and smoked salmon and blended them with the bits of scrambled eggs, using her little fingers. She spread the mush out on the plate. Then she gathered it up into a mound. She didn't touch the dish of fresh pineapple.

Matthew watched her and asked, "Why are you playing with your food? Mommy didn't prepare breakfast so you could treat it like finger paint. Eat up."

"I'm not hungry," she complained, and she quickly emptied the dish of pineapples over the mixture in the plate. She proceeded to knead the pineapple pieces into the existing mush.

"Hey, cut that out!" He picked up her plate and emptied the contents in the garbage. "That's food. You're supposed to respect food," he said as he placed the plate on the counter. "You know, I'm not the one who's going to be hungry an hour from now. Go ahead and starve. See if I care." He returned to the table, picked up her glass of milk, and drank it down. "Man, that was good. Too bad you weren't hungry. I hope you weren't thirsty either because that milk sure hit the spot. If it were up to me, you wouldn't be eating lunch either. I imagine, by lunch, you'll be really hungry. Gas will build up in your tummy, and you'll be farting all afternoon. No one will want to sit near you. Now get up and go wash your hands."

Katie eyed him with disdain. "You're mean," she said, crossing her arms in front of her chest. "I'm going to tell Mommy all the mean things you say."

"Did you forget? Mommy is not here to rescue you. Today, you're mine. You will do everything I tell you. After school, you'll start to clean everything up. Then this weekend, you and I are going to paint Mommy's bedroom. We'll make it very pretty because you're going to work very hard."

She pouted and gave him an evil look.

"Give me those dirty hands," he said, reaching for a napkin to wipe the grease off her hands.

"No!" she pouted.

"Once again, you lose. Keep wiping your hands on that pretty sweater. When mommy sees the grease stains on it and has to throw it out, she isn't going to be happy with you."

Katie offered up her hands, and Matthew sat down while still holding the napkin.

"Too late. You can wipe your own hands," he said, and Katie flashed him another evil look. She tried to reach one of the napkins on the table, but her arms were too short. "You'll have to get up and wash them. The bathroom is next to the laundry room on your left."

"I know where the bathroom is, smartass," Katie replied as she climbed out of her seat.

"Hold it right there," he said as he rose and blocked her path. "Calling me names isn't going to earn you any gold stars. Do you know why?" She glared up at him from her short height. "When people use bad words, they prove they aren't very smart. Bad words also make you look ugly. Is that what you want people to think of you? If that's the case, keep using words like 'ass', 'smartass', and all those negative words you know. People will just point to you and say, 'There goes that ugly, dumb little girl.'"

"I hate you," she said, and she pushed her way past him.

As Carolyn drove Katie and Stevie to Emily's Hope that morning, she was concerned about Katie's silence. Without interacting with the child, she checked Katie's face in the rearview mirror from time to time. Upon arrival at their destination, she freed Katie from the car seat and lifted her out of the car. Without uttering a word, Katie retrieved her book bag from the car's floor and started to walk toward the school.

"Katie, wait for me, honey. You can't go walking through the parking lot by yourself. You know better than that." Katie paused and hung her head. Carolyn walked up to her. "You've been quiet all morning," she said, squatting to be at eye level with Katie. "What's the matter?" Unable to express her emotions, Katie's eyes started to tear up again.

"Hey. Come here." Carolyn said and picked the child up in her arms. The gentle touch and concern was enough to open the floodgates, and Katie started to sob. Carolyn kissed her salty tears and held her mittened hand. "I'm sorry I wasn't home last night, sweetie. It's a difficult time for you. Are you angry with me?" Katie shook her head in negation. "Are you worried about Luis?"

Katie started to breathe in gasps, but she didn't know how to answer that question. She was concerned about Luis, but his welfare was not at the core of her present distress. En route to school, all she could think of was how she had angered God and Carolyn. According to Matthew, Carolyn was not there to rescue her today. She started to hiccup as a car pulled up alongside their parking spot. Sean and Ellen had arrived.

"Luis will be okay, Katie," Carolyn continued to console her. "He'll be in the hospital for a few days, but he'll be fine."

"I'll clean your room, Mommy," she finally said between hiccups as Sean and Ellen exited their vehicle. "I'm sorry. I didn't mean to be bad."

"Is that why you're so upset?"

Her brow furrowed; she nodded in affirmation and said, "Daddy made me spit into a bucket. I was bad. I'm sorry I messed up your bathroom."

"Daddy made you spit in a bucket? What else did daddy do?"

"He said I fart too much and nobody wants to sit next to me because I stink."

"What else did he say?"

"He called me stupid."

"He did?"

"Aha."

"Good morning, clan," Sean said at the top of his lungs. "It's time to start a brand-new day." Carolyn acknowledged his greeting and turned to greet Ellen as well.

Momma soon noticed Katie's wet face. "Are you feeling a bit sad this morning, young Kate?"

"She's feeling remorseful about her actions yesterday," Carolyn replied, reminding her of the information she had shared with Ellen during the phone conversation the previous evening. In Irish, she added, "I believe your son rode her a little hard this morning. I guess there's nothing worse than having to pay the piper."

"I understand," Ellen replied in Irish. "I guess she's learning the meaning of tough love. Grandmother can ease her pain if you like."

"She's all yours until class starts. I have to free Stevie from the car."

"Katie," Ellen asked, "do you want to come with Momma?" She extended her hands out to the child.

Katie studied her a moment, ignored Ellen's extended arms, and turned her attention to Carolyn. "Mommy, I'm hungry."

"You're hungry? Didn't you eat your breakfast?"

Katie shook her head. "It didn't taste good," she replied.

"Humble pie never tastes good, honey."

"There was no pie. It was egg and fish," Katie said.

"Well, it's too late to get breakfast in the cafeteria. Snack time is at ten o'clock. When we get to my office, I can give you a granola bar or fruit. You can also drink one of Stevie's milk bottles if you like. Is that okay?"

"Yes," she said in a babyish fashion because she knew she would actually be drinking Carolyn's breast milk. She was finally getting the attention she had been craving.

Ellen, who had stood by after being rejected, said, "You take care of young Kate; I'll deal with Stevie." She turned to her husband. "Please get the baby's stroller out of the boot, Sean." She was referring to the car's trunk. After all the years of living in the States, she still fell back on British or Irish terminology from time to time. "Let's give Carolyn a hand."

After Katie basked in Carolyn's attention while chewing a granola bar and sipping breast milk, she went off to class. It would be her first day there without Luis. Sean accompanied her down the hall to her class while Ellen remained in Carolyn's office with Stevie in her lap. Ellen picked up a picture of Stevie from Carolyn's desk.

"How old was he when this was taken?" Ellen asked. In the picture, Stevie was dressed in Yankee pinstripes and cap.

"He was three months old," Carolyn replied. "That's the uniform my mother bought for him."

"Good Lord," Ellen said, "I hope Margaret isn't entertaining dreams he'll be a ball player someday."

"What's wrong with being a baseball player? As long as he's happy and is a person of integrity, he can be whatever he wants."

"Well, I don't care for baseball. It's a boring game. You don't want to be a baseball player, do you Stevie?" Stevie, as usual, listened to his grandmother attentively. He responded by rattling off a few words in baby gibberish. Then he stuck three fingers in his mouth. As Ellen continued to speak to him, he started to drool. "So," Ellen said to him as if she had understood every word, "you agree with me. After all, if you were to become a baseball player, you would probably be a pitcher—a southpaw, just like your mother. I can see you now. As you get ready to pitch, you look left. You look right. You're chewing tobacco or gum—whatever strikes your fancy. You spit into the wind. You can't be a baseball player unless you're chewing on something like a cow and spitting. If you're not too bright, the spit blows back in your face or onto your uniform."

Carolyn had been resting her chin in her hands while she watched Stevie's attentive face and listened to Ellen interacting with her grandson. "Oh, gross," she said.

Ellen ignored her and continued her narration. "You raise your right leg to establish your balance as the left hand moves back. You extend the arm forward and re-lease the ball at ninety miles per hour. The right leg comes down, and right there on national telly, you proceed to scratch your balls."

"Momma!" Carolyn complained. "Have you no shame. What kind of role model are you for my son?"

"Carolyn," Momma argued with a hint of amusement in her voice, "the lad has balls. Eventually, he's going to figure it out. If he becomes a ball player, he is going to scratch them in public. If he doesn't do that, he'll surely scratch his..."

"Don't say it. I have enough problems trying to get Katie to behave like a proper young lady."

"Katie isn't here, dear. I'm discussing anatomy with my grandson."

"Well, stick to baseball, Momma. Besides, don't you have work to do?"

"Actually, no," she said as she lifted Stevie above her head and brought him down again. "I was planning on spending the day with the children today. The puppeteers are performing this morning, so I'll be there for that. I like watching the tykes being mesmerized by the performers. In the meantime, I can take this young man off your hands and take him for a walk in the park. We can be back in time for the show."

"It's cold out there."

"A little fresh air never killed anyone. It will strengthen his lungs. Besides, he may want to be a hockey player or a mountain climber. Get me his coat, dear. Stevie and I are going to enjoy the crisp morning air."

Carolyn rose to get Stevie's winter gear. "I appreciate you taking him off my hands. I'm sure he'll enjoy his day, but don't teach him any more anatomy."

"Carolyn, you don't want the child to grow up ignorant. You teach him to be a little gentleman, and I'll teach him how to deal with the real world. Maybe he should go to Chicago with me."

Carolyn laughed and said, "I don't think so, but you can dream."

Within a short time, Ellen was pushing Stevie's carriage down a path in the park. She parked it next to a bench. She then secured her shoulder bag strap across her chest, making her bag rest against her upper back. With it out of the way, she lifted Stevie out of the carriage and onto the ground. She held his hands as he attempted to walk in front of her.

"You need to strengthen those legs, my little man," she said as she guided him up the path. "Let's see if you can walk all the way to the pond. We'll watch the ducks." Slowly, Stevie kept walking up the gradual incline. "Very good," Ellen said, continuing to encourage him. "We can walk on the grass. If you fall, you'll have a soft fall. Let me hold just one of your hands to test your balance, my little man." Stevie continued to walk while she held his hand. He made it a few steps before his legs gave way, and he started to topple sideways. Ellen caught him in time. "You've done well, my little man. You can sit and rest awhile. Then, I expect you to get up on your own power." She allowed him to drop to the ground and squatted next to him. Stevie then started to crawl away on all fours. Ellen grabbed one of his legs. "That's cheating, my little man. Come on—get up." As she rose with him in her arms, she saw what appeared to be a homeless man walking away with Stevie's carriage.

"Hey, hey!" she called out, and the man started running with the carriage. "Stop!" With Stevie in her arms, she chased after the man, constantly yelling, "Stop, thief!" She put Stevie down and found a rock on the side of the road. With rock in hand, she continued to chase the man while passersby cleared the way. She threw the rock, landing it squarely between his shoulder blades and knocking the wind out of the perpetrator's lungs. She watched for a moment as he fell and appeared to writh in pain. "Oh, my God—Stevie," she said and started running back to her grandson.

"What was I thinking?" she said as she picked him up. "I chase after a carriage and leave you behind. You better not utter a word to Carolyn; she'll kill me. It's a good thing you can't say anything."

She returned to get the carriage and noticed a police car arrive and the injured offender attempting to get up. The patrol car was by his side as he rose to his feet.

The officer got out of the vehicle. "Well, if it isn't Kenny. Why am I not surprised? I hear that you're now stealing stuff from babies?"

"Officer," Ellen inquired, "do you know this man?"

"Are you the victim, ma'am?"

"Hey, she hit me with a rock," Kenny complained.

"Shut up, Kenny. No one is talking to you." He turned his attention back to Ellen and repeated. "Are you the victim, ma'am?"

"In a manner of speaking, I guess I am. He tried to steal my grandson's carriage."

"Well, ma'am, I'm officer Paulson. This poor excuse for a thief is Kenneth Spaulding. He does these things so he can get a night in jail. If you file a report now, ma'am, you'll be doing me a favor. That way, I can arrest him sooner rather than later."

Ellen studied Kenny and noticed he was wearing a tattered military jacket with medals over layers of old sweatshirts. "Are you a vet?" she asked him.

"What's it to you?" Kenny replied.

"Watch your mouth!" Paulson admonished him. Then he answered Ellen's question. "He's a Vietnam vet, ma'am. Will you be pressing charges?"

"Apparently, he wants to go. If I don't have to take time out to appear in court, arrest him. However, young man," she said, turning to Kenny again, "I can offer you an alternative if you're willing to accept it."

Ellen secured Stevie in his carriage and started to fumble through her shoulder bag. Kenny eyed her suspiciously. Then he asked, "What's on the table?"

Ellen was now thumbing through a wallet, and she finally retrieved three cards. She handed them to Kenny. "The top card," she explained as Kenny examined it, "belongs to my son, Father Patrick O'Gorman."

Kenny handed the cards back to her. "I ain't seeing no priest," he commented.

"Oh, picky are we?" Ellen replied without accepting the cards. "My son is a Vietnam vet. Before he became a priest, he was a man and a vet, and he's still a man and a vet. He's not going to convert you or preach to you, but he will provide you with a warm place to sleep, some decent food, a much needed shower, and a change of clothing. And if you're willing to go there, he can probably help you change your life. Of course, if you want to continue smelling like a skunk and resembling a ragamuffin, you can go to jail with this nice young officer. You can then continue to inconvenience people like me when you force them to chase after you. If you had succeeded in running off with my grandson's carriage, you would have left me in a lurch while you satisfied your own selfish needs. Is that what you plan to do with the rest of your life?"

"Let me see those cards," Officer Paulson said to Kenny as he reached for the business cards. Paulson thumbed through them. When he was done, he ordered Kenny to get in the car. As Kenny started to open the door, the patrolman turned to Ellen and said, "I'll see to it that he meets your son, ma'am. Are you Mrs. O'Gorman?" he asked, looking at the second card.

"Yes, I am," Ellen said extending her hand.

Paulson accepted it. "It's a real pleasure to meet you, ma'am; I've heard a lot about you. I work out of the same precinct as Esposito and Garrity. Speaking on behalf of myself and my fellow officers, we appreciate what you and your family are doing for the community."

"Well, thank you, Officer Paulson. We too appreciate what you and your fellow officers are doing for the community. If you are ever in the vicinity of Emily's Hope, stop by. I'll give you a tour and treat you to lunch."

"No need to treat me to lunch, Mrs. O'Gorman, but I'll take you up on the tour. What's the third business card for?" he asked, examining it and noticing it belonged to a realtor.

"It's a friend's card. She flips houses. If Kenny has any skills, she can use a painter and/or handyman. He can learn the trade and earn some money."

"Thank you, ma'am. Kenny is a nice guy. He puts on a front—perhaps because he's had a few tough breaks. Hopefully, you're the break he needs. Have a nice day, Mrs. O'Gorman." He tipped his hat as Ellen returned the farewell.

She watched as the patrolman drove off and decided it was best to return with Stevie to the school. As she pushed Stevie's stroller, she said, "You know, Stevie, I didn't know I could pitch a rock with such accuracy. Perhaps your grandma Margaret is right. You should be a baseball player. You never know when you might need the skill to knock down a mugger. Then again, you might prefer a contact sport, so you could tackle the misfit to the ground." She continued chatting to Stevie all the way back to Emily's Hope. She excused herself as she reentered Carolyn's office. Carolyn, Dr. Holder, and three other staff members were seated around the conference table discussing business.

"Care to join us?" Carolyn inquired as Ellen removed Stevie's coat.

"What's on the table?"

"These fine people and I are discussing how we can get the adults more actively involved in their children's education and welfare while improving the quality of their own lives."

"That's a tall order, dear," she said as she placed Stevie in his walker.

Stevie quickly started moving about and bumping into office furniture. Ellen pulled out a chair and joined the group discussion.

"I'm all ears if someone cares to summarize what you've discussed so far."

At ten, the children received their snacks from the cafeteria. About ten minutes later, Katie popped into Carolyn's office with a half-empty bag of trail mix in one hand. Carolyn rose from her seat with Stevie in her arms and handed him to Ellen. She excused herself from the other people present and walked over to Katie.

"What's up?" she asked her.

"It's boring in there without Luis. He's my best and only friend. I have no one to talk to because he's sick."

"I know he's sick, Katie, but you don't come to school to talk. You are here to learn and listen to your teacher. You can't walk out of class every time you want to talk to me. Come with me," she said, extending her hand. "I'll walk you back to class." Katie accepted her hand and accompanied Carolyn out of the office. As they walked together, Carolyn said, "The most important thing for you to do is to be a good student."

"Why?"

"It's your job. Everyone has to have a job."

"I'm a little kid. Little kids don't have jobs."

"Well, you're wrong. You have three jobs."

"I do?"

"Yes, you do. Job number one: be a good student. Job number two: follow the instructions of the person in charge. Job number three: be happy."

"I can't be happy if I'm bored."

"Oh yes, you can. When you think you're bored, use your imagination. We've done that before, remember?"

"You mean like when we went to the park and made believe that lions were hiding behind the trees?"

"Yes—that's using your imagination."

"Well, it would have made more sense if leopards were hiding behind the trees. Lions live in savannahs, you know. They would have been hiding in the tall grass."

"Well, I stand corrected," Carolyn replied while smiling down at Katie. "Anyway, you can think of an adventure or something that makes you happy. Then you'll forget you're bored." They arrived at their destination. Carolyn squatted down to Katie's eye level. "In a little while, we'll be entertained by the puppeteers." Katie's eyes lit up. "I know that will make you happy." Katie agreed. "Now give me a kiss and get back to class. I'll see you later."

When Carolyn returned to the group meeting, she said, "We discussed offering a class on parenting and discipline—I'll be the first to sign up for that."

They all laughed, and Ellen inquired, "Is young Kate running you ragged, dear?"

"Young Kate has me in tatters, Momma." They all laughed again.

It was a small enough group of children and adults for all to sit in the first few rows of the auditorium to enjoy the puppet show. Ellen was in an end seat of one of the side rows with Carolyn and Stevie seated next to her. Sean was in the row behind them. Carolyn was bouncing Stevie on her lap when Katie's class walked in. As soon as Katie spotted Momma Ellen, she ran over and climbed into her lap.

"Are you behaving yourself, young Kate?" Ellen asked.

"Yes, Momma," she replied as she made herself more comfortable in Ellen's lap. "I can write my whole name, Katharine Erin O'Gorman. I wrote it in my notebook. Then we all wrote a story together about a dog and a cat."

"You did all that, did you now?"

"Yes."

"Does that cat play with a big fat rat who has a bat?"

"No," Katie said, and she giggled. "That's funny, Momma. But cats don't like rats, you know."

"Well, maybe the dog met a hog and a frog when he fetched a log from the bog in a fog," Ellen replied.

Katie giggled again and said, "That's funny too. What's a bog?"

"That's a place where the ground is wet and as mushy as brown slushy."

Katie smiled. "You talk funny, Momma. My teacher Mary read us a book like that. I can write the words, but I can't make up a story like that."

"You'll learn. That's why you're in school—so you can talk and write smooth and cool while you snooze by the pool."

"You can't snooze and write at the same time, silly."

"Well, it was worth a shot," Ellen commented as she pointed to the stage. "The show is about to start."

"There's Fluffy," Katie said excitedly as she pointed to the squirrel puppet that had popped her head out from the stage prop. The audience quieted down as the introduction music filtered through the speakers. A dog and a parrot soon appeared, and the show began.

The children listened attentively as the parrot and the dog complained that their mean siblings treated them poorly by referring to them as stupid or ugly. Fluffy the squirrel said, "Nothing could be further from the truth." She reminded the parrot that she had beautiful feathers that pleased the people she encountered. She gave the dog an equally uplifting approval by complimenting him on his arithmetic skills.

After the performance the children in the audience were encouraged to discuss their pet peeves. They enjoyed this interaction as much as they enjoyed the show. Hands went up throughout the audience, and each child waited to be acknowledged. Finally, Katie was chosen to speak. She stood tall next to Momma Ellen as she addressed Fluffy.

"My daddy is mean to me," she said. "This morning, he embarrassed me. He did not let me use my toilet and he made me potty like a little baby. I'm not a baby. While we were having breakfast, he said I'm ugly and stupid and I smell bad. He wouldn't give me a napkin to wipe my hands. I told my mommy. Right, Mommy?" she said as she turned to look at Carolyn.

Carolyn had stopped playing patty-cake with Stevie as soon she heard Katie utter the first phrase "My daddy is mean...." As Katie continued the narration, Carolyn was stunned. When she heard "Right, Mommy?" she was flabbergasted and visibly embarrassed.

Ellen filled the nervous second of silence by saying, "Sometimes we need to examine a situation before we say anything. Katie, your mommy and I are going to look into this because I am not happy."

"Tell Daddy not to be mean, Momma," Katie insisted.

"I will check the facts, young Kate."

"Are you going to tell Daddy to stop being mean?"

"Absolutely, my love. Now come sit in Grandma's lap, dear."

After the discussion, the children were led to the cafeteria for lunch, and Katie left with her group. Ellen carried Stevie as she and Carolyn returned to the office. As soon as Carolyn closed the door, she burst out into laughter.

"If that wasn't embarrassing, I don't know what is. Of course, you know I'm going to kill your son."

"Oh, let me, dear," Ellen retorted. "Once I'm done with him, he's going to learn to choose his words very carefully when he's around children."

"This morning, Katie told me a few things, but I didn't say anything to her."

"Why not?"

"Momma, in my mind, I weighed the information. I intended to discuss it with Matthew. I suspect Katie could have taken something out of context. He's innocent until proven guilty. I can't imagine what he could have said to her. Matthew can't be that stupid."

"Well, I'll soon find out," Ellen commented as she placed Stevie down near a stack of toys. She then called Matthew.

"I never said that," Matthew said defensively.

"Think very carefully, Mattie," Ellen continued. "Perhaps not in the context I've related to you, but think—did you ever use any such words?"

"Well, yes, I did. I think I said she was going to get gassy because she didn't eat her breakfast, and if she farted in class, no one would want to sit near her. There's nothing wrong with that, Momma. She needs to learn that there are boundaries, something that Carolyn doesn't seem to provide for her. Now I'm being perceived as the bad guy here. Katie is out of control, Momma. She's almost six, and we can't allow her to do whatever she feels like doing."

As Matthew checked his watch numerous times, Ellen gave him a twenty minute lecture, reminding him that he needed to choose his words carefully when dealing with his vulnerable daughter. She also praised Carolyn for what she had done for the child, and concluded with, "When the task of parenting is in your hands, it's in your hands. You don't shift blame to someone else. You're the adult, so set an example by words and action."

When Ellen concluded the phone call, Carolyn defended Matthew with, "He's trying so hard, Momma. I guess it hasn't been easy for him."

"Rearing children isn't easy, Carolyn. I know he's trying, and so are you. Matthew simply needs a reality check now and then. Basically, we are all trying to be good parents. Sometimes we get it right; sometimes we don't. Sometimes it's more than we can handle. I pray the Lord wraps my young Kate in His arms to guide her on the right path. So far, He has done some of that. My Emily was taken from me. Then He brought me you to look after my little Kate.

I'm also aware that Mattie has been wonderful, but even I know that there is a time and a place for lightheartedness."

Carolyn wrapped her arms around her shoulders. "Thank you, Momma, for your guidance, love, and support."

Ellen padded Carolyn's hand and said, "We better get to the cafeteria before there's nothing left to eat. Where's my little man?" she added, looking down to find Stevie, who had crawled under the table.

That afternoon, Matthew arrived at three o'clock to retrieve Katie from school. The children were often at the school for extracurricular activities and socializing until five o'clock or later, depending on a family's individual needs, and Carolyn sometimes stayed until five. However, that afternoon, after learning that the completion of Luis's medical procedure was long overdue, she left early to be at Nydia's side, and Matthew arrived at Carolyn's office to find his mother there with Stevie. Ellen was playing with the baby and a toy train when Matthew entered the office.

"Hi, Momma," he said with his arms loaded with roses. "I'm here to pick up Katie. Where's Carolyn?"

Ellen explained Carolyn's whereabouts and referred to the flowers by asking, "Are you feeling guilty about something, Mattie?"

"Me? No," he lied, and he separated one bouquet from the other. He handed it to his mother. "This is for you. I simply want to tell my girls that I love them and that I'm often thinking of them. You're my number-one girl, Momma."

"Of course I am," she said, accepting the flowers and rising from the floor. "Nice touch, Mattie. They're lovely. Thank you."

Matthew placed the remaining bouquet on the conference table. "I'll get Katie," he announced as he turned to leave.

"Relax, she'll be along soon. We'll all leave together, except for Sean. He's too busy enjoying himself with the afternoon kids. I'll keep an eye on Stevie while you discipline young Kate. I want to see what she did and watch you in action. I hope you don't mind me tagging along."

"No, I welcome your wisdom," he said as Katie pushed the office door open. He turned to greet her. "Ah, here's my little princess now."

"Hi, Daddy," Katie greeted him joyfully and ran up to hug him.

Matthew picked her up and kissed her on the cheek while he thought, *She's certainly happy.*

He put her back down on the floor and said, "I have something for you." Katie watched him with expectation as he reached into his coat pocket. He handed her a small box. "Open it."

When Katie saw the gold pendant and chain in the box, her eyes opened wide. "This is pretty, Daddy."

"Well," he said, taking the box from her and freeing the pendant, "this is to let you know that you are my very special girl. I love you, and I will never say mean things to you again. Turn around; I'll put it on for you."

After he secured the pendant, Katie lifted it to admire it. She rotated it until the initials K.E.G. were right side up. It had a small emerald on either side. She was mesmerized by the sparkle. "I accept your apology, Daddy."

And the little keg of dynamite calls me a smartass, Matthew thought whimsically. *I have to hand it to her—she knows how to make a connection.* He said, "Thank you, Katie. Now we need to get home and clean up the mess you made."

That evening, Carolyn called from the hospital to check on the progress at home. After speaking with her husband, she spoke with Katie.

"Hi, Mommy," Katie announced, starting an excited monologue. "Daddy bought me a necklace. He and I are having a good time. Momma is here too. Daddy let me put the soap in the machine and we washed the bedcovers. He made the bed. We took all the toys out of the toilet. He showed me how to use an auger; it's a snake, but not a real snake. Your toilet is broken, Mommy. A toy is stuck in there, and we can't get it out. But don't worry. Daddy is going to buy a new toilet, and he's going to show me how to put it in. Some toys are wet, and we threw them out. The ones that aren't wet, I'm giving them to poor children who don't have any toys. I have too many toys, Momma said so. When are you coming home? Is Luis okay?"

"Luis is sleeping, honey," Carolyn responded as she recalled seeing him in the recovery room, attached to various tubes. "When I get home, you'll probably be sleeping too. Make sure you do your homework and go to bed early."

"I will. Momma is making dinner."

"Where were you during lunch today, Katie? I didn't see you in the cafeteria."

"I was there, Mommy. I had lunch with my new friend Rina. She's nice; she's in second grade. Her daddy is mean to her, but she is very nice."

"I don't know anyone named Rina."

"That's her nickname, silly," Katie responded as Carolyn noticed an orderly pushing Luis's gurney down the hall.

"Katie, honey," she said, "I'll talk to you tomorrow, okay? I have to go now because they're moving Luis to a new room. I have to see where they're taking him. Be a good girl, honey. I love you."

Eleven

◇◇◇

2005

Katie sat in the kitchen with her broken leg propped on an adjoining chair while she shared arepas, a type of flatbread that Nydia had prepared, and omelet with Stevie. Stevie related the conversation he had with Carolyn the day before, informing her that he no longer wanted to pursue a law career. He wanted to attend seminary school.

"I'm guessing Mom said, 'We have to talk,'" Katie interjected.

"She did say that, but she's okay with my decision," Stevie said and then bit a piece off the reheated arepa. "This is good," he commented with his mouth full.

"Stevie, I know Mom. 'We have to talk' means she's not letting you off the hook. You're going to law school."

"You're saying that because she convinced you to pursue the three master's degrees. Mom knows I'm not you. Compared to you, I'm a moron. You and Luis were in college by age fourteen. At fourteen, I was struggling to get a C in algebra."

"You're not a moron. 'There are different types of intelligence, sweetie,'" she said, quoting Carolyn.

Stevie laughed and almost choked on his breakfast. After a couple of coughs, he said, "You sound just like her." They both laughed.

Luis walked in wearing his boxer shorts and flip-flops. "What's so funny?" he asked.

"Katie is imitating Mommy."

"I thought you had already left for work," Katie said as Luis opened the refrigerator and grabbed the orange juice. "Where have you been, and why aren't you dressed?"

"Where have I been? See this?" he asked while pulling on the elastic of his briefs to display a bruise on his hip, a bruise which was difficult to discern because of preexisting scar tissue from his childhood trauma.

"What happened to you?" she asked with concern.

"That's where you kicked me in the side and onto the floor last night. I thought I had been hit by a tank, woman. You almost killed me in your sleep. I actually felt sorry for that poor bear. I probably have a broken hip, and the bear needs facial reconstruction."

"How you exaggerate and whine," she teased him while he poured the juice. "Is that all you're having for breakfast?"

"I'd like some green juice," he said and winked at her, "but I didn't see any in there."

"There are eggs, bacon, and a whole lot of other things in there. My mom would never let you leave the house without a high-protein breakfast."

"I'll get something at work. Stevie, drive me over to my house so you can get your books and I can get some clothes."

"Sure thing, Luis," he said, wolfing down the remainder of his eggs.

"You're not going out in your underwear!" Katie protested.

"Who's going to see me? This is private property. Stevie will drive me up to the porch, and I'll run inside."

"It's not summer yet, fool. The temperature dipped last night; it's cold out there."

"Who's whining now? By the way, when am I supposed to take Lolo and Lolita to the vet? I'll need to ask someone to take my patients that day."

"Tuesday at ten o'clock."

"Luis, I'm ready," Stevie said while getting up with the plate in his hand. "Katie, can I just stick these in the dishwasher?"

"Put everything in the sink. I'll wash them while I wait for you to return."

"Put them in the dishwasher, Stevie," Luis said. Then he turned to Katie and asked, "What part of 'keep the leg elevated' don't you understand? I'll take care of the kitchen duties when I get back from work. Maybe you should hire extra help."

"I already told you, I don't need extra help, except for a driver for work. Come here," she said, beckoning him for a good-bye kiss. He complied and gave her a peck on the lips. Stevie looked on and smiled.

As Stevie approached Luis's house, they were surprised by a few reporters who were staked out in front of his house.

"What's going on here?" Luis asked as soon as he saw them. Aware of his nakedness, he said, "Now, this could be embarrassing."

"You go inside as planned," Stevie offered as he steered the car toward the porch. "I'll handle this." When they arrived, Stevie rolled his window down.

"Dr. López?" someone asked.

"What can I do for you folks?" Stevie asked as he stepped out of the car. The other reporters quickly surrounded him, and Luis took the opportunity to rush to the house.

"We heard one of your guests was attacked by a five-hundred-pound bear yesterday. Do you have anything to add, sir?" someone asked.

"What else have you heard?" Stevie asked.

"Animal control is planning to capture the bear and relocate him to the Adirondack area, sir. Can you tell us anything? We heard a young woman was hurt."

"Well, so was the bear," Stevie commented. "It took off whimpering in that direction after my sister landed a karate kick to its nose. She has a black belt in karate."

"How badly was she hurt?" someone asked. Another asked, "What's her name, sir?" A third inquired, "What prompted her to kick him?"

"One at a time, please," he said, holding his hands in front of him, enjoying the situation. "I'll gladly explain. My sister, Katie, was not pleased when she saw that big bear chasing my little brother, Kieran. Kieran is only twelve, and he was running up that incline with a bucket of fish, which he clearly did not want to share with a hungry bear. The bear was determined to get a free meal, and Kieran had his heart set on a Cajun fish fry." The reporters laughed. "Well, Katie came running out of nowhere and planted her three-inch heel in that bear's face. The shoe must still be around here somewhere. It's a green shoe, and we didn't take the time to look for it yesterday evening. Katie has a broken foot and a fractured calf bone, but we expect her to be okay. As a matter of fact, she's already up and about. She's a feisty lady."

"How old is Katie?" someone asked.

"I don't think she would want you to know that," Stevie responded. "I'll just say she's over twenty-one. It's been nice talking to you, folks. Now I need to get inside and get ready for the day ahead. You know, another day, another dollar."

"Nothing impresses a man more than a feisty lady. Is your sister cute? Is she married?" someone asked.

"Is my sister cute?" Stevie repeated with amusement. "Let's just say, many a man has been smitten by her. She isn't married, but she will be soon, so she's not available. Sorry, guys. Anyway, I've said enough. I have to go. Have a nice day."

Stevie and Katie finally left for Manhattan, aka "the city." They were just about to cross from the Bronx into Manhattan. Here the traffic bottlenecked. As Stevie stopped in the early morning traffic, he commented, "You should construct a heliport on the top of the building and fly to work each day. Then you would avoid all this traffic."

"That's not a solution. I still need to drive to the work sites to conduct my inspections. Sometimes I come straight home from one of those sites. If I flew, I would have to drive back to the heliport to get the copter before I could come home."

"I didn't think of that."

"Obviously. With Bert and Kurt, I can drive on the HOV lanes and save time."

"Until you get caught. Mommy will not be pleased."

"I suppose not. Mommy is always tightly strung, and you and Luis are always so moral about everything. Don't you get tired of behaving like a saint, Stevie?"

"I'm not behaving like a saint."

"Yet you won't break a little stupid law."

"It's not a stupid law. HOV traffic makes a lot of sense. It cuts down on congestion."

"I certainly wouldn't reach that conclusion from observing this traffic. You should climb on the shoulder and avoid all this. If I had to crap, I'd shit in my pants in this slow traffic."

"Behave yourself, Katie."

"See, that's what I mean. You're such a damn saint that you wouldn't shit in your pants. Do you ever even speak like a real person?"

"I don't have to be crude to be a real person."

"You know what you are, Stevie?"

"No, tell me."

"You're a mama's boy."

"Fine, I'm a mama's boy. I'm okay with that."

"Hang loose, oh brother of mine. Hang loose. You don't want to frighten the women away," she teased him.

"I haven't frightened anyone away."

"Do you have a girl, Stevie? I mean, have you ever been laid?"

"That's crude and it's none of your business," he said, turning crimson.

They finally arrived at her office suite.

"Dr. O'Gorman," Gwendolyn Chueng commented when Katie followed Stevie into the reception room, "what happened to you?"

Katie related the events of the previous day to her intern/secretary. She then introduced her and Stevie to each other. "Gwendolyn is majoring in electronics technology and plans to start at MIT next year," she added to her introduction. Then she offered information on Stevie. "My brother wants to study religion, but I suspect he's going to be a lawyer like my mother. The jury is still out on that." She turned to face Stevie and raised one eyebrow as she said, "I'm waiting by the sideline for the verdict."

He smiled in response and said, "I'll put the laptop and the rest of this stuff in your office and be on my way. Call me if you need me. My last class ends at two fifteen. Gwendolyn, it was nice meeting you." Because his hands were full, he bowed and said, "Forgive me for not shaking your hand." He turned and walked in the direction of Katie's office.

"Gwendolyn," Katie said, turning to her intern, "you're going out in the field beginning today."

"Really, Dr. O'Gorman?"

"Really, Gwendolyn. Get yourself a hard hat from supplies. I'll call Jack and ask him to outfit you. You'll need steel-toed boots and work gloves as well. You may want to get some jeans if you don't want to mess up those business slacks you're wearing. O'Gorman Enterprises will pick up the tab. Jack knows what to do. You'll be accompanying Mr. Ramírez. You can learn a lot from him, so pay attention and listen carefully to everything he does and says. Before you see Jack, do me a favor and look up the names of any contractors who are idling at this time. E-mail me that information and then head down to supplies as soon as you're done."

"How long will I be in the field?"

"That's up to you. If you do well, you could be there all summer. If you don't deliver, I'll pull you out in a heartbeat. As I explained at your interview, I don't hesitate to cut people at the knees when they need to go. Do you understand?"

"Yes, Dr. O'Gorman. I'll get that list right now. Thank you for this opportunity."

"I hope it's my pleasure, Gwendolyn. I'll check with you at the end of the day. Follow Mr. Ramírez's instructions."

"Yes, Dr. O'Gorman."

Stevie was back and heading for the exit door. "Katie, don't forget, call me if you need anything."

"Thank you, Stevie. Drive safely."

At her desk, Katie propped her broken leg up on a chair and called Jack in supplies. She informed him to expect Gwendolyn and to outfit her for field work. She assigned Eblin Santos to replace Gwendolyn at the reception desk. She informed Jacquelyn Gupta that she would be in charge for the day while Katie dealt with site inspections. She then called Jonathan Furman on speakerphone and invited him into her office. When he arrived, she buzzed security from her desk, activated the computer wall monitor with her remote, and advised him to observe and tell her what was wrong with what she was demonstrating on the screen. She showed him an outdoor air conditioning unit and waited for his response. When none came, she commanded him to take a second look. He failed to respond.

"Look at the vent, fool. What's wrong with the vent?"

"I don't see anything wrong with the vent, Katharine. It's not dented or anything."

"It's facing the wrong way, you idiot. How do you expect to cool down a room if you have the exhaust facing the building? Your crew installed this, and you signed off on it. Where were you when they were positioning it, and why did you approve it?"

He shook his head. "The unit was installed to cool a lower room. It's sitting on its roof, adjacent to that upper room; it's a veranda."

"I know that, Jonathan. The AC's exhaust is facing the upper room, thereby projecting hot air into that room. I wouldn't want to be in there in the heat of summer. You allowed your men to solve one problem and create another. What was the logic behind this? Did you want to save a few feet of conduit?"

"No—I know I'm not supposed to cut corners."

"But you did. Evidently, that's a poorly designed building; I would have discussed the options with the owner. If you indeed had to place the unit on the veranda, disabling usable space, the least you could have done was to place the exhaust away from the building. This is not acceptable; it has to be corrected."

"I didn't realize the ramifications."

"Evidently. Now look at this second set of slides." She showed him pictures of window fittings. "What's the verdict, Jonathan?" she pressured him.

At that moment, Stevie walked into the room. He walked up to Katie and stood quietly by, aware that something important must be going on. Katie paused and asked, "Why are you back?" He explained that she had overlooked giving him the SUV's registration. She gave him permission to go through the wallet in her purse, and then she turned her attention back to Jonathan. "Well? What's wrong in these pictures, Jonathan?"

"The surface wasn't properly prepared for caulking."

"Now, you see, if you had figured that out before the work was finalized, you would have gotten an A. It's a good thing I noticed this before the painters covered up the evidence. What's going to happen when the rain starts to leak in through those exterior walls, Jonathan?" When he started to open his mouth, she stopped him with, "It's a rhetorical question, idiot. A functional retard can figure that out. What's your excuse? You know, I can show you more, but I'm not going to waste my time. You've wasted enough of that for this corporation. It's also going to cost us to rectify the messes you have approved. You're lucky I'm feeling generous today. Despite the losses you are costing us, you will receive two weeks' severance pay."

"You're firing me?" he asked incredulously. "I've worked hard for this corporation. I've put in a lot of overtime."

"And you have been paid handsomely for it—too handsomely for the boorish final results," she said as two uniformed men took positions in front of her office's glass doors. "Clean out your office, and security will accompany you out. Leave now and you won't lose your severance pay."

"You think you can do a man's work better than a man?" he yelled, and Stevie paused in his search to eavesdrop.

"Did you notice that the name on the door reads 'O'Gorman Enterprises'? That's my name; I own the corporation. So if you're insinuating that only a man can do contracting, then I conclude that you're not a man. You failed to do your work properly."

"You bitch!"

"Hey," Stevie interjected, dropping the wallet back into the purse and taking a step forward. "Watch your mouth."

"Who the hell are you?" Jonathan inquired.

"Stevie," Katie said, "get the registration and leave. I can handle this." She grabbed her crutches and eased herself to her feet.

"No one talks to you in that fashion. I'm not leaving until he goes."

"New boyfriend, slut?" Jonathan asked as Katie positioned herself between him and Stevie. Katie threw her weight against Stevie to prevent him from reacting as Jonathan added, "He's a little young for you."

Katie gave no verbal reply. Instead, she gave him a victorious grin and waved security forward. They had been standing quietly by the doors, awaiting her signal.

"I'll sue you, bitch!" he protested as the men stood by his side.

"You're welcome to try," she countered. "You'll only waste money on lawyers because you don't have a leg to stand on."

"Mr. Furman," one of the men said, "please come with us."

"This isn't over, you know; I've worked hard for this company."

"Mr. Furman," the second guard said, touching his arm.

"Get off me," Furman protested, pulling his arm away. Then he took a deep breath and turned on his heel to leave.

Katie breathed a sigh of relief and turned to face Stevie. "It was sweet of you to intervene, but don't do it again, especially in my place of business. What was your plan? Were you going to rumble with that idiot?" She walked back to her computer terminal. As she propped her leg up, she informed him, "You saw the security guards. They get paid to get rough. I don't want you to ever put yourself in harm's way because of me; I can take care of myself."

"Of course you can," Stevie said, holding his hands up and returning to her purse. "Heaven forbid if anyone should give you a helping hand. However, I too have my code of honor. No one insults you, Mommy, or any lady in my presence. I only intended to lift him off the floor and glare into his face. He would have probably peed in his pants."

Katie laughed and agreed. "Maybe he would have. You're all man, Stevie."

"Does this happen often?"

"No—I don't usually hire assholes. But at times I have to fire someone. It happens." She shrugged. "I prefer to do my own dirty work, but I do it with a strategy. When we entered the building earlier, I informed security of my intensions. They were expecting my alert. I learned that while observing Mommy at Emily's Hope. Do you know how many lunatics walked into that old building? That's why we have so much security at the new facility. Mommy and Dr. Holder handled all those lunatics with finesse. I was in her office when a guy stormed in on her. He was menacing, and I really thought he was going to hurt her. I watched in horror, but she stood her ground. When it was over, I started bawling like a fire hydrant-slash-banshee. I'll never forget that. Mom must have been petrified, but she scooped me up in her arms. Man, that was something," she concluded as she got teary eyed remembering Carolyn's many comforting embraces.

"I guess it was," Stevie commented, watching Katie feel uncomfortable displaying her emotions in front of him. "Listen, I better get going." He was holding the car's registration. "I'll probably see you tonight."

"Yeah; thanks again for the lift," she said, turning to her computer terminal.

Stevie let himself out. Gwendolyn had sent the e-mail she had requested. There were two names on the idle list. From her computer, she contacted the first name on the list.

"Katharine, what's up?" Evan Ohkawa asked when he answered his terminal.

"According to the information on my computer files, you're idling."

"Well, your information is wrong. We're digging to replace several hundred feet of Orangeburg pipes with PVCs and install a proper bedding. The fiber is brittle with wood rot. We also need to correct the footing around this property, replace the curtains and mend the east wall."

"I knew it was too good to be true. You're my best engineer, Evan."

"I bet you say that to all the guys."

"Well, perhaps a handful, but you are good."

"What did you have in mind?"

"No sense discussing it with you if you're not idling; I'll call Muftah. He's also my best engineer."

"Muftah is working on that mansion in the Hamptons."

"You're right. I forgot about that."

"What do you need, Katharine?"

"I want a barrier built around twenty acres of my property."

"Well, I'm closer to you than Muftah. I'm working in Portchester now. I'm familiar with your property, so I'll swing by and take a closer look. Perhaps I can hire a few extra hands and do that for you."

"Great, I have a preliminary CAD on it. I drafted it this morning. I'll e-mail it to you."

"Is this because of the bear you attacked?"

"How did you know about that?"

"It's been on the news today. The first time I heard it, they identified you as Katie López. When I heard it the second time, they used the name O'Gorman. I concluded it had to be you they were talking about because they mentioned Byram Lake. I didn't know you have a black belt in karate. You go, girl!"

"I can't believe what I'm hearing. How in the world did they get all that information on me? This can't be good. I'll talk to you later, Evan."

Katie sat back and contemplated the day's events. Other issues popped into her head. Then she remembered she had to hire a driver. She had scheduled a site inspection for after lunch, and she needed a means to get there. She called one of the services that her company and the family often used only to receive bad news.

"Dr. O'Gorman," the lady on the phone informed her, "I wish you had called earlier. With this taxi strike, every limousine service in the tristate area must be overbooked. We don't have a single driver available. I'm so sorry."

She hung up and thought, *Taxi strike—damn it! I've been so busy that I don't even listen to the news. Oh well, there's more than one way to skin a cat.* She stood by the window and stared out into the Manhattan skyline and the streets below. The crowds of people on the ground looked like ants, scurrying about. It was a pleasant spring-like day. By now, the men had probably removed their jackets and flung them over their shoulders. From the height of the thirty-sixth floor, it was hard to tell. She turned away from the window and called Matthew.

"Daddy, could you modify my SUV so I can manage the brake and gas pedal with my left foot?"

"Perhaps. I'll have to take a look at it."

"Would you mind if Stevie took it to you this evening after work?"

"That will be fine, princess."

"Daddy, my name was mentioned on the news today; I just found out about it."

"I know, princess. Your grandmother Margaret already took care of it. She threatened the media with a boycott if they air the story again. They can mention the bear, but they can't ever mention any member of the O'Gorman family, or she will pull all her corporation's ads and will not sponsor any of their programs."

When Katie's biological father was arrested, Matthew's main quest was to protect Katie. Carolyn concurred, and their first endeavor was to stop the media from reporting the story. The second concern was to prevent Katie's paternal grandparents from staking a claim on the child. After all, her biological father was a monster. What if he had mirrored the actions of one or both of his parents? If he had been their victim, the O'Gormans didn't want any Lyman near Katie. In case the grandparents wanted to search Katie's court and adoption records, they had been sealed by court order to protect her identity. From the Lyman's perspective, they had no knowledge that Matthew O'Gorman had adopted his niece. With all those steps taken, Carolyn still insisted that her daughter should never be the subject of the news media. In the event that William Lyman was ever paroled, they wanted to make sure he would be unable to contact or communicate with her. If Katie ever had children, there was also the implausible possibility that a Lyman might want to contact them. Implausible or not, Carolyn was always meticulous about every project she undertook. Katie's welfare was certainly no exception. The best thing, Carolyn concluded, was to make sure that Katie was never in the public eye. "Out of sight, out of mind," Carolyn often told her and instructed her to always stay under the radar. Upon hearing that Katie's name had been mentioned on the news, Carolyn became very upset. She was relieved to know that a photograph of Katie had not been released. Because Katie looked like Emily's clone, someone could have recognized her. Carolyn was not pleased when she saw a segment of video tape with Stevie narrating details of Katie's encounter with the bear. "What was he thinking?" was all she could mutter.

Now Katie needed to get to East New York in Brooklyn to inspect one of her biggest projects: the construction of mixed-income housing with three shopping centers and a recreation complex. As soon as she finished the conversation with Matthew, she strapped her laptop and shoulder bag to her back, determined to get to the site by train. At the reception desk, she instructed Eblin Santos and informed her that Jacquelyn Gupta was in charge. "Please inform Mrs. Gupta that I have left for the day. She can reach me on the cell phone if she needs me."

"Yes, Dr. O'Gorman," Eblin responded. "How are you going to manage the subway steps with those crutches?"

"Where there's a will, there's a way. How are you doing in school, Eblin?"

Eblin was a part-time undergrad who worked for O'Gorman Enterprises three days a week. "It's going great, Dr. O'Gorman. I'm preparing for an exam in organic chemistry. I think I'll ace it."

"I'm glad to hear that. Did you complete the registration forms for next term?"

"I'm working on it."

"Next semester, you'll be officially a junior, right?"

"Yes," Eblin responded, sounding very pleased with herself. "I made it this far!"

"Well, next semester, O'Gorman Enterprises is reducing your work hours to only eight hours a week and giving you full scholarship and a stipend through grad school."

Eblin's eyes lit up, and she yelled, "Oh, my God. Oh, my God. Oh, my God." She started jumping up and down and rushed around her desk to hug Katie. Katie reciprocated the hug. "Wait till I tell my mother," Eblin yelled. "Oh, my God!"

Eblin had interviewed for a job at O'Gorman Enterprises fresh out of high school. At the interview, Katie had noticed her attire. The child was neatly dressed; the clothing reflected Eblin's poor and humble background. Katie browsed through Eblin's high school transcript, which she had included as a required part of her job application. Then Katie returned her gaze to the cheap clothes and shoes Eblin wore. She had good grades and was visibly enthusiastic about the prospect of getting a job. She had tried other companies, but she was rejected because she lacked experience. Katie made a note on the corner of Eblin's application. "What are your dreams, your future aspirations, Eblin?" Katie had asked her.

Katie noticed that the question touched a raw nerve, for Eblin's countenance darkened, and she swallowed to compose herself. "I want to be a doctor."

"Which college do you plan to attend?" Katie challenged her.

"I'm not going to college yet," Eblin said, sounding embarrassed. "I will work and save. I've worked in a pizzeria, but it doesn't pay enough. I need a better job."

"Did you apply for a scholarship? Your grades are excellent."

"I don't qualify for a scholarship; I'm not a citizen," Eblin confessed, staring at her lap. She sensed the interview would soon be over.

"Do you have a sponsor?"

"I don't understand what you mean."

"How old are you?"

"I'm almost eighteen."

Katie thumbed through her desk files and took out a card. "Here," she said, handing Eblin the card from across the desk. "As soon as you leave here, I want you to see this lawyer. She'll be expecting you. In two days, you report back here at exactly eight o'clock. You report directly to me. Your work hours are eight to four with possible overtime. You'll be on probation for two months. Then we'll sit and review your work. I decide if you stay or go. If you stay, we'll review your future duties. Your starting salary is ten dollars an hour, with time-and-a-half for overtime. We don't pay for lunchtime. You get a health and dental plan. Your duties will be diverse. This is a composite corporation that requires people of diverse talents. We'll see what you can handle. Are you up to it?"

"Yes," Eblin said meekly.

"I'll see you in two days then."

At the end of the two-month trial period, Katie approved Eblin for part-time college attendance, with the corporation paying half of her tuition and school expenses. During the probation period, Eblin had been assigned a sponsor and applied for citizenship. While working and attending school, she took the citizenship exam and received her green card. Katie followed her progress by checking her academic accomplishments, examining her credit reports, and prying into the child's personal life. The background investigations were carefully done to determine Eblin's worthiness and her ability to manage her life.

By following those steps, Katie was practicing a legacy started by the Reilly family. It was a legacy that Carolyn then imposed on Katie while she was getting ready to attend college and being indecisive about her future pursuits. Carolyn knew that Katie's floundering was partly due to the fact that she was starting college at a young age. Academically, she and Luis were prepared to attend college at age twelve, but after careful consideration, her parents decided to place her in a Catholic high school. They hoped that would make the transition easier. Nydia did the same with Luis by sending him to an all-boys prep school. Things did not go well with Katie. She was expelled before year's end; Carolyn decided to keep her at Emily's Hope with private tutors until she was a little older.

She spent her first few years of college abroad, or "across the pond" as Momma Ellen called it. Katie was academically prepared to start college at a junior level, which meant she could choose a major. Despite being academically smart, she was uncertain about making the right selection. "Select the subjects that most interest you," Carolyn advised her, "and do them all. You have plenty of time. I'm thrilled that you're interested instead of disinterested. However, I'm going to give you an additional challenge because I know you can handle it." Carolyn explained that the Reilly Foundation issued scholarships to underprivileged students. "Your father and I will pay for all your courses until age twenty-three. That's nine years of college if you need them. However, upon completion of your education or the nine years, whichever comes first, you will design your own scholarship foundation in order to pay it forward."

Katie protested, "Mom, I only need one major to graduate. I can do that in no time—I just can't decide which one to pick."

"Where are you going? To catch a freight train? You'll do them all because you have the capability of doing them all, and you're still a minor. That means you do what I say."

"That's child abuse, and you know it, Mom!"

"It's called doing something productive with your time and energy. If you think it's child abuse, go ahead and report me to the police. See how far you'll get with that."

Katie shrugged her shoulders and said, "Okay."

Katie was always willing to see how far she could push the envelope, so she attempted to file child abuse charges against her mother. The police officer laughed and turned to his partner to share what he perceived as a joke.

"Aren't you Sean and Ellen O'Gorman's granddaughter?" he then asked Katie. "I know your grandparents. Your grandmother and I go way back. We met in the park when your brother was a baby; someone tried to steal his carriage. Tell your grandparents Sergeant Paulson says hello. I also met your mother, so give her my regards as well. And for the record, making your kid study is not child abuse. I argue with my own kids about that all the time." He laughed again, and Katie fumed.

In college, Katie whizzed through her courses. University College Dublin was her first college, and the one she most favored. After seven years, Katie had three master's degrees and a doctorate under her belt. Upon completing her doctorate, she founded O'Gorman Enterprises and its foundation.

Eblin was the seventh recipient of an O'Gorman scholarship. Katie's scholarship program was done in stages. First, she advertised a job opening in publications that were distributed in depressed areas of the inner city. She selected the applications based on academic potential, a child's level of poverty, and good references. When the candidate presented him/herself before her, she scrutinized each in the same manner she had scrutinized Eblin Santos. The scholarships were then issued based on each individual's needs and their level of maturity with respect to handling finances and other criteria. No candidate knew how far they would be supported until they accomplished each level of Katie's personal evaluation. Based on their accomplishments, they might not be worthy of a full scholarship. If they were foolhardy, chances were that they would never get beyond stage one. Based on Eblin's progress, Katie was certain she would be funded through the completion of medical school. The young lady had kept a level head and maintained a 4.0 average until now.

Katie observed Eblin's reaction to today's news and advised her to consider next term's choice of classes carefully. "Don't overextend yourself with too many classes," she suggested.

"Yes. Thank you, Dr. O'Gorman."

"I'll see you tomorrow, Eblin. Do a good job."

Fifteen minutes later, Katie was hobbling down the subway steps, holding her crutches in one hand and supporting herself with the banister. Her progress was slow, but determined. She comforted herself by the fact that the next descent from the turnstiles to the subway platform was via escalator. She swiped her MetroCard at the turnstile and pushed her way through. She gingerly boarded and climbed off the escalator. Ten minutes later, the train arrived. The car had about ten passengers. She took a corner seat and propped her broken leg up across the remaining seats and sat back against the wall. She needed the rest; walking to the station and managing the stairs was harder than she had imagined. She listened to the train's rhythmic hum as it proceeded downtown. After three stops, only she and three other passengers were on board, leaving the car practically empty. At Fourteenth Street, the three other passengers descended and four boarded, along with a uniformed patrolman. As the train left the station, the police officer towered above her.

"You need to get your leg off the seats, miss," he informed her.

She looked up at him and immediately noticed his name tag, which identified him as Rafferty. She asked, "You're kidding, right?" She made a mental picture of his badge number.

"Seats are for sitting, not lounging, miss. Please remove your leg from the seats."

"Under doctor's orders, I'm supposed to keep my leg elevated. Besides, no one else needs to use it."

The officer pulled out a summons book and started to write her a ticket. "What's your name?" he inquired.

"Mary Whistler," Katie responded with defiance.

"Very funny," he countered. "Do you have ID?"

"You can't write me a ticket for resting a broken leg on seats no one needs. What the hell's wrong with you? Are you a functional retard?"

"Get up!" he ordered.

"You gotta be kidding me, *amadán*!"

"I said get up! My parents speak Irish," he said, "so I know what *amadán* means."

"You must have heard it a lot," she countered.

"Calling me an idiot doesn't go well with you, *soith*."

Katie didn't know enough Irish to realize he had just called her a bitch. Nonetheless, she sighed with disgust and rolled her eyes before she grabbed her crutches and stood up.

"Hands behind your back!" Rafferty ordered, reaching for handcuffs.

"Have you kicked any babies lately?" she asked, tossing her crutches, balancing herself on her left foot, and placing her hands behind her back.

At the next stop, the other passengers watched in disbelief as Katie was bullied into abandoning her crutches and made to hop off the train. After a while she was forced to use both legs to keep her balance.

One passenger had grabbed the crutches and tagged along behind them. He finally got up the courage to ask the officer, "Can I be of any assistance, sir? You'll probably need help getting her up the stairs."

The officer considered the situation and said, "Could you grab her other arm for me? We have a holding cell at the top of the stairs; we need to wait for a patrol car."

"Glad to help, officer." The stranger held Katie's right side, lifting her off her leg as he helped to lead her away.

Katie was fuming, but she was grateful for his help. The two men hoisted her up the stairsand she soon entered a dimly lit, smelly room. Before the door closed, she caught a glimpse of the stranger. He wore wrinkled khakis and a worn brown corduroy sport coat with a white shirt and had a satchel suspended from his right shoulder. He was looking in, perhaps making a mental picture of her. Rafferty closed the door. While Katie seethed in the dark holding cell, she could hear the two men speaking outside. The officer called on his walkie-talkie for a transport car. Katie heard a train enter the station. Then she heard the stranger say, "I can stick around if you need help getting her up the next set of steps."

"Thank you," the officer said. "I wish there were more concerned citizens like you."

After helping to carry Katie to street level, the patrolman shoved Katie into the car and took the crutches from the stranger. He rested them across Katie's lap and closed the door. At the precinct, Katie was relieved of her possessions and booked for violating transit law, resisting arrest, and misconduct. When she was allowed to make her single phone call, she decided that Carolyn was her best option.

"Hello, Mom," she said as calmly as she could. "Mom, can you spring me out of jail?"

Carolyn examined the number on her caller ID. "You're not kidding, are you?"

"No, Mom, I'm not kidding. I was arrested for resting my broken leg across two empty subway seats. I was also dragged in handcuffs up three flights of stairs and pushed into a police car." Carolyn requested to speak to someone in charge.

"My mommy wants to talk to you," she said, holding the phone out to the clerk across the desk.

The clerk provided Carolyn with the information she requested and handed the phone back to Katie.

"Well, honey," Carolyn said, feeling another migraine coming on, "hang in there while I set the wheels in motion. I hope it won't take too long."

"As do I, Mom. At this very moment, I realize how much I love you. You're also pretty and sweet."

"Cut the crap, Katie, but I'm glad you're maintaining a sense of humor."

"Yes, Mommy, so am I. What's the sentence for murder? That's what I plan to do to the bastard who put me here."

"It's twenty-five years to life, honey. I hope to see you sooner than that."

Two hours later, Margaret, Carolyn's mother, had sprung Katie out of jail. As Katie was handed her crutches, she asked the attendant, "Where's that bastard Rafferty?"

Margaret grabbed Katie's upper arm and said, "Let's not make a scene, Katie. Walk out of here quietly."

"I'm not making a scene, Grandma. I simply want to kill him!" she yelled. "Rafferty, I'm going to pound your goddamn testicles with a sledgehammer and infuse them with sulfuric acid, you fucking snake!"

Margaret shook her head in disapproval, pulled Katie's arm, and said, "Let's go, Katie. It's over. Come on."

Katie looked at her grandmother and decided to obey. As she got to the door, however, she yelled, "It ain't over! I'll kill that freaking bastard!" She then walked through the door that Margaret held open for her.

Katie made herself comfortable in the back of Margaret's limousine. "Got anything to drink in there?" Katie asked, eyeing the fridge.

"Want some apple juice?"

"That will have to do."

"Between yesterday and today, you're on a roll, Katie my love," Margaret said as she retrieved a bottle of apple juice. "I hope you don't need to make any stops along the way because I'd rather take you straight home."

"What a freaking day! I wanted to check the site in East New York, but I better go home before the earth opens up beneath my feet."

Margaret depressed the intercom button and instructed Simon, her driver. Then she asked, "You were planning to go to East New York by yourself, with crutches? Do you have a death wish?"

"I go there all the time. I enter all kinds of neighborhoods. East New York doesn't frighten me."

"It's one thing to enter East New York in your vehicle and a totally different thing to hobble through it while carrying a computer and purse on your back. You're a walking advertisement that says, 'Mug me. Take all I have.'"

"It's more dangerous to encounter a sadistic transit cop. How did you manage to spring me?"

"I called the mayor. You owe him for his next charity fundraising."

"You mean, I'm totally free?" She gulped the apple juice.

"You're totally free. He's asking the city council to look into the MTA's practices. It seems you're not the only citizen to be penalized for a minor infraction. Last week, a woman was given a summons for placing her grocery bag on a seat. Another one was ticketed for eating a banana."

"I was dragged off to jail for having a broken leg. That bastard is going to pay if it kills me. As for owing the mayor, Rafferty is the one who should contribute to charity. That twit is nothing but ..." she said, using a couple of x-rated expletives that shocked Margaret, and continued with, "I didn't do anything wrong, Grandma. I'm on a freaking crusade to dismember the S.O.B." She placed the empty bottle in the waste receptacle.

"You evidently need a bar of soap, Katie."

Katie smiled impishly. "I apologize. That son- of- bitch has me all wound up. I'm a good person, Grandma."

"Well, you can take up your crusade later. Maybe you should join the navy. We're stopping at Emily's Hope first. Your mother wants a word with you."

"I'm not surprised. Is she angry?"

"No, she's worried. That's what mothers do, Katie. They worry because they want the best for their children."

"Do you worry about Mom?"

"Of course I worry; I worry about all my children."

"What was Mom like as a little girl?"

"She was a good child. Also very inquisitive and altruistic."

"That hasn't changed."

"Harold and I used to drag our children all over the globe. My children were always fascinated by the locals; they befriended so many people. I'm proud to say they aren't snobs and display no signs of prejudice. To this day, they have continued communications with childhood friends. That's probably why Carolyn's fluent in so many languages; I still carry a dictionary wherever I go. Carolyn doesn't need a dictionary in Malaysia or in any Spanish-speaking country. Why she learned Irish is beyond me. One doesn't need to speak Irish to go to Ireland."

"She loves the culture, Grandma."

"Yes, she does. She loves dealing with people."

"You know, I give Mommy a hard time. I need to change."

"You're quick. It's taken you, what, twenty years to realize that."

Katie smiled. "Touché, Grandma. You know, after Kieran was born, I drove that poor woman crazy by pinching the kid to make him cry. She thought he had colic."

"You did that? Why?"

"Trust me, lately I've given it some thought. I believe I was jealous because he was taking the spotlight off me. We've been battling ever since."

"Kids do foolish pranks like that. 'It's time to put away childish things,' as the saying goes."

"I agree. The little Meerkat is a nice kid."

"Why do you call him Meerkat?"

"That was his doing. I believe he and Stevie were eating gummy worms one day, and Kieran said he was a meerkat. The truth is he looks like one. He's skinny and small, but kind of long. I don't know why he's so skinny. That child eats as if he's been starved since birth."

"I have noticed that, but he is an active boy."

"Anyway, when he was about three or so, if we called him Kieran, he insisted his name was Meerkat, so it stuck. Luis is the one who humored him the most. I'm tired," Katie suddenly complained while yawning and covering her mouth.

"Did you pinch Stevie too?"

"No," she said, sounding tired.

"Why not?"

"When I arrived, Stevie was already part of the cast. He was no threat to me. Stevie isn't a threat to anyone. He's milquetoast." She yawned again.

"Have you eaten anything?"

"Not since breakfast."

"No wonder you're tired. You must be hungry. I'll ask Simon to stop at your favorite drive-through. You can eat as we travel. Your mom is anxious to see you, so I don't want to tarry."

"Great—I'll have a mandarin chicken salad and a chocolate frosty." She yawned again.

"Take a nap. I'll wake you when we get to the drive-through."

They arrived at Emily's Hope. "Mommy, Mommy, Mommy," Katie said, hugging Carolyn. "I love this woman," she announced to Margaret as she hugged and kissed the amused and bewildered Carolyn.

"I'm glad you're so happy," Carolyn said, believing Katie had an agenda. "Now stop squeezing the life out of me."

"A few hours in the hands of the police has been a life-changing experience for her," Margaret said while observing the two of them together. "If you ladies don't mind, I'm leaving the two of you alone and heading back home. It's a long drive back to the city, and I'm sure Simon doesn't want to get stuck in rush hour traffic."

"Thank you, Mom," Carolyn said. "I've kept you very busy today."

"That's what family is for, Lyn. Katie, behave yourself."

"I'll try, Grandma. Thank you."

When Margaret left, Carolyn brushed Katie's hair away from her face and asked, "Are you all right, honey?"

"I am now." She then related every detail of her experience while Carolyn listened in horror. Katie then added, "I need to call Luis. I want his doctor buddies to examine me to document evidence of my trauma. I'm going to sue that sadistic SOB and make him lose his job. I want him blacklisted for life. He'll have to live in the park and eat out of garbage cans for the rest of his life."

"We'll get this documented, but you're not going public with this."

"What do you mean, Mom? I want to fry his ass."

"Let me handle this."

"Yes, Mom," Katie conceded. "I know you'll do the right thing. You've done precisely that so far."

"Luis's inexperienced buddies are not the ones who are going to provide professional testimony. I already have someone we're going to see."

"Mom," Katie confessed while Carolyn took a jacket out of the closet, "when Kieran was a baby, I used to pinch him to make him cry."

"I know that, Katie. You were a confused child with rotten tendencies. I used to punish you, but you always found a way around it. I tried everything I knew to force you to stop. I tried to reason with you. I took away privileges, but nothing fazed you. I had to pad the poor kid to keep you from hurting him. I even moved his nursery into my bedroom. You're a tough nut to crack. Are you finally feeling remorseful?"

"Yes, I am, Mom. I'm so, so, so sorry for all I've put you through."

"Maybe this means my blood pressure will finally fall back to normal. However, I'll wait and see because you are you. There's no telling what you will spring on me tomorrow. Come, my enigma," she said while grabbing her purse. "Let's go get the documentation you need."

"Why are you calling me an enigma?" Katie asked defensively. "Do you think I'm responsible for what happened to me today? That was not my fault. I was minding my own business."

"Ah, Katie, please," Carolyn uttered in frustration while leading her out the door. "I'm not blaming you for that. But you are an enigma: academically brilliant and also irrationally quixotic. Perhaps if you had stayed home as Luis and I advised, none of this would have happened."

Katie hobbled to keep pace with her. Carolyn stopped at her secretary's desk. "Annie, if I'm not back by the time Kieran arrives, please let him into my office so he can change into his karate clothes. If something comes up, call me on the cell phone. I will most likely be back before Kieran finishes his music lesson," she concluded, referring to Kieran's second extracurricular activity.

"I'll let him know, Carolyn," Annie responded.

Carolyn continued to the second door that led out to the corridor and lobby. She held the door for Katie as Katie complained, "So you're blaming me. I should have stayed home because you said so. Mom, I'm a grown woman. I don't need you to plan every detail of my life. You don't need to solve everything, you know. Do you perhaps have a cure for the common cold?"

Carolyn stopped short in front of her and said, "No, I don't have a cure for the common cold. But I'd first like one for insanity because you drive me crazy! What do you want from me, Katie? I worry about you. Bite me, why don't you? I'm concerned about your welfare." She continued yelling while the blood vessels popped in her neck and temples. Her head was throbbing, and she put her fingers over her left temple. "I have spent the morning dealing with legal issues, bothering Mother, and setting up appointments for you, and you are nitpicking and accusing me of interfering with your life? I'm sorry I've failed to please you!" Katie listened with surprise and a hint of fear, for she had never seen Carolyn explode in that manner. For what Carolyn believed was the first time in her life, Katie was speechless. Carolyn managed one final comment before they traversed the lobby in tense silence while security personnel watched in awe. Carolyn yelled, "Now move your sorry ass and follow me!"

That evening, Katie related her subway adventure to Luis, who listened with profound concern. "Are you okay, Katie?" he asked while examining her bruised wrists and hands. While restrained, her computer and purse had dangled from her shoulders and constantly pounded her hands and fingers. The plastic tie that served as handcuffs was so tight that it cut into her wrists and nearly impeded her circulation.

"I'm pissed, Luis. I'm simply pissed."

"Well, Stevie and I can find this Rafferty guy in a dark alley and educate him a bit."

"You're not the Godfather, Luis. Besides, I would get more satisfaction kicking his ass myself. However, I thank you for the offer. Mommy took me to one of her lawyer friends. She also had me buy new crutches because they're checking the other pair for fingerprints. Maybe we can find the mystery man who followed me off the train. Then she took me to see a doctor who specializes in giving court testimony. Mom will kick Rafferty's ass the legal way. When my mommy gets pissed, she's worse than any volcano."

"Last night, you were complaining about her, calling her pedantic, and today you're singing her praises."

"Well, she's all of that too," she said, thinking of how Carolyn had yelled at her that afternoon. "But she's the kind of person you want on your side when the going gets rough. I don't know—it must be me. I think I'm mentally disturbed."

Luis chuckled and said, "You've been mentally disturbed for years, baby."

"Luis, if I murder someone and go to jail, would you take care of our children?"

"What children? How many are you planning to have?"

Katie considered it for a moment. "We could have four, just like Momma Ellen. Four is a nice number."

"Does that mean you're going to marry me? You know, never mind. You don't have to marry me because if you go to jail, I'll be free to marry someone else. I'll get a brunette with nice curves because you'll be all out of shape from having four kids." She smacked him on the head.

"Augh!" he yelled. "That one really hurt. You're going to bust my skull open."

"That's the intent. Don't talk about becoming a player in my presence. I've never been with another boy or man but you, and you're talking about getting a brunette? Hell no!"

"But you'll be in jail for murder. By the time you get out, we'll both be too old to care."

She pinched him hard, and he yelled again. She responded with, "A romantic man would have said, 'Katie, I wouldn't let you go to prison; I'd take the rap for you.'"

"For murder? Oh no, Katie. I love you, but I also love fresh air. So make sure you don't kill anyone."

"Go home, Luis."

"I'm not going anywhere," he said, getting up. "I'm feeling good tonight. I can let you play with my peppermint stick. How are your leg and foot?"

"My foot is a bit sore from today's ordeal, but it's not sore enough to prevent me from having some fun. I'll meet you upstairs. And don't you dare drink any damn juice."

Later that evening, Katie felt content and relaxed with Luis's "peppermint stick" still encased in her birth canal. Their hearts were still racing. Katie sighed with relief and contentment. Luis grunted with similar satisfaction. "That was better than last time," he commented.

"Last time, you were in a rush, remember? You never reached the entry gate," she responded, stroking his hair. She contracted her abdominal muscles and squeezed his penis. "You're still hard," she said in a dreamlike state.

"Aha," he confirmed. "Want to do it again?"

"You're not in pain?"

"Not a bit."

"Well, go for it, big boy."

He started his rhythmic motions again while she encouraged him. When her overstimulated involuntary muscles took over and started to pull his penis further up her birth canal, he screamed in pain. "You're pulling my groin!" he yelled. "Ease up, Katie." Her inner walls continued to contract, and Luis's face was contorted. Katie willed herself to stop, and the contractions slowly diminished in strength.

"Are you okay?" she asked.

"I think so," he whined. "Katie, I need to pull out." He tried to retreat only to discover that he was stuck. "Katie, you need to ease up a little more." When he finally pulled himself loose, the disengagement produced a distinct suction *pop* and their humors spilled onto the bedcover.

"Baby, are you okay?" Katie asked with sincere concern while her innards cried for the second orgasm that never came.

"I think I'll live," Luis said, holding his groin and his throbbing penis.

Katie's tone suddenly changed to one of annoyance as she hit him over the head with a pillow. "I can't believe I have to leave the comfort of my bed to get your medication again, or, did you remember to bring it with you this time?"

"No," he cried.

She reached for her crutches and climbed out of bed. "I can't believe your stupidity, Luis. And you're supposed to be taking care of me? Damn you!" she yelled as she grabbed her robe. "You know what I think? You probably drank that damn green juice after I told you not to." He gave her a guilty look and she yelled. "You damn idiot! You drank it! Do you want to strangle your damn peppermint stick and incapacitate yourself for life? You'll be walking around with a plastic urine bag strapped to your thigh. I'll get you some damn ice. Then I have to drive to your stupid house…"

"Katie, you can't drive," he said, still holding his groin.

"Damn you, Luis!"

"Katie, calm down. None of this is my fault. It's no one's fault, so calm down."

She sat on the side of the bed and exhaled. "I told you last time to have the medication with you. Now I'm going to have to hobble all the way to your house..."

"Call Stevie. He has a key to the house. In the meantime, please get me a warm compress instead of the ice. It could help the circulation and allow the blood vessels to drain."

"You're just clutching at straws, aren't you? Some doctor. You know, every time this happens, you get me so damn nervous. We need to find a way to prevent this. I don't want to lose you, you damn idiot."

"I'm touched by your endearing words," he said with a touch of humor. "But you aren't going to lose me."

"How the hell do you know?"

"Want to get me a warm compress?"

"I'll get the damn compress," she said while rising to her feet again. "Then I'm going over to your house and getting every damn syringe you have in the place."

"What if I get horny when I'm home?"

"Restock or get yourself neutered, idiot."

"Ouch. How is that supposed to help?"

Twelve

◇◇◇

Earlier that evening in 2005

"How long has he been out there?" Matthew asked Carolyn about Stevie, who was sitting on the deck.

"About an hour," she said. "He probably knows that if he comes in, I'm going to wring his neck. He missed dinner. Three times today, I called his cell phone and he didn't pick up. He had me worried sick, so if he's thinking it, he's right; I'm going to wring his neck. Where was he? He's never done anything like this before."

"I guess it's up to me to go out there and find out. You go upstairs and relax. At least he's home, and he looks fine to me," he said, looking out the window.

In a short while, Matthew was outside, offering Stevie a mug of tea.

"Thanks, Daddy," Stevie said, coming out of a reverie and accepting the mug from Matthew.

Matthew sat next to him and gently slapped his son's knee. "You smell like horse manure. Have you been rolling in it?"

"No, Daddy. I was plowing it."

"That sounds interesting. When did you become a stable hand?"

"Just today, Daddy. I was repaying a favor. Daddy?"

"Yes, son?"

"Do you remember when you didn't allow me to enlist for the war in Iraq?"

"It wasn't that long ago, Stevie. The war is still going on. Why do you ask?"

"Why wouldn't you let me enlist, Daddy?"

"Does this have anything to do with you smelling of horse manure?"

"Sort of."

"Were you involved in a fight, Stevie?"

"Oh no, Daddy. I was helping a friend. How come you didn't let me sign up?"

Matthew smiled and sighed at the same time. "I had my reasons. One, I'm a selfish man. I love you and my wife too much to permit you to put your life in harm's way. Two, I strongly believe that we have to try to solve our conflicts through diplomacy first. If I thought it was a necessary war, I would have gone in your place. You would have had to stay here and look after your mother and your two siblings. I wouldn't have it any other way. Under no circumstances are you to engage in this war. In my heart, I cannot agree with it. Are you still thinking of enlisting?"

"No, Daddy." Matthew was visibly relieved. "Do you remember my friend Omid?" Stevie asked. "I brought him home a couple of times."

"The kid with a scar on his upper lip?" Matthew asked. Omid had cut his upper lip when he fell from his bike as a child. Stevie nodded in affirmation, and Matthew confirmed, "Yes, I remember him. Does he have something to do with you being a stable boy today?"

"Sort of. Omid is back from the war. My friend Darnell and I went over to his house to visit because we heard he had been wounded. He's real messed up, Daddy. He can't do anything for himself. His parents have to feed him and bathe him and everything. They're not rich or anything, but his father has to pay for everything Omid needs because the VA won't even pay for a therapist. That's not right."

"I know, son. I've been listening to the news. That's been happening a lot lately. Our soldiers deserve better."

"Well, Darnell and I helped Mr. Hassan unload and stock some supplies for his store, a novelty shop in South Yonkers. Then we offered to take Omid out for a little fun and to give his parents a break. We had to wheel him and secure his wheelchair inside Katie's SUV. We drove out to Riverridge and met this real nice couple who has a stable," Stevie said, and Matthew thought that his question about the horse manure was finally about to be answered. "We talked. It turns out, the man who owns the stable served in Vietnam. He let Omid, Darnell, and me ride horses for free. We had to hoist Omid on and off the horse and strap him into place. When we returned, they invited us to dinner, and we talked some more. It turns out, the guy knows me from when I was a baby. His name is Kenny Spaulding."

"That doesn't ring a bell," Matthew said.

"He knows Momma Ellen and Uncle Patrick. He said he was a drifter and an alcoholic after the war and that Momma and Patrick helped to turn his life around."

"It's a small world, Stevie."

"That's what Kenny said. Now he's married and has two little kids. He told me to give his regards to Momma and Uncle Patrick and said we could stop by to visit anytime."

"So you and Darnell helped him shovel horse manure."

"Yes."

"Where's your cell phone, Stevie?"

"It's right here," he said, reaching for his belt clip; he discovered that it was missing. "I guess I lost it somewhere," he said, examining his empty belt.

"If you had tried to call home to inform your mother of your whereabouts, you would have realized it was missing, and you would have used a pay phone to call her."

"I didn't see any pay phones; I think they're ancient history in most places, Daddy. Is Mommy upset?" he asked, sounding concerned.

"Well, she's upset enough to wring your neck. Why didn't you call?"

"I don't know. I guess I lost track of time. I'm sorry, Daddy."

"Don't tell me—tell your mother. But tell her after you've showered. You're so ripe that I probably smell of manure by association. I'm going in to calm your mother. Leave your shoes out here and toss your clothes in the wash; use the downstairs shower. I'll get you your pajamas."

"Thank you, Daddy."

"For what, son?"

"For being a selfish man and not allowing me to enlist. I could have come back like Omid."

Matthew shook his head and took a deep breath. Then he said, "Omid is one of thousands of brave men and women who have sacrificed all for an honorable belief. I don't agree with the foundation of the Iraq War, but I have profound respect for individuals like Omid. They deserve respect, dignity, and the honor they rightfully earned. We need to step forward with a hand of gratitude and charity."

"How do I do that, Daddy?"

"What you did today is a start. Now that you know what's happening, it's your moral obligation to contribute to a solution. Start with something small, and the path will open for you," he said, placing his hand on Stevie's shoulder and looking into his eyes. Stevie nodded in affirmation. "As you ponder what to do, don't do what you want—do what is needed."

"I don't understand."

"Well, take your friend Omid. He went with you and Darnell on today's outing because he probably wanted to do it and appreciated the company of friends. Sometimes people in that situation may want to be left alone, and you may need to give them some space. Another individual may need financial help to pay the rent or rear his children. It sounds like Omid needs a good therapist to help him get back on his feet. A blind vet might like someone to read to him. An emotionally disturbed vet may need a warm hug and a shoulder to cry on. Tragedy befalls people in many different ways. In order to help, identify the individual's needs and wants. Don't impose yours on him. Also, familiarize yourself with the culture of the person in need and respect it."

"I understand, Daddy. I shouldn't be the Boy Scout who drags the old lady across the street she just crossed. She'll protest and hit me over the head with her purse."

Matthew smiled and said, "That's right. Changing the subject, give me Katie's car keys."

"I think I have to drive her to work tomorrow, Daddy."

"Do you have school tomorrow?"

"No, Daddy."

"Well, speak with your Uncle Patrick. And if Omid and his family need and want you around, then spend some time with them. You're not driving Katie anywhere. She'll be better off if she stays grounded for the next few days, or she can find her own solutions."

Stevie reached into his pocket and handed Matthew the keys.

Matthew said, "I'll ask Kieran to program one of the old cell phones for you. Make sure you take it with you tomorrow, and put it in your pocket or dangle it from your neck so you won't lose it. If you don't plan to be home at a reasonable hour, call or I'll be the one who wrings your neck. While you live under my roof, you follow the rules."

"Yes, Daddy."

* * *

Matthew entered the master bedroom and found Kieran and Carolyn reading in bed. Kieran lay perpendicular to his mother, using her hip as his pillow in order to take maximum advantage of the lighting in the room.

"Half-pint," Matthew said while grabbing one of Kieran's bare feet, "are you sleeping with us again tonight?"

"No, Daddy," Kieran responded while closing his book against a finger. "I'm just hanging. Did you know they caught the bear today? They had to stitch his nose. As soon as he gets better, they're releasing him upstate."

"No, I didn't know that. Katie did some serious damage. What are you reading?"

"*How Green Was My Valley* for school."

"That's heavy reading for a kid your age, but excellent. Good for you. When you're done, can you program one of the old cell phones for Stevie? He lost his."

Upon hearing that, Carolyn set her book to one side while Kieran said, "Sure." He climbed out of bed in his bare feet and left for his room.

"Did he tell you where he's been?" Carolyn asked.

"He's been out being a good Samaritan and having an epiphany, so to speak. I have to get his pajamas because he smells of manure. I told him to toss the clothes in the wash and take a shower downstairs."

"So you're going to have my washer smell of manure. You should have told him to toss them in the trash," she said, getting out of bed. "Let me get downstairs before he actually contaminates my machine."

He held her back. "He doesn't want his mother to see him naked. I'll see what I can do. Relax. If he contaminates the machine, I'll run water with baking soda until it clears."

"Or you'll get me a new machine."

He bent his head to one side and said, "Or that." Then he turned and left the room in order to head Stevie off before he started the wash cycle.

Carolyn thought, *I still don't know where he's been.* Convinced that she would eventually be informed, she returned to reading her book.

Later that night, Carolyn rested her head on Matthew's shoulder while running her fingers along his hairy chest and tracing the scar near his right armpit. With the boys sleeping in their rooms, the house was very quiet. Matthew and Carolyn were sharing stories of their involvement with each of the children.

"I blew my top," she confessed to Matthew about her interaction with Katie that afternoon. "I almost said 'Shoot me,' but considering that she sometimes takes me too literally, I yelled 'Bite me.' Well, she was awestruck. After that, whenever I issued a directive, the only thing she could say all afternoon was 'Yes, Mommy.'" Carolyn laughed and continued. "I guess you've been right all along. I coddle her too much. I should be more forceful and hit her with a two-by-four once in a while."

"You're just saying that," he responded. "Tomorrow you'll go back to being all sweet and understanding. If you'll notice, she doesn't pull any of that crap with me because I believe in putting her soles to the coals. It's what she needs."

"Is that why you buy her little gifts from time to time?"

"No, I buy you and her trinkets because you tend to put my feet to the fire whenever you believe I've overreacted. I need to keep the peace with you, or you'll put me in the doghouse. I use the method known as tough love. You make me feel like I'm the bad guy."

"That's a canard; I don't do that," she protested.

Matthew laughed and said, "You're calling me a liar, woman? If you believe that, there is something seriously wrong with you. You're an enabler."

"I am not. I'm trying the best I can for you and our children. So I sometimes get it wrong. No one's perfect. What makes you so sure your methods are better than mine? Raising children is challenging. And you want me to have another child?"

"I thought you'd like another child before the clock runs out."

"Mattie, have you taken a good look at the two of us lately? Neither one of us is a spring chicken."

"You're not any kind of chicken. You're my beautiful Rua, Honey-Lyn. Whether you want to admit it or not, you are an overbearing mother, but I can overlook that because you are a caring, beautiful woman."

"How diplomatic of you. You insult and compliment me in the same breath. Some beauty I am," she responded with self-deprecation. "Every part of my body has gone south. My tits are nearly down to my navel. My vulva is dangling. If I have one more child, it will look like two pieces of lasagna noodle."

Matthew laughed and kissed the top of her head. "None of that is true," he said. "I should know; I have a better view of your vulva than you'll ever have. It's tight, baby. It knows how to hold me when I need a squeeze."

She smacked his chest. "Stop that," she complained.

"You started it," he said. "If you don't want to hear what you consider dirty talk, don't get me started. I can make you blush."

"Oh, Mattie," she said, holding him tighter and kissing his neck. "If anyone had convinced me that raising children would be so trying, I probably would have opted for none. When I finished attending to Katie's needs today, I ran into Kieran's accusative and pained, 'Where were you, Mom?' He learned that from Katie. It means, 'I needed you to be at my beck and call. How dare you not be here.' I don't think I ever spoke to my mother in that manner."

"Why did young master Kieran address you that way?"

"After school, the new school bus dropped him off at the bottom of the hill instead of driving up to Emily's Hope for his afterschool activities. That means he had to walk to the entrance gate and up the hill. Before he got to the gate, a strange man tried to stop him and ask questions."

"What questions?"

"He asked about Cheryl's son, Rasheed. So I concluded it must be Cheryl's ex-hubby, Arturo Santillana. Kieran got nervous and told him he didn't know anyone named Rasheed. Thank God for that."

"Did you report that to the police?"

"One of the security guards at the gate realized that something was going on, and he warned Arturo to stay away from our students. He walked Kieran up the hill and filed a report. However, the encounter frightened Kieran. That's why I was greeted with 'Where were you, Mom?' Now I have to worry about this guy Arturo. He better not bother my children or any of the kids at EH."

"You'll kick his ass," Matthew said, imitating Katie as he smiled and stroked Carolyn's hair.

"I'm definitely going to kick something. It may not be his ass," she replied. "Anyway, Nydia was still at the school. Thank God for that woman. She fusses over my children as much as she fusses over Luis. She calmed Kieran down and fed him walnut-carrot cake and milk. He wants the recipe; he claims he's going to bake it for us this weekend." She sighed at the duality of life: both sweet and challenging at the same time. "Having children makes life taxing, but I love having sex with my husband. Have you met him, my husband, I mean?" she joked.

"The handsome jock who turns even a gay man's head when he walks by?"

"That's the one. He looks like a Roman gladiator. He produces such handsome children. And although his body parts are also going south, he is so well endowed," she giggled.

"There you go talking dirty again. I may be heading south, but I can still perform. Besides, if my boys travel too far south, you can grab a needle and thread and stitch them back up again," he said while responding to her advances, and she winced at the thought.

Thirteen

◇◇◇

1990

"Mommy, look," five-year-old Stevie said, holding up his foot. "Luis teached me to tie my shoes."

"Luis taught you to tie your shoes?" Carolyn asked as she sat next to Nydia. They had been watching the children play after lunch. "You did that all by yourself, Stevie?"

"Yes," he lied.

"That means that from now on, you can put on your own shoes."

"He can't do that yet, Carolyn," nine-year-old Luis said. "He doesn't know left from right, and it took a lot of tries before I could get him to tie one shoe. He needs more practice. I had to tie the other one for him."

"Uh-uh," Stevie objected.

"Oh yes," Luis corrected him. "You didn't tie it right."

"Thank you, Luis," Carolyn said, and turned to Stevie. "I'm still proud of you for trying. You can practice some more."

"Stevie, now I'm going to teach you to throw and catch a ball. Come on."

"I know how to play with a ball, Luis."

"Not this way, you don't. Come on."

The two boys went off together.

"Luis," Nydia called, "hold his hand, and stay where we can see you."

Luis paused in his steps to take Stevie's hand. Then they both continued on their way.

"Where's Katie?" Nydia asked Carolyn.

"After her latest outburst yesterday, she's forbidden to be in the schoolyard for an entire week. She's supposed to be in my office reading. I hope that's what she's doing."

"You mean you hope she isn't talking to Rina."

"She can talk to Rina all she likes. At least it keeps her from getting into trouble. Ever since she befriended Rina, she spends a lot less time with Luis, and that's a positive. We don't have to worry about their desires to explore and experiment. And while she's in my office, she can't be picking fights and yelling epithets at everyone she disagrees with. She can tag the suffix 'ass' onto more words than anyone can imagine. Parents don't like their children being named asses, especially by the CEO's daughter."

"She isn't always talking to Rina. Luis and Katie spend hours talking on the phone."

"Phone conversations are fine because they keep their distance from one another. I just can't believe she managed to do that about-face and walk away from her sexual encounters with Luis. It was probably because you told them it made God angry."

"Well, I knew that comment would work for Luis. When I said it, his eyes almost popped out of his head. It's nice to be young, resilient, and able to forget."

"That it is, but my antennae are still up for Katie. And with the memory of what happened still in my mind, I've decided to enroll Stevie in St. Francis. He'll start next semester."

"But he'd have so many more opportunities here at Emily's Hope. Look how far most of these children have progressed. Their standardized test scores are above average. They also receive so much more extracurricular instruction."

"I know. We have good teachers and plenty of enrichment activities, but there is nothing wrong with mingling with the rest of the world's population. As a matter of fact, here Katie has a sense of entitlement. That's my fault, and I know it. I allow her to get away with too much because I'm so afraid I could cause more damage to her delicate sensibilities. Matthew and I get into arguments about that. I want Stevie to have a different experience. I shouldn't be around to wipe his nose over every little thing; I want him to be more self-sufficient, and going to a different school could be the right thing for him. He can still partake in the afterschool activities."

"I hope you're doing the right thing, Carolyn."

"So do I. Life is full of choices, and they aren't always easy."

When it was time to return to class, Luis brought Stevie back to his mother.

Carolyn examined Stevie. "You need to wash up. Come with me," she said while taking hold of his hand.

"Mommy, I ketched the ball this many times," he said, holding up his other hand.

"No, you didn't," Luis corrected him. "You caught it this, plus this," he demonstrated, holding up eight fingers. "How much is that, Stevie?"

"Twee. I ketched it twee."

"No, Stevie. You didn't catch it three times. This plus this," he said, displaying three fingers and five fingers, "is eight. Say it, Stevie."

The women looked on with amusement as Stevie replied, "I ketched it eight."

"Good for you, my little mathematician," Carolyn said. "Let's go now."

"Carolyn, I can hold his hand," Luis offered, taking Stevie's other hand. "I'll make sure he washes up."

"Thank you, Luis. I'll be right behind you. They look so cute together," she said to Nydia as she watched them walk away. "I'll talk to you later."

Carolyn and the boys soon returned to her office, which had been downsized to make room for Carolyn's secretary's office. As attendance at Emily's Hope increased, everyone's duties had also expanded, so Carolyn had hired the secretary and ceded a fourth of her office to her.

"Annie, thank you for keeping an eye on my little princess. Has she behaved herself?" she asked as she guided the boys to two seats.

"I kept the door open between us, and she hasn't budged from her seat."

Carolyn peeked into the office to catch a glimpse of Katie, who sat chewing on a pencil and moving her legs back and forth. "Katie," she called, "come on, honey. I'm taking you and the boys back to class. And stop chewing on that pencil's paint before you end up with lead poisoning."

Katie rose and entered Annie's office. "Why should you care if I get lead poisoning or not?" she asked defiantly. "You leave me here in jail, reading a stupid book, while everyone else gets to play during lunch. I didn't do anything wrong, you know."

"You hit Howie Benjamin and called him names. Nice young ladies don't do that. When you do something wrong, you pay the consequences. Let's go now." Carolyn placed a hand on her shoulder.

Katie pulled away and said, "Don't touch me. I know the way."

"Katie," Luis commented, "don't be rude to your mother."

"Shut up, you Benedict Arnold. I'm not talking to you," she yelled, and then she turned to face Carolyn while pointing an index finger at her, "or you."

Carolyn grabbed Katie's hand in midair and said, "You don't point your finger at me, young lady." Without taking her eyes off Katie, she added, "Luis, please take Stevie to his class and go to yours. Katie and I need to talk."

"Yes, Carolyn. Come on, Stevie," Luis said, rising from his seat and taking Stevie's hand.

"Get in my office," Carolyn said, dragging Katie behind her and closing the door. "Sit down," she commanded.

Katie crossed her arms in front of her chest and challenged, "Make me."

"Suit yourself," Carolyn countered, and she grabbed the nearest chair and turned it to face Katie. As she sat, she said, "You know, you can choose to live a happy life or a bitter one. People who are bitter never have any friends because normal people don't want to be around grumpy people. If you continue this way, you're going to be sad and lonely for the rest of your life."

"So what?" Katie responded with her arms still crossed in front of her chest. "What do you care?"

"I care because I love you, and I don't want to see you miserable. I want you to be happy. In order to be happy,

you have to be nicer to people. You can't be picking
fights with everyone all your life, and I don't want to fight
you. I'd rather spend my time hugging and loving you,
but you are not making it easy for me. You promise me
that you will behave, and then you go back and do the
same thing over and over again."

Katie exhaled and rolled her eyes.

"Katie, do you know what 'primogenitor' means?"

"Yes," she responded defiantly.

"Well, I have a story to tell you."

"Oh boy," Katie retorted sarcastically.

Carolyn ignored the comment and told Katie a story
about two princes to whom the king had willed equal
shares of his kingdom. The older brother thought that he
should have been the sole heir to the throne because
he was the primogenitor and hated that he had ended
up with half a kingdom. As Katie shifted uncomfortably
from one foot to another, Carolyn went on to say that
the younger king treated his subjects well and increased
his kingdom's wealth because his people loved him and
worked willingly. The older brother became jealous and
waged war against the younger king. His subjects didn't
fight well, and he lost his kingdom.

"You made that up."

"No, I didn't," Carolyn informed her. "I read the story
when I was a kid. Do you understand the moral?"

"Of course I understand the moral. You catch more
flies with honey than with vinegar. You could have just
said that. You didn't have to bore me with a lame story.
I'm not stupid."

"I never said you were. But you are an unhappy little
girl. I don't want you to ever be so unhappy and unfulfilled

that you risk losing the love of the people around you. I'd like you to find more joy in this world. You can find joy by being kind to people instead of offending them. A person who fills his soul with love grows stardust in his heart. A person who fills his soul with hate gets rocks within his gut."

Katie was feeling mellower, but she didn't want to let her feelings known. Instead, she said, "It was a lame story. Same as the flies and honey shit. Why the hell would I want to catch a dirty fly?"

"Flies and their maggots can be useful. I'm sorry you didn't like the story. Maybe you can write a better one someday. In the meantime, try not to be so angry. Since I'm not getting through to you, I'll walk you back to class. Come on."

Katie walked quietly as Carolyn accompanied her to class. When they arrived at the door to her classroom, Katie inquired, "Why don't you trust me?"

"What do you mean?"

"You keep escorting me back to class as if I were some kind of common criminal going to the gallows."

"I'm sorry you feel that way, honey. Nothing could be further from the truth. I enjoy walking with you, and I thought you wouldn't mind my company. I take Luis and Stevie to their rooms for the same reason. It gives me the opportunity to spend a little extra time with you and them. But I guess you think you're all grown up now. Well, you're still my little girl. Like it or not, I will continue to accompany you wherever you go. I do it because I love you."

"Yeah, sure," she retorted, opening the door. "Whatever."

Carolyn spent the rest of the afternoon playing host to administrators from the New York City Board of Education.

Carolyn's sister-in-law, Camille, was showing off the family's school as a model that could possibly help inner-city students, and Carolyn was happy to receive them and give them a tour. Camille had worked with New York City students for over fifteen years. Momma Ellen had asked her to work at Emily's Hope, knowing that Camille's expertise would be an asset, but Camille had politely declined, explaining that she enjoyed working with the city kids and that she encountered a similar need there. Today, however, she felt a certain pride showcasing Carolyn's and Dr. Holder's accomplishments. Emily's Hope had become the pride of the Westchester suburb neighborhood. As regular school let out and the afterschool students started to arrive for extracurricular activities, Camille and the guests departed. Luis was in a fencing class while Nydia turned over the reins of her kitchen to the afterschool dietician.

Carolyn sat outside, enjoying a late afternoon snack with Stevie while she kept an eye on Katie who was in the tennis court, apparently talking to Rina, her new confidant. Katie had informed Carolyn that the older Ekaterina had been abused by her biological father, and because he had been an illegal immigrant, the INS deported him after his arrest. Rina supposedly lived alone with her mother. Katie claimed she learned a lot from her, and she insisted on learning Russian so they could have more in common. Carolyn obliged by hiring a Russian tutor. As Katie prepared to play tennis while bouncing the ball on the clay court with her racket, Carolyn was called away from her observation post via the beeper she kept in her pocket. Papa Sean and Momma Ellen were beeping her from their office. She dropped her nearly empty salad bowl in the receptacle next to her seat while Stevie continued to munch on his own food.

"We have to go, Stevie," she said.

A few minutes later, Carolyn was speaking to Sean and Ellen. "I'm sorry to lay this on you. Katie is my responsibility, and the doctors explained that sexually abused children could behave like that. I've tried to come to terms with it, but what happened this weekend has heightened my level of concern. I'm perturbed! A nine-year-old child should not be masturbating. I don't even know how long this has been going on. What am I doing wrong?"

"A Rua, dear," Ellen replied, "you're not doing anything wrong. I've told you before that dealing with Katie's afflictions is not a burden for you alone."

"You acknowledge what the doctors said," Sean intervened. "It's probable behavior among children of sexual abuse. You can't be blaming and torturing yourself for matters over which you have no control."

"Do I allow this to continue to happen, to run its course? I can't do that! I always think of ramifications. What if she has children, will she…? Oh, God, I can't even say it," she said as tears welled in her eyes. "What if she teaches her own children to do that? This can be cyclical."

Sean walked over to her and caressed her back as the tears rolled down her face, and Ellen held out a box of tissues. Carolyn drew two tissues out and started to clean her face and blow her nose. "I'm sorry," she said, "I didn't mean to get overemotional."

"Katie's psychiatrist suggested hypnosis. Are you willing to try that, a Rua?" Ellen asked.

"I don't know, Momma. I'm so confused."

"Well, I don't totally agree with the shrink. Stop trying to correct everything you perceive to be wrong, dear. If I were you, I'd talk to Katie and let nature take its course. Some things are not meant to be *fixed*. They may simply need an adjustment—you don't carry a car on your back; you use the steering wheel to guide it in the right direction. I think you need a break from her. I heard she beat up Benjamin. What do you say if Sean and I took her for a week or two?"

"I'll still be worried," Carolyn replied.

"But your life will be a little easier for two weeks," Sean countered. "Ellen and I don't have much to do here. Sure, we oversee the afternoon and evening activities, but that pretty much runs itself. Ellen can take Katie out of school for a week and take a little trip with her. I can watch her the second week. If anything shocking comes up, we'll handle it. After all, we raised…"

"…four children of our own." Carolyn completed his sentence and laughed.

"Carolyn," Ellen volunteered, "go home and get some rest. Better still, go to the spa and let them pamper you. You deserve a little R & R. We'll deliver Stevie and Katie to you when they're done with today's activities. Then we'll pack a bag for Katie and bring her home with us."

"She can't leave this week. She hasn't completed her week of detention," Carolyn protested. "I don't want her to get the impression she's being rewarded."

"Fine, we'll steal her from you next week," Sean said. "In the meantime, do what Ellen recommends. We'll bring the children to you after eight o'clock. That way, you'll have a little free time with Mattie as well." Sean winked, and Carolyn laughed while still holding the two tissues.

After Carolyn left, Sean said to Ellen, "I love Carolyn, but she's wound too tightly. I didn't have the heart to tell her that sometimes children tend to masturbate without any outside contamination, as she perceives it. We can't always trust a shrink to offer the best advice."

"That's why I said she can't right what she perceives to be wrong. We all perceive life from different angles."

"And our little Katie is a master of perception."

* * *

Katie and Rina were in the park, holding their tennis rackets and picking dandelions and blowing the weed's fine white fibers into the wind as they walked.

"So," Katie concluded, "I confronted her and told her that she walks me to class because she doesn't trust me. She claims she does this because she loves me. Like I'm going to believe that. What the hell does she think I'm going to do as I walk from one room to another? It's not like I'm catching a plane to Nicaragua or something. The woman is certifiable."

"I know what you mean. My mother does the same thing to me. 'Rina, where are you going?' or 'Ekaterina, make sure you be home by six.' Give me a freaking break. The woman doesn't even give me a chance to breathe. Where the hell was she each time her husband was banging me?"

"Do you ever think that maybe she saw him doing you and didn't care?" Katie asked.

"The thought has crossed my mind. I can remember telling her about it, and she said, 'Stop making up stories, Ekaterina.' Like I'm going to make up a story like that."

"Sometimes, I can remember my father breathing on me with his hot breath," Katie said as she touched her cheek. "I can almost feel him touch me down there, and I get all hot. Do you ever touch yourself, Rina?"

"Well, yeah. I don't want to do it because it isn't right, you know. It's because of what I remember, but it doesn't feel the same, you know."

"Yes, I know. Rina?"

"Yes, Katie?"

"My mother caught me this weekend, you know. I was in my room, sitting on the corner of the bed. When I was little, I used to ride Luis's pecker, you know. But I don't do that anymore. It isn't right. We're too young to get married. But I read in one of those geographic magazines that the girls in one of those third-world countries get married when they're nine. They can do it with their husband and their husband's brothers because each brother has the right to consider her a wife. Can you imagine that?"

"Katie, that's awful!"

"Yeah, I guess, but that means they can do it whenever they want."

"You sound as if you would like that. That's not good, Katie. Sex like that can damage all your insides, and you can get very sick, especially at your age."

"That's what my mother said."

"You talked about the magazine article with your mother?"

"No, but that's what she said when she caught me in bed, trying to massage myself down there. She told me not to do it again because I could get an infection or something. Then she explained that little girls are not yet developed enough to have sex. If they have sex too early, all their insides could tear up. Also, if you have sex with a man, you could get pregnant, and when the baby is coming out, it can rip all your insides out. I guess you could die."

"If my mother caught me doing that, I guess I could die. Were you embarrassed, Katie?"

"Yeah, I was very embarrassed. I didn't expect her to come in like that. She usually knocks. I knock whenever I enter her bedroom. Why didn't she knock?" Katie cried. "I don't want to disappoint her. My mother is a nice lady, you know. I love her, but now, I don't know. I think I disappointed her, Rina. I could tell she was upset. I could see it in her face." She wiped a tear from her cheek. "When she gets upset, she has trouble talking. It's like the wheels in her head are going round and round, you know. She was upset. She hates me now—I know she hates me. She hated me when I rode Luis's pecker. Now she hates me again." She wiped another tear from her face. "It wasn't my fault, Rina."

"I know, Katie. Sometimes that idea comes into my head, and I can't get it out. I turn the radio on real loud, and I sing to get it out of my head. But it doesn't go away."

"No," Katie agreed, "it doesn't go away. I want it to stop, Rina."

"I want it to stop. We can work together to help us forget, Katie."

"How do we do that, Rina?"

"I don't know, but we'll figure it out," Rina said while checking watch. "Katie, I have to go; my mom will get angry if I don't get home on time.

"Okay, Rina. Maybe I'll see you tomorrow."

* * *

A half hour later, Momma Ellen spotted Katie along the footpath as she drove by and called the child over. When Katie sat in the car, Ellen asked, "Where have you been, Kate? I've been looking all over for you. Why didn't you go to karate today?"

"I went to the park with Rina after we played a couple of sets of tennis."

"Kate, you can't leave school grounds without permission. What if something happened to you? You know, I was about to call the police."

"I'm okay, Momma. Nothing happened to me."

"Nothing happened to you? Well, something happened to me, young Kate. You almost gave me a heart attack. It's a good thing Carolyn isn't here, or she would kill us both. I told her I'd keep an eye on you and Stevie."

"Where's Mom?"

"She had an appointment and had to leave early. You and Stevie are having dinner with Papa and me. Strap yourself in so we can get going." Katie obeyed and buckled her seat belt. "I don't know, Katie my love. Sometimes you can try a dead woman's soul. Don't ever leave school grounds again without consent or adult supervision."

"I was with Rina, Momma."

"Rina doesn't count, Kate. Maybe it's time you and she parted company because she certainly isn't helping. Find a hobby, Kate."

"Are you going to tell Mommy that I went to the park, Momma?"

"Kate, one way or another, she's going to find out you didn't go to your karate class this afternoon. So yes, I will have to tell her that you have behaved foolishly today."

"I'm sorry, Momma."

"Kate, sorry doesn't cut it. You know better than that. Carolyn is trying to be a good mother to you, dear. You need to shape up and toe the line."

"Yes, Momma. I'm trying, you know, but you and Mommy don't get it."

"Don't get what, Kate?"

"You don't understand that I'm trying. It's just very, very hard, Momma. And I want Mommy to like me. I don't think she likes me very much lately, but it's not my fault, Momma—it's not my fault."

Ellen paused a moment to look at Katie. Katie felt uncomfortable because she thought that Ellen was judging her with her gaze.

"Kate, honey," she finally said, "Your mother does not dislike you—no one dislikes you. We simply want you to make the right decisions. I hear you, dear. It's hard; I believe you. Maybe I'm expecting too much too soon, and I'm reacting because I was worried about you disappearing today. Try not to do it again, okay?"

"Yes, Momma. What are you going to tell Mommy?"

"Honey, I have to tell her the truth. She left you in my care, and I have to be honest with her. Don't be nervous about it. Sometimes being truthful is the best thing to do. I'm sure Carolyn will admire you for that. Maybe it's best if you tell her yourself. I'll let you think about it; you decide."

* * *

At eight fifteen that night, Ellen and Sean walked into their son's kitchen. Stevie was asleep, resting his head on Sean's shoulder.

"I'll take him, Papa," Matthew volunteered. He was barefoot and dressed in a T-shirt and striped pajama pants. "Thank you for babysitting tonight," he said as he eased Stevie away from Sean.

Matthew took the boy up to his bedroom while Carolyn entertained Ellen and Sean in the family room. The older couple declined an offer of a drink, explaining they weren't going to stay long. Carolyn, who wore a robe over her nightgown, asked Katie to get ready for bed.

"Mommy," Katie interjected, "I went to the park with Rina today without permission. I apologize, Mommy. I won't do it again."

Carolyn looked at her solemnly and thought, *It's Mommy time again.* Then she asked, "Why?"

"Why what, Mommy?"

"Why were you in the park by yourself without permission?" Carolyn asked while stressing each word.

"I wasn't by myself; I was with Rina. It was a beautiful day, Mommy, so we went for a walk."

"Listen carefully, Katie. You do not go anywhere without permission. The rules are there to protect you. Safe neighborhood or not, you and your friend Rina should not have been there alone. You never know what can happen to you while you're out of sight and earshot."

"Nothing happened, Mommy."

"That's not the point, Katie," she said as Matthew walked into the room.

"What's the problem?" he asked. Carolyn explained while Ellen and Sean watched.

"I see," Matthew commented while turning to Katie. "Princess, do you know that thousands of children disappear off the face of the earth because they do something thoughtless like that?"

"Matthew!" Ellen interjected.

"Let me finish, Momma," he said, holding up one hand in Ellen's direction, without taking his eyes off Katie. "Every day, children get kidnapped and never see their families again. Do you want that to happen to you, Katie?"

"Nothing happened, Daddy. Besides, no one can kidnap me. I know self-defense and karate."

"You know self-defense and karate. Well, I'm strong and played football. Even I can be someone's victim if he is determined enough to hurt me, and I weigh close to two hundred pounds. What do you weigh, squirt?"

Katie shrugged her shoulders and said, "I don't know. Mommy, how much do I weigh?"

"About ninety-five pounds, I guess," Carolyn responded.

Matthew looked at Katie and rubbed his hands together as he thought. He finally said, "Let's try a little experiment, Katie. Let's make believe you're walking in the park ahead of me. I'm the bad guy. I will come up behind you and kidnap you. I'll have you tied to a kitchen chair before you can yell, 'Dial 911.'"

"You're not tying anyone up in my house," Carolyn protested. "What's wrong with you?"

"Okay, okay," he capitulated. "I'll have you seated in a kitchen chair before you can say, 'Call 911.'"

Katie eyed him as if she were looking at a poker challenger. "You want to make believe you're kidnapping me?" she asked incredulously. "You can't kidnap me. I told you I know self-defense and karate."

"Isn't karate and self-defense the same thing?" he asked.

"No," she corrected him. "You don't have to know ka-rate to practice self-defense. Bill teaches us to do both. I bet you I can take you down, Daddy. How much do you want to bet?"

"Listen, Maverick, I'm not betting money with you. I'm betting I can teach you a lesson."

Within minutes, while Carolyn, Sean, and Ellen looked on, Matthew and Katie were role playing. As Katie picked flowers in the park, Matthew grabbed her from behind and pinned her to his side. Katie instantly started flailing her arms, squirming and screaming for help while Matthew ran with her toward the dining area. Her squirming was a calculated effort to position herself where she could do the most damage. Katie wrapped one arm around his upper thigh, and when he pulled his leg back, leaving a wider surface area between his leg and pelvis, she bit his testicle.

As Matthew fell on one knee, Katie loosened her grip and rolled to the floor. Matthew's face flushed with pain. Carolyn gasped and rushed to his side. Ellen uttered "Jesus, Mary, and Joseph" in a single breath. Sean cringed with sympathetic pain.

Fourteen

◇◇◇

2005

"Today," Luis announced to Katie as he shaved, "I'm buying you a wheelchair."

"Do I look like a paraplegic to you?" Katie asked with annoyance as she sat on the toilet seat cover giving herself a sponge bath. "I don't need a freaking wheelchair, you idiot. Do my back, Luis. I can't reach it." She extended the washcloth toward him.

He stopped shaving and took the washcloth. "You know," he said while scrubbing her back, "you have to start treating me a little nicer. I'm going to be a daddy soon, and I demand some respect when you speak to me."

"Well, I doubt that's ever going to happen, so stop trying to change me."

"You keep taking me for granted, and I'm not going to put up with that any longer. If I can change, so can you. Besides, you behave like a nice young lady when you're around other people. I don't want my child being raised in a negative environment and disrespecting me."

"You want negative, Luis? Shut the hell up."

"What's wrong with you, woman? Here," he said, tossing her the washcloth. "Scrub your own back. I'm going to finish shaving and go to work."

"You have to drive me to work," she protested. "Daddy told Stevie not to drive me."

"I'm not driving you anywhere; I have to get to work myself. Stay home and sulk. Maybe a little quiet contemplation will make you a better person. If you keep treating me like I have no feelings, I'm staying home—my home. Hire somebody to help you. I don't appreciate being taken for granted."

"Well, well, the lamb has claws. You know, I don't need you to drive me; I'll call Cheryl. After all, she has one of my cars. She needs to drive into the city, and she should be awake by now."

"She has that crazy husband after her. I don't think it's wise for you to be around her. Stay home or I'll tell Carolyn."

"Luis, I'm over twenty-one. My mommy can't tell me what to do," she said as she wrapped a bath towel around herself. "I'm calling Cheryl right now." She grabbed her crutches and started to leave.

"Katie," Luis said, holding her upper arm as she tried to walk past him, "be sensible, woman. You can do most of your work via the Internet; you don't have to be in Manhattan. Stay home and rest your leg. The first month or even three months, depending on your rate of healing, are crucial to developing bone tissue. You don't want to end up with a permanent disability, do you?"

She gave it some thought and said, "No, but I need to go in today. I'm meeting with the appliance and heating people to decide on what units we'll use on my next project. I like to make those decisions myself, one-on-one. There are too many variables. Beginning tomorrow, I can probably stay home."

"Why do rich people work?" he asked, releasing his grip on her arm. "You're rich enough to get a cruise ship and travel all over the world."

"Is that what you plan to do, Luis? How shallow of you. Where's the challenge? Where are the rewards?"

"There are plenty of challenges in the world and plenty to see. New sights are enough rewards."

"Are visions of sugarplums dancing in your head, Luis? If they are, I advise you to shake them out. We have a child on the way, so if you're thinking of becoming a beachcomber or sailor, forget it. We'll talk later. Let me call Cheryl before I run the risk of missing her. You keep talking like that, and you'll be the one dealing with my mother. If it comes to pass, I guarantee you are going to be one sorry ass."

"If you're concerned that I'm going to be foolish about my impending wealth, it's not going to happen. Carolyn arranged for me to see a financial advisor today. Susan Sheridan and that guy Haggerty agreed to wait until Monday to see me. I'm going to have time to think about my future."

"You do that," she said as she stepped into the bedroom.

* * *

Cheryl was delighted to return a favor. En route, the women spoke of various things, including Cheryl's unpleasant experience with her ex-husband, Arturo Santillana.

"When we first started dating, I was young and impressionable," Cheryl stated. "I believed all the sweet nothings that son-of-a-bitch said. I should have known better than to trust a man hungering for a green card."

"Well, I don't believe all illegal aliens are animals," Katie countered. "I know plenty of illegal aliens who are fine people. I also believe that degenerates are found in all walks of society. My biological father was a medical doctor—nothing illegal about him except his twisted, malevolent mind."

"I know that a beast can be found anywhere. There's good and there's bad, but if you encounter an individual who's lacking something, girlfriend, stay the hell away from him. If he needs a green card, walk on. If he's an alcoholic, wait until he's sober for ten years. If he loves his mommy too much, make sure the apron strings are cut. If he's a player, you're not going to change him. If he can't hold a job, look past him and keep on walking. Girl, since I've been kicked every way imaginable, I have my PhD from the school of hard knocks. If I ever hook up with a man again, he'll have to pass Cheryl's list of perfection from A to Z."

"How bad was your marriage?"

"It was *THE* nightmare from hell! First, he complained about my cooking. One day I snapped and told him to cook his own damn meal, and he dragged me by my hair and stood over me while I prepared his damn chicken and rice the way his mommy did it. The next day, I didn't go home. I went straight to my sister's house. The bastard came to get me and told me that if I didn't want him to murder my sister and her kids right there, I'd better go with him. Honey, when he showed me that gun under his coat, I thought I was going to pee right there. Naturally, I grabbed my things and left with him breathing down my neck. He changed all the locks on the doors to the type that open only with a key, and if he had to go out, he locked me in."

"How did you get to work?"

"I had to leave at the same time as he did. He issued me a cell phone to keep tabs on me throughout the day. I had to be waiting at the door to my house by a set time. If I arrived earlier, I couldn't get in. If I arrived later, he would beat me and threaten to kill my family. That animal raped me practically every night. I worked, and still do, for Child Protective Services, and I couldn't protect myself or my family."

"How did you get away, Cheryl?"

"I trusted a coworker with my story. While at work, she would photograph my bruises in the bathroom stall, and she kept a journal on me. I also had a very inquisitive doctor who suspected something was wrong. All that documentation was important for me to attempt to make a move. Rasheed was about three years old at the time. My sister and her kids took a trip to Florida. Her husband, Jerome, stayed behind, and I called him from work. That very day, he came to get me at work before noon. We picked up Rasheed and my mother and drove to Jerome's mother's house in Maryland. Knowing my mother and Rasheed were safe, Jerome and I came back to New York together and filed an official police report. They arrested Arturo that very night."

"Now he's back," Katie said.

"Yeah; he spent only three years in prison; the bastard is out on parole. Although he apparently followed me to Emily's Hope, there was no actual proof when they detained him the other day. Besides, he wasn't within the prohibited five hundred feet. Now we have the goods on that worm. I thank God I saw and recognized that detective friend of Luis's at the ceremony. He's a very nice man."

"Yes, he is."

"Once they officially connect Arturo to that cell phone, his ass is grass. Hopefully, the police have picked him up by now. In the meantime, I'm on pins and needles. However, I do look on the bright side. My sister and her family now live in Maryland; Jerome works in DC, so they're off Arturo's radar. It's a good thing my mother and I moved to Westchester County and learned about Emily's Hope. You guys have been a godsend. I can't thank you enough. I need to ask INS to revoke the bastard's citizenship and deport him."

"He'll only come back or victimize someone else. I believe the only way to deal with violent offenders is to kill or violate them back. Bullies are molded by bullies, Cheryl. If the mold isn't broken, they continue to be predators. If you want to keep a mosquito from stinging, you whack it. Sending him back to Latin America doesn't solve anything."

The traffic was horrendous. With the taxi strike, everyone from the suburbs and adjoining boroughs appeared to be driving into the city. There were also more bikes on the road than usual.

"Why don't these idiots take the train?" Katie asked Cheryl about the cyclists and new motorists.

She responded with, "They're probably psychic and afraid they may run into the same transit cop that busted you." They both laughed.

Two hours later, Katie was in her office with her leg propped on a chair when Efraín Ramírez knocked on her open door.

"I got your message," he said as he walked in. "What's up?"

"I need you to oversee the project in East New York," she said.

"Isn't Abisheck working that site?"

"And he will continue to work it. He's a good man. However, since I can't get around, you are now officially my eyes and ears for that site, if you're interested."

Ramírez shrugged his shoulders and said, "Fine. What do you want me to do?"

"The same thing you always do. Check and double-check that everything is up to code and that we're following every safety regulation. By everything, I mean everything. I'm talking scaffolding, cranes, and all machinery. I'm even talking about paint when we get to that point. I don't want to hear about any kind of violation or idiotic cost-cutting to save a penny at the expense of losing something else. A corporation is built on reputation and safety as much as profits. You lose your integrity, and you lose everything else."

"I understand. Do I continue working the Manhattan sites as well?"

"We'll need new people. You may need to move people around until you hire new personnel. Furman is gone."

"So I heard," Ramírez responded as he placed his right ankle on his left knee.

"Under no circumstances are you to overlook the safety issue. Case in point: On my way to and from one of our sites in Yonkers, I often passed a commercial development. They had brought so much gravel onto the site that the crane was literally perched at a ninety-degree angle on a precipice made of gravel. I shook my head and said, '*I know that cranes have good traction, but I have never* known any to defy the laws of gravity.' Well, perhaps on three different occasions, traffic was stopped and the area was cordoned off. I suspect that some poor crane operator had probably tumbled from the height of that gravel mountain to his death. If any of my supervisors or workers ever does anything that callous and stupid, he will never work again—at least not in construction. If he doesn't die on the job, he can spend the rest of his life selling donuts on a street corner."

"How long do you plan to be out of commission, Katie?"

"I don't know. Luis said it can take a few months for the bones to mend, depending on my rate of healing. My father is trying to fix my SUV so I can drive it with my left foot. As soon as that happens, I plan to be making my usual rounds. However, I won't be able to do everything I did before. So you'll probably be burdened with the extra work for a few months; maybe a whole year. Gupta is in charge of the office, and you're head of field work. How does that sound?"

"Sounds good to me. Get well soon," he said, rising from his seat.

"How is Gwendolyn Cheung working out, Efraín?"

"I only spent the one day with her. So far, so good. I'll take her to the East New York site and let her see what goes into a major project. I'll check in with you at the end of the day. If you need anything, give a holler."

After reviewing her voice and e-mails, Katie spent the morning talking to heating contractors. One young man intrigued her. He and his mother had a start-up company that had brainstormed alternative energy production and harnessing. He pitched his ideas to her, and she listened with interest.

"Most turbines and windmills," he said, "are immense and present a danger to wildlife. The cup design on this unit allows you to capture more energy with a reduced surface area. Because smaller particles can be moved faster and easier than larger particles, this unit will actually produce two hundred times more energy than conventional units. From here, they enter the pressurized collectors. It's like packing all the energy you can into a snowball. When it's released—*bang!* You can run a bank of elevators at a fraction of the cost. As the elevators run up and down, we harness that energy as well. So we're recycling it. The energy collected from elevators is enough to power a community laundry room. The energy produced in the laundry room is enough to heat a living area. This is harnessing at its peak, from raw energy and recycled energy, with reduced risk to wildlife."

"I like what you have, Mr. Leung," Katie complimented him, "and I'm envisioning additional applications. Do you already have a patent for this?"

"Yes."

"It's an intriguing model, Mr. Leung. I'd like you and your mother to visit me at my home, perhaps this Sunday, and we'll work something out. You discuss it with your mother and get back to me. I'll e-mail you directions to my house."

The young man could not contain his excitement. He had made an impression. "Yes, Dr. O'Gorman. I'm sure my mother will be glad to meet with you." He nearly leaped into the air. Katie smiled at his enthusiasm.

"Two more questions, Mr. Leung."

"Yes," he said with anticipation.

"What does your mother do for a living? Whom does she work for?"

"She's a quantum mechanics professor at the City University of New York."

"Public sector is good as far as patents are concerned, Mr. Leung. Sometimes private industry tries to claim a chunk of the pie."

"I don't understand," he said with a quizzical expression.

"If you work for the private sector, they might try to prove that your invention was conceived and produced during company time and on company property. If they succeed in proving that, they can steal your patent from under you. Generally, individuals in the public sector don't have that kind of ambition or logistics. So you may be safe. Don't worry—I'm not in the business of swiping patents. If it meets my needs, I'll license it from you or purchase the finished product. I hope to see you on Sunday."

* * *

Close to noon, Katie received a personal phone call.

"Hey, Katie baby. It's me, Rina; I got your number from Carolyn. I thought you might want to meet for lunch. We can catch up on old times."

"That sounds great. Is your friend Elena Morales with you?"

"No, she's visiting an aunt in Queens. It will be just you and me."

They arranged to meet at a nearby restaurant at one o'clock. They sat in a booth near the kitchen.

"So, Katie, what have you been up to since we last spoke?"

"Luis and I are expecting our first child," Katie said and smiled with delight.

"After all these years the two of you have decided to create a miniature of yourselves. Congratulations! Are you married?"

"No, I'm still ambivalent about that. How about you, Rina? What's new?"

"I like Luis, Katie. Why don't you hurry up and marry him? He's perfect for you. You'll never know another man as well as you know him. You're practically siblings and you know he can be trusted."

"I know—you don't need to tell me. You didn't answer my question. What's new with you?"

"Well, let's see," she said and started to count, using the fingers of her left hand. "My mother, aunt, and I moved to Florida. I graduated college. I met Elena while I was there, and now the two of us want to set up shop here in the fashion district. The one good thing is that I never heard from my father again. It's like the bastard fell off the face of the earth or something. No news is good news, you know."

"You're talking about the time he returned after the INS deportation?" Katie inquired suspiciously because she knew Rina was aware of what had happened to her father. As children, they never kept secrets from one another.

"Precisely—it took two or three years for him to find his way back. Do you remember, he followed me home on my way from school and raped me? I told you about that, didn't I?"

"Yes, you did. I was probably twelve at the time, but I remember," Katie said as the waiter brought bread and salad. "You told me you didn't say anything to your mother."

"I didn't want to worry her. With his deportation, she had turned her life around. She was working overtime in order to earn extra money. Then one evening she came home and found him in the apartment with me. That was my second encounter with him after he weaseled his way back. My mother was so upset she nearly killed him with an iron skillet. It was the first available weapon she saw, I guess. Surprisingly enough, he didn't put up a fight and left. She called INS and reported him. Maybe they deported him again. Who knows? Anyway, we moved to Florida with my aunt. My life has been normal and good since then."

"I remember when you suddenly left for Florida," Katie said while buttering her warm pumpernickel bread, and thought, *"Is it possible she doesn't remember what happened to her father, or is she trying to pull my leg?"* "What are you planning to do now, Rina?"

"Elena and I studied fashion design. We started an online company, and it's doing quite well. I figure, if we can manage to open a New York boutique, the physical location should give us a little extra edge. People like having Paris, New York, etcetera, attached to the threads they wear. Miami and Tampa don't have that same attraction."

"People are funny that way," Katie agreed. "Are you okay financially?"

"Yes, we're good. We researched everything before making a move. However, it still boggles my mind about how expensive New York has gotten."

"It's expensive to the middle class and the growing number of invisible poor, but it's a bargain for Europeans, Japanese, the Arab oil barons, and people like me."

"It's Charles Dickens's words come to life again: 'It was the best of times...'"

"Exactly. The rich get richer, and the poor get poorer. In this economic climate, my company is doing well. Although,

I don't know how much longer this realty and contracting bubble will continue. I hope people are saving in case things suddenly fall apart. When the poor get poorer, they start to steal or sharpen the guillotine."

When the main course arrived, they ate mostly in silence. At the conclusion, they promised to see each other more often and Katie returned to her office. She spoke with several appliance salesmen and selected the items she liked. By four o'clock, she was finished for the day. She called Cheryl at work and decided to meet her at her job in order to save time on the commute home.

To ease her walk, Katie again slung her laptop and purse against her back. She was wearing a trench coat over her suit. As sometimes happens during March in New York, the temperature was dropping and there was a little chill in the air. She gingerly, but steadily, walked one block south to the Thirty-fourth Street bus stop. She waited at the stop for the downtown bus to Battery Park and noticed a boy who was about thirteen or fourteen seated on a Siamese water pipe in front of the building near the bus stop. He was seemingly disinterested with his surroundings. Katie furtively observed that he had no schoolbooks and was wearing top designer clothes. She placed one crutch against the bus stop's post and drew her purse forward. She removed a flat wallet from the purse and tossed the purse against her back again. She placed the flat wallet in an inside breast pocket.

When she looked up the street, the bus was approaching. She reached into a front pocket, where she kept her cell phone, and removed the MetroCard she had placed there earlier. She boarded the bus while holding both crutches in one hand and pulling herself up the two steps, holding the handrail. The passengers behind her waited patiently as she lifted herself up and balanced herself back on her crutches. She swiped the MetroCard to pay for her ride and secured it inside the flat wallet she had previously withdrawn from her purse. The bus was full, and she started to make her way to the rear, where she believed her crutches would not be an impediment to others.

As she excused herself past the standing passengers and squeezed her way to the back, the remainder of the passengers finished boarding. Before the driver closed the doors, two additional passengers rushed to take the bus. One of those was the teenager who had straddled the Siamese water pipes, and the other was Jonathan Furman. They also walked to the rear of the bus. Katie had embraced a vertical standing pole with the crook of one arm for support. She saw the teenager squeeze his way past her. Without looking back, she knew the boy had stopped behind her. Then she saw Furman. He reached for the horizontal pole near the bus's ceiling and stood facing her. He smiled as he looked into her face. Katie stared at him without any visible expression.

"I saw you waiting for the bus from across the street," he said. She eyed him quietly as he continued speaking. "For a minute there, I thought I was going to miss the bus, but I made it."

"Evidently, you did. For some reason, I thought I wasn't going to see you again. However, you did say it's not over."

Smiling, he said, "Yes, I did say that, didn't I?"

"It seems that breaking up is hard to do. What's on your mind, Jonathan?"

"Actually, I want to apologize for my actions, Katharine."

"You do?" she asked cynically.

"Yes, I do. I was wrong to react the way I did, and you were right to fire me. Listen, you have been sincere and forthright with me from day one. You do and say what you mean. You're a no-nonsense lady, and I admire that." The bus hit a bump in the road, and Katie tried to balance herself. Furman braced her shoulder as she was nearly flung forward. "Are you okay?" he asked.

"Yeah, I'm fine," she responded, straightening herself up.

"As I was saying," he continued, "I was wrong about that, and I was wrong about my work. I should have handled things better, but I didn't."

"Are you trying to sweet-talk your way back? Because if you are, it's not going to happen."

"No, no," he said, holding one hand up. "I just want to apologize. I have issues, and I shouldn't have let them interfere with my work performance. I'm truly sorry I let you down. I also apologize for what I said; I was out of line. Honest—that's all this is about."

The teenager started to walk past Katie. At that point, she purposely tripped him with the crutch, causing him to lose his balance. Katie instinctively grabbed his hair and pulled him back to prevent him from tumbling forward.

"Grab my laptop, Jonathan," she instructed Furman.

Furman took a second to realize that the boy was holding Katie's computer bag. He snatched it from the boy's grasp.

"Empty your pockets!" Katie ordered the young man while still pulling his hair. When he didn't react, she pulled his hair with greater force, nearly lifting him off the floor. "I said empty your pockets."

Somewhat stunned, the boy proceeded to take items out of his pockets and hand them to Jonathan, who started to place them in the outside pocket of the computer case while the other passengers watched in silence. One of the items was the cell phone that Katie had stored in the right pocket of her coat. When the boy finished emptying his pockets, Katie told Jonathan to hold him. When Jonathan complied, she let go of the kid's hair. She quickly removed the flat wallet from her breast pocket and just as quickly flashed a badge in the kid's face.

"You're lucky I'm feeling generous today, you little punk," she said as she recalled a Clint Eastwood movie, quickly folded the wallet, and placed it back in her pocket. "Otherwise I'd slip my cuffs on you right now and run you down to headquarters. Get off the bus and go home before I change my mind! If I catch you again, I'll arrest you."

Perplexed by what he had just experienced, the boy walked quietly to the exit door and waited for the bus to stop. Before getting off, he studied Katie one last time. It was both a stare of disbelief that he had been bested and the look of someone who wanted to record her image in his mind. Aware of his gaze, she returned a stare of defiance and gave him a cunning smile. Everyone else on the bus had returned to minding their own business while Jonathan watched Katie's dueling engagement with the boy. When the boy left the bus, Jonathan smiled at her from ear to ear and said, "I can't believe you did that. How did you know?"

"Do me a favor and clip the laptop back onto the strap," she said, ignoring his question and referring to the computer belt that still hung from her shoulders. He did what he was told, and she thanked him.

"Is that a security badge from work?" he asked about the badge she had shown the boy.

"No," she said without further explanation. "What are you going to do now, Jonathan?"

"I'm checking my prospects; I needed a good kick in the ass. I'm thinking of heading to Nevada; that state is developing quickly. I won't make the same stupid mistake when I get there."

"Don't build or live below a dam. I heard they're made of sandstone. As soon as the work ends, I advise you to move to a state that doesn't have a water shortage or a dam that's begging to bust loose."

"I'll keep that in mind. Thank you."

* * *

Katie and Cheryl were on their way home. The days were gradually getting longer, and it was still light out. Soon they would reach the Cross County Parkway exit.

"I hate to be the bearer of bad news, Cheryl, but have you noticed what I noticed?"

"All I've noticed is you fidgeting around. Are you in pain or something?"

"No, I've been checking your mirrors and our back. Arturo's back," she sang like an actor in a B-rated horror movie.

"What?" Cheryl nearly screamed.

"Yes," Katie laughed. "He's been on our tail since we left Chamber Street. I recognize his blue SUV from the other day." Katie repeated the license number. "I love this. Is that guy an idiot, or what?"

"Katie, this is no laughing matter."

"This is fun; I feel like I'm in an action movie."

"Girl, you don't know what that man is capable of. What the hell are we going to do?"

"Relax, and do what I tell you. This little car handles very well."

"Are you planning to get us killed?"

Katie convinced Cheryl to calm down. They were approaching exit 2. Exit 4 led to the Cross County Parkway. Katie instructed Cheryl to slow down, and Arturo followed their lead, slowing to thirty-five miles per hour. Annoyed motorists passed them by. As they approached the middle exit, Katie instructed Cheryl to increase speed to sixty-five. Arturo did the same. As they approached exit 4, Cheryl slammed on the brakes as instructed, forcing Arturo to swerve to avoid hitting them. Cheryl then steered toward the exit as Arturo sped past them. "Hit the gas!" Katie yelled, and Cheryl propelled the car across three lanes of service road and onto a ramp leading to the Cross County Parkway, barely missing a couple of cars and the Bee-Line Bus's tail as it proceeded north on Central Avenue.

"Tell me that wasn't fun!" Katie yelled as they merged with the Cross County Parkway traffic.

"I can't believe I did that," Cheryl said. "Oh my God! I think I just had a menopause moment!"

"Keep your eye on the road, Cheryl. I want to get home in one piece," Katie teased her.

"Girl, you are totally nuts. Here I am sweating bullets, and you're as calm as a cucumber."

Fifteen

1991

Something was amiss, and Katie sensed it. She was almost eleven years old. People acted strangely when she walked into a room. Conversations stopped suddenly whenever they were aware of her presence. Doors were kept locked, including her parents' bedroom door. Carolyn seemed nervous and on edge, sometimes short-tempered or she wept and dried her face as soon as she sensed someone's presence. Matthew seldom said a word unless he and his wife were behind closed doors. Momma and Papa were also different. Momma looked pale, sometimes listless. Papa sometimes brooded, but he feigned cheerfulness when he was around the children. He or Momma would take the children to a show or a movie. Papa would fumble with the car keys or sometimes forget things. It proved to be a difficult year for everyone.

William Lyman was seeking an appeal. His lawyers claimed to have a witness and evidence that someone else had committed the crimes for which he had been incarcerated. The O'Gormans dreaded the possibility of such an appeal, and they spent endless hours meeting with attorneys. Later, as Matthew, Carolyn, Ellen, and Sean spent additional time arguing against the appeal, they were hit with more bad news. Matthew was diagnosed with breast cancer. Nearly a half century ago, his maternal grandfather had died of the same disease. Carolyn had discovered the lump during a moment of foreplay. It had suddenly appeared about an inch above his right nipple.

"It wasn't there yesterday," he insisted.

"It's about the size of a quarter," Carolyn said in dismay as she felt the lump again.

Between legal interactions to prevent an appeal and cancer treatments, the O'Gormans were put through the wringer. One night, Katie discovered her parents' bedroom door ajar. Stevie had an ear infection, and Carolyn had gone to put the drops in his ears. She then tucked him in and kissed him good night and was exhausted when she returned to bed.

"Did you take your medication?" she asked Matthew before kicking off her slippers.

"Yes," he replied. "Get some sleep, Honey-Lyn. We have to be in radiology by eight o'clock. Is Momma looking after the kids tomorrow?"

Carolyn got into bed and said, "Momma is meeting with the lawyers tomorrow. Papa is coming with us to radiology in case you need help getting back to the car. You're too big for me to handle by myself." She rested her head on the pillow and faced Matthew. "I hate to bring this up, Mattie, because I agree with you; I'd rather the kids not know because I don't want to worry them, but we may have to get you a couple of male nurses to help. I don't want to do it, but we may have to."

"And you're afraid the kids will figure it out. I'm sorry to put you through this, but I don't want them to know I'm this sick. Who's taking care of them tomorrow?"

"My mother said she'll be here by sunrise. She's taking the kids this weekend; she'll have them back Sunday night."

"How is Margaret going to get here before sunrise? She'll have to get up at three in the morning to drive all the way from Manhattan."

"Mom is right here in Bedford Hills. She attended a dinner party at the home of a corporate employee, and she'll be spending the night with her chauffer at the county motel."

"Do tell," Matthew teased her, trying to provoke her. "Your mother is shacking up with the chauffer?"

"Get your dirty mind out of the cesspool," she said, sounding annoyed. "You know exactly what I mean. My mother isn't shacking up with any chauffer. They'll be spending the night at the motel in order to make it here by sunrise."

"If there's no hanky-panky, why didn't she stay here? We have room."

"Why don't you ask her tomorrow when she arrives to do us the favor of looking after the children for the whole weekend? Go ahead, I dare you," she said, punching the pillow. "The nerve of you, suggesting such a thing."

"Don't get upset, Honey-Lyn," he said, pulling her hand up to his lips. "I was simply trying to have fun with you."

"Well, that's not funny, Matthew."

"I love you, Honey-Lyn," he said, crossing his arm over her chest. "I'm sorry if my attempt at humor offends you. I'm also sorry that I've complicated your life with my bad health. You've been great."

"Don't apologize to me for your health, Mattie. I married you for better or for worse. All I ask is that you don't get worse than this. I don't think I can handle it."

"I'm not going to die, Carolyn, if that's what you mean. I'm going to beat this cancer. I'm going to be with you for a long, long time—until you get sick of me."

"May I die first, Mattie?"

"Sure, if I'm over ninety, divorced, and married to a Playboy bunny."

Carolyn giggled and said, "You'll need to buy her a mansion. You won't be able to do that because I'll clean you out during the divorce proceedings."

"You are a very dangerous woman," he said as she snuggled close to him.

"I'm not dangerous, Mattie," she replied. "I just don't like to lose."

"How is the Lyman situation going?" he asked while stroking her hair.

"I'm still keeping my fingers crossed. If Lyman is granted an appeal and goes free, we're moving to Asia."

"We're not moving anywhere."

"You're so provincial, Mattie."

"If I were provincial, I wouldn't be going on all those trips you plan each time the kids have a vacation. I'm grateful you haven't made me climb Mt. Everest. Machu Picchu was enough for me."

"You didn't climb Machu Picchu."

"It's a matter for debate; I was in the general vicinity. Twelve-month-old Stevie weighed ninety pounds. Someone had to stay with him at a normal elevation. Neither one of us would have made it up that mountain with him strapped to our back," he said, exaggerating a point that was not lost on Carolyn.

"Liar," she said.

Ignoring the accusation, he continued. "I was thinking that the trip probably affected his brain," he laughed.

"What?" she asked.

"That's probably why poor Stevie is so slow. He was oxygen-deprived at such a young age." He continued to laugh. "You dragged that poor kid up to the Andes to touch the sky."

"I didn't drag him anywhere," she protested, sounding annoyed. "As you said, he stayed with you at the bottom. And my son is not slow. He simply likes to daydream. I will not have you place a guilt trip on me. Go to sleep, and be quiet."

"I was insane to let you talk me into that trip," he continued. "So no, I'm not going to New Zealand, Australia, Iceland, or any place but good old New York. You can take the kids, and I'll wait until you get back."

"What if I don't come back?"

"Oh, you'll be back. You can't resist not having little Mattie along for the ride."

Carolyn laughed and said, "You think very highly of yourself. Shut up and get some sleep." She kissed him on the cheek. "We need to be up early tomorrow. And don't call my son slow again."

As soon as Katie heard her parents snoring, she crawled out from under their bed and left the room.

* * *

"Grandma?" little Katie asked the next evening.

"Yes, honey?" Margaret replied. They were in the library of Margaret's Manhattan duplex. Stevie had abandoned his children's interactive notebook computer. He was standing by the glass slider, watching the large snowflakes as they danced in the air. A few landed and melted on the terrace floor. Both of his hands rested on the cool glass as he enjoyed the snow-dance in awe. Katie stood next to Margaret, who sat at her desk, trying to peruse the financial section of the newspaper.

"If heaven exists," Katie inquired, "why can't we see it? Why can't we see God?"

"Oh, my," Margaret said, setting her paper aside. "You ask some tough questions for a little girl. Are you studying theology?"

"No."

"Do you know what theology is?"

"Yes, Uncle Patrick studied theology. Now he's a priest. So it has something to do with religion, right?"

"It has to do with God and religious truth. So you're trying to understand religious truth. I know very little about theology."

"Oh," she commented with disappointment. "But you go to church, right?"

"Right, but I'm not an expert on theology."

"May I call Uncle Patrick? He's an expert, right?"

"Maybe. What's troubling you, Katie?"

"When people go to heaven, we can't see them anymore. I want to know why. Why can't I take a rocket ship or something and go to heaven? If heaven is real, then I should be able to go."

"Katie, the moon is real, but we can't go there. Well, I guess we can, but there are presently no flights to the moon. The earth and the moon are part of the heavens, so we see part of the heavens every day. The heavens are immense, bigger than any ocean. Come," she said as she rose and put a hand on her adoptive granddaughter's shoulder, beckoning Katie to follow her to one of the enormous bookcases in the room. She pulled out a book on astronomy. "This book contains what we believe to know about the heavens. I love it because it has beautiful photos and paintings of many galaxies. It will give you an idea of how big heaven is and why we don't yet know how to get from this part of heaven to there."

Margaret led Katie to a sofa, and they thumbed through the book. Katie was intrigued as she studied the beauty and immensity of the heavens. The book was soon transferred from Margaret's lap to Katie's.

"Heavens and galaxies are used in the plural, Katie. Why aren't they heaven and galaxy?"

"More than one," she simply said. Then she hugged the book. "When we were in Malaysia and Indonesia, you could lie down at night, and the sky was full of millions of stars, Grandma. They appeared so close, close enough to reach up and touch them. But I couldn't really touch them. They are too far."

"Billions of years away," Margaret added. "That is extremely far. They are so far away that you have to travel billions of years back in time in order to reach them. Today, it's impossible for us to do that. The best we can do is to see specks of them from here. And you're right. Sometimes it feels like you can reach up and touch them; distance can be an illusion."

"Maybe my mother traveled through time, and she is walking through one of those stars. That's awesome, Grandma."

"Yes, it is. You can keep the book if you want; there are others on the shelf. Write down the names of the ones you like, and I'll have copies of them shipped to you."

The following day, Margaret took the children to the planetarium at the Museum of Natural History. In the pitch blackness of the theater, they watched a show of the heavens. The children were mesmerized by the billions of stars, galaxies, and shooting stars that were displayed on the ceiling above their seats. Stevie pointed to the shooting stars and at times called out enthusiastically, "Oooh! Did you see that one, Grandma?" Katie, on the other hand, got lost in a world of her own. While seated in that auditorium chair, her mind was transported to the cosmos. She imagined herself swimming effortlessly through time and space. She touched stars and planets, grabbed the tail of a comet, and funneled through black holes. The memory of that moment soothed her soul, and it became the focus of her meditation for many years to come.

When they returned to Margaret's duplex that evening, they were greeted by Grandpa Harold. Margaret was surprised and delighted to find her husband home. He had been attending to business in Malaysia, and she did not expect him home for a couple more months. He had arrived with a guest.

After she hugged and kissed him, she said, "I called your office yesterday, and your secretary told me you were out in the field. You scoundrel! I'm so glad to see you. When did you arrive?"

"Well, it appears we just missed you as you left this morning. I thought I'd surprise you and Carolyn, so I told Noui to cover for me if you called. In the meantime, Xiang and I had a nice nap."

Margaret greeted and hugged Xiang, a family friend. She then turned her attention back to Harold. "Where's

Frank?" Margaret asked, referring to Harold's pilot. "Will he be having dinner with us?"

"You know Frank. He's already out and about, checking out the ladies. We probably won't see him again until it's time to leave."

"When are you leaving?"

"That's up to you. Xiang plans to stay about a month. You and I can relax."

Once again, Margaret turned to their houseguest and said, "Xiang, I'm so glad to see you. How are you? How's the family?"

"We're all fine, Margaret," he replied. "I'm glad to see you too. It's been a long time."

"Yes, it has. Children," she said, bringing the children forward, "this is Dr. Xiang Tieng."

Tieng looked down on the children and said, "They certainly have grown."

"I remember you," Katie said to him. Tieng and Margaret were impressed by her recollection because she was only seven when they first met. "We went to your house in Malaysia with my Uncle Donny. You have two children, a boy and a girl, just like Stevie and me. You also have an Australian Eclectus parrot named Squeak."

"You are right!" Tieng confirmed. "That parrot is older than you."

"You mean you haven't cooked him in peanut sauce yet?" Katie asked.

"Her. It's a she. And the answer is no," Tieng laughed. "My wife would kill me if I did that. She raised her from a chick, and she and the children love Squeak; she's a member of the family. My daughter dresses her and puts a bonnet on her head."

"How do you know it's a she?"

"She's red. The male is green."

"If you aren't going to stew her, you should get her a male. She may be lonely, you know."

"Squeak is fine," Xiang replied with a big smile. "She's already had three sets of chicks."

"You mean she has a mate?"

"Yes, she has mated. Luckily, I found a dealer who can take the chicks off our hands. We can't afford to allow them to multiply because many people consider them pests. They can destroy a farmer's crops."

"Then you should stew them. You can serve them with a side of vegetables and fruit. The farmers will have their revenge."

"I don't think my family would like that alternative," he said with a smile.

Finally Katie asked, "Are you a medical doctor?"

"Yes, he's a medical and nutritional doctor," Harold interjected. "The best doctor on the planet."

"Are you here to cure my father? He's very sick, you know."

The adults were surprised by her revelation because they believed the children to be ignorant of Matthew's condition.

"What makes you say that, Katie?" Margaret asked.

"I heard Mommy and Daddy talking. They want to keep it a big secret, but I know Daddy is sick. Is he going to die?"

Stevie reacted to the question and clung to Margaret's side while he silently looked at everyone around him. He was confused. He knew that "die" was not a good word. He didn't know what to say, so he kept clinging to Margaret's side, pulling on her blouse.

Finally, Harold said, "No, Katie. Daddy isn't going to die. He's just sick."

"Then why is everyone making such a big deal? Why is Dr. Tieng here? You said you wanted to surprise Mommy. Why did you say that, Grandpa?"

"I also said I wanted to surprise Margaret. My wife and daughter are the two most important women in my life. I haven't seen Margaret or Carolyn for a whole month now, so I hope they're as glad to see me as I am to see them. Now I'm especially delighted to discover that you have a keenly inquisitive mind. That's good. And yes, your father is sick, but he isn't going to die. We're making a big deal of it because it's a disease that takes a long time and a lot of effort to combat. And yes, Xiang is here to help. He graduated from Harvard Medical School. He's the best I know and I always want the best for my family. Does that answer your question?"

Katie eyed him with skepticism and said, "I know what cancer is, Grandpa. I looked it up. It's not a good disease."

"No disease is good, Katie," Harold replied. "Diseases make you feel lousy. Matthew is going to feel lousy for a long time, but he'll be okay. In the meantime, he doesn't want you to worry because he loves you and Stevie very much. That's why we didn't tell you."

"Well, I worry when I don't know what's going on," Katie replied.

"Grandma," Stevie said, "I want to go home. I want Mommy."

"Stevie, we're going to have dinner soon, sweetie," Margaret replied. "You can see Mommy tomorrow."

"Uh-uh," he disagreed, "I want to go home now. I want Mommy."

Oh boy, Margaret thought. "Come on, Stevie. We're going to call Mommy right now." She took his hand and led him to the library while Katie continued her showdown with Harold.

"Mommy cries when she thinks no one is looking," Katie said. "I don't know what to do," she confessed, "because everyone wants to keep secrets. If Daddy is going to be okay, then don't make such a big deal of it. I worry too, you know."

"Okay." Harold surrendered with a smile. "I understand you want to be part of the process. It sounds to me like you want to act like an adult. If that's what you prefer, when you see your mother crying, I suggest you do what she would do if she saw you cry. Tell her it's okay to cry and comfort her. Sometimes, crying is the best thing to do in a bad situation; a good cry cleans the worry out of you."

Katie pondered his words for a moment. Then she reached up and hugged him. "Thank you, Grandpa," she said.

Margaret returned from the library and announced that she had called Carolyn, but no one was home; Margaret had left a message.

"Why do you want to go home, Stevie?" Katie asked.

"I don't know," he said. Then he quickly added, "I want to see Mommy."

"You can see Mommy tomorrow night. If you leave now, we can't go to the skating rink tomorrow. Grandma is taking us there."

"We're going ice skating?"

"Yes, tomorrow. In the meantime, I can show you some pretty books in the library. Come, Stevie," Katie said while taking his hand and thinking of Margaret's astronomy books. Then she turned to Margaret and said, "Mommy said Stevie has a short attention span. It's easy to distract him. All you have to do is read him a story or give him something to do. He'll soon forget about going home tonight. I don't want to go now, Grandma."

"I don't want you to go either. We'll be having dinner soon; Laura will call us when it's ready," she said, referring to the cook.

Katie and Stevie were soon lying on the library floor with an open book. She showed him the planets and stars and reminded him of the wonderful sky show they had seen at the planetarium.

"When I grow up," Stevie said, "I'm going to take a rocket ship and visit different planets all over the world."

"You visit different planets all over the universe, Stevie. You don't visit them all over the world."

"I'll visit different planets all over the universe, Katie. You and Luis can come with me, all right? I'll be the captain."

She looked at her little brother with genuine affection and said, "You be the captain, Stevie. I'll be the first mate, and Luis will be the engineer. Aye, aye, Captain Stevie. What are your orders, sir?"

"Go to the stars, Katie. Go up, up." He made an upward hand motion.

* * *

On Sunday evening, the Reillys returned the children to their parents. Carolyn was delighted and surprised to see Xiang Tieng with them. "Oh, my God, Xiang," she said, hugging and kissing him on the cheek. "What a wonderful surprise! Are Lin Yang and the children with you? How are you? When did you arrive?"

Soon they were seated in the family room, catching up on old times. In Malaysia, Xiang's father had worked for Reilly Pharmaceuticals for years. Xiang had been a classmate of Carolyn's older twin brothers, Donny and Danny. He had been Carolyn's first crush. His dark hair, tan complexion, and his lively, dark Chinese-Malaysian eyes had made her young heart go pitter-patter. It was a secret she tried to contain, but her siblings, especially her twin sister, Marjorie, knew of her feelings toward Xiang, and they often teased her. Because of the teasing, Carolyn soon learned to turn her attention to other things until Xiang's presence no longer had an effect on her. As for Xiang, he was totally unaware of the child's feelings toward him. To him, Carolyn had always been his best friends' younger sister. However, they had all spent intermittent years together as friends, schoolmates, and playmates. Because they had been in the same grade, Donny, Danny, and Xiang had successfully completed the Panilaian Menengah Rendah (PMR), the lower secondary assessment examination, together. Later in life, Xiang and the Reilly children resumed their friendship as the boys attended college in the States, and Xiang was often their dinner guest. By then, Carolyn could look at the handsome islander without feeling flushed.

After Carolyn sent the children to bed, the adults conferred.

"I'll be with you for at least two weeks," Xiang said to Carolyn and Matthew. "If necessary, I'll stay longer. I'll meet with you and the doctors in order to decide on a plan of action. Matthew, on the surface, you appear fine."

"Well, the treatments sap all the energy out of me. Now I know what they mean by a beached whale. That's how I feel after radiology or chemotherapy. I thank God for my family and Carolyn every day of my life," he said, squeezing Carolyn's hand and looking at her lovingly.

"People who travel to the South Pacific for treatment say that they feel invigorated. Maybe it's the climate, or maybe it's the diet, or the lower impact on your wallet, but the medical results are impressive," Xiang said. "We will try to work on a diet to bolster your immune system. Several of the conventional oncology treatments require that you stay away from certain nutrients like vitamin supplementation. It makes no sense to me, and there are plenty of studies out there indicating that the opposite route is the way to go. We will find something that can help you get stronger without interfering with your treatments. No offense, but if you are one of those guys who indulges in American fast food, you are not doing anything to help yourself."

"I'm guilty of that," he confessed. "Carolyn goes all out to shop at the organic market. She prepares beautiful exotic stuff, but I do like pizza, bagels, pasta, pie...I can go on and on. She hates me because I don't gain weight and because she has to dump the vegetables I don't eat."

"Well, you won't be doing any of that anymore," she said as she pinched him.

"No, you won't. For the next two weeks," Xiang announced, "I will be overseeing or preparing everything you eat."

"Can I still have a hamburger?"

"We'll see," Xiang said.

"Carolyn," Harold interjected, "the children know Mattie is ill. Katie said she overheard you, and she's very worried about you and the situation."

"How did she overhear?" Matthew asked with dismay.

"Matthew," Margaret added, "Katie is growing up. You cannot shelter the children from everything; I think it's time you involved them as a family."

"Stevie is barely seven; he's still a baby," Matthew protested.

"Even seven-year-olds like to feel useful, Mattie," Margaret replied. "As you get better, the children will feel a sense of accomplishment if you allow them to contribute. It doesn't have to be anything outrageous. Ask your son to bring you a glass of milk. Ask him to read to you or accompany you to a movie. It isn't a great change, but a change to make him feel needed and involved. It will take some of the burden off you and Carolyn. Children understand more than you can imagine. Allow yourselves to be human and vulnerable around them. Just as you say 'I love you,' you can also say 'I hurt.'"

"I guess you're right," Matthew commented as he stroked the back of his head. "We'll see what happens."

"Well, we better go," Harold announced while getting to his feet. "We'll be in touch, Mattie." Margaret and Xiang also rose from their seats.

"Xiang," Carolyn inquired, "where are your bags?"

"Margaret already set me up at the county motel. I'm not staying here with you guys; I don't want to cramp your style. You have enough problems without having me underfoot. I'll call and probably see you tomorrow. I'd like to examine you, Mattie, and run some blood tests. In the meantime, have a good night."

"Xiang," Carolyn said, "you're always welcome to stay with us. We have two extra bedrooms with their own bathroom."

"Thank you, Carolyn, but I agree with Margaret and believe it's best for you to have your privacy. I'll be here as long as you need me."

"You will at least come to dinner," Carolyn objected.

"Carolyn can cook practically anything," Matthew said, "and I can flip you a few burgers."

"I'll come to dinner," Xiang replied, "but I don't know about the burgers."

* * *

The next time Katie sensed that Carolyn was down in the dumps, she sat next to her and hugged her mother. The two sat quietly in each other's arms for a while.

"Mommy, it's okay to cry," Katie said, planting a kiss on her cheek. "I love you; I love you," she repeated, and Carolyn did burst out into tears. The little girl she had struggled with for nearly seven years had finally sincerely acknowledged her love for her. She was growing up, and at that moment, Carolyn believed that there could be a light at the end of the tunnel.

That year, Carolyn watched as her children handled themselves as responsible members of the family. When Matthew felt weak, Stevie helped him with minor chores. He combed his father's hair. He helped him put his shoes on, served him his green juice, and helped Carolyn prepare his salad.

"Come, Daddy, we have to take a walk. The doctor said it's good for you." He grabbed his daddy's hand and led him out the door.

"Do you still think he's slow?" Carolyn inquired one evening.

"No," Matthew replied, "he's a very sweet kid. You named him well."

"I had a hunch," she replied. "A mother knows. Oxygen-deprived my ass."

"You sound just like Katie," he retorted, "and you don't forget the things I say."

"Make sure you remember that. You said it yourself—I'm a dangerous woman."

Xiang Tieng had been a godsend. He spent over a month working with the O'Gormans and Matthew's doctors. He perused every medical chart and lab analysis, including his own medical lab tests. He constantly examined Matthew and drew fluids. Strongly believing that the best defense against any malady is a strong immune system, Xiang worked with the other doctors to prepare Matthew's unique diet. While there was no discernable change in the short time Xiang spent the O'Gormans, he urged them to continue the regimen. After six weeks, he returned to Malaysia and continued to monitor Matthew via long distance. Carolyn and the children did everything they could to help Matthew on the road to recovery.

While Katie helped out at home, she stopped picking fights at school. She saw Rina less and spent more time doing chores. She and Stevie learned to separate and do laundry. By the time the weekly housekeepers arrived, there was little for them to do. When Matthew started feeling better, the children took pride in helping him construct a new bookcase. For him, the activity was a type of victory celebration.

* * *

Katie turned twelve. While Katie's biological father was still pushing for an appeal, Kieran Emmanuel O'Gorman was born shortly after Matthew was diagnosed cancer free. It had been a difficult pregnancy for Carolyn. Matthew's illness and Katie's apparent maturity convinced Carolyn that the time was right for a new baby. If the cancer treatments did not go well and she lost Matthew, she reasoned that she would at least have one more child by him. However, she had not expected to lose Kieran's fetal twin. She started to blame herself for choosing the wrong time for the pregnancy, and that thinking added to the stress in her life. Kieran's arrival overwhelmed her with emotion and she shed tears of bliss. To her, he was the most beautiful baby ever. Eight-year-old Stevie, one of several people assembled in Carolyn's bedroom, took one look at Kieran in his basinet and said, "He looks like a long, skinny raisin, Mommy."

"He's right," Matthew agreed. "He needs some meat on him, Honey-Lyn."

"He looks like a little alien," Katie interjected. "Maybe you should send him back."

Carolyn didn't know whether to be annoyed or amused. She gingerly picked up the baby and cradled the little child in her hands. "He looks perfect to me," she commented. "Don't pay them any mind, my little angel," she said to the infant and kissed him on the forehead. Then she turned to all who were assembled in her bedroom and said, "We all looked just like him at one time."

"I looked like a raisin?" asked Stevie.

"You looked like a prune," Carolyn said. Everyone laughed as she added, "I love prunes. They're delicious. I can eat one now." With that comment, she positioned the newborn to one side and bent down to feign nibbling at Stevie's neck. He giggled, and Carolyn said, "You were as wrinkled as this baby is, except you were bigger. That makes you a prune, not a raisin. You weighed an extra four pounds, six ounces. This little angel is the smallest baby I've ever had. My little Kieran Emmanuel weighs only six point two pounds, and he is gorgeous."

"Is that the name you've chosen for his baptism?" Nydia asked.

"Indeed it is," Carolyn replied, proudly holding Kieran in front of her.

"Excellent choice," Nydia said in approval. "'The Lord is with us.' Excellent choice to acknowledge the end of a difficult year. May our Little God bless you and your family from this point on," she said, admiring the tiny infant.

"From your mouth to God's ears," Carolyn interjected.

"May I hold him, Carolyn?" Luis asked.

"Luisito," Nydia admonished him, "he's too fragile for you to hold."

"Come, Luis," Carolyn invited him as she went to sit on her vanity bench and motioned him to sit next to her. When Luis sat down, she instructed him on how to hold the newborn. She got up and gently transferred the infant to him.

Luis studied all the baby's facial features—his ruddy color, the tiny slits he had for eyes, and the miniature nose and mouth. Kieran had thin, dark hair. He yawned, and Luis giggled with delight. "He's beautiful," he proclaimed. "Hey, Kieran, I'm Luis. How are you, little buddy?" Kieran moved his tiny arms about and started to cry. Luis got nervous. "Did I do something wrong?" he asked fearfully.

"No, sweetie," Carolyn assured him. "He's probably hungry. I'll take him now," she said as she gently took the infant from him. She climbed into bed with the infant and started to nurse him. Stevie climbed in next to her and snuggled next to his mother as he watched the hungry Kieran nurse at his mother's breast. Katie sat at the foot of the bed with Luis next to her. Everyone was in awe of the moment.

Momma Ellen popped into the room. "Lunch is ready," she announced to all present. "Better get it while it's hot. Patrick has whipped up a feast." Then she noticed everyone gawking at Carolyn and the baby. "For God's sake," she said, "give the woman some privacy. Move it!"

"It's okay, Momma," Carolyn announced. "I don't mind at all. It's comforting to have the people I love around me on this wonderful day."

Sixteen

◇◆◇

2005

Luis normally attended church with Nydia and Felipe. But today, he was off to Matthew and Carolyn's place of worship. He walked down the private road, dressed in a dark blue suit, tie, and polished shoes. When he didn't see Katie outside the house, he called her on the cell phone.

"I'm almost at the garage," he said. "How long is it going to take you to get out here?"

"I'll be out in a minute; I'm almost dressed," she responded.

"Almost dressed? Woman, get jiggy with it; I don't want to be late for Mass."

"Get jiggy with it? You try getting jiggy with a broken foot. I'm moving as quickly as I can, you moron!"

"Again with the acrimony. When are you going to start being nice, my love?"

"I'm always nice, you twit. Now hang up the damn phone so I can get dressed."

Luis opened the garage and selected a car. The sports car offered enough front leg room for Katie to be comfortable. Besides, he thought Sunday was an excuse to be stylish. He sat in the car until she finally arrived, wearing a bright pink coat over a pastel pink modern design dress and hobbling on her crutches.

She stood by the passenger side door and inquired, "Aren't you going to open the door for me, Sir Galahad?"

Reluctantly, Luis got out of the car and walked around to open the door for her. "With a broken leg, you take a New York City subway, board a New York City bus, and you can't open a car door?"

"That's not the point. You're supposed to be a gentleman," she replied as she sat down and made herself comfortable.

"Oh boy!" he said as he closed the door, thinking she wanted him to be a gentleman, but she didn't behave as a proper young lady toward him.

"Oh boy, what?" she asked.

"Nothing," he said. "I'm not going to say another word. Luis," he told himself aloud, "sometimes it's better if you just shut up and go with the flow. Don't make any waves. Be quiet. Don't talk. Zip it." He sat behind the wheel and started the car.

"What the hell's wrong with you?" she asked.

"Not a thing. Nothing at all." He looked back and eased the car out of the garage.

"It must be your time of the month," she retorted.

By the time they arrived at church, Luis was in a better mood. The O'Gormans had arrived ahead of them, and he soon recognized the family as he entered the church and saw the backs of their heads from where he stood. He and Katie made their way into the row of pews behind the O'Gormans just as Stevie turned around and saw them. Luis held a finger to his lips, signaling Stevie to be quiet. Stevie turned his attention to the altar as Katie and Luis sat directly behind Matthew and Carolyn, respectively.

Luis removed the handkerchief from his breast pocket, unfolded it, and playfully placed it on Carolyn's head. A startled Carolyn reached up to remove the intrusion as she glanced behind her. As soon as she saw Luis's grinning face, she crumpled the handkerchief and flung it at him. He caught it in midair; she smiled and playfully admonished him, "Have you no respect for the Lord's house? Behave yourself, you overgrown child." Stevie and Kieran chuckled while Matthew cleared his throat.

"A woman should cover her head when she enters the Lord's house," Luis retorted jokingly.

"Have you been in a time capsule?" Carolyn asked him. "We're past that. Besides, you should mind your own business."

"Oooh, feisty, just like her daughter."

Carolyn smiled at him again, and Katie smacked the back of his head.

"I'll just let Katie deal with you," Carolyn said as she winked and turned away.

After the service, the family gathered outside the church.

"The caterers are coming in less than an hour," Carolyn said, glancing at her watch. "We better get going. Luis, Katie, we'll meet you at the house."

"Yes, Mrs. G.," Luis said. "Come on, Katie."

"I'm going home, Mom," she announced. "I'm having a business meeting at one o'clock."

"What do you mean? How could you be having a business meeting when you knew the family was meeting today?" Carolyn said, recalling that at the Emily's Hope II opening ceremony, she had sensed that Katie could be headed for a train wreck. At the time, she had also felt a sense of urgency and believed that a family intervention was necessary.

"I never said I'd be there, Mom," Katie objected. "I'm meeting with a client."

"You don't wait until today to tell your mother that," Matthew interjected. "She has gone to all this trouble to arrange this day for you."

"I didn't ask her to do that," Katie replied. "As a matter of fact, she didn't ask me."

"Don't pull that stunt with me, Katharine," Matthew said. "This is not a game."

"It's okay—it's okay," Carolyn said, getting between the two of them.

"No, it's not okay, Carolyn, and she knows it. She's pulling the same nonsense she always pulls, and I'm sick of it."

"Mattie, please, not here," Carolyn said. "We're in front of the church. Katie, go home. Do what you need to do. Luis, please take my daughter home. We'll talk later. Mattie," she said, pulling his hand, "let's go home, honey. It's okay."

* * *

Later that day, Luis arrived at his parents' house. "Are you making Indian food?" he asked. "I can smell curry from the driveway."

"Curried chicken with rice and palaak paneer," Nydia responded. "Come into the kitchen and eat some."

"I'm laying off the spinach, so forget the palaak, Mami. Katie thinks I'm consuming too much green food. She's even forbidden my intake of green juice."

"Well, Katie may be right. Green juice is very nourishing, but you should be careful with it. Remember, everything in moderation."

"Well, I do listen to Katie. Besides, if I don't, she'll smack me. She sure likes the back of my head," he commented while touching his head.

"Carolyn told me Katie refused to go to her intervention. Where is she?"

"She's home."

"Is something wrong, son?"

"I don't know," he said with a shrug as he dropped into one of the kitchen chairs. "Where's Papi?"

"He's working today, as a favor to a coworker."

"How did you know about Katie's intervention?"

"Well, Carolyn asked me to go, but she called me today to inform me it was off. Why didn't Katie go?"

"She claims she has a business appointment. Matthew was really angry; I've never seen him that angry. So I took Katie home and came here. I don't know what to make of all this. I mean, Katie is twenty-five years old. Should Carolyn still be involved in her life? On the other hand, Katie is...I don't know."

"A lost soul?"

"Perhaps. You know, on Friday she had lunch with Rina."

"Oh, my God! I thought Rina was in Florida. She's been gone for over a decade. Does Carolyn know she's back?"

"Katie claims Rina was at the EH ceremony and Carolyn gave Rina the number to Katie's job; Rina called Katie at work. I haven't spoken to Carolyn about it."

"You see, son. That's why Carolyn is so worried about Katie. She may be over twenty-one, but she isn't going in the right direction. I love Katie, Luisito. Underneath the bravado, she is a frightened little girl. She's also a loving and caring young lady. She loves you and has always been good to you as well as done good for you. I also know how much Carolyn cares for her. The Reillys and the O'Gormans have had so much pain in their lives. Carolyn is trying the best she can to steer Katie in the right direction and offset another tragedy."

"Mami, Katie is a little nutty at times, but she's not going to do anything stupid. Besides, I'm always with her."

"You're not always with her, Luisito. You are not her conjoined twin. Parents worry about their children in a way you cannot understand. Katie may be over twenty-one, but Carolyn will always be concerned about her well-being."

"Are you thinking of Carolyn's sister Marjorie?"

"Precisely. According to Carolyn, no one saw that coming. Yet the poor girl killed herself with a drug overdose. Perhaps she fears the same for Katie."

"I don't think Katie will ever do anything like that, Mami. It's a sin against the Church."

"I know that, and you know that," Nydia said as she peeled a green banana-like fruit called a plantain. "We both accept it as Church law. Did Marjorie accept it as dogma? Does Katie?"

Luis rose from his seat.

"Where are you going, son?" Nydia asked.

"I'm going to talk to Carolyn. Then I'm going home to Katie."

"Aren't you going to eat? I'm going to make you some mangú as a side dish. You won't have to eat the spinach."

"Thank you, Mami, but I'm not hungry enough to stuff myself with mashed plantains and bacon bits." He kissed her and left.

Seventeen

◇◆◇

1992

"Please accept my condolences," twelve-year-old Luis said to Margaret and Harold. "I didn't know your daughter Marjorie, but Carolyn said she was a wonderful person. She said I would have liked her."

Margaret and Harold listened to Luis's expression of sympathy. Harold shook his hand and thanked him. Margaret bent down and gave Luis a long, affectionate hug, followed by a kiss on the cheek.

"Thank you," she replied. "You have certainly grown into a wonderful little gentleman. Harold and I accept your condolences." She then turned to his foster parents and said, "You must be very proud of him."

Nydia and Felipe beamed, and Felipe said, "We certainly are, Mrs. Reilly." He stroked his son's hair to stress the pride and affection he felt for the child. "Please accept our condolences as well. We are deeply sorry for your loss."

They exchanged a few additional phrases of polite conversation and moved on, allowing others in line to express their sympathy.

Luis and the other children found each other in the sea of sympathizers and distracted themselves while the adults stood around sharing memories, sampling the food, and discussing matters that did not interest children.

"Did you know your Aunt Marjorie?" Luis asked Katie.

Katie was wearing a small navy blue top over a white dress with a white and pastel blue floral lace bodice. She carried a navy blue shoulder bag to match her shoes and jacket.

"Of course I knew her," she responded to Luis's question. "Sometimes we saw her when we went on family vacations. I saw her when we went to Australia, as well as Greece. I showed you her picture once."

"I don't think so," Luis replied. "I would have remembered."

"Well, didn't you see her picture when you came in? It's near the entranceway when you first walk in. You can't miss it."

"I didn't notice anything."

"You must be blind. Come, I'll show you." She grabbed his hand and dragged him to the lobby while Stevie followed close behind.

Given the size of the place, a very modest twelve-by-fourteen photograph of the departed sat on an easel by the entrance. An adjoining table held Marjorie's Mass cards and a duplicate ceremonial urn. Marjorie's actual remains, cremated according to her wishes, sat on a mantle in the family room until a family member could fulfill the second part of her wish, to have the ashes scattered at a fjord in New Zealand.

"Wow," Luis said, staring at the photo. "She looks just like Carolyn."

"Of course, silly. They were identical twins. However, Marjorie's right eye was different. It was kind of droopy. She had to wear a patch over the other eye when she was younger in order to correct the droopiness and make the eye stronger, but it didn't help," she said as she pointed at Marjorie's eye. "You know, not all identical twins are one hundred percent identical. If you look closely, you're bound to find a minor difference. One may be a little fatter than the other or have a slight imperfection. It has to do with how they develop after the egg splits; I read about it. Kieran could have been identical too, but his other half died. I guess you could call that a major imperfection."

"That's a cruel thing to say, Katie," Luis objected.

"But it's true," Katie countered.

"Here, Luis," Stevie said, handing him a Mass card. "This is supposed to be a souvenir. It's like a baseball card or something. You can keep it; I took a few of them."

"Thanks," Luis said, accepting the Mass card, but not knowing what to do with it.

"It's not a baseball card, Stevie," Katie corrected him. "You can't trade it."

"But you can keep it," Stevie countered. "You can take as many as you like. There must be about a hundred of them there," he said, referring to the contents of the table. "I'm going to take some more." He turned and grabbed a handful of cards.

"Jesus, Mary, and Joseph," Katie muttered, imitating Momma Ellen's brogue as Stevie struggled to stuff the cards in his pockets. Later that night, Carolyn would be amused after discovering the Mass cards in his jacket.

In the meantime, Katie said, "The kid has a few screws loose. Come, Luis, I have something else to show you." She grabbed his hand, and he pulled away. "What's wrong with you?" she asked.

"Where are we going?"

"Upstairs. I'll show you my bedroom. It's where Stevie and I sleep when we stay here with Grandma Margaret and Grandpa Harry."

"We're not supposed to be alone together. You know that."

"It's not that, Luis; I promise. Come. It's okay. You can trust me. Besides, we can bring Stevie."

"Are you sure?"

"Yes, I'm sure. Come. Stevie, come on," she commanded Stevie while she grabbed Luis's hand again and led him to the stairs. In a few minutes, they entered an upstairs bedroom. "When I stay with Grandma Margaret," she said, "this is my room. Do you like it?"

Luis looked around and said, "Yes, this is nice."

"This used to be Marjorie's and my mother's room when they lived in the city. Now Stevie and I sleep here when we stay with my grandparents."

"This is a big room," Luis said while looking up at the tall ceiling with the stucco reliefs. "Actually, this whole place sure is big for an apartment. My uncle has an apartment in the Bronx, and it's nothing like this. Your grandparents' apartment is as big as a museum. I bet you can get lost in here."

Katie guided him to a seat. "No, I already know every room in here," she said, standing next to him while he made himself comfortable. "You can't get lost. If you want to talk to someone in another room, you simply pick up the phone and dial that room. Stevie and I talk on the phone all the time, and we can call downstairs to the kitchen or the library. Or we can walk. But that's not why I brought you here. I want to show you something." She slipped her little purse from her shoulder and removed an item from inside.

"What's that?" he asked as she held the tool out for him to see.

"It's an awl," she said.

While they talked, Stevie had taken an interest in another part of the room. He pushed a mahogany panel to one side, revealing a vault he had never seen before.

"What's an awl?" Luis asked.

"It's like an ice pick. It's used for making holes in leather. You can also thread it like a needle and sew pieces together."

"Where did you get it?" he asked while taking it from her for closer examination. The wooden handle was stained from years of handling. The tip was sharp from overuse.

"It belongs to Papa Sean."

"You stole this? Why?"

"Give me that," she said as she snatched it out of his hands. "You immediately jump to conclusions. How do you know I didn't borrow it?"

"If you had borrowed it, you wouldn't have brought me up here to show it to me. It's like it's a big secret or something. You stole it. What are you going to do with it?

"None of your business!" she snapped and stored it back in her purse. She then changed the subject. "How do you like your new school?"

"It's okay. How do you like yours?"

"Actually, it's kind of dull. Luckily, I can see Rina. She's in my language class. Sometimes we eat lunch together. The other girls are like really boring, you know. I miss you, Luis. I wish we were still together. Do you miss me?" she asked, holding his hand. He pulled his hand free and got up.

"Yes, I miss you, but we're not supposed to be alone together. We better go back downstairs."

"Luis, come take a look at this," Stevie invited. He had been exploring the vault's contents.

"What is it?" Luis asked, looking in Stevie's direction.

"It's a toy room," Stevie announced. "Come on. This is cool."

Luis went to see, and he was amazed to find shelves with toys neatly displayed. Katie stood next to him andwas also impressed by the display. It wasn't a storeroom of exclusively girlish toys. Luis walked past numerous crafted wooden items from around the world, polished porcelain eggs and other figurines, gold crested containers, and numerous other wonders.

"This is awesome," Luis said. He paused near a wooden object, a polished pudgy doll. "Can I touch this?" he asked.

"Sure," Stevie said, grabbing it off the shelf and handing it to him. "It's a Russian doll. Mommy has one at home." Luis studied it for a few seconds, admiring the lacquered colors. Stevie took it back from him while saying, "You can open it up like this." He showed Luis how to take the matryoshka doll apart, displaying the other small dolls within it, and handed them back to Luis. "The pretty eggs do almost the same thing," Stevie informed him, referring to the Fabergé eggs that were further up. "Go ahead and try one."

"No, no," Luis said. "I don't think that's right. All this stuff must be worth over a thousand dollars. Man, your family sure is rich. They must have like a million dollars or something."

"Mom says we're comfortable," Katie interjected. "If you have a roof over your head, you're comfortable. That's what she says."

"We have a roof," Stevie said. "You also have a roof, Luis. That means you're comfortable, too. Here, check this out." He handed him a wooden analog clock. "This is really neat. It's my favorite. You can take the whole thing apart and put it back together again."

"It's a three-dimensional puzzle, Stevie," Katie said. "It just has a few simple gears. That's not worth much."

"It's a neat toy," Stevie said. "I like it."

Someone knocked at the door to their newly found treasure room and entered after a pause. It was Uncle Daniel, Donovan's twin and Carolyn's older brother. He walked into the vault. "Why didn't you respond when I knocked?" he asked.

"We didn't hear you knock," Katie said.

"Katie, Carolyn and I have been looking for you. What are you doing here?"

"I'm showing Luis the toys," Stevie said.

"We were just talking, Uncle Danny," Katie added.

"Well, you can talk downstairs," he said and turned to walk to the room phone. He dialed the number to the family room. When Carolyn answered at the other end, he said, "I found them, Sis. They're in your old bedroom."

"Are they behaving themselves?" Carolyn asked in Malay while struggling with three-month-old Kieran in one arm and handling the phone with her other hand.

Danny looked at the kids, who were still in the toy room, and responded in Malay, "Yes, they're behaving themselves. They're playing with your old toys. They probably think they found Ali Baba's cave."

"You mean, they opened the vault? How did they do that? It has a passive alarm."

"I didn't ask, but it's open."

"I'm coming up," Carolyn announced. She then turned to Nydia and said, "I suggest you come with me, Nydia.

Our children just broke into my old toy room. You're going to enjoy this."

In a short while, she was in her old bedroom with the kids.

"How did you children get in here?" she asked.

"It wasn't me," Katie responded. "Stevie opened it."

"I'm not blaming anyone," Carolyn assured them. "I simply want to know how you managed to do that."

"The wall moved," Stevie said.

Carolyn laughed and repeated, "The wall moved. How did the wall move, honey?"

"I guess I pushed it like this," he said, and he demonstrated by pushing the panel. "And it moved."

"Well," Carolyn concluded, "I guess I better tell Mom. Evidently, the passive alarm is deactivated and needs to be repaired."

"Is this stuff expensive?" Stevie asked. "Luis said there must be a thousand dollars worth of stuff in here."

Carolyn was amused by the modest assessment and laughed. "Yes," she said, "there must be at least a thousand dollars worth of stuff in here. Do you like it?"

"I think it's cool," Stevie said. "But why do you keep it all in here instead of playing with it?"

Soon, the children were seated on the floor, surrounded by a few of the old toys while Carolyn sat in a chair and told stories or gave a history of each item as she cradled Kieran in her arms. It was a bittersweet moment for her, for several of the items had belonged to Marjorie. Now they served to recall a childhood memory.

"What about this?" Katie asked, holding up a music box.

"That was a gift from my Uncle Brendan. As the plate spins, the Chinese fisherman travels up the river and lifts the rod with the little fish attached. It's an ancient Chinese toy with an ancient Chinese melody; it's very soothing. I used to wind it up before I fell asleep."

"Mommy, can I take the clock home with me?" Stevie asked.

"You can take whatever you want, honey. It's probably about time I moved everything out of here. Mom probably needs the room for something else."

"Can Luis have one of the eggs? I think he likes them."

"I didn't touch the eggs, Carolyn," Luis said defensively, sensing that they could be very expensive.

Carolyn smiled down at him on the floor where he sat a couple of feet away from her. "It's okay, Luis. You can have an egg. I insist."

His eyes opened wide. "Really?" he asked. "An egg like that is probably worth a hundred dollars; they're very pretty."

"If you say so," Carolyn replied. "I suggest you take good care of it. Maybe someday you can pass it on to one of your children. Which one would you like?"

"I don't know," he said, looking at Nydia for permission to accept the offer.

"Carolyn," Nydia said, "Luis is just a child. Are you sure you want to give him such an extravagant gift?"

Carolyn smiled again and said, "It's okay, Luis. Now go and pick one." Luis did not move, and Carolyn added, "Nydia, I insist you take one as well. They aren't benefitting anyone by sitting in that closet. It's time someone enjoyed them. Life is definitely too short. Maybe Marjorie deactivated the alarm for this very purpose."

"You mean there's a ghost in here?" Katie asked.

"I don't know, Katie," Carolyn said, rubbing her brow. "It's odd that the alarm decided to malfunction at this time. A supernatural explanation is as good as any when we don't know the reason why. I would gladly get rid of all this stuff if it would bring Marjorie back."

"Carolyn," Nydia interjected, "don't make a decision based on grief. I refuse to take advantage of a sad occasion."

"Art should be enjoyed. Luis, go ahead, honey," Carolyn said.

Luis turned to Stevie and said, "Stevie, pick one for me."

"Okay, Luis," he said and returned moments later with an egg.

"That one belonged to Marjorie," Carolyn said. "Father bought it at auction in Austria. It was a high school graduation gift."

"What did you get, Mommy?" Katie asked.

"I got the pearl necklace I wanted."

"Is that the one with the pink pearls?"

"Yes, that's the one."

"It's a pretty necklace," Katie commented. "I believe you got a better deal."

"No, we each got what we wanted; a perfect gift."

"But," Katie protested, "an egg doesn't do anything except sit there."

"Beauty, purpose, and usefulness are all in the eye of the beholder, honey."

"Who owned the clock?" Stevie asked.

"I don't remember," Carolyn said. "It's a very old clock, but it's still a good toy."

"It sure is. I bet I have the best gift."

"What do you want from all this stuff, Katie?" Carolyn asked her.

Katie smiled back at Carolyn and said, "I'm okay, Mommy. Like you said, it's just stuff."

Carolyn gazed lovingly at her. She then turned to look at Stevie and Luis, who had opened the egg to reveal an elegantly detailed cathedral. She held Kieran closer and a little tighter while she observed the children.

That evening, Carolyn placed her pink pearl necklace in Katie's hand and said, "It's just stuff, but giving and receiving are ways of saying you love someone. So I want you to have it."

Katie looked up at her and said, "Thank you, Mommy." Carolyn hugged her tightly.

Eighteen

1992

Little Katie had stolen an awl from Papa Sean. One evening, Katie sat outside the family home on the deck, overlooking Matthew's shed. Her feet dangled over the side of the platform. She lifted her blouse and proceeded to poke a hole above her navel with the awl's tip. Matthew surprised her, interrupting the procedure. She hadn't seen him walk out of the shed in her direction.

"What do you think you're doing?" he asked, looking up at her from below. He was almost at eye level with her torso. She looked at him and rolled her eyes. "Give me that!" he insisted and snatched the awl out of her hand. Katie got up and started to walk away. "Sit," he commanded.

"I'm not a dog, you know," she yelled down to him from the height of the deck, refusing to sit.

"Well, stay right there. I want to talk to you." He started to walk toward the steps to get to her level. She entered the house and hurried past Carolyn, who was storing pans in a kitchen cupboard.

Katie rushed into her bedroom, looked about, and quickly grabbed a Queen Anne chair to barricade the door. Matthew was soon knocking on her door as she sat staring at it from within. "Katie," he called as he turned the doorknob, and she remained silent, wishing he would go away. Matthew pushed the door and encountered the blockade. He started banging. "Open the door," he ordered several times. When he got no response, he started to throw his weight against it. Katie continued to stare at the door with her arms crossed in front of her chest as Matthew then proceeded to kick it.

She then heard Carolyn's voice. "Matthew, what are you doing?" she inquired in dismay.

"Isn't it obvious?" he asked in kind as he gave the door another kick. One of the chair's legs broke.

Katie steeled herself for the inevitable. With a final kick, the chair crumbled, and the door flew open. Katie looked at him with dread. She noticed Carolyn standing next to him and Stevie peering from the hall. Her eyes went back to Carolyn, and she hung her head in shame.

Matthew soon towered over her and ordered, "Carolyn, check her torso."

Carolyn was bewildered and asked, "What's going on, Matthew?"

"Check her torso, and you'll see," he replied while glaring at Katie. "She has cuts all over her abdomen, and I caught her trying to poke a hole in her navel with this." He opened his hand to display the awl. "Check her torso," he repeated.

Carolyn placed her hand on Matthew's shoulder and proceeded to caress his back. "Thank you, Mattie," she said calmly. "Please take Stevie downstairs, and the two of you can finish emptying the dishwasher for me. I'll talk to Katie."

Matthew turned and looked at Carolyn incredulously. In a tone he couldn't resist, Carolyn said, "Please," while she continued to caress his back.

Before Matthew yielded to his wife, he muttered, "I think she needs a new therapist. I don't think Dr. Quack is helping."

Carolyn kissed him as if to say, "I'll take it from here."

Matthew took a deep breath. He was playing the role of the disciplinary parent, but he was deeply concerned for Katie's welfare. He had developed a deep affection for his niece-turned-daughter. The love he felt for her was now expressed by the fear he felt for her. *She can't do this to herself*, he thought. His soul ached with the thought of Katie hurting herself. The pain turned to anger. He turned on his heel and motioned to Stevie to follow him out of the room. In the kitchen, he let out his frustration by banging pans and dishes as he forcefully removed them from the dishwasher and relocated them in their cupboards. He banged a drinking glass on the counter and shattered it; a shard embedded itself in his palm. "Damn it!" he said. He pulled out the shard and applied pressure to the heel of his hand.

Before Matthew left the room, Katie had been breathing tensely. When he walked out, she knew she wasn't off the hook, but she appreciated the turn of events and almost breathed a sigh of relief. Carolyn sat next to her and wrapped an arm around her shoulder.

"Have you been cutting yourself, Katie?"

Katie broke down and wept. Carolyn held her and stroked her hair.

"You're my little angel, honey. Don't ever forget that." She kissed the top of Katie's head. "You're too precious to be hurting yourself. I love Katie," she cooed. "I want you to love Katie too."

Katie continued to sob. Carolyn rocked her in her arms, but Katie only sensed a void in her soul. She wanted to believe she was loved, but something was preventing her from feeling that warmth. This world was unreal. It was devoid of tenderness. It was empty. It had no tactile matter. She wept to unearth a sense of emotion, but in the end, there was nothing but an abyss. Her cries became a wail. The wail morphed into an uncontrollable fit of despair.

That was the evening she was rushed to a psychiatric emergency room for the first time.

* * *

Matthew paced nervously back and forth as he waited for the doctors who wanted to speak to him. He worried about his wife and children at home and decided to call to check on Carolyn. He was surprised and relieved to hear Papa's voice at the other end.

"Are you okay, son?" Sean inquired.

"As okay as I'm going to be. I'm so worried about Katie, Papa. I love my little baby girl. This feels like another nightmare."

"Katie will be okay, Mattie. We are all praying for her, son."

"I hope you're right, Papa. Thanks for looking after Carolyn."

"It's the least I can do, Mattie. Ellen is upstairs in the bedroom with her. Carolyn is edgy, but Momma will calm her down. Those two ladies have an affinity for one another, thank God. All will be well, son. We'll be here all night."

"I'll be home as soon as I see the doctors."

"How is young Kate now, Mattie?"

"She's asleep. They'll be keeping her for observation, but I need to meet with the doctors before I head back home. Don't wait up. Get some sleep. I'll grab a cab as soon as I'm able. I want to get a few hours sleep before I come back again. I want to be here when Katie wakes up, in case she needs to see a familiar face."

"Well, your mother and I are not going to sleep until you get back You can go to work tomorrow; I'll be there when Katie wakes up. I'll talk to you later, Mattie. Right now, I have to get back to Stevie," he said while watching Stevie feverishly coloring with a bold red crayon. "I'm drawing pictures with my favorite grandson. He's quite good. Maybe he'll be a craftsman like his granddaddy."

Sean was true to his word. When Katie woke up the next morning, he was standing right by her bedside. Katie looked about and soon realized she was in a hospital. Silently, she stared up at Sean.

"Top of the morning to you, Katie, my love," he said. "How is my little gem?"

"Put a sock in it, Papa," she responded, pulling the covers over her shoulder and turning to face away.

"Is that any way to talk to your grandfather?"

"Go away and leave me alone."

"And I love you too. Get up. I brought your toothbrush and everything else you need. You have two jackets in the closet. The rest of your clothes are in that suitcase," he said, referring to a suitcase that was on a chair within her line of sight. "Carolyn packed it for you."

"Where's Mommy?" she asked, facing him again.

"She'll be by to see you this afternoon."

"That's not what I asked. Where is she now?"

"At this time, she's probably driving Stevie to school."

"That figures," she said as she kicked the covers off. "She has time for everyone but me. Well, I don't want to see her. I don't need her anyway."

"Stop behaving like a spoiled brat. Your mother cares a lot about you."

"Well, she's not my mother—not my real mother, anyway. If she were, she would be here. Where is she?"

"I already told you—she's driving Stevie to school."

"I know that! It was a rhetorical question."

"Rhetorical, is it? The little girl uses big words."

"I'm not a moron, you know."

"You could have fooled me because you are behaving quite poorly, Katie. If you were smarter, you would have a little compassion for others, especially your mother." Katie glared at him. "That's right, your mother. Carolyn Josephine O'Gorman is your mother. Despite what you may think, she is the woman who loves you unconditionally as a real mother would. So don't you ever say she's not your real mother. Carolyn has two biological children, but she chose you. There are millions of children out there in need of a parent. Carolyn chose you because she loves you. You've made a selfish comment, Kate. I expect better of you. Carolyn has sacrificed a lot for you. But that isn't what this is about," he added, looking pensively at her. "Get up and wash up. Your breakfast is getting cold, and we have all day to talk."

Katie got out of bed and modestly held the back of her hospital-issue robe to keep her buttocks from showing. She placed the suitcase on the bed and retrieved a toiletry bag from it. Then she locked herself in the bathroom. When Sean turned to face the room door, he noticed Carolyn standing on the threshold with the baby in her arms. A baby bag hung from one shoulder and a purse from the other.

"How long have you been there?" Sean asked.

"Long enough," she replied as Sean stepped out into the hall with her, "to know my daughter's in pain."

"She's jealous," Sean said.

"I'm flattered," Carolyn added. "Whether she's aware of it or not, she's paid me quite a compliment. She expects a lot from me—perhaps more than I can deliver."

"Heroes are usually bigger than life. However, don't sell yourself short. You've done a great job."

"Not good enough. This past year, I've placed a lot on her little shoulders."

"She's not that little anymore. She's nearly as tall as either of us. She's almost a young lady."

"Well, she was younger last year, and she did help a lot while Matthew was sick. I leaned on her while she still needed to lean on me," she said as she shifted Kieran about.

"Let me hold him," Sean volunteered. "I'm aware he can get quite heavy after a while even if he is small." Carolyn handed him the child. "Come into the room and sit; you'll be more comfortable. You can put the baby's satchel on the window ledge."

Carolyn hesitated. "I'll probably upset her more if she sees me."

"Come," Sean coaxed her, "she has to face you sooner or later." Carolyn walked into the room. Sean took the diaper bag off her shoulder and placed it near the window. She sat in the closest chair, and Sean soon dragged a second chair to sit next to her. He said, "You are a very charitable woman. You too need a reality check because whether you're aware of it or not, in my book, you are indeed bigger than life."

Carolyn smiled politely and said, "Now you flatter me as well."

"It's not flattery. It's the truth. Mattie knows it too. He calls you Honey-Lyn. I'm glad he met you."

"Thank you. I'm glad the bus ran me off the road and into his arms," she said, referring to the way she ran into Matthew the day they first met. "I'm also glad I didn't run him over with my bike."

"If you had, he would have thought Cupid's arrow packed a wallop."

Katie came out of the bathroom and nearly froze when she saw Carolyn seated in the chair and Sean holding Kieran.

"Good morning, Katie," Carolyn greeted. "How are you feeling, honey?"

"I'm fine," Katie responded as she walked toward the suitcase, holding the back of her robe.

"Let me help you put the clothes in the closet," Carolyn volunteered.

"I can do it myself. How long do you expect me to be in this prison? There's enough clothing in here to be on safari."

"I don't know how long you'll be here, sweetie. The nurse advised Matthew to bring you regular clothes because they don't want you to spend the day in PJs. I packed only three sets and a pair of pajamas."

"Well, from the looks of it, it looks like you want me to camp out here."

"On the contrary—I'm hoping you'll be home soon."

"I shouldn't be here at all. I told you I'm fine."

"We'll let the doctors determine that," Sean interjected. "I didn't hear you thank your mother for packing the clothes for you."

Katie rolled her eyes and started going through the clothes. She selected an outfit. "I guess I'll wear this one today." She also removed underwear and a pair of shoes and went back into the bathroom to dress.

In the meantime, Carolyn checked the breakfast tray. "She's not going to eat this," Carolyn commented. "The boiled egg is cold, and I never feed my children overprocessed toasted grain. I'm going to see if they'll permit me to take her to the hospital cafeteria. She can order a nice warm meal. I also need to see the dietician. If they can't provide better fare, I'll arrange for her to receive outside delivery." She turned to Sean. "Are you getting tired of holding the baby, Papa? I can take him."

"Are you kidding? I'm fine, he's fine, and you fuss too much over Katie. There's nothing wrong with that breakfast. You spoil her too much. When I was in the army, we scraped cold salty rations out of a tin can or ate shit on a shingle. I'm still alive. She'll survive on that," he concluded, referring to Katie's breakfast.

"What's shit on a shingle, Papa?"

"It's the army's version of lasagna, except it's made with greasy slivers of potatoes, equally greasy ground meat, and greasy welfare cheese."

"Sounds delicious," Carolyn laughed. "What's welfare cheese?"

"I guess you're too young to know these things. The government used to issue surplus orange American cheese in brick-shaped boxes that were about fourteen-by-four square inches in size to poor families. The box must have weighed about five pounds. They received that along with big cans of processed ham, powdered milk, peanut butter, bags of flour, and I can't remember what else. Well, the army also received crates of all that stuff. It was food that stuck to your ribs."

"I'll bet."

"You either got severely constipated, or all that grease helped the waste come out in one smooth package," he said. Carolyn covered her mouth and laughed at the thought.

A short time later, Katie came out of the bathroom wearing a skirt and blouse.

"You certainly are a pretty young lady," Sean commented. "One of these days, you're going to break a fellow's heart, but that may be after your personality catches up with your looks."

Katie rolled her eyes and sucked her teeth in disapproval of his opinion of her.

Sean countered with a smirk. "Now you can eat your breakfast," he said and eyed Carolyn as she was about to protest. She had not sat since she inspected Katie's breakfast so before she could say anything, Sean distracted her with, "Why don't you sit down, Carolyn? Get the load off your feet while Katie enjoys a nice cold breakfast. I love crunchy cereal—don't you, Kate?"

"It's okay," Katie replied as she pulled the seal off the plastic cereal bowl. "How long do you think I'll be here?"

"Only the doctors can answer that," Sean replied. "Hopefully, you'll be home before the week is up."

"I'm not sick, Papa. I told you I shouldn't be here," she said as she poured milk over the cereal.

"Oh, so you're a doctor now. When did you get your degree, young Kate?"

Katie smacked her lips in protest. "I don't have a degree, but I know I'm not sick," she said as she scooped a mouthful of the wet cereal. She looked at Carolyn, but

Carolyn had chosen not to contribute to the conversation. Katie was unable to read anything into her demeanor. In her defense, Katie stated, "If you people put me in here because I want to have a navel ring, it's not grounds to commit me, you know. Lots of kids have navel rings." She stirred the cereal and scooped another mouthful.

"So, one, you think it's fashionable to accessorize with a hole in your abdomen," Sean replied. "And, two, you're not fooling anyone with that nonsense. Or, perhaps, you actually believe we have committed you on account of that lame excuse. It's okay to pierce your delicate skin with a filthy tool. Don't worry because infections are a myth," he added sarcastically. "No one develops gangrene and dies. Three, I enjoy seeing you committed. It works for me." Katie rolled her eyes as Papa continued, and Carolyn listened without interfering. "Why doesn't it work for you? I have a friend who often says, 'Wrong and strong.' That's what you are, Katie my love. You are strongly committed to following the wrong path. You don't poke a hole in your belly because everyone else is doing it. Only sheep follow a blind path. Call me a fool, but I thought better of my granddaughter. I didn't expect her to be a brainless follower. On the contrary, I hope you will blaze trails of creativity. That's the Katie I'm rooting for because that is the young lady I know. A lovely, intelligent young lady like that doesn't do foolish things. A nurtured and beloved young lady respects the life and the body God blessed her with. Human beings cannot improve God's work; they should accept His gift unconditionally. You want to poke it full of holes. Why?"

Katie had stopped eating and stared at him solemnly. She had no reply. A young woman knocked on the open door. Carolyn and Sean acknowledged her presence and she stepped into the room.

"I'm Dr. Lieberman," she introduced herself. Sean and Carolyn rose to greet her and introduced themselves. "I spoke with Mr. O'Gorman last night," Dr. Lieberman continued. "He signed the releases for Katie's medical records. I perused what we have received so far from Dr. Peterman, and I thought we might have a chat," she said while drawing up a third chair to form a circle. She looked at Katie, who was seated on the bed, and asked, "How are you today, Katie?"

"Fine," Katie said dryly.

"Lovely baby," Lieberman commented, looking at Kieran. "Well behaved, too."

"Yes," Sean said, "he's a quiet little fellow." As usual, Kieran had been looking about alertly while sucking on his pacifier. Whenever he heard a voice, he moved his head and eyes to look in the speaker's direction. Sometimes he flailed his arms.

"Yeah, right!" Katie protested.

"I see you disagree, Katie," Lieberman observed.

Katie eyed her suspiciously and said, "Don't try that trick with me, lady. I've seen enough shrinks in my life to know when you're fishing. I've also read shrink books."

"Oh, you believe I'm trying to trick you. What have you read, Katie?"

"I've read Freud and others. In my opinion, he needed a shrink himself. I've read childhood psychology, adult psych—normal and abnormal. I've read critiques by and on the so-called experts. I've read up on various disorders like bipolar and split personalities. Some of those shrinks really come up with some lame ideas. Some of those suggestions can actually be harmful to your health. There's an idiot out there who suggests that a cure for colic is to wrap the kid up tightly in a blanket. He calls it swaddling. I call it damaging the kid's joints and constricting his breathing—small wonder he stops crying. The poor kid can't breathe, he's in shock, and is probably saying, 'Is this really happening to me? Is my mommy trying to kill me?'"

"I'm impressed. How old are you, Katie?"

"Why don't you read the chart and figure it out?"

"I suppose I could do that, but here's the deal. I ask questions and you answer them. Based on your answers, I make an evaluation. I have the pen. Your parents are paying good money to see good results. If you don't cooperate, I can't make an intelligent decision."

"Can you do that? Can you make an intelligent decision, Doc?"

"Kate," Sean interjected, "stop the insolence!"

"I'll stop being rude when you take me home. I don't belong here. I'm sick of shrinks. They must sit up at night making things up while fondling in the dark."

"You're not going home until you behave and cooperate," he responded. "The insolence stops now, or we leave. We're not coming back unless you change your ways. Do you want to spend a year in here? Does that sound reasonable to you?"

"You can't make me spend a year in here. Besides, I'll bet the doc breaks before I do. Go home—see if I care!"

"Fine," Sean said, getting out of his seat. "Carolyn, Dr. Lieberman—my granddaughter wishes to be alone. Perhaps we should all go."

Carolyn retrieved Kieran's bag from the window ledge. Katie watched fearfully as the three adults proceeded toward the door. "I didn't say I wanted to be alone," she protested. "I said I want to go home." The adults continued walking. "Mom, you can't leave me here. I want to go home." The adults walked into the hall and turned right. Katie rushed out, calling, "Mom, no. Mom, don't leave me." She quickly caught up to Carolyn and nearly pulled her arm out of its socket as she screamed, "Mommy, no! Mommy, no!" Katie soon had her arms wrapped around Carolyn's neck, pulling her down toward her. Carolyn wrapped her arms around her daughter as Katie continued to yell. "Don't leave me; please don't leave me. I want to go home. I promise I'll be good. I promise!" she screamed. As the crescendo grew, the doctor consulted Sean, and she soon administered a tranquilizer. Katie's screams and pull on Carolyn's neck diminished as the drug took effect. Her legs started to give way. An orderly caught her and transferred her to a gurney. Carolyn was as red as a beet and exhausted. The tears streamed down her face. Sean handed her a handkerchief, and she mopped her face as the orderly wheeled Katie back into her room.

"Are you all right?" Dr. Lieberman inquired as she touched Carolyn's arm.

"I'm fine, thank you," she said as she dried her eyes. She tried to smile as she said, "It's not easy."

"No, it isn't," Lieberman agreed. "Would you folks like to come down to my office? We can continue to chat."

"I can't leave Katie," Carolyn said, feeling guilty. "My baby needs me."

"She'll be fine," the doctor assured her while holding her hand. "She'll be out for an hour or so. The nurses will monitor her."

"Can we talk in her room? I don't want to leave her."

"Fine, we'll talk in her room."

Carolyn stood by Katie's bed and confessed. "I feel like it's an invasion of privacy, but my husband said he noticed scars on her torso. He believes she has been cutting herself. I just want to see while she's asleep. May I see?" she inquired as if asking for permission. She was afraid to confirm Matthew's allegations, and she was also afraid to violate Katie's privacy.

"It's okay," Dr. Lieberman said. "Legally, I'm bound to investigate because I could be charged if I don't report something that might be considered a crime. I'll unbutton her blouse, and we can all see." Carolyn nodded in affirmation. She understood the letter of the law, but this was a personal matter. Her emotions and the law were in conflict with one another. She didn't want to invade Katie's privacy, but she needed to know. Lieberman peeled back Katie's blouse. Carolyn and Sean observed with great sadness. Katie did have scars all over her torso. Some were scratches. Others were deep lesions. Several had healed over.

Carolyn's tears flowed silently. "How could I not have known this?" she asked aloud. "How long has this been going on?"

"Apparently, several weeks, judging from the healing," the doctor replied.

Sean caressed Carolyn's back. "Papa," she said, "I've failed my little girl. I want to take her home."

"That's a mother's reaction," Lieberman said, "but she can't go home. She is apparently a danger to herself. I need to hold her for the required seventy-two hours."

"She's afraid to be here. I can't let her stay."

"Mrs. O'Gorman, listen to me. We will work around this. Trust me—she'll be okay."

"Papa, I can't leave her here like this. She's terrified."

"Then we'll stay, Rua my love."

In a time of crisis, a family's ability to stay afloat depends on its ability to come together. People have commitments; people have impediments; people have excuses. Katie had a family of people who were dedicated to one another, and that is what helped them stay afloat during each whirlpool they encountered in their lives. They had many such bumps in the road; some were bumpier than others. Legally, Katie needed another sixty hours of observation, Papa decided not to leave her alone, Carolyn agreed, and the O'Gormans followed their instincts. That morning, Ellen had taken Stevie to school in order to permit Carolyn to arrive earlier at the hospital. When Matthew left the hospital the night before, he left with an assurance that his daughter was sleeping safely. And now Sean spent the rest of the morning reaching out to his wife and sons to share the burden of the sixty-hour vigil that lay ahead. Within the O'Gorman extended family, Camille pitched in. Harry and Margaret Reilly were willing to drive north from the city in order to contribute. A timetable was agreed upon, and little Katie had her sixty-hour round-the-clock surveillance team to reduce the stress of the hospital stay for her. Beginning at four that afternoon, Katie would also have round-the-clock private-duty nursing.

While Katie slept, the O'Gormans and Dr. Lieberman shared information. Carolyn and Sean filled the doctor in on Katie's personal and medical history. From them, Dr. Lieberman gleaned information that wasn't in the notes she had received from Katie's therapist, Dr. Peterman. Dr. Lieberman offered suggestions and spoke of the long-term effects and scars of childhood sexual abuse. When Katie awoke the second time, Sean and Kieran were gone. Carolyn had been sitting nearby, observing her sleep. She quietly smiled at Katie when the child woke up.

"You didn't leave," Katie observed groggily.

"No, I didn't leave," Carolyn assured her.

"I had a dream, but I can't remember. Oh, yes. I was on a boat, drifting out to sea. I kept calling you, but you couldn't hear me."

"I can hear you, honey. I'm right here. Are you hungry?"

"I don't think so." She focused on Carolyn's face. "Are you hungry?"

"No. I'm not hungry. Would you like to go for a walk?"

"Where can we go? I guess going home is out of the question, huh?"

"I'm afraid so, sweetie. You need to be here a couple of days. It won't be so bad. You can meet a few of the other children who are here. We'll try to make the best of it between therapy sessions. Let's take that walk. We're allowed to walk within the grounds of this hospital wing." Katie got out of bed, and Carolyn soon had her arm around her shoulders. "You'll need your jacket. It's a little chilly out there."

Most of their walk was quiet and contemplative. Carolyn was grateful that Katie was now subdued and hoped the mood would last. Katie felt oddly happy. Throughout her life, moments like this were like cotton candy at a state fair. However, like cotton candy, they were sweet moments that melted too soon. As a result of sessions with health care professionals and augmented reading, they each knew that the wounds of childhood abuse were the exact opposite of cotton candy. Such wounds tended to fester and travel through time. In Katie's case, there were times when she believed she had swatted the troublesome memories away like pesky mosquitoes. Then she discovered they would return to drain her again. Sometimes her head felt like it was doing summersaults, racing from one thought to another. At times, she was confused. Subconsciously, she developed coping mechanisms. Carolyn had once advised her to use her imagination to combat boredom and Katie did that and more. She had also grown to depend on Carolyn as her mosquito net. Mommy kept the pests away, but Mommy wasn't always there to protect her. Lately, Mommy had been swatting mosquitoes of her own and caring for the baby.

"I'm sorry, Mommy," she said as they walked arm in arm.

"For what, honey?"

"For being a pain in the ass."

"You're not a pain in the ass. You're my baby."

"I thought Kieran was your baby."

"Haven't you noticed?" Carolyn asked while pausing to look Katie in the eye.

"What?" she asked, squinting at the nearly midday sun as she looked up at Carolyn.

"I have three babies, Katie," she said, hugging Katie's head against her chest. "In order of age and size, you're my first baby, honey. And you will always be my baby."

"If I'm sixty and you're eighty-three, I'll be your baby?" she asked as they parted.

"Always."

"We'll both be very old. And Stevie will be fifty-six."

Carolyn laughed. "Imagine that. Thank God we have a long way to go." She looked lovingly at Katie and added, "I love you, kiddo, with all my heart. Please don't forget that, Katie."

Dr. Lieberman met with them again, and Katie was more cooperative.

"I noticed you don't take any medication. Have you ever been medicated?"

"She's never had any need for medication, Dr. Lieberman," Carolyn interjected. "Normally, we have counseling sessions much like this one. Katie has an occasional mood swing, but never anything like what she had last night or today."

"It may be anxiety," Dr. Lieberman volunteered. "Is something bothering you, Katie?"

"I don't like the school I'm at."

"What don't you like?"

"At my old school, Emily's Hope, I knew everyone. I don't know too many people at St. Lucy's. The rules are different, too. At Emily's Hope, I could come and go as I pleased. At St. Lucy's, I have to be in my seat all the time. I'm not a freaking mannequin, you know."

"What else bothers you?"

"I don't know."

"Does something bother you at home?"

"No, nothing."

"Katie, be honest with Dr. Lieberman. She's trying to help," Carolyn advised her. "Would you be more comfortable if I left?"

"No! I mean, no," she said, lowering her voice. "Don't go."

"I'll only be out in the hall or in the lounge."

"No, you can stay. I'll answer the questions if I can go home."

"By law, you're required to be here the full seventy-two hours, honey."

"But then I can go home, right?"

"Yes," Carolyn responded reassuringly.

"Okay, so ask me another question, Doc."

"Your father informed me that you had cut yourself with an awl. Why did you cut yourself?" Doctor Lieberman inquired.

"I've never cut myself."

"Katie," Carolyn admonished her, "you have to answer truthfully so we can help you."

"Mom, I have never cut myself! I wouldn't do a stupid thing like that."

"Katie," Carolyn replied, "look at me." Katie looked her squarely in the eye, and Carolyn said, "I know you have scars all over your abdomen. How did they get there if you didn't cut yourself?"

"I don't know. Maybe I had an itch, and I scratched," she said, glaring at her. "I did not cut myself."

"Katie," Dr. Lieberman asked, "how do you feel about your father?"

"Is this a Freudian question, Doc?"

"Katie, the lady's name is Dr. Lieberman. Please address Dr. Lieberman properly. Dr. Lieberman asks the questions, and you answer them. You need to answer truthfully. Don't try my patience, and don't waste Dr. Lieberman's time."

"What was the question, Dr. Lieberman?"

"What is your opinion of your father?"

"He's mean." Carolyn felt ill at ease by her reply, and Lieberman noticed the reaction.

"Please define mean," the doctor said.

"That's not a question, Dr. Lieberman, ma'am."

"Katie!" Carolyn admonished her.

"Okay, okay, Mom. My father won't allow me to go to the movies with my friends until I turn fourteen, but not with boys. He said that if I go with a boy, he'll be seated right behind me. Actually, he doesn't want me to go anywhere unless I'm with the family."

"It sounds like he's trying to protect you."

"Well, I don't need protection; I can take care of myself. He doesn't even want me to go to the park with my friend Rina. My mother is the same way. She shadows me wherever I go. Well, she used to shadow me. Now I go to St. Lucy's, and she's too busy."

"You don't look like someone who is cooped up at home and school," the doctor observed. "Are you involved in sports?"

"Yes."

"What do you do?"

"Track, karate, tennis, basketball, volleyball, swimming, soccer, yoga. Yoga isn't a sport, but it helps to keep you fit. Mom and I do yoga at home, but not anymore."

"You're very active. That's good. Why don't you do yoga anymore?"

"I do yoga; I do it all the time. It's important for sports. I don't do it with my mother anymore."

"Would you like to do yoga with your mother?"

"Not necessarily. She doesn't have time."

"Why do you suppose that is?"

"I don't know. Ask her. She's right here."

"Well, I want to know if you understand why your mom doesn't have time. You're a smart girl. I think you can figure it out. What is different now as opposed to before? If you understand why A plus B equals C, you can resolve your own problems or correct a situation. You're young, but put yourself in your mommy's shoes, if you can, and tell me what's different now."

"You mean like role play."

"This is analyzing the role play. Analyze the situation. Look at your mother's life, and identify what's different from say a year ago."

"Well, my father was very sick. We all helped out, including my little brother Stevie, but Mom did what she always does, except Stevie and I helped her cook because sometimes my father couldn't do that."

"Your father used to cook when he was well?"

"Yeah, sometimes; but when he was sick, we did laundry, vacuumed, went to school, washed dishes, and did homework."

"Your mother went to school and did homework?"

"No, she doesn't go to school," Katie said and thought, *"Idiot, you're pissing me off."*

"What did your mother do that's different?"

"She had a skinny baby."

"She had a skinny baby. Does the baby bother you?"

"Well, yeah. He cries all the time. And he poops a lot. He can stink up the whole house."

"Do you resent the baby, Katie?"

She thought for a second and said, "No. I shouldn't resent him."

"Does that mean you resent him?"

"No, but he stole my initials, you know."

"What do you mean?"

"K.E.O.G., those are my initials. My name is Katharine Erin O'Gorman. Now that poopy kid has my initials, K.E.O.G. Some people drop the O. I have a pendant that says KEG. It's mine."

Carolyn was visibly upset by what she heard. "Katie, I named Kieran. He didn't steal your initials. I didn't even

stop to think they were the same. You're not the only person in the world with those initials. I always liked the name
Kieran; I have a great-uncle named Kieran. The baby's
middle name, Emmanuel, was appropriate for the occasion. Katie, the name Emmanuel is a symbol of what his
birth means to me. No one stole your initials. They're still
yours. You and Kieran share a common bond."

"Whatever," Katie replied, looking away. "If you liked
the name Kieran so much, why didn't you give it to Stevie,
before I met you?"

"Stevie was named to honor Momma. I didn't give
birth to a girl, so I couldn't call him Ellen. He's named for
Momma's father, except the spelling is different. His name
was Patrick Stephen."

Dr. Lieberman continued her line of questioning. "Can
you forgive the fact that your brother shares your initials,
Katie?"

"I guess so."

"Katie, you need to forgive the matter so you can feel
better and move on," the doctor advised her.

Katie didn't understand. "What do you mean?" she asked.

"You need to understand that you're blaming a baby
for something he hasn't done. Think about it. Did Kieran
name himself?"

"No."

"Precisely. He didn't do that in the same manner that
you didn't name yourself Katharine. The name was chosen
and given to you. Kieran's name was chosen and given
to him. Evidently, each name has a special significance.
The person who receives it is being given a legacy. He or
she becomes the new standard-bearer. Why were you
named Katharine?"

"It's my great-grandmother's name. Momma calls me young Kate because my great-grandmother is older than me."

"You were given a name to honor your great-grandmother. It means your mother had fond memories of her, and she wanted to preserve those memories through you. She named you for someone she cherishes and loves. That is what you focus on—the fact that you are a vessel of love. You are not a vessel of resentment. Resentment breeds bad feelings. Love breeds good feelings. Focus on the love. Carolyn loves you very much. If she didn't love you, she wouldn't be sitting here right now. While she's loving you, you're telling her you don't like her baby. How do you think she feels when she hears that?"

Katie was visibly embarrassed by the question, and her face flushed. "Not good," she replied.

"Well, when you feel resentment toward the baby, you don't feel good inside either. That's called jealousy. Apparently, you also dislike something about the baby. When your insides are busy feeling jealousy or dislike toward him, you are harming yourself. I recommend that you start looking at your brother differently. He is a projection of your mommy. When you do not like him, you are also hurting your mommy. Do you want to do that?"

"No," Katie said as a tear rolled down her face.

"If you want to feel better, Katie, find what you like. Concentrate on that. Don't concentrate on the dislike. Think—what do you like about your mommy? See the baby as a projection of her. What do you like about Kieran?"

"He's Mommy's baby. He is a vessel of her love," she said, but she had difficulty accepting it.

"Good, Katie. That's a start. You know what? I'm going to leave you a little notebook, and I'm going to give you a homework assignment. I'd like you to make a list of the people and things you like and the people and things you love. It's an assignment to help you concentrate on the positive things in your life. As you write each item or name, try to explain why you feel like or love toward it or the person. Can you do that?"

"Of course I can do that. I like pie because it tastes good," she said dryly.

"You can start your list now if you like, Katie," Dr. Lieberman said as she handed her a miniature notebook. "I'd like to speak to your mom alone if you don't mind."

Katie accepted the notebook and said, "Sure. Do I get a pen?"

Carolyn checked her purse and handed Katie a retractable pen. She hoped the child didn't decide to use it as a weapon on herself. "I'll be right back," she informed her daughter, but what she wanted to say was, "Don't get any dumb ideas." Then she and Dr. Lieberman walked out the door and down the hall.

A few feet down the hall, Dr. Lieberman paused and asked, "Are you okay, Mrs. O'Gorman?"

Carolyn crossed her arms in front of her chest and ambivalently said, "Yes, I'm fine."

"It's seldom easy for a loved one to hear the thoughts that race through a confused or troubled mind. What you hear may not always be true. It's a perception or interpretation, so I hope this conversation wasn't too painful for you."

"I'm fine, Dr. Lieberman. I've already been informed that children of abuse can face a lifelong journey. As Katie struggles with all of this, she has put up many defense mechanisms in order to cope. My husband and I try to keep her on a steady course, and I agree it isn't easy. I constantly need to remind her that I love her and that she is loved; I hope she hears me. She did get my attention when she called my baby 'that poopy kid,' but I have to shrug that off along with all the other irrational comments she sometimes makes. Nothing I hear or see could possibly compare with the horrors she endured. I pivot my feelings around that gruesome memory."

Lieberman smiled. "So you have your own defense mechanisms. That's good. If you ever need a sounding board, feel free to call me." She fumbled through her book bag and handed Carolyn a business card. "I gave your husband one as well. I'm licensed in therapy and psychiatry, but if you ever have a need to chat woman-to-woman, off the business clock, feel free to call."

"Thank you, Dr. Lieberman."

"My name is Odette. I was named for my grandmother Olga. In Jewish tradition, we use the first letter of the deceased loved one's name."

"I'm Carolyn. Pleasure to meet you Odette."

"Likewise. You know, if it isn't easy for us, it's probably ten times more difficult for the patient. I've seen it a number of times. Just as you think you have them walking a steady tightrope, they slip and fall. Refractory depression is particularly difficult to treat."

"I've experienced the tightrope slippage with Katie. She gets mood swings. The best my husband and I can do is to try to put her back on the rope."

"I wish science could offer more, but biological chemistry and neuron triggering are still an enigma. We don't have all the answers. We were taught, above all, do no harm. I share your belief. You don't want her to take drugs;

I read it in Dr. Peterman's report. I apologize for injecting her with a tranquilizer, but I believe it was justifiable, and Mr. O'Gorman approved."

"Well, I don't disapprove of a sedative. I disapprove of antipsychotic drugs for children, from fluoxetine and beyond, because I am aware of the science. Unlike the gurus who sit on the FDA committees, I won't allow efficacy to be outweighed by risks. My daughter is not an inanimate statistic."

"I understand. As you most likely know, in the nineteenth century, they discovered that pellagra could be cured with a B-vitamin and a protein. Until then, people were locked away in insane asylums. I wish we could cure other disorders in a similar manner. Only time will tell. In the meantime, we experiment with different techniques. One of my colleagues is experimenting with exercise and coordination techniques. It doesn't involve drugs. I know someone else who is doing holistic studies. There's a third study involving light and color frequencies. Finally, there are studies involving music, dance, and tai chi. If you are interested in any of that, I can offer you a referral."

"We teach tai chi at the academy. However, I am leery of making Katie a test subject. On the other hand, I would like to know what treatments look promising. I will try practically anything that isn't harmful in order to have a contented child. I'd like to meet with these doctors. Thank you. If they offer anything positive, I'll have Katie choose an activity. Hopefully, she won't feel like she's being coerced into something if she has a choice."

"Katie also suffers from an emotional disconnect." Dr. Lieberman was referring to commentaries made by Katie's therapist. "According to Dr. Peterman, Katie has difficulty giving or receiving affection. Did he mention that a pet, such as a puppy or a kitten, can probably help her make that connection?"

"No, I can't recall him making such a suggestion. If this were a few years ago, I would say great idea, but right now, I don't know if I want to entertain the notion of getting up earlier to walk a dog. I know it would be Katie's responsibility to do that, but there is no guarantee she would do it. Perhaps a few months from now, when the baby is older, we can get her a kitten or a small dog."

When Carolyn returned to Katie's room, she was looking out the window at the grounds below.

"Did you finish writing your list?" Carolyn inquired.

"Yes. A lady came in and asked me to select from a list of activities to participate in."

"What did they have to offer?"

"Not much. Lame stuff, mostly. I can watch an old movie. She left the list on the night table. They have a gym downstairs; I can use a treadmill or something."

Carolyn picked up the list as she said, "Let's go check out the gym."

"I don't have any sneakers."

"I'll have your father bring you what you need tonight," she said as she skimmed the list. "There's no harm in checking it out. You can also volunteer to read to younger children or help them with their schoolwork." Katie had already met a few of the children during their morning stroll.

"Don't they have audio tapes for that?" she asked, referring to Carolyn's reading suggestion.

"If you read to them, it's interactive. It's also a nice act of charity. We can both read. It's a way to shorten your days here, and you'll probably enjoy it."

Carolyn expected Katie to say something sarcastic like, "Yeah, right," but she was surprised when Katie said, "All right. I'll give it a shot."

Katie's first nurse arrived at four, and Carolyn introduced her, Mrs. Agbenya, to Katie. Camille, Carolyn's sister-in-law, arrived a few minutes later to relieve Carolyn.

"Thank you so much for coming, Camille," Carolyn said. "The nurse is here, but if Katie sees a familiar face, it helps to keep her calm. If you can only stay a few minutes, it's okay. Matthew will be with her after work, and Patrick will spend the night. She's already interacting with the other children, so it's a good sign." As the two women spoke, Katie was playing a board game with three other children.

"I'll stay until seven. Courtney can take care of herself until Neil gets home." Courtney was the youngest of Camille's three daughters; she was fourteen. "She has a swim meet today. I'll call home around six to make sure she arrived home all right. As long as I know where my girls are, I'm okay." Camille's other two daughters, eighteen-year-old Elizabeth and twenty-year-old Shannon, were college students. "Go home and try to get some rest," she advised Carolyn.

When Carolyn informed Katie that Camille would keep her company until Daddy came, Katie asked, "You're going home? I thought you were going to stay with me."

"Katie, I need to go home. Aunt Camille will keep you company for a few hours."

Katie looked at Camille, who was standing next to Carolyn. She looked back at Carolyn and asked, "What if I need you?"

"Honey, you can call me. You won't need anything. You have everything here, including a nice open kitchenette in case you need a snack. This is a very nice hospital, and you're not alone."

Katie eyed Camille again. She then turned to Carolyn and asked, "When will you be back?"

"I'll come tomorrow, as soon as I can. Tonight, Daddy will bring you the things you'll need for the exercise room. I'll see you tomorrow, okay?"

Katie looked at her sullenly and said, "Okay."

"Don't you have anything to say to Aunt Camille?"

Katie looked sullenly at Camille and unenthusiastically said, "Hello, Aunt Camille."

"Good afternoon, Katie. How are you feeling?"

"I'm okay. I shouldn't be here, you know. This place is for crazy retards."

Camille smiled and said, "I don't think it's politically correct to use that term."

"Well, if people keep inventing new words based on stupidity and political concerns, we'll never understand each other anymore. Trust me, Aunt Camille, they're crazy retards. See that kid over there?" She pointed to a small boy in jeans and sweatshirt who had a nervous tick and bald spots on his head. "That loony pulls his hair out and eats it. That's not all he does. He also eats his boogers and the stuff that comes out of his eyes. Tell me that isn't retarded and crazy. He's downright demented."

"Katie, I don't think Aunt Camille needed to hear that," Carolyn said.

"Well, it's better to be forewarned. If you're smart, Aunt Camille, don't look at him, especially when you're eating. I'm waiting for him to cough up a fur ball like Mr. Spats." Mr. Spats and Miss Ghillie were Camille's cats, so named because they had white feet that accented their dark gray fur.

Camille laughed at Katie's comments and said, "Thank you, Katie. I'll keep that in mind. Oh, I brought you a few books. I hope you like them." She handed Katie a bag with four paperbacks—two activity books, a biography, and a novel.

"Thank you," Katie said, accepting the bag.

"Katie, I'm leaving." Carolyn kissed her on the cheek and said, "I love you, honey. Behave yourself. The onus to prove you're ready to go home is on you, so don't antagonize anyone. Go finish your game. Your friends are waiting."

As Katie went back to join her new acquaintances, Camille commented, "It looks like it's going to be a fun evening."

"From your mouth to God's ears," Carolyn replied. "Sometimes Katie can shock you out of your socks."

"Well, you're patient with her."

"God must have given me that as a gift, knowing I was going to have her in my life. Do you know anything about dogs? The doctor suggested I get her a dog or a cat."

"With a new baby, I don't think you want a litter box in the house, Carolyn. Cat feces can be very harmful to babies. Do you want to walk a dog each day?"

"Not really. I have to think about it because it's a big responsibility."

"Well, just like humans, pets need doctor visits, grooming, and many other interactive activities. I heard that Chihuahuas and poodles don't shed, so they may be a good option to avoid allergies."

"Oh, God, I don't think this is the time. I've never had a pet. As a child, my family was always traveling, so I guess it was never an option."

"Well, you travel now, and, even if you're home, pets can get lonely. That's why I've always had two cats. If one dies, you have a new set of issues to consider."

"This is definitely not the time. Thanks for the info, Camille," Carolyn concluded.

She left the hospital and was anxious to get home in order to milk her breasts. She had changed the pads on her nursing bra four times already, and her breasts were aching. However, on her way home, she spotted a small church. She walked in and lit a candle for each of her children, alive and deceased, and one for Marjorie. She knelt in prayer and asked the Lord to protect and heal her loved ones of their ills. Finally, she asked for God's guidance in dealing with the problems she faced. As she rose from prayer and turned to leave, she heard someone ask, "Carolyn? Is that you?" It was Father Patrick, Matthew's oldest brother.

They each asked, "What are you doing here?"

Patrick kissed her in greeting and said, "This is my friend's parish. I figured I'd kill two birds with one stone. I'm having dinner with him, and then I'll scoot over to the hospital center and keep Katie company. What's your story?"

"I was on my way home; I noticed the church, and I suddenly needed to come in and light a few candles."

"That many problems, huh? Why don't you come into the office with me and have a sip of wine and a chat? Father Warren is at the hospital, seeing to his parishioners before dinner. You can keep me company for a few minutes."

"I can't stay. Papa is looking after the boys, so I need to get home before he starts to worry. I shouldn't have come in here in the first place."

"Papa and the boys will be fine. We'll call him and explain you'll be a little late."

Carolyn considered it a moment. Her breasts ached. She finally said, "I appreciate the offer, but I really need to go. Besides, I can't have any wine; I'm nursing."

"In that case, I'll accompany you home. I'll drive your car and take a cab back. It will give you a chance to rest your eyes a bit."

"You don't know how much I appreciate that. If I were able, I would gladly have a nice glass of wine right now."

"You are so careful about everything," he said as they walked. "Ask Momma, and she'll tell you. When we were babies and were teething, she used to take a cotton swab and rub a little brandy on our gums. It tastes better than oil of clove."

"I agree it tastes better," Carolyn replied while keeping pace with his stride, "but is it safe?"

"Well, I think I turned out okay, and I still like a nice brandy to chase away a cold. Is oil of clove safe for babies? Brandy is a good antiseptic, it's delicious, and it's all natural. Now that I think of it, I think I'll use it the next time I get a toothache."

"Let me know if it works. I've gotten quite an education today. First, it was Papa with his story about shit on the shingles."

"He told you about S.O.S?" Patrick asked as they reached Carolyn's car and she handed him the keys. "That's what we call it, S.O.S. After eating it, you might need to send out a distress call."

"That's not what Papa said."

"Oh, I know what he said—I can imagine. Actually, S.O.S isn't that bad. It kind of grows on you," he said as Carolyn strapped herself in. "I plan to grab a nap while I'm sitting Katie tonight because I have to be back early to see about a parishioner's will." They were soon on their way.

"Actually, you can take the whole night off. Katie seems to be doing all right. She has round-the-clock nursing. Camille is with her now. I needed someone she feels comfortable with to be with her until she falls asleep. Matthew will relieve Camille, and Katie should be asleep by then."

"In that case, I'll take Matthew's shift and save him the trip. Maybe I can relieve Camille a little earlier. I'll stay with Katie until she dozes off."

"I accept your offer. There's one more thing."

"Name it."

"Could you deliver her gym clothes to her? I'll pack them as quickly as I can when we get home."

"No problem."

"The will you're handling—is the person deceased?"

"No, but she soon will be. I'm her executor. She's an elderly lady; lovely woman, very stoic. She has all her faculties, but she has terminal cancer. My main concern is her two little Chihuahuas. I need to find them a home."

"Oh, God, no," Carolyn said through her teeth.

"What's the matter?"

"God has a very wry sense of humor, that's all. I just wish He would stop picking on me. I'm juggling enough clubs already."

"What do you mean?" he asked, and Carolyn told him about the doctor's suggestion of a pet. She also told him about the conversation she had with Camille, who recommended dogs that don't shed.

"So," Patrick commented, "you think God is clearing the way for you to get a couple of Chihuahuas?"

"I wouldn't use the word 'clearing.' He hasn't cleared anything off my plate. He's adding to my list of chores. I'm in no mood to care for another one of God's creatures. I have my family to look after, I think I'm stressed out, Katie had a nervous breakdown, except they now call it an anxiety attack, and I'm highly ticked off at Lyman for pursuing an appeal. Every time I think of it, God help me, I want to kill the bastard."

"God has cleared your plate a bit, you just don't know it," Patrick said as he stopped at a stop sign, and then he continued.

"Please enlighten me."

"No one walks alone, Carolyn. What you perceive as a lightning bolt could actually be a night light to guide you on your way."

"I've heard that one before. Today, I can't buy it, but thanks for trying."

"Come with me tomorrow to Mrs. Shultz's home. That's the lady who owns the Chihuahuas."

"I'll have to think about it."

"Okay. Why did you walk into that particular church today and find me in it? Was it a coincidence? Remember what happened to Jonah? He decided to hightail it out to sea, and the leviathan decided to become his own personal ferry. The fish coughed him up right where he didn't want to be."

Carolyn sighed and said, "I sympathize with the poor soul. Do I smell of fish to you?"

Patrick laughed and said, "That's a loaded question, but here's one answer. We're all God's fish, Carolyn. You can swim all you want, but He decides which waters are best for you."

Nineteen

‹›◇‹›

2005

Katie resigned herself to running her business from home via computer, Internet, and phone. She often thought back to the lunch conversation she had with Rina a few days earlier. During that conversation, it was obvious that Rina had failed to recall a very important factor about her past with her father. Katie knew that Rina's father had died brutally shortly before her friend and her mother had moved to Florida. During their recent conversation, Rina had said, "It's as if he disappeared off the face of the earth." Katie would continue to recall that conversation and ask herself the same questions repeatedly, *"Is Rina in denial? Did she forget? Is she hiding something?"* To Katie, nothing seemed to make any sense.

* * *

Katie's SUV was parked in front of Matthew's shed, waiting for him to determine what was needed to customize it for her needs. On Saturday, Matthew finally found the time to do that. While he was working, Carolyn brought him hot tea and a slice of the walnut-carrot cake Kieran had baked. She sat with him, straddling the van's rear bumper as he ate cake and sipped his tea. She stared into the van's back storage area and caught sight of Bert and Kurt, Katie's two mannequins.

"What on earth is Katie doing with those?" she asked aloud.

"I don't know." Matthew shrugged and continued enjoying his cake. "This is good. Kieran should become a chef."

On Monday, Carolyn had received an e-mail from her investigators, indicating they had found a match for the prints on Katie's crutches. They belonged to a Lawrence Quinn, who was assigned to the mayor's office of New York City. *Interesting*, she thought as she read the memo.

In addition to school, Stevie was spending a lot of his time with Darnell and the Hassan family in South Yonkers. Carolyn and Matthew were impressed and proud of his newfound awareness and efforts to be a good Samaritan to his injured war veteran friend Omid.

On Tuesday, March 15, an overbooked Luis postponed Lolo and Lolita's trip to the vet for their annual checkup until the following week. He was also scheduled to meet with Susan Sheridan, attorney at law, on the twenty-third in order to finalize the sale of his Web site.

Before midday Tuesday, Katie had finished her work. She hobbled to Luis's house and poured fresh water for the dogs, Onyx and Amber, and tossed a Frisbee with them for a while. When she tired of the game, she locked the gate to Luis's property and returned home. She noticed that Luis had not yet changed the gate lock that Amber had gotten so adept at opening. After lunch, Katie grabbed her crutches and hobbled through the woods in order to reduce the two-mile trek to Emily's Hope. The academy had St. Patrick's Day decorations on most of the bulletin boards. She entered the cafeteria and found her way to the dietician's office.

"Katie, my love. How's the new mommy to be?" Nydia asked, hugging her. "I haven't seen you since opening day."

"I'm fine, except for the broken bones," Katie replied. "How are you and Felipe?"

"We're fine, sweetheart. We're getting ready to become grandparents," she said, touching Katie's flat abdomen, "even if you have a while to go. What brings you this way?"

"I was getting restless at home, so I decided to take a walk. I need to find something to keep me occupied in the afternoons. I already miss traveling from site to site."

"Have you seen Carolyn?"

"No—besides, I think I better lay low. She's probably still annoyed with me."

"What did you do now, Katie?"

"It's what I didn't do. I didn't attend my own intervention."

"Why didn't you go, Katie?"

"I believe I already know what was going to be said and not said. I don't want to go there; I'm tired of the same old same old. I settled into my own home for a reason. Mom needs to understand that I'm no longer a child and that I'm capable of deciding my own destiny."

"She's simply showing her concern. Carolyn wants nothing but the best for you, Katie. You're going to want her around as soon as the baby comes."

"Well, I'll cross that bridge when I come to it."

"It's interesting how life unwinds," Nydia commented.

"What do you mean?"

"Well, as a little girl, you followed Carolyn everywhere and sought her attention. Then you started becoming more and more independent. Now you think she's interfering with your life."

"Isn't that the way life is supposed to be? How old were you when you left home?"

"I never left home. I attended City University and left home as a married woman. If my mother were still alive, God rest her soul, I would still worship the very ground she walked on. My father returned to the Dominican Republic after she passed away and I call him every week."

"It sounds like you had good parents."

"So do you, Katie. Treasure and love them while they still live. You can follow your destiny and still involve them in your life; don't push them away. Don't do anything you may regret later, love. It's funny. Do you know what I was thinking about the other day?"

"No."

"Well, I was thinking about that last day in New Zealand and your adventure in Orlando, Florida. Do you remember those trips?"

"The New Zealand trip was the most awesome trip ever. Of course I remember that."

"I agree. It was awesome, but I remember the last day there. It wasn't that awesome for Carolyn and Matthew. You gave them the scare of their lives. I think Carolyn aged ten years that day. I hated to leave her there under those circumstances."

"Was she that upset?"

"Katie, you have no idea. You disappeared and the poor woman was so worried when she couldn't find you, that she looked visibly ill. Of course, that wasn't the first or last time you pulled a stunt like that. I hoped you would never do anything like that again, then came the Florida incident. Felipe and I were equally worried for your safety."

Katie mulled it over and said, "Hmm. I didn't know it was that big a deal. In NewZealand, I was just having fun; I prefer to forget about Florida."

* * *

The St. Patrick's Day celebration at Emily's Hope was sensational because as Momma Ellen pointed out, in New York everyone is suddenly Irish on St. Patrick's Day. She and the rest of the family, minus Katie, watched the parade on a TV in her office. Nydia and her staff served a lunch of mussels, shepherd's pie, corned beef and cabbage, soda bread that was sliced and shaped as a shamrock, and all the other traditional Irish fare.

Luis arrived dressed in his kilt as the dishes were being passed at the table reserved for the family. "Where's Katie?" he inquired.

"She didn't come," Stevie replied.

"I'll get her," Luis said, rising from the table as he pulled out his cell phone.

"What do you mean you're not coming?" Carolyn heard him say into the phone as he passed her seat. "The whole family is here. I'm coming to get you." After a brief interchange, he finally hung up and announced, "She doesn't want to come. I'm sorry; I guess I better go home. I don't want to leave her alone. Stevie, I'm sorry, but I guess you and the guys will have to play the pipes without me."

Luis found Katie in her lab, seated in front of one of her laptop computers, working on an art program while she munched on soda bread and sipped red wine.

"What are you doing? This is more important than a family celebration?" he asked, sounding annoyed and looking at the full-screen image of a cartoon figure she had drawn. "Everyone was wondering why you weren't there."

"I doubt that." She zeroed in on the image's face. She concentrated on one of the figure's conical teeth and reshaped it to be larger and more rectangular in shape. "What do you think?" she asked Luis for his opinion.

"About drinking while you're pregnant or about you shunning the family?" He asked, sounding annoyed.

"Never mind. With that attitude, I don't want your opinion. I think this is pretty good," she said as she viewed a three-dimensional animation of the computer figure. "I think I'll make the hair a little longer." She proceeded to do just that. "And a tad darker." She clicked the mouse a few times. "There. That's perfect. Now, what's your problem?"

"My problem? I don't have a problem, Katie. What the hell are you doing?"

"I was creating, Luis."

"It's St. Patrick's Day, Katie. St. Patrick's Day is family day. And I'm supposed to be performing with the rest of the guys."

"So who's stopping you? Want some soda bread and a little vino?"

"You shouldn't be drinking alcohol."

"It's just a little vino, Luis. It's the lesser of two evils, you know. If I take my medication, there's a chance the kid will be born dead or with a brain deformity. Either way, the little bastard is screwed. I have to celebrate St. Pat's one way or the other. I can't go to Emily's Hope because

Mommy is annoyed with me. She has every right to be annoyed, you know. I've been a pill. Have some bread. See, I'm celebrating."

"Katie, you're drunk. Come on. Get up," he said, helping her out of her seat. "We're going upstairs so you can flush the vino out of your system."

"Flush the vino, Luis," she replied, not being very steady on her feet. "You know, that's counterproductive, Luis. You're spoiling a good drunk."

* * *

On March 22, Luis took the dogs Lolo and Lolita to the vet for their annual checkup. Katie communicated with Ramírez and her other engineers to see how work was progressing at the company. After checking on Amber and Onyx, she decided to head to Emily's Hope and pay Carolyn a visit. She again hobbled through the woods in order to save on travel time.

When she entered Carolyn's outer office, Annie, the secretary, was working at her computer. A man in full NYPD uniform with three stars on each shoulder was seated opposite Annie's desk, thumbing through a child's book. His NYPD dress hat was on the table next to him.

"Hi, Annie. Is Mom in?" Katie asked Annie while eyeing the man in uniform. He looked up from his book when he heard her voice.

"Hi, Katie," the older woman replied. "Carolyn is on her way. This gentleman is waiting to see her." As if on cue, Carolyn walked in as Katie's eyes made contact with the uniformed man.

"It's you," Katie said, staring at him while leaning on her crutches.

"Yes, it's me," he confirmed as Carolyn witnessed the interaction. Carolyn thought she had seen sparks fly between them. "I see you have new crutches—different, anyway, because the other set was new too."

"Yes, they were new," Katie said while staring at him for a moment. "Mom, this is the man who helped me up the stairs when I was arrested two weeks ago." She turned back to face the uniformed man. "You're a cop."

"Yes, I am," he agreed and smiled. He introduced himself as Chief Larry Quinn and shook hands with Carolyn as he said the obvious: "You must be Mrs. O'Gorman."

"Yes, I am. What brings you here, Chief Quinn?" she asked while lacing her arm in the crook of Katie's elbow.

Chief Quinn noticed the protective motion. "Well, ma'am, at least two things bring me here."

"At least two things," Carolyn repeated. "You drove all the way up here from One Police Plaza for two things. They must be important."

"Yes, ma'am. I believe them to be important, but I'm not from One Police Plaza. I'm assigned to the mayor's office."

"Which is practically across the street from One Police Plaza," Carolyn replied.

"I guess that's one way of looking at it, ma'am."

"Well, let's discuss those two important things in my office," she said while coaxing Katie to follow. "It's approximately a two-hour drive from the mayor's office."

"Yes, ma'am. It is," he agreed while following the two women into the office.

Inside, Carolyn offered Quinn a seat at the conference table. He sat and placed his hat to one side; Katie sat opposite him while Carolyn remained standing.

"Would you care for a cup of coffee, tea, or other refreshment, Chief Quinn? You must be parched after such a long drive."

"No, thank you, ma'am. I'm fine."

Carolyn sat next to Katie. "Is there something I could help you with, Chief Quinn?"

"Well, ma'am, first, I'll inform you that the man who arrested your daughter on Thursday has been suspended without pay, effective immediately."

"Yes, I know that, Chief Quinn." She almost asked him why he didn't share the information via telephone, but she thought better of it. Quinn swallowed uncomfortably.

"Mom, why didn't you tell me?" Katie interjected. "That's great news. Well, it's great for me," she gloated. "I guess it's bad for demented Rafferty. Do you have any more great news, Chief Quinn?"

Quinn looked her in the eye and said, "The department apologizes to you for any discomfort and time wasted as a result of Officer Rafferty's actions. When the investigation is over, his position will most likely be terminated."

"I understand there are numerous complaints against Rafferty," Carolyn commented, "and that's why you were investigating him in the first place. While on duty, he assaulted a young woman in the presence of her two toddler children. That happened on Fifty-ninth Street and Columbus Circle in August of last year."

"You're well-informed, Mrs. O'Gorman, but I can't comment on that, ma'am. That brings me to the second matter, however." There was a pause while Carolyn waited in anticipation of the second matter. "Personally, ma'am, I wondered how a woman with a seemingly innocuous profession like education could gain access to a police database and track down my fingerprints."

"You're misinformed, Chief Quinn," Carolyn objected while Katie's eyes darted to Carolyn's face.

Are you in trouble? Katie thought while looking at Carolyn's cool demeanor.

"How so, Mrs. O'Gorman?" Quinn asked.

"There's nothing innocuous about education, Chief Quinn. On the contrary, we teach our children that education is empowering."

"I stand corrected then. But education is not your first profession."

"No, it isn't. Are you here to interview me, Chief Quinn? Normally, I don't grant interviews."

"No, Mrs. O'Gorman, I'm not here to interview you. I know enough about you already. I'm also not here as an adversary. I was impressed by what you did, and I was curious."

"I didn't do anything impressive, Chief Quinn."

He smiled. "It's been a pleasure meeting you, Mrs. O'Gorman. Please try not to impress me again. We have two things in common: we both know the law, and I understand why you did what you say you didn't do. An eagle needs to protect its hatchling, but be wary of the hunter." He rose to his feet.

"We both read *National Geographic*," Carolyn concluded.

"Apparently, we do."

"Have you any daughters, Chief?"

"As a matter of fact, I do. I have two daughters, eight and twelve. You probably knew that too."

"Maybe. Your wife and you must worry about them all the time."

"Yes, we do." He shifted uncomfortably from one leg to the other and changed the subject. "Have a nice day, ma'am. Mrs. O'Gorman, Dr. O'Gorman. If you ladies are ever in the Park Row area, perhaps you can join me for a cup of coffee. My office is on the first floor, but you probably already know that, Mrs. O'Gorman." He handed each of them his card and reached for his hat.

"Chief Quinn," Katie said, "thank you for your help last Thursday."

"It was my pleasure, Dr. O'Gorman. If I can be of any further assistance, please feel free to call me; NYPD is here to serve. Unlike Officer Rafferty, most of us have manners. Our motto is courtesy and respect."

"It's a shame you're not a member of the Westchester PD. You could have had a shorter trip," Katie commented.

"Well, NYPD does service Westchester County from time to time, especially after 9-11. We've responded to several of your emergency calls."

"NYPD services Westchester this far north?" Katie inquired. "If my memory is correct, I've seen a few of your patrol cars in the border communities like Mt. Vernon or South Yonkers, but I haven't seen you this far north until today."

"Our special services units are available whenever and wherever you need us. Westchester police and EMS have also crossed into New York City borders from time to time. As brothers and sisters in uniform, we help each other."

"That's interesting," Katie commented while subconsciously twirling her hair with one hand and resting her other arm on the back of her chair.

"Well, I'd better be going," Quinn commented as he shifted his weight from one leg to the other and interpreted Katie's actions. "It was nice to see you again, Dr. O'Gorman. Pleasure to meet you, Mrs. O'Gorman." Carolyn rose to see him out.

After Quinn left, Katie said, "Way to go, Mom. I can't believe you hacked into NYPD computers without a warrant."

Carolyn glared at her and walked to her desk. As she sat in her chair, she asked Katie, "And what were your goo-goo eyes all about?"

Katie shook her head in negation. "Mom, you're imagining things."

"I'd better be. You're expecting a child, and that man is divorced."

"How do you know that?"

"I just know; that's all you need to know." Carolyn had no evidence of her suspicions, but judging from Quinn's body language she believed she was correct.

"Well, if he's divorced, he's fair game."

"There are reasons why men divorce, and none of them are any good—trust me. Whatever happened in the first marriage is bound to happen in the second and third. I see that happen with the women here all the time. Each successive wife thinks she can reform the man or be better and more attractive to him than the previous Mrs. Clueless. I expect better of you."

"You always expect better of me. Mom, did it ever occur to you that I'm human? I feel the same desires as any other human being, and I'm not perfect. I'm allowed to make mistakes."

"No one is perfect, Katie, but this is not the time to make mistakes."

"Don't worry; I'm not going to make any. I see attractive men all the time. I can look."

"Make sure that's all you do."

"Mom, I don't get you. When Luis looks at another woman, you defend him. It's perfectly all right. I sit across from this guy Quinn, and in your mind I'm jumping into bed with him. What's your hang-up? I'm never going to see that guy again."

"From your mouth to God's ears. He drove all the way up here to say something he could have said over the phone. He came in full uniform to impress someone. Trust me—he didn't drive up here and get all dressed up for me. He's not concerned about someone looking at his fingerprints. That's a matter of public record. 'Dr. O'Gorman, the department apologizes to you for any discomfort it may have caused you.' Oh, please. He could have sent you a letter. He's very much interested in you. He drove all the way from Park Row because he has the hots and he'll come looking for you again. Maybe unmarried pregnant women turn him on."

"Mom, you're paranoid. He came to see you. He couldn't have known I was going to be here, so how could he have come to impress me?"

"Impress the old lady, and then impress her young daughter," Carolyn responded as Katie shook her head. Carolyn continued with a few observations. "He made a few mistakes, however." Katie twitched an eyebrow as if to say, "Name them," and Carolyn continued. "First, he came in here dressed like a penguin. As I said, he could have called. Secondly, his eyes and body language gave him away. He struggled to keep his eyes off you. Third, he ticked me off by trying to inform me he was in control and therefore had the upper hand. Evidently, he doesn't realize I wasn't born yesterday. I'm old enough to have changed his diapers while I read Supreme Court dissents. However, he's too old for you. He must be ten years your senior."

"If he's that old, you couldn't have been reading Supreme Court dissents while changing his diaper. You're simply exaggerating because you obviously don't like him."

"The man is an arrogant fool who thinks he's smart. As Momma Ellen says, 'Don't ever delude yourself into believing you're smarter because there will always be someone who can crush you with one knowing look.'"

Katie smiled and asked, "Are you smarter, Mommy?"

"I'm not smarter than many, Katie, but I'm smarter than that arrogant fool."

"If he annoys you that much, maybe I should have coffee with him. Do you think he's a player, Mom?" she teased Carolyn.

"Shut up, Katie," she said with a smile and changed the subject. "Why are you here? Don't you have work to do?"

Katie smiled and said, "I miss my mommy. I haven't seen you since, what?—Two Sundays ago?"

"Don't remind me. If I hadn't been standing in front of the church, I would have wrung your neck."

"There you go making idle threats again, Mom. You're incapable of violence, and you know it. Actually, I came to chat and bring you this." She reached into her jacket pocket and presented Carolyn with a security badge.

Carolyn took the badge and examined it. With a trace of amusement, she said, "Badge 1152. This has been missing for years." She shook her head. "You stole this from my safe. What else have you stolen?"

"How do you know I didn't find it? I could have found it."

"But you didn't; you stole it. What else have you stolen?"

Katie shrugged and shook her head. "I can't recall. Maybe that's all."

"I doubt it," Carolyn replied. "I hope you haven't done anything stupid with it."

Katie shrugged, considering that she had impersonated a police officer and surmised that Carolyn would blow her top. "Nah," she said. "Why is it badge 1152? You don't have eleven hundred and fifty two security guards working for you."

"Well, at the time it seemed silly to start with a single unit number. So we started with number 1130 and used only even numbers. This badge goes back many years. You were probably seven at the time. How does a seven-year-old become adept at breaking into a safe?"

"Maybe the safe wasn't locked and your back was turned. Which reminds me, did Kieran help you hack into the NYPD computer?"

"I didn't hack into a computer, Katie. That's illegal. Chief Quinn was trying to impress you. I'm not an idiot."

"I didn't say you are. Anyway, I think Kieran broke into my computers again. When I checked the duty list on Thursday, a few of my engineers were listed as not having an assignment, it's what I call idling. It turns out they weren't idling. I think Kieran changed the information."

"Then I suggest you talk to him. You can handle your own problems."

"This is one for the books. Are you finally admitting that I'm old enough to make my own decisions? Gee, thanks, Mom. In your eyes, I'm finally over twenty-one."

"No need to get sarcastic about it, honey. And don't start celebrating yet," she said while thinking of the conversation she had with Luis on Sunday afternoon. "I reserve the right to change my mind. It's hard to change old habits; I need a withdrawal period."

"Mom, how long do you need? I'm twenty-five. Twenty-five and pregnant."

"Being pregnant doesn't mean you've acquired wisdom. It could mean you lack it," she said matter-of-factly.

"Was I supposed to wait until I turn thirty to have a child?"

"No, honey. I'm glad you're pregnant. Having a child is a wonderful experience. Sometimes difficult, but wonderful. And I'll be a grandmother. I like that too." She sighed. "Time marches on; I remember when I first saw you. You were tiny—probably malnourished. Now you're a woman. But you're still my baby," she said, feeling a bit melancholy and overprotective. She wondered if this was the time to bring up what she had learned from Luis, and she shook it out of her mind. Katie was speaking with her, actually communicating with her, and this could be the wrong time. Yet she desperately wanted to alert her to the potential dangers ahead. Katie was pregnant and she had not taken her antipsychotic medication for at least four months now. According to Luis, Katie had spoken to Rina twice that week, and Rina alleged that Carolyn had given her Katie's phone number at work, which was no true. Rina was a major part of Katie's problem and Carolyn hoped her daughter would break ties with her. Again, she shook it out of her mind as Katie responded to her comment.

"Thanks, Mom. I'd better be heading back home. Luis took my dogs to the vet, and he should be home soon."

"Did you walk here?"

"Yes, I cut through the woods."

"Why? What if you had stumbled and gotten hurt? Katie, please don't do that. You get me nervous, honey. Next time, call me or call a cab. Come, I'll drive you home. Promise me you won't cut through the woods again," she said, and Katie sighed. "Promise me, Katie."

"I promise, Mom," she said halfheartedly.

"Say it and mean it, honey."

"I promise. Really, I promise."

"You need to mean it because now your actions impact two, not one. If you put yourself at risk, you put the baby at risk. The first trimester is the most vulnerable."

"I know that, Mom. Besides, nothing is going to happen."

"You always say that. Considering the misadventures you've had in the past few days, I wouldn't be that sure. Don't push it, okay?"

"Yes, Mom," she replied.

Carolyn drove her home, and they sat in the car for a while. "Do you want me to stay with you until Luis gets home, Katie?"

"I'll be okay, Mom. You can go back to work. Thanks for the ride, and I'm sorry about what I did two Sundays ago. You know, I believe I'm thinking a whole lot clearer these past few days. You may think I don't hear you, but I do. I've put you through the mill, and you've been very patient with me. Thank you."

"You're welcome, honey."

"Let me finish while I'm still thinking clearly. I thought about what you said. You said you'll always be with me and that I'll never be alone. However, I know that isn't possible. Eventually, one day, I could be all alone." A tear trickled down her cheek, and she wiped it away with her bare hand. "Kieran is still a child, and he should be your primary concern, not me. And Mommy, I'm sorry I haven't been nice to him. He's a good kid—I know that. Sometimes my head doesn't work right, and I don't mean to do the things I do, but I do." Another tear rolled down her face, and again she wiped it away. "They say you always hurt the ones you love, but that cliché isn't totally true. It should be, 'You always hurt the ones who love you.' If you didn't love me, you wouldn't hurt because what the hell do we care what people we don't love do or don't do? I know you love me. You tell me all the time, but I can't feel it; it's not your fault. It's me; it's like trying to pick up water with my fingers. It's almost the same with Luis. He loves me, but I can't feel the love. I can't reach it. It's there, but I can't touch it; it eludes me, Mommy, and I'm frightened. So, you see? You can't always be with me because I'm already alone. Do you know what drew me to Luis? The first day I saw him, he cried my pain. Do you remember that day?"

"Yes, I remember," she said sadly as she remembered Luis as a five-year-old child crying in Sean's arms. The pink birthmark on the child's neck had turned crimson as he sobbed uncontrollably.

"Well, I was already alone," Katie continued to say. "I had been alone for a long time, and I was sad all the way down to my gut, and that day Luis cried my pain of loneliness and abandonment. With each wail, I felt a connection, but it didn't last long. Sometimes I think I have that connection, I think I feel a catharsis, and I'm able to touch the love, but in the end it's an illusion. I can't feel it; I can't really touch it. I'm just a cold, hollow human being. For this I'm sorry, Mommy, because you deserve better than me. Luis deserves better. I know it."

Carolyn reached out and touched Katie's hand. "Katie, honey, what makes you think that you aren't better? Baby, I wouldn't trade you for anyone else; I love all my children. At times, you've been a challenge, but I love you all the more because, despite the pain, you sparkle."

"You were upset with me during the opening ceremony at Emily's Hope; you said that I didn't understand what it means to lose a child. You're wrong, Mommy; you are so wrong. I lost me a long time ago, and I can't find me, no matter how hard I try. I died when I was two, or maybe even one; I died because I was alone, and no one cared. I've been trying to find me, Mommy, but I can't; I just can't. That child is gone. How do you grow, and become a woman, if the child was never there?"

"Oh, my darling Katie," Carolyn said as her own tears flowed and she caressed Katie's shoulder. "You're here, baby. Pull back your armour and expose your loving heart; I see it, and I see my loving child."

"Huh, what love, Mom? I didn't get pregnant because I love Luis. God knows I've tried and I tell him I love him, but I don't believe it's true. I became pregnant because I've heard about that fetal imprint. Maybe it can help me make the connection and become a better human being. I know that's a tall order to place on an unborn baby's shoulders. And it's wrong for me to do that, but I don't know what else to do. I need to be a whole person, Mommy. I can't find the other part of me. I'm sorry. I'm so sorry because you've invested so much in me, and I've failed you."

Carolyn looked at her silently, but she felt profoundly sad because of what she had just heard. When she knew Katie had nothing further to say, Carolyn responded, "You haven't failed me, Katie. Over the years you have brought me great happiness. You filled a tall order for me as well. Before I met you, I had lost two children, Seán Patrick and Harold Ignatius. You helped to fill that hole in my heart. But most importantly, I fell in love with a beautiful little angel."

"There's nothing angelic about me, Mom."

"You're wrong, honey. You can't be held accountable for actions you can't control and for developing a shield to protect yourself. And you don't need to rely on this unborn baby to make you whole. You need to concentrate on who you are and love yourself for it. When the baby comes, he or she will be your love's overflowing fountain."

"Part of me is William Lyman," Katie said, thinking of her biological father.

"No, honey. You're wrong about that. He lost the right to be a part of you the day he decided to hurt you. He most definitely lost any hold the day he decided to extricate himself from your life and leave you for dead. You were the lone living shoot of a dying plant. Momma, Papa, Daddy, and I pruned you. We planted you in fertile soil to allow you to live and to bring me the pleasure of enjoying your beautiful soul. You have blossomed for me numerous times, honey. Don't sell yourself short. You love more than you know. The fact that you get jealous is an indication of that. You've been jealous of Kieran for most of his life. You don't need to be. I guarantee that I love you. My love for Stevie and Kieran doesn't lessen my love for you. I know you love Luis because you can't stand for other women to look at him. You don't need to keep him on a tight rein. His heart belongs to you."

Katie wiped her eyes with the back of her hand. "It's been an eternity, Mommy. How can I succeed at feeling whole? God doesn't hear me. I've asked numerous times, and He continues to ignore me. I can't be real. He isn't real either. I'm keeping you too long," she said suddenly, changing the subject. "You need to get back to work." She opened the car door.

"I can't go and leave you feeling like this."

"I'm fine, Mom. I was just rambling. Please go." She stepped out of the car and balanced herself on her crutches. "Luis will be home soon."

Carolyn watched her as she walked toward the house deck and hobbled up the stairs one step at a time. Carolyn shut off the car's ignition and got out of the car. She caught up with Katie, who had reached the landing and was fumbling through her purse for her house keys.

"I see you're not leaving," Katie observed.

"No, I'll wait until Luis returns. Let's talk."

"What do you want me to say? I've said enough already." She found her keys and looked at her mother.

"Anything you want. What's new at work?" Carolyn asked.

"Nothing much. Oh, one of my engineers came by yesterday because I want to build a wall around twenty square acres of this property." She unlocked the door and pushed it open. "It'll keep the bears out. Unfortunately, it won't be ready for your anniversary dinner on the twenty-sixth. This is quite a month—four celebrations in one month."

"Yes, it is," Carolyn agreed, following Katie into the kitchen.

"Why did you decide to marry in March, Mom? March is a crazy month. Sometimes nice, sometimes cold and dreary. Why weren't you a June bride?"

Carolyn smiled. "Is that what you want to talk about?"

"You said 'anything.'"

"Indeed I did. You're always so literal, Katie."

"Are you trying to avoid the question, Mom?"

"No." Carolyn flailed her arms defensively. "Of course not. I got married in March because I was so much in love that I couldn't wait until June after Mattie popped the question."

"How does it feel to be so much in love, Mommy? I need to know."

Suddenly Carolyn became starry-eyed, and then she focused on Katie again. "Well," she said, "at times, it almost feels like you're ill. I certainly was lovesick. You get feverish and nearly lethargic. You can't sleep; food doesn't matter much. You daydream a lot. In my case, I couldn't get Matthew out of my mind. No matter what I tried to do, thoughts of him kept coming up. He was one of the reasons I couldn't sleep. I would lie in bed and think of him."

"Do you still think of him that way?"

"Sometimes, but much of that has waned. Now I have other things on my mind. It isn't that I love him less. Now, I remember how much I loved him and still love him. I'm very much aware that I am definitely a part of him. Now I worry about him as much as I worry about my children, especially during and after the cancer. That's the other side of love; I want my children and my husband to be safe. I worry that something might go wrong. I want time to stand still and keep you all with me always." She purposely did not mention that she worried Matthew would follow his male DNA and pursue other women. She recalled a conversation she'd had with Momma Ellen years ago when Momma had said that all men strayed because of their male DNA. Carolyn had called Momma a liar and didn't believe Matthew to be capable of such a thing. She thought of Matthew cheating on her and shook the thought out of her mind, almost saying no out loud.

Then Katie said something Carolyn did not expect. "I don't want to be a constant disappointment to you, Mommy."

"Why would you think that, Katie?" she asked with alarm. "You're not a disappointment to me. On the contrary, I'm very proud of you."

"At times, you've said I disappointed you."

"Honey, I cannot think of saying any such thing. When have I said anything that hurtful? You might have disappointed me by not completing a chore or by doing something irrational, but you are not a disappointment. That's a totally different matter. Don't confuse an act with a human trait. You have never been a disappointment. That's not what defines you."

Katie paused before she responded. She was listening for something. Finally, she asked, "Do you hear that?"

Onyx and Amber were barking out of control. Both women paused. Katie opened the kitchen door, and they could hear the barking louder. They started to walk down the steps in response to the persistent noise.

"Did they spot another bear?" Carolyn asked as they reached the bottom.

Thinking a bear might be the cause of the barking, she ordered Katie into the car. She planned to drive down to Luis's house to check. If it was a bear, they would remain in the car and call 911. As Carolyn walked to the driver's side and Katie started to open the passenger door, someone grabbed the back of Katie's hair and just as quickly slapped her to the ground.

"Katie!" Carolyn yelled as she ran to Katie's defense.

Carolyn immediately recognized Arturo Santillana. Before she took a single step, however, Santillana kicked Katie in the side as he said, "That's what you deserve for getting into my business, bitch."

Carolyn had no fighting skills, but she jumped onto Santillana's back and held onto his neck with the crook of her arms. He slammed her back against the car door with all the force he could muster. Carolyn felt the impact and released her hold on him. She fell off his back and onto the ground.

He headed back to Katie and said, "I'll kill you, bitch. I've been watching you."

He kicked her again as Onyx and Amber came racing up the path. Amber got to him first, throwing him to the ground as she pounced on him. He screamed as the dog started to maul his head. Onyx bit into his leg.

Carolyn dragged herself to Katie's side while Katie writhed in pain from the blows she had received. "Oh God, Katie," Carolyn said.

At that moment Luis arrived with Lolo and Lolita. He brought the car to a screeching stop near the house deck and ran out. As he sprinted toward his dogs, the car continued to roll until it was stopped by the housedeck's beam; he had forgotten to set the vehicle on "Park". He called off the dogs. Santillana was a bloody mess; he lay moaning. Luis ran to Katie's side as he pulled out his cell phone and dialed 911. He gave Katie and Carolyn cursory checkups as he held the phone to his ear.

"Can you talk?" he asked Carolyn.

"Yes."

He handed her the phone and said, "Speak to 911."

Onyx and Amber were pacing back and forth around the two women. Luis walked back to Santillana and pulled him up by the collar with his right hand and planted a fist in his face with his other hand. "That's for hitting women, you son of a bitch." Santillana groaned. Luis hit him again and let him flop to the ground. His hand drenched with blood, he walked back to Katie's side.

"Let the dogs out," Katie said, grimacing, for Lolo and Lolita were barking inside the car.

The dogs soon joined the other two that were milling around Carolyn and Katie.

Twenty

◇◇◇

1992

Katie was in the children's psychiatric wing of the Westchester County hospital fulfilling her mandatory seventy-two-hour observation stay. She had finished a board game with the other children and was now flipping through TV channels in her room while Camille read and graded her students' reports and Katie's nurse read a magazine.

"This is a total bore and a waste of time, Aunt Camille. I could have been out playing soccer or something."

Camille looked up from her papers. "Nothing interesting on TV, Katie?"

"If you consider listening to thirty-second sound bites about all the woes of the world interesting, then there's plenty of that boring shit. What are you doing?"

"I'm grading my students' essays."

"How many students do you have?"

"Only thirty-four."

"Only thirty-four? That's a lot."

"It's not a lot in New York City. Thirty-four is one class. I'm a supervisor, so I teach only one class. Most teachers teach five classes."

"We don't have that many kids in my classes. The most we ever had was maybe twelve or fifteen at St. Lucy's.

At Emily's Hope, we had like half of that. If you like, I can help you grade some of those papers. What's the topic?"

"The topic is 'What would you do to improve the environment?' but I think I better grade them myself."

"I know how to grade papers. When my teachers grade my reports, they make comments in the margin. I can do that; trust me. Give me one."

"Knowing a student's potential is one variable to consider when you grade a paper. Thank you for offering to help, but you don't know my students. I need to do this myself. Why don't you read or do the crossword in today's paper?"

"Can I go to your school?"

"You need to be a New York City resident to attend my school."

"I don't mean attend. Can you take me for a visit? You visited EH with your friends. I should visit your school."

"So, you want to do research. I guess you can visit, but you'll have to clear it with Carolyn first. You'll also need to behave."

"I behave well most of the time. I get into trouble because people provoke me."

"Have you ever thought of being diplomatic or turning the other cheek for the sake of peace?"

"That's no fun. Besides, if you smack someone because he's a jerk, he won't do it again."

"If life were that simple, we wouldn't have any war."

"It's not as simple as turning the other cheek, either," Katie said, thinking of her biological mother, Emily. "That's what my mother used to do, and what did it get her? She's pushing daisies at Hope of Heaven Cemetery. She should have killed him, you know. I would have. I was too little then, and I guess the thought never entered my mind. But now I know better. She never helped me, either. I would have waited until he was asleep, and I would have plunged a knife right in his throat. He would have suffocated, just like that," she said as she snapped her fingers.

"Do you still remember what happened, Katie? You were only four years old."

"I remember. You say four years old as if it were a point in time. It wasn't a point, you know. It was more like a thread. I was four, I was three, I was two, and so on."

"And you can remember that far back?"

"I've been remembering a lot lately," Katie said, and then she suddenly changed the subject. "Do you know that Rina's father molested Rina when she was little?"

"Yes, you have told me that before. You also said they deported him."

"Yes, they did, but they should have killed him, you know. People who get deported come back. It isn't safe, you know."

"What isn't safe, Katie?

"Nothing is safe. I'll bet you he comes back. They always do. Rina now lives in a building with her mother. She doesn't live in a house like me."

"Have you ever been to her building?"

"No, Mommy would never let me do that. I know about the building because Rina told me."

"What does Rina's father look like?"

"He's tall, about Daddy's size. He has dark hair and blue eyes. He has a small brown mole right here," she said, pointing to the bottom of her left eye socket, "and a small scar above his left eye, like someone hit him with something and it never healed properly."

"When did you see him?"

"He came to school one time when Rina and I were playing tennis."

"How did he get past security?"

"I don't know."

"Did you tell Carolyn or anyone?"

"I told Mommy. She told me she would talk to security about it. He never came again. Just that one time. I think I'll get a snack. Do you want something, Aunt Camille?"

"Katie, they're serving dinner. I can hear the attendants pushing the carts, and I can smell food. Be patient, and you'll soon be eating."

"What about you. Aren't you hungry?"

"I'll wait until I get home, honey. Perhaps you can get something for Mrs. Agbenya," she said, referring to and looking at the nurse who had been quietly listening to their conversation as she pretended to read a magazine.

"I'm okay," the nurse responded. "I brought my own food from home."

"So can I go to your school, Aunt Camille?"

"I have to ask Carolyn. If she says it's okay, I'll see what I can do. I also have to get an okay from my supervisor."

"I thought you were a supervisor."

"Every supervisor has a supervisor. Even the president of the United States has to answer to someone."

"Are you coming back tomorrow?"

"I believe your grandmother will be here tomorrow."

"Which one?"

"Margaret."

"Well, can you call Mom now and ask her if I can go?"

"Carolyn is probably getting dinner ready now, Katie. I'll call her when I get home."

"Then you'll be getting dinner. She said I could call if I need anything. Then you can tell her I've behaved myself. I did behave, didn't I?"

"You're not behaving when you insist on having things your way. You're not autonomous, Katie. You need to respect other people's time and space. I'll call your mother when I get home."

"Well, I'll call her now. Mom said I could call."

"Katie, I know you do things by design. I can play that game too. If you call Carolyn now, you're not coming to my school." Katie glared at Camille and pouted. Camille added, "Someday you will understand that the world does not revolve around you, Katie. You will hopefully understand that your mother works very hard and she can't spend every moment of the day catering to your every whim. I suggest you read something while you wait for your dinner to arrive. I'm grading my students' essays."

"Mom doesn't have to work. Why do you and Mommy work if you don't have to? You probably have more money than the queen of England."

Camille wanted to say, "It's no one's business what we do." Instead, she said, "I don't think that's true, and I don't see how it matters. When you grow up, you'll understand why. Read a book, Katie." She wanted to say, "You're getting on my nerves." When she noticed Katie was still pouting, she added, "Katie, life isn't always going to be gray, honey. Try to think positively, and your light will shine through."

Katie glared at her and then she suddenly pointed her index fingers at Camille and released a couple of pretend shots in her direction. After blowing pretend smoke from her fingertips, she started singing "This Little Light of

Mine." She walked past Camille and out the door. Katie's nurse followed her out. About three seconds later, Katie paused and peeked back in. "Are you going to be here when I get back?" she asked, and she walked off again without waiting for a reply. She continued singing as she walked down the hall.

* * *

Later that evening, Carolyn was lying on the sofa in the family room, blowing bubbles for baby Kieran, who was propped up against her raised thighs as she held him in place with one hand and held the bubble hoop with the other. Pacifier in his mouth, Kieran watched the bubbles float up. He smiled with delight while the drool slid down the sides of his mouth and the pacifier fell out, landing between his legs. At that moment, Stevie walked in with a sealed jar in his hands.

"Mommy," he said, presenting the jar, "look what I have."

"Give me a moment, honey," Carolyn said. "I have to close the soap solution so it won't spill."

"I can do that," he said, taking the soap bottle and handing Carolyn his jar. "Look at what I found; I'm going to use them for my science project. Do you think I'll get an A?"

Carolyn examined the contents of the jar and said, "Jesus, Mary, and Joseph. Holy Mother of God! Where did you get these, honey?"

"I got them in the backyard. There's a whole mess of those insects near the shed."

"Honey, these are not insects. It's autumn. There are no insects around when the weather is this cool. Go get your father and tell him to come here quickly." As Stevie left the room, she said, "Oh dear God, what now?" She placed the jar on the floor and sat up. Looking up to heaven, she spoke to God and said, "This isn't funny, you know. You're supposed to protect children and fools."

About two minutes later, Matthew and Stevie walked into the room. "What's up?" Matthew asked. "I was just setting the table."

"Dinner will have to wait, Mattie. Stevie has been collecting ticks from the backyard."

"He's been collecting what? You're kidding, right?"

"No," she said, handing him the jar. As Matthew studied its contents, Carolyn added, "Get the tweezers. Please take him to the bathroom. Strip his clothes off. Check every crevice and orifice of his little body; check his head and fingernails. I hope he didn't bring any of them into the house. I'll put his clothes, shoes, and jacket in a trash bag; I'm not taking any chances. Make sure he showers, and check him again. I'm calling the doctor, the gardener, and the exterminator. Then we need to sit down and teach him the difference between an insect and an arachnid and define 'disease carriers' for him. That, Stevie," she said, looking at the befuddled Stevie, "will be your science lesson for today. The joy never ends."

Later that evening, Stevie sat at the table. He had a unique way of eating. He held a meatball between two fingers as he cut into it with the fork. He then used his fingers to gather a few strands of spaghetti squash onto his fork. He chose the right piece of broccoli and skewered it on the fork's tips. Finally, he placed the meat on top of the sauce-covered squash. As he completed the task, he responded to Matthew's question by saying, "I understand, Daddy."

"Then repeat it for me, son," Matthew insisted as Carolyn, who sat next to Kieran's basinet, observed Stevie's table manners and quietly listened to their conversation.

"Ticks are not insects," Stevie replied. "They're tiny spiders that can cause many diseases. But Daddy, what am I going to do for my science project?"

"You still have a science project. I'll fill the jar with alcohol and seal the ticks inside."

"You mean you're going to kill them."

"Yes, I'm going to kill them. That way, they can't escape and hurt anybody. You can write a report about what you learned today about ticks, and you have a science project. It's that easy."

"That's not easy. I don't like to write."

"What did you plan to do for your science project?"

"I was going to take the jar to school."

"And?" Matthew asked in anticipation.

"Nothing," Stevie replied. "I was going to take the jar and show it to Sister Agnes."

"Did you hear that, Honey-Lyn?" Matthew asked, and Carolyn nodded in affirmation as she chewed her food. Matthew turned to Stevie and asked, "And you thought you were going to get an A for that?"

"Yes. I worked hard to get those ticks."

"Not as hard as I worked checking your hair for them. It wasn't easy to pull that one out from behind your ear," he replied, alluding to the tick he had placed in a jar for the doctor to analyze. "I think we should shave all your hair off to make sure you don't have any more of them hiding in there."

"You mean I'm going to be bald?" Stevie asked, and Matthew nodded in affirmation. "No," Stevie protested and turned to his mother for support. "Mommy, are you going to let Daddy shave my head?"

"Daddy is teasing, honey. You know he likes to tease. He's not going to shave your head. However, you are going to read about ticks, and you are going to write a report."

"Sister Agnes didn't say anything about a report," he protested.

"Well, Mrs. O'Gorman said you have to write a report," she replied.

"Who's Mrs. O'Gorman?" Stevie asked, and Matthew spat out his drink as he burst into laughter. "I don't have a teacher named Mrs. O'Gorman."

"Stevie," Matthew interjected as he wiped his face, "your mother's name is Mrs. Carolyn O'Gorman." He proceeded to clean the areas where he had spewed his milk.

"I know that, but she confused me! Why didn't you say that you want me to write a report?" Stevie asked Carolyn. "You're Mommy."

"Yes, I am. I am also Mrs. Carolyn Josephine O'Gorman. I'd like you to meet your father, Mr. Matthew Thomas O'Gorman."

"I told you I know that, but you confuse me. My name is Stevie Christopher O'Gorman."

"It's a pleasure to meet you, Mr. Stevie Christopher O'Gorman," Carolyn said with amusement. "Mr. O'Gorman, when is your science project due?"

"You mean me?" he asked, and he suddenly realized that she was indeed addressing him. "Oh," he said, giggling, and then he added, "You did it again. Stop confusing me. I don't know when the project is due, Mrs. O'Gorman. Now I can confuse you."

Carolyn chuckled. "Well, when you finish eating, Mr. O'Gorman, go upstairs, slip an encyclopedia or a *National Geographic* disk into your computer, and read about ticks. I'll be up to check on you. Tomorrow, I'll help you write a report."

"That's a lot of work for a few little ticks," he protested as he scooped more spaghetti squash onto his fork.

"Stevie, don't eat with your fingers, honey," Carolyn said. "You're getting spaghetti sauce all over yourself."

"It's easier this way. This stuff is tricky."

"Well, use your napkin, honey. Wash up when you finish so you won't smell of spaghetti sauce."

"I already took a shower. How clean do you want me to be?"

"Clean enough to keep the giant cockroaches away from your bed tonight," Matthew teased him. "They come in the middle of the night and steal little people who smell of garlic. They carry you back to their nest and start licking your face and hands before they eat you all up."

As Stevie's eyes opened as wide as saucers, Carolyn admonished Matthew, "Stop lying to him, Mattie. You're worse than a little child; grow up."

Stevie laughed. "Mommy told you to grow up, Daddy. Maybe the giant roaches will carry you away. They'll probably bite your tongue out for lying." He laughed again while Carolyn and Matthew smiled to see him so happy. If he hadn't been across the table from her, Carolyn thought, she would have gathered her son in her arms and loved him to death for being so cute and gullible.

As if on cue, Matthew, who was seated between the two, got up and enveloped his son from behind. "I'll eat you first," he said as he feigned nibbling Stevie's face.

He paused and said, "Actually, you taste more like sweet cherry pie to me. I love pie," and he continued to nibble Stevie's face. The child laughed, partly at the playfulness and partly because of the itchy stubble from Matthew's evening shadow.

After dinner, Stevie went to read about ticks, and Carolyn said to Matthew, "I'm having him tested for learning disabilities. He seems to behave like a much younger child. I also believe he has a problem with context. 'Who's Mrs. O'Gorman?' he asked."

"Are you saying he's slow?" Matthew asked as if to say, "I told you so."

She glared at him. "I'm not saying any such thing. He's just a child. Maybe it's a phase. He could also be as immature as his father."

"Yeah, Mommy is always the last to know or to admit something is wrong. Trust me—it can't be normal for someone to be that clueless. However, if you think he's as immature as his father, give him back to the milkman."

Carolyn glared at him again. "That isn't funny, Matthew. Seriously, though, he's just a kid. Maybe he wasn't focused on the conversation. But I'll have him tested, and if you're right, we'll deal with it. Either way, it's not a laughing matter."

"I'm not laughing. I'm simply making an observation and reminding you that I tried to warn you earlier. You didn't want to accept it."

"If you felt so strongly about something being wrong, why didn't you arrange to have him tested? I'm not the only parent here, you know."

"True, but that kind of stuff is a woman's responsibility. I wouldn't dream of overriding or undermining you."

"Why? Are you afraid I'll crush you?"

"No, I'm not afraid of you," he teased.

"Well, you better be. First, I'll start by making one thing clear. It's our equal responsibility to see to our children's needs and welfare. If you remember that, you don't have to worry about anything else."

"On the contrary. From experience, the first thing I need to remember is not to cross you or Momma, so I always have something to worry about."

"So you are afraid."

"Maybe." He shrugged and added, "A little. I think I'll go upstairs and help Stevie. That way, I won't get into trouble. Sometimes I feel like I can't win."

"Come here," she said, pulling on his collar. She kissed him affectionately. When they parted, she said, "To me, you're always a winner. Sometimes you behave childishly, but you're always a winner." Matthew smiled, and she added, "Thank you."

"For what?" he asked.

"If you don't know, you must be a little slow," she teased. "Now go upstairs and bond with a father's son, and let me clean up in here."

"Can a son's father bond with a son's mother a little longer?" he asked and wrapped his arms around her. Hands on her buttocks, he pulled her closer.

"That depends on how well he bonds with the son," she said, fighting the desire to give in.

"I prefer unconditional love."

"I'd like to sprout wings and fly, but it's not going to happen," she said, belying her desire to give in to him. "However, you already stole my heart. Isn't that unconditional enough? If you're patient, we can continue this discussion later. It's getting dangerously warm in here."

"How warm?" he asked, rubbing himself against her. "We can lock ourselves in the laundry room."

"Oh, God, Mattie," she said in response to his actions. "We can't do this now. We just ate. What if Stevie walks in on us?"

"That could be a damper. But look on the bright side. He'll have a new science project."

She smiled and said, "Behave yourself and go upstairs. We'll both have to suck this up until later."

"How much later?"

"You know the drill—until they're asleep."

Matthew sighed with disappointment. "Little Mattie is not happy, you know. He was all set to go. In your next life, I hope you come back as a lecher so you can understand how I feel right now."

Carolyn laughed and patted his butt. "Get some ice," she suggested and released herself from his grip. "Let me tell you something. If you're implying that your desire is greater than mine, you have nothing to base it on."

"I got all knotted up, woman. Little Mattie is set to go."

"But you have no basis for comparison. You were never a woman, man."

"How would you know that? I was probably a very hot chick in my last life."

"Mattie, if you're all knotted up, as you put it, get the ice and let me get some work done. We'll continue this dis-cussion later." Disappointed, Matthew took a deep breath and started to walk away. "Mattie, don't fill Stevie's head with any more tall tales about giant cockroaches or any other monster. I don't want him waking me up with a nightmare in the middle of the night."

He smiled impishly and said, "I'll try."

"God, you can be a pest sometimes."

"But you still love me."

"Get upstairs and behave yourself."

After checking on Kieran, Carolyn called Katie, who had also finished dinner at the hospital.

"I'm okay, Mommy," she said in response to Carolyn's inquiry. "At what time are you coming tomorrow?"

"I don't know, Katie. I need to report to work to see if I need to do anything, and I want to go to St. Lucy's to pick up any assignments you may need to do. I also have to take Stevie to the doctor for a checkup."

"What's wrong with Stevie?"

"Nothing, I hope. He got into a ticks' nest, so I want to make sure he'll be okay. What have you been up to?"

"I watched one of those ancient classic movies for about two minutes; it was all I could stand, Mom. I'm going nuts in here. Maybe you can bring me a 'heater' so I can spring out of this joint," Katie said, tossing in slang terms, Cagney-style.

"I don't subscribe to violence, honey. What else have you done?"

"I'm finishing my arts and crafts project. It's a vinyl wallet; I'll give it to Stevie when I get out. When are you coming, Mom?"

"I hope to be there by lunchtime. Daddy will be there in the morning. Do you need anything, honey?"

"I want to go home, Mom. This place is getting on my nerves."

"I know, honey. Just hang in there; you'll be home soon. Is Aunt Camille still there?"

"Yes, but she's getting ready to go. She's taking me to visit her school in the Bronx."

"That's nice, honey. I have to go now, Katie. Please tell Aunt Camille I said thank you, and I'll speak to her later."

"Okay, Mommy. Bye." Katie hung up and turned to Camille. "Aunt Camille, Mommy said thank you, and she'll speak to you later. You should go home and get dinner."

"Will you be okay, Katie?"

"Yes, Aunt Camille. Thank you for coming, and thanks for the books. I apologize for my bad behavior. You're right—I'll try to be more respectful of other people's time and space. Besides, I'll be going home soon. I think being in here has me frazzled."

"Well, try to stay active, Katie, and the time will appear to go faster. I'll see you in a couple of days." She kissed Katie on the cheek. She then turned to the nurse and shook her hand. "It was nice meeting you, Mrs. Agbenya."

"Likewise, Mrs. O'Gorman. Good night. Safe home, ma'am." Mrs. Agbenya said as Camille admired the charming rhythm of her speech. Perhaps it was an accent from northwest Africa, but she wasn't sure.

As soon as Camille left, Katie grabbed one of the activity books and a pen Camille had given her and started to work on a crossword puzzle. One of the entry words was "light," and she started singing, "Light the footpath of my life and guide me gently away from strife," as Mrs. Agbenya smiled, surmising that Katie's song choice meant she was perhaps a fine or dedicated Christian child.

Later that evening, Carolyn received a phone call.

"Mrs. O'Gorman, this is Sara Agbenya, Katie's nurse. You asked me to call if something important transpired, ma'am."

"Is my daughter okay?" Carolyn asked with concern.

"Oh, yes, ma'am. Your daughter is fine. I am home now. The new nurse is with her, and I apologize if it is too late to bother you, ma'am."

"It's fine," Carolyn assured her. "What is the purpose of your call, Mrs. Agbenya?"

"Well, you see, ma'am, I always take a meal with me to work because I do not like to leave a patient alone while she is under my care. Please forgive me, ma'am, but when I came home and took my things out of the bag, I found a wallet inside the bag, ma'am. It is not my wallet. I do not carry a wallet with me for obvious reasons, ma'am. This is the wallet of your sister-in-law. I can assure you, ma'am, I did not take your sister-in-law's wallet. I would not do such a thing, ma'am. Everything is in here. I did not touch anything." Mrs. Agbenya was talking very quickly in the accented rhythm of her native tongue.

Carolyn sensed her nervousness and sympathized with her apologetic tone. "I am so sorry, Mrs. Agbenya. I know you didn't steal the wallet." An involuntary sigh of disappointment expelled from her lips as she spoke.

When Carolyn shared the information with Camille, Camille said, "Katie never seizes to astonish me. As punishment, I could deny her the anticipated trip to my school."

"That's not enough. She totally upset poor Mrs. Agbenya. Sometimes I think Katie thrives on being punished. Don't take her to school, but I have to think of something that can make a dent. At the moment, I don't know what to do. I'll have to talk to Mattie. Maybe he can come up with something."

By the time Katie was released from the hospital, Carolyn had dealt with the backyard tick infestation by calling in the gardener and the exterminator. The only thing that needed to be done was to clean and paint Matthew's shed before winter set in. That weekend, Matthew and Carolyn sat in the yard, keeping an eye on all three children while Katie removed everything from the shed. The only time Matthew gave her a helping hand was when an item was too high above her head for her to safely remove or too heavy for her to handle by herself.

"I guess you won't be stealing any more wallets anytime soon," he said, rubbing it in as Katie struggled with a sledgehammer. She rested the heavy hammer's head on the ground as she paused to give him a dirty look for a few seconds. Then she continued to move the sledgehammer by dragging it across the ground. "This is the fun part," Matthew said. "You still have to scrape the old paint, plaster, and slap on a new coat. Then you can move everything back. I'll be enjoying a slice of pie; I love pie."

Katie thought she had heard those stupid words about him loving pie too many times before. She displayed her displeasure with a second glare and a huff.

"Matthew," Carolyn admonished, "stop tormenting her. Behave yourself."

"Heckling is part of the fun, Honey-Lyn."

"The purpose of this is to teach her a lesson—not for you to have fun. So, save it for a hockey game." Carolyn then turned her attention to Katie, who had just finished dragging the sledgehammer across the lawn.

"I hate Aunt Camille," she said as she let the hammer's long handle drop next to the pile of tools that were accumulating on the lawn.

Carolyn was within earshot of what she had said, and she replied, "You're placing your anger where it doesn't belong, Katie."

"Well, it's her fault I have to do all this shit! I hate her!"

"Come here," Carolyn said, reaching out to her from her lawn chair. She invited the child to sit in a chair next to her. Katie sucked her teeth as she reluctantly sat down, and Carolyn enumerated a few matters for her.

"Aunt Camille is not responsible for your recent predicament, Katie. You are the author of this situation. When you ended up in the hospital, Aunt Camille was very concerned about you; she took time out of her busy schedule to visit you. She also brought you a few books. How did you repay her for her kindness?" Katie rubbed her arm and looked sullenly at Carolyn, who didn't wait for a reply. "You took her wallet and inconvenienced her and Mrs. Agbenya. Mrs. Agbenya was very upset and embarrassed by your actions. That evening, Aunt Camille couldn't purchase the gas she needed for her car. The following day, she had to take a cab to and from work because she didn't have her license to drive. She normally drops Courtney off at a friend's house when she leaves for work at six in the morning, which she was unable to do because you apparently thought it was funny to take her wallet."

"I didn't think it was funny."

"Then what were you thinking?"

Katie shrugged her shoulders and said, "I don't know."

"Well, the next time, think about your actions and their consequences. Aunt Camille tried to do you a favor, and you betrayed her, Katie. You're not doing yourself or her any good by hating her as you muttered a moment ago. What's the point of that?"

"I don't know," she said, pouting.

"Well, think about that too. Hating doesn't help. On the contrary, while you hate, you only harm yourself. Remember what Dr. Lieberman said. How do you feel when you hate? Do you feel good?"

"I don't know," Katie replied, shrugging her shoulders again and rubbing her arm as she looked away.

"Well, I'm willing to bet you don't feel well. On the contrary, you stew in your own bitter juices. The other person doesn't know you hate him or her. Aunt Camille doesn't feel your hate, but I guarantee that you feel it. It's not in Camille's nature to be that primitive. Hate churns your stomach and makes you feel as if you were going to pop like a volcano. It doesn't bother the other person until it makes you strike out at him or her. Then it takes two victims—you and her. In the meantime, it can torment you. The word itself is negatively charged. Don't let it get a hold of you, honey."

Katie looked down. "May I go now?" she asked.

"Yes, you may go now," Carolyn replied. As Katie got to her feet again, she added, "Katie."

"Yes, Mom?"

"When you're done here, we need to talk."

Katie sighed and said with annoyance, "Fine; we'll talk."

Katie eventually received the dreaded lecture, and she listened impatiently as Carolyn related another boring anecdote. A few days later, Camille informed Carolyn that she had received a nice letter of apology from Katie, where Katie expressed contrition. Katie also reminisced about Camille's kindness toward her. Carolyn was surprised and hopeful when she learned about the letter's contents.

* * *

The week after young Katie was released from the hospital, she stood at the top of the stairs and overheard Momma say that she hoped the judge would not rule in Lyman's favor and grant him the request to appeal. The other members of the O'Gorman family who were present concurred and went on to comment that Lyman's parents had been pushing hard for that appeal.

Carolyn commented, "I don't understand how his mother could have raised such a monster and be totally in denial about his guilt. After all, the evidence was and is quite clear."

That night, young Katie tossed and turned in her sleep. Troubling images sped through her synapses like a speeding train out of control, sending sparks of electricity that lit the inner darkness of her mind. The train screeched. There was red all over the canvas of young Katie's mind. It was blood. The blood cascaded through dark cisterns and bubbled in a fiery hell. She screamed.

When she opened her eyes, she was still screaming and Matthew was trying to calm her down. "It's okay, princess," he whispered in her ear. "You were having a bad dream." He held her and caressed her slender, trembling back. "It's okay, baby. Daddy's here."

"I'm okay, Daddy," she said.

"Are you sure?" he asked as he felt her shaking.

"Yes," Katie said and looked at the LED clock on her nightstand. Matthew relaxed his hold on her. "I'm late for school. Why didn't anyone wake me? Where's Mommy?"

"It's only ten thirty, Katie," he replied as he released her. "It's still Wednesday. Mommy is downstairs tidying up for the night."

"I thought I had slept the whole night. I'm not sleepy anymore."

"What was the nightmare about?"

She thought a moment. "There was a lot of loud noise. Maybe someone was yelling, or machine guns were firing. Then there was a lot of blood. It's like when you travel through those water pipes in an amusement park, but it was blood instead of water. I was burning, Daddy. I think I saw hell."

"That's definitely a nightmare, princess. Put it out of your head."

"Daddy, if William Lyman wins his appeal, will I have to be his daughter again?"

"How do you know about that?"

"I hear things. I know he and his parents have been seeking an appeal for over a year now. Mommy calls him a monster. She also calls him a bastard. What does 'jawl' mean? That's what Momma calls him." She had pronounced *diabhal* phonetically, as she had heard it from Momma's lips.

"I don't know," Matthew replied. "I don't speak Irish."

"I think it means 'devil.'"

"You're learning Irish?"

"No, I'll stick to Russian; I've learned a lot of Russian from Rina. I can figure out some things when Momma and Mommy speak because they switch back and forth between Irish and English. They have a new language; I guess you can call it Engrish or Ireng. Anyway, will I have to live with the devil?"

"No, that will never happen."

"How can you be so sure?"

"Your mother will never allow that to happen and neither will I. You're my princess. Besides, Lyman has been petitioning for a retrial for some time now. I doubt he'll get anywhere with that. Come downstairs. I'll nuke some frozen cherries in the microwave for you. That and a glass of almond milk should put you back out like a light."

"I don't know if I want to go out like a light again. I don't want another nightmare."

"We will have none of that. I'll sit and guide you through meditation before you doze off. It's something Mommy taught me. It really works."

"We do meditation at EH."

"Well, I know a few meditation exercises that are excellent for sweet dreams. Let's go downstairs, princess."

Katie ate the cherries, drank the almond milk, and did breathing and meditation exercises. However, her mind couldn't calm down. She futilely tried to visualize pleasant images and relax her mind and body, but the screeching and sparks she had heard and seen in her dream kept interfering. Matthew placed a meditation disk in her CD player and suggested she concentrate on it. Eventually, she decided to do the breathing exercises alone; Matthew dimmed the lights and left. Katie spent the night tossing and turning as numerous thoughts raced through her young mind.

One day after school, Rina informed her that her father, Pinkhosof, had returned. He forced her to have sex with him. The two young girls walked and talked, confiding in each other.

"Are people capable of loving one another?" Katie asked. "Is there really such a thing as love?"

"I love my mother and my aunt," Rina responded. "Love is like a warm baby blanket. It feels nice; it's soft; it smells nice. It makes you feel good."

"I don't know if I've ever felt like that," Katie responded. "Sometimes I think I remember something like that. But sometimes, when Mommy hugs me, it feels like she's hugging me through a box; I can't feel the hug. I know she loves me, but I can't feel it. I want to love her, but I can't. Does that sound weird?"

"No, it's not weird. I understand what you're saying."

"You're the only one who understands me. My father Matthew, he's mean sometimes."

"Not as mean as my father. Why do you sometimes refer to your father as your father Matthew?"

"That's so I won't confuse him with my real father. My real father may soon get released from prison. He has appealed his case."

"Do you remember him, Katie?"

"I don't know," she said with a shrug, brushing a thin, dry leaf off her sleeve. "He killed my mother—my real mother. I remember that. I can't picture him, but I think I know his eyes. Mommy says that if they turn him loose, she doesn't want him coming after me."

"Do you think he would?"

"I don't know. I hope not. I guess it wouldn't be good."

"Do you like your new parents, Katie?"

"I guess so, but they don't have time for me. I guess I'm just the adopted kid. That baby sure cries a lot. One of these days, I'm going to smash his head in."

"Katie, he's just a baby. Maybe he has colic."

"Well, it's annoying."

"My mother said that I used to cry a lot as a little baby because I had colic. My father would get upset and beat her because she couldn't keep me quiet. Now he beats and rapes me."

"How did he get back here after they deported him?"

"I don't know."

A couple of days later, Rina's father raped her again. The following day, the two girls sat under a willow tree that was losing its leaves to the autumn chill as Rina recounted her ordeal. Katie looked at her solemnly as a tear rolled down Rina's cheek.

"Do you think he'll hurt you again?" Katie asked.

"My mother chased him out of the house. She beat him with a pan and called the police. Hopefully, he'll stay away, but I can't be sure."

"God should strike him dead," Katie replied vehemently.

That night, Rina called and informed her that she had seen her father in front of the deli on her way home. He was there with friends while he drank a few beers and vodka. Rina sounded worried, and Katie tried to reassure her. The next morning, Carolyn dropped Katie off in front of the school and drove away. As soon as Carolyn's car was out of sight, Katie and Rina walked off in the opposite direction; they didn't go to school. The two girls sat vigil across the street from the deli where Rina had seen her father. It was almost noon, and they were getting hungry. Katie volunteered to enter the deli for food. As she was exiting the store with lunch, she ran into Pinkhosof.

"I know you," she said in Russian to Pinkhosof after she got over the initial shock. "You're Rina's father. She and I go to school together, and she's told me a lot about you."

Hands in his pockets, Pinkhosof looked down on the sweet young girl. "What has my daughter told you?"

Katie responded, "She said you like little girls."

"You speak good Russian," he said. "Where did you learn to speak Russian?"

"In school and from Rina. Do you like me, Mr. Pinkhosof?"

"I don't know you, little girl."

"I know you, Mr. Pinkhosof. I can like you. I play grown-up games. Maybe you would like to play with me."

Pinkhosof eyed the child suspiciously and said, "You talk like a woman."

"I am a woman. I can prove it to you." Pinkhosof sneered, and Katie continued, "If you want to play with me, meet me at the park in an hour. Follow the north entrance path about six hundred meters, and I'll be waiting for you."

Pinkhosof looked at the girl dressed in the tartan blue parochial school skirt. He suspected that under her blouse she had lovely pink nipples or her breasts were probably starting to form and he licked his lips. She looked delicious, and he found it difficult to keep his eyes off her. Her skirt was above her knees, displaying slender, firm legs. He continued to watch her as she crossed the street and entered a building across the way. Katie felt his eyes on her back. She finally entered the building and breathed a sigh of relief.

"Are you okay?" Rina asked.

"I'm fine, I think," Katie said as she took a deep breath. "I spoke to him."

"Yes, I saw. Did he fall for it?" Rina asked, inquiring about the plan the two girls had forged earlier.

"I think he did. God, I'm nervous. I need to calm down. We need to get to the park. I think he'll meet me there."

As soon as the girls arrived at a preplanned spot Katie had in mind, they dropped their knapsacks and got to work. It was a fair-sized clearing a few meters away from the footpath. At fifteen minutes to the designated hour, Katie sat on a tree stump near the footpath and waited for Pinkhosof. A few minutes later, the man came walking toward her. She rose from the stump and met him halfway. She slipped her hand into his and led him into the clearing. They arrived at a blanket that the girls had spread out earlier. Katie invited him to sit. She took his hand and placed it on her pelvis and invited him to fondle her under her skirt. She then urged him to unbuckle his pants, and she started to fondle him. As she gazed into his eyes, he reminded her of her biological father, William Lyman. She saw Lyman's eyes in his as she massaged his foreskin with both hands.

"You know a lot for a little girl," he said.

"I can undress now if you like," she said while still fondling the foreskin on his penis and getting close enough to almost kiss him. She was nauseated as she visualized him as the *diabhal*, the devil. It was at that instant that Rina plunged an ice pick into the back of Pinkhosof's neck as Katie simultaneously ruptured his testicles with the tightest squeeze she could muster. A scream was caught in Pinkhosof's throat. He remained in an upright position as Rina unsuccessfully struggled to pull the ice pick out of his neck. She had to wiggle it back and forth to finally free it. She then plunged it into the small of his back and struggled with it again until she dislodged it a second time.

Rina and Katie wasted no time in completing their task. They repositioned Pinkhosof in the middle of the blanket and folded his legs and arms over his torso. They wrapped the blanket around him. Rina poured nail polish remover over the blanket, and Katie lit it with a disposable lighter. They watched long enough to confirm ignition. Later that afternoon, en route to her apartment, Rina discarded the ice pick into a sewer drain.

Promptly at three that afternoon, Carolyn picked Katie up in front of the school. Baby Kieran was asleep in his car seat in the back, and Stevie, who got out earlier from school, was strapped in next to him. Katie got into the passenger seat and strapped herself in.

"Did you have a good day, Katie?" Carolyn asked as she steered the car back to Emily's Hope.

"It was okay."

"Where's your book bag?"

Katie almost panicked. She had forgotten her school bag. "I lost it," she said calmly.

"That's the third book bag you've lost so far. Since you didn't go to school today, I guess you left it wherever you went; I bet you had a blast," Carolyn said.

Katie's blood ran cold, but she concealed the discomfort. She wondered how Carolyn had found out about her cutting school, and she concluded the woman had spied on her. The truth was that the mother superior at St. Lucy's ran a tight ship, similar to Dr. Holder's ship at Emily's Hope; parents were immediately called when a child was absent. Katie had not counted on that. She held her breath and waited for the other shoe to drop.

"Care to tell me where you've been all day?" Katie pouted and turned her head toward the passenger window while Carolyn continued speaking. "So the cat has your tongue. Well, I'm glad you're okay. I guess I was a fool to be concerned about your welfare. From now on,

I'll be marching you into your class each morning. If I have to, I'll hire a bodyguard to sit next to you." Katie turned to face Carolyn and glared at her. Keeping her eyes on the road, Carolyn said, "Let me guess; you're giving me the evil eye. But trust me—heed my words—if I can't trust you to do the right thing, I will watch every step you take. It's not a threat, Katie—it's a promise." Then Carolyn caught a glimpse of Katie's tartan skirt and hair. They had bits of dry leaves. "You've either been in the park or rolling in hay. Which is it?" Katie kept her silence.

* * *

That night, a rain storm moved through. The strong autumn wind shook tree branches and scattered their leaves. Lightning lit up the sky and thunder roared. Young Katie spent the night tossing and turning while Rina, her mother, and her aunt went to the scene of the crime and managed to move the victim's body. Katie got out of bed and sought shelter in her closet. She wept and trembled until she finally fell asleep, huddled in the corner.

Katie continued to experience restless nights and troubled dreams. The crime replayed as an endless loop in her mind. One night, before three in the morning, she felt wet. Thinking she had wet herself, something she had not done in years, she walked into the bathroom and turned on the lights. Her pajama pants were stained with blood. Katie started to screech. Carolyn rushed into the room and turned up the light. Matthew followed behind her. Katie was huddled on the floor, screaming and trembling. Carolyn noticed the stained pajamas. She bent down to comfort Katie, but the child lifted her forearms defensively;

then she started to push herself away from Carolyn and further into the bathroom.

"Go away," she screamed repeatedly as she continued to tremble. Then she started to claw at the air. "Stop it; stop it. Leave me alone." Her eyes were open, but glassy. She wasn't focusing on anyone. The screaming and defensive actions continued. Then she lay in a supine position, and her entire body heaved as Carolyn and Matthew looked on.

Afraid she might hurt herself, Matthew picked her up. She continued to squirm in his grip. "Dial 911," he ordered Carolyn as he walked past her. He sat with Katie on the edge of the bed, struggling with her as she clawed at him. "God, help my baby," he cried. "Stop it now. This isn't right."

"My husband is trying to calm her down," Carolyn was yelling into the phone. The yelling wasn't simply due to the noise in the room; Carolyn was very nervous.

Sleepy-eyed Stevie walked in. He watched fearfully as Katie squirmed and screamed in Matthew's arms. He inched his way toward his mother, pulled at her nightgown and rested his head above her waist, seeking comfort from the frightening scene.

Carolyn continued to yell the address into the phone. Then she said, "She was released from the psychiatric division over a week ago. She was fine until now." Then she asked, "How soon," and concluded with, "Thank you." When she clicked the phone off, she discovered she couldn't move because Stevie was still gripping her nightgown tightly. Carolyn caressed her son's head. "It's okay, Stevie," she comforted him. Stevie couldn't take his eyes off Katie. Luckily, Katie started to calm down. Then she appeared to pass out in Matthew's arms. The struggling had caused her to hemorrhage further; Matthew's pajamas were also stained.

Stevie noticed the blood and asked, "Is Katie going to die?" Both his voice and eyes were filled with fear.

"No, honey," Carolyn replied. "She'll be okay. Daddy and I are going to clean her up. Could you go into my room and watch the baby while he sleeps? Let me know if he wakes up, okay?"

"Okay, Mommy." He finally released his grip.

When Stevie left, Matthew said, "She really cut herself badly this time. This isn't good."

"She hasn't cut herself, Mattie. Our little Katie has reached puberty."

The revelation shook him. He started to stutter. "I...I thought...well, I'm wrong." His face flushed. Then he said, "I thought you had the grown-up talk with Katie. Why would she freak out like this?"

"Katie and I spoke about all of that, Mattie. Obviously, the process of menstruation isn't the only factor at play here. Something else caused her to freak out. You said she was inquiring about William Lyman. Maybe she experienced a flashback. Take off her PJs while I get some pads and fresh clothes. The ambulance will be here soon."

"This is woman's work, Honey-Lyn. I can't do this."

"Close your eyes then. Sometimes you don't have a choice."

"I thought girls as active as Katie menstruated later in life," Matthew commented.

"Well, apparently the research is flawed, or she's an exception to the rule. Remove her PJs. I'll be right back."

A repeat performance of Katie's psychiatric stay in the hospital netted her an almost three-week stay during the second time around. She spent the first two days in a fetal position, apparently unaware that anyone was around, and was placed on intravenous feeding. At Dr. Lieberman's insistence, Carolyn agreed to the administration of a low-dose antipsychotic drug. By the third day, Katie started to show slight signs of improvement. By the fourth day, she could walk outside her room with some assistance. By the fifth day, she was behaving more like herself. She sat and chatted with her visitors and behaved courteously.

Noting Katie's minor alertness, Doctor Lieberman started the therapy discussions with her. During one such session with Carolyn present, Katie disclosed her dark secret. She wept openly as she mentioned every detail of her crime. Carolyn was stunned into disbelief and fear for her daughter. Matthew and Sean investigated the alleged scene of the crime. Moist autumn leaves covered the ground. They found Katie's seared bookbag at the site, but no sign of a body.

"Did you talk to Rina?" Katie asked. "I think she moved the body."

"That's impossible," Carolyn said as she looked worriedly at Matthew.

Sean scratched the back of his head and said, "She must have stashed it in her knapsack." He and Matthew chuckled.

"Papa, you're not funny," Katie challenged him.

"Katie, none of this makes any sense," Carolyn said. "You evidently had a night terror."

"I didn't imagine this, Mommy. I know the difference between reality and imagination. Am I going to jail?"

"Don't jump to any conclusions, Katie. There's no corpse."

"Maybe they'll send you and Rina to a home for juvenile delinquents," Sean added. "Don't worry; we'll visit you. I'll put a file in the cake for you. With any luck, you can file your way out by Christmas. Wrong and strong I always say, wrong and strong, Katie my love."

"Papa," Carolyn said while placing her hands on Katie's ears, "please don't say that to her again. She's not responsible for her actions. My baby cannot be wrong and strong if she doesn't understand what she's doing." She gazed up toward the ceiling. "God, please take this cross from her. It isn't fair; she's just a child." She pursed her lips and the tears welled in her eyes.

"With all do respect, Carolyn," Sean said, "Katie knows the difference between right and wrong, so she needs to be reminded and face the consequences of her actions. We didn't find a corpse, but she has been explicit. In the event that she did kill some poor unsuspecting devil, we need to look into the matter. Better that she faces the consequences sooner than later. We need to turn the crime scene over to professionals."

"You're going to have me arrested, Papa?"

"We need to do what's right, Katie my love. You'll talk to the police."

"Papa," Carolyn protested, "let's not go overboard here."

"It's time Katie's held responsible for her actions, Carolyn. You and Dr. Lieberman can continue to hold her hand and not hold her accountable for anything. I, on the other hand, believe she needs a wake-up call. We need to consult the police. If necessary, I'll also hire investigators to sift through all those leaves. That's all Mattie and I saw, a bunch of wet leaves."

* * *

By the middle of the third week, Matthew stood against a wall, holding a cup of coffee and feeling very relieved to see Katie interacting with the other children as he watched her play a board game. When he had first arrived with her at the hospital because of this recent episode, he had spent much of the morning standing by her bed for hours, watching every breath she took. He thought he could will her to get better. Now she was sitting and chatting with the other kids as they took turns trying to form words on the game board. He wondered about the alleged corpus delicti when he spotted Momma Ellen walking toward him and instinctively pushed himself away from the wall where he had been resting his back. Momma stopped to chat briefly with Katie and Matthew waited patiently, knowing she would soon come to speak with him.

"How are you holding up, Mattie?" she inquired when she stood facing him.

"Fine. I'm glad to see her behaving normally and up and about, Momma. I hope this doesn't happen again."

"So do I, Mattie. Why don't you go home and get some rest?"

"I'll stay a while longer. She's happy, Momma."

Ellen turned to look at the smiling Katie and said, "Yes, she is."

Katie was well enough to return home. A week later, one of Katie's schoolmates cut her off while she waited on line for lunch. It had happened twice before. Each time, the young lady spotted a friend on line and took advantage of the situation by cutting in front of the other girls. During the second incident, the intruder was a few people ahead of Katie. The other students were as irate as Katie, and protested. The offender ignored them and continued to talk to her accomplice. Katie got off the line and verbally confronted the interloper. Verbal protest was the closest she could come to turning the other cheek. The antagonist claimed she had been there before and her companion had been holding her place in line. Katie walked away in disgust and resumed her place on line. On the third day, the adversary's friend was standing in front of Katie while Katie wrote in the small notebook that Dr. Lieberman had given her and the cheat cut the line again. Once more, she and Katie exchanged words. The opponent had her say, turned her back in a huff, and pushed her long hair back over her shoulder. The hair hit Katie in the face. Katie grit her teeth, her brow furrowed, and her eyes narrowed; it was obvious to her that diplomacy did not work. Without giving it any further thought, her writing arm appeared to involuntary draw itself back for momentum, and retaliated by plunging Katie's stick pen into the young woman's buttocks. Mother Superior was not pleased. Katie was expelled, and the O'Gormans faced a legal lawsuit, which they settled out of court. Carolyn and Matthew decided it was best to keep Katie at Emily's Hope until they believed she was mature and stable enough to attend college. That did not happen for two more years.

Twenty-One

◇◆◇

March 15, 2005

When Katie and Carolyn were attacked by Arturo Santillana, Chief Lawrence Quinn was the second responder to the scene. He had driven to Emily's Hope that morning for his meeting with Carolyn and was still in Westchester County at the time. The paramedics, followed later by the Westchester police and state troopers, were the first to arrive at the scene of the crime. They were attending to Arturo and Katie when Chief Quinn pulled up in his NYC police car. He spoke with Carolyn first.

"Mrs. O'Gorman, I heard the call on my radio and thought I could be of some help." He noticed the paramedic conferring with a plainclothesman near another woman who was on the ground. "Is that your daughter, Dr. O'Gorman?" he inquired about Katie.

"Yes," Carolyn replied. "The assailant caught her off guard." She pointed in Arturo's direction.

Quinn walked over to Katie and asked, "Are you okay?" Katie was holding an ice pack against her left jaw. She looked both annoyed and distressed. She knew the encounter with Santillana could mean the loss of her baby. Luis and Carolyn were thinking and worrying about the same possibility.

"I believe it's obvious she's not okay," Carolyn interjected.

The paramedic walked off to get a gurney, and Luis squatted next to Katie. He held her hand and kissed her on the forehead while Quinn spoke to Carolyn. "Dr. O'Gorman has had a rough week," he said.

"Yes, she has," Carolyn agreed. Defensively, she added, "Chief Quinn, I'd like you to meet my godson and future son-in-law, Dr. Luis López."

Quinn raised one eyebrow and looked at Luis as they each extended a hand in greeting. Quinn noticed a twitch in Luis's face as he said, "Pleasure to meet you, Dr. López. I didn't know Dr. O'Gorman was engaged to be married. Are you a physician?"

"Yes, I am. Could you excuse us please?" Luis said, getting up. The paramedic was returning with the gurney. "We need to get Katie on the gurney."

"Can I be of any help?"

"I think we can handle it," Luis replied. "Thank you."

"Perhaps you should start back for city hall, Chief Quinn. It's a long ride. Your wife must be worried," Carolyn said, believing he was divorced and hoping to see how he would react.

"I doubt it," he replied, looking uncomfortable. "You're right, however. I should start back. I see I'm not needed here." He turned to Katie. "Dr. O'Gorman, I hope you will mend soon."

"Thank you, Chief Quinn."

"If I may, I'll call you in a few days to see how you're doing."

"That's very thoughtful," Katie replied. "Have a safe drive home."

After he walked away, Carolyn asked, "How did he get past the gate?" She was referring to the computer-activated gate that led from the road into Katie's and Luis's property.

"Perhaps the same way Santillana got in; I'll have to look into it. I hope Kieran didn't mess with anything," Katie said.

"He wouldn't do anything as irresponsible as that," Carolyn replied, "but I'll ask him."

"Who was that guy?" Luis asked when he returned.

"Someone who is obviously interested in our Katie."

"Mom, don't jump to conclusions." She then addressed Luis. "He's the man who helped me up the subway steps when I was unjustly arrested."

"I believe he's being more than just a good Samaritan," Carolyn concluded.

* * *

At the hospital, Katie received the bad news they had all anticipated. She had lost the baby. At first, Luis held her as she wept with despair. Later, he stood sorrowfully by her gurney as she balanced herself on one leg and dressed to go home.

Carolyn silently helped her daughter with her jacket. She straightened Katie's collar and instinctively hugged her. "I'm sorry, baby," she said.

Katie did not reply and the three returned home in silence.

Matthew wasn't home. He would most likely return late from work; it wasn't the first time. Carolyn was upset and fuming. She went upstairs and allowed a hot shower to loosen the muscles in her back. They were tight for various reasons, including the blow she had received when Santillana threw her against the car's side door, and her back shattered the door's window. When she fell to the ground, she had felt a jarring pain in her buttocks that traveled up her spine. Fortunately, at the hospital the doctor concluded she had not broken or dislocated anything. She was bruised, but not as bruised as poor Katie, she thought. She worried about how this was going to affect her daughter mentally, and she was annoyed with Matthew for being late and not being there when she needed him. She came out of the bathroom, wearing a robe, and headed down to the laundry room. She had a desire to hit something, throw something, or kill Santillana. He had murdered Katie's baby. However, Carolyn knew that in New York State, murdering a fetus was not considered a crime. He would probably be charged with assault and battery combined with trespassing. The mere thought of less egregious charges caused her to thrust dirty laundry into the washer and shove it tightly into its spin barrel. She picked up the heavy bottle of detergent and thrust it against a wall. The bottle spewed blue detergent all over the place. It was on her hair, face, and robe. With her back against the dryer, she dropped to the ground and started to cry.

* * *

Luis and Katie quietly took the elevator to the upper floor of her house. They stepped into the bedroom. Katie lay down; Luis sat in a chair. They remained there until the sun went down. Luis stepped outside to check on the dogs. Accompanied by the animals, he walked up and down the lake, as if he were serving sentry duty for the night. Later, he examined the car that had been stopped by the house deck's post because he had failed to put the car's gear in park and remove the keys when he returned home from the veterinary clinic. The post was fine, but the car's fender was dented. He moved the car into the garage. As he was about to close the garage entrance, he noticed a car pulling up. It was Sean and Ellen.

"We spoke with Carolyn, Luis," Momma said as she stepped out of the sedan. "How are you and Katie holding up, dear?" She handed him two large bags. Judging from the smell, Luis concluded it was cooked food.

"I'm okay, Momma—just angry. Katie is upstairs in her room. You can go up through the garage. I'll tell Papa to bring the car inside."

"Fine, why don't you and Sean set up for dinner? Kate and I will be right down."

Ellen followed Luis's advice and walked into the garage to get to the upstairs bedrooms. As she walked past one of the downstairs rooms, she could hear and feel the exhaust fans sucking air out of the garage and passing it into the side vents. It was part of the home's security system. That particular unit only came on if there was the slightest trace of carbon monoxide in the garage. Ellen turned back and informed Luis. He checked the CO monitor, and it indicated the air was normal.

"Well," he said, "Katie and Carolyn suspect someone messed with the security system. Apparently, the CO vents are also out of whack. I'll call Matthew. Maybe he can check it out tomorrow. In the meantime, we'll leave the vents on; better safe than sorry."

Ellen went up to see Katie. Upstairs, Katie was in a fetal position, staring into the darkness. Ellen walked into the room and asked, "Young Kate, are you asleep?"

"No, Momma," she replied, turning toward the voice and sitting up.

"Have you eaten anything, dear?" Ellen asked as she flipped on the light.

"What's the point?" Katie asked as she squinted.

"Do you plan to stay up here and starve yourself, Kate?" Without waiting for a reply, she added, "Come on, get up, dear. Sean and I brought you some nice hot soup from the diner. We also have roast beef and spuds; join us for dinner. Come on—shake a leg. I will not have you sitting up here wallowing in self-pity." Katie reached for her crutches and got up. Momma said, "You know the old saying: 'When you fall off a horse...'"

"Yeah, yeah. I've been doing that all my life, Momma. There's the other cliché: 'You can't win for losing.' Lately, I've been riding nothing but broncos." She followed Momma out of the room. "It isn't fair, Momma."

"That's the cliché I don't want to hear, young Kate. I'd like you to see this as an opportunity, love."

"Snuffing out the life of a harmless, helpless being is not an opportunity, Momma. It's an abomination. And what were we doing, Momma? We were helping Cheryl and her family. My baby got caught in the crossfire. What did I do to that man, Momma? Nothing. I've been in the crossfire of too many lunatics, and that isn't fair! I don't care what you say. Opportunity, my ass!" She started to follow Momma down the stairs. "That jackass deserves to be skinned alive!"

Momma paused and faced her. "The Lord gave His only begotten Son to save us from our sins, young Kate. It is painful to lose a child, but we need to look beyond that to carry out the Lord's work."

"And what is the Lord's work, Momma? He certainly hasn't been working for me. If He weren't asleep at the helm, He would have burned that bastard's ass a long time ago."

"We work for Him, dear," she replied while looking up into her eyes. "By standing between Cheryl and her ex-husband, we probably saved three lives. We have protected Cheryl, her mother, and her ten-year-old son. Individuals like Santillana will always be among us, young Kate. We battle them any way we can, but we never stoop to their level because we don't want to be as troubled as they are. That's why we try to forgive and move on. We may not succeed, but we must try."

"I'll forgive him after I slash his throat."

"That won't bring back your unborn child, and it will rob me of a granddaughter while you serve your sentence. Sean and I are getting too old to trek back and forth to visit you in prison, dear. Don't be unfair to senior citizens, Kate. And don't break your parents' hearts. Let's have some chicken soup, and we'll continue this conversation later."

They joined Luis and Sean in the kitchen. After saying grace, Katie said, "God did not give His only begotten Son, Momma. I don't understand how I have fallen for that line all these years." She reached for her bowl of soup.

"What are you talking about, Katie?" Sean asked, not realizing that Katie had been following a train of thought.

Ellen attempted to correct Katie and answer Sean's question at the same time by interjecting, "We were speaking of John 3:16 earlier. 'For God so loved the world that He gave His only begotten Son, that whosoever believeth in Him should not perish, but have everlasting life.'"

"That's wrong," Katie objected.

"What do you mean that's wrong, Kate?" Momma challenged.

"How can you not see?" she inquired. "He didn't give Him up. He simply gave Him a temporary change of address on earth, and then He called Him home again. He didn't give Him up. He called Him home. John is wrong!"

"John is wrong," Ellen said to humor her. "If you say so, dear. Drink your soup."

"God didn't lose His Son, but my child was taken for no reason. He was murdered. That bastard! It's unpardonable. Santillana should burn in hell, and I'll fan the embers for him."

Ellen looked at her granddaughter with a mixture of concern and affection as Luis added, "Katie is right. God gave His Son a change of address; he went home. Katie, I don't understand why this happened, and I'm mad too. But I'm trying to take comfort in what I believe. Our son or daughter has also been given a change of address. Our child was also called home. I don't know why. This is incomprehensible. I'm perplexed; I'm trying to make sense of it, but I need to believe what I believe. Can you believe with me?" He placed his left hand over hers.

Katie noticed the bruises on his knuckles and said, "Right now, I don't know what to believe, Luis." Then she added, "You need to put some ice on that."

"I'm okay," he said, withdrawing his hand.

"Kate, dear, drink your soup," Momma reminded her, and Katie obediently scooped up the broth.

"Pass the bread," Sean requested. "Soup always tastes better with some nice Italian bread with plenty of butter. Katie, eat some bread. We'll all think better once we've eaten," he concluded as Luis handed him the bread basket.

"Luis," Momma commented, "it's impossible to make heads or tails of a crazed mind. Santillana is not only deranged, but he is also apparently saturated with hate. You're perplexed because your mind doesn't function that way. That's your blessing. You have a loving heart and an unclouded, pure mind. Don't try to reason this out; you'll never succeed, dear. Look to your blessing, and you will find peace."

"Have you found peace, Momma?" Katie inquired. "William Lyman murdered my mother and destroyed our lives. Have you found peace with that, Momma?"

Momma paused and looked her granddaughter in the eye. She said, "Yes, Kate. I have found peace. Lyman destroyed my life for a while. Then I realized that if I continued to believe that he had destroyed my life, he won. As I stopped allowing his actions to take over my life, I realized how much I've won. I have a wonderful family, health, and peace of mind. He didn't only lose—he's lost. He's damned. I don't know why I'm blessed and he's not. I pray for him, and I will continue to do so. I can be charitable because I'm a winner who is numerously blessed. After the nightmare, I regained a lovely and vibrant granddaughter. I also have Sean and my three sons and a positive nature. I have formed a bond with Carolyn that can never be broken. I still love my Emily, and I rejoice that she has been called home. I believe that her spirit has been instrumental in providing you with a family life that many would envy. I see the positive forces that surround you, and I am grateful for the many angels who are with you. You have your parents, your uncles, your Aunt Camille, Luis, etcetera. You also have Sean and me, dear. Perhaps, you're not yet ready to acknowledge us and your blessings, but you will; I know you will. So yes, I am at peace, young Kate. I'm very much at peace."

Katie took a moment, attempting to process what Momma had said. She couldn't wrap her mind around it. Finally, she asked, "What about you, Papa? Are you at peace?"

Ellen waited for his reply with anticipation because Sean seldom spoke of his feelings in the matter.

"I will always miss my Emily, but I take what I can get. I find peace in my dreams because she often comes to me. At times, I can touch her, but it's not the same. I resent that I no longer hear her voice. However, you don't only look like Emily, you sound like her. You have a combative nature. Emily was sometimes headstrong. That's one reason why I can't understand how that man got the best of her. I've decided not to give Lyman a moment's thought. He's not that important. I focus on the living and not on the living dead. I look at you, my dear Katie, and I know that I still have God's blessing. You have inherited attributes from Emily, and at times you emulate Carolyn's nature. Those are two good gifts."

* * *

When Matthew came home, Carolyn was upstairs banging drawers and doors shut as she angrily tidied up. Stevie and Kieran had given her a wide berth. They stayed inside their rooms playing video games and listening to the occasional *bang* or "Damn it!" They heard Matthew calling her. They heard his footsteps up the stairs. They heard him call out, "I'm sorry, Honey-Lyn. Momma called me and told me what happened. If I had known, I would have come home earlier." The boys heard her yell, "You shouldn't have bothered to come home! You should have stayed wherever the hell you were!" The boys then heard their parents' bedroom door click shut, and they suspected that Matthew was about to be sorry he ever came home. They had never seen or heard Carolyn that angry before, and it frightened them a bit. However, they were also amused because they suspected that Matthew was about to face an execution he didn't deserve. They knew this because behind Carolyn's back they had been conspiring with him and other family members for several weeks.

Matthew placed a sympathetic hand on Carolyn's shoulder. She shrugged him off and told him to leave her alone. He tried to kiss her, and she said, "Don't touch me," between clenched teeth.

"Carolyn, I'm sorry. Honey, you should have called me. I didn't know." She glared at him. He looked lovingly at her. "You have gunk on your face and hair," he said playfully, noticing the dried detergent. He reached out to touch her hair. She pushed past him and started to undress the bed down to the bare mattress.

She tossed a pillow at him. "Maybe you should go downstairs and make yourself comfortable on the sofa."

He looked at her incredulously. "What's wrong with you?"

"There's nothing wrong with me; I'm fine. What the hell's wrong with you?"

"I don't understand," he said, placing the pillow back on the bed. "I suspect this isn't just about what happened today. What's the matter?"

"You weren't here, Matthew. You weren't here! Where the hell were you? Katie lost her baby. Do you know what that feels like? No, you don't know. You couldn't possibly know. You don't even care!"

"I care, Honey-Lyn," he said and started to walk toward her.

She put both her hands up defensively. "Don't touch me. I don't want you to touch me, you lying bastard."

"Carolyn?" He was taken aback by her comment. "You're behaving irrationally. When did I lie to you?"

"I went to your job on Monday. I left Kieran in the car while I went to take you some dinner because you were working late. There was no one around. The business was empty, and the door was locked. I called you on the cell phone. Do you remember?" He looked at her sullenly. "I asked you, 'How much longer will you be at work?' Do you remember that?"

"Yes, I said I'd be another hour or two."

"And you weren't even there. Where were you?"

Matthew gauged the seriousness of Carolyn's emotions and still decided to have some fun at her expense. "I've been working with a few women after hours—three of them are quite young and pretty. But, it's not what you think, Carolyn."

"What am I thinking, Matthew? Today we needed you, and you weren't here. You weren't at work, either. I know because I dialed your landline and the answering machine picked up. Now you tell me you've been working with young women."

He smiled and said, "I know this looks bad, Honey-Lyn, but I have a good alibi. I haven't done anything wrong. I lied about being at work, but I would never do anything to hurt you. I'm sorry I wasn't here." He pointed to the phone. "Dial Felipe's house. I don't want you to get the wrong impression.

He'll vouch for me, I swear. So will Nydia." She stared at him suspiciously. "Go ahead. Dial their number. I'm sorry I wasn't here for you and Katie. If you think I'm having an affair or something like that, you're wrong. I don't do trysts; I would never do anything like that. I love you; I love my family. Besides, who would want me besides you? My testicles have gone south. You said you'd stitch them up for me."

Carolyn slumped onto the side of the bed. She sighed and disagreed. "I never said that. You're the one who brought up the needle and thread. You've put me through all this, and you claim you're innocent."

"It's my constitutional right," he said as he sat next to her. He smiled and said, "I guess that's why you've been coming to bed after I've fallen asleep for the past few nights. I'm innocent until proven guilty. You had a rough day, huh?" He looked into her eyes, and she peered into his as if trying to read something in his gaze. "You still have doubt," he observed.

"Circumstantial," she said, continuing to study him. "Can you blame me?"

"No. Again, I'm sorry. And I do understand about Katie. I'm not a woman, but I do sympathize. I think I know how much it hurts. Today, you relived a part of your history. Your history is my history, Honey-Lyn. Katie could have a tough road ahead; I hope she'll be strong."

"Me too. My mind has been racing. She gave up her medication in anticipation of this pregnancy. Evidently, she wanted a baby that badly. But I don't know. If she had continued with the pregnancy, it could have been a disaster. Now that she lost the baby, it can still be a disaster. See, that's why I needed you here today; I needed a sounding board. And Katie—poor Katie."

He wrapped his arm around her shoulder and held her for a while. Then he said, "Well, I'm here, and Katie and I both have you. Without you, we'd be totally lost, Honey-Lyn." He gazed in her eyes again, and she suddenly felt embarrassed for wrongly accusing him. "What's wrong?" he asked.

"If I'm wrong, I apologize," she replied.

He smiled and felt the urge to say, "Oh, you're wrong all right." Instead, he decided to change the subject. "How's Luis taking this?"

"He didn't say a word all the way home, but I could tell he's as angry as I've been today. I think I frightened the boys; they're hiding in their rooms. I forgot to pick Kieran up at EH; Momma dropped him off. Oh God, Matthew! I don't even know if they've had dinner. What time is it?"

"It's after eight. I'll go check on them. Besides, they know how to take care of themselves. If they haven't eaten, I'll call for Chinese. What do you want?"

"I don't know," she replied as he touched the smudges on her face and hair.

"Get cleaned up while I check with the boys and order something. What's the gunk?"

"It's detergent. It's all over the walls downstairs."

"Is that a new beauty treatment?"

"Very funny."

"Are you going to call Nydia and ask her about me?"

"I'll ask her tomorrow," she said, and Matthew smiled with delight.

"So you still don't trust me."

"If I didn't trust you, I wouldn't be speaking to you right now."

"Well, Nydia isn't going to say much. We have an agreement. I believe I've said too much already. You'll find out the rest on a need-to-know basis."

Carolyn shrugged and said, "Fine." As an afterthought she added, "...a few women and three of them are young and pretty, Matthew?"

"Ravishing, Honey-Lyn," he said as he turned to face her from the threshold.

* * *

Later that night, Luis awakened and did not find Katie in bed. Lolita, who had been in the room with them, instinctively went to the slider and started pawing at it. Luis glanced out. Katie was seated in the balcony, stroking Amber behind the ear. Lolo lay a couple of feet away, perhaps sleeping. Luis pulled the slider door open and stepped into the chilled air while Lolo rose to his feet. Katie turned to look at him and then went back to gazing into the starlit sky.

"Why are you out here? It's freezing."

"I needed to see the stars," Katie replied without facing him. "They're not as bright as I hoped they'd be."

Luis gazed up into the night sky. "It's a clear night, though. How long have you been out here?" He had his arms crossed in front of his chest and was shivering from the cold.

"I don't know."

"You were gurgling in your sleep earlier and cried out like a little girl," Luis said.

"What did I say?"

"You called out, 'Mommy, make him stop.' Then you turned on your side, whimpered, and then you appeared to be fine. I decided not to wake you."

"It's the same old, same old, Luis. I dreamt Carolyn was Emily and she refused to help me when I called. Rina's father, Pinkhosof, was my biological father. Did I tell you that Rina doesn't seem to remember what happened to her father?"

"Yes, you did." Katie felt Luis's warm lips as he kissed her cool cheek. "Why don't you come inside? You're as cold as ice."

She smiled and thought, *If you only knew.* There were times that her soul felt as cold as ice, incapable of loving. However, she also knew that over the years Luis had been a true friend, a caring lover, and a faithfully loving companion. *Do I love you, Luis?* she asked herself. *Or have I just grown comfortable? When we make love, is it love, or is it lust?*

He managed to coax her into the room and she sat near the slider. He draped a blanket over her and sat to face her in the dark.

"Why do you suppose I have such crazy vivid dreams, Luis? I can't seem to escape them? The meditation exercises they taught us at EH don't always work."

"You've always had a very active mind, Katie. You must have a leaky pipe somewhere in there. It's a shame we can't find it and mend it. Maybe your subconscious is trying to tell you something."

"This dream I had tonight, do you suppose my mother allowed my father to hurt me? In this dream, Emily became Carolyn and Carolyn was indifferent to my cries."

"The mind plays all sorts of tricks on us; sometimes dreams are total nonsense. Sometimes they aren't. Only Emily and William know the truth and neither one of them can help you find the answers now. I don't want to malign Emily because she is not here to defend herself. Knowing what I know, I'll defend her."

"Why would you do that?"

"I will do anything if it will help you to stop looking back and start living in the present—looking forward to a fulfilling future. Let's suppose that Emily refused to help you. How and why would a mother reach that point?"

"I've asked myself that countless times, Luis. I understand the battered woman syndrome."

"You have knowledge of it, Katie. I don't think you or I understand it because we haven't lived it. We can't relate to that type of life. I imagine the beatings and control that William inflicted on Emily started long before you were born—perhaps shortly after they married or while they were dating."

"She could have left."

"Not if he managed to physically and emotionally beat the will out of her. Now, imagine that same battered woman, who couldn't care for herself, being repeatedly raped. Drained of all willpower, she gives birth. She falls into postpartum depression. We lost our baby, so we're sort of feeling a type of depression now."

"I suppose it's not of the same magnitude as Emily's."

"I agree. Her magnitude must have been greater. I don't believe either of us could understand how great, but it must have been immensely disabling for her. Katie, please forgive Emily so you can move forward with your life. Forgive Emily and love her for giving you life. Forget Rina; she's been nothing but a bad influence on you. Forget Pinkhosof. Forget William. As Papa said—they're not important. *Tell yourself* they don't exist; they're not real, and believe it."

In the darkness of the room, Katie looked at him pensively. "You know, Luis. You're right. I should be nicer to you. Let's go to bed," she said reaching out for his hand. "I promise I won't rape you."

Twenty-Two

◇◇◇

Autumn 1992

When life became less hectic, Carolyn decided to take Patrick up on his invitation and accompany him while he visited Mrs. Shultz, the ailing parishioner who owned a pair of Chihuahuas. Without mentioning the true purpose of her visit, she took Katie and the boys with her. She wanted to see how the dogs reacted to the children and how Katie reacted to them.

Mrs. Yung Shultz was a Korean widow. During the war, Yung Kim had met an American soldier named Ronald Shultz. The old silver-based black-and-white photographs of Yung and her husband displayed a young couple who were very much in love. He was a handsome Caucasian who stood with an arm wrapped around her shoulder, posing with her cheek to cheek. There was another photo of him behaving like a proud papa while holding a Korean baby. The child was neither his nor Yung's. After they married in Korea against Ronald's commanding officer's wishes, the newlyweds found a baby orphan and adopted him. Ronald devoted nearly two years desperately trying to get his young wife and child stateside. When he finally succeeded, he moved his family to his native Ohio, close to his parents. Cultural and personal differences between

Ronald's mother and his young wife grew into animosity. Ronald moved his family to New York, where he started a successful advertising business and where he and Yung had two more children. Ronald died at the age of forty-nine from an undiagnosed congenital heart condition and Yung continued to run the family business on her own. She never remarried. Her three children were grown now, with families of their own. She had her two long-haired Chihuahuas and a house full of memories. Her home was tastefully decorated with Eastern and Western accents.

When Katie arrived, she noticed everything around her. No stranger to Asian art or culture, she recognized the artistic nature motifs that she saw displayed on the walls and shelves. Bright colors made the living room inviting and comfortable. Katie instinctively bowed from the waist when Uncle Patrick introduced her to Mrs. Shultz. She noticed the two little dogs by Yung's feet that had come forward to examine the new arrivals. Katie smiled as she stood tall to face Mrs. Shultz. The old lady had thinning hair and droopy brows, but her eyes twinkled like the stars in the sky. She had an inviting smile, which motivated Katie to say, "It's an honor to meet you, Mrs. Shultz."

At that moment, Carolyn felt immensely proud of Katie; she was behaving like a proper young lady. Mrs. Shultz invited them to sit. Katie bowed again and thanked the old woman. She then sat and rested her hands on her lap. Yung had already put out finger sandwiches, cookies, milk, and tea on the coffee table and invited the O'Gormans to share the fare with her. Katie and Stevie politely accepted, and Mrs. Shultz started to pour a cup of tea for Patrick while the children continued to admire the dogs. Carolyn surreptitiously eyed Katie. The dogs ignored Patrick and unabashedly gazed at and sniffed the four strangers while Carolyn sat baby Kieran up on her lap.

"Do you like dogs, Katie?" Yung asked, handing Katie a cup of tea.

Katie accepted the tea and said, "I don't know; I've never had a dog."

"Anthony and Cleopatra are very friendly. They seem to forget they're Chihuahuas. Normally, Chihuahuas are snappy little things. Not Anthony and Cleo. I take them with me for my clinic visits, and they cheer everyone up. They love being the center of attention." As if on cue, Cleopatra stood on her hind legs. "She's asking to be picked up," Yung observed. "You can hold her; she loves it."

Katie didn't know what to do with the teacup, and Carolyn said, "Place it on the table, Katie."

Katie put the cup down and used both hands to scoop up Cleopatra. Anthony stood on his hind legs as well and started to whimper. "Wait your turn, Tony," Yung admonished him.

"She feels strange," Katie commented. "I mean, I didn't expect her to be so solid. She has good muscle tone and is heavier than I expected."

"They run around a lot, chasing each other throughout the house, so they are quite fit. They also wrestle each other and play tug-of-war and hide-and-seek."

"Are they allowed on the furniture?" Carolyn inquired while brushing Kieran's hair to one side.

"Oh, yes—they think they're human, you know," Yung replied. "When we're home alone, they snuggle with me while I read or watch TV."

"In that case, Katie, place the dog next to Stevie and pick up the other one," Carolyn instructed Katie.

Katie obeyed. The two dogs walked back and forth on top of Katie and between Carolyn and Stevie. The male dog started to sniff the baby, and Kieran gurgled with delight as he tried to grab the dog's ear. He didn't succeed because Anthony's reflexes were quick. On Stevie's lap, Anthony stood on his hind legs and quickly pulled Kieran's pacifier out of his mouth. The dog jumped off the sofa and took off with his booty.

"Anthony, come back here, you rascal!" Yung called, rising to her feet. It was a useless call because Anthony had already disappeared from sight. Katie and Stevie laughed with delight while Kieran had been left flabbergasted. His baby brain said, *I've been violated.*

Yung apologized. "Oh, I'm so sorry. He has never done anything like that before." The children continued to laugh while Yung called Anthony, and he chose to ignore her. Yung gave up and sat back down while she once again apologized to Carolyn. Anthony then peered into the living room from behind a wall near the threshold. He cautiously stood at the entrance without the pacifier. Patrick observed the developments without comment.

"There he is," Stevie giggled. "Mommy, he's fast. Did you see that, Mommy? He grabbed Kieran's pacifier, and *zoom!* He was out of here like a flash. Look! Look! He doesn't have it. He hid it somewhere." Anthony backed up behind the wall near the doorframe. Stevie started to laugh again while he rocked back and forth in his seat.

Well, Carolyn thought as she observed the children's amusement, *the dog has certainly made an impression.*

Yung apologized again as Anthony peered into the room a second time. "It's no big deal," Carolyn assured her as she noticed Kieran sucking on his index and middle fingers. "The baby already found a substitute."

"I can hold the baby," Yung volunteered, "while you help yourself to some tea and sandwiches or cookies."

"That sounds like a wonderful offer," Carolyn replied as she watched Stevie and Katie pet Cleopatra together. She got up and transfered Kieran to Yung's waiting arms.

"How old is she?" Katie asked, inquiring about Cleo.

"She's six, and Anthony's five. I picked her up at the animal shelter. Someone had abandoned her because her legs were too weak to stand. She's fine now. My son brought me the little guy as a gift in order to keep Cleo company."

"Did you get her as a puppy?" Katie inquired.

"She was about four months old. Anthony, the little thief, was so small that he fit in my hand." Anthony peered in again.

"Come here, Anthony," Stevie called. "May I get him, Mommy?"

"Ask Mrs. Shultz, honey," Carolyn replied, and Stevie quickly turned to Yung with anticipation.

"You may go, young man, but he will probably keep you chasing him all afternoon. He has a lot of energy. You better take a few cookies with you."

"I can catch him," Stevie replied with confidence. "When I play football with my friend Luis, I run fast." He quickly got to his feet.

"Stevie," Carolyn said, holding his arm, "be gentle with the little dog. He's not a toy."

"I'll hold him like cotton candy, Mommy. I'm careful."

"No running; I don't care how fast you are."

"Yes, Mommy," he replied, and she let go of his arm. Regardless of what he heard, he dashed out of the room.

"Walk, Stevie," Carolyn instructed him as he turned left near the door.

Katie continued to play with Cleopatra and giggle with delight. Yung handed her a pull toy, and Katie and the dog were soon involved in a tug-of-war while Katie munched on a cookie. Then Stevie returned holding Anthony under one arm.

"Good boy, Stevie," Katie commented. "How did you catch him?"

"It was easy. I made believe I was a dog and got down on all fours. I looked him in the eye and asked him if he wanted a cookie."

"No cookies for him," Yung interjected. "Some of them have chocolate, and chocolate can be deadly to dogs."

"Do you mean Anthony could die?" he asked, looking at Yung with saucer eyes.

"He could, or he could get very sick," Mrs. Shultz replied.

"Well, it's a good thing I didn't give him a cookie. I don't have any."

"Yes, it is a good thing," Yung agreed. "Dogs eat dog biscuits, and people eat cookies."

"Do you have a dog biscuit? I sort of promised him, and you're not supposed to lie, you know; it's a bad thing."

"Anthony will get a dog biscuit later," Yung assured him. "He understands; he has a routine. But you can have cookies. Help yourself, young man; I'll pour you some milk."

"Stevie," Katie informed him, "the dog doesn't understand what you say, you know. So how can you promise him anything? He speaks dog, and you speak people."

"But she says he understands, didn't you?" he turned to ask Yung.

"Oh yes, they both understand. Dogs understand us more often than we understand them."

"You see. Anthony is a smart dog and he feels nice," he said, petting Anthony behind his ear. "Mommy, can we get a dog like Anthony?" He walked up to Carolyn and held the dog out to her. "Touch him, Mommy; he's very soft. He looks like a little mouse."

"He's too large to be a mouse, honey, but he is cute," she said as she held her teacup.

"Touch him," Stevie insisted while stroking the dog's long hair.

Carolyn stroked the dogs head. "He is soft," she agreed.

Stevie drew the dog back and kissed him on the head. He turned to Mrs. Shultz again. "Do you have any puppies? If you have a puppy, I can take him home and take good care of him. I promise."

"Aren't you putting the cart before the horse?" Uncle Patrick finally spoke. It's a good thing he did because Katie was about to start with, "Honestly, Stevie, sometimes you certainly say the strangest things. If there were any puppies, you would see them."

Stevie looked dejected. He said, "But I can take care of a puppy, Uncle Patrick."

"You probably can, but first you need permission. Taking care of a puppy isn't easy. It's a lot of hard work."

"I work hard."

"What kind of work do you do, Stevie?" Katie asked him as she scooped Cleopatra up.

"I don't know." He paused to think, but nothing came to mind.

"Well, you can't say you work hard, if you don't do anything."

"I work; I work. Tell her Mommy—I work."

"You do work. You study. That's work. You help Daddy, and you help me with the housework."

"You see," he retorted to Katie. "You don't know everything, you know. You didn't know that Anthony understands people talk."

"I didn't say I know everything. No one knows everything."

"Well, I know that I work hard. I should have a puppy, right Mommy?"

"I think it's a little premature for that, honey," Carolyn replied, "but I'll think about it."

"Well, if he can have a dog, I should have one too," Katie interjected. "I've never had a pet, and I'm older than he is."

"Katie, I haven't made a decision. And I agree with Uncle Patrick; caring for a living creature isn't easy. We also need to consider logistics. What happens to the dogs when we go on vacation?"

"We take them with us. They don't require much room. Besides, we'll travel in Grandpa's jet," Katie said.

"What happens if Grandpa's plane isn't available?"

"Why don't you buy a plane, Mom?" Katie asked.

"Oh, sure," Carolyn said, sounding amused. "I should buy a plane to accommodate a couple of dogs."

"These are people dogs, Mommy," Stevie informed her. "We can get two people dogs just like Anthony and Cleopatra. Or you can buy a little dog plane."

Carolyn laughed at the prospect. She had to set the teacup down as she continued to laugh. Yung, Patrick, and Katie were equally amused. Stevie looked around, not understanding what was so funny.

"Will the dogs fly the plane?" Katie asked him.

"Dogs don't fly planes, Katie. Only cartoon dogs do that. I'm not stupid, you know."

"No one is calling you stupid, Stevie, but a little dog plane is funny. How little should the plane be?" Katie asked.

"I don't know. Little enough for Mommy, Daddy, Luis, you, the baby, the dogs, and me. They have little planes; I've seen them at the airport. I know. It doesn't have to be a real big plane."

"You know, he's smarter than he looks," Katie commented jokingly.

"I don't care how smart you both think you are, we're not getting a plane," Carolyn informed them.

* * *

Carolyn had Stevie tested for learning disabilities. Dr. Ernestine Holder gave him a battery of tests and placed her findings on Carolyn's desk as she sat next to her.

"Here's what you asked for," Ernestine informed her.

Carolyn opened the folder and started to read. "Why don't you give me a summary; I'll read it later," Carolyn said as she closed the folder.

"You have a perfectly normal kid."

Carolyn smiled with pride and relief. Then she asked, "Why does he act so spaced out?"

"He's not spaced out; he's very innocent. How else can I put it? He's pure. Stevie is an adorable child who is incapable of corrupt thought. He can't think like the rest of the world because he doesn't live inside that box. His cognitive skills are normal. He can solve problems; he can deduce; he can extrapolate and conclude based on his own level of innocence."

"He doesn't seem smart. At times, he doesn't seem to be all there."

"He's probably focused on something else. And in his defense, at any given moment, anyone can tune out of a situation," Ernestine replied.

"I don't know," Carolyn said, sounding unconvinced. "He still counts on his fingers. Sometimes he says the strangest things."

"Grown people still count on their fingers; I've seen them. The important thing is that he understands what to do when he's given a problem. Before he encounters any major difficulty, get him the right tutor."

"Education is not my field of expertise. Who is the right tutor?"

"Someone who can teach him proper study skills. Someone who understands mnemonics. To improve his mathematical skills, someone who can unlock the wonders of numbers for him. If you want him to develop better skills, I suggest you speak with Karl Malburg. If he isn't available, I'll see who else I can get for you."

"Thanks, Ernestine. I hope my little boy wonder will blossom a bit."

"You know, forgive me if I'm out of line here, but I suspect you've been comparing Stevie to Katie. Stevie is precious and special. Katie is a different kind of special. Emily's Hope has had a few extraordinary children pass through its doors. Katie and her two contemporaries, Zoe Epstein and Luis Walker, are remarkable kids. Academically, they are way above average. Stevie is average, pure of heart, and very sweet. You are one lucky mommy."

Carolyn pondered the comment with mixed emotions. "I hope you're right about me being lucky. Historically, the pure of heart become the victims of dark souls. I don't know whether to cheer or cry. I don't want Stevie to remain innocent, but I don't want him to be cynical or fearful of the world."

"Achieving that balance is never easy," Ernestine commented.

"How are your kids, Ernestine? You seldom speak of them."

"I'm afraid I may jinx a good thing."

"How so?" Carolyn asked, raising an eyebrow.

"Well, Parker will be finishing at MIT this year. He has decided to do his doctorate at Berkeley. He believes that variety is better than a homogeneous education; he's probably right. Beverly will continue at Julliard."

"I envy you that. You have already seen how they're turning out. My children have a way to go."

"You'll be surprised how quickly time flies. Before you know it, they'll be away from home and you'll be fiercely missing them. I already miss Beverly, and she hasn't left New York. She's a young woman who is bound to fall in love and move away."

"Well, they're entitled to do that. We did it."

"Indeed, we did," she said and then paused a moment. "I wonder if my mother was as heartbroken about my parting as I am about my children's parting."

"I believe it must be a universal woe. I can tell you miss your mom. That's another universal woe."

"Indeed I do. She died much too young. I was completing my junior year at Princeton. I dropped everything and came home. I don't think I ever got over that. However, I left journalism and decided on educational psychology. I strongly believe her spirit guided me here. Anyway," she said, rising to her feet, "I came here to discuss Stevie. He's a sweet kid. I still believe you can count your blessings."

"I do. Thank you, Ernestine."

That evening, Carolyn left Stevie's evaluation results next to Matthew's pillow.

* * *

Carolyn and the children visited Yung Schultz and the dogs periodically. The children loved Anthony and Cleopatra. On nice days, they played with the dogs in the yard. Sometimes, Katie was entrusted to visit the Schultz home alone with Stevie. Yung enjoyed having them, and she knew that as potential new masters for Anthony and Cleopatra, the children and the dogs needed to get used to each other. Carolyn or Patrick sometimes dropped the children off at Yung's house with instructions that they were to behave and be helpful while there.

Due to the cancer treatments, Yung had her good and bad days. Sometimes the treatments left her feeling too weak to leave her bed. She had always been a proudly independent woman and was reluctant to hire anyone to help her with daily tasks. She finally gave in and hired an attendant who helped her with her meals and other chores and humbly accepted the gifts Carolyn sent. The two women became quite fond of one another.

When Carolyn was unable to visit, she informed Yung to send the children home if she was unable or unwilling to have them around during any given time. She also explained those conditions to her children and gave Katie cabfare. Katie and Stevie understood their responsibilities and were glad to help; they looked forward with anticipation to seeing the dogs and the kindly old Mrs. Shultz. However, Katie took advantage of the situation by boarding return buses and pocketing the cab money. One day, Carolyn was worried because they had taken too long to return home.

"The children left over an hour ago. I'm so sorry," Yung said when Carolyn called. "Katie assured me that it was okay to take the bus. I should have seen to it that they got in a cab."

"No need to apologize, Mrs. Shultz; you didn't know." Just then the children walked in. Carolyn finished her conversation with Yung and was soon having words with Katie.

"You're putting your safety and Stevie's at risk by taking buses?" she asked with disbelief. "I'm trying to give you certain liberties, Katie, but this is irresponsible."

"Nothing happened, Mommy. Most of the kids I know take buses all the time."

"Yes, a school bus. Besides, in better populated areas where there are sidewalks, yes, children ride buses all the time. You are not going to walk and stand on the side of a narrow rural road waiting for a bus. The walk to a bus stop is too long and hazardous, especially for a little child like Stevie. What if a car loses control and crashes into you? What if someone decides to kidnap you?"

"Mom, I swear, you worry too much. That isn't going to happen."

"If you weren't doing an act of kindness, I'd ground you."

"Why don't you just shackle me and throw me in a tower until I turn eighteen? I swear—you're so unfair. I can't even walk down a street."

"Don't tempt me. I'm concerned about your safety. How can I make you understand, Katie? Maybe I should shackle you until you turn thirty."

"Go ahead—see if I care."

Twenty-Three

◇◇◇

1992

Late in 1992, the court awarded Nydia and Felipe permission to adopt Luis. No one had stepped forward to claim him during all those years. His last name was officially changed from Walker to López, and Carolyn and Matthew became his godparents. These landmarks in his life were cause for celebration, and the festivities were held at the country club.

While everyone was involved in conversation or dancing, Katie pulled Luis aside. "Come, Luis," she said, and she led him down a hall near the coat room, in a dark corner not too far from the pay phone. She wrapped her arms around him and kissed him. Luis was astonished when she forced her tongue into his mouth. She separated from him and gazed at him.

"What do you think?" she asked.

"I don't know," he said, wiping his mouth with the back of his hand. "Why did you do that?"

"Maybe I didn't do it right," she said, and she kissed him again, reintroducing her tongue. When they separated, she asked, "Was that different or better?"

"Different or better than what?" He wiped his mouth again.

Katie sucked her teeth in disapproval and said, "You suck, Luis. I thought it was about time we started practicing. Older people kiss, and they seem to like it. I just wanted to see why it seems so good in the movies. It should have been a good way to congratulate you on your adoption."

"You could have sent me a card. You didn't have to stick your tongue in my mouth."

"It's an experiment, stupid. I figure you're my only choice."

"Is that supposed to be a compliment?"

"No. I have no one to practice with. You go to an all-boys school, so you don't have anyone either."

"I know other girls besides you."

"Does that mean you'd prefer to kiss someone else?"

"Well, my cousin Jasmine is pretty."

"Jasmine is older than you, stupid. And she's not really your cousin."

"She is now. I'm officially Luis López."

"Well, cousins shouldn't marry cousins. They have idiot kids."

"I didn't say I was going to marry her. Besides, I can too marry her because we're not blood related."

"Do whatever the hell you want. Like I give a shit." She turned to leave. Then she paused and said, "I'm probably the best you'll ever have." That said, she continued to walk away.

"Come back," he said. When she faced him, he said, "Do it again. I'll try to concentrate."

"Go to hell."

Later that night, he lay in bed and thought of Katie and him together. Katie thought of him, but she didn't approach him again. Luis started to have wet dreams, and Katie had daydreams.

* * *

In February of 1993, Carolyn convinced Nydia and Felipe to join the O'Gorman family on a winter recess trip to New Zealand. The purpose of the excursion was to release Marjorie's ashes into a fjord, and they planned to spend a whole month, enjoying the warm weather. It was also an opportunity for the children to learn about a different culture. Margaret had made most of the arrangements for close family members and friends. Unable to attend for the entire month, Camille and Neil would entrust young Courtney to Matthew and Carolyn as they had to return stateside in less than a week. Their other two daughters, Elizabeth and Shannon, didn't go because they couldn't afford to take time off from their university studies. Carolyn's twin brothers, Donovan and Daniel, also planned to stay a week.

The Reilly family jet took them to New Zealand. The next day, they boarded a chartered cruise ship to Te Anau, a small town in the heart of Fiordland, and headed to one of the fjords. They were joined by Father David Flannigan from the Diocese of Dunedin, who, along with Patrick O'Gorman, conducted Marjorie's memorial Mass on board ship. Among the participants, Dr. Xiang Tieng's wife from Malaysia, Lin Yang, sang "Ave Maria", and Luis sang Psalm 20. After he finished and before he could take his seat, Margaret grabbed him from an aisle seat, pulled him toward her, and planted an appreciative kiss on his cheek. He smiled proudly because he believed the kiss affirmed that he had done an excellent job.

The time came to release Marjorie's ashes into the base of the fjord. Water cascaded from the top of the precipice and sprayed and foamed out into the waters below. The spray engulfed them in a mist as the congregation stood in yellow raingear, trying to take in the majestic sight while squinting in the fjord's rain and feeling the icy water hit their exposed faces and hands. A seaman hung precariously over the bow as he emptied Marjorie's urn into the waters below, and the Reilly family huddled closely as they witnessed the act. Momma, holding baby Kieran, and Papa had remained as far from the spray as they could. Kieran was as alert as the other spectators. Katie was huddled in front, near Margaret and Carolyn. She glanced away from the seaman and surreptitiously studied the two women's faces as he released the ashes. Their tears were whisked away by the fjord's spray, but the telltale pain on each of their faces could not be washed away by all the waters on earth. Later, the seaman handed Margaret the empty urn, and she caressed it against her chest. The deed was done. The urn and ash residue was all she had left of her beloved child. She wept openly, and Harold drew her closer. His face was also furrowed with pain. Carolyn and the two male twins hugged each other for support. Then they each turned to hug and kiss their parents. Carolyn finally sought and found Matthew's support. Marjorie Louise Reilly's story had finally ended.

It was incredibly hot and humid when the boat returned to port. There was plenty for the children to enjoy in summery Te Anau and the not too nearby townships. The towns were walker friendly, with plenty of shops, attractions, and restaurants. The younger crowd enjoyed jet-skiing while the older adults tried to stay cool in the shade or tour the shops. Donny, Danny, Matthew, and the children headed for the nearest coffee shop as soon as they finished skiing.

"Stevie, what are you doing?" Katie asked as he tried to stuff his pockets with tea biscuits.

"The waiter said these are biscuits."

"So? Why are you putting them in your pocket?"

"I'm saving them for Anthony and Cleopatra. Mrs. Shultz said they can eat biscuits."

"Put them back on your plate, oh brother of mine. These are not dog biscuits. They're people biscuits."

"People eat biscuits too?"

"Yeah, back home we call them cookies. Eat up."

"These are some big cookies."

"Large enough for a German shepherd," Katie said as she munched on hers. "Anthony and Cleopatra's mouths aren't large enough to chew on these."

"That's probably why they call them biscuits," Stevie concluded. "They're too big to be cookies."

"Stevie, you're funny," Courtney commented. "You better clean the crumbs out of your pockets before ants get in your pants."

Stevie laughed. "I'll leave the crumbs there in case I get hungry later. Hey, look," he called out as he saw the view out the window, "there goes Mommy."

Everyone turned to see Carolyn, the other ladies, Sean, and Felipe walking on the opposite side of the street. Donny got up, left the café, and was soon across the street talking to his sister. Katie and the others observed as Uncle Donny pointed to the café from across the street. Soon, they were all reunited and enjoying their afternoon snack.

"What are we going to do for the rest of the day?" Katie inquired.

"Haven't you done enough for one day?" Carolyn replied. "Don't overdo it. We have plenty of time. Besides, we have something special planned for tomorrow, and you'll be very disappointed if you're too tired to move."

"Where are we going?" Luis asked.

"It's a surprise," Camille responded. "It's something I need to do before I leave, and you're all going to enjoy it. At least, I hope so. Nydia said she'll need to bring her rosary beads." The women laughed.

"Are we going to the top of the fjord?" Stevie asked.

"According to the brochure, it takes about a week to reach a fjord on the Dusky Trail," Katie interjected. "Can we go, Mom?"

"If it takes a week," Margaret interjected, "it should take me a month to get there. We don't have enough time."

"We'll catapult you up, Grandma," Stevie said as he motioned with both arms and laughed.

"That will be a pretty sight," Margaret replied, "and I'm not talking about the fjord. I thought you loved me."

"I do," Stevie replied and continued laughing. "I'm just helping you to get there faster."

The next day, as soon as the morning mist cleared, they waited to board float planes in order to get to their destination while permitting them an aerial view of the surrounding area. The children were very excited when they saw the planes.

"We're taking a little plane," Stevie yelled excitedly. "Oh boy!"

"This is better than a catapult," Luis said as he grinned from ear to ear.

"Mommy, Mommy, can we take one home for Anthony and Cleopatra?" Stevie asked.

"No," she simply replied as she adjusted his knapsack.

"I can learn to fly it."

"Of course you can. Now, repeat the rules for me."

"Always stay with the group. Protect my eyes, head, and neck from the sun," he said, touching the sunglasses, blue Yankee cap, and white towel he had draped along the back of his neck. "Refresh the sunscreen every hour. Keep my pants inside my boots. Don't pick anything up from the ground. Don't touch or bother the animals. Protect the environment— what goes in with me comes back with me."

"And don't put anything in your pockets," Carolyn reminded him.

"Oh yeah, I forgot. Don't put anything in my pockets unless it's clean."

"You modified the rule."

"If it's clean, it should be okay, right?"

"Well, I guess so. Now go with Daddy; I'll see you when you get back."

"You're not coming with us?"

"No—my parents, the baby, and I are staying here. Your plane will be back by five o'clock, and I will be right here waiting for you. How about a hug?" Stevie complied, and Carolyn returned the hug and kissed him on the cheek. "I love you, kiddo," she said. "Stay close to Daddy, okay?"

"Okay," he replied.

Carolyn then approached Katie and Matthew and said their farewells. The Reilly-O'Gorman party, including the Tiengs and the Lópezes, boarded their individual planes. Carolyn and her parents watched as each plane left the dock, gained altitude, and got lost in the distance. The fleet was soon flying over open water. Katie was the first to notice a pod of dolphins below. Stevie stretched across her lap to get a better view from her side of the plane.

"It looks like they're feeding on a bait ball," the captain commented as they flew past them.

"What's a bait ball?" Stevie asked.

"It's a large school of fish that swims round and round," the pilot replied.

"That's a dumb way to swim," Stevie replied. "How do they get anywhere?"

"Well, they do get right into the dolphin's mouth for lunch," the pilot replied.

"Now that's really dumb," Stevie said.

"Well, you're not a fish. I suppose it makes perfect sense to them. They probably think they look menacing to their predators if they form a bait ball. Hold on," the pilot announced. He then doubled back.

Stevie felt the sudden turn and giggled with delight. Matthew craned his head to catch a glimpse of the children in the backseat and smiled. They all had a better look at the feeding frenzy below.

The pilot resumed his course and pointed out a penguin colony on the distant shore below. They were soon over a fjord with a cascading waterfall. Everyone was in awe as the plane flew through the gully. Now they saw nothing but white water rushing past naturally precariously placed rocks. To everyone's delight, the plane gained altitude again. They flew over snow-covered mountains. At a lower altitude, they flew past spindly brush. The pilot purposely tipped the wings up and down, giving the plane a rocking motion, and the kids cheered. Stevie said, "Do it again!" The pilot obliged. Now they were over lush green grass. They passed a couple of sheep farms. The plane finally landed in a lake, and they felt the impact as it touched down. The pilot eased the plane across the lake and toward the dock. They were the first to arrive at their destination.

"That was fun," Katie commented as Matthew helped her and Stevie onto the dock.

"Yes, it was," Stevie agreed, "but it was too short."

"Well, we have to fly back to town after we complete the day trip," Matthew said as he grabbed their supplies from the pilot and handed Katie her knapsack.

"I'd rather fly instead of walk," Stevie commented as the next plane pulled in. "I can walk any time."

The first pilot boarded his plane and started back for home base to pick up another load of tourists.

"Well, this is a special kind of walk," Matthew replied. "When our guides arrive, we're supposed to climb to the top of one of these ridges. That's what they call 'exercise.' It's supposed to be good for you. We have to be back down here by four thirty at the latest."

"What happens if we're not back by four thirty?" Stevie asked.

"We'll be eaten by giant birds."

"Daddy, stop messing with the kid," Katie admonished him. "He's liable to believe you."

"I don't believe him anymore, Katie. He's always trying to pull my leg."

Matthew gave him his knapsack as he said, "Well, since you don't believe me anymore, I see no need to speak to you ever again. I'm your father; you're supposed to believe me."

"A father shouldn't make up stories," Stevie replied. Camille, Neil, and Courtney had stepped out of their plane and were walking toward them as Stevie added, "You should be setting an example."

"Let me see something," Matthew said as he checked Stevie's knapsack. "Did you pack your mother in here?" Stevie laughed as Matthew added, "The two of you are beginning to sound just like her. I swear, a man can't have a little fun. But that's okay. As you get older and wiser, I still have Kieran coming up the ranks. And Santa doesn't bring gifts to children who don't believe their parents."

"Well, Santa believes me," Stevie countered. "And he always brings me whatever I ask for."

"Stevie, oh son of mine, you are as precious as gold. I see there is still hope."

"Daddy, you're lame," Katie commented as she adjusted her knapsack. "Stop needling that poor child." She then acknowledged Camille. "Aunt Camille, this is an awesome trip. The plane ride was short, but terrific."

"I noticed the dips, turns, and accelerations your pilot was making, and my heart was in my throat," Camille replied.

"That was great, Aunt Camille," Stevie interjected excitedly. "I'm going to fly just like that. Mommy said I can."

"Well, remind me not to get in your plane," Camille replied. "I like to keep things smooth and simple."

"No, it was fun, Aunt Camille," Katie replied. "We should switch pilots on the way back so you can experience it."

"Don't do me any favors," Camille replied as she adjusted her own knapsack.

The second plane left as Donny, one of Carolyn's twin brothers, arrived with his two tow-haired sons. The family started to walk off the dock and onto the lake's bank. As each successive plane arrived and left, the crowd was getting larger.

Matthew noticed three men walking toward them with rustic staffs in their hands, and he gave Donny a nudge. "They must be our guides," he said.

He was right. With the help of their guides, Frank Flynn and his two sons, Andrew and Liam, they walked through prairie, forded streams, marched downhill and up, and scraped their clothing on spindly brush. The path became a bit more difficult as they stepped over overgrown roots, slipped on slimy mulch, and sometimes crawled under uprooted trees. There were plenty of easy paths in New Zealand's Fiordland Park, but the purpose of this hike was to have the children and newcomers experience what a pioneer might have experienced. The birds chatted in the background, and the travelers sometimes swatted annoying insects, but the participants enjoyed the good and the bad. As Katie tried to straddle a mud puddle by skirting it through the rise along the side, she lost her footing and landed on her butt within it.

Matthew heard the splash, and returned to assist her. "Are you okay?" he asked with concern as Stevie chuckled with delight.

"Who fell?" someone asked.

"Me! I'm fine, Daddy," she said, grabbing his hand to climb out. Stevie continued to chuckle. "You think this is funny?" Katie wiped her muddy hands on him. "Now that's funny. You're lucky I don't toss you in. My panties are wet." Stevie laughed heartily as Courtney was passing above the mud. "Hold onto the tree roots," Katie advised her, "or you'll end up like me."

"There's another stream up ahead," Andrew Flynn informed Katie. "You can either allow the mud to dry on you and flake it off, or you can sit in the stream to wash it out."

"I don't think I'm going to sit in any icy water, thank you. I'll wait until it flakes off. I can also rub it off on my little brother," she said while wiping her muddy hands again on Stevie's jacket.

"Hey," Stevie complained. "Cut it out, Katie."

"It's sunscreen, oh brother of mine."

"The hell it is. You're getting my jacket dirty. Daddy, look at what she did," he said, holding out his jacket sleeve.

"Katharine, behave yourself," Matthew admonished her.

"Yeah, Katharine, behave yourself," Stevie echoed.

As they resumed the walk, Katie started to feel the clothing clinging to her. As the mud caked, the clothing's rough texture chafed her skin. The terrain got steeper and had less dense growth. When they reached the stream, she washed her hands in the cold water. After deliberating a few seconds, she decided it might be better to sit in the cold stream to release some of the mud, which was getting extremely uncomfortable with each step. She yelped as she felt the cold water filter through her clothes. She proceeded to pat and rub her trousers to release the mud. Nydia stepped into the stream and helped her wash off most of the remaining soil while the rest of the group waited patiently. After a few minutes in the stream, the water didn't feel as cold as before. With most of the mud gone, Nydia and Katie returned to the trail. As they continued, the sun beat on them and once again Katie's clothing became stiffer with each passing minute. Fortunately, it wasn't as uncomfortable as before. Katie attempted to flake the residue off her hips, but it was saturated into the fabric, creating a permanent stain on the lightly colored cloth.

"It's better if you beat it," Stevie volunteered, smacking her on the butt three times with his open palm. "No, it's not working." She glared at him. "I was only trying to help," he said defensively. "It's not coming out; your pants are like thin cardboard."

"No kidding," she said between her teeth. "Don't help."

"You've got a brown butt," Luis said as he walked past her. She took the opportunity to smack him on the back of the head.

"It's mud, you damn idiot," she said.

"Well, don't take it out on me," he said, stroking the back of his head. "I didn't cause it."

"No, you're just an idiot. Come on, Stevie," she said, nudging Stevie's shoulder as she continued ahead. Stevie rushed to keep up with her, and Luis followed close behind.

They arrived at the most difficult upgrade. Flynn instructed them to put on their harnesses. Matthew tethered himself to Katie, and Katie latched onto Stevie.

"What happens if you both fall?" Stevie inquired as she fastened the buckle. "I'll be a goner."

"Well, you'll have a soft landing if we both end up on top of Daddy."

"Make sure you use the handholds," Flynn was saying as he continued his instructions. "We'll be at the summit in no time."

The climb wasn't as difficult as Katie expected. It was simply long and upward, allowing the hamstrings and glutei to get a good workout. The footpaths were dry and easy to trek. A few times, they crawled on all fours. No one slipped, and Katie suspected that the harnesses were basically props.

As they trecked upward, a kea sank its talons into Stevie's blue Yankee cap. The parrot pulled the cap up and yanked his hair. Not knowing what was attacking him, Stevie fearfully cried, "Get it off me; get it off me!"

Katie rushed to his side as he started to cry. She wrapped her arms around him as the rest of the party watched. "It's okay," she assured him as she caressed his back. "It was just a parrot. He's gone now." Matthew came forward and put his hand on Stevie's shoulder. The boy started to calm down.

"Why did he do that?" Stevie asked incredulously, feeling violated. "I didn't do anything to him. He pulled my hair."

Katie examined his scalp and noticed beads of blood forming on the top of his head. It didn't look too bad, however. She took off her safari hat and placed it on his head. As she adjusted the chinstrap, she said, "You need a tissue, oh brother of mine. You have a runny nose."

Stevie retrieved a tissue pack from his jacket pocket and blew his nose. He then took out the garbage bag Carolyn had given him, recalling "What goes in with you comes out with you," and he placed the tissue inside.

Katie wiped the tears off his face and said, "You'll be fine, kid. Come on." She coaxed him to follow.

They reached the top, and their guides set up camp while they enjoyed what appeared to be the top of the world. In addition to the hour and a half already traveled, it took an extra two hours to reach the plateau. Katie unbuckled her tethers. She stood at an edge and looked down a gorge to the sea, where waterfalls cascaded into mist as they met the water below.

"Oh my God, this is amazing," she said. "Aunt Camille, you have to see this."

"Don't stand too close to the edge, Katie," Camille cautioned her, but Katie had already sat with her legs dangling over the side.

"Do you think we can walk down there?" Katie asked, pointing to the gorge.

"I don't advise it; the trail doesn't go far," one of the young Flynns informed her. "It becomes a sudden drop. If you miss your footing, you'll splash like a watermelon."

"Katie, come away from there," Matthew called.

"Daddy, this is awesome. Come look."

"Get over here," Matthew replied.

"We came to see the fjords from the top. That's what I'm doing. This is great."

Luis walked over and sat next to her.

"Luisito!" Nydia cried out with alarm when she noticed what he had done.

"It's okay," Donny assured her. "I'll take care of this. They'll be fine." He then turned to Patrick and said, "Give me a hand. I did exactly the same thing when I first came here. My father found a solution without depriving me of the moment."

In the meantime, Luis looked at Katie and smiled. "What are you looking at?" she asked, feeling uncomfortable with his gaze.

"I'm looking at you. I can look."

"Well, look somewhere else."

Donny and Patrick latched tethers to Luis and Katie's harnesses and ran them about three feet, anchoring them to the foot of an outcrop. Katie watched them as they ran the spikes into the ground.

"Hey look," she observed. "It's an outcrop. I didn't notice it. We can go higher."

"You can check it out later," Patrick informed her. "Stay put for now.

"Can I try that?" Courtney inquired.

"I don't see why not," Donny said. "Let me anchor you first."

"It's okay," Katie said, rising to her feet. "She can have my spot. It's getting kind of crowded here anyway."

"Anchor me, Uncle Donny," Stevie asked.

"Me too, Daddy," one of his children said.

"I'll tell you what," Donny replied. "Let's eat first. Then you can all take turns."

They ate sandwiches, gulped beer or soft drinks, and savored the local fruit. The combined hunger and the day's exercise made everything taste extra good. Stevie topped off the fare with a box of Anzac biscuits.

"Where did you get these?" Katie inquired.

"Mommy bought them for me this morning," he said, grabbing one from the box. "Take one and pass them around. There're seven pounds of biscuits."

"Seven pounds? You carried seven pounds of biscuits in your knapsack?" she asked incredulously.

"I carried a lot of stuff," he said with his mouth full.

After lunch, Katie climbed the outcrop and looked about. It was a full 360-degree view from sea to land and back. She saw the lake from here. It looked like a basin full of pristine water. There were forests of pōhutukawa trees, which are native to New Zealand and produce clusters of red flowers while at the peak of the season, rivaling the red hues of a Christmas poinsettia plant. Katie admired the trees for a while, and then she turned her attention to a ranch. With her naked eyes she couldn't tell if the tiny specks were cows or horses. She used her small binoculars and focused on a brown horse with a long black tail. As she continued to survey the area, she realized someone was standing next to her. It was Luis.

"You again?" she inquired. "What is it with you?"

"Katie, you can't be mad at me forever. You've been avoiding me ever since that night at my party. I want to talk."

"You're talking," she said, sounding annoyed.

"Well, I've been thinking, I liked the kiss. I like you. Maybe we can try it again sometime."

She scrutinized him. She liked him too, but she didn't want to admit it. The fool had gone out on a limb, she thought. She realized she was holding his heart in her hands and the ball was now in her court. She hoped she would not mess this up. *What would Mommy do?* she asked herself as she gazed at him.

Luis waited anxiously with bated breath. Then he said, "My prom is this semester. I was wondering if you would come."

"You want me to go to your prom?"

"If you want to come...yes. Well, I'd really like you to come with me...if it's okay with you." He looked down toward the ground. The brim of his hat concealed his flushed face from her.

"Come, Luis," she said, grabbing his hand. She walked him down from the outcrop and proceeded down the slope. When she believed they were out of view of the group, she pressed herself against him and sucked his lips. This time he felt it, and she did too. He returned a warm smile.

"Did you like it this time?" she asked.

"Yeah," he said dreamily.

Katie kissed him again. She was into the moment when they both heard a surprised, "Luisito!" coming from a much alarmed Nydia. They looked up to see several people staring down at them.

Katie and Luis spent the rest of the trip giving each other furtive looks as Nydia and Ellen conspired to keep them apart. While most of the group spent time taking photographs and posing in front of marvelous views, Luis and Katie were blind to the bucolic countryside. Eventually, they made their way back to the lake and waited for their planes to arrive.

As soon as Stevie arrived back at Te Anau, he ran toward Carolyn, hugged her, and handed her a bag. "What's this?" she inquired, knowing she was holding the garbage bag she had given him. Katie and Matthew stood behind him, waiting for their turn to greet Mommy.

"It's my poop bag," Stevie announced.

"Your poop bag?" Carolyn inquired, holding the bag.

"Ah-huh," Stevie replied. "You said what goes in with me comes out with me. Let me tell you, those biscuits travel fast."

"I see," Carolyn said, laughing uncontrollably as she handed him back the bag. She supported herself against Matthew's shoulder as she continued to laugh and turn red as a beet.

Matthew and Katie joined in the laughter as Margaret, who pushed Kieran's stroller closer to them, inquired, "What's so funny?" Carolyn could not respond. It took her a while to regain control.

Finally, Matthew said, "Most men bring their women flowers, and Stevie brings poop. Nice going, son. You're an ace—a hole in one. You've made my day."

"Well, I did what she told me," he said defensively.

The child was telling the truth. Each of the novice explorers had received a sanitation pack from Reilly

Pharmaceuticals, which was an ideal solution for relieving oneself in the bush. Each kit contained sealable pads that absorbed one hundred percent of the moisture. They were contained in an odor-free zip bag. The user could later dispose of the pad in a toilet and add a few drops of Reilly solvent. In a few minutes, the pads degraded for flushing.

"You're right, honey," Carolyn said apologetically. "I just wasn't expecting this. Wait until we get back to our suite, and I'll show you how to dispose of your poop." She laughed again and kissed him on the forehead. "Daddy is right—you're an ace, honey."

"I have a rock," he replied, digging into his pocket. "It's clean; I washed it in the stream," he added as he handed it to Carolyn. "You can have it."

"Well, thank you," Carolyn said enthusiastically as she examined the dark spear-shaped rock.

"The man said it's probably a meteor rock," Stevie said excitedly. By "the man" he meant Andrew Flynn, one of the trail guides. "That means it fell out of the sky. It may be valuable."

"I'll treasure this always," Carolyn replied as she slipped it into her shoulder bag.

Carolyn looked up at the other members of the family and noticed that Katie had a towel wrapped around her head like a turban and realized that Stevie was wearing her hat. "What happened to his cap?" she asked.

"He lent it to a bird," Katie replied.

"Uh-uh," Stevie objected. "The bird came and stole it, Mommy. I wasn't bothering him or anything. He came out of nowhere," Stevie explained excitedly. "It was a big parrot. He pulled my hair and it hurt." He removed the safari hat for Carolyn to see.

Carolyn tousled his hair instead of giving him the anticipated inspection, and she said, "Well, keas and crows can be little hooligans. It's their nature."

"He has little specks of blood on his scalp," Katie volunteered.

"I have blood? Why didn't you tell me?" Stevie asked, sounding alarmed.

"Everyone has blood, Stevie. Without it, you'd be dead."

"I know that—you know what I mean. Why didn't you tell me the bird cut my head?"

"I didn't want to freak you out, kid. It's just a little blood. You'll live."

"You've had an exciting day, my little prince," Carolyn said. "I'll check you out after you've cleaned up, and I'll put some antiseptic on it. Let's go 'home' and get ready for dinner." As they turned to go, she noticed the seat of Katie's pants. "Did you roll in mud and sit in pomegranate juice, Katie?"

"She fell, Mommy," Stevie blurted out. "You should have seen it. She went *swoosh*, right into a pool of mud. It was funny," he laughed.

"Yeah, funny to you. I got wet to my skin. Coming back, I sat under a pōhutukawa tree. The blossom mulch was damp, so now I have a brown and red butt. I'm not the only one. Luis and a few others also sat under the trees."

"Did you have fun?" Carolyn inquired.

"It was the bomb, Mom."

"Then that's all that matters; I'm glad you enjoyed it."

At dinnertime, the explorers ate heartily. It was a family-style dinner. The first course was succulent chunky lamb stew. The main course was comprised of huge prawns and blue cod served with sweet potatoes with a side of stir-fried cucumbers with seasoned tomatoes and onions. Huge slices of pavlova arrived for dessert.

"It says here," Matthew commented, reading a menu card, "the pavlova, a baked meringue covered with whip or Chantilly cream and topped with a variety of seasonal fruit, such as kiwi, strawberries, bananas, and mango, was named for the 1920's Russian ballerina Anna Pavlova." He downed his first mouthful. "Oh, my God; I'm in heaven; this is great!"

As most of the crowd retreated to the bar, Carolyn and Ellen herded the children to Carolyn's suite. The group of children included Carolyn's three kids, Courtney, Luis, Donny's two sons, Danny's daughter, and four other children of the Reilly-O'Gorman party. Several of the adults were departing the next day. An evening of drink, play, and conversation before parting company made for a fun farewell. Carolyn called room service for extra pillows and blankets, and the children were soon lying all over the floor, enjoying each other's company as they watched a movie. Courtney was entertaining Kieran, who was in his playpen. Ellen and Carolyn watched over the group of children as they discussed the day's activities. Carolyn smiled when Momma told her about Luis and Katie being caught in a lip-lock. Carolyn looked at Luis and Katie, who were staring at the large television screen as they rested their heads on floor pillows placed at opposite ends of the room. As if on cue, Katie looked back at her. She got up and came to sit at her mother's side. She kissed Carolyn on the cheek and rested her head on her shoulder.

"Did you have a nice day today?" Carolyn asked her for the second time that day as Ellen watched the two of them together.

"Yes, thank you, Mommy. This has been the best trip ever," Katie replied.

Carolyn thought of Katie's amorous actions toward Luis, gazed at Ellen, winked, and said, "Well, you can thank Grandma Margaret for this trip."

"I already did, and she told me to thank you because you planned the itinerary."

"Well, Grandma and I planned it together. We've been here before, and I suspected you guys would love it as much as Marjorie and I did."

"I'm sorry about Aunt Marjorie, Mommy. Although we met only a few times, I liked her; she was really nice. I still have some of her letters."

"You do?"

"Yeah—she sent me a few letters. I thought she had an awesome life, Mom. I guess I can let you read them sometime. Except some of them are personal."

"Well, I suggest you keep them that way. I have my own memories of Marjorie. They go way back, but I thank you for the offer."

"May I go with you to Winton tomorrow? I'd like to see that old church." She was referring to Father David Flannigan's church. Father Flannigan and Patrick had conducted Marjorie's memorial Mass on board ship.

"Well, we can all go."

"No—just you and me and Uncle Patrick."

"Okay, just you and me and Uncle Patrick if I can convince Daddy to take care of Kieran and Stevie."

"I'll look after the boys," Ellen volunteered. "Sean and I can take them to the wildlife park. We'll also take Mattie off your hands," she added jokingly.

"Will you and Papa be able to walk tomorrow after today's trek?" Carolyn asked.

"Honey, Sean and I headed straight to the spa as soon as we parted company with you. That's why we arrived a little late for dinner. It was worth it. That masseuse loosened every muscle in my body."

"I took a warm shower," Katie said.

"Well, you're young and more resilient. My old bones need something more invigorating."

"May I get a massage, Mom?"

"Only if one of us is there with you. I don't want anyone trying any funny business. You never know."

"What do you mean?" Katie asked.

"Forget I said it," Carolyn replied in an attempt to retract the statement.

"Fine. Will you take me to the spa when we return from Winton?"

"I don't see why not," Carolyn replied. "Why don't you go ask the kids if they want a snack or something? I'll call room service." As Katie left to query the children, Carolyn said, "How about a nightcap, Ellen?"

"How about some wine?"

"Any particular type?"

"I'm not picky; I'll try a local vintage. Will you join me?"

"I'll settle for a soft drink."

Katie returned with a verbal list of items and Carolyn called room service. When she hung up, she said, "I figured the kids would eat again about now. A good hike always stimulates the appetite."

"Where did you go today, Mommy?" Katie asked, snuggling next to her again.

"Your grandparents and I hit the Kepler Trail. It's an easy walk. We walked for about an hour. If you get the pictures from my purse, you can see what it's like."

"I'll look later," she said as she stretched out on the couch and rested her head on Carolyn's lap.

"Are you tuckered out, young Kate?" Ellen inquired.

"Yes. Mom walked only an hour. How long did we walk, Momma?"

"I don't know. It took three and a half hours to reach that summit, but it felt like we descended faster than that."

"I agree." Katie yawned. "I think I better hit the sack if I can find the strength to get up. Stevie is still all bright-eyed and bushy-tailed. I'm getting old, Mommy."

"Well, get up, old lady. I'll walk you to your room. This is payback time for not going to bed early last night like I told you."

"I wasn't sleepy then. Let me stay here; I can't move."

"Well, you'll have to; I can't be your pillow all night. Get up."

Katie forced herself to sit up, and Carolyn helped her to her feet. "And you said the young are more resilient," Carolyn chided Ellen as she guided Katie to bed. "She feels like a drunken sailor."

Katie turned and faced Ellen. "I have a few suggestions for you, Momma," she said, looking bleary eyed. "Take the boys to a petting farm tomorrow. It's less walking. Oh, and tie a bandana around Stevie's head. And don't accept any bags from him. Don't say I didn't warn you. Good night, Momma."

"Good night, young Kate," Ellen laughed.

Twenty-Four

◇◆◇

2005

Katie had a swollen black-and-blue jaw, which she had received at the hands of Cheryl's ex-husband, Arturo Santillana. Despite her unsightly appearance, she and Luis went to an early morning appointment at Susan Sheridan's office, where Luis completed the deal to sell his Internet Web site for $175 million. Upon signing the papers, it was agreed that he would receive four separate wire transfers to his account within two years.

After their business was completed and Carolyn's agent left, an astonished Luis turned to Katie and said, "I can't believe this. The man didn't give me seventy-five million. He gave me one hundred and seventy-five million. I misunderstood. How is this possible? I have to call my mother. I have to tell Carolyn."

"Calm down, Golden Boy," Katie advised him. "You're not going to climb on the rooftop and announce to the world that you're one hundred million dollars richer than you expected. Put a sock in it!"

"Katie, Katie, Katie, I'm rich. I'm richer than rich."

"I said, calm down! Better still, shut the hell up!"

Susan Sheridan strongly advised him to seek financial advice to manage his assets.

"You sound like my godmother," he said, shaking Susan's hand, "and she's already signed me up for financial help."

"Well," Susan responded, "most people who come into sudden wealth believe they have come upon a perpetual cornucopia. Unfortunately, evidence indicates the opposite to be true. It doesn't matter if it's the wealth of ten dollars or ten billion, frugality and wisdom must be practiced in order to hold onto your money and help it grow. In other words, don't blow it, grasshopper."

He smiled and said, "I'll try not to."

Katie smacked him on the back of the head and said, "You'll have to do better than that, or Mom will have your liver for breakfast."

He stroked his head and said to Susan, "I put up with this all the time. The first thing I'm going to do with my money is buy a padded helmet before she gives me a concussion."

"If I didn't smack him, he wouldn't have any sense at all. Do you know he wanted to be a rock star?"

"Well, I would have probably become a millionaire sooner rather than later," Luis interjected.

"Or an unemployed musician, begging for change in the subway," Katie teased him. "Susan, thanks for everything. Are you coming to my parents' anniversary celebration?"

"My parents and I will be there. I'll probably talk to you before that." The two women kissed each other good-bye. Susan patted Luis on the shoulder and reminded him, "Be frugal and wise, Luis."

Once outside Susan's midtown office, Katie asked him, "Hey, Golden Boy, would you like to go for some coffee and cake to celebrate before we head home?"

"I wish it felt like a celebration. This is the only good thing that's happened all week," he said while gently stroking her jaw and examining the bruises on her face. "I'm sorry, Katie."

"You have nothing to be sorry about. The ill turn of events is not your fault. I've been too hard on you. Let me make it up with coffee and cake," she said, gazing into his eyes. "You deserve a little celebration, Golden Boy. Come, Luis."

"Come, Luis" was always hard to resist. He smiled and agreed to her offer before heading back to work.

"This is nice," Katie said after sipping the hot coffee. "It's been a while since we've been downtown together."

"Well, yes," he agreed. "We've been busy."

"Well, I'm done with the construction of Emily's Hope. Why don't we take a vacation together, Luis? My parents and the boys are going to Costa Rica this summer. Why don't we join them? It will be like old times. Remember the trip to New Zealand?"

He smiled. "How could I forget? I was following you around like a lovesick puppy, and you agreed to go with me to the prom. We were the youngest kids at that dance, and you were beautiful. You still are."

"You know, we can try again."

"Try what again? Going to New Zealand?"

"That too, but I was thinking we can try to make another baby."

"You would do that?" he asked, looking at her longingly.

"Of course I would do that," she said, holding his hand with both of hers.

His countenance suddenly changed; he looked sad. He was torn between his religious beliefs and creating another illegitimate child. He suspected that if he voiced his concerns, Katie would get angry.

"What's wrong?" she asked.

"Nothing," he lied.

"Spill it, Luis. I know you. What's wrong?"

"When I heard you were pregnant, I was ecstatic. I thought, *She's carrying my baby.* I can't tell you what a high that is, Katie. It's wonderful; it's amazing. You were carrying my child. You chose me."

"Of course I chose you. Who else would I choose? You're the only logical choice."

"I'm a logical choice?" he stammered. "I love you, Katie. But I'm a logical choice. Do you love me, Katie?"

"I want your child, Luis; I guess that's love. I felt your presence in me. You were embedded in me. It felt nice. Is that love, Luis? I want to be honest with you; I don't know. Have you ever felt empty, Luis?"

"I don't know what you're talking about, Katie. Do I make you feel empty?"

"No—oh God, no. It has nothing to do with you, Luis. I just feel hollow, so I need to rely on logic. We've discussed this before. For instance, there are times I resent my mothers. I resent Emily, and I resent Carolyn. That doesn't make sense, does it? I was too young to really know Emily. And I shouldn't resent Carolyn. That makes absolutely no sense. I have to love Carolyn. That woman has done everything for me, but I can't feel the love. Over the years, I've given her hell; I know that. I can't help myself. I'm hollow, Luis; I'm empty. I don't understand this, and it infuriates me because I don't want to be like this. But I want you. I don't want a life without you, and I'm so worried I'll lose you. I hate it when other women look at you. It's insane; I can't make any sense of it," she said with tears welling in her eyes. "Why should you risk being with a crazy woman, Luis? I know women want you." She took a tissue from her purse, wiped her eyes, and blew her nose. "Now I'm just being stupid, and I look a mess."

"You're not stupid, and you look fine, Katie. I don't understand the emptiness you speak of, so I agree it doesn't make sense. I have a few things racing through my head too." He looked at her intently. Among the things on his mind was the knowledge of Katie's discontinuance of her prescription drugs. He suspected that she was probably voicing her present feelings because of the lack of that medication. On the other hand, her present behavior could be independent of that fact. If they were to try for another child, she might have to continue drug free. He mulled all of that in his mind as he studied her flushed face. He searched for the proper words and said, "Maybe the reason why I don't understand the emptiness is because I'm a blessed man. I'm blessed because each day I notice the good and wonderful things in my life. I'm not a psychiatrist, Katie, but if you can feel hate, a sense of loss, and emptiness in your life, then the opposites are also within your grasp. Concentrate on them and you will hopefully replace the sense of emptiness with one of fulfillment."

"I've been there, done that. Odette Lieberman once gave me a notebook to write down the good things in my life. It doesn't work."

"Don't write them. Feel them. Or do both—write and feel them."

Katie stared at him dismissively, as if to say, "How stupid is that?"

She didn't have to speak. He knew that look and understood it. He shrugged and tilted his head to one side, as if to say, "I'm sorry; I tried."

"Let's just go home," Katie said aloud.

Upon arriving home, Katie attended to her corporation's business via computer and Internet. All appeared to be going well at work. Ramírez decided it was prudent to hire another engineer and asked for her approval and input, and she sent him the draft for an employment ad. Later that morning, she received get well flowers from Chief Lawrence Quinn. *Maybe Mom is right*, she thought. *Quinn is probably interested in me. Why would he send me flowers? He doesn't know me.* She tossed the card in the garbage and left the flowers in the box. As Lolo and Lolita looked on, she turned her attention to her property's security system. She needed to check why Quinn's NYC car had managed to pass through the entrance gate. His license plate was not programmed into the security system to allow that entry. From her home computer, she ran a diagnostic. It would take several minutes for the computer to complete the test, so she used the time to call Phil Garrity on his cell phone.

"Listen," she said to him, "in case you don't know, Cheryl's ex-hubby came onto my property yesterday and assaulted my mother and me."

"Yes, I know about that. I was planning to call you and Carolyn today to see how you're doing."

"Mom says she's fine, but I don't like showing my face in public. People probably think I'm a battered wife. My jaw is bruised and puffy."

"Well, if it's any consolation to you, the guy is finally in lock-up, and we have a warrant to search his property. If he doesn't make bail, he should be in for a while," Phil said. "I'm sorry about what happened. We've gotten crazed individuals from Emily's Hope before because they like to track down a spouse who's benefitting from the services you folks provide. I was shocked to hear that you were the target and that he did it at your home."

"I'd like to know how he got past security. The only thing I can conclude is that he hired a boat and came from the lake—the same way those reporters gained access a few days ago. Presently, because the lake is owned by the township, I have no control over lake traffic; but I'm working on that flaw."

"We already have someone inquiring about boat rentals. As soon as we know something, I'll let you know."

"That's what I was hoping you would do. That could be evidence, right?"

"Absolutely. Have you checked the premises to see if he left a boat on or near your property?"

"No, I haven't had a chance to do that yet."

"That's our job. I don't want you touching anything, Katie. I'll ask the sergeant to send someone over and do that for you."

"Thanks, Phil. The entry gate is malfunctioning. If the investigating officer can't get in, tell him to enter 7549 as the manual code. Thanks for your help."

As soon as she hung up, she hobbled outside on her crutches. Accompanied by the German shepherds, she walked along the lake's bank to see if she could find anything. A hundred feet from her dock, she noticed furrows along the ground. Without trampling it, she followed the path with her gaze and saw a small motorboat that had been dragged into the brush. She didn't bother to approach it.

She turned and walked back to the house, concluding that the computer had completed the diagnostic report by now. It did; there was a "system failure" in port three. The computer asked if she wanted to correct the failure. She selected yes. The computer blinked and reported, "Unable to correct system failure." She grabbed the manual and studied the schematics for port three. She sighed with exasperation when she saw the point of origin.

With the dogs following close behind her, she walked back outside and down the road toward Luis's house. Amber and Onyx greeted her at the gate and joined the procession as she opened Luis's garage. She grabbed a long ladder and proceeded to drag and pull it with one hand while laboring to keep her balance on one crutch. Tired and perspiring, she had managed to get the ladder to the road when Matthew's car pulled up.

He rolled down the car window and asked, "What in the world are you doing?"

"I need to check the computer system at the gate," she replied. "There's probably a short in the system."

"And you were planning to climb a ladder with a broken leg with no one around to hold it for you? Did your brain check out when you broke your leg? Put that damn thing down. Either call a technician or wait until Stevie gets home so he can hold the ladder while I check it. Sometimes you're unbelievable. Get in the car!"

"I can't leave the ladder out here."

"Get in the car, Katharine!"

As he argued with her, Sean and Ellen arrived. "What's this, a family reunion?" Katie inquired. "No one calls anymore?"

Ellen and Sean stepped out of their car. "Are you okay, young Kate?" Ellen inquired.

"And good morning to you, Momma. Yes, I'm okay. You were just here last night. Did you come to bring me lunch?"

"Oh no, dear. Are you hungry? I'll make you something."

"No, I'm not hungry. I'm trying to get some work done. My security system is malfunctioning."

Matthew had also stepped out of his car and announced, "She was going to climb that ladder to fix it. Maybe the two of you can hold it for me while I climb up there to check it."

"Well, I did say she's headstrong," Sean said. "Mattie, I'll help you move the ladder, and Ellen and I will be happy to hold it. *Wrong and Strong*," he added altering Katie's name, "you can sit and watch."

In no time, they set the ladder against the gate, and Matthew climbed up for a visual inspection. He climbed down and announced, "It's obviously been tampered with, but I can't touch anything until Phil gets here."

"Phil?" Katie asked. "You mean Garrity?"

"Yes."

"I was just on the phone with him. He said he was going to ask the sergeant to send an officer to check for a boat. He didn't say he was coming."

"Well, I asked him not to say anything to you until I got here. Phil and James Esposito are on their way. Phil called me an hour ago."

"What's going on, Daddy?"

"We need you to pack your bags and come with me."

"Why?" she asked while the others looked at each other with obvious unease. "What's going on?" she asked again.

Matthew sighed and confessed. "The attack on you and Carolyn apparently had nothing to do with Cheryl."

"What do you mean? When Santillana hit me, he said something about me getting into his business. I don't remember his exact words, but I'm sure he meant that I was interfering with him and Cheryl."

"Maybe he wanted you to believe that. But the truth is, he's been fixated on you long before we found the cell phone in Cheryl's car. It's probably a coincidence that he was checking on Cheryl as well. He's deranged."

"I know the man is deranged, but how do you know all that other stuff?"

"This morning the police found photographs of you in his apartment. There are photos of you near the old Emily's Hope, at your job sites, and here by the lake. In some photos you're alone. In others, you appear with different individuals. If that lunatic is able to make bail, I don't want you here alone. I want you to come home with me, princess."

"Daddy, I can't just leave everything. What about my dogs?"

"You bring them with you," he said, placing his hands on her shoulders.

"Does Mommy know?"

"No, I haven't told her yet. I didn't want to upset either of you. Now you know. I can't leave you here, princess. You have to come with me."

"Daddy, calm down. So he has a few photographs. So what? That's no reason for me to leave my house. I have the dogs, and Luis is usually here with me."

"Not always, Katie. Until you return to work, you're here alone. I want you home."

"I am home, Daddy. This is my home now."

"Kate, listen to Mattie," Ellen pleaded with a furrowed brow.

"Well, we need to wait for Garrity and Esposito. Let's wait," Katie said. "Let's go to the house and start lunch. We'll make enough for everyone. I need to get my other crutch," she said, heading toward the garage.

"Where did you leave it?" Sean asked.

"It's in Luis's garage."

"Get in the car with Mattie, and I'll bring it to you."

"We're going to my house, right?" she asked Matthew.

"Only until Garrity and Esposito get here. I want to show them the entry gate and the rest of the security system. We can also discuss what they've found. Then you're coming home with me. Carolyn will never forgive me if I leave you here."

"Mommy doesn't have to know anything. You're making a mountain out of a molehill. Besides, Luis's house is also within the security parameters of the entry gate. If I leave, then he'll be here alone. Who'll take care of him if someone trespasses? I can defend myself."

"Just like you defended yourself yesterday," he said sarcastically.

"He sucker punched me, Daddy."

As they were in the middle of the bickering, James Esposito arrived, followed close behind by Phil Garrity and two other patrol cars.

"What's this, a convention?" Katie asked Esposito when the other cars arrived. A fifth car pulled up.

"We'd like your permission to search the premises, Katie," James Esposito announced.

"Knock yourselves out," Katie responded.

"I left the ladder up by the gate," Matthew interjected. "The intruder apparently made modifications to that unit."

He pointed to the surveillance hook-up at the top of the entry gate.

"I'm not surprised. Barry, you and Seth check up there." James pointed to the top of the ladder as he called to one of the officers. "We also need to check the inside of the house."

Katie wanted to know why, and Garrity said, "The perp has been inside your home. We have evidence of that."

"That can't be," Katie said incredulously. "The dogs are always here. The house has a security unit."

"Do you always set it?" Garrity inquired.

"Well, no. Sometimes when I'm home, I don't always set it. But the dogs are always here," she repeated, not wanting to believe what she heard.

As the other officers fanned out throughout Katie's property, James Esposito sat with the family at Katie's kitchen table and showed them the evidence they had gathered so far. The pictures were extremely disturbing. There were pictures of her at home, including pictures of her in the bathroom. There were photos of her and Luis being intimate. Other photographs had been doctored with magic marker, depicting phallic symbols near her face. Katie was both shocked and embarrassed by what she saw. This was the ultimate violation; her family and strangers at the police station and at the DA's office would also thumb through this personal evidence.

"I believe this guy probably went to EH looking for Cheryl," James said, "and he happened to see you there. He obviously developed an unhealthy interest in you and has been following you ever since. You said you noticed him following you and Cheryl when the two of you were returning home the other day?"

"Yes, I first noticed his car when we turned on Chambers Street."

"Did anything else happen that day? Did you see or notice anything odd?"

"A well-dressed teenager tried to pickpocket me while I was on the bus, but I got everything back."

"Did you file a police report?"

"No, I just frightened the crap out of the little shit and let him go."

"Have you ever seen Santillana hanging around here or at EH?"

"No, not that I can recall. This is all very embarrassing," she said, shaking her head. "I can't believe all this could have happened and I haven't been aware of it."

"You have people working for you here from time to time, right?" James inquired.

"Yes. I have feed delivered for the fish. I have a housekeeping service maintain the house. It's an entire crew; they come every other week. The gardeners do landscaping. Contractors are in and out for various reasons. It's a big place, and it's basically just Luis and me. So yes, I have help maintaining it. My parents' anniversary celebration will be held here, so I've had consultants in and out."

"Well, I want a list of everyone who's been in and out of here. Maybe someone hired Santillana to work for them, and he's been here as a member of one of those crews. That could explain why the dogs weren't a first line of defense. He probably befriended them with doggy treats. If he was part of a housekeeping crew, he had the opportunity to be indoors and install cameras in here."

"Why, why, why?" Katie asked, holding her head. "This is unbelievable."

"I know," James added. "It's hard to fathom. Psychotic behavior never makes sense. You know, I was thinking of putting in for retirement. Now I've decided I'm not leaving until this is behind me."

"I appreciate that," Matthew said. "You and Phil have been good friends all these years, so that means a lot to me. I can never repay you and the department for everything you guys do."

"That's not true. We're like family. So Katie, your neighbors will have to get used to seeing us around because we're not leaving until this is settled."

"My neighbors are probably sick of me already. This is the third time in a week that Westchester's finest have been in my yard."

"I also want full details concerning that teenager. We'll track him down in case there's a connection."

"I made him empty out his pockets and I believe I have his school ID among my things."

"James," Momma Ellen interjected, "call your crew in. Lunch is ready. You'll love Sean's chili."

After lunch, James Esposito and his men went back to work, combing every inch of Katie's property. Momma and Papa tidied up while Matthew watched Katie scan appointment files for people who had worked on her property since its construction until present day. As he observed Katie, Matthew tried to convince her to come home with him.

"The parts for your SUV are supposed to arrive today, Katie," he said. "Why don't you come by tomorrow and help me make the modifications?"

"If that's your ploy to get me to leave my house, you're as transparent as glass."

"I thought you liked working with me."

"Yes, but I know that isn't why you're extending the invitation. It's okay, Daddy," Katie insisted. "I doubt that Santillana is going to make bail anytime soon. Luis's dogs are out and about, so I have plenty of protection. If anything happens, I'll call you. If Phil or James hears anything about that deviant's bail, they'll let me know. I'm just sorry you, Momma, and Papa had to see those pictures of me. Please don't say anything to Mommy."

"Your mother and I don't keep secrets, Katie. Eventually, I'm going to break or she's going to notice something."

"You would have made a lousy war prisoner."

"If your mother were the jailer, yes. There are two people I don't mess with, Katie."

"Yes, I know—Momma and Mommy. Please try, Daddy," she pleaded. "Don't say a word."

"I'll try, but I can't guarantee anything, Katie."

"Are you going to try to impose a gag order on Ellen and me?" Sean asked from the doorway. "Don't try it, Katie. It isn't going to work"

"And they say women like to blab. You men are worse," Katie commented.

"It has nothing to do with gender, Katie my love," Sean replied. "The truth always gets out. If she doesn't learn about it now, Carolyn will be furious about the cover-up when she eventually finds out. Mattie, talk to your wife."

Twenty-Five

◇◇◇

Stevie was studying the contents of the refrigerator while his friend Darnell waited expectantly.

"We have cold cuts," Stevie announced, grabbing a few things from the refrigerator. "Grab the bread out of the cupboard, Darnell. We're going to make us some sandwiches. I also saw a pie in there. What do you want to drink?"

"I don't know. What do you have?"

"Check the fridge, my man. We can also heat up some soup."

"That sounds good. Soup and sandwich it is. Where's the soup?"

"My mother keeps the jars in the upper left hand cabinet. The bowls are near the stove."

"What are you boys doing?" Carolyn asked as she walked in with Kieran.

"We're getting some food. I'm making sandwiches. Do you want one?"

"I'll have one," Kieran said.

"What about dinner, Stevie?" Carolyn asked.

"Darnell and I are hungry now, Mommy—not later," Stevie replied. "Besides, we're going over to Omid's. I know you don't want me to eat them out of house and home."

"How's Omid doing?"

"He's still messed up, Mommy. The poor guy can't even take a leak without someone's help."

"Is the VA doing anything for him?"

"Yes," Darnell replied, "they gave him an appointment for four months from now. The guy can't get out of bed, and they want him to schlep all the way over to the VA hospital. He needs home health care, not a VA appointment. Stevie, do you want chicken noodle or minestrone?"

"Chicken noodle," Stevie replied.

Kieran went over to see what else was available. "Mommy, don't we have any chunky beef?"

"I don't know, honey. Look," she suggested.

"I don't see any," he said.

"Grab something else, Kieran," she said.

"Oh, man," he complained.

Carolyn continued to address Stevie. "Would his family object if I had Sheridan's people look into that for him?"

"That would be great, Mommy. It isn't fair, you know. Omid did his part to defend this nation. Uncle Sam should be more sensitive to his needs."

"I found chicken and stars," Kieran announced. "Darnell, pass me a bowl, please."

"Give me the jar, little man," Darnell said. "I'll nuke it for you."

"Thanks," Kieran said, handing him the soup jar. "I'll help Stevie with the sandwiches." As he tried to reach for the bread, Stevie slapped him gently on the hand.

"What was that for?" Kieran complained.

"You're not putting your dirty little hands on my food. Go wash up," Stevie admonished him, and Carolyn smiled.

"Well," Carolyn continued, "if it's okay with Omid and his parents, I'll ask Sheridan to bring the press into it. Good press coverage always gets the ball rolling faster. Give me Mr. Hassan's number and I'll call him."

"It's number eight on my speed dial, Mommy. The phone is on my belt," he volunteered, sticking out his hip in her direction.

She noticed that the phone was strapped to his belt with a shoelace. "Is this a new fashion statement?" she asked.

"Daddy warned me not to lose it again."

"I see," she said while untying the lace, remembering how upset she was a few days earlier because she couldn't reach him by phone. She left the room with the phone in hand as the boys continued to prepare their meal.

"Mommy," Kieran called after her, "what do you want to eat?"

"Nothing, Kieran," she yelled back. "I can wait till dinner."

Darnell started placing the warm bowls of soup on the kitchen table as Stevie distributed the sandwiches. Kieran sat next to his bowl of soup.

"Did you wash your hands?" Stevie inquired.

"Yes, I washed my hands," Kieran responded, reaching for his sandwich.

"I didn't see you leave the room."

"Well, I did," he said, holding his hands out. "See. You don't know everything, you know."

"Shut up and eat, half-pint."

"I'm being abused."

"You don't know what 'abused' means," Stevie teased him. "Eat up."

"This sandwich tastes great," Darnell commented. "Does your mother buy anything that isn't organic? I noticed the label on the soup jars."

"Sometimes she does," Kieran said, "but not stuff we eat. Mommy says the stuff in the supermarket is only good for corpses."

Matthew arrived with Katie. "Early dinner?" he asked as he placed his jacket on the wall peg.

"We were hungry," Kieran said after sipping his soup. "Hi, Katie."

"Hi, squirt. Hello, Darnell, Stevie." The boys waved at her because they were busy chewing. "Bon appétit," she commented.

"Where's Carolyn?" Matthew asked.

"She's probably in the den," Stevie said. "She's on the phone. A package came for you, Daddy. It was on the deck when I arrived. I think it's the stuff you ordered for Katie's SUV; I put it in the shed for you."

"My whole family is here," Carolyn commented as she walked in. She kissed Matthew and asked, "You're not seeing your mistress tonight?"

He smiled and said, "I probably saw her earlier today."

As Carolyn handed Stevie his cell phone, Kieran asked, "You have a mistress, Daddy?"

"Your mother is joking, sport. I can't afford a mistress."

"How expensive are they?" Kieran asked.

"Expensive enough to cost me my life," he said as Carolyn spoke with Katie. "I'm too young to die."

"I have an uncle who cheated on his wife," Darnell said. "She set fire to all his clothes and hammered his car until it resembled a crushed tin can."

"Well, it's better than killing him," Kieran said.

"My father thought it was funny," Darnell commented.

"If your uncle litigated it, she would have been liable for the damages," Stevie interjected. "Did he sue her?"

"I don't know," Darnell replied. "If he didn't sue her it was probably because he feared the worst. Anyway, my father said it served him right for being such an idiot, and it's his own brother he's talking about."

Carolyn reached over Kieran's shoulder and took half of his sandwich.

"Hey," he protested, "that's mine. You said you didn't want anything to eat."

"Well, I changed my mind." She bit into the sandwich.

"But that's my sandwich. I litigate this. Besides, did you wash your hands?"

"What do you know about litigation, oh little boy of mine?"

"Plenty. I have rights, you know. You better make me another sandwich."

"I better what?" Carolyn challenged him.

"You better quit while you're ahead," Stevie advised him. "You can't talk to Mommy that way."

"It's my sandwich!" Kieran protested. Stevie bent over and whispered something in his ear. Kieran's face contorted, and his combative attitude disappeared. He suddenly looked embarrassed. He placed what was left of his sandwich back on the plate and dropped his head.

Carolyn looked at Stevie and wondered what he had said to his brother. She then hugged Kieran from behind and said, "I love you. Thank you for the sandwich."

"You're welcome," he said submissively. "I was wrong."

Matthew and Katie observed what had transpired, and they also wondered what Stevie had said. In the moments that followed, everyone was silent until Carolyn invited Matthew and Katie to sit so they could all eat together. They each grabbed a couple of slices of bread and proceeded to the cold cuts that were on the table. During the meal, Carolyn glanced at Stevie several times. He continued to eat silently, his face unreadable. When he and Darnell finished eating, Stevie rose, tousled Kieran's hair, and announced, "Darnell, it's time to go."

Kieran looked across the table at his mother. When their eyes met, he dropped his gaze. "May I be excused?" he asked.

"You're excused," Carolyn replied. He looked pained as he left the table. Carolyn felt guilty about taking his sandwich.

"That was strange," Matthew commented after Kieran left. Observing Carolyn's demeanor, he added, "He was insolent and out of line, Honey-Lyn. Whatever Stevie said, he probably needed to hear it."

"I'm an adult; I can suck it up. Children sometimes say things they don't mean. They speak from their gut. He looks so remorseful and appears ill. Besides, you know how sensitive he is—he tends to be jittery and overreacts to the slightest thing. Excuse me. I need to speak to my son."

She left the table and was soon in Kieran's room, sitting next to him. His face was wet. She handed him a tissue from the side stand.

"What did Stevie say to you?" she asked earnestly.

"He said, 'Honor thy mother,'" he replied, and the tears welled in his eyes.

"That's it?" she asked incredulously, suspecting that he was holding something back.

She was right because Kieran had resented her actions. He almost said, "How can I honor you when you don't even acknowledge me? It's always Katie this and Katie that. You never seem to care what I think; it's open season on Kieran and okay to invade my space. It was my sandwich." Instead, he nodded and said, "It's the way he said it."

"Well, there's no need to cry over that, honey. I love you."

"Yeah," he hiccupped. "I guess I was being stupid."

"I don't understand, honey."

"I do," he said, looking away. "You know when it's dark and you suddenly see the bright sun?"

"Your eyes hurt?" she asked.

"No. It's like when you eat hot sauce and you were expecting ketchup."

"Your throat and nostrils burn?"

"No, you don't understand. Go away and leave me alone, okay?"

"I'm not going to do that," she said, hugging his shoulders. "You know, I know you better than you think; I believe you're annoyed with me. I was wrong to take your sandwich. I apologize, little baby of mine."

"I'm not a baby! You treat me like a baby and like I don't know anything and like I'm not here, but I'm not a child, you know."

"I'm your mother; I love you. You'll always be my baby. You know something?"

"What?" he asked, sounding annoyed.

"When you hurt, I hurt. That's why I'm not leaving you alone. Do you remember how the bear frightened you?"

"Yeah."

"What did Daddy do? He let you sleep with us. He didn't do that because you're a baby; he did it because he was concerned and he loves you. Well, right now I'm very frightened because I can see you're hurting. I can't leave you alone, and I'm asking you please, don't leave me alone," she said as she hugged him tighter.

He struggled and pulled away. He ran to the bathroom and heaved before he reached the toilet. Carolyn was alarmed and wondered if she had hit a nerve. She rubbed his small back until he finished emptying the contents of his stomach. She hugged him; he was shaking.

"I'm so sorry," she repeated twice as she held him. She wondered how a perfectly fine evening had come to this.

As his trembling subsided, she led him to her bedroom and advised him to wash up in her bathroom. Wearing one of Matthew's sweatshirts that was too large for him, he later climbed into her bed. They talked awhile; he insisted he was fine, and she suspected that he wasn't being honest. When they stopped talking, he snuggled close to her, smelled her fragrance and drifted off to sleep. After listening to his calm breathing for a few minutes, she got up and tucked the covers under his chin. At the door, she paused to look at him in his slumber. Then she went downstairs. Matthew was savoring a piece of pie while Katie set a sandwich down in front of Luis, who had arrived a few minutes earlier. Carolyn greeted her godson and turned to Matthew.

"Mattie," she said, "go upstairs and stay with Kieran while I clean his room."

"What happened?" Katie asked.

"He expelled his dinner all over the carpet."

"I'll give you a hand," Katie volunteered.

"Mattie," Carolyn ordered, "I need you upstairs now."

Matthew pushed his pie to one side and complied with her demand.

"Do you need me to check the little Meerkat, Carolyn?" Luis asked.

"No, eat your sandwich, honey. Kieran is asleep, and he doesn't have a fever. He was upset. It's a long story. I need to get the wet-dry vac and carpet cleaner."

"I can do that for you," Luis volunteered and got up. "It's in the laundry room, right?"

"Yes, but I'll get it. Katie, warm up a jar of soup for him," she suggested.

"I'm on it, Mom. But he doesn't need to be catered to. He has hands."

"And he's my godson."

"So what? That doesn't make him special."

"Kieran is asleep," Matthew announced, returning to the table.

"I know he's asleep," Carolyn protested. "I want you to keep an eye on him."

"What's the point? Do you want me to chart his dreams?" he asked, picking up his pie. When Carolyn glared at him, he said, "Fine, I'll go watch him sleep. It's not for me to reason why." He turned to Luis and asked, "Did I tell you women are crazy?" Carolyn pinched Matthew's arm, and he yelped.

"Now I know why Katie is always smacking me on the head," Luis commented.

"Why are you here?" Carolyn said, suddenly confronting Luis as if perceiving something was amiss.

"I came to pick up Katie."

"Why is Katie here?"

"I came to visit my mommy."

"Why? Because you haven't seen me since yesterday? Normally, you shy away for weeks. Now all of a sudden you're here. Again."

"What do you mean 'again'?" Katie asked defensively. "I wasn't here yesterday; I was at EH. You drove me home."

"You know what I mean. Do you need something? Do you want something?"

"I'm offended by the interrogation," Katie said light-heartedly. "Apparently, everyone here is nuts. Can't a daughter visit her mother?"

"If my daughter were Mother Theresa, I wouldn't wonder about the purpose."

"Well, it so happens that Luis and I want to know if we can join you on the trip to Costa Rica. You know, it's a family matter, all us lunatics traveling together." Carolyn looked at Luis, who didn't say anything. Katie continued, "We were reminiscing about the trip to New Zealand, and we thought it would be nice to do another trip like that again."

"Why, so you can send me on another goose chase?"

"That was not my fault, Mommy."

"What do you mean it wasn't your fault? On the day we were supposed to return to Christchurch to catch the plane, you decided to go whale watching. We didn't know where you were. Courtney was the only one who saw you leave the suite early that morning."

"Courtney has always been a snitch."

"Is that all you can say in your defense?"

"Mom, that's ancient history. I'm not a little kid anymore."

"Do you know that we spread out throughout Te Anau looking for you? We didn't know where you were. I didn't know if you were alive or dead. Matthew and the others left because the kids had to return to school. Papa, Momma, and I were beside ourselves when you finally turned up as fresh as a cucumber at the end of the day. Our return was delayed until we could acquire commercial reservations because Dad's plane was already committed to a previous engagement. I came this close," she said, holding up her hand measuring a space between her thumb and forefinger, "to murdering you and serving a life sentence. My vacation plans were never the same after that."

"So I guess you're saying no."

"You can go to Costa Rica if you want. You're simply not coming with me; I wouldn't walk from here to the corner with you. Excuse me, I have to get the vacuum."

"I love you, Mommy," Katie called out as Carolyn walked toward the laundry room.

"You love torturing her," Luis said.

"No, I don't. I'm trying to make amends. Besides, I had forgotten all that business about the whales. God, that woman can hold a grudge."

"It isn't about the whales, Katie. She's telling you that you frightened the living daylights out of her, and you fail to see the point. I'm amazed she hasn't had a nervous breakdown already. Are you unaware, or are you insensitive?"

"I'm not insensitive. I already told you I know I've put her through hell. Heck, I could write a book about Mom and me. I'm trying to put out an olive branch. I thought it would be nice to have another family trip à la natural. Your soup Is ready," she announced as the microwave beeped. "Get it. I'm going to help her clean the room. She'll change her mind about Costa Rica; she always gives in. Besides, the Costa Rica bullshit suddenly popped into my head. For a moment there, I was beginning to think she was onto me about something more serious than that and I would have to spill the beans."

"You're unbelievable," Luis replied as he got up to get the soup.

* * *

The next morning, Carolyn sat alone in the kitchen enjoying a cup of hot ginger tea with honey when Kieran walked in, looking as if he had just rolled out of bed. His hair was unruly.

"You didn't wake me," he complained as he walked into the kitchen. "Now I'm going to be late for school."

"There's no school for you today, my absentminded genius," Carolyn corrected him. "That's why I let you sleep in."

"That's right; I forgot. It's Holy Thursday. Where is everyone? Can I have eggs?"

"You can have whatever you want. Stevie is out with Darnell. They're helping Omid's father do inventory today. Then they're going horseback riding with Omid. Daddy took Katie's bus to his job where someone can help him with the modifications."

"You mean the SUV."

"Whatever."

"Are you going to work?"

"Yes—EH is a secular school. How do you want your eggs?"

"I can make them. I want lots of butter," he said, opening the refrigerator. "Do we have Italian bread?"

"I can make them with lots of butter," she offered. "How about home fries?"

"No, just Italian bread with lots of butter. It's faster. And hot cocoa with milk, no water. I like it the way Meema Nydia makes it."

"And hot cocoa with milk," she repeated as she started gathering the ingredients. "So you're on a dairy kick today. How are you feeling?"

"I'm feeling fine, except I'm hungry."

"Good. I can make you a western omelet. I also have a surprise for you today," she said, snuggling her cheek against his. She kissed him.

"If the surprise is that I have to spend the day at EH, I already know that."

"No—I'm going to EH," she said as she cut the bread. "You're going with Katie."

"That's not a surprise. That's a nightmare. I can go with Luis."

"Luis is probably on his way to work already. You're going with Katie. You'll like it—I promise."

"That's like telling the chicken he'll enjoy having lunch with the fox. If the vixen is full, it's okay. But if she's hungry, I better watch out."

Carolyn laughed as she removed the bread from the toaster oven and handed it to him. "Where are my eggs?" he asked.

"They're coming. Butter the bread," she said as she walked to the stove. "You certainly are a bossy child."

"What do you want from me, woman? I'm hungry! I was fainting in my sleep upstairs, and you didn't wake me," he whined.

"Well, be patient," she said as she transferred the omelet from the pan to a plate. The microwave was beeping. "And I'm not your woman; I'm your mother. Your cocoa is done," she said while placing the eggs in front of him. "See, it didn't take that long, your majesty."

"We need to develop a system," he commented with his mouth full of bread.

"Chew, swallow, then speak," she said as she sat across from him and picked up her teacup. "You don't say grace anymore?"

"I said it silently while you were getting the milk. It saves time. We need to develop a system, wo...I mean, Mommy." He repeated. "We need a replicator, like the ones in those science fiction movies. As soon as I open my eyes in the morning, I should be able to say 'bread,' and the bread comes out just as I like it: toasty warm and oozing with butter."

"Do you know what 'science fiction' means? It means it isn't going to happen now. Of course, you can sleep with the bread strapped to your abdomen. That will keep it warm. The butter could be messy. That's as close as you'll get to a replicator in your lifetime. Let me know how it works out for you. Want some fruit?"

"May I have ice cream?"

"No, you need fruit."

"I'll tell you what—I'll take the fruit with a scoop of pistachio ice cream."

"You'll take the fruit with a scoop of fruit. There is no ice cream."

"Is too."

"Is not," she lied, enjoying the banter and getting up to get him a serving of melon. "I can tell you're related to Sean O'Gorman. You both love dairy and grease. The two of you are a couple of heart attacks waiting to happen."

"Papa is still alive and perfectly healthy. I am too—you said so yourself. I have a clean bill of health."

"Well, Mr. Clean Bill of Health, here's your fruit," she said, placing the bowl in front of him.

"One scoop?" he pleaded, looking up at her with pitiful blue eyes. "Besides, ice cream is a food group—it has
calcium and protein. And, you said I could have whatever
I want."

"Fine, one scoop," she said, picking up the bowl.

"Thanks, Mommy, you're the best."

The day wasn't as bad as he had imagined. He thought
he might have to spend the day at Katie's, being vigilant of
another bear visit. Instead, they met Katie at church. After
church, Katie and he boarded a cab back to his house.
While Katie finished her morning chores via computer, he
played a video game. After lunch, they boarded a cab
and ended up at a local animal shelter.

"Mom said you can pick out a couple of whatever
you want as long as the creatures don't grow up to be
larger than a poodle," she said as they stepped out of
the taxi.

"Is this the surprise?" he inquired.

"Yes, this is the surprise."

He was visibly pleased. Then he said, "I thought Mommy
said no more pets after Anthony and Cleopatra died."

"Well, that's because she was heartbroken when they
had to be put to sleep. Pets age too quickly and eventually need to be humanely taken care of. Mom got too
attached to Tony and Cleo."

"Were you too attached?"

"I liked having them around, and I miss them. Anthony
was a little rascal. He used to steal everything that wasn't
tied down. Cleo was more like a philosopher."

"Do you think they'll have a couple of Chihuahuas like
Anthony and Cleopatra?"

"We'll find out when we go in," she said, hobbling along-side him on her crutches.

A Mrs. Telma Howard, an elderly retired schoolteacher who, along with her two dachshunds, Niña and Pepita, volunteered two or three days a week at the local shelter, greeted them at the front desk. The older of the two dogs, Niña, was nearly blind with retinitis. Whenever people entered the rescue shelter, Niña sniffed the air and just as promptly laid her head back on the cool floor, adjacent to the small bed her mistress provided for her, but which the dog totally ignored. Pepita was younger and rambunctious. Before Katie and Kieran entered the facility, nine-pound Pepita rushed out from behind the tall reception desk and started barking. The noise alerted the other dogs at the shelter, who increased their own level of anxiety by increasing their usual bark by several decibels. When Katie and Kieran entered, Mrs. Howard was admonishing Pepita to calm down. The dog had a mind of her own and continued to bark at the new arrivals. Regardless of the dog's miniature size, Kieran wasn't about to put himself in harm's way, so he stepped behind Katie and eyed the exit door.

Mrs. Howard sensed the boy's nervousness and smiled because she knew Pepita was all bark and no action. She picked up the small brown dog and said, "I told you to hush. What's wrong with you? This isn't your house. Behave yourself." Then she said to Kieran, "If you let her smell you, she'll calm down. She's just showing off because she thinks she owns the place."

Mrs. Howard held the dog to sniff Katie's arm as Katie held it out for her. Kieran cautiously stepped out from behind Katie. Pepita sniffed his arm as well and then barked twice. Kieran retreated again behind Katie.

"The dog must be detecting the smell of mischief on you," Katie needled him as Mrs. Howard admonished Pepita once more. When the lady set the dog down, the canine stepped forward to smell Kieran's foot. "Don't move," Katie told him, and he obeyed while watching the small dog and feeling somewhat uneasy. Pepita smelled between and around his feet. She then sat on her hindquarters, barked once, stood on all fours, and turned to walk away with her tail high in the air. The dog's final act gave Kieran a sense of rejection.

"I don't think I want that dog," Kieran said as he stepped forward. Katie smiled.

"Fortunately for you, she already has an owner," Mrs. Howard replied. "Or let's say she owns me because she never listens to a word I say. However, because of her loud mouth, she does make a good guard dog."

Katie then explained the purpose of their visit and that they were undecided about the type of pet they wanted. Mrs. Howard introduced them to Quincy, a longtime handler at the shelter, who guided them through the facility.

Kieran was overjoyed as he examined one cage after another. The sound of the barking dogs was deafening, but he didn't stop smiling as he placed his hands over his ears. Sometimes he stopped and sat in front of a cage as Katie and Quincy waited patiently. Then they moved on to the room where they kept the felines, rodents, reptiles, and other animals. It was quieter in that room. He studied each subject with equal interest. Quincy handed him a mouse, and he was thrilled as the mouse climbed up his arm and tickled the back of his neck. Katie handed the mouse back to Quincy. There were two parrots on their perches near the window and a cage of finches. Kieran moved on to the snakes.

"Can I try the snake?" he asked, and Quincy retrieved a small garden snake for him. Kieran allowed the animal to travel from one hand to the other several times. "I don't know," he said, returning the snake to the man. Then the last cage caught his attention.

"Oooh. Can I touch them?" Quincy retrieved a black and white kitten for him. "He's very soft," Kieran commented, holding the tiny feline between his cupped hands. He lifted one hand, and the cat started to walk up his jacket sleeve. "Ouch. His claws are like needles."

"So are his teeth," Quincy said. "You can clip his claws, but you can't do anything about his teeth except brush them from time to time. Eventually, they won't be as sharp as they are now. When they're this small, the teeth feel needle thin."

"Cats brush their teeth?"

"No, we brush their teeth in order to keep them healthy," Quincy replied.

"I like him," Kieran announced. "Mommy said I can have two. Katie, I like them all."

"There are six cats in there, Kieran. Two means a pair, a couple; dos or deux," she repeated in Spanish and French. "Make up your mind, kid, because Mommy will show you the high road if you go home with more than two."

He looked pained and looked at her with the same pitiful eyes that had gotten him the scoop of ice cream that morning.

"Don't give me that look," she admonished him. "I invented it. If the gentleman doesn't mind, you can sit here and decide, but you're only leaving with two."

They left him alone while he played with each cat for several minutes. He finally reached a decision. He approached the front desk holding a kitten in each hand.

"I'll take these two," he said to Mrs. Howard while trying to reach up to place them on the tall counter.

"Who gave you permission to carry them out here?" Katie asked him, sounding irritated. "You're not at a supermarket checkout."

"But these are the ones I want. I can take care of all of them, you know."

Katie took both cats from him and gently handed them over to Mrs. Howard. Then she reminded Kieran, "I already told you Mom said you may have two, not six. As soon as we're done with the paperwork, we'll take them home. Then we have to shop for their food and stuff."

"They can drink milk."

"They need a feline diet."

"And feline toothbrushes," Kieran added.

"Here," Mrs. Howard said to him, handing him a list of what the cats required. "If you get them the items on that list, they'll be happy cats. We'll give you a week's supply of cat food, a cardboard carrier, and a cat box with litter."

"Thank you," Kieran said.

By the time they got home, he had already named the cats Spotty and Blacky. While Katie confined the cats to a safe spot in the laundry room, he ran up to his room to save the adoption papers. Then he rushed back down, excited about going shopping for their needs.

After they returned from the store, Katie helped him set everything up. Then she dropped him off at Emily's Hope for his afterschool instruction in martial arts and music. Kieran ran into Carolyn's office and spoke excitedly about his day. She was pleased to see him so cheerful. As soon as he left for karate, Carolyn thanked Katie via cell phone.

"No big deal," Katie said. "Good luck with your new wards, Mom."

"Why didn't you or Matthew tell me about what happened yesterday?"

"Who told you?"

"Papa," Carolyn replied. "Is that why you came over yesterday?"

"Yeah, we were going to tell you. Then we saw what happened with Kieran, and we thought it was best to hold off."

"Papa said Mattie wants you to return home. I agree with Mattie; I want you home, Katie. I'm worried about you, honey."

"Mom, you didn't raise me so I could be dependent on you all my life. We've discussed this before. Do you go running back to your mommy every time something goes wrong? I'm a woman now."

"As am I, and yes, I do turn to both of my parents as well as to Sean and Ellen whenever I need help. That's what family does."

"And yet, you don't want me to go with you to Costa Rica."

"I regret saying that, honey. I spoke out of context. I want you home, please."

"You spoke within context, Mom. You reminded me what a prick I was as a kid. I'm not a kid anymore. I'm changing; I'm evolving."

"And yet dinosaurs walk the earth," Carolyn said, mocking her. "How long is it going to take you to evolve, Katie?"

"Well, I'll admit I'm a little slow in that field, but I am trying."

"While you work at that, come home. I've kept your room just as you left it."

"I noticed that, and you know, it looks too small for me."

"If you come home, you can go with us to Costa Rica."

"That won't work, Mom. Besides, I won't have the privacy I've become accustomed to."

"Judging from what Papa told me about the pictures, you haven't had much privacy, Katie."

"Don't rub it in, Mom. Besides, that's not the kind of privacy I'm talking about. What if I feel the need to hump Luis? Where am I going to do that?"

"Oh, Katie! Is that evolution exclusive of evolving into a lady?"

"What? Don't you hump Daddy?"

"Stop being the shock jock. It doesn't become you, and it's offensive, Katie. If Santillana makes bail, he's bound to come around again. For God's sake, Katie, when they checked the boat he rented, they found duct tape, handcuffs, and a knife. His intentions were not good. He could have killed both of us, honey. I don't want you in that house by yourself."

"Mom, I'm out of the bottle. You can't force me back in. I have to go now, Mom. I'll talk to you later. Bye."

Twenty-Six

◇◆◇

March 26 finally came, and Matthew and Carolyn's anniversary dinner was being held at Katie's house. It was scheduled early enough for the younger members of the family to partake in the celebration. The festivities got off to a rough start as Nydia, Camille, Margaret, and Carolyn stood on the house deck overlooking the lake. Luis made a grand entrance when he drove up in a huge military vehicle. Most of the people who had gathered for the day's festivities had watched as the enormous automobile came into view.

"What in the world is that?" Nydia asked as she stood by Carolyn's side.

"It's a Hummer," Carolyn commented.

Luis parked the vehicle next to the deck and stepped out of it. Wearing a full grin of complete satisfaction on his face, he said, "Mami, look!"

When Nydia realized that Luis was the owner of the monstrosity, her response was an incredulous, "What the hell?"

Carolyn turned to her and said, "If you don't smack him, I will."

"He's your godson," Nydia replied as Luis skipped up the steps to greet the women. "Be my guest. I'm liable to kill him."

Luis reached the landing with both arms extended like a performer about to embrace his audience. "What do you think?" he asked, smiling from ear to ear.

He was astonished when Carolyn smacked him on the head and biceps.

"Fight, fight!" a very pregnant Courtney announced as Carolyn placed both hands on his chest and pushed him.

"Have you learned nothing?" she asked him as he steadied himself on his feet.

He turned and ran down the steps as a blue shoe flew past him. The children were laughing hysterically while a few adults tried to control their laughter to a giggle. Carolyn was now minus a shoe and was forced to remove its partner to ease her walking.

Katie instructed Kieran to go into her bedroom to get Carolyn a replacement set of footwear. When he arrived upstairs, he was pleasantly surprised to find the four remaining kittens from the animal shelter confined to a corner of the bedroom. They had a cushioned bed, a scratching post, and a few toys. He sat next to the makeshift kennel and forgot about his mother's shoes. A short time later, Momma was in the room with him in order to fulfill the task he had failed to do. After speaking to him, she grabbed a pair of espadrilles from the closet and left Kieran alone with his newfound treasure.

After Carolyn donned Katie's shoes, Luis approached her with the blue shoe in hand and offered to return it if she didn't hit him.

"Are you familiar with the phrase 'A fool and his money are soon parted?'" she asked, glaring at him.

"What? It's a great car. I'll be able to drive through any winter storm. It's a full-terrain vehicle."

"It's a tank," she said, snatching her shoe out of his hand. Katie eased her way toward them and rested her hand and chin on Carolyn's shoulder as she listened to the interaction. "Actually, it's worse than that," Carolyn continued. "It's the most expensive shed ever invented. No, I'm wrong—it's the most expensive heap of scrap metal you'll ever own."

"I told you so," Katie reminded him because she had indeed warned him when he expressed a desire to own a military vehicle.

"Mrs. G., it's not a shed, and it's not scrap metal. That little baby can go anywhere."

"And be a menace to everyone else on the road," she explained. "You don't need a monster gas-guzzler, Luis. We don't live in the wilderness, fool. What the hell were you thinking? Are you planning to join a road crew and plow the roads in winter? That's all it needs—an industrial size plow."

"He also bought a two hundred and eighty-five thousand dollar Bentley," Katie informed her. "It will arrive next week." She gave Luis a grimace that again said, "I told you so," and added, "Let him have it, Mom," urging Carolyn to give him a tongue lashing.

Nydia was the one who intervened in rapid-fire Spanish that most people did not comprehend. Those within earshot did understand "military" and "normal," and they concluded that she must have said, "What the hell does a military vehicle do that a normal vehicle doesn't do?" Katie snickered with complete satisfaction.

The ballroom in Katie's home was decorated and filled to capacity. The caterers bustled about as the guests enjoyed the food and drink and occasionally hit the dance floor. After learning of Kieran's whereabouts, Stevie went upstairs to retrieve him. As they reentered the ballroom, Carolyn was dancing dreamy-eyed in her husband's arms as the band played a slow dance. When the selection ended, he walked her back to her seat and said, "Now it's time for me to embarrass myself."

"What do you mean?" she asked.

"You'll see. After I'm done, you'll probably be embarrassed too," he said with a smile. "I'm not going down alone." Then he turned to Luis and asked, "Are we ready?"

"Of course, Mr. G.," Luis replied. Not knowing if Carolyn was still annoyed with him or understanding the belligerence she had displayed, he gave her a wary look and then said, "Follow me, Mr. G.; Stevie, Kieran," he called, "it's time."

The four of them walked to the stage. Kieran sat behind the drums. Stevie picked up a saxophone. Luis and Matthew strapped on guitars. Seeing Mattie with a guitar surprised Carolyn because he had never displayed any ability as a musician.

"You'll have to bear with me," Matthew said after he had the audience's attention. "Today, my wife Carolyn and I are celebrating our twenty-fourth wedding anniversary. I thank you for coming, and for what you are about to endure. My coconspirators and I have been working on this presentation for the past three months. I not only thank the boys who are about to help me get through this," he said as he turned and introduced Kieran, Stevie, and Luis, "but much to Carolyn's chagrin, I also thank Nydia and Felipe, who have painstakingly tried to teach me a few guitar chords. I thank lovely Shannon, Courtney, and Katie for their candid advice. You see, when I kept arriving home late after practice, Carolyn thought I was seeing another woman."

Laughter erupted as all eyes turned to Carolyn. She hid her flushed face with her hands. As Matthew waited for the audience to calm down, she uncovered her face and mouthed, "I'm going to kill you," to Matthew while good-naturedly slicing her hand across her throat.

"She even threw a pillow and blanket at me, trying to relegate me to sleeping on the couch," Matthew continued to address the audience. Carolyn covered her face again as the laughter repeated itself. "Well, Honey-Lyn, for twenty-four years, twenty-five years if you count from the day we met, I've only had eyes for you. Besides, I know that looking at another woman could be detrimental to my life. I'm not a poet, but with Luis's help...by the way, Luis is the kid you almost killed outside with your shoe earlier today..." He paused as the audience laughed again. "I hope there are no hard feelings. With Luis's help, I did the best I could to compose this song for my Honey-Lyn. Happy anniversary, my one and only love..."

Matthew and the boys started playing the introduction. Carolyn was thrilled to witness Matthew's newfound talent. With Luis leading him on, he nervously broke into song:

Carolyn, lovely and classy, is definitely the wisest lassie. Carolyn, saffron gold, has helped me to be strong and bold. It's always nice to hug and kiss my one and only Carolyn. I can shake off all my woes when I'm home with Honey-Lyn.

The amateurish song went on to describe Carolyn's other attributes and Matthew's love for her. When the artists finished the serenade, Carolyn clapped with enthusiasm and climbed on stage to hug and kiss a very nervous Matthew.

"The things I do for love," he muttered as she kissed him again. Clinging to him, she turned to thank his band.

"Hold on, hold on," Matthew said, trying to get the audience's attention as he placed an arm around Carolyn's shoulder. "I have a question for my wife." Everyone quieted down. Matthew held Carolyn's hand and got down on one knee. He wet his lips and asked, "If you had it to do over, would you marry me?"

"In a heartbeat," she replied in a choked voice.

"Will you marry me now?" he asked. Carolyn nodded in affirmation, and Matthew stood up. "Patrick," he yelled, "she said yes!"

Patrick, Katie, and Shannon soon joined them on stage. Shannon pulled Carolyn aside and adjusted a veil on her head that matched Carolyn's light blue dress while Carolyn enjoyed being the center of attention. Katie handed her a bouquet. Patrick and Kieran took their places next to the couple, and Patrick guided them through the marriage ceremony as they exchanged vows.

As Kieran held out the rings, Matthew removed the old claddagh wedding ring from Carolyn's finger and replaced it with a new one. It was modified with a setting of six diamonds on the band side of the ring. The inscription read "love bliss 25." His ring was similar. Sensing she knew the symbolic interpretation, Carolyn nonetheless inquired about it later. She was right. He said, "I've loved you for a quarter century." He looked into her eyes as if to cushion a blow and said, "There are good and bad memories, but you have been mother to our six children. One didn't cross the threshold to us, but we've gotten to know the other five." He continued to gaze at her as the tears welled in their eyes. To lighten the moment, he pointed to one of the diamonds and said, "That one is Katie. It's probably the sharpest of the six." Carolyn laughed and gave him a loving kiss.

"I love you, Mattie," she whispered hoarsely.

"Are you sure you don't want to have another bundle of bliss?" he asked her.

"Oh, I'm very sure," she insisted with a laugh.

After the wedding kiss and cheers from guests, the festivities continued.

Luis sat near a window, watching the people mill about. Margaret sat next to him. "Are you here to beat me too?" he asked.

"No, my young prince," she replied. "I don't believe in pummeling."

"I'm used to it. Katie loves to pummel. I had never been pummeled by Carolyn, though. That's a first."

"Are your feelings hurt?"

"Only if Mami and Carolyn stay angry at me. What did I do wrong? That's a nice vehicle," he said, thinking of his new acquisition.

"They're not angry. It was their way of letting you know they believe you've made a bad decision. By now, it's over."

"Do you think I made the wrong decision?"

"It doesn't matter what I think. But if it will help you feel better, I'll say no."

"Do you believe that, or are you humoring me?"

"I say what I believe. We don't all think alike or enjoy the same things. That's why we have diversity in the world. It gives us the freedom to choose and make decisions."

"Do you think I can return it and get my money back?"

"Luis, I don't think automotive dealers have return or exchange policies. Once you sign your name on the dotted line, it becomes a used car—your used car. Why do you suddenly want to take it back? You obviously like it or you wouldn't have purchased it."

"I don't know," he said, having his doubts. "It seemed like a good idea at the time, but Carolyn is right—it could be a menace to people on the road."

"The cow is out of the barn, Luis. Besides, people drive behind trucks and buses all the time. Your vehicle could fit that category. It probably gives you a nice view of the road."

"Yes, it does," he said with a smile.

"You're a medical doctor, so you can think like a scientist. One of the things we do in science is to see a hypothesis to the end, right or wrong. We won't know which way it's going to go until we get there. You drove that special SUV on the road in order to satisfy an end."

"That's one way of looking at it," he agreed.

"Did you enjoy the analysis of the subject?"

"Yes," he said, grinning.

"Have you concluded your experiment, or do you need further investigation of the data?"

"Further analysis would be nice," he replied, smiling. "Would you like to go for a spin, Margaret?"

"Let's go, Luis."

"I can take you home, if you like."

"That means Harold and Simon will have to leave without me. Let me inform them, and we can get a head start. Perhaps Katie or the boys will join us so you won't have to return home alone."

"I'd rather take the boys if it's okay with Carolyn. They don't hit me."

"I can't believe she has encouraged him," Carolyn commented as she leaned against Matthew and watched Margaret and her sons climb into Luis's vehicle.

"Well," Katie added as she looked on, "I guess he's entitled to make a few mistakes. I just hope he doesn't destroy anything on the road—like the pavement, for one. It must be the curse of the Midas touch."

Twenty-Seven

◇◆◇

1992

After spending several frantic hours searching for Katie, those left behind in New Zealand were relieved when Katie finally returned from her impromptu whale-watching trip. Carolyn hugged and kissed her daughter with tear-filled eyes. Then she suddenly became enraged. She grabbed Katie by both shoulders and shook her as she delivered a severe tongue lashing. Ellen and Sean had similar feelings, but they contained themselves as they separated mother and daughter from one another.

When Ellen had Katie over to one side, she held her forefinger in front of Katie's face and said, "Don't you ever pull a stunt like that again because, God help me, I will dismember you myself. Have you any idea what you've put us through, young Kate?"

They were able to get commercial reservations to leave a week later. It was a very tense week for all of them. Sean and Ellen had to cancel a planned detour through Ireland. They had planned the trip for themselves and Katie and it would have been an opportunity to see Ellen's elderly mother. However, they didn't believe Katie needed to be rewarded with an additional trip, and they didn't want Carolyn to return home without their assistance.

Upon arriving home, Patrick looked in on Mrs. Shultz. She was in very poor health. By the time Carolyn arrived with the children, Mrs. Shultz was hospitalized. The cancer had spread to her lungs. Despite learning the painful truth about Mrs. Shultz's condition, Katie and Stevie were happy when she gave them Anthony and Cleopatra. Mrs. Shultz's three children were now at her bedside practically 24-7, for they knew the end was near. As they waited for Yung to be transferred to hospice, she died during the early morning hours, two days shy of her birthday.

Stevie and Katie were saddened by the news. "She was a very nice lady," Stevie commented with genuine sincerity. Katie remained silent and spent most of the day brooding in her room. In the evening, she stared up at the stars and wondered which one had become Yung Shultz's new home. Katie thought that Yung probably met Emily up there and Emily probably said, "Welcome to Heaven, Yung." Then she imagined Marjorie flying on a comet and saying, "I'm Katie's aunt, Carolyn's twin sister. Come, I'll show you around."

The phone rang. It was Rina calling from Florida: she and Katie were soon talking and giggling. Rina said she had seen an alligator down by the canal. She had watched as the police tied him up with duct tape and tossed him into the back of a flatbed truck.

"I guess they'll release him in the swamp," Rina commented. "That sucker was big. On the news they said he was seven and a half feet."

Katie shared her recent adventures in New Zealand and informed her, "They have a lot of weird animals down there, but they don't have any crocodiles, alligators, scorpions, or snakes. I did see a snake at the zoo and a big lizard, but you don't see any snakes in the wild."

"Well, we have snakes in Florida, big copperheads. When and if you come, I'll show you," Rina offered.

"Maybe I can go sometime this year," Katie replied as Carolyn knocked on the door and let herself in.

"It's time for dinner, honey," Carolyn said. Then she asked, "Whom are you talking to?"

"I'm talking to Rina, Mommy."

Carolyn shook her head in disapproval and sighed. "Well, say good-bye and come down. Daddy and Stevie are waiting. After dinner, we have to walk the dogs, honey."

Prior to the New Zealand trip, Luis and Katie had mailed their college applications. They each received their letters of acceptance and needed to make their final decisions. They attended their first prom together. Luis was one of the youngest students to graduate from his prep school, and he had accepted the offer to attend Fordham University in the Bronx. Katie had set her sights on a school further away from home. When University College Dublin accepted her application, Carolyn was beside herself.

"She can't be going to school across the pond," she complained to Momma. "She's only thirteen. I can't uproot the children and take off to Ireland. Besides, Matthew isn't going to leave New York."

"She'll soon be fourteen. I was thirteen when I came across the pond," Momma reminded her. "I stayed with my uncle and his wife, and I got a job."

"But we're talking about Katie, Momma. She's book smart, but incredibly irrational. We can't just turn her loose thousands of miles away from home. She needs to attend a local school."

"Didn't you travel the world when you were considerably younger than she, a Rua?"

"With my parents, Momma. I landed wherever they went."

"What if Sean and I went with her, Rua? Would that be okay?"

"What about your job?"

"I think I'll ease up on that for a while."

"You're going to retire?"

"Perhaps take a rest; Sean can do the same. It's a risk. Once you leave the entertainment business, it may be hard to return. However, this could be an excellent opportunity for young Kate. Perhaps we can find a flat near my mother. I hear she's getting a bit senile, and this could be an excellent opportunity for me to be with her."

"How old is she?" Carolyn asked, sounding concerned. She had met the older Katharine a couple of times when she visited with Ellen and the children, and Carolyn had noticed that Katharine hadn't shown any signs of mental decline at the time. The elderly Kate was a good-humored woman of limited education, but she was very clever.

"Seventy-four, going on seventy-five."

"It would be nice if you spent some time with her," Carolyn agreed. "I'm fortunate to be close to my mother. However, Katie is still too young to leave home."

Ellen laughed and said, "This isn't about Katie, a Rua. It's about you. You don't want to let go." Carolyn blushed. "I'm right," Ellen said victoriously. "You're having separation anxiety."

"Katie is just a baby," Carolyn said defensively.

"Some baby. She's nearly as tall as you and still growing."

"Well, I worry about that too. What if one of those college freshmen tries to get fresh with her?"

"The attraction of the sexes is as old as time. I think Katie can take care of herself. Come on, Rua, cut the cord. It hurts less if you do it in one stroke."

"That's easy for you to say. If you go with her, you won't be cutting any cord."

"That's a low blow, dear. I've already cut it four times. You walked off with Matthew, the final tear."

"You see him practically every day, so don't rub my nose in it," Carolyn replied. Then her brow furrowed. "I'm grateful for the offer, but if she goes to Ireland, she'll be so far and I'll miss her, Momma. And she needs to take her medication. Her doctor is here."

"They have doctors and meds in Ireland. Think about it. You have a few months to get used to the idea."

And so Carolyn got used to the idea. At the airport, she started reciting a list to Ellen. "Make sure she dresses warmly. Don't let her stay up late. She likes her eggs over easy. Try to buy only organic foods for her."

"A Rua, will you relax!" Ellen scolded her. "She isn't going to Mars. We'll be a phone call away, but don't annoy me by flooding my phone with calls, or I'll disown you." Then she gave her a farewell hug. "I love you, dear. Look after my Mattie and the children."

Carolyn turned to Sean and said, "I know she listens to you. Don't let her get away with anything. She knows she has to be in bed no later than ten. She needs a full night's sleep to function properly. Call me if you need anything. Oh, I'm going to miss you, Papa."

"Like Ellen said," he replied, "we're just a phone call away. You can call me anytime. I'll pick up; I won't disown you, I promise."

"I love you, Papa," Carolyn said, kissing him good-bye.

Then she turned to Katie. First she looked at her intently. Then she hugged her and kissed her several times. "Be good," she reminded her as she brushed Katie's hair back. "Call me if you need anything. Are you sure you have all the phone numbers?"

"Yes, Mommy, I know them all by heart."

"Winters in Ireland can be harsh because of the dampness. Make sure you bundle up. Wear your hat, and don't eat too much junk food. Take your medication on time."

"Bye, Mommy. We have to go. We'll be the last ones on board. I'll miss you."

"I'll miss you too," Carolyn said, giving her a final hug and kiss. "I love you, baby. Bye."

She watched forlornly as Sean, Ellen, and Katie disappeared into the plane's walkway. She dragged Matthew and the children to the observation window and didn't detach herself from it until the plane was in the air and out of sight. As baby Kieran watched from Matthew's arms, he pointed up and said, "Ayee."

"Oh my God. Did you hear that?" she exclaimed turning to Matthew. "He made a connection. He said 'Katie.' Say it again, sweetie. Say 'Katie.'"

"Ayee," Kieran responded. Then he started sucking on his two fingers.

"Yes, Ayee. She's gone," she sighed, and Matthew chuckled as she wiped the tears from her eyes. She pushed him. "That's for snickering."

He put his arm around her shoulder and continued to laugh. "I think we can go home now. She'll be okay, Honey-Lyn."

* * *

Katharine Sr. had been living in Dublin for nearly twenty years. Contrary to the country life she had known most of her life, everything was more convenient here. She was a highly independent woman. Although her bones were showing the signs of age, she was a very active woman who enjoyed an occasional trip to the cinema or theatre. She was also active in her church, where she was the treasurer of the senior activities, which sometimes included out-of-town excursions. When Ellen, Sean, and Katie arrived at her flat, she was bustling around in the kitchen. As Ellen observed her, she concluded that her siblings had misled her. There was nothing senile about the white-haired, porcelain-skinned old lady. She had all her marbles, Ellen observed.

"I figured you'd be hungry after your trip, Ellen. I've made watercress sandwiches to tide you over until dinner, a Cocán Róis," she added, using her pet name "rosebud" for Ellen and uncovering the sandwich platter she had set on the table. "The tea is almost ready, dear. Sit, sit. Kate, my love, would you prefer some milk, dear?"

Up until now, Katie had been very quiet. However, she did observe everything around her. It wasn't the first time she had met her great-grandmother, but time and distance away from relatives tends to turn them into strangers. Katie was using the observation time to acclimate herself to her new surroundings. Compared to home, Katharine's flat seemed small. The kitchen table was also a small four-seater. Everything was neat and in its place. As Katie concentrated on the ambience and her great-grandmother's appearance—her hair and eyebrows were so white and thin, her skin flawless and beautiful despite her age—Katie almost missed the question. "Tea is fine," she finally said as she pulled out the chair to sit.

"I've been making inquiries in church, Cocán Róis," Katharine said to her daughter, "and I believe I've found the perfect flat for you; it's within walking distance of the church. It has three bedrooms, a kitchen, one full bath, and a water closet. It's very airy, dear, and you'll get the sunlight in the afternoon. The kitchen gets the morning sun, which is good because it will be cool in the evening when you have to cook. I know you Yanks like a heavy meal in the evening. As you know, I'm fine with tea and biscuits, dear. We can take a walk over there before dinner if you like."

"That sounds good, Mamaí," Ellen replied.

"Eat up," she insisted. "Help yourselves. I discovered this nice shop a few blocks away from here. They sell all sorts of international foods, including organic. We've become quite universal in Ireland with all sorts of people from so many different countries. At the shop, I met this nice young man from a place called Sri Lanka; I had to look it up on a map. I'll get the tea; it's ready."

After the tea was served, Katharine sat between Sean and Katie. "So, Kate, you'll be going to university. Good for you. I've never had much schooling, so I'm happy to see that the young ones are going upward and onward. Education is a wonderful thing, you know. Oh, I wish I had the opportunity when I was growing up. I would have probably run for Parliament, you know. I do have the gift of gab, and that's all those politicians do. They don't do much for the common man, but they sure do love to gab. Do you like politics, Kate?"

Katie had been hypnotized by Katharine's beautiful brogue, and she smiled inwardly. Ellen's brogue wasn't as pronounced as Katharine's. However, they were both pleasantly melodic. Katie set her teacup down and replied, "No, Mamaí. I don't think I do."

"Well, I can see you don't talk much," Katharine observed.

"That's because you don't know her well," Sean warned her. "Wait until she gets her bun in a tizzy. You may have to stand back."

Katie took a polite bite of her watercress sandwich and returned to quietly assessing the situation until the flavor of the sandwich awakened her taste buds. It was pleasantly delicious.

They viewed and accepted the small apartment that Ellen's mother had found for them. The apartment would be furnished while they remained at the hotel. They also took time to visit University College Dublin's new and still expanding campus and met with the headmaster of the engineering department. He was very impressed by Katie's young age and knowledge, and he informed them that his door was always open if they needed anything.

As the campus tour progressed, Katie observed the few locals who had also apparently come for a rehearsal look at the campus. A handful of young men and women had blue, green, or pink spiked hair. The girls wore black lipstick and mascara, short skirts, fishnet stockings, and ankle-high boots. The boys wore tight jeans with similar type boots as the girls. One of them also sported black mascara, a leather neck collar that was attached to a chain leash his girlfriend controlled, and a large silver safety pin through his nose. Their belts were fashioned from leather and/or chains. Either gender wore leather or denim jackets with metal studs. They had earrings, nose rings, lip rings, eyelid rings, and tattoos.

Ellen eyed the youngsters and muttered, "Jesus, Mary, and Joseph. What is this world coming to?"

Sean snickered at her reaction and said nothing. Kids stateside sported similar fashions, but Katie concluded that the degree of creativity appeared to be more prevalent in Dublin.

Upon arriving home, Ellen agreed to take Katie shopping the next day.

"Thanks, Momma," she said, practically skipping toward her room.

Once Katie was out of earshot, Ellen said, "Now I'm beginning to realize what we've gotten ourselves into."

"What would that be?" Sean asked.

"Well, the closest eatery to that school sells alcohol. She's bound to make friends. Should I follow her around that enormous campus to make sure she stays out of trouble?"

"Are you concerned she'll become a lush?" he asked, sounding amused.

"Well, you never know. And the kids have pink and green hair, Sean."

"It's called funk, Ellen. Don't tell me it's news to you. You're a film producer."

"Yes, but I didn't think I was going to enter a movie set. Good God, if Rua saw this, she would probably have a conniption."

"Well, relax. I suggest you offer Katie a visit to the hair salon. Ask her if she wants a makeover, goth or funk, and get it over with once and for all. If she knows the option is on the table, she can't use it as a tool of rebellion. After she dyes her hair pink, we simply make sure she becomes a blonde again before she heads home."

"You're incorrigible."

"I'm a pragmatist, Ellen."

The next day, they shopped for furniture. Sean returned to the hotel, leaving the females to shop for girl stuff. As Katie searched the racks for a jacket, she chose both a leather and a denim. "What do you think, Momma?"

"Have you been inspired by the locals, young Kate? If you have, those are much too tame, dear; they need studs and chains. We need to visit an establishment that caters to the younger generation," she said, and then she suggested following Sean's recommendation. "Perhaps you should cut your hair and tint it with a few of those rainbow colors."

"Momma, are you serious? I don't think I want my hair to look like corn silk protruding from its husk. But the jackets are kind of neat, don't you think? They remind me of an old-fashioned style."

"Do you mean James Dean, *Rebel Without a Cause*, or Hell's Angels? If you're going for the Hell's Angels look, you probably need studs."

"You know what, let's just look around some more. I'm not exactly sure what I want. I don't want to overextend myself and look like I'm desperately trying to fit in."

"We should have checked with the concierge at the hotel before venturing out. They're usually the best source of advice."

They window-shopped for about an hour before Katie decided to purchase a pair of the ankle-high shoes she had seen the young ladies wearing. "Momma, I think these will make me look less foreign. What do you think?"

"I think it's a good start, Kate. Footwear is important."

"Do you still think I should change my hair, perhaps wear it up?"

"The decision is yours, dear. Do what makes you comfortable. However, in case it's crossed your mind, you already know my stance on body piercing, Kate."

"I certainly know Papa's opinion of that. When I was in the hospital, he said I was wrong and strong. Do you suppose he still feels that way? Besides, I don't cut myself, Momma. Maybe I can get a clip-on nose ring."

"Make sure you don't accidentally breathe it up your nostril. It may take some doing to dislodge it."

"So I can get one?"

"I didn't say that. You'll have to clear that matter with your parents and perhaps Sean. I suggest you ease into it. Besides, you came to Dublin to get an education. You didn't come here to compete in a fashion show."

"I have to get an education because Mom insists on it."

"You have to get an education because it's part of the demands society places upon us. The more credentials you have, the further you'll go. As soon as we get back to the hotel, review your syllabi and complete at least one task on a list."

"I already completed a unit last night while you and Papa were watching the boob tube. I'm going to build a bridge," she said with a sparkle in her eye. "I mean a real bridge, not a model."

"Where, exactly, are you going to build this bridge, Kate?"

"I don't know yet, but I'll find the perfect place. I was thinking in a rustic area. We're in Ireland, for God's sake. I'm going to find a spot, maybe in a public garden or in the countryside where they need a bamboo bridge for the right ambiance."

"So now Ireland needs ambiance. Just make sure Sean and I don't have to trek too far to find this perfect spot.

Let's pay for your shoes and head home. We've done enough shopping for one day."

They grabbed a cab back to the hotel. Later, Katharine Sr. joined them for dinner.

"The only problem with this arrangement," Katie commented, "is that it will limit my sports participation. I doubt they'll let me participate in university sports because I'm younger than the other students. Track should be okay, but soccer may be a problem."

"The church has girls' junior football and rugby, Kate," Katharine replied. "I'll speak to Father Brien about that. Perhaps they'll allow you to play or practice with a team."

"I've never played rugby, but I'm willing to try. I think that would be awesome."

"Are you enjoying yourself so far, dear?"

"Yes, Mamaí. It's nice to be a little laid back and not rushing from one point of interest to another like we usually do when we're on vacation. I mean, it's not too bad to do that either, but sometimes it's nice to chill."

"Did you hear that, Sean?" Momma asked. "Katie feels this is a relaxing trip. My dogs are still barking from yesterday, and she's feeling laid back."

"Well, unlike you, Ellen, I know when to quit. While you two were out shopping for shoes, I was reshaping the hotel soap into works of art. The hotel maid is impressed with my work. I think I swept her off her feet with my talent."

Katharine Sr. responded to Katie's comment with, "Well, you'll have enough time to chill during the winter months, and I literally mean chill, dear. Ireland isn't as cold as New York—it's more temperate here—but the cold humidity could take a toll on you. This will be your first winter experience in Ireland. Then you'll understand what I mean."

"Well, I would have been here last year, but something came up."

"Indeed, something did come up," Sean interjected. "We almost attended Katie's funeral after she disappeared on her own whaling expedition. I don't know who would have killed her first, me or Carolyn." He laughed.

"Oh, yes," Katharine Sr. said. "I remember that. I was so looking forward to that visit. I was hoping you would have stayed long enough to celebrate St. Pat's Day with me. Well, hopefully we can do it this coming year. As for Kate's expedition, we've all been young and foolish at one time or another."

"Some are more foolish than others," Sean added. "But then again, God does protect children and fools."

Katie looked at him and gave him an impish smile. She didn't mind Sean's sense of humor, and she knew she had been foolish. However, not one to hold anything back, she said, "I'm still a child, Papa. What's your excuse?"

"Will you listen to the mouth on her? I told you she isn't as quiet as she appears," Sean warned the older Katharine. "Have you no respect for your elders, Katie?"

"I respect you, Papa. But I couldn't resist, and there are plenty of old fools in the world."

"So are you calling me a fool, Katie?"

"I wouldn't dream of doing such a thing, Papa," she said while maintaining the impish grin that was accompanied with a wink.

* * *

As Sean and Ellen got to know UCD better, there was no doubt that Katie had chosen an excellent university, but their faith in Katie's future actions was definitely in doubt. With the help of the headmaster at the School of Engineering, Ellen and Sean volunteered their services at the university in order to keep an eye on Katie. Never being overbearing, it gave them comfort to know they were nearby in the event of an emergency. Ellen helped out at the arts and theatre division. Sean decided to take a class in Celtic history. When he wasn't in class, he took on the duties of groundskeeper. He enjoyed the hours of exercise and fresh air, and Katie carried a mobile phone with her to allow her grandparents to stay in contact with her.

A few days after arriving, Katie called Carolyn and enthusiastically announced, "Mom, I'm on the rowing team. They've also accepted me for rugby. This is the bomb, Mom. If it's too cold to row, I can do aikido. And the track, Mom. You have to see the track; it's awesome; I've run it three times already. When you come, I'll take you to see it."

The stay across the pond gave Ellen an opportunity to rekindle her relationship with Katharine Sr., and it gave Katie a chance to get to know her great-grandmother on a more personal level. Carolyn and the family spent as many family holidays with them as she could squeeze in. At times, they arrived via Harold's personal jet, and other family members as well as Nydia and her family joined them.

Between Thanksgiving and Christmas, Katie had familiarized herself with Dublin's public transportation, which was extremely efficient and easy to navigate. She went Christmas shopping on her own. On her way home, she stopped off at Katharine's flat. The white-haired woman opened the door for Katie and gave her an unpleasant shock.

"*Dia duit, a Gráinne*," Katharine welcomed Katie, speaking in Irish.

"I'm sorry, Mamaí," Katie replied. "I don't understand Irish."

To Katie's dismay, the old lady continued to address her in the unknown tongue. By her actions, Katie understood she had been invited to sit. She also understood the constant referrals to Gráinne.

"I'm not Gráinne, Mamaí. My name is Katie."

Katharine continued the one-sided conversation. In desperation, Katie called Momma Ellen.

"Apparently," she explained, "she thinks I'm somebody named Gráinne, but I don't understand anything else, Momma. Please come quickly; I don't know what to do, Momma."

And so Katie and Ellen were now aware that Katharine Sr. tended to have bouts of dementia.

Twenty-Eight

◇◇◇

2005

Easter Sunday was the last March celebration of the devout Irish Catholic O'Gorman families. It was a low-key day. After church services, the O'Gormans met at Momma and Papa's house. Shannon and Elizabeth's children entertained themselves in much the same way they had played when they were children. Sean played with the latest generation by showing the little ones how miniature cars gained momentum on a downward path. These days, it was harder for him to get down and up from the floor, but he ignored his arthritic knees as he sat and played with the children. Elizabeth's baby drooled onto his bib and onto a little car as he sucked on its bumper or pounded it against the floor and tried to make sense of it. Katie and Luis took turns at the piano as they attempted to outdo each other with a tune. Nydia, Momma, and Camille played a board game. Neil, Kieran, Felipe, and Patrick were at another table playing cards. Carolyn snuggled next to Matthew as they watched Papa with the children. Young Courtney and her husband played a video game. Stevie sat in a corner reading a book on Church history. What seemed to be a boring picture for an outside viewer was a much-cherished and comfortable tradition for the O'Gormans.

* * *

Katie finished speaking to her head engineer, Ramírez, and as she hung up, Matthew arrived. He found her in the garage lab, looking through carefully categorized integrated computer circuits. She looked up and asked, "Did Mommy send you?"

"No, I sent me," he replied. "Judging from what you're doing, I believe I arrived on time. Are you planning to repair the security unit?"

"Yes, but I don't think I have the right parts."

"Good, because you're not going to foolishly climb any ladders today. Do you really believe you're invincible, or did your brains leak out your ears?" After Katie glared at him, he added, "Stevie and I will replace the SU for you this afternoon. I brought a whole new unit. When we take down the old one, you can knock yourself out repairing it on level ground." When she didn't reply, he continued with, "We're still welding a few parts on your SUV. You can probably get back to work in a few days."

"Thank you, Daddy; I'm looking forward to being free. However, I probably won't be using it much for work."

"What do you mean?"

"I'm thinking of selling the business. I'm thinking of putting feelers out there."

"What made you decide that? I thought this was your love and life's work. Besides, weren't you thinking of hiring a new engineer?"

"That's scrapped, as of today. I like what I'm doing, but there are different facets to anything you do. Evolving is essential to staying afloat and fresh. I'm also a finance major. Last night, I started thinking. The housing industry is doing great, and I wondered, what if this is the apex? What if it starts going downhill tomorrow? Mommy has also taught me not to get too greedy and to have foresight. I think this is the right time to sell; I can feel it in my bones."

"Well, Mommy will be delighted to hear you've been listening to her. Sometimes we wonder if your ears are clogged. What will you do if you find a buyer?"

In response to his question, she turned his attention to a computer and opened a new CAD window. "What do you think?" she asked. She invited him to sit and flip through the files.

When Matthew finished looking at the diagrams, he said, "That's impressive. The greenhouse and hydroponics lab are a nice touch, but I'm confused. First question: if you plan to continue to construct on this property, why sell your construction company now?"

"You're right. Maybe I should complete this first," she said, pointing to the computer screen. "Then sell. That means I'll have to hire an engineer after all. What's the next question?"

"Why are you building two more homes?"

"That's a 'probably,' and it depends on you, Momma, Papa, and Mommy." When Matthew gave her a quizzical look, she said, "I want to build those for you and them. I was thinking of how difficult it got when Mamaí Katharine became ill and how fortunate it was for Momma to be near her. You and Mommy want me back home, but Daddy, I can't go back; I like my independence. If you move here, we can be together and still have plenty of space. I have seven hundred acres. Part of that went to Emily's Hope. For my personal use, I'm only enclosing twenty acres;

wildlife can have the rest. In some places, twenty acres holds as many as eighty homes. If you move here, you'll have amenities you don't presently have. I can include an elevator for you. I can even design separate apartments above or adjacent to you for Stevie and Kieran if they want to fan out."

"Your mother and I have a lot of memories in our home."

"Bring the memories with you. You don't have to decide now. You can even keep the old house while you give the new one a trial run."

"Carolyn chose that house because it was ideal for us to raise a family. She said she likes the cozy feel."

"I don't have to build the one I designed. I can make a replica of your present home, except it will have amenities you don't have now and be more fuel efficient, if you like. I bet Mom will like LED track lighting. It will give the place a cheerier look. Think about it; discuss it with Mommy. We can put our heads together. I've even considered asking Luis to move in with me permanently, and his parents can move into his house. Or, we can design one for them as well. I'll bet Nydia would love that."

"So you're making plans for everyone," her father countered.

"You sound upset. Don't be, please. It's a proposal. I don't want to be presumptuous. Will you consider it?"

"Listen, princess, it's a nice thought. However, sometimes distance can be a good thing. Yes, I want you home, but I'm not so sure I want to move from my home."

Katie tapped him on the shoulder and smiled. "I understand," she said. "You don't like change. Whenever you came to visit in Ireland, you didn't always appear comfortable."

"You noticed that, huh? Well, I'm set in my ways. But I was always happy to see you. I just liked it better when you came because it meant I didn't need to go. However, e-mail me a copy of this and I'll show it to your mom. I'll try to keep an open mind, I promise. So you're thinking of having Luis move in permanently?"

She gave him a nervous smile and nodded.

"I know you don't want my advice," he said, "but I suggest you marry the poor guy already and get it over with. He's a good kid. He's also been very patient."

"I know that. Marriage is a huge step, Daddy. What if something goes wrong?"

"I believe sometimes you think yourself into an abyss, Katie. Life can be a great thing. You should jump in and enjoy it. Maybe that's why I don't see much sense in traveling. I'm perfectly happy right where I am; I enjoy the little things in life. When you kids were young, I loved watching you. You were cute little people. Kieran is still a cute little person. I love the fragrance of Carolyn's hair. I love the smell of a summer breeze. I love pie."

"Yes, I know you love pie. There's a frozen one upstairs. Copy or e-mail yourself the files while I tidy up down here. Then we can go upstairs and whip up something to eat, including pie for dessert."

As they started to do their individual tasks, Katie heard a car pull up. She stepped outside to see Camille and Courtney step out of the car. "There's Katie," pregnant Courtney commented as she struggled to get out of the car.

Katie walked up to the two women and greeted them.

"No work today?" she asked Camille as she kissed her on the cheek.

"It's Easter week, love," Camille replied. "The schools won't close until Passover, April 24. I can't wait that long to extend the weekend. I've been spoiled into having Easter week off. Now the department of education has changed the rules and today, I decided to stick to the old rules. I hope next year Easter and Passover fall early and during the same week. That way, I won't feel like I need to play hooky. So on my self-proclaimed day off, we decided to stop in and see how you're doing. You're getting to be a pro with those crutches."

"Yes," Katie agreed. "Maybe I should enter a marathon."

"Do you always leave that garage door open, Katie?" Camille inquired.

"So this isn't a social visit, Aunt Camille. You are literally here to check on me and perhaps babysit. Well, Daddy beat you to it; he's inside. If I wait long enough, the rest of the family will probably start filing in. I'm going to start charging admission."

"Well, I'm not paying anything," Courtney said. "The swelling on your jaw has gone down I see."

"Yes, it has, but the bruise is still visible. Come on in." She invited them to follow her into the garage. "We're going up soon to start lunch. Stevie will be coming by later to help Daddy with the brawny part of the security system. I suspect Mom and Kieran won't be far behind."

After they were inside, Camille locked the garage door. "This is how it should be while you're inside," she instructed Katie. "You need to make sure you're secure in your own home. That way, no one can walk in and surprise you. As soon as Matthew repairs the security unit, make sure it's always activated whether you're home or not."

"James Esposito already told me that," Katie replied.

"And yet, I arrive and find the garage door open," Camille admonished her. "Don't get careless, Katie. Besides, keeping it shut also keeps the wildlife out."

Events turned out as Katie had predicted. Family members continued to arrive throughout the afternoon. Stevie secured the ladder for his father while Matthew replaced the damaged unit with the new one. Nydia arrived with a box full of cranberry tarts. Carolyn arrived with Kieran carrying two cat carriers.

"Why did you bring your cats?" Katie asked him.

"They're family," he responded. "They're entitled to visit their siblings; they probably miss each other."

"Well, the next time you come, you leave them home," Katie countered.

"Uh-uh," he objected. "They have a right."

"I make the rules here, kid."

"Mommy," he said, turning to Carolyn, "I need you to petition the court to allow Spotty and Blacky to visit their siblings. Katie is being uncooperative and denying them their rights."

"You both stop the nonsense," Matthew interjected. "Kieran, take your cats upstairs for their visit and help me reprogram the security system."

"Well, he better clean up their poop when they're done. He didn't bring their litter box."

"I'm not cleaning anything up. Besides, how am I supposed to know whose poop is whose?"

"Get a DNA marker."

"I said quit it," Matthew interjected again. "Kieran, move those legs! Katie, act your age. They must do this to irritate me," he said to Carolyn, who merely gave him an understanding smile.

Luis arrived sporting his brand-new Bentley, and Stevie, Courtney, and Nydia went out to examine his new car. He explained it had arrived earlier than expected and took them for a spin around the neighborhood. After the novelty wore off for the new admirers, Luis went inside the house and brought Carolyn out to see the car.

"Do you approve of this car?" he asked as he wiped a fingerprint on the door handle with the hem of his shirt.

"At least it's not a tank," she commented while studying the car's exterior.

"Get in," he invited.

They both sat in the car while he showed off the amenities. "The leather is as soft as a baby's bottom. Feel it." He ran his hand over the seat.

"It's nice," she agreed.

With that encouragement, he proceeded to enthusiastically show her how to adjust the automatic seats. He gave her a full functional tour of the dashboard and steering mechanism. Then they sat quietly for a moment.

"Did my mother enjoy the ride in your tank the other day?" she asked him while settling back in her seat.

Luis almost chuckled and said, "Margaret is a good sport. She had a hell of a time climbing in and out of it, but she didn't complain. And unlike you, she didn't hit me or refer to it as a tank or a shed."

"Well, sometimes you need someone to pound some sense into you. You're lucky I didn't do what Matthew suggested I do to Katie."

"What would that be?"

"Hit you with a two-by-four."

"You wouldn't do that to me; I know you love me. Besides, I'm your godson, so you have to behave in a godly way toward me."

"Even God sends thunder and lightning sometimes, Luis. That lightening can can knock your shoes off," she teased him. "It's a nice car, Luis. Congratulations. However, please follow your financial advisor's advice and invest the remainder of your money wisely. Where's your tank?"

"It's at the dealership. I figured Stevie and I can go pick it up later. I needed to drive this new baby home first."

"I'll go with you, if you like."

"In that case, let's go now with my new baby, and you can drive her back for me. This way you'll get to see how nicely she handles."

"Compared to your tank, she should feel like a docile cantering pony."

While on their return trip from the car dealer, Carolyn gave Luis a ten-minute head start with his military vehicle while she drove the comfortable Bentley. She explained to him that she didn't want to be in front of or behind his "bus." As she pulled next to his transport in Katie's driveway, Kieran and Matthew were still inside programming the security system. The rest of the family members were enjoying the afternoon outdoors. The women were sitting on lawn chairs near the deck while Stevie and Luis were throwing Frisbees for the dogs.

"What do you think of the car?" Luis ran up to ask Carolyn when she got out of his automobile.

"It's fine," she replied.

"Fine? Is that the best you can do?"

"What do you want me to say? It handles well. The seats are very comfortable. I got a good view of the road. For that price, it should do all that and more. Thanks for the test-drive."

Luis rejoined Stevie while Carolyn positioned a chair next to the other women. When the boys tired of throwing Frisbees, they proceeded to wrestle. Stevie knocked Luis to the ground. Luis got up, and the two locked shoulders together and started to have a feat of strength.

"Look at those two," Camille commented. "They remind me of a couple of wildebeests in heat."

"Why should they be any different from the rest of the male kingdom?" Nydia inquired. "Nature gave them the testosterone to do precisely that."

"Oh, Nydia, what a sheltered life you live," Katie interjected. "That's not its primary purpose."

"Katie, don't start," Carolyn admonished her, believing she was going into a shock jock routine. "We get the picture," she added before changing the subject. "Why don't we go for a walk? It's getting a little nippy sitting out here. A walk will invigorate the muscles."

"Good idea, Aunt Carolyn," Courtney said as she struggled to get to her feet. "I'll join you."

"How far do you think you'll get with that big belly of yours?" Katie inquired.

"Hey, I may not have my shapely form, but I can still get around. My only problem is that I need to pee every fifteen minutes."

"Well, come on then. If you get the urge before we return, you can baptize a shrub."

When they returned from their walk, Matthew was standing on the deck contemplating the lake.

"Did you finish programming the security system?" Carolyn asked him as she snuggled next to him.

"Yes, we transferred the entire database from the other drive and added additional codes."

"Where are the boys?"

"They were playing Frisbee. Then I saw them take off in that direction," he said, pointing into the woods, "with the dogs."

"Did Kieran go with them?"

"Yes."

"I'm surprised he would venture into the woods. I think he's still afraid of bears."

"Well, he went. And I'm going back to work; I need to finish with Katie's SUV. I'll see you tonight," he said as Carolyn accompanied him to his car. He gave her a peck on the lips. "Love you."

Carolyn stood by her car as she watched Matthew drive off. She started to walk away when she heard Luis calling, "Carolyn, start the car, start the car," as he and Stevie ran toward her, flailing their arms.

"Mom, bear!" Stevie yelled.

Carolyn entered and started the car as the boys caught up. Once inside, Luis ordered, "Go, go!"

Carolyn obeyed, but after driving a few feet, she realized Kieran was missing and doubled back. She stopped the car at the incline, facing the lake, while Luis and Stevie burst out laughing. The three of them exited the car while Stevie and Luis continued to laugh and Carolyn fumed, suspecting the boys had played a practical joke on her. She spotted Kieran sullenly walking toward the lake, a few feet ahead of them.

"You should see the look on your face, Mom," Stevie said.

"She really thought it was a bear," Luis laughed. "I need a camera."

Carolyn glared at the two of them and said, "You two morons think this is funny? Get the hell out of my sight!" She went to meet up with Kieran.

Kieran had almost made it to the lake bank when Carolyn caught up to him. Carolyn fanned her face and turned her head away in disgust because the child reeked of skunk spray. As she turned her head, she saw the car rolling toward them. She turned again and like a football player rushing toward a tackle, she hoisted Kieran on her shoulder. She ran with him, clearing the car's path as it rushed past them and crashed into the lake. Camille, Courtney, and Nydia had also come running and now stood frozen and horrified as they realized Carolyn had succeeded in avoiding a tragedy. Carolyn dropped Kieran on the muddy bank and instantly embraced him. She started kissing his smelly face as her face flushed. She then turned to Luis and Stevie. She released her wrath on the two terrified young men as she rushed up the hill. She pounded and kicked the two contrite boys as everyone looked on with mixed emotions. Stevie and Luis instinctively put their arms up in defense but received each blow in silence. "And I don't want to see either of you two jackasses anywhere near me! He could have been killed," she yelled while pointing at Kieran. "Kieran," she added without altering the tone of her voice, "we're going home!"

"I'll drive you home," Camille offered.

"Thank you," Carolyn replied as the etched lines on her brow started to relax. "Kieran, honey, come on."

"What about Spotty and Blacky?"

"I'll ask Daddy to get them later," Carolyn replied as she guided her smelly son toward Camille's car. "We need to get home now."

All the way home, Kieran was buffeted by the cold March air as Camille kept the windows rolled down. While Camille completed her act of altruism, back at Katie's, Courtney went into labor. Luis rushed her into the back of his Bentley while Stevie took the wheel and Nydia sat next to him in the passenger seat. Courtney's amniotic fluid broke before they reached the hospital, and Luis guided baby Heather into the world. His new Bentley's interior with the leather seats as soft as a baby's bottom was now covered with amniotic fluid and afterbirth blood. None of that mattered as Luis cleaned Heather with his shirt and wrapped her up in Nydia's jacket. "She's beautiful," he told Courtney as he handed her the infant.

After receiving the good news, Katie rang Carolyn's cell phone and then realized the phone was probably in the lake with the car. "Well, there's little hope of that," she concluded as she noticed the car was almost totally immersed in the lake. She called Camille, who had already dropped off her passengers and was now en route back to Katie's house.

"Congratulations, Grandma. Courtney had her baby," Katie informed her.

Camille laughed with delight as Katie gave her the details. "It's been an eventful day," Camille concluded. "I'm glad I played hooky from work."

Early that evening, Katie and Nydia arrived at Carolyn's house with Kieran's kittens. They entered the house through the kitchen as Carolyn came in from the main part of the house to greet them. Nydia set the cat carriers down, and Katie placed a plastic bag on the counter.

"We're here to return the cats and pick up Stevie's belongings," Katie announced.

Carolyn picked up a cat carrier as she asked, "Why are you picking up Stevie's belongings?"

"He's afraid to face you," Katie replied. She reminded Carolyn, "He claims you said, 'I don't want to see either of you two jackasses near me.'" Then she drew Carolyn's attention to the plastic bag. "Your wet wallet and your car information are in that bag. I suggest you air everything out to dry."

"That sounds about right," Carolyn said about Stevie's comment, "but you're not going to make life easy for him. Access denied." She placed the cat carriers against the wall. "I may not want to see him, but he still has to face me. Call Kieran and tell him to get his pets comfortable," she instructed Katie.

Katie complied by hobbling out of the kitchen. Carolyn turned her attention to Nydia.

"Camille suggested tomato juice on our way home. We bought eight large cans, but the kid was still ripe; so I caked him and me with baking soda," she informed Nydia as she emptied the contents of the plastic bag. "Camille probably needs to deodorize her car or torch it. Now that I look back on it, the entire incident is kind of funny, but those two clowns aren't getting off that easy."

"I don't think it's funny. They need to be taught a lesson. How long are you going to remain angry?"

"I figure a week or two of giving them the cold shoulder should be punishment enough. Those two seem to be cut from the same cloth. Luis doesn't like rejection, and Stevie cowers whenever I blow my top. Two weeks of alienation sounds very good."

"I don't believe you can hold out for two weeks," Nydia replied.

"Oh, I will. They need a good lesson. Would you like some tea and cookies? Salad, yogurt maybe? Kieran usually has a snack around this time. If he doesn't get fed like clockwork, he gets as cranky as a newborn infant."

"He must burn it all up because he's so thin and small."

"I agree, and he's getting self-conscious about it. I told him Luis was small too. Look at him now. Stevie grew at a steadier pace, so I'll probably get Kieran checked out," she said as she handed Nydia a yogurt.

"You and Kieran enjoy your snack. I'll pass, thank you." Kieran walked in and Nydia said, "Here's our little angel."

Kieran smiled from ear to ear. "Hi, Meema," he greeted Nydia and planted a kiss on her cheek.

"How are you feeling, adventure boy?" she asked him.

"I'm okay, but I'm staying clear of skunks."

"We should wrap you in a bubble and roll you from place to place," Nydia commented. "That way, you'll stay out of trouble."

"I don't look for trouble, Meema. It looks for me. There I was, walking along minding my own business. Stevie, Luis, and I were just looking for the Frisbee. This cute little thing walked out. I thought it was a cat, honest. If it had been a cat, I would have had three."

"So it was greed that did you in," Katie interjected. "You tried to pick it up, didn't you, Einstein?"

"That's not being greedy. I was going to give him a home."

"He already has one. It's called free range. Besides, you're not supposed to pick up wild animals. How do you know it isn't rabid? If a nocturnal animal is out and about during the day, you should suspect something is not right, so leave it alone in case it's sick. Mommy said you could have two pets. What part of the word 'two' don't you understand?" Kieran gave her the evil eye and she asked, "Did the skunk spray you in the face or an open wound?"

"No—my lower body got most of the force. He didn't allow me to get that close."

"And the *lovely fragrance* enveloped you. Lucky for you that's all it was or you would probably need a few rabies shots. Next time, don't be stupid."

"Kieran, take the kitties into the den," Carolyn instructed him before he could reply. "Make sure they have food, water, and a clean box. Then you can have your snack."

"I thought you were keeping them in the laundry room," Katie commented.

"I don't think they should be exposed to the smell of detergent. They look and feel so tender and fragile. He'll have to keep them in the den until they're big enough to stay out of harm's way."

"Courtney had the baby," Katie said. "I tried to call you, but your cell phone died in the lake. The tow truck already came and pulled your car out and the rest of your personal belongings are drying in my garage. I figured you would need the wallet and this other stuff for the insurance claim. You should take Luis's military vehicle until you get a car."

"I wouldn't take that house on wheels if my life depended on it."

"Take his Bentley," Nydia suggested. "If he and Stevie hadn't pulled that stunt, you would still have a car. But I forget, the Bentley had a mishap," Nydia laughed.

"What happened to the Bentley?" Carolyn asked.

"It was Courtney's birthing room," Katie said.

"You should see the mess," Nydia added as the three women laughed.

"Talk about poetic justice," Carolyn said. "Well, unlike Luis, I have a modest taste in automobiles. If I were a gambling person, I would bet the Bentley will be stolen before I start speaking to him again. Thieves like flashy and expensive cars, and I prefer a car that will still be there when I come out of a store. It's a matter of convenience instead of a matter of frustration. How is Courtney doing?"

"She's fine," Katie said. "The baby's name is Heather Marie, and Luis said she's as cute as a button."

"I agree," Nydia commented.

"You saw her?" Carolyn asked.

"I was there when she came out. That's how I know about the car."

"I'm going to see them tomorrow," Katie said. "Want to come, Mom?"

"We'll all go," Carolyn said. "It's fun to see and handle a new baby."

"I made her the usual knit combo: hat, leggings, booties, and sweater," Nydia commented. "I hope Courtney likes it."

"I still have the set you made for Kieran. I'm going to give it to him for his first son."

"If he ever has one," Katie muttered. "He'll probably have all girls like Aunt Camille and Uncle Neil."

"I'm finished," Kieran announced as he walked in. "Where's my food?"

"Then again," Katie added, "his wife will probably divorce him before he procreates."

"Well, thank you for giving him the benefit of the doubt and allowing him to at least have a marriage ceremony," Carolyn replied, sounding hurt.

"Speaking of ceremonies, Mom, will Stevie ever be an ordained priest, or is he going to be a lawyer?"

"He can be both, if he wants. It's his life, his decision."

"That is so unfair. I wasn't given a choice. You mapped out my life."

Carolyn glared at her as Kieran complained from his seat at the table. "I'm hungry here. I brushed and fed the cats. Who's feeding me?"

"Well, you did," Katie said in response to Carolyn's glare.

"I'm not going to dignify that with a response," Carolyn countered.

Kieran got out of his seat and opened the refrigerator. He grabbed a bowl of grapes and cold chicken. He started munching on the grapes as he transferred the chicken onto a plate and into the microwave. As he downed the fruit, the chicken popped and spattered in the microwave for seventy seconds. He grabbed his chicken and returned to the table.

"In most worlds, a loving mother cares for her children," he complained. "In this world, Kieran gets ignored. You're lucky I don't starve to death!" Nydia heard him and laughed. Carolyn and Katie were still bickering and missed his comments. He continued to gripe. "No one feeds me. Sometimes they forget to pick me up after school. I must be transparent."

* * *

That evening, Matthew showed Carolyn Katie's CAD blueprints. Carolyn was impressed by them and Katie's suggestion.

"You mean you would consider moving?" Matthew asked.

"Well, I do like that greenhouse idea. We could grow our own fruits and vegetables year round. I could probably import seeds from Asia. However, we may have to sell Kieran on the idea of moving near the woods."

"What about Stevie?"

"At the rate Stevie is going, he may be living with us until he turns sixty. He'll go wherever we go. That poor child will never be a priest; he never goes anywhere unless he's with us. Can you imagine if he did become a priest and the Church sent him to the most remote area on earth? He wouldn't last a day. Of course, that's between you and me; I don't want to discourage him. He's such a sweet kid. He would be a good family man. He's too much of a bleeding heart to listen to the woes of his parishioners. He'll be graduating soon, and he's never brought home a girl."

"Maybe he's shy."

She looked at him intently. "I remember," she said, "how shy you were. I did everything I could to get you interested. Whenever I looked at you, your eyes flicked and you would stare at your feet. I was head over heels in love with you, and I thought you weren't interested."

"How could you assume that? We dated. Besides, I loved you as soon as you crashed into me, but you were out of my league."

"That shows how much you know," she said, snuggling against him. "Why don't you talk to Stevie and inform him that girls don't bite. If he finds a nice girl, he may get married and give us a few grandchildren. Camille and Neil are grandparents four times over, and we don't have a single one."

"Well, Camille and Neil have older kids, and they're all girls."

"What does that mean?"

"Girls have it easy. They wait for the man to approach. We ask them; they turn us down; we get crushed. Look at that poor fool Luis. He knows what he wants, but Katie keeps him flapping in the wind."

She sat up and faced him. "First, sexually, Katie hasn't turned Luis down, so he's not flapping in the wind. Secondly, are you living in 1492? Girls don't have it easy now, and we didn't have it easy then. I'm the one who chased you. God, you were dense. I remember the first time I asked you to join me for coffee, you said, 'I don't know,'" she quoted, imitating a dunce. "I would have had an easier time getting a root canal."

"I don't speak like that," he said defensively, "and you never invited me for coffee. We exchanged numbers, and..."

"You never called. I called you. We exchanged numbers after you said 'I don't know.'"

"I called several times; the words wouldn't flow; I perspired like a pig; I hung up."

"Are you perspiring now?"

"No."

"Explain that to Stevie, then," she said, lying back beside him. "I want grandchildren."

"Is that your new bliss?"

"Hush and go to sleep."

"What, no sex for little Mattie?"

"Listen, Mr. 1492, I did my part twenty-five years ago. Hoist your sail and see if you can shoot for a brave new world," she said, getting out of bed to get her diaphragm. "If you want to continue entering the Bering Strait, you should consider navigating a clipper ship."

"What do you mean by that?" he asked.

"I told you I'm not having another child. The pill has complications, and contraceptive inserts are a nuisance. Vasectomies are fashionable."

"Ouch! I'll do anything for you, Honey-Lyn, but I don't know if I want to clip little Mattie. What if I ever find that younger model and she expects children from him?" he asked while staring at his pelvis.

"You were too shy to speak to me. What makes you think you'll have the courage to talk to a younger model?" she asked as she disappeared into the bathroom.

Soon the busy month of March became history and a few tumultuous months followed.

Twenty-Nine

◇◆◇

Based on the evidence against him, the district attorney argued that Arturo Santillana should not be given bail. In his petition, the DA argued that Arturo had a proven record of potentially deadly algolagnia and sadism toward women. He was charged with trespassing, breaking and entering, several counts of illegal surveillance, attempted kidnapping, as well as assault and battery. Releasing him prior to trial could put his victims and the general public in danger. He had also violated the terms of his parole and was considered a flight risk. Carolyn, Katie, Ellen, and Sean were present at the indictment. They were happy to report to the rest of the family that bail was denied. As Arturo was led away, the DA, Carolyn, and the Sheridan team of lawyers huddled in the corridor. They were already fast-tracking to make sure Santillana would spend the rest of his life in prison.

"If we can't get that type of sentence," Carolyn said, "we'll work with INS for deportation after whatever sentence is served. It's a shame we don't have a death penalty for people like him. Deportation goes on the table only if we can't get a life sentence. If we obtain it, however, there is no guarantee he won't return."

"He could fall off a cliff on a moonless night," Sheridan joked, and they all laughed at the wishful thought.

Carolyn was the only one present who was visibly troubled by the idea. She said, "I wish we knew why certain minds work like his. Were such people ever the product of a loving mother? Why do they have an insatiable need to be violent and to turn the world upside down? My brain feels like it's in a food processor whenever I try to make sense of this insanity."

"Don't waste your time thinking about any of that," Sheridan advised her. "When it comes to understanding evil, there isn't any logic."

* * *

Katie had her modified SUV and her freedom to drive shortly after the arraignment. She drove to her job in Manhattan and also inspected her pet project in East New York. Efraín Ramírez was glad to see her back and to return the reigns of managing back to her. She was pleased with the progress engineers Efraín and Abisheck had made. The two young student interns, Eblin and Gwendolyn, were doing well. She got Evan Ohkawa and Muftah Aggarwal on conference call. Ohkawa was at the Portchester site, and Aggarwal was working in Southampton.

"Muftah, I hope you're almost done out there. If not, I'm replacing you because I need you and Evan at my place. I have a large project I want done right, and you two guys are going to do it for me in record time."

"You're the boss, Katharine," Muftah replied, "although, I am enjoying the ocean air. How soon will I be relieved?"

"I'm e-mailing the new blueprints to you and Evan. Evan, are you there?"

"I'm here," he said, waving at her from the computer screen.

"Well, you guys study the prints. On Friday, you can work out the kinks. And hopefully a week from now, we can get started."

"You're not kidding about fast-tracking," Muftah said. "You're talking lightning fast."

"That's why I chose you two brainiacs," Katie said. "I have faith in you."

"My own mother doesn't have that much faith in me," Evan interjected, "but I'm willing to prove her wrong."

"Thanks, guys. We'll play it by ear."

Katie also met with Rina and her partner Elena Morales at Rye Beach Playland. They walked along the boardwalk with the wind of the Long Island Sound buffeting their hair and ears. The amusement rides were still closed for the winter season, but a few people were braving the April winds. People walked, jogged, or sat on boardwalk benches. Others were walking or playing on the sandy shore. Katie, Rina, and Elena walked and talked while the seagulls flew overhead or skipped along the beach.

"How's your fashion business going?" Katie inquired.

"So far, so good," Elena replied. "We've lined up a few customers."

"We're launching a children's line," Rina said. "As a matter of fact, we don't simply have that. We have mother-daughter and father-son lines. The youngsters will be dressed just as spiffy as the elegant parent; I'll send you a few pics. We just put out the June wedding theme."

"And the Academy Award presentation will soon follow," Elena added. "In this business, you always need to be months ahead of what's coming. Then there are the in-betweens like bat or bar mitzvahs, back-to-school and work, etcetera."

"I'm thinking of selling my business and marketing a doll," Katie said. "On St. Patrick's Day, I made a caricature with an elongated canine tooth. I was as drunk as a skunk, but when I revisited it a few days later, I realized it has a meerkat-like cuteness to it. I think it's appealing enough to be sellable."

"You were drunk?" Rina asked. "I thought you couldn't drink because of your meds."

"It was that one time—besides, I'm not taking my meds."

"Why not?"

"I have issues. I need to take care of something, and the meds are getting in the way."

* * *

During the two weeks following the skunk incident and the car plunging into the lake, life was not easy for Stevie. Whenever he walked into a room, Carolyn left, except during family dinners. Stevie made sure he arrived on time for those. At the table, the serving plates were passed from person to person, but there was no interaction between him and his mother. When she suspected he wasn't looking, she studied his face, and he did the same with her. He welcomed his time out with Darnell. Otherwise, he would hang out with Luis and Kieran, or he would shut himself up in his room. He and Luis often compared notes about the progress they failed to make with Carolyn. Luis had tried to make amends by calling, but when Carolyn examined the caller ID, she ignored the calls. One evening, Kieran picked up the phone, spoke with him for a while, and handed the phone to Carolyn, explaining, "Luis wants to talk to you." Carolyn took the phone and pressed the off button. Finally, one morning, Carolyn asked Stevie to pass the milk. He looked at her and a sigh of relief spread over his face. He knew she had finally forgiven him for the stupid prank that had almost cost hers and Kieran's lives. His sentence was over.

"Bye, Mommy," he said as he left for school. "Darnell and I are going to Omid's this afternoon. I'll call you if I'm delayed."

"Have a good day, Stevie," she replied without making eye contact. Her good wishes, however, lightened Stevie's heart. He smiled as he left.

After school, Darnell and Stevie showed up in Mr. Hassan's novelty shop. They greeted him and proceeded to the rear of the store that connected with the Hassan's upstairs home. Mrs. Naghmed Hassan and Omid's younger sister were keeping Omid company in the living room. The lovely hazel-eyed Shirin was working on her eighth grade homework while Mrs. Hassan fed Omid. She waited patiently as Omid struggled to keep the yogurt within the confines of his mouth without drooling it out the sides. If he didn't succeed, Mrs. Hassan wiped him clean with a paper napkin. As the boys approached the upstairs dwelling, they called up the steps ahead of them because Mrs. Hassan always kept the door open. That way, if Amir Hassan ever needed anything while he worked in the store below, he could call his wife or daughter from the foot of the stairs.

"Mrs. Hassan," Darnell called out, "we're here. May we proceed?"

"Welcome, welcome," they heard her call out from Omid's side. "Come forward."

Darnell and Stevie soon joined them in the living room.

"Sit, sit," Mrs. Hassan invited them as she continued to feed her son. "Omid will be with you soon. Shirin, get the boys some refreshments." Shirin complied while Mrs. Hassan inquired, "Where will you boys go today?"

"That's up to Omid," Darnell replied.

"A man from the Veteran's Administration came today," Mrs. Hassan said. "Tomorrow they start coming to give Omid his therapy here at home. Stevie, please say thank you to your mother for the work she and her lawyers have done. Without this help, no one probably give my Omid therapy. I send her letter, but my English is not too good to write. Shirin write letter for my husband and for me, but you tell your mother thank you. I am very happy," she said with tears welling in her eyes.

"You speak English well," Stevie replied. "I don't speak a word of Farsi, and you communicate effectively in English. I studied Spanish, but I was never good at it."

Shirin returned with a platter of almond honey cakes and tea. She set the platter down on the coffee table and poured the tea for Darnell and Stevie.

"What are you studying today?" Darnell asked her in order to make conversation.

"It's my science homework," she replied in a tender voice as she gave him the tea. "When I finish that, I have to do social studies. Help yourselves to the cakes."

"I liked science," Stevie said, "but Darnell and I are now concentrating on law."

"Law is a good thing," Mrs. Hassan interjected. "It is your mother's lawyers who help Omid. I hope you and Darnell will be good lawyers."

"He wants to be a Catholic priest like his uncle," Darnell replied.

"Allah's work is good too," Mrs. Hassan replied. "I believe it will suit you."

The boys drove up to Dobbs Ferry and transferred Omid to his wheelchair. They positioned the chair to allow him to see the Hudson River and the Palisades across the way. After a few minutes of watching the boats travel through the water, they pushed Omid's chair up and down the walkway until Stevie announced that they better start back.

"I can't be late for dinner," he said. "My mom finally spoke to me today; I don't want to upset the cart."

"You're a real mama's boy," Darnell commented.

"Indeed I am," Stevie agreed. "Besides, she had every right to be angry; Luis and I made her so nervous that she forgot to set the brake. When that car started rolling down that incline, I thought for sure it was going to kill them both. I froze, and at the same time, I thought I was going to shit in my pants."

"Is she talking to Luis?"

"I don't know. But if she's forgiven me, I'm sure she's forgiven him. Luis and I are like brothers."

"And we're like twins," Darnell said.

"Indeed we are. Let's take our other brother home," he said, grabbing Omid's chair.

They entered the Hassan property through the rear gate. Darnell pushed Omid's chair up the walkway and rang the back doorbell. After a couple of minutes, Shirin unlocked the door. "It's the boys," she yelled up to her mother as she held the door open. Stevie heard Mrs. Hassan's footsteps as she rushed downstairs to greet them. Together, Stevie and Darnell hoisted Omid out of the chair and struggled with him up the stairs. Mrs. Hassan and Shirin followed behind them with the wheelchair.

"Mrs. Hassan," Stevie inquired, "would you mind if I asked my sister to install an elevator for you?"

"I wouldn't mind at all," she replied, "but this is not our property. My husband and I pay rent here. I will need to ask the landlord."

"Well, please ask him or her. Those steps are a killer."

"You boys will stay for dinner, yes? I am making American food today, spaghetti and meatballs."

"No, thank you," Darnell replied. "My man and I need to get home, or his mother will disown him."

"You are joking—his mother will never disown him. You are both very good boys. Stay and eat with us. Stevie, you can call your mother."

"Did you hear that?" Darnell asked.

"Darnell, we can't stay," Stevie replied.

"No," Darnell held his hand up. "Quiet," he cautioned them. "Listen."

They heard yelling coming from downstairs. Darnell ran to the threshold and heard someone ask, "Who the hell do you think you are, Osama Bin Laden?"

"You don't know what you are talking about," Amir Hassan replied as Darnell started down the steps. "Leave my store now."

Stevie followed at Darnell's heels, and the two of them were downstairs within seconds.

"What's going on here?" Darnell inquired as he faced Amir and three strangers. Stevie was behind him.

"These gentlemen are leaving," Amir replied with determination.

"The hell we are," the stockier one said. "You're the one who should be leaving. We don't want no Al-Qaeda in this country. We're sick of seeing this damn Taliban here."

Mrs. Hassan was now standing next to Stevie.

"Mr. Hassan is not Taliban," Darnell replied. "You're making a big mistake. Please leave."

"I said, I ain't leaving," the stocky fellow replied and pulled out a gun.

Mrs. Hassan gasped and held her hands up to her mouth.

"Georgie," one of his companions objected, "what the hell are you doing with a gun, man? Put that away."

Stevie stepped forward and said, "Please listen to your friend, Georgie. Put that away. You're making a mistake, man."

"You don't tell me what to do, man. You don't know me."

"And you don't know us," Stevie replied. "Mr. Hassan is not Taliban. His son fought in the Iraq war. He almost died fighting for this country."

"Don't tell me they ain't no Taliban. Look at her with those damn sheets she's wearing," he said, referring to Naghmed's hijab, her headdress, and loosely fitting clothing. "Why the hell don't she take that off? You're in America now, lady. Dress like an American."

"Georgie," his companion begged him, "put the gun down, man. I don't want no part of this."

"Guys," Darnell said, "please turn around and leave before someone gets hurt."

"I told your friend not to tell me what to do. Don't you tell me either."

"Georgie, listen to Jake, man," the third stranger said. "Let's go."

"Thanks to you two idiots, they now know our names," Georgie replied. "We can't go now."

"Put the gun away, Georgie!" Jake bellowed.

Georgie cocked the gun and said, "Don't tell me what to do!"

"Give me the damn gun!" Jake argued, and he started to reach for it.

Later, Jake realized it was the most stupid move he had ever made. Georgie squeezed the trigger. A deafening blast was heard, and Stevie fell.

They say that when you're about to die, your whole life flashes in front of you. Stevie was a baby in Carolyn's arms. She handed him a cookie. Matthew carried him on his shoulders. He was a toddler. Sean and Ellen were with him at the Bronx Zoo. He was seven; Luis threw a football and he caught it. Margaret, Luis, Katie, and Stevie were at a Yankee game. He was eight; Katie placed her safari hat on his head. Then he was sitting in the kitchen at home and three- year-old Kieran was chewing gummy vitamin worms. As he chomped off the worm's head, he announced, "Look, I'm eating bugs. I'm a meerkat, Stevie. I'm a meerkat, Luis." Stevie was now taller than the rest of the kids in his class, and he felt lonely being the only boy at the back of the line. He had no one with whom to hold hands. Then he was outside, running with Anthony and Cleopatra. He fast-forwarded to the whole family riding horses along the steep Irish coast. He lingered there for a while because it felt so good. He was older and he took his first solo flight in a plane. Now he was running across campus with Omid and Darnell to get to the next class on time. Then he was listening to Matthew. His father didn't let him go to war and said, "Don't break your mother's heart, son." Stevie placed his head on his mother's chest and heard her heart beat. He looked up and couldn't see her face. He could barely focus on Darnell's face. Darnell cradled Stevie's head with one hand and extended the second hand to cover Stevie's wound while Mrs. Hassan slipped her hijab under Stevie's head. Amir Hassan rushed to apply pressure to his side while his blood kept rushing out.

Stevie tried to say, "Tell Daddy I'm sorry I let him down; I think I broke Mommy's heart," but he couldn't speak. Then he felt very cold. He started to tremble violently before his entire body went limp.

Darnell sobbed, "No, Stevie, no," while Mrs. Hassan started to produce a cry that sounded much like a yodel. It was the sound of mourning.

Thirty

◇◇◇

1994

Katie had been looking forward to her family's arrival in Dublin. She was visibly excited as Momma watched her vacuum and dust in anticipation of the visit. Christmas was a week away, and Katie had already spent one full year at UCD. Sean had gone out to get refreshments and last-minute things. Mamaí Katharine was behaving normally today, and she was entertaining herself with her knitting as she sat near the window facing the park. Katie enjoyed the periods when Mamaí was lucid because the old lady liked to reminisce about her past. Not only did Katie learn family history, but little seeds of wisdom filtered from her great-grandmother's mouth and down to Katie's level. Katie had developed a great affection for the elder Kate. Aware that the white-haired old woman was getting on in years and that she might not be with them much longer, Katie hung on her every word. She sometimes recorded the stories on her microcassette recorder. At other times, she wrote them in her journal. She learned about her great-grandfather Patrick Stephen Connelly who had died of breast cancer when Momma Ellen was ten years old. Patrick had worked and toiled at many jobs to keep his family afloat. He checked the postings every morning and showed up wherever they were hiring. He cleared debris after heavy storms. He paved roads, thatched homes, and groomed horses. He was a man of limited education, much determination, and endless common sense. He had a quick head for learning new tasks, but little luck at finding lasting jobs. Such misfortunes usually occur when the economy is poor and a person has "little book learning," Patrick sometimes reasoned. He was right about both situations.

"Paddy once apologized to me for being a failure," Mamaí Katharine said to Ellen, Sean, and Katie as they listened to her recollections. "We had six babies to feed, and sometimes we would go without so our children would have what little we could provide. He had such affection for his children. I have had plenty of time to contemplate his agonizing words. I've come to only one conclusion. And that is this: A man who toils day after day and never seems to make ends meet is never a failure. He is a man blessed with the gifts of love and endurance. He worked himself to exhaustion, but it was not because he was a failure. He did so because he loved too much. I miss him terribly, for he was a good and honorable man," she concluded as the tears welled in her old eyes. "Paddy finally moved us to Waterford, where he found a per-manent job in the old crystal factory. That too was not for the dear man, for he died two years later. I believe sometimes God forgets that we are mere mortals and places too many burdens on our shoulders. He probably mistook Paddy for his right-hand man and gave him too many duties to fulfill. Or you could say the luck of the Irish is ten percent good and ninety percent toil, tears, and sacrifice."

Katie had finished the house work and looked out the window every ten minutes. The rain was coming down in buckets.

"They won't get here any faster if you keep looking out that window. You miss them, don't you?" Mamaí observed as Ellen dried her hands with a kitchen towel and eavesdropped on the conversation.

"Yes, I do," Katie admitted.

"Sit here by me and help me make a ball from this skein of wool," Katharine invited Katie in order to distract her from her nervous anticipation. "Did I tell you about the time my mother had us make Christmas decorations with plain old straw?" Katie sat on the floor and reached for the skein. "We didn't get store-bought stuff back in those days, so we used whatever we could find inside or outside the house. Perhaps I can teach you how to make those old-fashioned things. All you need is a little creativity."

"I'd like that," Katie said as she positioned her hands inside the skein and Katharine started to unravel the thread to form a yarn ball. "Did your mother speak Irish, Mamaí?"

"Of course. Whom do you think I learned it from, dear?"

The bell rang, and Katie jumped to her feet. "They're here," she announced, freeing herself from the skein and handing it to Katharine. "Momma, they're here!"

"I hear the doorbell too, Kate," Ellen announced.

It was Scan with the groceries. A disappointed Katie went back to staring out the window as Katharine transferred the roll of yarn to a template. After a few minutes of staring out the window, Katie resigned herself to sulking on the couch. The phone rang andSean picked it up. It was Matthew calling from the plane, Sean explained. The plane had been detained at JFK in New York due to an ice storm. Matthew had been concerned they'd be rerouted to Shannon Airport; but it looked like they were finally being cleared to land in Dublin. He didn't know how much longer they'd be, perhaps another two hours before they arrived at the flat. Momma and Papa were both worried about the Dublin weather and its possible adverse effects on the travelers.

"I'll be in my room," Katie announced, feeling dejected.

"No," Ellen said in order to distract her. "Come help me ice the cupcakes and prepare the salad."

"Fine," Katie said disappointedly.

Knowing the guests were still en route, they ate at the usual time. After Katie helped to tidy up, she shut herself in her room and played a computer keyboard program. In the parlor, Mamaí expressed a desire to return to her flat.

"I suggest you spend the night, Mamaí," Ellen said. "It's pouring buckets out there, and you'll be soaked to the skin."

The doorbell rang. A very excited O'Gorman family arrived at the little flat. Matthew and Stevie were loaded with Christmas packages. Carolyn carried Kieran's diaper bag and her purse while she led the little toddler into the flat. Everyone and their packages were drenched.

"We finally made it. What unfriendly weather!" Carolyn said as Sean picked Kieran up in his arms.

"This is the Emerald Isle. How do you expect it to remain green without a little water? How's my boy?" Sean asked Kieran as the toddler surveyed his surroundings. "Do you remember me?"

"Papa," Kieran replied, and everyone laughed.

"Where's the rest of the gang?"

"Nydia and Luis headed straight for the hotel," Matthew replied. "I don't blame them. We're all exhausted."

"Well, I've been keeping dinner for you," Ellen said. "You can all eat and warm up. Then we'll decide whether you'll all bunk on the floor, walk to Mamaí's flat, or head for the hotel."

"I'll probably sleep leaning against a wall," Matthew replied.

"Where's my other baby?" Carolyn asked. "Is she here?"

"Herself has been staring out that window," Katharine replied, pointing to the window, "as if she were expecting Old St. Nick himself. She finally gave up and locked herself in her room."

"Excuse me," Carolyn said, and she headed for Katie's room.

Katie had her back to the door. She was wearing her headset as she played the keyboard and watched the computer graphic equalizer display kaleidoscope color patterns on the screen. She didn't hear Carolyn when she knocked on the door and didn't see her when she entered. Carolyn watched her for a while when Stevie came running in.

"Katie, Katie," he blurted out as he touched her shoulder.

The three of them immediately exchanged excited greetings.

"You've gotten taller," Katie said to Stevie.

"So have you," Carolyn interjected. Katie and she were now the same height. "You'll soon be taller than me. We've missed you so much, honey."

"I've missed you too."

"Why don't you come home?" Stevie asked. "They have schools in New York, you know."

"I know," Katie replied as Kieran made his way into the room, "but I love UCD. It has everything. We were out rowing last week, despite the cold. It was great."

Kieran steadied himself by holding onto Carolyn's pant-suit and studied Katie from a distance.

"Hey, squirt," she said, bending down to greet him, "how are you? You've gotten tall too."

Kieran continued to study her in silence.

"Do you remember me?" Katie asked.

"Aytee," he replied, and he looked up at Carolyn while continuing to tug on her pants.

"He remembers everyone," Stevie said. "We look at the pictures, and he knows everyone's name. What's my name, Kieran?"

"Seevee," Kieran replied.

"See? He's really smart," Stevie said. "He can play with the computer. He does Simon Says. I'll show you later."

"Is Daddy here?" Katie asked.

"Of course Daddy's here," Carolyn replied. "Come and say hello." She beckoned Katie out of the room as she picked Kieran up in her arms.

"Are Uncle Neil and Uncle Patrick still coming?"

"They'll be here next week, honey. We'll have a regular family Christmas; at the hotel, of course. How's your bridge coming along?" she asked as they walked back to the living room.

"Good. I'll take you to see it tomorrow, if you like. We can take the tube."

"Oh, yes," Stevie said, "I love riding the train, and the bus, and the plane."

"You love anything that moves," Carolyn replied. "We'll drive."

The next day, Dublin's weather was cooperative. Matthew's family had spent the night in Sean and Ellen's little flat because Ellen didn't want them venturing out into the ice-covered roads. Matthew didn't put up an argument because he had no desire to combat the elements. Mamaí Katharine slept in the guest room. Katie insisted that her parents use her room. Carolyn then insisted that Matthew take the bed and she spread blankets on the floor for herself; the carpet afforded her sufficient cushioning to have a fairly comfortable sleep. The three children shared the pull-out couch in the living room. Carolyn awoke the next day to find Kieran huddled so close to her that he was nearly on top of her. As the morning progressed, most of the ice melted. Mamaí left early to attend to her duties at church, and the O'Gormans picked up Nydia and Luis at the hotel. Matthew had his rental car, and Sean had a leased Land Rover.

They drove to the warehouse where Katie and five of her classmates were working on a combination spandrel-braced arch bamboo pagoda-covered bridge. Matthew was impressed by the work they had done so far. The model displayed a bridge that gave them reasonable shelter from precipitation, but allowed the pedestrian to enjoy the surrounding scenery while standing on the bridge. The students were building the segments at the warehouse. They would later be transported via flatbed lorry and assembled over a stream in a Dublin park. Bamboo was not an easy medium to work with. It was strong, but difficult to shape once it was fully grown. If they had the luxury of time to shape the bamboo as it grew, the project would have been easier. However, in order to get credit for their project, they needed to complete the work before the end of the school year. Despite the challenges, they were doing "a bang-up job," according to Matthew. The non-engineers in the group were also impressed. "We'll have to come back and try it out after they move it to the park," Nydia said. The students were glad to hear the accolades and hoped their professor would be equally impressed.

After leaving the warehouse, they attended a matinee Celtic Christmas performance at the Olympia in city center. Luis and Stevie came out dancing while holding onto each other's shoulder.

"Mommy, Mommy, check this out. What do you think?" Stevie asked as he tried to imitate a dancer leaping into the air. He landed with his arms extended like a cross and placed his feet in an awkward ballet third position.

"Don't quit your day job," Katie interjected. "I've seen penguins do better."

"Penguins can't do a split leap," Stevie replied.

"Exactly," Katie replied. She then turned to Carolyn and asked, "Where to now, Mommy?"

"I've had enough excitement for one day. I'm still jet-lagged," Carolyn replied, looking exhausted. "I think I dozed off in there."

"It was a beautiful show," Nydia commented. "I loved everything."

"I mostly saw a blur. You were smart to head directly for the hotel yesterday," Carolyn said to Nydia. "I'm sleepy, and the kids are feeling chipper."

"I never thought I'd see the day you would run out of steam," Matthew said.

Ellen took one look at Carolyn's tired face and advised her and Matthew to get some rest while she looked after the children. The couple returned to the hotel, and the rest of the group headed for Trinity College to see the famous Book of Kells.

After the Trinity tour, Nydia and the children went to Ellen and Sean's flat. Stevie downloaded a problem-solving game for Kieran and proudly showed Katie what the baby was capable of doing.

"Isn't he amazing?" he asked Katie after Kieran solved one challenge after another. "How do you suppose he does it? I can't do that."

"Considering he can't speak, that is impressive," Katie agreed. "I don't know how he does it. Maybe he isn't human."

"Aytee," Kieran said, looking away from the computer screen. He continued speaking in a high-pitched voice that only he could understand.

"He speaks," Stevie said, contradicting Katie's opinion of the child. "We just don't understand what he says."

"Well, I'll leave you and the performing monkey to your entertainment. I have work to do," she replied, opening a book.

"Aytee," Kieran replied and uttered a few more incomprehensible sentences while Stevie had his own reply for her.

"He's not a monkey, you know. He's my brother, and he's very smart. He's probably smarter than you because he doesn't go around offending people."

"Well, that's your opinion. Besides, I'm not having a personality contest."

"Maybe you should. It might smooth some of your rough edges, Katie."

"Well, look at you. You've become a philosopher."

"I don't know what a philosopher is. Right now, I don't care. We came all this way to see you. We were all excited to come. I missed you, Katie. But I don't like you when you behave like this. Don't ever call him a monkey again. Come on, Kieran," he said, coaxing the baby away from the computer. "Katie needs to study."

That evening, Ellen and the boys visited Mamaí Katharine while Katie and Sean remained at their own flat. Ellen followed Kieran about as he sampled the wares in Katharine's flat, and Mamaí entertained Stevie with a craft lesson. With pipe cleaners, navy beans, and macaroni shells, he fashioned and painted a tree that was balanced on a knoll made from a larger macaroni shell. She advised him to leave his tree overnight to allow everything to dry properly. Before leaving, he proudly examined his tree one last time. He believed it to be a magnificent work of art.

"I'm going to wrap it and give it to Mommy for Christmas. Do you think she'll like it, Mamaí?"

"It's a lovely tree, dear; I'm certain she'll love it. I'll wrap it for you, if you like."

The next day, as Nydia, Carolyn, and Matthew were exiting Iveagh Gardens with their three children, Carolyn said, "We have to hurry, boys. Katie will be out of school soon."

"I want to go home," Stevie protested.

"We can't go back to the hotel now, Stevie. Momma and Papa are expecting us, honey," Carolyn replied.

"I don't like it here. I want to go home—our real home, not the hotel. This was a dumb old trip. You go to the flat. Kieran and I are going home!"

"And how are you going to do that, little man?" she asked him while fully aware that he wasn't little at all. He was only ten, but he was nearly as tall as she.

"I'm taking a plane, and I'm going home!"

"Well, I hate to rain on your parade, but you can't do that. You're too young to buy a ticket and travel on your own."

"Then I'll go back to the hotel! I don't have a monkey!"

"Do you want a monkey?"

"No! I want to go home," he cried. "Let's go home."

"I don't understand. You were all excited about coming to Dublin, and now you want to go home? What's wrong?"

"Nothing."

"Well, since there's nothing wrong, we're not leaving until December 27. Now let's go back to the flat."

With a furrowed brow, he reluctantly followed her. He spent the rest of the evening sulking and avoiding eye contact with Katie. Carolyn kept observing him and noting his body language. The next day, he didn't want to leave the hotel and refused to get dressed.

"Do you think we're fooling around here?" Matthew asked Stevie, sounding annoyed. "Your mother told you to get dressed. Don't make me come back into this room. You better be dressed and out that door before me, or there will be hell to pay."

"Something isn't right," Carolyn said when he returned and sat next to her on the sofa. "He never behaves like this. He was fine yesterday until I said we had to return to the flat. You know what?"

"What?"

"You can spend the day with Katie and your parents if you like. Nydia and I will take the boys and meet you back here tonight."

"Where are you going?"

"On a short cruise, hopefully. I need to call Brian Mulkeen."

"Is he the *don Juan* I met in Galway, the guy with the boat whom you see whenever you know he's in town?"

"Mattie, Brian is simply a family friend who owns a boat. Are you jealous?"

He studied her a moment and said, "No, I'm not jealous. I don't believe he's your type. I wouldn't mind a cruise, though. Maybe the boat will go under a bridge with mistletoe. I'll call Momma and tell her not to expect us. So you think something or someone upset Stevie back at the flat?"

"What makes you say that?"

"By now, I think I know you. Last night, I was watching you watching him, and I could sense your wheels turning. What do you think happened?"

"I don't know, but..."

"You'll figure it out," he completed her train of thought. He winked as if to say, "I have faith in you."

When they arrived at the quay laden with bags of groceries for the trip, Brian Mulkeen and his crew were already busy on board ship.

"Some boat," Matthew commented when he saw the ship. "I had something considerably smaller in mind."

"From late January until the end of November, Brian conducts cruises on this thing," Carolyn explained. "He and his crew lie low during this time of year. He said I was lucky to have gotten a hold of him at this time."

Carolyn and the family boarded the ninety foot yacht, and a crew member directed her to Brian. She thanked Brian for agreeing to take them on such short notice. He led them to the galley, where Cook relieved them of their parcels.

"Well, I don't normally get any requests for the boat at this time of year," Brian said. "I usually shelter her in the Canaries by the end of November. This year, we went as far as the Spanish coast and headed back north. I'm going to leave her here while me and the lads go up to the Highlands for a couple of weeks. So everything works out well."

Carolyn thanked him again and reintroduced him to Matthew, Nydia, and the children.

"We've met before," Brian said to Matthew. "You folks were up at Galway a few years ago. There was a fund-raiser to eradicate land mines in Cambodia. You were there with your mom and dad, Lyn," he said, turning his attention again to Carolyn.

"I remember that and so does Mattie," she said.

"Harold introduced us," Brian said. "You don't always come to the Emerald Isle with Lyn, do you Matthew?"

"I come as often as I can, if my job permits," Matthew replied. "Sometimes Carolyn and I have different interests. At the fundraiser, you had a foxy blonde with you, but Carolyn wasn't with me at the time. It was just us men, except for your lady companion. Carolyn was probably in a huddle with other ladies at the time."

"Perhaps you were too busy looking at the foxy lady," Carolyn interjected.

"Well, if I was, I wasn't the only one. If I remember correctly, she was very attractive."

"Well, whoever she was," Brian commented, "I don't remember. Four or five years is a long time. I'm not a man who makes commitments. I'm in love with freedom and open space. Where do you want to go today, Lyn?"

"Just up and down the coast. If we can hit some choppy water, the boys would love that. Don't make it too choppy, though; I want to keep my food down."

"Semi-choppy it is then," he replied. "Nice meeting you again, Matthew. If you and the kids want to join me at the helm, you're all welcome. Otherwise, you're welcome to explore around deck. Carolyn knows her way around. But first, let's make sure everyone has a life jacket."

Carolyn went into the dining area and kept Kieran entertained while the rest of the group joined Brian at the helm. Stevie was impressed with the state-of-the-art control panel, and Brian allowed him and Luis to play with the knobs, levers, and toggle switches that they were able to reach while Brian explained the purpose and the handling nature of each item. Then Brian turned the controls over to one of his men, and he addressed Matthew.

"I heard Lyn's sister Marjorie passed away," he said to Matthew.

"A couple of years ago, yes," Matthew agreed. "You knew her too?"

"I've known the whole family since we were kids. I don't know what to say to Lyn. I'm not good at offering people my condolences. 'I'm sorry' is an insipid comment to use when you're referring to the loss of a life."

"It's a gracious start. What more can you do? It's a comment that also makes us realize how powerless we are in the face of death. Carolyn has had more than her share of it. We lost two boys when they were three months shy of their first birthday."

"Another set of twins?" Brian said, biting his lower lip. He wondered if he should say, "I'm sorry," but he held back.

"Yes. They resembled their mother."

"I was in love with Marjorie," Brian confessed. "She could have been the one, you know. But she disappeared off the radar. The Reillys travel a lot, and so do I. That's all I do now. I'll probably continue traveling until I'm old and gray, blind and lame. I heard Marjorie died in Italy."

"Yes, she did. We spread her ashes in New Zealand. She loved the fjords."

"They are beautiful. Would you mind if I have a word with Lyn? I think it's time to use that insipid comment," he said with a pained face. "I'm glad she called me today."

During part of the voyage, the boys found a spot near the portholes. Stevie held Kieran up by his waist in order to allow the toddler to enjoy the view. They giggled every time the yacht bumped up and down. Brian put on some music, and soon Stevie and Luis were kicking up their heels, imitating the Celtic dance. The little toddler joined them, hopping up and down on both feet and taking a spill now and then. After a few minutes of their antics, Nydia called Luis. She conferred with him, and he ran back to Stevie.

"Stevie," Luis called, "Mami and Carolyn said we can go on deck."

"You can go on deck as long as each of you stays near an adult," Nydia corrected him.

And so the boys spent time looking out from the deck, where they had a better view of the choppy sea and the Irish coast. Despite the cold wind, they enjoyed the speed. When Carolyn thought it wise to return to the dining room for shelter, Nydia and Matthew soon followed her with Luis and Stevie. She placed Kieran down and encouraged the boys to move about to raise their body temperature.

"Mommy," Stevie said, "this is the best trip ever."

"Do you still want to go home, honey?"

"No," he said excitedly. He then gyrated and tapped his way across the floor.

"It's nice to be young and energized," Carolyn said to Nydia as she watched him enjoy the moment, glad not to see him troubled anymore.

They were back at the quay before sundown. "Brian Thomas Mulkeen," Carolyn said to Brian as they parted, "New York isn't that far across the pond. If you're ever in my neck of the woods, make sure to pay us a visit."

He studied her face a moment and replied, "Thank you. I will gladly do that."

"Did you find out what was troubling Stevie," Matthew later asked.

"No," Carolyn replied. "It's okay though. He's forgotten and moved on. Little things annoy us, and little things make us happy. In the end, for good or bad, they're all forgotten."

In the early morning of December 24, Patrick, Felipe, and Neil and his family arrived at the hotel. The large suite was filled with all the family members. A piano had been brought in the night before, and Katie played Christmas carols while Shannon and Elizabeth sang with her. Luis and Stevie decorated a tree, and toddler Kieran helped by handing them ornaments and getting himself tangled in tinsel. Occasionally, he rattled off baby jargon. Stevie gave him an angel and instructed him to place it on the top of the tree while he held the toddler up. Kieran made several attempts. In his final effort, the best he could do was to hold onto the tip of the tree as he tried to fit the ornament on its apex. By then Stevie was tired of holding him and started to lower the child to the ground. The entire tree came crashing down. At first Kieran appeared dismayed, but when he noticed Luis and Stevie laughing joyfully, he joined in, screeching with delight at the top of his lungs.

"Look at this mess," Nydia said disapprovingly as the boys continued to laugh.

They attempted to straighten the tree. Patrick came up behind Nydia and lifted the tree with little effort and placed the angel at the top. Everyone helped to get the tree functional and lit, and Kieran clapped with delight when he saw the lights flickering on and off.

"Merry Christmas," Stevie said to him as he picked him up to permit him a better view. "Look at the tree, little buddy. Merry Christmas."

"May Kiss," Kieran repeated as he clapped and chuckled. Stevie kissed the baby on the cheek.

Thirty-One

◇◇◇

2005

While Darnell, Stevie, and Mrs. Hassan went down to Amir's store to check out the commotion, little Shirin had the presence of mind to dial 911. That was before she heard the shot. Mr. Hassan and Darnell had taken turns applying pressure to Stevie's wound. Mrs. Hassan took off her headdress and placed it under Stevie's head and tenderly caressed the young man's face, which had become pale and lifeless. The police and fire department ambulance arrived as Georgie and his friends fled, and Mrs. Hassan was grieving aloud, producing a hooting sound that made Shirin uneasy as she stood in the rear of the store, watching from a distance. FDNY paramedics assessed the situation while Mr. Hassan continued to apply pressure to the wound and give the police an excited description of the perpetrators.

Within seconds, the paramedics concluded that Stevie had lost a lot of blood, was probably still bleeding in as well as out, and his heart had stopped. If the heart was stimulated, the bleeding would definitely intensify. The paramedics needed to stop the bleeding, replace lost blood and fluids, and attempt to revive the victim.

"Emilio, get an IV, ice, cortisone, and Factor 7," one paramedic called to the other as he instructed Amir to retain the pressure while he reset the defibrillation unit. He then asked Mr. Hassan to stand clear of Stevie's body. Emilio rushed out and back with the necessary supplies. The two paramedics and police worked rigorously on Stevie until they managed to get a weak pulse going. They wasted no time in using that window to pump him full of drugs and fluids and gingerly lifted him onto a gurney while applying ice pads to his spine, where they had noticed an exit wound. Before they could transfer Stevie to the ambulance, his heart stopped again. The first paramedic continued to feverishly work on him as he was raised into the ambulance.

At the hospital, Darnell McCullough nervously pressed speed dial on his phone. He couldn't stop his bloody hands from shaking. His face and cell phone were smeared with blood; his eyes were red and his complexion ashen. This was the second hardest thing he'd ever do. The first was holding Stevie as his life seeped away.

"Mrs. O'Gorman?" he asked when he heard her voice. "This is Darnell. Is Mr. O'Gorman home, ma'am?"

"No," she replied, sensing a weighty tone in his voice. "He'll be home soon."

"Mrs. O'Gorman," Darnell cried because he couldn't contain himself any longer. "Something bad happened to Stevie." There, he said it—or he thought he said it. He held his breath and dropped into a nearby chair. He believed she was supposed to reply, but she didn't say anything.

"What do you mean?" she finally asked.

"We were at Omid's house, and three guys came into the store and got into an argument with Mr. Hassan, and one of them shot Stevie," he said without taking a breath.

"Is my son okay," she asked, not wanting to comprehend. Darnell didn't reply, and she yelled, "Is Stevie okay?"

"We're at the hospital," Darnell finally said. "The doctors are working on him, but he wasn't breathing when we came in. There's blood—there's blood everywhere. Oh, God. I'm sorry, Mrs. O'Gorman; I'm so sorry. I love Stevie. I'm so sorry."

"What hospital, Darnell? What hospital?" she yelled at him.

"I don't know."

"What do you mean, you don't know? Ask someone!"

Darnell turned to Mr. Hassan and inquired. Amir Hassan took the blood-stained phone from him and said, "Mrs. O'Gorman, we're at Montefiore Trauma Center in the Bronx. It's near I-87." Carolyn hung up the phone without saying another word.

* * *

Carolyn came close to making her new Nissan Maxima car fly as she raced down the expressway as fast as she could go while struggling to maintain control of the automobile. She parked illegally outside the emergency room. Darnell saw her when she rushed in, and she noticed the caked blood on his pants and the blood on Mr. Hassan's shirt and pants. They both rushed to meet her.

"How is he?" she asked.

"Apparently, they're still working on him," Mr. Hassan replied. "I interpret that as a good sign because it means there's hope."

The news was too overwhelming for Carolyn. She fainted and Darnell grabbed her before she could hit the floor. The two men placed her in a chair as a triage nurse came to check her vitals.

"What's her first name?" the male nurse asked as he monitored her pulse.

"Carolyn," Darnell replied.

The nurse popped a vial of smelling salt and held it to Carolyn's nose while he gently slapped her and called her name. "Carolyn, Carolyn, wake up." When she came to, he proceeded to test her blood pressure, which was very high. He shone a light in her eyes and examined them carefully. "Mrs. O'Gorman," the nurse said, "I need you to lie down."

"I need to see my son," she protested. "I need to know how he is."

He held her hand and said, "I know, but first I need you to lie down."

"Where's my son?" she asked as she attempted to get up. She was unable to lift herself out of the seat. Her head felt heavy, and everything around her looked like a Cezanne painting sitting under ebbing water.

Within minutes, the nurse and an orderly transferred her to a gurney and wheeled her into the ER.

"Do you suffer from high blood pressure, diabetes, or respiratory problems, Mrs. O'Gorman?" the nurse asked as he drew the curtains for privacy.

"I came here to see my son. Why are you asking me these idiotic questions? There's nothing wrong with me.

My son has been shot. Where is he?" she asked and attempted to get off the gurney. Her legs were too heavy to move.

"You'll see Steven soon," the nurse assured her.

"You know my son?"

"Yes, I was here when they brought him in. We've been waiting for you. He's in good hands, Mrs. O'Gorman. But first I need you to answer my questions because you're not looking too good right now. Do you suffer from high blood pressure, diabetes, or respiratory problems?" he asked again.

"I'm perfectly healthy. There's nothing wrong with me."

"I'll be the judge of that, Mrs. O'Gorman. Now I need you to stay here. Don't go anywhere. I'll be right back." He disappeared behind the curtains and returned a couple of minutes later wheeling an EKG monitor. He helped her remove her upper garments and pantyhose and hooked her up to the machine. As soon as he acquired the printout, he left with the information and the machine, leaving her with the same instructions as before. Carolyn put her blouse on. The nurse returned a few minutes later, carrying paraphernalia to draw blood and a couple of legal forms.

"You don't need to do all this," Carolyn protested. "How's my son?"

"He's in good hands," the nurse replied as he again shone the light in her eyes.

"You already said that. I need to see him."

The man looked at her intently. "Mrs. O'Gorman, I'm not going to lie to you. Steven lost a lot of blood. We have the best trauma team in the city. They're working in there, feverishly trying to keep him alive. I understand they've lost him twice already, but he's a strong young man. He's fighting to stay with us. You need to give the doctors time. In the meantime, I want to make sure you're okay. Sign these please," he said, handing her two emergency room forms.

"I was wondering when we were going to get around to this," she said, taking the forms.

"It's legality."

"I know," she said. "You've been holding me against my will. You've put the cart before the horse, sir."

"Are you a lawyer?" he asked.

"Indeed I am, sir."

"Then you'll want to read them. Fine, I'll just wait here while you gamble with time," he replied, crossing his arms across his broad chest. "Here we err on the side of caution, Mrs. O'Gorman. Do you know how many people I see fall like flies when they enter through those doors in response to a catastrophe? There was one guy who collapsed like a fallen tree before anyone could catch him, and he cracked his skull on the floor like an overripe melon. I'd rather see you alive to sue me than dead to cause your family further grief."

"I want to see my son."

"You'll see him as soon as the doctors are done with him and as soon as you permit me to do my job. I want to make sure that fainting spell you experienced out there wasn't due to a heart attack or stroke, Mrs. O'Gorman."

She suddenly remembered a conversation she had with Kieran a few days earlier. He wanted Italian bread oozing with butter, and she mentioned he was a heart attack waiting to happen. "Jesus, Mary, and Joseph," she said with dismay.

"Don't worry. If it's a heart attack or stroke, you're in good hands, Mrs. O'Gorman."

"Oh, it's not that," she said worriedly. "I left my other son home alone. Oh dear God. I wasn't thinking. I rushed out of the house; I forgot him. Oh dear Lord," she said, trying to get up. Her head was pounding.

"Is there someone you can call?" he asked while guiding her back against the pillow.

"Please hand me my purse," she said. He bent down and retrieved the purse from where he had placed it earlier, on a railing at the bottom of the gurney. She quickly retrieved her cell phone.

"I'm sorry—you can't use that in here. The microwaves may interfere with our equipment," the nurse said.

"But I need to call my son."

"I'll bring you a landline." He left and returned a short time later with a land phone, which he plugged into a nearby jack. "It's all yours," he said, handing it to her.

When she had Kieran on the line, he asked, "Where are you, Mommy?"

"Is Daddy home, honey?"

"No. Where are you?" he asked again.

"I'm out on an errand, honey. I forgot to turn off the oven and the stove. Can you do that for me?"

"I already figured that out, Mom. The smoke alarm went off, and the rice is burned to a crisp. I like crispy rice, but these are black pellets. What are you trying to do—burn the house down and kill me?"

"I'm sorry, honey. Thank you for turning the stove off. Did you turn off the oven?"

"Yes. The brisket is a little overdone."

"I'm sorry, Kieran. I'll make it up to you, I promise. I won't be home for a while. You wait there until Daddy gets home. Don't let anyone in unless it's family. I'll talk to you later."

When she hung up, the nurse asked, "Is everything okay now?" She nodded in affirmation, and he said, "Please read and sign the forms."

"I'm a perfectly healthy woman, but if signing this will allow me to get out of here sooner, fine." She started to read. A few seconds later, she signed the forms. "You'll want my insurance cards," she said, retrieving her wallet from her bag. "My son is on the same plan, so you may as well transfer the information to his forms."

"By the way, my name is Stephen Cullen," the nurse said as she handed him the insurance cards. "You'll need that information in case you decide to sue me."

Her eyes welled with tears, and she said, "That's my son's name."

"Mine is spelled with 'ph,' Mrs. O'Gorman."

"It's a pleasure to meet you, Mr. Cullen."

"Now, you see," he replied as he stuck a butterfly needle in her arm, "we may get to be friends yet."

Stephen left her alone after he completed his task. A few minutes later, a doctor appeared.

"Mrs. O'Gorman," the doctor said, extending her hand in greeting, "I'm Dr. Karen Johnson. I know you've been waiting awhile. I apologize for the delay. The good news is that your son Steven is out of the OR. We stopped the bleeding." Tears rolled down Carolyn's face as she waited for Dr. Johnson to continue. Johnson paused, giving her a moment to reply. When Carolyn said nothing, the doctor handed her a tissue and cautiously continued. "He's in recovery and will be asleep for a while. In the meantime, I'd like to discuss your test results with you. You're lucky Mr. Cullen has been looking after you. He's an excellent nurse-practitioner."

"Mr. Cullen has been very attentive, Dr. Johnson. Will my son Stevie be all right?"

"We need to monitor him for the next twenty-four hours. We're hopeful because the bleeding has stopped."

"Will he be all right?" Carolyn asked again while trying to remain calm.

"He's weak. He needs time to recover, and we need to watch him for any complications."

"I need to see him."

"Is anyone with you, Mrs. O'Gorman?"

"If you mean family, no. I came alone. Stevie's friends are in the waiting room. I haven't called my husband yet; I must see Stevie first. I need to be able to tell my husband he'll be okay. If he's not okay, it will break my husband's heart. He must be okay," she said as if willing it to happen.

"I'll take you to him myself," Dr. Johnson said while undoing the brakes on the gurney. She drew the curtains open, pushed Carolyn's gurney out of the ER, and guided it through several corridors while Carolyn felt foolish being dependent on another soul. They started to board a service elevator as an orderly greeted Dr. Johnson while they crossed paths. "You're in good hands," he said to Carolyn, holding two thumbs up as the doctor guided the gurney past him. "Dr. Johnson is the best cardiologist in New York. She stitched me up real good last year."

"Thank you, Joel," Johnson replied as she pressed a button on the console.

She wheeled Carolyn into the recovery room, placing her gurney flush, with headboards reversed, against Stevie's gurney. Carolyn faced her sleeping son and fear, hopelessness, and sadness overtook her as she examined his pale face, the tube in his nose, the IV in his arm, and the monitor that beeped with every beat of his heart. This was her gentle giant, a young man who had never done anyone any harm, a soul with a pure heart. *How could God allow this to happen to him?* The question exploded in her mind. She found the strength to sit up and hold his hand. She held it tenderly, and she started to weep. Guilt overpowered her because she had chosen to ignore him for two weeks. *For what, to prove a stupid point?* she asked herself. This morning, she didn't look at him or kiss him good-bye. *How heartless,* she thought, *how heartless and stupid I have been.* Then she took a deep breath and composed herself. She held his hand up to her lips, and she telepathically prayed her soul into his. "I love you so. You must do this," she said aloud with determination as she concluded her prayer for him to stay alive. She turned to the doctor and said, "Thank you for looking after him and bringing me here. He's such a good boy—if you only knew. He's always brought me joy. Thank you."

"Is there anything I can do for you, Mrs. O'Gorman?" Dr. Johnson asked.

"No. I needed to see him. You've done that. Now it's God's turn to do the right thing. He shouldn't be like this. It's not fair."

"I need to discuss the results of the tests that were run on you, Mrs. O'Gorman." She paused, expecting a comment from Carolyn. Carolyn didn't reply. "It appears you've had a heart attack, perhaps a mild stroke."

"That can't be. I rarely get sick. I've had a cold now and then, but other than that, I can't remember ever being ill."

"I'd like to make sure everything is okay. I'd like to do further tests to look for a possible blood clot. It's a simple test. I'll inject you with a dye and place you in an MRI, if it's okay with you."

"How long will it take?"

"Not long." By that she meant forty minutes. "I can do it right now. Perhaps you'd like to call your husband first."

"I'm not looking forward to that, but I guess I better do it now. Matthew wanted to have more children," she said, not knowing why she said it. She suspected that information wasn't of any interest to this woman who didn't know anything about her, but she continued to say, "I told him I didn't want any more children. Now it seems like a selfish thing to say."

"How many children do you have?"

"We have three," she replied while fiddling with her wedding ring. "Two boys and a girl. We would have had six, but the twins died of meningitis; a third was stillborn. Do you suppose I'm too old to have another child? I'm forty-eight."

"You look young to me. We hear of women in their forties having children, but statistically, it can be heartbreaking. Perhaps you should discuss it with your ob-gyn to make sure your eggs are viable."

"I need to call my godson before I speak to Matthew. Stephen Cullen told me I can't use my cell phone in here."

"I'll take you to the nurse's station. If it's okay with you, I'll prep you for the MRI while you're on the phone. It will take a few minutes. After the test, you can return and sit with your son."

"I need to see his friends. They've been waiting downstairs."

"I'll call downstairs and have them come to you," Dr. Johnson said as she started to wheel her gurney out.

* * *

Luis picked up the phone and was surprised to hear Carolyn's voice because the caller ID displayed an incomplete "Montefiore Med..."

"I think Katie's out by the dock," he said when asked. "Do you want me to get her?"

"No, I want to speak to you," Carolyn replied. "I have very bad news. First, I apologize for ignoring you."

"That's okay; I had it coming. What's the bad news?" he asked while sitting down.

"Stevie's in the hospital."

"At Montefiore?"

"Yes. They just brought him out of the OR," she said and paused.

"Say it quickly, Carolyn; I'm ready."

"He was shot, and it doesn't look good," she said, her voice cracking. "I need you to go over to the house and tell Matthew. I don't want him to find out about this over the phone. Could you and Katie go over there and see him?"

"Of course we'll go. Is there a doctor there?"

"Yes, a Dr. Karen Johnson. Do you want to speak to her?" When he replied, she turned to Dr. Johnson. "My godson would like to speak to you. He's a medical doctor."

Luis went over the technical aspects of Stevie's case. Carolyn heard the medical jargon, but she didn't understand much. Apparently the bullet had pierced the abdominal artery and continued its trajectory to nick the fourth lumbar bone of the spine.

Luis understood the implications and asked, "Is he really asleep?"

Dr. Johnson negated that while she looked at Carolyn.

"So he's comatose," Luis concluded.

"Yes," Dr. Johnson replied.

"Well, don't say anything else to her, please," Luis said. "I'll handle it when I believe the time is right."

"Who's comatose?" Katie asked as he put the phone down. She had arrived while the phone conversation was in progress.

"I have bad news. Come here," he said, guiding her to where he had been sitting. After she sat down, he looked her in the eye and said, "Stevie is comatose. He was shot."

"Stevie was shot?" she asked incredulously as the blood drained from her face.

Luis waited for her nerves to settle and then said, "Listen to me. Your parents don't know he's comatose. Carolyn is at the hospital with him and she thinks he's sleeping off the anesthesia."

"So how do you know?" she asked, sounding shocked.

"I spoke with his doctor. She couldn't be more candid with me because Carolyn was present and the doctor is worried about Carolyn."

"Why is she worried? Mommy can handle anything."

"Not this, Katie. Her children are her life, so this is beyond her. The doctor is running some tests on her because she believes Carolyn had a stroke."

"No, no, no. Mommy would never have a stroke," she said. "Not Mommy. She's tougher than nails. And who would shoot Stevie? He couldn't hurt a fly."

"Listen, I need to see Matthew and break the news to him. I'll have to take him to the hospital. He won't be able to drive once he finds out. Will you be okay here, or do you want to come with me?"

"You can't leave me here. What's wrong with you?"

"Nothing's wrong with me. I just need to figure out what I'm going to do first. I need to call my parents. You call Uncle Patrick, but be careful about what you say and how you say it. When we see Matthew, let me do the talking, okay? I don't want to upset him."

"You mean you don't want me to upset him. How the hell can he not get upset, you idiot? His son is in a coma."

"Don't mention the coma to anyone yet. Carolyn thinks he's asleep. Until we can break the news gently to everyone, he's asleep."

"When do you plan to tell them? Next year? By then they'll figure it out."

"I'll tell them tonight, when everyone is present. That way, we'll have each other. Are you ready?"

"Are you?" she asked emphatically while grabbing her crutches. "I'll call Uncle Patrick and your mother while you get the car. We also need to see Momma and Papa. Which hospital are they in?"

Sean and Ellen were still at Emily's Hope. Luis spoke with them while Katie waited in the huge military vehicle. Ellen and Sean headed straight for the hospital while Luis and Katie went to see Matthew. Matthew appeared to be quiet and calm when he received the news. Inside, his stomach churned and cramped. The words he heard were surreal. He was no longer sitting on his sofa at home; he was in a cold, dark place. The words he heard were being distorted by a tunnel. Kieran had been sitting next to him, and he huddled close to his father, gathering Matthew's shirt in his fist and pulling it as if it were a security blanket.

"Is that why Mommy left?" he asked Katie, who was looking at them intently.

"Well, she's at the hospital with him," Katie replied. "Now we need to go too."

"Is Stevie going to die?" Kieran asked.

"They're taking good care of him," Luis replied. "He'll make it."

Montefiore was a teaching hospital and had conference facilities for its staff. As soon as Luis arrived, he huddled in one of the conference rooms with Dr. Johnson and the other attending physicians. After they conferred, they waited for the rest of the family to arrive. Practically every member of the extended family was there; Margaret and Harold were the only two missing. Two days earlier, they had left for Paris. The entire family, Amir Hassan, and Darnell filed into the conference room to meet with the doctors. Kieran walked in holding Carolyn's arm tightly. His eyes were wider than normal. It was evident he was as frightened as a baby deer lost in a forest. He sat next to his mother and rested his head on her upper arm. The doctors explained that Stevie had lost a lot of blood, a bone in his spine had been hit by the exiting bullet, but no nerves were damaged. He had received several units of blood and Factor 7, a fairly new medication used to prevent bleeding but which presented a risk of clotting. The patient was in a coma. He would remain that way until he hopefully regained his strength.

Kieran raised his hand, and Luis asked him, "What's the matter, Meerkat?"

"You said Stevie isn't going to die. He said," he said, challenging Luis and pointing to Dr. Punjab Ansari, one of the other two doctors, "Stevie's in a coma until he *hopefully* regains his strength. Does that mean he could still die?

And don't you lie to me. I'm not stupid, you know. Stevie is my brother, so he better not die!"

A hush fell over the room as Carolyn gathered her son closer to her. Dr. Ansari conferred with Luis a moment. Ansari then turned to Kieran and said, "I won't lie to you, Kieran. When a person is in a coma, it can go either way. However, during that time, the brain does everything possible to help heal him. The brain also learns from us. We can send information into his brain to help it with the process of healing."

"You mean like a computer?"

"Yes," Luis replied, "exactly like a computer."

"How do you do that?"

"We provide him with the drugs and nutrients his body needs," Dr. Ansari replied. "We exercise his limbs so the brain will not forget how to do certain things. You can help by talking or reading to him about things he knows and likes. You can gently move his fingers and toes. The staff will provide him with the more difficult exercises. Have him listen to music, but also allow him to rest. When he's asleep, he can process what he's done and heard."

"When do I talk to him?"

"You can start talking to him tomorrow. Right now, we would like him to rest," Dr. Ansari replied. "You ask very good questions, young man. Is there anything else you need to know?"

"How can Stevie eat with that tube down his throat? He needs to eat."

"He's being fed," Luis replied. "I'll show you how when we get back upstairs."

"Okay," he said, resting his head back on Carolyn's arm. She caressed his face and kissed the top of his head.

The doctors made a request for friends and family to donate blood. When the conference was over, Patrick led the family in prayer. Mr. Hassan, a devout Muslim, bent his head and joined them. In the brief time he had known Stevie, he had developed immense respect for the gentle, tall Christian young man. Now he felt he was forever indebted to him and his family. "If he had not stepped forward between me and the gunman," he explained various times, "my children would probably be without a father today." He envisioned the further hardship his wife would have to endure if she was left to take care of Omid and raise Shirin by herself. It would be too much for her. He also thought of Omid, who had been born and raised in this country and had served it well; however, he and his family were viewed as outsiders. He quietly thanked Allah for Stevie, Darnell, and the kind Mrs. O'Gorman, who did not think like the vehement Georgie, the man who had pulled the trigger.

"You should both go home," Carolyn told Darnell and Mr. Hassan after they finished praying. "We appreciate you being here, and I thank you for staying this long. However, Darnell, your mother needs you home, and Mr. Hassan, your family must be equally concerned."

Matthew insisted that Darnell take a cab, and he placed the necessary amount of money in the palm of the young man's hand. Darnell and Stevie used each of their cars alternately to travel to and from school. The evening of the incident, they had used Stevie's car, and it was left in Yonkers.

"You can always come back tomorrow, if you like," Matthew said to Darnell, "but now you need to get some rest. While en route, I suggest you call your parents and explain what happened so they won't be shocked when they see you caked in blood." He then hugged Darnell and said, "Thank you for looking after Stevie."

After leaving the hospital, Sean and Luis drove Carolyn, Kieran, and Matthew to the impound lot, where her car had been towed for illegal parking. The area was a seedy, isolated section of the Bronx. Even Sean, a seasoned veteran, was ill at ease in that neighborhood. Once they had the car, the caravan proceeded to the northbound I-95 New England Highway, thankful to be out of there and on their way home.

"I never thought I'd say this," Carolyn said to Matthew as she sat next to him and he followed Luis's SUV out of the uninhabited neighborhood, "but I somehow feel safe with that tank in front of me."

* * *

"So how many strokes have you had?" Matthew asked her later that night.

"According to the medical test results, I've had three."

He looked at her intently and asked, "And you didn't feel anything wrong?"

"Not that I can recall, but today I could barely move; I felt heavy. The doctor injected me with some type of anticoagulant, and I'm fine now."

"You can't be fine," he said worriedly.

"No, really, I'm okay. Dr. Johnson gave me a prescription, and I've agreed to see a colleague of hers every three months. His office isn't too far from here, and she claims he's excellent. She said I have above normal levels of homocysteine."

"What's that?" he asked.

"It's a protein; I need to take vitamin B to bring it down. I also need vitamin D."

"I don't understand it," he said. "You eat well. You avoid all those so-called wrong foods. You don't smoke or drink. It doesn't make sense."

"Well, maybe I should be eating what your father eats. Perhaps I'll cook up a batch of shit on the shingles."

He laughed. "Where did you learn about S.O.S?"

"Where else? Your father told me about his days in the army. But that's enough of that," she said while her thoughts drifted back to Stevie. She tried not to cry. "This is so wrong. He was out doing a good deed. It never should have happened."

"I know," he said, holding her close. "Stevie will recover. We'll get over this, Honey-Lyn."

Thirty-Two

"Hurry up, Mommy!" Kieran urged Carolyn as he gathered his book bag and Matthew waited by the door. "Stevie is probably awake by now and he's wondering why we aren't there."

Stevie wasn't awake, and Kieran was disappointed to see that nothing had changed. He watched as Carolyn brushed Stevie's hair back and said, "Stevie, it's Mommy. Daddy, Kieran, and I are back." She kissed his forehead. "I'm very proud of you, baby." She caressed his face. His stubble had grown in. "You need a shave."

"I should have brought his razor," Matthew commented as he stood next to her.

"I brought him his iTunes music player and one of the books from his room," Kieran said. "We can read to him; I'll start." He drew a chair up to Stevie's bed. "Maybe this will wake him up."

Matthew and Carolyn listened as Kieran started to read a biography of Ruth Bader Ginsberg. Matthew wrapped his arm around his wife's shoulder and whispered, "He's handling this well." Carolyn caressed her husband's forearm as Katie walked in.

"You beat me here," she said.

"Quiet," Kieran said, "I'm reading to Stevie."

"Let's go outside." Carolyn motioned to Katie, and the three of them stepped into the corridor.

"Luis is downstairs," Katie said. "We both went to give blood, but the blood bank won't open for at least another hour. He went to see if any of Stevie's doctors are around. How's Stevie doing? Any change?"

"No change," Matthew replied. "Now that you're here, could you stay with Kieran? Your mom need to find the chapel and say a prayer for Stevie."

"Why don't we wait for Luis," Katie replied, "and we'll all pray for him right here?"

"That's a good idea," Carolyn said, turning to Matthew.

Nurse Stephen Cullen came down the hall.

"You're here bright and early," he said to Carolyn.

She was surprised to see him and quickly introduced him to Katie and Matthew.

"If you don't mind," he said, "I came to look in on my namesake before my shift starts. If everything's going well, they should be moving him to ICU today."

The three of them followed Stephen Cullen into the room and watched attentively as he read Stevie's chart and examined the numerous attachments. Kieran stopped reading as soon as he was aware of Mr. Cullen's presence. He watched Stephen's every move. Knowing that at times the relatives of a comatose patient need to be involved in his care, Stephen acknowledged young Kieran's curiosity. He explained the technology as Kieran and the others watched and listened attentively.

"What's that?" Kieran inquired, pointing to a transparent sack of yellow liquid hanging by the side of Stevie's bed.

"It's a catheter and artificial bladder," Stephen replied as he reached for an empty graduated pitcher on the nightstand. "He can't go to the bathroom, so this tube is attached to his bladder to collect the urine." Stephen drained the contents of the plastic bladder into the pitcher. "We measure it," he said, showing Kieran the markings on the pitcher. "It's one way of us knowing whether his kidneys and bladder are working properly. We also test a sample of the urine to make sure there's nothing in there that shouldn't be there."

"What if he needs to poop?" Kieran asked with innocent inquisitiveness.

"That's also taken care of," Stephen explained. "There's another attachment on his intestines; I won't show you that. We need to maintain the patient's dignity, so some things are best kept private. That's one of the times we use those curtains," he said, pointing up to the curved curtain rod that circumvented the bed. "If you'll excuse me, I'll do that now. So I'd like you to wait outside, please."

"Okay," Kieran replied.

That afternoon, Carolyn was pleasantly pleased to see Margaret and Harold walk into the intensive care room where Stevie had been moved. They had cut their Paris trip short after receiving a call from Donny. Only two people at a time were allowed in Stevie's unit while he was in ICU. The family members had taken turns moving back and forth between the waiting lounge and ICU. After learning that Margaret and Harold were Stevie's maternal grandparents, the desk nurse made an exception and allowed them entry. Prior to the grandparents' arrival, Katie had been watching her mother fussing over the unconscious Stevie. Carolyn almost lost her composure when she received a loving hug from her father. They discussed the history of events up until then, and Margaret inquired about the prognosis.

"It's too early to tell," Carolyn replied as a tear betrayed her composure.

Margaret gave her a comforting hug and wiped her cheek with her thumb. "He'll be okay, baby," she reassured her daughter. "We must not give up hope."

The Hassans stopped by and again expressed their appreciation and lamentation to Matthew, Carolyn, and the family. It was a meeting that sparked a lifetime friendship between them. Due to regrettable situations, they now shared a common bond; their children were damaged, but thankfully still alive. One had lost his ability to move due to love of country and loyalty to duty. The other was immobile due to friendship and sense of duty toward his fellow man. Each had been caught in unfriendly crossfire.

Nydia and Felipe came every evening. During her second visit, Nydia used a yellow ribbon to tie a ceramic figurine of her "Little God" to the headboard of Stevie's bed. Later that week, she secured a St. Christopher's medal next to it. She knew the Church no longer recognized Christopher as a saint, but it was hard to let go of old beliefs. St. Christopher had guided her father safely home during the Korean War. She hoped he would do the same for Stevie. During each visit, she and Felipe fingered their rosary beads and prayed in quiet desperation. At night, she lay awake thinking of the young man. She had watched the boy grow up, and she knew his weaknesses and strengths, his wit and his charm, and his loving, generous heart. "Little God," she pleaded, "please let him stay. Don't take him from us now."

A week later, Stevie was moved to an upstairs private room. Margaret used her influence to make sure it was one of the best available rooms with amenities for the comatose patient and the visiting guests. Each one settled into a routine as they played the waiting game.

After the end of the first three days in the new room, Matthew decided that it was best for Kieran to return to school. Until then, they had allowed him to tag along and spend the long waiting hours at their side. At first, he actively participated in the daily care of his brother. He read to him, adjusted his iPod music player, and helped to sponge bathe him. Under the exterior, Kieran was getting impatient because God had not answered his prayers.

"How long is he going to be in this coma?" he asked both God and anyone he encountered. Then he became totally disappointed and disinterested in the lack of progress. For reasons he couldn't explain himself, he suddenly became mischievous. One day, he approached each adult who came to visit Stevie. "May I have twenty dollars? I want to go down to that Spanish restaurant and buy some mofongo; I love that mashed plantain with garlic sauce." A few of the numerous people who heard the same line were his father, Nydia, his grandparents, Donny and Danny, and Katie. Luis was the only one who replied, "That's a great idea. I'll join you," and the two walked off together. Luis paid for both meals and returned to the room with food for the others who kept vigil over Stevie.

By the end of the day, Kieran had grossed two hundred dollars through the art of deceit and panhandling. He didn't count on being found out. When someone inquired of his whereabouts, Katie said, "He went down to that Spanish restaurant. I gave him twenty dollars to buy mofongo."

"Twenty dollars?" Sean inquired. "That's an expensive mofongo; I gave him ten and asked for change."

"I gave him twenty," Matthew said.

"So did I," someone else interjected.

Katie laughed and said, "The little Meerkat is more cunning than me."

"Well, as soon as he returns, he's about to meet Carolyn O'Gorman's version of the IRS," Carolyn said while clipping Stevie's toenails.

* * *

Late one evening, as Luis got ready for bed, Katie observed him quietly while she rested her head on her pillow. "I miss you," she suddenly said.

"What do you mean?" Luis asked. "I'm right here."

"Yes, I know. I was thinking. If Stevie doesn't make it, I'll miss him. I know what loss feels like, Luis. I would miss you too."

Luis became sadly pensive. He nodded his head and said, "I know what loss feels like too, Katie. It's an abyss and an absence of tangible love."

"I think I'm ready to marry you, Luis. I don't want to lose you."

"You think?" he asked, raising one eyebrow as if to ask, "Is that the best you can do?"

"Will Stevie be your best man?"

"Assuming you'll marry me, yes, Stevie will be my best man."

"Well, when he's ready to stand at the altar, I'll marry you."

"Fine," Luis replied, crossing his arms in front of his chest.

"Fine," Katie agreed.

Luis sat on the bed facing her. "I spoke with Garrity today. Esposito and he checked the list of service providers and found that Cheryl's ex-husband was employed by your home cleaning service for nearly a month. That's how he gained access to the house. They fired him because a client filed a complaint against him."

Katie rested her chin on her knees. "Well, Esposito suspected that would be so. From now on, I shall have to carefully observe everyone who comes in and out of here. If I weren't used to my lifestyle, I would move into a studio apartment in Manhattan and do my own cleaning."

"Perhaps you should have more than one video camera in each room. That way, you can maintain varied video records of everyone who comes and goes."

"That's no solution," Katie said, sounding frustrated. "That translates into miles of tape or digital storage space, and a waste of valuable time. In non-Western cultures, the solution is easy. People who break the law are punished so severely that they never consider breaking it again. Somebody should have dismembered Santillana and people like him a long time ago. Imagine what an economic dive the video industry would take if we did that."

"Well, if we start cutting limbs, the market for machetes and chainsaws might go up," he said as he rested his head on the pillow and pulled the covers over his legs. "Oh, Esposito said that they were able to track down that teenage kid you encountered on the bus. He said it was a piece of cake because the kid and his mother have a long history with the law. You said the boy was well dressed in designer clothes?"

"Yeah, very expensive threads."

"His mother is a member of a drug cartel and she and Santillana are *friendly* with one another."

"Huh! Go figure."

* * *

The weeks passed; fewer visitors appeared at the hospital. During the first few weeks, Carolyn always arrived bright and early. The others took turns retrieving Kieran from school and bringing him to the hospital when they came to visit. Carolyn made an effort to make sure his needs were met; it was a challenge as she worried about each of her children who faced different needs. There also was the other job of attending to two small cats, for Kieran often forgot to clean their litter box and provide them with food and clean water. She noticed that he sometimes sat listlessly looking out the window in Stevie's hospital room. He appeared to be easily bored with his electronic toys and would sometimes wander the hospital's numerous corridors.

Because of Stevie's condition, the hospital staff was lax about visiting hours. After he was first moved upstairs, Carolyn or Matthew slept in the room with him, keeping vigil as they hoped for the best and expected the worst. Noticing the effect all that attention had on Kieran, they stopped the overnight stays. When visiting hours ended at eight, they headed home, arriving there a little after nine; Luis and Katie left at the same time. One night, Luis was called away to attend to one of his young patients who had suddenly developed a high fever. It had been the usual exhausting day for everyone. Katie went to bed. As she lay there in total darkness, her thoughts were on Stevie and her family. She prayed for him and asked God to wake him soon. She also asked Him to watch over each family member and close friend. She then spent almost an hour tossing and turning, unable to sleep. She finally grabbed the crutches and went down to the kitchen; Lolo and Lolita were there. As Katie placed a bottle of milk on the counter, Lolita started to pace nervously back and forth. Then she started to scratch at the kitchen door and proceeded to bark.

Katie drew the door's curtain and peered out. It was pitch black outside; nothing was visible. If something or someone were out there, it or he would have triggered the flood lights, she thought. The lights were off.

"Settle down, Lolita," she told the dog, but she too was uneasy. "There's nothing out there."

The dog continued barking. Katie activated the manual switch for the flood lights, but the lights failed to go on. Lolo started to bark as well. Katie turned to scold him and found herself face-to-face with Arturo Santillana.

"Good dog," he said, calming Lolo down while holding dog biscuits in each gloved hand. His arms and legs were well padded with protective clothing. If either dog attacked, they wouldn't have been able to penetrate down to his skin.

"You're supposed to be in jail," Katie said, trying not to sound as astonished as she felt.

Santillana chuckled. "After the arraignment, those idiots locked me in a room at the courthouse while we waited for the prison bus to arrive. I scorched my hands, but I burned those plastic cuffs off with the radiator and jumped out a window. Sorry I couldn't come see you sooner," he grinned devilishly from ear to ear. "I sprained my ankle, and needed a little time to heal. You're mine now, bitch."

Katie hobbled backward toward the kitchen counter, hoping to get hold of a knife or any available weapon. Trying not to take her eyes off the intruder, she grabbed a cast-iron pan. Then it all happened too fast. He came toward her. She dropped the pan and her crutches. In that final second, she placed her weight on her good leg. Using her aikido training, she grabbed Arturo's left arm and used his momentum to slam his head into the refrigerator's handle.

Lolo stood nearby, chewing his dog treat, and Lolita was apparently confused and whimpering. "Some guard dogs," Katie said disapprovingly as Arturo lay unconscious on the kitchen floor and she grabbed the pan again to smash his head a few more times. Regardless of their evident shortcomings as guard dogs, Katie employed her pets to help her drag Arturo to her basement lab.

In the laboratory, Katie had an enormous machine that she used to grind beef bones that she converted to fish grub, which she hadn't used in months. Arturo Santillana was about to become fish bait.

A few minutes later, Matthew was awakened from a troubled sleep by a ringing phone. He unsuccessfully tried to pick it up before it disturbed Carolyn.

"What is it?" Carolyn asked worriedly, expecting bad news from the hospital.

"It's Katie," Matthew replied. "She said she killed Arturo Santillana."

"That's nice," Carolyn replied and rolled back to sleep.

"I'll be there as soon as I can," Matthew said into the phone as he reached for the pants he had discarded earlier. "No, don't call the police," he replied. "I want you to wait until I get there."

"Give me the phone," Carolyn said as she sat up. While reaching for the phone, she muttered, "Jesus, Mary, and

Joseph, when it rains it pours." Matthew handed her the phone as she calmly eased her feet into her slippers. "Talk to me, honey," she said to Katie. "I want you to stay on the phone with me until Daddy gets there." She placed one hand over the phone's receiver and addressed Matthew. "Mattie, call a cab. I don't want you driving at this hour of the night while you're sleep-deprived."

"I can drive," he said.

"Call a cab," she insisted and turned back to addressing Katie. "I know, baby," she said to Katie as she walked out of the room and down the stairs to the kitchen. By the time Matthew finished dressing and calling a cab, Carolyn had coffee ready to go as she continued to talk calmly to Katie. She had already learned that Katie was alone in the house because Luis was out attending to a patient. "I need you to listen to me, honey," Carolyn said as she handed Matthew a cup of coffee. "Yes, yes, Daddy is on his way. He's taking a cab." She paused while Katie asked her about the cab. "Splendid, honey," Carolyn replied after sipping her own coffee. "Don't worry about the police. Just stay on the phone and talk to me until Daddy gets there." She handed Matthew several bills to cover his cab fare, reminded him to carry the remote for Katie's entry gate, and turned her attention back to Katie.

As Matthew's cab reached the entrance to Katie's property, the new computer system announced the car's arrival by sounding a low buzz throughout the exterior of the homes on the premises and within each room of both Luis's and Katie's homes. From the cab's interior, Matthew pressed the remote to open the gate. Inside the house, the buzz altered to an intermittent beep, indicating that the guest at the gate was a family member who had gained entry. By the time Matthew's cab pulled up to the side of the house, Luis was waiting for him outside.

"She's okay," he reassured Matthew as he stepped out of the cab.

"Could you wait for me?" Matthew asked the cab driver. "This will take a few minutes," he said confidently as he was reassured by Luis's presence.

When the cab driver agreed, Matthew asked, "What happened?"

"Come into the lab and I'll show you," Luis said, leading the way.

"Did you speak to Carolyn?"

"Yes. She was going to call you on the cell phone to let you know, but I convinced her not to. You really need to see this."

"Where's Katie?" Matthew asked as he followed Luis.

"She's sleeping. I gave her a mild sedative. She'll be okay."

He led Matthew into the lab and the two of them stood in front of Katie's bone churner.

"What's this?" Matthew asked as he picked up what appeared to be shreds of fabric and batting from the machine's receptacle.

"That's either Bert or Kurt," Luis replied. "I get them mixed up."

"Who are they?" Matthew inquired as he set down the wads of fabric.

"They're dummies Katie uses to get her through the HOV lane on the highway. She keeps them in her SUV."

Matthew chuckled and said, "I remember them. I found them in the back of the van when I was working on it. Did you explain this to Carolyn?"

"Yeah. She had a good laugh and said that it was nice to find something to laugh at during these trying times."

"I agree," Matthew said. "We can take a look at the surveillance tapes tomorrow and see what actually happened."

"She apparently had a night terror, and poor Bert met his demise," Luis chuckled.

"Well, I want this glorified wood chipper out of here," Matthew said while he glanced at the industrial-size bone crusher. "She's lucky she didn't fall in with poor Bert while she was sleepwalking. I'll come over with a few of my men tomorrow and drag it out of here. This is one of the numerous reasons why she should have never left home. She's a bright young lady, and I can understand her wanting to be independent, but she can still be a danger to herself."

"I have her back, and she has mine," Luis replied.

Matthew gazed at him and said, "I know." He paused and then asked, "Doesn't this frighten you, Luis?"

"What do you mean," Luis asked, sensing that Matthew's query was a loaded question.

"I mean, why do you choose to be with Katie, knowing all you know about her? I know it's not her fault that she's the way she is. Are you happy, son?"

"Yes, I am; I love Katie despite all this. She loves me despite the fact that I'm deformed from the waist down. Katie is struggling to understand the concept of love, but I know she loves me. And in the end, there is no other logical choice for the two of us. She said she'll marry me when Stevie is able to stand next to us at the altar."

Matthew placed a hand on Luis's shoulder. "If she doesn't change her mind, congratulations. I love you like a son. She's my daughter. I love you both, and logically you're right. You are right for each other. I just needed to know for sure. Sometimes I hurt for you, Luis. At this moment, however, I realize that God has indeed given you a cross you can bear. I'm rooting for you, son." He pulled Luis toward him and gave him a forceful hug. "I don't hug my children enough," he said hoarsely. "I want you to know how much I love you, and I'm immensely proud of you, Luis. Well," he concluded, separating himself from Luis, "I better get back home; Carolyn is probably waiting up for me. Get some sleep."

"I love you too, Matthew. I don't have a cross. I'm immensely blessed."

* * *

When Katie entered Stevie's hospital room the next evening, Sean, Carolyn, and Nydia were already there. Sean was in one of the two leather recliners that Margaret had purchased for the room. Nydia was on the matching leather couch, and Carolyn was examining Stevie's IV drip. Katie guardedly looked at each of them, surmising they knew what had transpired the night before, and sat at the opposite end of the sofa.

"So I guess you all know," she said.

"Of course they know," Carolyn said, sitting next to her and wrapping her arm around her shoulder. "Where your welfare is concerned, we don't keep secrets from one another."

"So my life is an open book."

"Don't worry about that, Katie," Nydia said. "It's a good book."

"The whole thing was so real!" Katie said.

"You remember everything?" Nydia asked.

"Yes, I explained it all to Mommy and Luis."

"You do understand why it can't be true?" Carolyn asked.

"Santillana is still behind bars," Sean said. "He never escaped or jumped out a window as you imagined. Besides, radiators don't melt plastic handcuffs. And, with all the security improvements done to your property, and no rental boats available at night, how could he infiltrate the safeguards?"

"I don't know, but it made perfect sense as I was imagining or dreaming it."

"Well, dreams can unravel themselves in strange ways," Nydia said. "Thank God that's all it was."

"Amen to that," Sean said. "Katie, love, perhaps it will help you to know that there's a pattern to these visions you have."

"It's called night terror, Papa," she corrected him.

"It's not just night terror, Katie my love," he replied. "The visions you experience happen whenever you feel threatened. That lunatic Santillana gave all of us a scare. And now we're all knocking on the Lord's door asking him to help Stevie. It's no wonder. These two incidents are triggers for your visions, night terrors, hallucinations, or whatever you choose to call them. They're interrelated."

"I've never had a hallucination before," she corrected him.

"And here we go again," Sean said calmly when in truth he was near exasperation.

"What do you mean by that?" Katie asked.

"You've had hallucinations before, honey," Carolyn said.

"When?" she asked defensively.

"Several times, Katie," Nydia replied. "For some reason, your mind resets itself, and you apparently forget. Then the pattern repeats itself or surfaces in a different format. Dr. Lieberman has explained it to all of us before."

"How old was she when she killed her first victim?" Sean asked Carolyn.

"She was about Kieran's age," Carolyn said.

"Where's the squirt?" Katie asked.

"He's either buying mofongo or exploring again," Sean said and continued his train of thought. "So, you were about twelve years old when you allegedly killed, what was his name, Pink something."

"Pinkhosof," Nydia said. "He was Rina's father."

"You know about that?" Katie asked, sounding shocked. "Rina doesn't remember."

"Rina doesn't remember because Rina doesn't exist, Katie," Sean said, trying to keep a straight face, but unable to control a few chuckles.

"This is a serious matter," Carolyn said, hugging Katie closer to her. "I'm sorry, Katie, but Papa is right. We've been down this road before, and as Nydia informed you, honey, your mind keeps resetting. We found out about Pinkhosof's murder during a therapy session. When Papa and Matthew checked the area where you allegedly killed him, they found your partially charred schoolbag. It's a good thing we had plenty of rain that fall, or you would have probably burned everything in that park."

"That's insane. I remember being interrogated by the police about his murder."

"They were actors Ellen hired," Sean explained. "As usual your mother wanted to shelter you and I believed you should be taught a lesson. So, Ellen hired actors to put the fear of God into you, hoping that would knock some sense into that dense head of yours. It worked to some extent because Rina suddenly *moved* to Florida."

"But, I spoke to Rina a few days ago. We met at Rye Playland."

"Listen to me, honey," Carolyn said, caressing her face. "Please, please, understand this, baby, and God, I pray that you allow me to get through to her," she said as she glanced upward. "Listen to me, Katie. Who or what is Rina? It's a derivative of Ekaterina. What's your name in Russian, honey?"

"I'm Rina?" she asked incredulously as she attempted to connect the dots. "You mean I've been talking to myself?"

"Sort of," Carolyn said while she smiled sympathetically and brushed Katie's hair back. "It all started when you were five or six, and Luis was rushed to the hospital. You missed him, and I suggested that you use your imagination to fill the void. I didn't know it was going to get out of hand."

"You give yourself too much credit, Carolyn," Sean said. "I suspect Katie would have gone down that road without your help."

"We also suspect that the name Pinkhosof is Sean's contribution," Carolyn added, ignoring his comment.

"How so?" Katie asked.

"In my day," Sean said, "there was a TV program called *All in the Family*. The main character, Archie Bunker, used to call the Communists pinkos. When you decided to learn Russian, I said you were learning a pinko language."

"But Pinkhosof is a real name," Katie said.

"Perhaps it is," Sean said, "but you have to admit that my take on this is interesting."

"And offensive," Katie replied. "That's a pejorative."

"Subconsciously, we believe you intended it to be exactly that," Nydia said. "You invented Rina; who would Pinkhosof represent in your life, Katie?"

"Pinkhosof is my biological father," she said as she connected the dots again.

Carolyn hugged her closer. "You described him to Camille when you were hospitalized. Pinkhosof is definitely William Lyman. I hope you can concentrate on that realization, honey, and move on from here. You've accomplished so much. Don't let this be a perpetual hurdle for you. Arturo Santillana will no longer be a threat to you. Your biological father is ancient history. I know you're worried about Stevie; we all are. I have faith that God is going to come through for him. You need to move on."

"Mom, I've been trying to do just that. It isn't easy."

"I know, baby," Carolyn replied with tears welling in her eyes. "We'll all keep trying until we succeed. We will succeed; you have to believe that."

"Think of your life as a metaphor," Nydia suggested. "You were adrift at sea, and now you've reached the rescue dinghy. Don't jump back in the water, Katie."

"I'll try," she said. She drew her crutches toward her and added, "This conversation is giving me the creeps. I'll go look for Kieran."

"Don't you get lost too," Sean said.

"I won't," she replied as she got up to leave.

"He keeps wandering off, and security must be getting sick of me by now," Carolyn said. "One of these days, they'll ask us all to leave. He can't keep doing this, and I'm an idiot for permitting it; he keeps pulling the wool over my eyes."

"Tough love, Carolyn, my love," Sean replied.

"I know," she said as she wrung her hands.

"When I was a boy, my father would smack the crap out of me, and it straightened me out. Today, children are treated with kid gloves or they'll cry child abuse. I promise to look the other way if you give him a good spanking."

"I can't punish him for dealing with this situation in his own way," Carolyn replied. "He's very confused and upset by all this."

"Well, he's old enough to understand consequences; I'm going to have a good talk with him when he returns," Sean said. "If my foot kind of slips up his ass, I'm sure God will forgive me."

Carolyn gave him a stern look and said, "Are you sure your arthritic knees are up to it? The shock may backfire, Papa."

A few minutes later, Katie returned, walking alongside Kieran. "You can't do that. What if you encounter a rapist or a kidnapper?" She was aware that she was starting to sound like Carolyn. "Do you know where security found him?" she asked Carolyn. "He was in the basement; it's drafty and spooky down there. The child has no common sense. You can't trust him to be by himself."

Carolyn hugged Kieran and planted a kiss on the top of his head. She asked him if he was all right.

"Try not to wander off like that," she said when he replied he was fine.

In the meantime, Sean reacted to Katie's statement. "Is this the pot calling the kettle black? Kate, my love, do you remember Florida?" he asked.

Looking painfully embarrassed, Katie admitted, "I was hoping no one would bring that up. Anyway, the kid needs to be tethered."

"What happened in Florida?" Kieran asked.

"When you were a baby," Carolyn replied, "Katie wandered off and got lost in Disney World."

Sean and Nydia looked on solemnly, aware that Carolyn had given a very abridged version of what had actually happened. When Katie was in her second year at University College Dublin, Mamaí Katharine suffered another memory loss and disappeared shortly after New Year's Day. Ellen had filed a missing persons report on her. The authorities found Katharine's body early the next morning in Merrion Square, among one of the shrub beds. Momma Ellen concluded that she had apparently suffered a moment of dementia and had wandered off into the night. The autopsy revealed that Katharine had suffered a massive stroke, which caused her to tumble into the shrubs. Momma Ellen was grief-stricken and heartbroken. Katie was so upset that she boarded a flight to Florida to confer with Rina. Unfortunately, no one knew where she was until she called home; she was frightened and lost somewhere in Orlando and never set foot in Disney World. By then, the entire O'Gorman family was in Dublin, mourning Katharine's loss and planning a funeral. Matthew contacted the Orlando police and arranged for them to place Katie in a hospital. Carolyn called Dr. Odette Lieberman, and Odette agreed to meet them in Orlando the very next day. When Katie was well enough to travel, Matthew returned with her to Dublin while Odette and Carolyn returned to New York. Carolyn and Matthew missed Katharine's funeral, and, excluding the two young children that accompanied them, they logged close to twenty thousand travel miles in less than a week.

As Sean looked at Katie that evening in Stevie's hospital room, he simply said, "You are loved, young Kate."

Katie looked at him remorsefully and said, "I'm beginning to understand that, Papa. I love you too, and I'm sorry for all the headaches and heartaches."

* * *

The older adults now worried about a hurting and troubled Kieran. They knew that in his young mind, he was struggling with various emotions. He feared his brother might die and felt helpless in his presence. That's why he detached himself from the situation and chose to wander through the hospital's numerous corridors and strayed into service elevators and locations that were off limits to non-hospital personnel. By now, most people knew him, and they would patiently return him to his worried family.

Kieran also found himself forgotten and unwanted. From his perspective, no one seemed to miss him when he was away. At times, he wandered the neighborhood and sat on a bench while he watched the students from a nearby high school do things they shouldn't be doing in public, such as smoking pot and drinking vodka out of Poland Spring water bottles. Kieran had the presence of mind not to watch too closely in order to avoid an altercation with the oddly dressed youths.

The approximately three thousand teenagers who attended each of the public non-charter high schools in the city displayed varied fashion choices, reflecting their social standing within the diverse communities that each group represented within any given school, and this school was a sample of the whole. Kieran was intrigued by the students' creative attire and studied them with fascination. Several wore the conservative, well-tailored look of the time. Within any given population, however, a few hundred female students wore their unfastened short jackets to display the sexy blouses that strategically ended just above the navel. Their short skirts or tightly fitting slacks started an inch or two further down. Others dressed with loose-fitting clothing. The boys who chose that type of roomy attire paraded about the streets with their baggy jeans at mid-thigh, exposing their boxer shorts. The cascading folds of the pants' denim fabric and the hems of their jeans showed signs of wear from scraping the New York pavement. It was the beltless cell block style of the time that had become popular with gang rap artists and had originated in American prisons, where the inmates had been deprived of belts and shoelaces in order to humiliate them and to reduce mischief and attempted hangings. The free-roaming, streetwise teenagers embraced the jailhouse policy as high fashion. However, the oversized mid-thigh beltless jeans and shoelace-free sneakers made walking and running precariously difficult.

In contrast, Kieran's designer clothing, including his jeans, had a tailored look. With his fine clothes, the young boy stood out like a beacon in a fog. As he observed the teenagers, they occasionally observed him watching them. However, as he sat in the small park across the street from the large high school with its small patches of lawn, no one bothered him. A few girls thought the small child was cute, and they occasionally struck up a friendly conversation with him. Because he was so young, most girls inquired why he was there, and he answered truthfully, giving the entire story of Stevie's history while the girls listened sympathetically. "*Que carita y ojos bellos tiene el nene,*" he overheard one of the girls comment as they walked away. "*M'ija si fuera máh grande, me lo llevaría pah casa.*" Kieran knew enough Spanish to understand that the young woman had said, "What a beautiful face and eyes the boy has," and he blushed. However, he didn't know enough of the dialect to understand the second comment: "Girl, if he were older, I'd take him home with me."

Kieran spent a lot of time sitting on a park bench, munching on a bagel or hamburger and occasionally feeding the pigeons and squirrels as he studied the students or passersby. On one such day, he had convinced Carolyn to allow him to miss school, for he was anxious to see Stevie. He wasn't at the hospital long before he wandered off again. The usual high school hooky players were doing their thing, and the passersby were mostly elderly people pushing their partially filled shopping carts as they traveled to and from the local markets. Unlike Kieran's home in the suburbs, here everything was very convenient. There were numerous small shops and restaurants within short walking distances of one another. One could purchase anything from a nut and bolt to a T-shirt and sneakers. Watching the high school kids, he knew a person could also purchase illegal alcohol, cannabis, and other drugs. One could occasionally see a soiled condom or little empty vials of crack-cocaine throughout the tiny park. Kieran found one such vial at the base of the bench where he sat. He examined the curious little clear cylindrical container with a red lid and placed it in his pocket.

There was a gas station nearby and elevated train tracks. The trains emitted a rhythmic white noise as they entered and left the station every half hour. Katie had in-formed Kieran that the train traveled into Manhattan and Brooklyn. Maybe he could ride it all the way to Grandma Margaret's house in Manhattan, he thought. He made a mental note to find out about its specific route.

It was a strange, new, and fascinating neighborhood, he thought one day as he leaned back on a bench, fac-ing the narrow path that connected the school to the commercial community. He had traveled to many foreign countries, but he knew little of his own backyard, so to speak. This little community was as foreign as any other place he had visited, and yet, he was still in New York. Then something else struck him. He was a tourist. He was not only a tourist, but he was here by himself; there wasn't a family entourage with him. He was a lone traveler.

He got up and ventured further from the park. Before he realized it, he had traveled past a reservoir, down a steep hill, and into a residential community. There was one block of shops that included a Chinese take-out restaurant, a locksmith, and a grocery store called a bodega with the sign so prominently displayed that Kieran mistook Bodega for the store's name. He entered the Chinese restaurant, which was just opening to get ready for the lunch patrons. It was a quarter to eleven. Kieran ordered a half dozen steamed pork dumplings and cabbage and waited patiently on a window seat while the order was prepared. When he obtained his food, he walked a few feet down the block and sat on a building stoop. He placed the dipping sauce next to him on the white concrete step and proceeded to pick and dip his dumplings with the chopsticks as he watched the few pedestrians who lived or worked in the area. After he consumed all the dumplings, he poured the remaining tamari sauce over the steamed cabbage and chewed the stringy leaves. When he was finished, he tossed the empty containers into the bag and walked on until he found a corner trash bin.

He made an arbitrary right turn and continued his exploration. He came upon another commercial community with a theater, a food mart, a bookstore, and a Jewish kosher restaurant. He entered the restaurant and ordered a hot dog with mustard, onions, and sauerkraut and an orange soda. The place was bustling with patrons, and rightly so; the hot dog and soda were a delicious combination in his mouth. The beefy, paprika-flavored hot dog danced on his taste buds as it enticed the spicy mustard to caress the vinegary sauerkraut and tangy onions to twirl with the sweet and bubbly orange soda through his papillae. He smacked his lips with delight. Before he left, he downed a broccoli knish, half of it with ketchup and the other half with mustard.

A few blocks further down, amidst all those small shops was an International House of Pancakes. He stepped in and ordered an apple crepe à la mode and a glass of milk. After paying for his order and leaving the tip, he realized he had only a dollar and fifteen cents left, not enough to buy a pretzel if he needed it. Maybe he should start back and get some more money from his mother, he thought. But curiosity got the best of him, and he trekked on. He walked up and down hills. When he reached the next community with its own high school and plenty of nearby shops, his crepe à la mode was already wrestling with the hot dog and steamed dumplings and cabbage. Perhaps it was time to return to the hospital before he had a problem. He knew he had followed another elevated train trestle most of the way to his last food stop. Or maybe it was the same train trestle as before and they connected somewhere. He didn't know. He was lost.

He decided to cross the street to the high school. Before he could place one foot in the gutter, a school safety van pulled up and an officer got out. A female officer, followed behind him.

"Why aren't you in school, kid?" the first safety officer inquired.

"My brother is in the hospital," he said. "I was there and went for a walk."

"We're nowhere near a hospital," the female officer said.

The woman continued to grill him with numerous questions while his face reflected the discomfort that he felt in his intestines as everything percolated like a bubbling volcano. After getting all the information she needed, the officer placed a call to Carolyn and informed her that her son had been detained by the NYPD school safety patrol. She finally concluded with, "You ain't got no sense, boy. Your mother is worried sick and you're sightseeing."

"So what do we do now?" the first officer asked.

"You let me go, right?" Kieran replied.

"No," his female interrogator replied. "Kids! If you were my child, I'd knock you senseless."

"But you already said I have no sense. How can you knock me senseless?"

She looked him right in the eye and said, "I'll rephrase it for you, Einstein. If you were my child, I would knock the blue right out of your eyes, boy. Now get in the van so your mother can deal with you. I have no patience for sassy kids. I really need to get another job before I knock them all senseless. Damn fool."

"Do you think maybe I could use the bathroom in there," Kieran asked, pointing to the school and looking pale, "before we go? I have a pressing matter."

She eyed him suspiciously. Then she said, "Vinny, escort him in there, but don't let him out of your sight. You better make it quick, boy. Your mother is waiting for you. I swear—God help me!"

Vinny escorted Kieran into the boys' bathroom, and the child rushed into the closest stall to relieve himself none too soon.

"My God, kid," Vinny said fanning the air. "What have you been eating?"

From behind the stall door, Kieran had no difficulty enumerating the food list. "It was damn good," he concluded. "It's a shame it traveled so fast."

As hurtful as it was, Carolyn cut her visits to her comatose son to Saturdays and Sundays. She knew she needed to devote more time to Kieran, for she believed the boy probably felt abandoned as well as grief-stricken and helpless about Stevie's situation. At night, he often had nightmares and started to display signs of sleep deprivation. At Emily's Hope, he started seeing a therapist. Carolyn comforted and reassured him during the sessions that she was invited to attend. She picked him up from school on time and made certain he didn't miss his extracurricular activities. She knew that those distractions were important to his mental well-being.

Thirty-Three

⬦⬦⬦

The first week in May, Carolyn started the spring cleaning. She sorted the winter clothing that was being sent to the Salvation Army. As she rummaged through the pockets of one of Kieran's lightweight coats, she found an empty vial of crack.

"Oh Lord," she said aloud, thinking the worst possible scenario. She immediately called Matthew at work.

"Don't worry about it," he advised her.

"What do you mean, 'Don't worry about it'? I'm talking about crack and a twelve-year-old, Matthew. Jesus, Mary, and Joseph!"

"Let me finish," he said calmly. "You were thinking of taking him to a doctor because of his height problem. Well, take him to the doctor under that pretext and have him checked out for drugs. Frankly, I don't believe he's doing anything that stupid. He looks fine to me. Don't say anything to him until we see the blood results. Kids put all sorts of things in their pockets; he probably found that somewhere."

When Luis heard of the situation, he offered to conduct Kieran's medical tests himself. "I'll forward the results to his doctor," he said to Carolyn. "Bring him by my office tomorrow."

Carolyn and Kieran were relieved to hear that the tests were fine and there was nothing medically wrong with him.

"But when am I going to grow?" Kieran asked Luis.

"When God permits you to," Luis replied.

"Can't you give me a shot or something?"

"If you were a racehorse, maybe. For you, I wouldn't recommend it. As a matter of fact, it's morally and ethically wrong, even for a racehorse. I don't believe in messing with God's work. If I were you, I'd enjoy the perks of looking so young for as long as I could. Consider it a blessing."

"Some blessing. This is embarrassing. I bet those two school safety officers would never have busted me if I had been taller. That lady clearly did not like me. She said I had no sense."

"Amen, to that," Carolyn said from her seat, where she had been watching and listening to them.

Kieran ignored the comment and continued venting to Luis. "The high school kids play hooky all the time, and no one seems to bust them. That woman busted me; she didn't believe I was twelve. A fool in my school called me little Napoleon. How embarrassing is that?"

"It's embarrassing only if you permit it to be," Luis replied. "What did you say to the kid?"

"Nothing. I simply grabbed him and tossed him like a bag of beans." He displayed his karate moves, and Carolyn smiled. "I didn't hurt him or anything. I tossed him down gently, but not gently enough so he wouldn't forget whom he was messing with. I really need to grow, Luis" he said in exasperation. "At this rate, I'll never be a basketball player, so I may as well be a racehorse. Inject something up my butt—it may be my only hope!"

* * *

It pained Carolyn to spend less time by Stevie's bedside. One afternoon as she rummaged through the gadget drawer, she found a rock. It was the rock Stevie had given her when they vacationed in New Zealand many years ago. She kissed the rock, sat down, and wept silently; she forgot about what she had been looking for in that drawer. She went up to the attic and rummaged through the plastic containers until she found the one she was seeking. It was filled with the children's trinkets from years ago. She dragged the box down to her bedroom and immersed herself into a world of her own. Time stood still as she held a macaroni tree that Stevie had given to her during a Christmas in Dublin.

"Are we ever going to eat today?" Kieran inquired as he popped his head into her bedroom. "It's almost eight o'clock, Mom." That broke her reverie.

"What's all this stuff?" he asked, sitting across from her on the bed and picking up an old card made of construction paper.

"These are all the gifts you guys have given me over the years," she replied as she placed the macaroni tree on her dresser.

Kieran fumbled through a few items and immediately understood what she had been doing. He would occasionally sit in Stevie's room and go through his brother's books, baseball cards, and other little treasures. One night, he fell asleep wearing Stevie's football jersey. It almost suited him like a blanket, but it failed to cover his feet.

"Mommy, do you think Stevie will ever wake up?" he blurted out. "I miss him."

"I miss him too, honey. Yes, I believe he'll wake up. What do you want for dinner, baby?"

* * *

Guitar or flute playing were among the activities Luis did when he visited Stevie. Within a couple of days of Stevie's injury, Luis wrote a song that took him a few minutes to compose. He called it "Having Our Jamboree." It had a folksy, playful beat that any child would enjoy skipping or hopping to, and he played it routinely for Stevie. As he strummed and played the guitar, passersby lingered by Stevie's room. At times, staff members found themselves humming or whistling Luis's playful tune.

It's just Stevie, Katie, Kieran, and me
Heading for a jamboree
Skipping stones, getting tall
Eating scones, climbing walls
My lover, my brothers, and me
Sailing out to sea
Flying high, touch the sky
Ride our bikes, this is nice.

It's just Stevie, Katie, Kieran, and me
Heading for a jamboree
Our lives are cool as ice
Perhaps Katie will be my wife
Everything will be all right
If you stay out of the light
Stevie please come with me
Watch out for that stinging bee.

It's just Stevie, Katie, Kieran, and me

Heading for a jamboree

Kieran is chasing after fishes

If I only had three wishes

We'd be shooting at the dishes

Or windsurfing in St. Paul

When Carolyn invites us all,

Stevie, don't accept this call.

It's just Stevie, Katie, Kieran, and me

Heading for a jamboree

Stevie, brother, watch the pony

If you ride it, we'll be lonely

Don't be fooled by what's phony

Clap your hands, stamp your feet

Life down here can be a treat

It's time to rejoin the jamboree.

It's just Stevie, Katie, Kieran, and me

Having our jamboree.

One month and two weeks to the day after the writing of that song, a janitor was mopping Stevie's room while whistling "Having Our Jamboree." Stevie started to produce guttural sounds. Katie was the only other person in the room. She had been sipping apple juice and looking at the dreary urban scenery outside the window when she heard him.

"Oh my God," she cried out in jubilation as she spilled the apple juice on her blouse and onto the clean floor. "I think he's trying to talk!"

The janitor paused and listened to the sounds. He smiled and walked over to examine the patient. "He's waking up," the janitor diagnosed.

Stevie opened his Vaseline-lubricated eyes and looked about the room. "Stop singing that irritating song! I can't get it out of my head," he complained with a hoarse voice.

Katie and the janitor laughed, and she planted a big kiss on Stevie's cheek. "Welcome back, oh brother of mine! We're having our jamboree."

"Katie," he said, "Omid needs an elevator. I need you to go over there and install it for him."

"Mom," she later yelled into the phone, "Stevie is awake!"

Carolyn broke down and cried as she sank into a seat, and Kieran took the phone from her.

Not knowing whom to expect, he spoke into the phone and said, "This is Kieran."

"Is Mommy okay?" Katie asked.

"She's crying," he said matter-of-factly.

"Squirt, Stevie's awake!" she blurted out.

He smiled and asked, "Did he say anything?"

"Yes, he complained about Luis's annoying song," she laughed. "And he said he wanted corned beef and spuds."

"Mommy," Kieran said to Carolyn, "Stevie wants corned beef and spuds."

Carolyn composed herself and took the phone from him. "I'll bring him his food," she said to Katie.

"No, you don't have to do that. As soon as the doctor said it was okay for him to have it, the janitor went across the street and bought it for him. Now we need a bottle of champagne, streamers, horns, and an Irish jig," Katie said joyfully. "Mommy, I have to call Luis and Nydia. You call Daddy and everyone else. You don't need to call Momma; we just finished talking to her. Stevie needed to say something to her before he forgot. I'll see you later. Wait, your son wants to talk to you!"

"Hi, Mommy," Stevie said in his still dry, hoarse voice.

"Hi, honey. How are you feeling?" she asked with a mixture of concern and jubilation.

"Is that Stevie?" Kieran asked

Stevie said, "I'm a little groggy, Mommy. I heard I've been sleeping for a while."

As Kieran continued to hover over her, Carolyn replied, "One month, two weeks, and four days, honey. Kieran wants to say hello," she added. "I'm going to call Daddy. We'll see you soon, baby," and she handed the phone back to Kieran.

* * *

"I missed Mother's Day," Stevie said as Carolyn and Matthew flanked his bed on either side, and Katie, Luis, Kieran and the others crowded around. "I'll make it up to you, Mommy."

"Oh God," she said, caressing his face and five o'clock shadow. "You already have, honey. I couldn't have asked for a better gift."

"She likes cards made of construction paper, roses made of tissue paper, and trees made from macaroni," Kieran commented. "Mommy is a cheap date."

As the family and close friends listened, Stevie related his recollections.

"Then I kept hearing that annoying song about chasing fishes, going to a jamboree, and staying out of the light. If that ridiculous song couldn't wake me, nothing could," he laughed. "I needed to wake up or that stupid song would have killed me; I still can't get it out of my head."

"So you're saying I saved your life," Luis interjected.

"No, no, no. You made my head ache. I needed to wake up and kill you," he teased him.

"That's going to be the theme song at my wedding," Luis said as he drew Katie closer to him. "She said she'll marry me if you can stand next to us at the wedding. You're my best man."

"Not if that tune is playing, oh brother of mine! Help!" he cried, and they all laughed.

"Stevie," Luis added, "I heard you saw the light."

"Well, I saw something. I spoke with Mamaí Katharine; she spoke Irish, and I understood every word. Tell him what she said, Momma," he said, turning to Ellen. "I kept referencing that part so I wouldn't forget."

Ellen said, "According to Stevie, Mamaí said, '*Caith siar é agus ná lig aniar é*,' which basically means 'Drink it and don't let it come back up.' Mamaí used to tell us that whenever she gave us bitters to ward off a cold."

"I bet they also say that at the local pub," Katie commented. "Were you having a snort with Mamaí, Stevie?"

"Well, that would explain why he slept so long," Kieran interjected. "What else did you see, Stevie?"

"Well, I kept going back to those days when we rode horseback along the steep Irish coast line. Do you remember that, Daddy?" he asked his father, and Matthew nodded in affirmation. "The first time we went, you told me we were going to ride the ponies. When we got there, I was disappointed because they were regular size horses. You lied to me."

"Well, you were easy, son," Matthew replied. "Besides, when people go to the racetrack, what do they bet on? They bet on the ponies. I've never seen a pony at any racetrack. So technically, I didn't lie."

"Well, anyway, in my coma, I kept going back there. It felt good, very comforting. Mamaí kept telling me to get off the pony because it was phony. It was a lie, and she kept trying to pull me off. I wanted to keep riding because we were all there. The air was sweet, the scenery was awesome, and it felt like a warm blanket."

Katie looked at Luis and sang:

Stevie, brother, watch the pony
If you ride it, we'll be lonely
Don't be fooled by what's phony
Clap your hands, stamp your feet
Life down here can be a treat.

"Baby," she said to Luis, "did you write the song, or did Mamaí use you to communicate with him? Or did he hear you and then dreamt that Mamaí was speaking to him?"

"Those are good questions," Stevie said, "but I still can't figure out how I understood and spoke Irish; I don't know any Irish. I first saw Mamaí Katharine after the light; she was sitting under a star. She *was* there, and she *did* speak Irish. You can't convince me otherwise."

"Did you see anyone else?" Kieran asked.

"I kept seeing Luis holding a baby," Stevie replied, and Katie whirled to look at Luis.

Luis looked back at her and shrugged. "He probably remembers seeing me with one of my patients. I hold lots of babies."

"I saw and remember a lot of stuff," Stevie continued. "I need to write it all down. Mommy, can you bring me a notebook tomorrow?"

"You can use my laptop; I have it right here," Katie offered, walking toward a case she had placed near the sofa. "You can e-mail whatever you write to your own account."

"Do I need a password?" Stevie inquired.

"It's 'rugby € star 317,'" Kieran replied. "The letters B and S are uppercase. She reprogrammed the keyboard and placed the euro sign on shift F6."

Intending to smack him, Katie whirled in his direction, but Kieran reacted quickly. He hid behind Carolyn and said, "You can't hit me. I'm a minor. Besides, I stand behind the law." He hugged his mother's waist from behind and popped his head out from under her arm.

"I'm going to skewer you and feed you to the fish," Katie said vehemently, "you little twit. Mommy, you see what I have to put up with? He did it again. He hacked into my computer. Eventually, I'm going to figure out how you're doing this, and you're going to pay."

"You should be paying me," he replied. "I'm providing you with a service by showing you the weaknesses in your system. If I can do it, anyone out there can do it. By the way, do you really believe you're a rugby star?"

"Mom, I'm going to kill him, I swear!"

Carolyn smiled at their antics and caressed her son's soft face. Later that evening she made him promise to stop hacking. "Find another outlet to amuse yourself. If you can't come up with anything, we'll work at it together. Your sister is entitled to her privacy."

"But this is so much fun, Mom, and the internet is sort of intended for that."

She gave him a stern look and said, "You need to abide by and respect the law, young man."

* * *

As soon as Darnell informed them that Stevie was awake, Amir, his wife, and little Shirin Naghmed stopped by for a brief visit. Shirin had taken a liking to Stevie and was happy to hear he had finally awakened from the coma. They walked alongside Stevie as he struggled to walk down the hall. After lying in bed for a month and a half, his muscles and chipped spine bone limited his abilities to do much. Sean and Ellen later helped him back into bed while Katie and the Hassans watched. The Hassans had an animated conversation with Stevie and the others, for they were all thrilled that he had cheated death. Stevie once again mentioned the elevator for Omid. Amir said he appreciated his concern, but it would not be possible to install an elevator. Not only was the landlord opposed to it because it could raise the already exorbitant property tax, but Amir could not afford such a modification.

"Why?" Katie asked. "I don't wish to pry into your personal life, but if you explain why, maybe there's a solution. Your son obviously needs such an amenity, so we need to determine how it can be done. Is money really an issue? Would you be willing to move to another location? If you don't want or cannot relocate, what alternative modifications does the law allow to be made to the present space? Do you see what I mean?"

"Yes, I see," Amir replied, holding his chin. "Despite the terrible thing that happened to your brother, I would like to keep my business in the same location. Those men who did this terrible thing do not represent the entire community. People have been very kind since all this happened. Stevie," he said, looking at the young man, "in case you did not know, the three men who did this have been identified, thanks to concerned citizens and the police. They will face justice."

"After the people in the neighborhood heard what happened and why," Naghmed said, "they now stop by and help Omid with his therapy. There is a big man, much like Stevie, who carries him up and down the stairs and helps him to do his exercises in the backyard. We have many good neighbors. If we move, we do not know how things will be. If there is no other way, I will do whatever is good for Omid. But we do not have much money. Rent for business and apartment is eighteen thousand dollars a month, and this is very cheap for a business in Westchester. Rent and everything in New York and Westchester is very high—as high as the sky. It is crazy."

"It's more than crazy—it's outrageous," Katie said. "I didn't think you could have an eighteen-thousand-dollar profit margin by selling novelties. I suspect you're working just to keep a roof over your heads, and it sounds like you're in debt. But you have answered my questions; I need to see the property. Then I will deal with your landlord, and maybe we can find a solution."

By the end of the next day, Stevie was moved to a rehab center in Westchester County. There, before and after a massage or chiropractic adjustment, he spent practically every waking hour exercising. He had lost weight while in his hospital bed; most of it was due to muscle atrophy. The chipped bone in his spine caused excruciating back and leg pain. Nonetheless, he rose each morning and went into his daily workouts as soon as he finished breakfast. A young woman named Sheeva Syedullah was one of his therapists. An orderly would deliver Stevie to the gym, and the young man patiently sat in his assigned location until Sheeva was ready to start him on his next routine. As he became acclimated and more comfortable with his surroundings, he would claim an unoccupied therapy area and start doing an exercise. When he first arrived, however, the pain and stiffness in his lower back and leg made it difficult to maneuver a walker, so he sat and waited for Sheeva to coax him. As he sat, he studied the photographs on the desk that was flush against one of the corner walls. There was a picture of Sheeva and a baby who was a few months old. There was also a picture of a young man proudly posing in a Marine uniform in front of an American flag, andStevie concluded that the man was her husband.

"I have a friend who was in Iraq," Stevie said to her as he studied the pictures. "Where is your husband stationed?"

"My husband was killed in Afghanistan," she said matter-of-factly while gathering the contents of the patient information folder that was on her desk. "How are you feeling today, Mr. O'Gorman?"

"I'm sorry," he replied clumsily. "I didn't know."

"Of course you didn't know. That's why you asked. How are you feeling today?" she asked him again.

"I'm fine."

"Good," she said. "Let's get to work. Today, I want you to walk all the way around the gym three times without any prodding. Do you think you can do that?"

"Sure," he said contritely. The truth was his leg hurt like hell, but he concluded that it didn't compare to her pain. He grabbed the walker and started the excruciating trek. *You should learn to keep your mouth shut*, he chided himself as he took each step. *Stop minding other people's business. She sure is feisty, though.*

After that incident, he found himself studying her from afar as she worked with other patients. One afternoon, he made eye contact, and he thought he caught a slight glimpse of a smile. Then she brushed her hijab back as if it were her hair. One morning, as she leaned over to adjust the tension on his bike, he caught a whiff of her hair. The fragrance was intoxicating.

"Did you hear what I said, Mr. O'Gorman?" she asked him.

"No," he admitted. "I'm sorry. I think I'm still hungry. They only give you two small eggs for breakfast. That's not enough protein to keep me going until lunch."

"Tell that to the dietician then. I want you to do two miles on this setting. It's the next-to-lowest setting. After that, take it up a notch and do two more miles. Call me as soon as you're done."

"I'll definitely need more protein for that."

"Very well, I'll call downstairs and ask them to bring you a sandwich. What kind would you like?"

"What kind of what?" he asked, sounding confused.

"Never mind, Mr. O'Gorman. Do your exercise."

"Stevie," he corrected her, "my friends call me Stevie. My father is Mr. O'Gorman."

"I'm not your friend, Mr. O'Gorman. I'm your therapist." She turned and walked away.

Stevie hadn't noticed that Matthew, Carolyn, and Kieran had arrived for a visit. They had witnessed the entire interaction while they stood behind him. Carolyn poked Matthew, aware that Stevie had taken an interest in the stern young woman.

"I think there's hope for him yet," Carolyn whispered. "God works in mysterious ways."

She walked up beside him and startled him with her presence. "Mommy, where did you come from?" he asked, looking flushed.

"We've been standing right here," she said as Matthew and Kieran made their presence known.

"Are you hungry, son?" she asked mockingly, raising one eyebrow.

"No," he said as he peddled on. "Why do you ask?"

"Well, I don't know. I thought you might like a sandwich or perhaps some cherry pie."

"I'd like some cherry pie," Kieran said.

During another exercise session, the Hassan family, minus Shirin, came to visit. Omid was looking much better. He was still confined to his wheelchair, but he was able to maneuver it by himself. He couldn't yet lift himself in and out of it without assistance, but he was progressing well. He said he had visited Kenny, the owner of the horse stables, a couple of times and had helped him feed the horses. His entire upper body was starting to look less flabby. During the months of neglect and indifference Omid had received from the military, his once buffed upper body had diminished to stringy biceps and a sunken chest. Stevie was pleased to see the physical improvement. Omid now looked happy and confident. When Sheeva came to check on Stevie's progress, he introduced her to the Hassans. Sheeva was wearing a white Muslim headdress and tunic. Mrs. Hassan said something in Farsi to the young woman. Sheeva smiled and replied courteously.

"I wish she were that nice to me," Stevie said when Sheeva had walked away.

"Perhaps you do not understand, young Steven," Amir Hassan said to him. "In our culture a young woman cannot be forward in the presence of a young man."

"Oh, she's forward, all right," Stevie said, playing on Amir's words. "She's downright curt. But she is pretty."

"You like this young lady?" Mrs. Hassan asked him.

Stevie grinned, blushed, and dropped his chin. Mrs. Hassan understood the body language. Stevie, she concluded, had a crush.

Stevie made it home in time for Father's Day. They had a heartfelt and joyous celebration. The entire Hassan family was present. Darnell and several of Stevie's other school buddies hugged and patted Stevie on the back. Stevie still needed a cane to support his painful leg and walked with a slight limp. To the guests, he told and re-told the dreams he still remembered from his coma. As the celebration progressed, they enjoyed good food and dance. Stevie, pivoting on his cane and to the entertainment of those present, performed an Irish slip jig with Luis. Everyone clapped, and Sean challenged Stevie to a hop jig; Camille and Carolyn joined in. They stomped their feet and smiled joyfully until they were winded. Despite his bad back and uncooperative leg, Stevie endured. "Bring it on," he said. "At rehab I had a drill sergeant," he said, thinking of the dark-haired Sheeva. "After her torture, I can do anything." Despite his bravado, the next dance was slow, so he sat it out and enjoyed excited conversation with his friends.

Later that evening, he was in his room, sorting through get-well cards and other memorabilia people had sent while he was in the hospital. He came upon the St. Christopher's medal Nydia had attached to his headboard. He examined it, holding it between his thumb and index finger. Katie knocked on his door while he was contemplating the little medallion.

"What are you doing, oh brother of mine?" she inquired from the doorway.

"Do you know who left this for me?" he asked her as she sat on his bed.

Katie took the medal and examined it. "I don't know," she said. "It was either Nydia or Aunt Camille. They often stood by your bed with their rosary beads and prayed. And they're the only two I know who carry those little religious trinkets. This is St. Christopher."

"I know," Stevie replied. "When I was in a coma, I remember an old woman with a bandana wrapped around her head. She gave me a St. Christopher on a gold chain; she pressed the medal into my hand. I wrote about it in my journal. The piece appeared to be solid gold, and the circumference was filigree. It was about the size of a nineteenth-century silver dollar, and it had some kind of strange writing along the inner circumference. It was probably Greek or Hebrew."

"Did the old woman say anything to you?"

"She said, 'God bless you, my son.' I'm not her son."

"Nydia left this for you," Katie said with conviction. "'God bless you, my son,' is commonly used in Latin countries after a salutation or a request for a blessing. Let's download a computer facial-imaging software program from the Internet. Maybe you can reconstruct the face of the old lady who gave you the medal. Wouldn't it be awesome if Nydia recognizes her?"

That being said, they started surfing the Net for such a program.

"Katie," Stevie asked as they searched, "are you really going to marry Luis?"

"Yes," she replied without looking up from the computer screen. "I made a promise."

"To whom?"

"To God and then to Luis. I promised God that if he allowed you to live, I'd take the plunge and marry Luis. I told Luis that if you were able to stand with us at the altar, I'd marry him."

"So you're marrying him because of a promise. It sounds like a contractual agreement. Is Luis okay with this? I mean, it sounds so cold. Do you love him, Katie?"

She looked at Stevie right in the eyes and said with conviction, "Yes, I love Luis. It's been quite a journey for me, bro, but I do love Luis. I've been in love with him since I first met him."

"What made you finally realize that?"

"Several factors, but it was mostly you."

"Me?" he asked.

"Yes, you. When you were shot, I realized how much I love you."

"You love me?"

"Yes, you damn fool; I love you. The day they shot you, my gut was in my throat. My head exploded and I couldn't imagine life without you or Mommy or Daddy or Luis. My world would be empty without you guys. You are my tether to earth."

"What about Kieran? You didn't mention him."

"I couldn't imagine my life without him, either. He can be annoying at times, but I haven't been a picnic either. Do you know about me and Rina?"

"Of course I know about you and Rina. You hadn't spoken of her in a while."

"What do you know about me and Rina?"

"Well, she's your friend. You've known her for as long as I can remember," he said as he surfed the Net. "Mom told me she came to visit during the grand opening of Emily's Hope Academy. Why do you ask?"

"Rina isn't real. Do you know that too?"

"Of course I know that," he said in a noncommittal tone, wondering why she had brought it up. "I wasn't sure you knew."

"The matter was brought to my attention while you were sleeping. Nydia and Mommy said that I've known Rina is a figment of my imagination, but I keep blocking out that fact. How does it feel to have a crazy sister, Stevie?"

"You're not crazy, Katie."

"How do you figure that, Stevie? It isn't normal to invent people and situations."

"What's normal, Katie? When we were kids, Daddy was diagnosed with cancer. Is it normal to be physically ill and normal to cope with one's illness? I'm sure you guys worried and loved me while I was comatose and we each coped with the situation. Having a mental illness is no different," he said as he stopped fiddling with the computer and turned to face her. "To those of us who are allegedly normal, the person with the mental illness appears to behave oddly. However, underneath the scar of the illness, you are still you, and you are coping to rectify the plague within you. A lame person uses a cane to get about; you use Rina. It's unfair to give you a label that is considered negative, so I would never call you crazy, Katie. I love Daddy with or without cancer, and I love you with or without Rina. We've all been trying to tell you that all these years. I pray you can finally say good-bye to her and stay on this path."

"So do I. I also want to be able to stay off the medication. I want to marry Luis and have a family; I can't do that if I have to rely on meds."

"Are you taking your medicine now?"

"No, I haven't had anything in a while. I'd like to stay like this. However, I murdered Kurt; I put him in the bone cruncher."

"Why did you do that?"

"It's a long story. Mommy or Daddy can bring you up to speed; it will make for an entertaining dining experience. Now let's get to work on this," she said, turning back to the computer. "Rina is ancient history."

They were able to make a composite drawing of the woman in his dreams. Days later, Stevie handed Nydia the picture.

"Who is she?" Nydia asked him.

"I don't know," he said and explained his dream. He then showed her a picture of a St. Christopher's medallion. "I gave the tin one you left at my bed to a friend of mine and asked him to paint me a gold one with filigree, using yours as a guide. That's not quite it, but it was the best he could do. The one I saw had a bigger image of Christopher with Little God on his shoulder. Does it ring a bell?"

"No," she replied. "I've never seen anything like that. Can I keep these?"

"Sure," he said, looking and sounding disappointed. He had hoped his dream had an ethereal reality or some kind of earthly meaning. He instead came upon an unexpected dead end.

Thirty-Four

Rental property in New York was high, and small businesses were being hit hard by the rocketing inflation. While doing business, Katie made a profit, but she tried to be fair with her clients. Upon inspecting the premises where the Hassans lived, she told them that she believed that they had been victims of extortion, for they had paid the landlord enough to purchase the property five times over. She also informed them she didn't understand why the landlord hadn't been fined by the fire department because she found thirteen fire code violations and a few structural problems. She took her findings to a friend at the Buildings Department and asked him to conduct his own official inspection. Then she checked the landlord's and property's histories.

Katie and her employee Ramírez knew their way around the laws and regulations of the real estate business. They discovered that the present owners had considered selling in order to relocate closer to their son who lived in North Carolina. Within weeks, Katie and Ramírez used their skills to negotiate a reasonable price for the out of code property. Margaret's corporation offered the Hassans an excellent mortgage rate and they were soon real estate owners who would eventually be able to save money instead of owe it to an unscrupulous landlord.

Ramírez and his crew knocked down an outside wall to extend the rear of the building a few feet. They constructed a shaft that was large enough to hold an elevator for six occupants and enclosed it with insulated brick walls. Katie advised the Hassans on what to do to give the store a less cluttered appearance, allowing them easier and safer access to the merchandise. The Hassans were delighted with the new turn of events.

Darnell and Stevie continued to visit Omid, although their presence wasn't needed as helpers; Omid was working hard at becoming independent. The boys continued to drive Omid to different locations in order to entertain him. They returned him home and occasionally stayed for dinner; Mrs. Hassan always insisted. More often than not, Stevie declined.

"What, you don't like my cooking?" Mrs. Hassan challenged him.

"Your cooking is fine," he replied. "But I don't like to miss dinner at home when my mother is expecting me."

"Well, you tell your mother not to expect you for dinner next week Wednesday. Next week you two boys dine with my family; I make something special for you. If you like, I make American food."

"We'll eat anything you decide to cook, Mrs. Hassan," Darnell said with a big smile. "We eat American food every day; I'm game for something new."

"Good, good. I will plan something nice."

When the three young men returned from their outing the following Wednesday, Stevie gaped and blushed when he discovered Sheeva Syedullah, his former therapist, seated in the living room with her hands folded over her lap. She wore a lovely blue silk dress that complemented her beautiful brown eyes and hair; she wasn't wearing the hijab.

Dinner was served in the backyard. The days were longer, and a gentle summer breeze blew Sheeva's long, wavy hair across her face. She was lovely; Stevie forgot to breathe. His heartbeat slowed, his eyes drooped, and he sighed. The succulent lamb stew over a bed of nutty flavored basmati rice, the spiced roast chicken, the savory eggplant and sweet potatoes, the warm naan, the aromatic tea, and sugary dates were nothing compared to the sweet smile Sheeva displayed across the table from him. Each dish was served in individual small plates, but Stevie hardly noticed as each course came and went. After dinner, he was not aware that the table had been cleared and the two of them had been left alone.

"Mrs. Hassan told me you're a law student," Sheeva initialized the conversation.

He was going to respond, but nothing came out of his mouth. He cleared his throat, wet his dry lips, and felt embarrassed. He finally said, "Well, I'll be getting my bachelor's degree. I'll still need to work toward my master's, so I have a bit to go before I can be considered a true law student. The university is allowing me to make up the exams I missed for the bachelor's degree. My family cancelled a trip to Costa Rica so I can do that. I'll get my degree, but without the graduating class. I missed that. Of course, I can attend a summer graduation if I want. But there's really no need for that. It's the sheepskin that's important."

"I attended my graduation," she replied. "It's a nice experience. My family was there to cheer me on, and that felt good. Maybe you should reconsider."

"No, it's okay. I already graduated from eighth grade and high school. Graduations are all the same. I already discussed it with my parents, and they're okay with it, except my mother said she was looking forward to seeing me in the procession."

"Well, there you go," she replied. "You're depriving her of her moment of glory. Parents are as proud of you as you are of your accomplishments. I suggest you reconsider and revisit the matter."

"Would you come to my graduation if I participated?" he asked.

"Well, graduations are for family and friends. We don't know each other that well."

"What made you change your mind about me?" he asked pointedly. "At rehab, you tried to ignore me whenever you could."

"Mrs. Hassan has informed me that you have a kind, loving heart. She has assured me that you are a good person, and she insisted that I give you a chance and get to know you. She also told me you want to be a priest. I am Muslim, and you want to be a Catholic priest. So we can be friends."

"Well, I have a confession," he said.

"Yes?" she asked.

"Now that I know you—well, now that I've met you—I'm not so sure I want to be a priest. Besides, when I was in a coma, my great-grandmother appeared to me in a dream. She said I needed to get off the pony. That means I had to live because I needed to care for my family and become a statesman. According to her, I will personally meet the president and the pope. It's not everyone who meets the pope. In my religion, that's a big deal. I talk too much, don't I?"

"No, you're doing fine, Steven."

"Ah, you called me Steven. No more Mr. O'Gorman."

"How old are you, Steven?"

"I'm twenty-one. I'll soon be twenty-two, though."

"How soon, Steven?"

"About seven months from now."

"You're very young. I'm twenty-three, and I have a son."

"I saw your son's picture on your desk. Anyway, twenty-three is young. My sister is twenty-five. She's getting married soon to my brother."

"Your sister is marrying your brother?"

"Well, Luis isn't really my brother. We're like brothers because we all grew up together and he's my parents' godson. My little brother calls his mother Meema Nydia. 'Meema' is my brother's version of 'mommy.' That's how close we are. Anyway, Luis and my sister Katie are getting married. Maybe you can come as my date. You don't need to bring a gift or anything. Luis and Katie aren't accepting gifts. Instead, they're asking the guests to make a donation to Injured Veterans of War. That was Katie's idea."

"That's a noble act."

"I guess she decided that on account of Omid. We're always talking about him. He got messed up during the war, and then the military wasn't helping him with anything. Through IVW, anyone who finds himself or herself in a similar situation can receive the help they need," he said as he watched her brush her hair away from her face. "The general public needs to do more to reach out to those individuals; our veterans are getting a raw deal. Do you know that when they get furlough, they have to pay and find their own way home and back to duty again? Now that's totally unfair and ridiculous. If we ship them off to war, then we should provide timely, free, and safe transport home when they're on leave. Then there's the matter of housing for their spouses and children while they're away risking life and limb."

"You already sound like a statesman, and I know about all that."

"Of course you do. Your husband was a marine. I apologize; I talk too much. Why don't you tell me about yourself?"

"There's nothing much to say."

"How old is your son?"

"He's ten months old."

"Who cares for him while you're at work?"

"He goes to baby daycare. This evening, he's with my mother."

"That must be hard on you," he observed. "My mother works, but she never had to place us in daycare."

"How did she manage that?"

"She took us to work with her. She still does that now. My brother is twelve. A car service picks him up after school, and he spends the remainder of the day at the academy where my mother works. I used to do the same thing when I was younger, except my mother drove me to and from school because the school was closer then. The academy has since moved to a new location. At the academy, there are lots of things to do. I studied music and art. I learned fencing. I played football and tennis, and there are lots of other things. Before you know it, the day is over. And you get to meet a lot of people."

"Is that where you met Darnell and Omid?"

"No, I met Darnell in parochial school; we went to St. Francis together. I met Omid at Fordham University. Then he dropped out to go to war. The recruiters used to come by and talk to us as we left campus. They nailed Omid. My father didn't allow me to go, but Omid signed without consulting his parents."

"But you were over eighteen. You could have gone if you wanted to."

"Not in my family. My mother says the laws of society apply to her children when they are out the door. As long as we live under her roof, we abide by her laws. The laws are simple; my parents have the final word. It's not that I'm a coward or anything. I would have gone, but I was raised to abide by my parents' laws. In their absence, I answer to my grandparents, my uncles, my Aunt Camille, Nydia, and Felipe. We are a very close, very tight family. It may be old-fashioned by today's standards, but I'm okay with it."

"Who are Nydia and Felipe?"

"They're Luis's parents. Luis is my sister's fiancé."

"Right," she recalled.

"I apologize again. I don't normally talk this much, honest. It's getting late. May I see you home?"

"I have my car," she replied, meaning that she could see herself home.

As if on cue, little Shirin arrived with a tray of fresh tea and two large slices of walnut and blueberry honey cake garnished with wedges of mandarin oranges.

"Where did everybody go?" Stevie asked her as he helped her lift the tray onto the table.

"Omid and Darnell are playing a video game," Shirin replied. "I was helping my mother."

"Did you make this?" Stevie asked about the cake.

"I prepared the tea, but I know how to bake a cake, if that's what you want to know. My mother made the cake and the naan. She wanted everything to be perfect."

"And it has been," Sheeva commented.

"I agree. Your mother is an excellent cook. Why don't you sit and join us? We can share my cake," Stevie said as he pulled a chair out for her.

Shirin accepted the invitation. When she sat down, she said, "My father made the stew. He always makes the stew. My mother's stew never turns out this good."

"Can you make stew?" Stevie asked her as he sliced the cake.

"Yes, but not as good as Baba. He makes the best stew. Do you cook, Stevie?"

"Yes," he said as he transferred his half of the cake onto a napkin. "My mother says, 'Every healthy human being is born with three assets: limbs, a heart, and a mind. In life you don't waste any of them.'"

"What does that mean?" Shirin asked.

"It means you learn to do everything you need to survive and you don't shy away from work. That way, you will succeed at practically anything. So based on that, yes, I cook, and I do everything else I need to know. If you can't afford something, you work for it. There's always work to be done, no matter how insignificant it may appear to be. It's our responsibility to do it, or we waste the assets God has given us." He handed her the plate with her half of the cake.

"Is that why you help my brother?"

"Partly, but I also help Omid because he's my friend."

"Would you collect garbage for a living?"

"Good question, and the answer is yes because it needs to be done. If we didn't clean up after ourselves, we'd be into our necks in vermin and disease. It's also an honest way to make a living. If I believe I'm too good to collect garbage, then I'm cheating and deluding myself. In my religion, the man whom we believe to be God washed his disciples' feet. If God can humble himself to do that, then why shouldn't the common man do the same? Eat your cake."

"Why did he just wash their feet? Why didn't he just give his friend a bath?"

"Well, that was the custom back in those days. They wore sandals and washed the dust off their feet. I guess today, you could just turn on the hose in the backyard and hose the guy down from head to foot."

Shirin laughed and said, "But he'll be naked for the whole world to see. You're funny, Stevie."

"Who said he had to remove his clothes? You're jumping to conclusions."

"You don't take a bath with your clothes on, silly. You won't be clean. You'll just be wet and yucky, especially on a hot, humid day."

"You're right, Shirin. Why are we talking about baths anyway?"

"I don't know. We were talking about washing somebody's feet," she said, laughing.

On the way home, Stevie got into a discussion with Darnell.

"So," he said to his friend, "you knew she was going to be there, and you didn't warn me?"

"Would you have come if I said something?"

"Maybe not, but a heads-up would have been nice. Then you guys walked off and left me alone with her."

"How did it go?"

"How did it go? I'll tell you how it went. I couldn't shut the hell up. I was so damn nervous I couldn't stop talking."

"Did she say anything to you?"

"Not much. I don't know any more about her now than what I knew before. I'm so damn stupid! When Shirin arrived with the cake, I tried to use her as a shield. I asked her to join us, but I still couldn't shut up."

"What did you say?"

"What the hell do I know? I just rambled on about nothing. Man, she must think I'm a total idiot. I blew it; I know I blew it. Why didn't you warn me? Why did you leave me alone with her?"

"Don't beat yourself up, and don't beat me. Maybe she'll give you another chance."

"I doubt it," he sighed. "I'll never ever see her again."

"Let me ask you something. How many girls have you dated?"

"None. You know that. How many have you dated?"

"None, but that's not the point. The point is we shouldn't jump to conclusions. Call her and invite her to a movie or a concert. If she accepts, then we can conclude you didn't blow it. If you watch a movie or some type of show, you can't talk. That will put a sock in your big mouth. Before or after the movie, you treat her to a nice meal, and you keep telling yourself, 'Stevie, chew and shut up.'"

"Then what do we do? We sit there and stare at each other?"

"No, before you call her, make a list of things you want to know about her. Or ask her impersonal stuff so she won't feel like you're prying."

"Like what?"

"Start with the weather. I'll be her and you'll be you. Go ahead, ask or say something." There was a pause. "Well?" Darnell said, trying to coax him on.

"I've got nothing, man," Stevie replied, and they both cracked up.

"You picked a fine time to be quiet," Darnell said. "We'll think of something and work at it. We are two sorry asses."

"We certainly are."

Thirty-Five

◇◇◇

It was a lazy summer Saturday. Katie, Carolyn, Ellen, Nydia, and Camille were in Katie's den enjoying the cool air-conditioned air. Camille held her youngest granddaughter, Courtney's infant baby, in her arms while Nydia kept a watchful eye on Elizabeth's baby. He was crawling better these days, which meant he could find trouble anywhere. Courtney and her sisters Elizabeth and Shannon had borrowed Katie's boat and were out on the lake with their older children. The men were outside barbecuing or playing ball. The dogs couldn't make up their minds about where they wanted to be. Amber knew how to open and close the kitchen door, so the dogs were in and out. When the heat outside was too much to bear, Amber obliged her companions by letting them into the air conditioned house.

"Momma," Katie asked Ellen as she thumbed through a brochure of wedding invitations, "what do you think of this one?"

Ellen peered over her shoulder and said, "It looks too busy. I like to keep things simple and to the point."

"Do me a favor," Katie replied. "Pick one for me."

"It's your wedding, Kate. Why can't you choose your own invitations?"

"Just choose something you'd like to receive. It's no big deal. I'm going to look at the gowns. That's the big deal.

I need to spend my energy on looking good for my big day. Invitations are just paper."

"For heaven's sake," Ellen said as she took the brochure from her. "I suppose I'll have to mail them as well."

"No, the publisher will do that. All I have to do is give them the address list. That's enough tedious work right there."

"What a generation!"

"I agree," Katie replied. "It was much easier when we were living in caves. They didn't send invitations, and all I would have needed was a smelly dead skin wrap for a gown."

"And a club over your head," Carolyn interjected.

"Now that's where I can thank God for progress," Katie replied. "These days, a woman turns the tables and uses a frying pan."

"These days, you do no such thing," Nydia objected. "Abuse is wrong no matter who does it. You're not going to hit my Luisito with a frying pan."

"Oh, that's right. I use the palm of my hand for that," she said as she smiled at Nydia devilishly. Nydia furrowed her brow and gave her a mocking evil eye. "Don't worry, Nydia, I've cut back on that. I'm really getting better with those anger issues. By the time I walk down the aisle, I'll probably be totally cured."

"Smacking Luis over the head is not an infirmity, Katie," Carolyn said. "It's just plain disrespect."

"No, it isn't. It's a reaction to a stimulus," she objected.

"Katie," Camille asked, "how many guests do you plan to have?"

"As many as we can fit into the courtyard and beyond. After all, it is a fundraiser."

"What happens if it rains or if it gets nippy?" Nydia asked. "October can be iffy."

"That's the same thing I said to Mommy about her wedding month. I guess history repeats itself. Anyway, we have that covered. If there's any chance of rain, we'll extend a canopy above the courtyard, anchored to the extensions on the roof. It's a piece of cake."

"What kind of cake are you having?" Camille asked.

"That's Luis's department. Ask him and Stevie; they met with the caterer."

"Is Stevie still pining after his therapist?" Nydia asked.

Carolyn smiled and said, "I'm amazed he can function and put one foot in front of the other. He was probably better off when he was in a coma. He was never interested in girls before. Now, all of a sudden, he has fallen off his horse like a knight in heavy armor. He sits up there in his room, under the pretext of studying, but when I go up to check on him, he's staring into space. He'll probably flunk every test."

"The poor kid is under a lot of stress," Katie said in his defense. "Before he took Sheeva on their first movie date, Luis and I had to role play with him in order to get him to loosen up."

"I hope you didn't do anything X-rated," Carolyn admonished her. "You have to remember the poor kid is still a virgin."

"Well, maybe he needs a little outlet," Camille interjected. "Let's chip in and get him a nice escort."

"You're not doing any such thing for my son," Carolyn laughed. "Besides, the men probably took care of that angle for him. I'd rather he didn't, though. There are too many diseases out there. If this is the girl for him, then he should wait and do the right thing for both their sakes. Besides, she's a widow; she can teach him what he needs to know. All Matthew and I can do for him is talk and guide him in the right direction."

"Mommy, you act as if the kid were totally ignorant. Trust me, he knows he didn't get here via immaculate conception, and he knows what his penis is for. Maybe when you think he's upstairs studying, he's..."

"Don't you dare say it," Carolyn said, glaring at her.

"What, you never masturbated? Come on, Mom," she said, winking at Carolyn. "You're among friends. Share your innermost secrets."

Carolyn pursed her lips and glared at Katie with disapproval.

"Stevie will be fine," Nydia said in an attempt to cut the tension. "He's a good boy, and God will lead him where he needs to go. Maybe it's time you spoke to this young lady's parents. I understand that is the proper course of action in these matters within Islamic society."

"But Sheeva and her parents are Americans," Camille said. "Maybe they don't adhere to ancestral tradition."

"Well, excuse me for bringing this to your attention," Nydia advised them, "but we are all Americans. Yet you ladies haven't let go of your Celtic ancestral traditions, and Felipe and I haven't let go of our Dominican traditions. My son has grown up around you, and he can't decide if he's Irish, Dominican, Puerto Rican, or Scottish. He plays the bagpipes and dances salsa and merengue. Although we live in a secular society, we are devout Catholics. I say it's time to talk to Stevie and Sheeva. If the young lady feels the same as he, then it's time to call on her parents. From what I've learned, you meet with them alone, without the children being present. It's worth a shot."

"You're right," Carolyn agreed. "Perhaps we'll be planning two weddings soon. Then maybe Stevie can study for his exams. Oh God," she suddenly said.

"What's wrong?" Ellen asked.

"It suddenly dawned on me. I feel like a kid on graduation day," Carolyn cried. "You look forward to that graduation, but when it finally comes, melancholia sets in. Two of my children are finally getting married. Before you know it, I'll also be a grandmother."

"You're putting the cart before the horse, but welcome to the club," Ellen said, laughing and patting Carolyn on the back.

"Hey, Mom," Katie said, "why don't we make it a double wedding? That ought to rock your boat."

Carolyn smacked her on the back of the head, and Katie cried, "Ouch! What was that for?"

Carolyn replied, "That's me reacting to a stimulus."

* * *

Stevie sat, waiting for Sheeva to finish with her last patient of the day. They were going to see their third movie together. Because Darnell was right, Stevie didn't want to give up on a good thing. During the movie, he didn't talk. They had dinner before each movie started, and he sat across from her and said what Katie had advised him to say. The first couple of dates were a success. After Sheeva finished with the last patient, a teenager who could hardly walk, Stevie quickly rose from his seat and helped the young woman and her parent out the door.

Sheeva observed the care he displayed. "Mrs. Hassan is right. You are a nice young man, Steven O'Gorman. I apologize for being so curt with you."

He smiled a shy, humble smile and said, "Thank you. You are a nice young lady."

Stevie discovered that Sheeva's parents were both doctors. Her mother was in pharmaceuticals and her father was a medical doctor. Sheeva wondered if she hadn't shortchanged herself by not pursuing a similar path. Stevie convinced her that despite having a child, she could return to school.

"In ten years, you can continue to voice the same regret or you can have a whole new career and feel a sense of fulfillment. Either way, ten years will come and go. There are plenty of government loans for single mothers; maybe you should look into it."

She studied him for a moment. "I like you, Steven; you're very mature."

"I like you too. And, well, I was thinking," he said haltingly. "I was thinking that maybe this could get more serious between us."

"How serious?"

"If you feel the same way I do, maybe you would like to meet my parents."

"I already met your parents, Steven. We met at the hospital."

"You're not making this easy."

Sheeva leaned over and kissed him on the lips. It was a friendly kiss. Stevie touched his mouth and looked a little bewildered.

"What's the purpose of this meeting you speak of, Steven?"

"Well, I told my mother that I like you a lot. She said that if I'm certain of my feelings toward you, she wants to meet with your parents. Before she does that, she wants to know if it's okay with you. If it's okay, she knows that my father must talk to your father."

Sheeva smiled at him and asked, "What do you really want to ask me, Steven O'Gorman?" He blushed and dropped his chin as she continued to speak. "In Muslim culture, when two parents meet, they do it to arrange a marriage. Is that what you want to ask me, Steven O'Gorman? If that's the case, I'll bring my parents to your house this weekend. Or your parents can go to my parents' home. Which do you prefer, Steven?"

Steven gulped and said, "I'll ask my parents."

* * *

"You write music and lyrics, and you don't want to write your own marriage vows?" Katie asked Luis as she rested her head on his shoulder.

"I'm a traditionalist," he replied. "I see nothing wrong with the priest reading the conditions from the book. Besides, no one is really interested in what we have to say unless we can come up with something humorous."

"Fine, we'll go with traditional as long as you understand one thing: I don't obey, so I'm not going to promise to obey. Children obey; dogs obey. I'm not a dog."

"No one says you are, and I know you don't obey," he said, kissing the top of her head. "Do you fetch?"

"Very funny, Luisito. I'll tell you what," she said as she sat up to look at him. "What if we promise to love each other, abide by the laws of the Church..."

"Abide means obey, Katie."

"Oh well, there goes that idea," she said and leaned back on his shoulder. After a few seconds, she said, "You know, you aren't as traditional as you claim to be."

"Enlighten me, woman."

"Well, men and women today are always testing new waters. Men, including you..."

"Thank you for including me in the definition of men."

"Could you just listen, please."

"I'm listening," he replied.

"Well, let me condense it. Men and women, you and me, do everything. We both tend to household duties, except that you never dust or apparently vacuum anything. And you're a medical doctor who should be concerned about cleanliness. Shame on you."

"I thought you were going to condense it."

"What if our vows say, 'Except for unforeseen circumstances, we promise to respect one another, share in our family duties, be good stewards to our financial obligations, nurture one another in sickness and in health, and bang each other at least three times a week.' That's all traditional, but at the same time it speaks to how we have evolved as equals despite our gender differences."

"Banging one another is not traditional wording," he said as he caressed her hair. "It isn't even proper wording to be used in public."

"You wanted humor. That's humorous."

"Not to me, and it won't be humorous to my parents or any of the other older folks we know. Come to think of it, you're the only shock jock I know."

"Do I really shock you, Luis?"

"No, you don't shock me, Katie. You try to shock people, but you don't shock me; I'm used to your shenanigans. It's all smoke screens, baby. In the vows you just made, you forgot 'love.' I promise to continue to love you despite your shenanigans. If you include 'love unconditionally,' we can go with that."

"Fine, I'll write it all down before I forget. One other thing—what is our married name going to be? If I take your name, will you take mine?"

"You mean O'Gorman-López or López-O'Gorman? In Spanish culture, the man's name is first."

"Well, we're not in Spain. Besides, you're wrong, fool," she replied. "In Spanish culture, your name comes first if you're talking about your offspring. I'm not your child. Either one seems fair to me, though," she replied. "We'll flip a coin to see who gets first dibs."

"Fine, we'll flip a coin after you write those vows."

Thirty-Six

The O'Gormans arrived at Sheeva's parents' home, located a mere three miles away from one another. Dr. Arsham Shahbaz answered the doorbell and welcomed them. Matthew presented him with a large package as soon as they entered.

"It's a hookah," Matthew explained as he transferred the gift to Arsham. "If you don't use it, it will at least be a nice conversation piece."

He didn't mention that Carolyn had bought the item a few years ago when they vacationed in Jordan. Although she knew no one who smoked shisha, she fell in love with the vase's intricate silver, gold, and turquoise craftsmanship, which continued throughout the quadruple-stemmed water pipes. She hoped the Shahbazes would enjoy the artful piece as much as she.

"Thank you," Dr. Shahbaz said, accepting the tall box. "Come in and sit. My wife will be back shortly. She had to drive my other daughter to pick up her car from the repair shop. They should be back soon." He led them into the living room and placed the box on a sideboard. "I have some tea steeping. Please excuse me. I'll be right back."

"They have another daughter," Matthew whispered to Carolyn after the doctor walked away. "Maybe we should make arrangements for Kieran while we're here."

"Stop your nonsense, and behave yourself," she admonished him. "Besides, the daughter is old enough to drive. Kieran still rides a bike. Remember, we're here to make a good impression. Act your age."

"I love you when you get bossy."

Arsham returned with a tray. "You have to forgive me. I can tell you right up front that I know I'm a lousy host. We'll sit down to dinner as soon as my wife returns. In the meantime, I don't know if it's proper etiquette to serve bread and tea before dinner, but I like both."

"So do I," Matthew said. "It smells like garlic bread."

"It is," Arsham replied.

"Then we're off to a good start. I promise not to tell the etiquette police on you."

"By the way," Arsham said as he placed the tray on the coffee table, "I don't know if Sheeva told you, my name is Arsham Shahbaz. My wife's name is Sarah."

"It's a pleasure to meet you, Dr. Shahbaz," Matthew said extending his hand. "Our son Stevie told us that both you and your wife are doctors."

"Arsham. Forget the doctor. Doctor is for work."

Carolyn and Matthew mentioned their first names.

"Nice to meet you. Now, let's eat the garlic bread before it gets cold," he said as he offered the bread dish and later poured the tea. "So, it's Matthew like in the New Testament."

"Yes, it is," Matthew replied. "You're one up on me because I know nothing of the Qur'an."

"Neither do I. I would like to study religion, but I can't seem to find the time. I'm not a religious man, but I get curious sometimes."

"I thought you were Muslim. Sheeva said she's Muslim."

"Perhaps she wants to be. Well, she tries to be. Her husband was Muslim, and I don't think his family was too happy she married him. I had nothing against him; he was a good man. Sheeva's given name is Rebecca Dawn. She unofficially changed it to Sheeva when she married Kaveh. I guess if my family still lived in the Middle East or Asia, I would be Muslim. Rumor has it that one of my great-grandparents came from Iran. We also believe one of them was from Afghanistan or India. I've never been to any of those countries; I was born in Queens. I come from an Episcopalian family, but I'm not involved with the Church in any way. My wife Sarah is a Baptist from Kentucky. People hear my name and immediately assume I'm Muslim. Arsham was my great-uncle's name. Today, Arsham Shahbaz is not a fun name to have. Maybe I should change it to Adam Smith. What do you think?"

"Me?" Matthew said. "I'm flabbergasted. Not about you changing your name. I'm flabbergasted about the information you've just shared. I don't think I would ever change my name because of politics. We are who we are."

"Sheeva speaks Farsi," Carolyn interjected.

"Yes, she does. She has always been interested in her Islamic roots, if there are any; I don't really know. These days, kids are usually trying to find themselves. I don't know why they feel this need. Rebecca, aka Sheeva, studied Farsi; I understand she speaks it quite well. I don't know a word of Farsi, except 'Farsi'. May I ask you something," he inquired. Matthew and Carolyn waited for his question. "What's a hookah?"

Carolyn broke into an instant fit of laughter. Given what she now knew about the Shahbazes, she believed the Mideastern water pipe she and Matthew had presented to Arsham was the most inappropriate gift she had ever given anyone. As her face turned crimson, she was unable to stop laughing. "I'm so sorry," she was finally able to say between gasps. Haltingly, she said, "Matthew" at least three times as she desperately tried to get him to explain what was going through her mind. Matthew simply sat quietly next to her, enjoying the moment. He gave Arsham Shahbaz an apologetic shrug of the shoulders while he patiently waited for his wife to regain control. She was finally able to say, "Explain to him what a hookah is, Matthew."

When Matthew finished describing the item, Carolyn said, "Given the circumstances, it's such a ridiculous gift. I'm so sorry; I didn't know. I honestly thought you were Muslim. So even if you don't use a hookah, you might still appreciate it as an art piece. I made my son go to Brooklyn to buy you some shisha; it's an aromatically sweet blend of molasses, fruit, and tobacco. You place it in the well of the pipe and smoke it."

"Well, forgive my ignorance, but I was trying to make sense of what Matthew said when he handed me the package. My mind had fun with it, and I thought you had managed to stuff a two-foot hooker in there. Then I figured it was probably some kind of knitting equipment."

"I'm truly sorry," Carolyn apologized again. "We'll take it back and get you something more appropriate. My God, what will your wife think if she sees it?"

Sarah Shahbaz and her daughter Jessica arrived home at that very moment. Carolyn composed herself as they were introduced.

"I know you," Sarah said to Carolyn as she shook Carolyn's hand. "I never forget a face. You're Harold and Margaret's daughter. Arsham, she's Harold Reilly's daughter."

"You're kidding," Arsham said in astonishment.

Carolyn was equally surprised.

"I saw you in person a few times. I work for your father in the New York office. You once came in while we were having a board meeting. You had a little boy and a girl with you. The boy was about eight or nine, and the girl was about twelve or so. That's when we had our offices in the Thirty-fifth Street building."

"That must have been years ago," Carolyn said. "You're talking about my son Stevie and my daughter Katie. I don't remember ever meeting you."

"You didn't. I saw you when you came into the board room; I wasn't the only one present. You had a short conversation with your father and left. The other times, we passed each other in the hall, but I never forget a face. Arsham and I have been to your parents' home a few times for dinner. They've been here; they've met my daughters. I also saw you a few months ago at the checkout in the supermarket. You were with another woman, and you had about three cases of tomato juice in your cart."

"That's amazing," Carolyn said, "and yet we've never met."

"Not officially until today," Sarah replied. "Now my daughter is in love with your son. He must be that little boy I saw several years ago. Life sure is interesting."

"It's a small world," Carolyn replied. "And Stevie is in love with your daughter."

"I'm sorry about what happened to your son."

"He's fine now."

"Sarah," Arsham interrupted, "the O'Gormans brought us a gift." He pointed to the large box.

"Oh God, no," Carolyn pleaded with him and she went on to explain the entire matter to Sarah.

"A souvenir from the Middle East; I think that's a lovely idea," Sarah said and tore the wrapping off the box. "It's beautiful; thank you. We gladly accept it."

Arsham examined the item. The snake-like stems, designed for the user to inhale the smoke, resembled a luggage cart's bungee cords, except these were adorned with silver and gold. He concluded that Sarah was holding a very expensive and decorative opium pipe, but he decided not to comment.

"After dinner, Arsham and I have something to show you," Sarah said to Carolyn while she still held the odd gift and before asking her daughter Jessica to help her in the kitchen.

"We can help," Carolyn offered.

"No, you sit and chat with Arsham. Jessica and I can handle this."

As they enjoyed dinner, Carolyn asked, "Isn't Sheeva going to join us?"

"You mean Rebecca," Sarah replied as she passed the mashed potatoes. "I believe she said she was going to meet Steven at a friend's house, a lady who lives in Yonkers."

"That would be Naghmed. They're at Omid's house; he's my son's friend, and Naghmed is his mother."

"My daughter is going through a phase," Sarah said almost apologetically. "I hope she comes down to earth soon."

"I think there's little hope of that," Arsham said.

"I agree with what you said earlier," Matthew said to Arsham. "Kids today are trying to find themselves. Stevie wanted to be a pilot. Then he decided to study law. Before he went into that coma, he wanted to be a priest. Now I don't know what he wants to be. He claims he's going to be a statesman. Tomorrow, perhaps he'll join NASA—his mind is usually in outer space."

"Well, both he and Rebecca will be circling the stratosphere," Arsham replied.

"Stevie sounds like a sensible young man to me," Sarah said. "To your son's credit, he has convinced my daughter to go to medical school."

"My Stevie did that?" Carolyn asked, feeling a mother's pride.

"Yes, he did. It's late in the year, but she has contacted a few schools in the area. With any luck, maybe she can start in September as a late admission. Perhaps if she had never met Kaveh, she would have continued with her education."

"Mom, Rebecca has always been a little flighty. I don't think it had anything to do with poor Kaveh," Jessica commented.

"I'm not blaming Kaveh; I'm blaming the situation. Love makes people do strange things. It would have been nice if she had continued with her schooling and not had a child at such a young age. Now she has a baby and no husband. I hope you will have more sense."

"Well, Becca appears to be happy, even if she is a little flaky. I think that's important. Maybe her life needed to be exactly what it is. So why don't we forget it and move on already? Could you excuse me? I'll be in my room." Without receiving a response, she rose to her feet. "It was a pleasure meeting you, Mr. and Mrs. O'Gorman."

* * *

Carolyn insisted on driving. She informed Matthew that he had drunk more than the legal limit of wine. "I would have been happier if they were Muslims. Then you would be sober," she commented as she strapped on her seat belt.

"Are we going to tell Stevie that his girlfriend is a little confused?" Matthew asked as he struggled with his own seat belt.

"We will do no such thing," she replied as she reached over to help him with his belt. "He'll find out soon enough. I don't want him to get the impression I might be critical of his girlfriend. That kind of tactic is counterproductive. Besides, who are we to judge? At least Sheeva or Rebecca, whatever she wants to call herself, is seeking answers in all the right places."

"How do you figure that?"

"Well, she has decided to return to school."

"You're short," he said as he tried to stretch his legs and discovered there wasn't enough room.

"Move the seat back or live with it," she commented. "You haven't complained about the length before."

"I grew," he said as he fumbled with the controls and managed to move the seat back a few extra inches.

Carolyn started the car and pulled out. "I hope Kieran hasn't driven Nydia and Felipe crazy."

"You should have left him with Katie and Luis."

"He prefers to be with Nydia; she spoils him."

"He eats the poor woman out of house and home."

"Well, they understand each other."

They heard music as they walked to the López's front door. Inside, the Lópezes, as well as Luis, Katie, and Kieran were having a jam. Kieran banged the bongos while Luis and Felipe played guitars, Nydia and Katie danced merengue and played maracas. Matthew rang the doorbell and pounded on the door several times. When no one answered, Carolyn dialed Nydia's number and got the musicians' attention.

"We were about to break a window," Carolyn said to Nydia when she answered the phone. "We've been pounding on your door. I'm surprised your neighbors don't complain."

"Our neighbors are worse than us. You should hear their heavy metal," Nydia said as she reached the front door to let them in. "Esposito, Garrity, and we have a blast every Thursday. Our neighbors retaliate every Friday or Saturday. We've been at it for years. Actually, sometimes they come and join us."

"What are you guys doing here?" Carolyn asked when she saw Luis and Katie.

"I came to visit my mommy," Luis replied as he put the guitar aside.

"We came to hear the skinny on Stevie's future in-laws," Katie interjected. "What's the verdict?"

"Their daughter is a fruitcake," Matthew said.

"Mattie!" Carolyn admonished him. "That's not true."

"What do you mean it isn't true? Katie, you have competition in the nut department."

"Don't listen to him. He had too much to drink. Mattie, go sit down somewhere and behave yourself," Carolyn said as she guided him to a spot on the sofa.

"Would you like some coffee, Matt?" Felipe asked him.

"No, don't give him any coffee," Carolyn said. "He's going home to sleep it off."

"So how did things go?" Nydia asked.

"Yeah, Mom, what happened?" Katie asked. "Don't keep us in suspense."

"You were Rina," Matthew said, "and Sheeva is Rebecca. Or is it the other way around?"

"Hush, Mattie," Carolyn said. "You're not helping." Then she turned to the others and said, "Sheeva's parents aren't Muslim; they're Christian."

"The father is none of the above. He's an atheist," Matthew said.

"He's probably agnostic, but he's not an atheist," Carolyn corrected him. "Sheeva is the only Muslim in the family. Her husband was Muslim, and she apparently converted to Islam. Sheeva is her Muslim name. Her birth name is Rebecca Dawn."

"Does Stevie know?" Luis inquired.

"I don't know," Carolyn replied. "However, if he doesn't know, nobody here is going to tell him. That matter is between him and Sheeva. Eventually, he'll find out."

"Why can't we tell him?" Katie asked. "That's no big deal."

"Regardless of that," Carolyn replied, "I believe Sheeva should be the one to tell him. If she had thought it pertinent to mention it earlier, she would have said something to Stevie. Unless they disclose it, what happens between them is their business, not ours."

"I still don't get where you're coming from," Katie said. "You've never had any problem telling me my business."

"You're my daughter!"

"And he's your son," Katie retorted. "What's the difference?"

"It's not about you, Katie. It's not about Stevie. It's about Sheeva. Apparently, she's in a very delicate situation right now. Stevie loves her. I'm happy he's happy. I don't want to do anything that could come between them. Sometimes the best way to get to where you're going is to do it slowly.

Sheeva will either share this information with him, or he will eventually meet the parents and the topic will be open to discussion. We don't know if Sheeva is going through a phase, or if she's grounded and committed to her beliefs. We're in no position to prod and pry."

"I'm confused," Katie admitted.

"I'm bemused you don't get it," Carolyn replied. "Just don't say anything."

"Fine," Katie retorted.

"Kieran, get your things. We're going home," Carolyn said, but when she turned, he wasn't in the room. "Where is he?"

Carolyn and Nydia found him in the kitchen eating a big slice of chocolate cake with milk.

"I was hungry," he complained. "All that exercise gives a man an appetite."

"Why didn't you warm up a chicken empanada instead of eating chocolate cake?" Nydia asked him. "All that sugar is going to keep you up tonight."

"I couldn't help it. The cake kept calling me. Besides, it would have taken too long to warm up the empanada."

"Carolyn," Nydia said mussing Kieran's hair, "are you sure he doesn't have a tapeworm?"

"I think he has a whole colony of them. I need to provide you with a food budget just for him. Mattie said he would eat you out of house and home."

"Baby boy can eat all he wants, and I wouldn't accept a cent from you," Nydia replied and planted a kiss on Kieran's cheek as he forked another mouthful of cake.

"Well, as you said, if baby boy eats all that cake, he won't sleep tonight and he won't be able to get up in time for church tomorrow morning."

"Food helps me sleep. Besides, you can take me to a later Mass," he suggested.

"You don't have personal chauffer service, mister." Carolyn admonished him. "You'll go to church at the same time we always go."

"Hey, Mom," Katie said, entering the kitchen. "Stevie and Sheeva are here, and they brought a baby with them."

"They have a baby out at this hour of the night?" Nydia objected. "A baby should be asleep by now."

"I want to see him," Kieran said, picking himself up with cake and milk in hand.

"Put the cake down," Carolyn admonished him. "You're not taking food into the living room."

"Oh, man!" he objected as he settled down again.

"Oh man, nothing," Carolyn replied. "You can join us after you finish eating and cleaning up in here."

The new arrivals greeted everyone and were soon seated and interacting with one another. Nydia was immediately taken by the baby and asked if she could hold him.

"Sure," Sheeva replied, "he's used to being handled because he spends his day at baby daycare."

Nydia placed the child on her lap and started to talk to him. She paused and asked, "What's his name?"

"Javeed," Sheeva replied. "It means 'lives forever.' I named him that because he was born after his father died. His father lives on in him."

"I think it's a wonderful choice," Nydia said. "I'm sorry for your loss."

"I'm getting used to it. I was two months pregnant when Kaveh died. It's been over a year now. I miss him and love him, but I hope to move on."

"So, Sheeva," Katie asked, "why did you decide to become Muslim?" She glanced up at Carolyn as she asked the question, and Carolyn glared at her.

"Well," Sheeva replied, "I always suspected my ancestors on my father's side were Muslim, so I studied Farsi. I don't know if it's the language my ancestors spoke, but it's a beginning. Then I started reading the Qur'an and the Hadith. On my way to school each day, I used to pass a gas station and a man there would always say very annoying things to me as I passed by. I resorted to going an extra block out of my way so he would not bother me. Then one day, in the Qur'an I found instructions on how women are to dress in order not to bring attention to themselves. With the proper dress, a woman can avoid being annoyed by men and their catcalls. That resonated with me and made perfect sense."

Katie smiled at Sheeva and Carolyn. She pressed on and said, "But you don't wear the hijab now. Why?"

Sheeva looked visibly uncomfortable and embarrassed. Noticing the young woman's discomfort, Katie withdrew her question with, "I'm sorry; I didn't mean to pry. Forget I asked."

"It's a pertinent question," Sheeva replied.

"Which is none of our business," Carolyn interjected.

"No; it's okay," Sheeva said. "For me, it's a personal question, which I have revisited numerous times since my husband died. Kaveh often said that I was more religious than he and warned me of the dangers of trying to speak for God. As for women covering up, he said, 'If Allah had intended to disguise a rose as a leaf, he probably wouldn't have bothered with the extra effort'."

"That's a good point," Felipe said. "We shouldn't be deprived of enjoying God's art, and it's up to us to behave like gentlemen toward our women; look and don't touch. Besides, cat calls say a lot about the man's lack of respect and character."

"Well, that may be true," Nydia interjected, "but I'm sometimes concerned about the provocative clothing that some young girls wear these days; it can be a bit much."

"I like the ladies in bikinis," Matthew said.

"You better be talking about the ones at the beach," Carolyn warned him.

"Is *Sports Illustrated* okay?" Luis asked.

"Ladies are not objects, Luis," Carolyn admonished him. "I don't object to women displaying their sexuality, if that is their choice, and I don't object to being admired. However, in this male oriented society, men don't always respect boundaries. That shouldn't be. I've never heard of a woman violating a man's space, but when men get carried away, they rape and beat women. In some countries, rape and mutilation are used as instruments of war. That kind of mentality is what forces us to want to hide in order to protect ourselves."

"The strong prey upon the weak," Nydia said, "and it shouldn't be; we aren't animals and shouldn't behave as such. Men rape women; women get pregnant, and we're left with having to pay the consequences, which are too numerous to mention."

"Well, ostracizing, blaming, and punishing the victimized woman and leaving her to care for the child are the most deleterious," Carolyn said.

"You're preaching to the choir, Honey-Lyn," Matthew said. "We understand and obey our women. I pray to live another day."

The men chuckled, and Carolyn gave him an amused look. As the adults talked, Kieran joined the group, and Carolyn changed the conversation.

"Sheeva, we had a wonderful time with your parents. As it turns out, they know my parents, so our families have known each other all along. And Stevie, they sent you something that you must return to them after you check it out. Hand me my purse," she said to Matthew, who was seated against it. "Sarah, Sheeva's mother, said she had something to show us after dinner, and she showed us this."

While Carolyn waited for her purse, she questioned Kieran about cleaning up in the kitchen. Then she handed Stevie a legal size envelope. He shook its contents out, and a gold medallion fell into his hand.

"Jesus, Mary, and Joseph," he said as he examined the medal and its gold chain. "Nydia, Katie, look at this."

The medallion was passed from person to person, and everyone was in awe of it. As Nydia passed it to the next viewer, she handed the baby to Sheeva, quickly got up, and went into her bedroom. The medallion was back in Stevie's possession when Nydia returned with a sketch in hand. She handed the paper to Stevie, and he examined the sketch he had given Nydia a few days earlier against the actual medallion.

"There's that writing I mentioned," he said as he held the St. Christopher's medal in one hand and the completed sketch in the other. "And it has filigree," he said as he smiled at Sheeva. "Did you tell your parents about my dream?"

"Yes, I knew about the medallion. It belonged to my great-grandfather. The engraving you mentioned," she said, referring to the Greek words □yio□ Xpiotó□opo□, "mean 'St. Christopher,' and the remainder says 'travel safely' or something like that. I don't speak Greek, so I don't know the exact translation."

"In my dream, a woman with a bandana on her head gave it to me."

"Was it Sheeva wearing a hijab?" Luis asked.

"No, it was an old woman," Stevie replied.

"Maybe the dream means that Sheeva will pass the medallion on to you when you're both old and gray," Kieran commented as he sat close to his father.

"No," Sheeva said. "We know how and why the medallion fell into my great-grandfather's hands. Old Greek women also wear bandanas or kerchiefs on their heads. I believe that's what you probably saw. There's an old World War II photograph with an old Greek woman that could explain this. You'll have to see it. I'll ask my mother to e-mail it to you."

"How did your great-grandfather end up with a Greek medallion?" Nydia asked.

"As I understand the story, he was in northern Africa during the war," Sheeva explained. "There, he rescued a young Greek soldier, who had his leg blown off from the knee down. My great-grandfather stopped the bleeding and carried the young man to safety. Before they parted company, the young man, knowing he was going home to his family, gave my great-grandfather the medallion. The Greek soldier said his mother had given it to him when he left for war. He told my great-grandfather it would protect him too until he could return to his family."

"Did the Greek soldier get home in one piece?" Kieran asked.

"Minus his missing limb, yes," Sheeva replied. "The photograph I speak of shows him back home with his mother."

"And," Nydia concluded, "she's wearing the bandana."

"She's wearing a scarf," Sheeva corrected her, "which Stevie perceived as a bandana."

Thirty-Seven

◇◇◇

Tuesday morning, Carolyn was in her office with Momma Ellen, explaining what had happened at the Shahbazes' home.

"It was a very interesting evening," she concluded, "to say the least. I went in there trying to make a nice impression for my son's sake, and I started to laugh like a lunatic because of that stupid hookah. In hindsight, it was always a stupid gift. Then Matthew got drunk sipping too much wine. He never does that, and he had to pick that night of all nights to get drunk."

"I'm sure he wasn't the only one, a Rua. How did the hosts hold up?"

"Actually, we had a fun evening; I just wanted Mattie sober. We sensed a little tension between the younger daughter and the mother."

"No family is perfect."

"Don't I know it. Katie and I have our moments at times, but she seems to be finally making a promising transformation. Do you know if she already gave the address list for the wedding to the publisher?"

"I certainly hope so. October will be here before you know it."

"Well, I'm going to see if she can include Rebecca and her family."

"She probably already has," Momma replied. "She said she wanted to squeeze in as many people as she could; she probably invited the mailman. I'll call her and find out if you want. She's home today, overseeing her construction project. I hope those people finish all that work before the wedding. There's nothing but dust all over the place; the noise is unbearable. She'll have to halt construction for at least a week in order to clean that place before the day of the reception, or people will be picking cement out of their cake."

"She'll do the right thing," Carolyn replied. "She's always been very meticulous about cleaning, thank God. I suddenly remembered the time she trashed my bedroom. God, she was a character when she was younger."

"She's still a character, but I'm keeping my fingers crossed. Is she still planning on selling the business?"

"Yes, she believes the market is going to take a dive. That's why she's rushing with this construction. When the housing market dips, construction costs will be lower, she said, but it won't be worth the wait. She has advised me to put my house on the market now while I can still get an inflated price."

"Are you going to do that?"

"I don't know, Momma. I also found out that Mattie was never overjoyed about moving. He hasn't said anything to me. As a matter of fact, I thought he was as excited as I am. I have to talk to him first; I don't understand why he hasn't said anything about that to me."

The intercom buzzed, and Carolyn responded. It was Annie, her secretary, "Carolyn, Luis is here to see you."

"Tell him to come in."

When he entered with the guitar case flung over his back and a folder in his hand, Momma asked, "How did your jam session go with the kids?"

"Fine," he said, freeing himself from the guitar case. He flopped into an armchair.

"I thought you were working today," Carolyn said. "Have you been here all morning?"

"Well, Katie took the day off; I decided to do the same. She claimed I was annoying her, so I decided to jam with the kids during their break. Siddharth is really smoking. That kid is going to make it someday."

"Do you still feel you should have been a rock star, Luis?" Ellen asked.

"No, I'm over that," he said, dismissing the idea with a hand gesture. "Besides, I got rich without even trying. I've always wanted to do something for Mami and Papi for all they've done for me. I can do that now. The problem is they don't want anything. Mami thinks I've been ostentatious with the military vehicle." Momma laughed, and Luis said, "Check out the watch," as he placed the folder on a nearby table and got up to display his new watch to them. "Nice, huh?"

"Yes, it is nice," Carolyn replied approvingly.

"What did you buy?" Ellen asked him reaching for his wrist to have a better look. "Rolex?"

"No, Patek Philippe. I bought Papi a Paget, but he hasn't worn it. I think he's happy with his Seiko."

"Have you picked out the engagement and wedding rings yet?" Carolyn asked him while flipping through her mail. "You were supposed to do that about two weeks ago."

"Shouldn't Katie give me the ring? After all, she's the one who finally asked me."

"It doesn't work that way," Ellen said.

"Why not? Of course, I prefer emeralds to diamonds," he said jokingly. Both Ellen and Carolyn sensed he was in a good mood. "I don't want to look too gay. I figure, an eighteen-karat gold setting with two parallel rows of emeralds would look quite nice." Ellen furrowed her brow and glared at him with a glint in her eye. Luis wrapped his arms around her and said, "I'm kidding, Momma. Katie and I already saw the rings we want, but we haven't had time to pick them up. She chose claddagh rings like her mommy. The engagement ring is a regular diamond, almost standard issue."

"Cubic zirconia?" Ellen asked.

He grinned and said, "Cracker Jacks."

"Sit down and stop acting like a fool," Ellen said, separating herself from him. "Besides, I want to hear the rest of what happened Saturday night."

"Did Carolyn tell you what she discovered about Sheeva and her parents?"

"Yes, the child comes from a Christian home," Ellen replied. "Now I'd like to hear the rest."

"Actually, I've pretty much covered everything," Carolyn said.

"I'd like to read that journal when Stevie finishes it," Momma said. "It was one thing when he spoke about Mamaí. He knew her, so that explains why she appeared in his dream. The message he gave me is definitely food for thought, but this business about the medallion is something else entirely. At the time, he had never met Sheeva, and he knew nothing of the medallion."

"His middle name is Christopher," Luis said. "Plus, while in his coma, someone may have mentioned the name.

My mother could have said something to him about the medal as she fastened it to his headboard."

"What about the woman with the scarf and his sudden ability to speak Irish?" Ellen asked.

"Our subconscious retains information—we may all have more knowledge than we need. Eventually, it bubbles to the surface of our mind. He's heard the two of you speak Irish; you do that every time you want to keep secrets. And it's not unusual for him to have seen or remember an image of a woman with a scarf," Luis replied. "Omid's mother wears a hijab. Maybe her face was one of the last things he saw before he passed out."

"That doesn't explain the details of the medallion," Carolyn said. "He mentioned the strange writing and the filigree periphery. How do you explain that?"

"Maybe he recalled a filigree design from one of the images in church or anywhere else, for that matter. Strange writing? There's strange writing right on Jesus's cross, 'King of the Jews.' We live in a society where we encounter people reading newspapers written in all sorts of different alphabets, including Greek. His mind made and remembered an imprint of that."

"Where is your faith, Luis?" Momma asked.

"I have plenty of faith. I'm also a pragmatist. Come on, I'm sure we've all done it. We work our experiences, desires, and day's events into our dreams. If my libido is heightened, I could dream I'm having sex with a famous model. Now that I'm rich, I can probably make beautiful music with a nice voluptuous model who has sensual lips of wine, as the song goes."

"Is that before or after Katie breaks both your legs?" Carolyn asked him.

"Before—I need to get there first."

They continued the banter until Ellen noticed the time. "Well, I'm going down to the auditorium," she said changing the subject. "I want to see today's puppet show. The children get such a kick out of them, and I like watching them reacting to it. Aren't you coming, a Rua?"

"Actually, I need to talk to you in private, Carolyn," Luis said, "if you have a moment."

"Of course, my love," she said as she sat back in her leather chair. "Momma, I'll catch up to you later."

When Ellen left, Luis picked up the folder he had brought in and sat in a leather chair, opposite Carolyn's desk.

"I was watching TV the other day," he said, "and saw a Reilly Pharmaceuticals' commercial. That's your father's corporation."

"Yes, I know; I'm his daughter."

"They used one of the animations I produced for that Web site that made me a rich man."

"And?" Carolyn asked him.

"Well, then I remembered that the wire transfers made to my account come from a financial corporation that is affiliated with GFS. That's your mother's corporation. Do you follow me here?"

"What's your point, Luis? GFS funnels money through diverse corporations. Everyone does that because one shouldn't keep eggs in one basket—you know that."

"I go back to my old college loans and the house mortgage that I'm paying to Kerry Credit Corporation. My parents' mortgage is also from KCC. It turns out that KCC belongs to GFS. You don't cover your tracks very well."

"I don't see what all that has to do with me," Carolyn said. "GFS probably handles millions of accounts and other corporations handle ours. Why did you get a mortgage from KCC? Was it because your parents already had one and suggested you do the same? Or did you subconsciously acquire it because of your college loans? Sometimes life is full of coincidences, Luis."

"You may have me with the financial jargon, Carolyn, but then there's this," he said, handing her the folder.

"What's this?" she asked, looking at the folder he extended in her direction.

"Read it," he said. His hand was shaking as he held the folder.

Carolyn accepted it and started to read its contents. As she read and flipped each successive page, her facial muscles started to droop; her Caucasian complexion became whiter. Luis observed that she did not look well. He didn't feel well either.

"How long were you planning to keep that from me?" he asked. "I'm over twenty-one. I have rights, you know."

"I know you have rights," she said as she closed the folder. "I didn't know how to tell you, but it's not what you think."

"What am I thinking?" he asked, looking directly at her but sounding nervous. His facial muscles were tense.

"I love you dearly, Luis. I love you as if you were my own son," she said, and Luis glared at her. "I would never do anything to hurt you; I want nothing but the best for you. According to your findings, you believe I could be your mother? I wish you were my son, but you're not. Once we crossed paths, I did everything I could to keep you close to me. How did you come upon this information?"

"When I went to donate blood for Stevie, I was told I was a perfect match for him. We are both universal donors.

That's O negative. When we checked Kieran out to determine if he had a medical problem connected to his lack of height, I asked you and Matthew to donate blood as well. Do you remember that?"

"Yes, I do. You told me everything was fine."

"Well, you have the same type O blood, same as Stevie and me. Kieran and Matthew are B."

"There must be millions of people with O negative blood, Luis."

"Six or seven percent of the population have O negative—very low odds."

"I read what you have there concerning DNA fingerprinting," she said tapping the folder. "So you decided to check our DNA prints against each other based on blood type? And you've concluded I'm your mother?"

"It was a long shot; I know that. As a med student, I did my own fingerprinting several years ago. When I saw yours, Stevie's, and Kieran's, I was struck by how similar they were to mine."

"How did you get Stevie's DNA?"

"That was easy. I pricked him while he was in the hospital. That was after I saw your DNA print. For Kieran, Stevie, and me, I get the same results."

"A 99.9% chance that I'm your mother," she said as she tapped the folder again, recalling what she had read. "Incomplete or faulty science can only lead you to incomplete or faulty results."

"There's only one chance in about three billion that I'm wrong. Do you understand the odds, Carolyn?"

"Yes, I understand the odds," she said as she stood up, "and I'm fascinated by the results and why you decided to pursue this. I also understand how you arrived at this stunning conclusion. But I assure you, I never gave birth to you; I would remember that. As a matter of fact, I wish you were right. This is fascinating. However, I do have your answer," she said as she leaned against the front of her desk, facing him.

"I know, and I suspect you've known for a long time. That's why you've been taking care of my financial needs through GFS. I've given it a lot of thought." he said, sounding disappointed. "Question is, why didn't you tell me sooner?"

"I wanted to, but I could never seem to find the right time. I was afraid I might hurt your feelings. As I told you before," she said with tears welling in her eyes, "I always tried to keep you close."

"Margaret and Harold, do they know? Do my parents know?"

"My parents know. Nydia and Felipe do not."

"How long have you known about me?"

"All your life. You came back into my life when Nydia interviewed for the job at EH. She brought you to the interview. You saw Sean and started to cry. You have a red birth mark on your neck, so I immediately recognized you. But I didn't know what to do. My parents didn't know until you were six, going on seven. By then, you were Nydia and Felipe's ward. Nydia and Felipe have always had a tremendous love for you, so we decided it was best to leave you with them."

"Who's 'we'?"

"My parents, Marjorie, and I."

"Marjorie never saw me. How could she decide for me?" he asked, sounding hurt.

"She saw you. She gave birth to you."

"I know that, but she abandoned me to a woman who scarred me for life. Why?" he cried. "Why didn't *you* keep me? You knew, and you abandoned me too."

A tear flowed down her cheek. "I knew the truth would cause you pain. That's why I could never find the right moment to tell you."

"You felt guilty, didn't you?"

"I am guilty. I'm sorry, Luis."

"Sorry doesn't cut it, Carolyn. You, Harold, and Margaret decided to soothe your guilt by handing me money."

"It's your part of your inheritance. You're entitled to it."

"No, no. I didn't earn it. I don't want it. Tomorrow, I'll wire what's left back to GFS. I'll find a way to pay off the rest." He got up, reached around her, and picked up the folder. He ripped it apart and tossed the shreds onto her desk.

Carolyn looked at him with tear-filled eyes.

"Do you know who my father is?" he asked with his fists clenched by his side.

"I don't know for sure, but I suspect he's Brian Thomas Mulkeen. You met him. You and Stevie danced on his boat when we were in Dublin."

With a stiff jaw, Luis said, "I guess it's a little late to call him Daddy. You cheated me out of a father and cheated him out of a son. I expected better of you. I don't know what to make of Marjorie; I never met her. That's the biggest cheat of all, Carolyn; I never met her. Do you know what that feels like? You've torn out my heart! My heart, Carolyn! Did she ever inquire about me?"

"It's complicated, Luis. Sometimes it's necessary to practice tough love and let go. She was a troubled soul."

"So the answer is no. But you knew me, Carolyn. Why didn't you...? Why didn't you...?"

"Keep you? Adopt you?" she asked. "I was young. I was a coward, and I was very frightened. I was Marjorie's accomplice in a crime against you and the Church. I'm sorry, Luis."

He glared at her and said, "You held me as an infant, didn't you?"

"Yes, I did. I'm sorry. We left you in what we believed to be good hands."

"I've loved you; I have revered you, Carolyn. You are my aunt; you are my godmother, for Christ's sake!"

"Luis, there's a lot you need to know. Marjorie wasn't uncaring or indifferent when she gave you up. She was concerned about you. When we've calmed down, we need to talk."

"I've heard enough," he said. "How can anyone pick up a little infant and decide it's okay to abandon him? Am I a trading card? Am I chattel? Then, years later, you decide it's okay to right the wrong with a monetary token. I'm a human being! I was cast out because I was seen as an embarrassment! Evidently, I must still be an embarrassment because even today, you try to cover up with that crap about multiple corporations. You had an out here and you missed it." He shook his head. His face was flushed, and his eyes reflected the pain of betrayal. He turned on his heel and left without remembering to take his guitar.

Luis didn't return home. After sundown, a worried Katie called Nydia to ask about him and informed Nydia that he wasn't answering his cell phone. Nydia didn't know where he was. Katie called her parents' home and inquired. Carolyn revealed what she knew.

"Why the hell would you do something like that?" Katie yelled at her. "What if he's hurt? He doesn't answer his phone, Mom!"

A very remorseful Carolyn then visited the Lópezes and revealed everything to them as well. "He's very upset," Carolyn concluded. "I already called the police and filed a missing persons report."

"What are we going to do?" Nydia asked in desperation.

"I'll hire investigators to find him," Carolyn said, but that didn't disquiet the worry they all felt.

Weeks later, Luis was still missing. Everyone was comforted by the fact that he had withdrawn enough cash from his account to keep himself comfortable for a while, but they still didn't know his whereabouts. According to GFS transcripts, he had wired most of the money back. The request for the wire transfer was traced to the computer in his medical office. The cash withdrawal was made in person from his local bank. After that, the trail went cold. Everyone went about their day mourning his loss, as if he were dead; Katie seldom spoke to Carolyn. The few times they did speak, Katie was curt and ill-tempered and blamed Carolyn for what had happened. The wedding was called off. Nydia met with Margaret and Carolyn and heard their sides of the story. She needed to fully understand why her boy went missing and had not bothered to communicate with anyone.

Six weeks later, Nydia visited Katie.

"You can't blame Carolyn for this," she told Katie.

"Luis was fine until he heard the truth."

"He searched for that truth himself."

"How do you know? You weren't there. You're going by what she said. There are two sides to every story."

"Well, I believe Carolyn; I've known her too long. She still has the folder Luis tore to pieces. He was angry; I understand that. However, as far as Carolyn is concerned, we all make mistakes. Do you know anyone who's perfect, Katie?"

"She thinks she is."

"That's your perception. It isn't easy being a parent. What a child perceives as a parent's fault may be an expression of love and guidance. You will understand that one day. Carolyn believes you're pregnant again. Is this true?"

"Yes, it's true. I swear that woman has radar. God, I hate her! She infuriates me!"

"You need to mend fences and bridges, Katie. Carolyn loves you with all her heart. Don't fault her for Luis's disappearance. He'll be back as soon as he figures it all out. He's confused. You're confused."

"I'm not confused; I'm pissed. She could have been honest with all of us earlier. If she had done that, he would still be here today. He doesn't know he's going to be a father. This time I'm taking care of myself. I don't want anything to go wrong with this pregnancy."

"Your misplaced anger isn't good for the baby. I spoke with Margaret, so I've heard two sides of the story. Like any mother, she has a forgiving heart."

"She's not the one who was hurt by all this," Katie retorted.

"Marjorie became pregnant, and she hid that information from her mother. So how do you figure she wasn't hurt? Margaret watched her grandson grow from afar. She did it because she didn't want to tear the bond he had formed with Felipe and me. She knew nothing of Luis until then. Marjorie and Carolyn kept that information from their parents."

"But Mommy knew. Everything would have been different if she had come forward with that information earlier."

"Many things could have been different. The way they worked out, we all benefitted."

"How do you figure that?"

"I raised Luis as my son. First, he was my ward. While interviewing for the post at EH, Carolyn suspected Luis was Marjorie's boy, but chose to say nothing, and I got the job. Perhaps it wasn't solely based on my skills and credentials. I was probably hired because Carolyn recognized Luis. As a second blessing, I met the entire family."

"How did she know?"

"When he cried his little heart out, she noticed the birthmark on his neck. She held him shortly after birth and remembered that birthmark; it's a trait he shares with someone she knows. She told me she remembers being nervous while we were at the table having brunch. Momma changed seats with her and offered to feed Stevie because her hand was shaking. Carolyn believes that Ellen must have noticed something was amiss. Ellen went as far as doing a background check on Luisito. Have you stopped to think about how one change of events influences another?"

"Yes, I have," Katie replied.

"Then consider this. Young Marjorie doesn't give Luis up for adoption. Luis grows up with his birth mother and doting grandparents. I never quit my job at the rehab center to raise Luis because he and I never meet. You never meet Luis. When you are orphaned after that terrible experience, Carolyn is not there to raise you. She's not there because she probably would have followed a different road in life and would never have met Matthew.

She's not there to protect you and chase after you through the four corners of the world while you are tortured with terrible memories. Your trip to Orlando, Florida, is one for the books, Katie. Just as my life changed, everyone else's life probably changed. If you look at the other side of the coin, we can't fault Carolyn for Luis's disappearance. We need to thank her for bringing him into our lives. She's hurting more than you know because she too faults herself. Sometimes she's afraid to look me in the eye. But I'm going to be in her office every day until she understands how grateful I am to her and her parents. They have sacrificed a lot."

"Has Mommy or Grandma explained how the son of Harold Reilly became an orphaned Puerto Rican named Walker?" Katie asked, looking Nydia in the eye.

"The girls were in college when Marjorie became pregnant, and they chose to hide that from their parents. We're old-fashioned, devout Catholics, Katie. You just don't have a child out of wedlock."

"That's no big deal. Women shack up and have children all the time. I'm pregnant."

"It's no big deal to you, but for Margaret it would have been a scandal back in those days. Marjorie and Carolyn felt the same way, but abortion was also out of the question. A nun hooked them up with a Catholic family in Puerto Rico. The Walkers had been unsuccessfully trying to have children for years. I also understand that under Puerto Rican law, no child can be considered a bastard, or illegitimate, as we call it. The girls enrolled at the University of Puerto Rico and finished their studies there. Puerto Rico was perfect. It was out of the way, but the child would still be a U.S. citizen and be legitimately entitled to all the law allows. In simple terms, that means he cannot be disinherited; he will always be an heir of the Reilly estate and any other existing assets."

"When Momma did the background check on Luis, they found out the Walkers were Scots or Scottish. There was no record of adoption," Katie said.

"Carolyn said it was easy to list Lucy Walker and her husband as the birth parents."

"Hmmm," Katie said. "Do you suppose Mommy bribed somebody?"

"Perhaps. If she did, she did it to protect Marjorie. The girls continued to communicate with the Walkers. Carolyn has pictures of Luis as a baby; she gave me copies. I'll show them to you the next time you come over. However, before he started walking, the Walkers suddenly stopped communicating with the girls. Apparently, that threw Marjorie further into the deep end. Carolyn said Marjorie was never very stable."

"She appeared fine to me. Despite being a jet-setter, she always took time to write to me. I need to reread those letters. How did Grandma Margaret find out about Luis?"

"You remember when Luis was taken to the hospital because he couldn't pee? While at the hospital, they discovered his heart condition. Carolyn was worried he wouldn't make it and relayed that information to Marjorie. She told her she couldn't continue the charade. She convinced her to call Margaret and tell her."

"But you and Felipe kept him."

"We didn't know. We recently learned of Luis's true history after he disappeared."

"Why didn't the Reillys claim him as their grandchild? Why didn't they contest his custody?"

"Harold and Margaret considered that. In the end, they concluded that Luis had suffered enough and that he was in a safe and stable environment. They visited Luis at the hospital a few times. I didn't think much of their visits at the time, except that I was impressed by their kindness. Harold wanted to pay for the medical care, but I told him Medicaid took care of that because, technically, Luis was still a ward of the state. Nonetheless, he talked to the hospital administrators and insisted that if there was anything the state didn't cover, they were to bill him directly. A staff nurse told me that. Carolyn had also provided insurance for him, especially when we traveled. The rest is history. They have always been there for him. He's received an excellent education and extravagant gifts."

"Luis went to school on a student loan."

"Yes, and who gave him the GFS loan? Harold and Margaret; Carolyn made the arrangements. Whenever we had family gatherings with Margaret and Harold, they always acknowledged him. It's interesting how the universe conspires to define our lives. I prayed for one child—just one, that's all I wanted. I received an incredibly wonderful family. I'm humbled by Little God's generosity," she concluded, choking on her words.

* * *

That evening, Katie went to see Carolyn and noticed that her mother appeared to have aged. She threw her arms around her mother and squeezed her tightly. "I'm sorry, Mommy," she said. She kissed Carolyn on the cheek and brushed her hair back with one hand. She studied Carolyn's eyes; her eyelids were beginning to droop, resembling her twin sister Marjorie's right eye. Katie noticed the crow's feet at the corners of Carolyn's eyes and hugged her again. "I've been such a lousy daughter," she said.

Katie surmised that this final episode in Carolyn's life was probably too much for her to bear. The truth was that Luis's disappearance was as hard on Carolyn as Stevie's recent fight for his life.

"You've been trying to find your way, honey," Carolyn replied.

"You've been very patient with me. I would have kicked my ass a long time ago."

"Kicking your ass is not a solution, Katie. I fell in love with you the moment I saw you in that hospital room. As you grew, you reminded me a lot of Marjorie. You weren't related by blood, but you faced similar demons, so kicking your ass was out of the question."

Once again, Katie examined Carolyn's tired face as if trying to find an answer within the lines of wisdom. "What were Marjorie's demons?" she finally asked.

"I wish Luis were here so I could make him understand," Carolyn replied. "I don't know how many children are sexually abused and they're able to move on with their lives. Others have a lifelong struggle."

"Marjorie was abused?"

Carolyn nodded in affirmation. "We were probably six," she said. "We were in Malaysia and had an American teacher. Pedophiles are everywhere, but they are apparently drawn to Asian or third world countries where it's easier to victimize children. He was an old man, from a child's perspective. He gave the children lollipops and toffee. I thought he was a nice man. I later found out that he had taken advantage of Marjorie, not once, but several times. When you're that young, you don't fully understand the ramifications. She didn't know; she was a child."

"What about Grandma, Mommy. Did she know?"

"I don't think so. You can look for telltale signs in a child's behavior and clothing, but if you don't know what the signs are, how could she know. You can check the child's underwear, but we always had servants. Marjorie and I were independent enough to undress ourselves, and the maid did the laundry. I don't believe Mother knew. As Marjorie got older, she was more withdrawn. The depression set in, and she looked for happiness in the wrong places."

"She became a world traveler."

"After college, yes. Prior to that, she had turned to drugs and alcohol. While we were in school, she was careful to maintain a façade. When she became pregnant, she confided in me and asked, 'If I can't take care of myself, how am I going to care for a little kid?' We spoke about an abortion and concluded it was out of the question. We turned to a young nun we knew. She was hip and in touch with the world, and she gave us what I believed to be good advice."

"What did she say?"

"She knew the Walkers in Puerto Rico. They had been trying to have a child with no success. The rest is history."

"Do you still believe you received good advice?" Katie asked while she sat, resting her head on one hand.

"Well, everything fell nicely into place. In retrospect, if I had known then what I know now, I would never have left Luis with the Walkers. I wish I had called Mother and confided in her. Luis would have grown up in a sheltered world."

"That world didn't help Marjorie. Although you had everything as children, Marjorie was still victimized. There's no guarantee that Luis would have lived a charmed life. Look at me—my father was a doctor, an educated man. Despite his education, he tormented my mother and me. We don't have the answers. I love you, Mommy," she said rising from her seat to hug Carolyn. "I love you. For me, you made the right decision. Do you remember the day you drove me home, the day Santillana attacked us?"

"Who can forget?" Carolyn said, looking into Katie's eyes.

"I said a lot of things that day; I rambled on about not being able to find myself; I said I died when I was two."

"I remember that too," Carolyn said. "I'm sorry, honey; I wish I had the power to make it all right. No person, especially a child, should be denied a life, and that's exactly what was done to you. He stole your life; he stole your childhood and your happiness."

"I've been looking at this all wrong, Mom. I'm still here; I'm a survivor. That," she added, pointing back, "happened a long time ago. There are children who do not survive, all the more tragic. It's heinous to torture and kill an innocent being or to suck out his spirit, but I'm here. I have you; I am more fortunate than anyone can imagine; I'm alive; I breathe; I am blessed, and I can move on, thanks to you and Daddy. I have a loving family, Mommy; I have two terrific brothers. How lucky is that? I live! Luis loves me; now he's just a little lost, and I love him, and I'll wait."

"I'm glad you believe, honey." Carolyn reached for her hand.

"There's something else, Mom."

"What's that, honey?"

"Now that I know I'm a survivor, I almost feel whole. Luis and a sense of duty are the only missing pieces.

While I wait for him, I need to be public about my life. I don't fear Lyman, so you don't need to worry about me. I need to go public so people, especially potential victims, can learn to recognize a predator. Laws need to be changed to protect the weak and punish the aggresors, Mom."

"Are you sure you want to go public? That's a big step."

"People who abuse children need to serve life sentences without parole. People who abuse animals need a minimum of five or ten years of confinement in prison or a mental institution because such people eventually go on to commit heinous crimes against children or anyone whom they perceive as helpless. The culture won't change if I, and others like me, continue to cringe. I must do something so no other innocent being will experience the nightmare we've endured."

"Well, if that is your decision, we will walk that road together," Carolyn said, holding Katie's hands. "Katie, there's something you should know."

"What, Mommy?"

"I received an e-mail from Brian Mulkeen. You remember him, don't you?"

"Yes, I've seen him a few times."

"Well, I told Luis that Brian might be his biological father. Luis has met with Brian."

"Luis is in Ireland?" Katie asked.

"No, he's probably in Italy. Brian gave him the names of mutual friends he and Marjorie had in Italy. Of course, those mutual friends go back years, so I don't know what kind of success Luis will have in contacting them. I forwarded that information to the investigators. I'll give them your e-mail so you can get information in real time, just like me."

Katie nodded her head and said, "I appreciate that, Mommy. During all these years, did Brian know anything about Luis?"

"Yes, he knew that Luis might be his son. Why do you think I sought him out whenever it was possible?"

"He knew that Luis might be his son and he never tried to claim him? I don't understand."

"If you knew where to find Luis right now, Katie, would you go get him?"

"Yes, Mommy, I would. I love him."

Carolyn smiled. "I'm glad you do, honey, and I'm glad you know that. Marjorie and I made an astronomical mistake when we conspired to give him up at birth. However, when my parents found out, Luis was already about six years old. He had already suffered greatly, and Brian didn't know anything. That's when my parents stepped in and assessed the situation. Dad spoke with Brian; I don't know how the situation was handled, but it was handled. The bottom line is that my Dad said to me, 'If you truly love him, Lyn, you'll leave him in the safe and stable environment where he is.' I believe my parents made the right decision. Years ago, Patrick said two things to me and I took them both to heart."

"What did he say?"

"He said that God had cleared some things off my plate, but that I simply didn't know it. He also said that only God knows which waters are best for us to swim. God sent Luis to Nydia and Felipe—he answered her prayer and cleared my plate so I could look after my family. We are all swimming where we should be. Right now, Luis is doing what he needs to do. The only thing

I can do to keep my sanity is to keep tabs on him and hope for the best."

"Do you think I should let him swim where he needs to swim and not go after him?"

"Listen to your heart, Katie."

Thirty-Eight

The construction work on Katie's property was progressing nicelyand she started to plan the sale of her corporation. She gave Ramírez and the other two engineers who were working on her property the option of staying on with her under a new corporation, which she named Reilly Construction Engineers (RCE). She concluded that when the market dropped, she would still be able to sustain a smaller crew until the market improved by using the profits she made from the sale of O'Gorman Enterprises. RCE would be less diverse than the previous business. She decided to maintain the East New York project and the student scholarship fund regardless of what happened to O'Gorman Enterprises.

As she made plans for herself and the corporation's future, she sat at a New York restaurant entertaining a potential buyer. She was four months pregnant and beginning to show. As the pregnancy progressed, she was becoming more enamored with this child and its absentee father. She rubbed her abdomen and lost herself in a temporary reverie while her client cut into his T-bone steak and savored the beef's juices. *Luis would be home if he knew you were coming*, she said telepathically to the fetus. She remembered what Carolyn said the night she had made peace with her mother.

The two women had spoken late into the night. They wondered about Luis, his safety, and his whereabouts. They spoke of motherly love. Carolyn informed her of how much she loved her children, born and unborn, and Katie was beginning to understand what her mom meant. They spoke about a person's perspective of pain and suffering. Wherever he was, Luis was dealing with his pain and suffering. Whenever Kieran felt neglected because Carolyn had somehow forgotten him, he dealt with his pain and suffering. A child who couldn't get the fingering right on his violin was tormented by his pain and suffering.

"In the final analysis," Carolyn had said, "I wonder how we would have held up during the potato famine. Would we have had the fortitude of the Lost Boys of the Sudan? Could we have survived the torment of a slave who was separated from her family and raped by her masters? I lost three of my children, but how many mothers lost theirs before they too were gassed by the Nazis during the holocaust? Imagine sitting in that oven and perhaps wondering if the child who was separated from you is in an adjacent oven being gassed just like you. Yet the survivors, having lost their loved ones, and knowing how they were tortured, somehow managed to go on with their lives. As Americans, many of us live such pampered lives that we don't know what real pain and suffering is. Every night I pray that Luis can put his pain and suffering into perspective and return home to meet the child he has sired."

While in that reverie, someone tapped Katie on the shoulder. She looked up and recognized the man with the affable smile.

"Chief Lawrence Quinn," she said in acknowledgement. "How are you?"

"I'm fine. I'm here with my date," he said, drawing attention to an elegant young woman who was standing a few feet away. He was dressed in civilian clothes. "I noticed you when we came in, and I had to stop and say hello. I hope you don't mind if I say what's on my mind and say you look radiant."

"Thank you," Katie said, and she introduced the man at her table as a business associate. The men shook hands and exchanged pleasantries.

"I don't see a ring," Quinn said, turning his attention back to Katie. "I thought you and the doctor might have tied the knot by now. I received your thank you note for the flowers I sent. I called your office several times, but you were never available; I assumed you were very busy."

"I was. I am. Shortly after my incident, my brother ended up in the hospital and the family and I spent most of our time by his bedside."

"I'm sorry to hear that. I hope he's well."

"He's fine, thank you."

"Well, have a nice evening, Dr. O'Gorman," Quinn said. "I need to get back to my date before she gets upset. Perhaps you can join me for dinner sometime."

"Thank you, but I'm afraid I'll have to decline. I don't think the doctor would like me dating other men. We're expecting our first child in February."

"Well, congratulations then. It was nice running into you. You'll make a lovely mother."

That evening, Katie shared Quinn's encounter with Carolyn. "I guess you were right about him," she said to Carolyn as her mother sat petting Spotty the cat. Blacky, the other cat, was dozing and purring in Katie's lap. "The man is definitely a player. There he was with his date patiently waiting by the entrance, and I believe he was trying to hit on me."

"Honey, he wasn't trying; he was hitting on you. I told you I've seen enough gigolos hovering over the women at Emily's Hope. If it's not there, it's in church. They seem to know where vulnerable women hang out. They can't help it; it's a male's nature to pursue a female, especially one that appears helpless. We would feel dejected if they didn't do it, and they know that."

"And the dance goes on."

"Exactly," Carolyn responded as an eavesdropping Kieran perched himself on the sofa's armrest, eased his buttocks into the adjoining cushion, and finally dropped his head into his mother's lap, displacing Spotty, who was clearly irritated and voiced it by letting out an objecting meow. Kieran reached down and back, scooping the cat up with one hand; he placed him on his chest and proceeded to pet him behind the ear.

"What have you been doing, mama's boy?" Katie asked him.

"Nothing," he responded.

"So you admit to being a mama's boy."

"I'm not admitting to anything, but I'm the only boy here."

"Did you finish your homework?" Carolyn asked him.

"Yeah. It was easy. Did you tell Katie about me?"

"Yes," Katie replied. "Congratulations, squirt. Maybe this will keep you out of trouble."

Kieran smiled with pride. He had been offered an afterschool job with the Westchester County DA's office. Phil

Garrity had shown them the work Kieran had done for the police, helping them in their arrest with Arturo Santillana. At first, Kieran wasn't interested. Then Carolyn told him it would be a good intern experience for him and an excellent reference for his future endeavors. So, he accepted the job, which meant working a few hours a day, twice a week. He would train select members of the DA staff to understand the hacking process and obtain valuable information.

"I'll have my own desk and an official police computer," Kieran informed Katie.

"Now that you're on the side of the law, I hope you'll stay out of my business." Katie replied.

"He promised me he isn't going to do that anymore," Carolyn interjected. "My little baby is growing up and assuming responsibilities of his own."

"Does that mean you'll stop whining?" Katie asked him.

"I don't whine. Whining is for losers. I'll admit, sometimes I'm a victim of circumstance, and I'm inclined to state my case, but that doesn't make me a whiner."

"Whatever. You need to put little boy things aside, Meerkat. You'll soon be my daughter's uncle. She'll be looking up to you."

"No one asked me if I wanted to be an uncle."

"Are you feeling old, little man?" Katie asked him.

"No, but uncles should be old; I'm just a kid. And how do you know you'll have a girl? You haven't done a sonogram yet to determine gender."

"Well, in reply to your first concern, you won't be a kid forever. Secondly, I want a girl. Boys are a pain in the ass. They're too damn sensitive, vulnerable, and needy."

"If that's what you believe, I won't be an uncle. I'll remain noncommittal, thank you, Miss Perfect."

"Squirt, I'm far from perfect; I've been very unfair to you for something that's not your fault; I apologize. You'll make a good uncle. I promise not to needle you anymore. Besides, sometimes it's nice to be sensitive."

* * *

Katie diminished her travels throughout southern New York and parts of the tristate area. She confined her business solely to Westchester County and a biweekly trip to East New York, where she continued to oversee the progress of her other pet project. She spent most of her days walking with the four dogs and conferring with Carolyn and her grandparents about educating the public about child predators and animal abusers. She was five and a half months pregnant when she received an envelope from South Africa that was from a Father Wilfred Yussef-Harper. There was a handwritten note inside and another envelope from a charity organization. When she read the letter, she broke down and cried.

Dear Miss O'Gorman,

I have been asked to forward a message to you from Dr. Luis López. I met him while I was in Sudan. He asked me to say he loves you and he shall try to be home by next spring. He wrote your address on the back of the enclosed envelope. Please read...

She turned the enclosed envelope over and recognized Luis's handwriting. Under the address, he had scribbled, "Ask Carolyn to forgive me." Katie opened the envelope and shook out a *Doctors Without Borders* brochure, which had a picture of Luis with his head wrapped in a ghudrah for protection against the burning sun. He was administering a vaccine to a small Sudanese child. Katie rubbed her belly and said, "Daddy is coming home, baby." Then she called Carolyn and yelled, "Mommy, call Nydia and tell her Luis is coming home. He wants you to forgive him. He'll be here in the spring. Yes, I received a note from South Africa from a priest who saw him in Sudan. He's coming home, Mommy."

* * *

In November 2005, Rafferty, the transit policeman who had dragged Katie off the train, was officially fired from the NYPD and was sentenced to six years for abusing his powers as a civil servant and assaulting several women.

In December 2005, the men who had entered Amir's store the evening Stevie was shot were tried and sentenced. Georgie, the man who fired the shot, was sentenced to two years in prison for a hate crime and attempted manslaughter. The other two received three months' probation. All three men had to attend a human relations course dealing with ethnic, racial, and religious tolerance. The O'Gormans were disappointed with the sentences and immediately started to discuss new strategies to correct the court's ruling.

Arturo Santillana's trial started in February 2006. He was found guilty on all counts, and he received consecutive sentences that totaled thirty-five years. The Sheridan lawyers had successfully argued against deportation for fear that the felon would reenter the United States illegally and commit further crimes.

Carolyn Josefina López-O'Gorman was born that same month, on February 15, 2006. Katie sat in her hospital bed cradling the small infant. She soon transferred her to her proud grandmother. Carolyn, Nydia, and Momma Ellen took turns holding, admiring, and cooing the new arrival. Kieran asked to hold her, and he was given careful instructions as Nydia transferred the newborn to him and Carolyn looked on nervously.

"She looks just like you when you were this size," Nydia said to him.

One evening in March 2006, a week before St. Patrick's Day, Luis rang his parents' doorbell. It was Thursday night, and Esposito and Garrity were there. Felipe answered the doorbell and was extremely happy to see his son again. He yelled back into the house, jubilantly announcing Luis's arrival. As Luis stepped in, the others joined him by the doorway. Luis looked thinner and more resolute. He had an eighteen- or nineteen-month-old child in his arms. Felipe and Nydia looked at the little girl and said nothing. They studied Luis momentarily and embraced him while he still held the small toddler. They wept. Luis also noticed the change in them. They appeared older, fragile, and beautiful. Holding the baby in one arm, he firmly shook Garrity and Esposito's hands. The men followed each handshake with pats on the back and strong hugs.

Luis finally introduced the child. "This is Florence Teresa. She's the reason why I was held up in Darfur. I had to wait for the adoption papers to come through. I found her."

"What do you mean you found her?" Nydia asked as they sat in the living room.

Luis held the child in his lap. "I found her lying between her parents' mutilated bodies; she's been with me ever since. Flo," he said to the toddler, "say hello to my mami and papi. These are the people I told you about; they're your grandparents." He pointed to each of them as he spoke. "I bet you thought you'd never be grandparents, huh?"

"No, I never did," Felipe said, rubbing the back of his head.

"I named her Florence for Florence Nightingale and Teresa for Mother Teresa. It's because you help Daddy, right?" he said to the child. Florence nodded her head in affirmation. "You should see her. In the middle of all that suffering, she would hug the other children who were hurting and bring them water or food. There are so many children, Mami and Papi. I wish I could bring them all home with me, but I chose Florence because she followed me everywhere I went. We help each other, right Flo?" he asked the child.

She said yes in a low child's voice, and Felipe and his wife chuckled with delight.

"Have you seen Katie yet?" Esposito asked.

"No, I came here first," Luis replied. "I want to see Carolyn next. Then I'll go home."

"Has she been baptized?" Nydia asked, looking at Florence.

"Of course she's been baptized. I took care of that in Kenya. However, we can redo the ceremony to your satisfaction, Mami. I can't stay long," he said apologetically. "Papi, may I borrow your car? I need to see Carolyn."

"Yes, my son. Of course," Felipe responded in Spanish and went to fetch his car key.

"Mami, could you call Carolyn and tell her I'm on my way? I don't want to startle her. Tell her I need her forgiveness."

"You can't leave yet," Nydia objected. "This baby has traveled a long way, and I'm sure she must be tired and hungry. You may be a doctor, but you have a lot to learn about nurturing children."

"I've done okay so far," he said, but he knew better than to argue with her.

"Felipe, get Luis's old car seat from the attic while I prepare something for the baby."

Felipe handed Luis the car key and immediately went to find the baby chair.

"You still have my car seat?" he asked incredulously while he followed his mother into the kitchen, and Florence held his hand. Esposito and Garrity followed closely behind them.

"I have practically everything you've ever owned," Nydia said. "The car seat may not be up to code, but it will do until you get her a replacement. It's a good thing you were a tiny little thing when we first got you."

Within minutes, Nydia whipped up a western omelet and toast for little Florence. The baby dug right in. As Nydia poured a glass of vegetable juice for her, she said, "See, I knew she'd be hungry. Now what do you want to eat?"

"Nothing—I'm fine."

"Jimmy, Phil," she said to Esposito and Garrity, "why don't you guys help yourselves to cake; I'll brew some coffee. You know, Florence is such a big name for such a little girl," she said to Luis as she retrieved a carrot cake from the counter and placed it in front of Phil.

"She'll grow. Besides, I sometimes call her Flo," Luis said as he watched Florence take a small bite with her big fork. "She needs smaller tableware."

"I have that too," Nydia commented. "It's probably in the back of one of these drawers. I'll find it for the next time she comes. Mind if I call her Teresita?"

Luis smiled and said, "Teresita does sound nicer than Flo. Okay, we'll call her Teresita, but she's already used to Flo. Flo, do you like the name Teresita?"

Flo shrugged her shoulders while she chewed on her food and the adults laughed.

Felipe brought the carseat and proceeded to remove the old, dusty transparent cover; Nydia told him to get the vacuum cleaner. As soon as Teresita finished eating, Luis whisked her off to his next stop while Phil, James, and Luis's parents enjoyed their snack and a game of dominoes.

Thirty-Nine

The boys were delighted to see Luis back. They almost knocked him off his feet as Florence stood beside him holding his index finger. There were hugs, kisses, and plenty of enthusiasm from everyone present.

"You grew," Luis said to Kieran.

"Nine whole inches and counting," Kieran responded.

"Hey, Matt, is that a potbelly I see?" Luis asked Matthew.

"It's probably gas," Matthew lied while rubbing his belly, "but you're looking like spaghetti, boy. We'll need to fatten you up."

Carolyn wrapped her arms around her nephew and had a tough time letting go.

"You were my candle home. I was so wrong, Aunt Carolyn. *Bendición. Perdón*," he said in Spanish, asking her blessing and forgiveness, remembering what she and Nydia had taught him of Latin tradition.

Carolyn choked up and held him tighter. She was finally able to respond, "God bless you, my son. I ask your forgiveness for not being forthright with you."

Excitedly, everyone soon bombarded him with questions that he answered with equal exhilaration. He introduced Florence to them in much the same manner he had introduced her to his parents.

"Mami wants to use the diminutive name Teresita," he explained enthusiastically.

"Hello, Teresita," Carolyn said, and Florence returned a shy glance as she clung to Luis.

"It will take time for her to get used to it," Luis explained. "I've been calling her Flo. Flo, don't be shy," he coaxed the child. "Say hello to Auntie Carolyn."

"Hello," Florence said in a tiny voice.

"You have a lovely voice," Carolyn said as the others looked on.

"She's a regular chatterbox when she gets going," Luis said proudly. "We even sing together. Let's sing for Aunt Carolyn, Flo," he said, picking her up in his arms. "I'll start. 'The teeny tiny ant....'"

"Toy day, toy day, toy day," Florence joined in. Luis allowed her to complete the song on her own.

"That was wonderful," Carolyn complimented her. Florence smiled shyly and hugged Luis's neck.

"What was she singing?" Kieran asked. "I didn't understand any of it except toy day."

"She mondegreens it," Luis explained. "It's a song I taught her, 'The teeny tiny ant toils all day.'"

"Children always mondegreen stuff," Stevie said to Kieran. "In Scotland, instead of singing 'They have slain the Earl of Murray and laid him on the green,' they say 'They have slain the Earl of Murray and Lady Mondegreen or Mandagreen'. I remember when you used to call me Seevee."

"Seevee, Aytee, Eewan, me," Florence sang, "head boree."

Stevie burst into a hearty laugh and said to Luis, "Oh, no you didn't!"

"Oh yes, I did. She knows the whole song. 'It's just Stevie, Katie, Kieran, and me, heading for a jamboree.' Flo, this is Stevie," Luis said, placing his hand on Stevie's chest. And that's Eewan." He pointed to Kieran. He then reintroduced Uncle Matthew and Aunt Carolyn.

The family settled down in the family room, and Florence sat close to Luis on the sofa.

"I've missed you all so much, and I was such a self-centered fool," Luis said. "I need everyone's forgiveness, but I know I don't deserve it."

"You're right about that," Kieran replied. "You left us high and dry; I would have never left me without saying good-bye. We thought you might be dead or something."

"Well, I'm not, and I sincerely apologize. That's what happens when you're a self-centered jerk; I didn't think of anyone but me."

"What did you do all that time?" Kieran asked.

"I saw a lot of pain, and I realized how insignificant my little troubles were. Someone pricked me with a pin, and I reacted as if I had been sliced in half."

"Who pricked you?"

"Carolyn, Marjorie, Harold and Margaret, Momma, Papa, and my adoptive parents. They pricked me with their love. Now I understand," he said, gazing directly at Carolyn. "Thank you for loving me enough to let me go. I saw... I saw a lot of terrible things in Sudan."

"What did you see, Luis?" Stevie asked him with concern.

"I came upon the rotting corpses of men who had been hacked to death. I saw women and children who had been raped and tortured so badly they couldn't walk. Many had deep, infected wounds. Limbs had been chopped off. There were so many people dying of starvation. Abuse doesn't just happen here; it happens everywhere, perhaps more intensely," he said as he leaned forward in his seat. "There I was among them, feeling sorry for myself. At night, I stared at the stars. They twinkled back at me and said, 'You complain about not having ketchup for your fries, and these people weep as they see their children's heads chopped off. You choose to be dung on gold.' That's what I am." He looked at Carolyn.

"You've never been dung, Luis," Carolyn said. "You and my children are diamonds in the sun; our children are our greatest treasure. You're our future's hope."

He nodded and said, "I understand; I have Flo. You also said that I have three assets: a mind, a heart, and functional limbs. Several of those people had no limbs. If they didn't die, a loved one cared for them. If a woman or child was missing his or her legs and couldn't find a staff or other means of support, he or she crawled. Despite all that pain, they still found a reason to chuckle and have a good belly-laugh. I have all my assets; I intend to use them. If Katie takes me back, she's my fourth asset. This little jewel," he said, hugging Florence closer, "is my fifth. She is so loving and resilient."

"She's adorable," Carolyn responded while admiring Florence and her big, gorgeous, almond-shaped brown eyes with long black lashes, which reminded Carolyn of an Egyptian princess. "Katie has been waiting for you ever since she received a note from a priest in South Africa," she interjected without taking her eyes off Florence. Florence was wearing a lilac dress with a white pinafore and a purple woolen sweater. A floral pattern adorned the collar, cuffs, and hem of her attire.

"How's Katie?" he asked.

"She's fine," Matthew replied. "She was upset and angry with Carolyn when you left. She blamed Carolyn for your disappearance; I wasn't happy about that. We had our words, but she finally came around."

"I'm sorry, Carolyn," Luis said to her. "I was hurt and overreacted."

"That's ancient history, honey," she replied. "This was a test for all of us. Although Katie was upset, she held her own. She hasn't taken any medication for over a year, and she's fine. She's calmed down considerably, and she doesn't talk to any imaginary people as far as we know."

"Why didn't you write?" Kieran asked.

"There are no post offices in the middle of Darfur. I had to wait until I met a passerby like Father Yussef-Harper."

"What, you couldn't drop us a postcard from the airport or something?"

"You're right. I have that coming to me."

"That's not all you have coming to you. Man, I looked up to you and considered you to be my older brother. Then you go and disappear like that. What the hell were you thinking?"

"Kieran, that's enough!" Matthew interjected.

"No," Kieran objected. "It's not enough. Who gave him the right to do that, Daddy? You don't just walk off and leave. We were all worried. Even Katie was worried, and she's as tough as nails. You were wrong, Luis. You were wrong, and somebody needs to call you on it."

"I know. You're right. If I could undo it all, I would. I sincerely apologize to you, to everyone. I wish it never happened."

"Kieran," Carolyn said, "Luis had to go, honey. I want you to look on the bright side of this."

"What bright side?" he asked. "There is no bright side."

"The bright side," she said, "is sitting right there next to him. He needed to bring Florence home."

"He never even met Florence until he left."

"Exactly," Carolyn replied. "He needed to go and meet her. Now Florence is our responsibility. She'll need a big brother, and I expect you to be there for her. Do you understand?"

Kieran looked at the toddler with renewed interest. "Yes, I understand."

Luis looked at Carolyn and said, "I decided to return via Kenya because things are a bit calmer there, and I went into a bank to see if I could arrange to have funds transferred. I needed cash to return home, and I did leave a few thousand bucks in my account."

"Yes, I know," Carolyn replied.

"Well, then perhaps you also know that the balance was increased to its maximum of a hundred thousand dollars. You didn't have to do that; I owe you considerably more than that. I bought a lot of senseless stuff before I left, and I did equally selfish things."

"I didn't deposit any money into your account. I didn't know," she replied. "I do know that you returned most of your funds to GFS."

"So who transferred money to my account?" Luis asked, looking perplexed.

"I suppose it was Mother," Carolyn replied. "Luis, honey, you are her grandson. The money you received for the Internet site came from your grandparents. Regardless of what you may think, as a Muir-Reilly heir, they believe the money is rightfully yours. They never wanted to cheat you of anything. Mother's the one who decided that buying your Internet company was a good way to transfer those assets to you; I was simply the intermediary."

"I believe I understand how Grandma Margaret feels," he said, looking into her eyes, "but I like where I am right now. You were right about a lot of things, Aunt Carolyn. I understand why you like the life you've made for yourself. I don't need all that stuff. You've chosen to live without the trappings of wealth; I sold my watch and used the money to hasten Florence's adoption. I'm going back to work, and I guess I'll buy a new watch at the drug store."

Carolyn smiled and said, "It's your money, and you're legally entitled to it. And, although I'm not fond of military vehicles, you can do whatever you want with it. I suggest you talk to your grandmother, and I'll give you a novelty watch for your graduation."

"I graduated a long time ago," he replied.

"And you just graduated from the School of Life's Lessons. Congratulations, and thank you for bringing Nydia and me a granddaughter," she said, looking affectionately at Florence. "Are you going to open your practice again?"

"I don't know. I was thinking of devoting some time to my music; I can write children's songs. It cheers them up, you know. Music is a different type of medicine."

"I understand; you need to follow your bliss. Perhaps you should be heading home now. I expect to see you and Florence tomorrow."

"Stevie will take you home, Luis. We'll call Katie and inform her you're on your way," Matthew said. "I'll return Felipe's car; he'll need it for work tomorrow."

On their way to Katie's house, Florence sat quietly in the child seat, hugging a stuffed toy that Kieran had given her. Luis asked Stevie, "Did you ever figure out if the woman with the bandana whom you saw in your dreams was the same one who gave the Greek soldier his medallion?"

"I took a look at the Shahbaz's WWII picture, but it's too old and blurry to tell for sure. However, although I couldn't see the details of the women's face, she was wearing a scarf in the same manner I remember from my dream, so I believe what I dreamt was real."

"It's nice to believe. Are you and Sheeva still a couple?"

"Her name is Rebecca," Stevie replied, "and the answer is yes. We plan to marry when I finish grad school; I passed all the undergraduate exams."

"I'm glad to hear that. So Sheeva is no longer Sheeva?"

"No," Stevie said as he stared at the road ahead. "She realized she wasn't Muslim material. She said she had done it for the wrong reasons, to satisfy a personal need. She thought she was being selfish because she hadn't done it to honor God, and she's torn about her Christian upbringing."

"So what is she now?"

"She doesn't know yet. She still wears the hijab from time to time; she likes it. Now she's studying Buddhist meditation whenever she can spare the time, which she mostly spents caring for Javeed and studying."

"Have faith, my son. She'll figure it out."

"Yes, my brother," Stevie replied. "You figured things out."

"Yes, I did," Luis agreed.

"While you were away, Kieran, Katie, and I had a lot to discuss with Mommy over dinner. Do you know what I learned?"

"No—tell me."

"Your name, Luis José, is derived from Louise and Josephine. According to Mommy, the proper concordance for your name in Spanish should be the opposite, José Luis. Like Cleopatra's Mark Anthony is Mark Anthony and not Anthony Mark. The names sound kind of strange if you flip them."

Luis nodded in affirmation. He then finished Stevie's train of thought and said, "Josephine is Carolyn's middle name. I guess Louise was Marjorie's middle name, so it came first."

"Exactly," Stevie agreed.

Luis shook his head and sighed as his head spun to connect the dots of his life. "Life is good," he finally said. "Strange, but good. Did Carolyn tell you anything about Brian Mulkeen?"

"She believes he may be your father."

"Well, I tracked him down. After hearing my story, he agreed to a paternity test. He is my father. We met again on my way back from Africa and spoke about my mother."

"Why did you go to Africa, Luis?"

"Marjorie had been there. I needed to follow the roads she had traveled."

"What did you learn?" Stevie asked.

"I'm not quite sure. It's a lot to assess. She was well liked. Perhaps, I will continue to wonder why we never met face to face—I think it could have been nice. Who knows? I also learned something about Brian. On the way back from Africa, he took me to meet his mother. Talk about life being strange. She's from the Highlands of Scotland."

"So you are partly Scottish, me lad," Stevie said, trying to imitate a Scottish accent.

"Aye, indeed I am. Brian's mother is a sweet old lady, and she claims I resemble her son, my uncle Edward Mulkeen.

So I've made an ancestral connection. It feels good to know my roots. I'm following the thread of life, brother."

"Your thread gets better with time, Luis," Stevie said while thinking of Katie's baby, but choosing to disclose nothing. "As we were leaving the house, Mommy called Katie. She's expecting you and little Florence."

"Well, that's good. I really missed her while I was away; I had no one to smack me senseless."

"A lot has changed since you left. You're not going to recognize your old digs when we arrive. By this summer, we'll all be living in our own little community, which Katie has named Margaret's Quay. She's made a lot of improvements to the place. The winter snows interfered with the work, so it was slow going. We attached a shovel to your military bus and used it to clear a lot of snow along the side streets so her crew could get in and out. Katie taught me how to drive that monster—it was fun. However, I did total someone's Toyota on my maiden run."

"Too bad for the Toyota. Bus and monster, huh? You sound like Carolyn." Luis changed the subject. "I remember that Katie was making changes in her life. She has apparently become more family oriented. What about that big project in East New York? That was her pet."

"It still is. Grandma Margaret's financial firm is managing that for her. So far, they have sold or leased two hundred and twenty-five million dollars worth of affordable condos and commercial space to the lower middle class in that area. The place is a dream come true for everyone. And you know Katie—deep down under her belligerent façade, she's a soft touch. She'll make good to all those investors."

"I'm sure she will," Luis said, and he started drumming on the car's dashboard as he sang:

It's just Stevie, Katie, Kieran, and me	My lover, my brothers, and me
Heading for a jamboree	Sailing out to sea
Skipping stones, getting tall	Flying high, touch the sky
Eating scones, climbing walls	Ride our bikes, this is nice.

Florence Teresita accompanied him from the backseat.

Alerted by the security system, Katie knew that Stevie's car had entered the premises. She was on pins and needles as she waited for the car. She was standing on the house deck when Stevie stopped the car at the foot of the steps. It was dark out, but her home's flood lights lit the immediate surroundings. As soon as she saw Luis step out of the car, she screamed with delight, ran down the steps, and wrapped her arms around his neck.

"You're home!" she shrieked.

"Yes, I'm home," he said as he laughed and unlocked her arms from around his neck. "Let me look at you, woman."

Katie stepped back while holding both his hands and each of them grinned from ear to ear as they studied each other. Then she leaped forward and hugged him again.

"I've missed you," she said as she kissed him several times. "You don't know how much I've missed you. I love you; I love you." Then she pushed him. "Don't you ever frighten me like that again, you damn fool!"

"Hey, they told me you've changed. Do I need to buy some body armor?" he said rubbing the shoulder that had received most of the force while Katie looked at him mischievously.

"Tell me you didn't deserve that!" she challenged him.

"Well, if you plan to continue to abuse me, I may as well go back to Africa."

He turned away and started to open the car door. Katie smacked him on the back of the head and Luis turned to face her again, with a gleam in his eye. Katie backed away. He charged forward and quickly lifted her off the ground and onto his shoulder.

Katie shrieked with delight and laughed as Luis spun her around. "Put me down!"

"I can see you haven't changed at all, but I have," he said as he continued to spin and Katie shrilled. "And I'm not putting up with anymore of your nonsense, woman."

"Who's that?" Katie inquired as she caught sight of a child who was walking toward them, holding Stevie's hand.

Luis put her down and wrapped his arms around her waist as they faced Florence and Stevie. They both needed to steady themselves for a few seconds.

"That's Flo, my daughter."

Katie took a moment to calculate a few matters in her head, reasoning that Luis had not been away long enough to have fathered Flo, but she did not dismiss the possibility that he could have cheated on her before he left. "What do you mean?"

"I adopted her. Flo's my daughter."

"Oh," Katie said sounding relieved while she studied the child who stared back at her with bewildered eyes. "You adopted her. I guess that's okay. Yeah, that's okay."

"You don't sound convinced," Luis replied sounding hurt.

"I'm convinced, Luis; I'm convinced. I'm just surprised. For a moment there, I thought you could be her biological father. In which case, I would have to kill you, you know."

He smiled and said, "Yes, I know. But, if I were Flo's biological father, do you think I would have returned to face certain death?"

"I guess not, Luis. However, just to be certain, are you willing to submit to a paternity test?"

"For you, Katie, I'll submit to anything."

Katie freed herself from Luis's embrace and walked up to the child. She squatted to get a better look at her. "Hi; I'm Katie."

Florence nodded in affirmation. "I know. You're my new mommy."

Katie turned and smiled at a beaming Luis. She faced Florence again. "Yes, I am. Did Daddy tell you that?" Florence nodded again, and Katie could not resist the urge to scoop her up in her arms. "Daddy's a wise man." With Florence in her arms, she faced Luis again. "Come, Luis, there's someone I want you to meet. I too have a little surprise for you." She tucked at Luis's sleeve.

Within minutes, Luis was gazing down at his sleeping infant daughter. "She's mine," he whispered with pride as Stevie held Florence in his arms and he and Katie happily observed the tiny baby.

"She's ours," Katie corrected him as she got closer to him.

"She's ours," he agreed. "She looks like Kieran at that age."

"Yeah, I sort of noticed that, but she has your birthmark on her neck."

"She does?"

"Yeah."

"Well then, I guess I won't need to do a DNA test to make sure she's truly mine."

"Don't even go there."

"You're not going to hit me?"

"Never again. I promise. I also promise not to insult you anymore."

"Katie, Katie, Katie."

"Luis, Luis, Luis," she laughed and leaned her head on his shoulder.

THE END

A Bug's Pantry

◇◇◇

The teeny tiny ant toils all day
Over hills of clay (2X)
To gather sweets and treats
Of beets, leafs, twigs, and meat
And takes them to her nest
For her family to taste and eat.

The wispy, fuzzy spider spins and dips
Weaves and swings (2X)
Laces and shuttles a very fine web
To trap a little pest
And suck him till he's good and dead.

Oh, the dung beetle pushes and rolls
Shoves and crawls (2X)
Tucks and packs his ball of crap.
Through valleys and dunes,
He struggles and moves
To stash a mighty fine snack.

The skinny mosquito flutters and flies
Dives and strikes (2X)
As you snore inside your warm hut.
She'll definitely suck your blood
From your neck, your thigh, and butt.

Acknowledgments

Acknowledgments traditionally appear at the beginning of a book; I choose to be different. I surmise that if the reader got this far, he/she may be interested in how the characters were developed. The tragic case of Lisa Steinberg haunted me for years, until she inspired the creation of Katie O'Gorman. I often lament that so many children are murdered and robbed of what could be a very productive and inspiring life. I see their lovely faces in the newspapers and I cannot comprehend how a grownup decides that it's okay to use a child, who is a fraction the size and weight of an adult, as a human punching bag. I am also aware that we as humans seldom stand alone; at times, we may be inspired by a stranger, celebrity, neighbor, teacher, friend, or relative. Therfore, Katie had to be a survivor who is surrounded by supporters and individuals who admire her. Her story became an unlikely fairy tale in a world of illogical evil.

In addition to addressing the lasting damages of child abuse, I wanted to present intelligent and strong female figures. I wish to acknowledge the following individuals and media for directly or indirectly sharing their knowledge and for making it easier for me to compose *Emily's Hope* and develop the characters.

Telma Howard, née Russell, retired teacher and counselor, for her amusing thoughts and religious information.

Catherine J. Crowley, retired school teacher, and Ellen (Eileen) McCarthy, business administrator, who enriched my knowledge of Irish culture.

Aileen Mangione, (née McCready), who is the inspiration for Carolyn, Nydia, and Luis.

My brother and dad, two loving fathers, who are the inspiration for Matthew O'Gorman.

The Sue sisters, Ivy, Nancy, Anne, and Noreen, and Catherine J. Crowley, Carmen Iris Díaz, and Cynthia Griffin, who, much as the people in this tale, joined as family to help while my youngest sister fought a losing battle with leukemia in 1974.

Della, who hung out with me on Tiebout Avenue, entertained me with humorous monologues, and is the inspiration for Momma Ellen.

Camille Quinn, hairdresser, for discussing Irish folklore with me, and my co-workers Kathleen Reilly and Mary Spellman, the ladies who serenaded my soul with beautiful brogue.

Virginia Jordan, co-worker, for sharing her Irish music collection.

Dr. Odette V. Callender, ophthalmologist, whom I still remember as a very precocious and talented teenager and who, like her mother, Barbara Thomas, usually voiced excellent opinions, and partly inspired Katie's outspoken nature.

Dr. Marlene D. Galizi, gastroenterologist, who partly inspired Katie's endearing nature and answered the following question for me in 1997— "How does an educated person, who should know better, beat up an innocent child?" I had been thinking of the lawyer who had tortured and subsequently killed six year old Lisa Steinberg in 1987. Dr. Galizi's response was, "It has nothing to do with education; it's about control." I had spent a decade analyzing the tragedy through the wrong end of the telescope. I understood bullying and control and thought of the teacher who ridicules and whips his young student, Huw Morgan, in Richard Llewellyn's 1939 novel *How Green Was My Valley*. Twenty years after Lisa's brutally senseless death, I decided to write *Emily's Hope*.

Total strangers: Oprah's educational forums and guests, especially Dr. Mehmet Oz for sharing information on male concerns; Ms. Gloria Vanderbilt for her expression, "Follow your bliss."

John Bradshaw, author and counselor. As the reader follows Katie, the main character, they will recognize "the little child within", who was inspired by Mr. Bradshaw's PBS series. You can learn more about Mr. Bradshaw at http://www.johnbradshaw.com/johnsbio.aspx. Or, you can read about healing the inner child at Robert Burney's site: http://www.joy2meu.com/innerchild.html.

Jessica, for her outstanding editing skills in dealing with this tome.

About The Author

Ms. Rosa is a retired New York City teacher who taught for thirty-two years, and has called New York home since January, 1952. She enjoys being a part of New York's diverse population and entertains herself with several hobbies, including writing about her perceptions of the individuals and situations that she has encountered.

CPSIA information can be obtained at www.ICGtesting.com
Printed in the USA
LVOW012220080112

262955LV00008B/203/P